SECRET PACK
THE COMPLETE TRILOGY

I0722466

Ember Blaze also writes as R. A. Steffan:

The Last Vampire: Book 1-3
The Last Vampire: Books 4-6
(with Jaelynn Woolf)

Vampire Bound: The Complete Series, Books 1-4
Forsaken Fae: The Complete Series, Books 1-3

Circle of Blood: Book 1-3
Circle of Blood: Books 4-6
(with Jaelynn Woolf)

The Complete Horse Mistress Collection
The Complete Lion Mistress Collection
The Complete Dragon Mistress Collection
The Complete Master of Hounds Collection

Her Band of Rakes

Antidote: Love and War, Book 1
Antigen: Love and War, Book 2
Antibody: Love and War, Book 3
Anthelion: Love and War, Book 4
Antagonist: Love and War, Book 5

SECRET PACK
THE COMPLETE TRILOGY

EMBER BLAZE

Secret Pack: The Complete Trilogy

Copyright 2022 by OtherLove Publishing, LLC

All rights reserved. Printed in the United States of America. No part of this book may be used or reproduced in any manner whatsoever without written permission except in the case of brief quotations embedded in critical articles or reviews.

This book is a work of fiction. Names, characters, businesses, organizations, places, events and incidents either are the product of the author's imagination or are used fictitiously. Any resemblance to actual persons, living or dead, events, or locales is entirely coincidental.

ISBN: 978-1-955073-33-2 (paperback)

For information, contact the author at
http://www.rasteffan.com/contact/

Cover art by Ember

First Edition: March 2022

Table of Contents

BOOK ONE:

HIDE OR DIE

2

ONE

Leona

CONSIDERING I'D risked my life to be here, I wasn't enjoying this party at all. The ballroom inside the Hotel Epoque in Bucharest had been decorated to resemble nothing so much as an explosion at a wedding cake factory. Around me, the other VIPs who would be attending the upcoming Transatlantic Summit on Alphomic Policy were mingling politely, drinks in hand.

Like everyone else present, I was dressed to the nines. My forest green velvet evening dress had been chosen to highlight my fiery red hair. Makeup thick enough to hide my nervous pallor presented a facade of approachable feminine beauty to the outside world. Jewelry hovering just on the right side of gaudy dripped from my earlobes, throat and wrists, as I cradled the martini I was pretending to nurse and smiled pleasantly at everyone who greeted me.

Inside, I was waiting for the metaphorical ground to crumble beneath my four-inch designer stilettos. It was a feeling I'd grown used to over the years, since it was almost always present, hovering in the background of my sham of a life. Tonight, however, I had more cause than usual to worry.

Kameron Patel hurried toward me through the crowd, trying valiantly not to *look* like he was hurrying. Lithe and graceful in his tailored tuxedo, he slipped through gaps in the throng like a shadow, ignoring the appreciative looks he garnered from most of the female guests and more than a few of the male ones as he passed.

4

I smiled blandly as he reached my side and cupped his hand beneath my elbow — the small point of contact easing a fraction of the tension from my shoulders. Placing my untouched martini on the tray of a passing waiter, I allowed myself to be herded subtly toward the dance floor.

"He's just arrived," Kam murmured in my ear, his light, Indian-accented voice too low to be heard by anyone else above the rising hum of conversation.

I gave a tiny nod to let him know I'd understood, and settled into his arms. We smoothly inserted ourselves into the glittering whirl of other couples waltzing around the floor to the accompaniment of a string quartet playing Tchaikovsky.

"They say he has the sharpest senses of any beta alive," Kam said, still too low for any other ears but mine. "Leona, I'm scared for you. This was too risky."

Anyone watching us would see nothing more than a short, curvy, redheaded beta woman dancing with a black-haired, olive-skinned beta man of average height and slender build, but with an unusually beautiful face.

They'd be wrong on both counts.

Since the Purge began more than a century ago, omegas like us had three choices. Submit to slavery, undergo sterilization and become second-class citizens, or hide in plain sight as betas and take our chances in a world that despised us. Thanks to rich beta parents who'd cared more for their child's freedom than their own safety, I'd had the luxury of the third option. The omega in my arms — who now played the role of my trusted colleague — had, in succession, experienced all three of those things during the course of his thirty-five years.

That we'd achieved as much as we had was almost unheard of in a world run by betas. Thanks to a combination of ambition and the subtle evolutionary advantages conveyed by my omega status, I'd enjoyed a meteoric rise through the diplomatic corps in the United Federation of North America. Black market heat blockers and pheromone suppressors had so far prevented anyone from detecting my ruse. Of course, that toxic cocktail also practically ensured that I'd succumb to one form of cancer or another within the next couple of decades, if I didn't somehow manage to get off them soon.

Kameron, meanwhile, had escaped his fate thanks to help from the secret underground that acted as a support system for alphas and omegas lucky enough to find a contact there. Inserted into a new life stolen from a random dead beta, he was now my diplomatic attaché. Both of us had found a place in the UFNA's new liberal administration, shaping policy that might one day help our kind escape from beneath the bootheel of the global beta supremacy movement.

I squeezed Kam's hand, trying to convey reassurance as we whirled effortlessly around the dance floor. "It'll be fine," I murmured. "We knew the bastard wouldn't let something as important as this summit happen without showing up in person to try and thwart it."

"He's a monster," Kam whispered, barely audible even at such close range.

"Yes," I agreed. "He is."

⸻◆⸻

Kostya Nikolayev was a familiar figure in the news media. Tall and broad-shouldered, his very presence seemed to draw all the air from a room. Even from across the dance floor, the effect was far more overpowering in person than it was when experienced through the filter of a television screen—

unsurprising, since one did not rise to the top echelons of an influential worldwide para-governmental organization by being a wallflower.

As the newly installed head of the Euro-Soviet branch of the Committee on Alphomic Suppression, Nikolayev had a vested interest in ensuring that the upcoming summit didn't strip any power from his organization. For decades, most of the world's major nations had allowed the Committee to take the lead in defining policy related to the subjugation and eradication of alphas and omegas.

Apparently, our very existence perverted the natural order of things, or so the argument went. We flew in the face of beta religious teachings about the roles of men and women in family and childbearing, with our polyamorous mate-bonds and 'unnatural' decoupling of the concepts of sex and gender.

Never mind the fact that alphas and omegas had been around every bit as long as betas. Female alphas had been siring pups on male omega carriers—and vice versa—since before humanity started banging rocks together. For us, gender didn't matter—only reproductive plumbing. Alphas sired pups. Omegas carried them. Mated packs formed on the basis of emotional compatibility, regardless of the number or gender of the pack members involved.

The perennial hostility of those in power toward beta homosexual liaisons was multiplied a hundredfold when it came to alphomic social structure. Betas feared alphas as being generally stronger and more dominant. Meanwhile, they secretly desired omegas, seeing us as both inherently submissive and inherently corrupting.

Alphas were mindless brutes that would take over if given the chance, immediately hurtling humanity back to the Stone Age. Omegas were weak slaves to their own sexual natures, who would drag good, upstanding betas into their sinful ways like sirens luring sailors to their doom. Those were the old slurs… the old lies. For millennia, the push-pull of hatred and reconciliation had rolled over human civilization in never-ending cycles. For a few generations peace would reign, until eventually some group needed a convenient scapegoat and turned on alphas and omegas to provide it.

The latest round of persecution—and the rise of the Committee—had started some eighty years ago in response to increased global poverty, climate change, and the mechanization of jobs at the turn of the century. *'Alphas are stealing all the good jobs!'* came the rallying cry. *'Look at all these good-for-nothing omegas squeezing out pups! They take resources and give nothing back!'* And so began the calls for ever-more repressive laws and ever-more stringent penalties, until it became a full-blown witch-hunt of anyone with a knot or a mating gland.

People whose parents would have loudly proclaimed against the evils of slavery began clamoring for controlled breeding programs to produce chemically castrated alphas for use as unpaid labor. Laws requiring omegas living outside of the breeding plantations to be permanently sterilized became commonplace. In most parts of the world, being an unregistered alpha or omega was now a capital offense.

At the heart of it all stood the Committee. And at the heart of the Committee stood Kostya Nikolayev—a beta renowned for his cruelty. He was said to have personally tortured and executed his adolescent female omega sibling when she refused to report to the slave camps. According to those who'd confirmed the death, the body had been barely recognizable after he'd finished with her.

The fact that he was from an impure beta bloodline—one that had historically interbred with alphas and omegas—should have been an obstacle in his rise to power. His reputation for ruthlessness ensured that it hadn't been.

And now he was here, in the same room as me. The same room as Kam. A man who was said to be able to sniff out any omega within twenty paces, regardless of pheromone suppressors.

It was probably an exaggeration.

Almost certainly.

I hoped.

"He looks like a Bond villain," Kam muttered, *sotto voce.*

I elbowed him as discreetly as I could manage. It would be more accurate to say that Nikolayev was feared by those in political power than to say that he was liked—but there was no reason to tempt fate by saying things like that in public.

Not that Kam's observation was entirely inaccurate. Broad shoulders... iron-gray hair streaked with silver... thick, neatly trimmed salt-and-pepper beard... two-piece charcoal suit at odds with the sea of black tuxedos around him... he looked like a man who considered this entire soirée beneath him. It was clear that he'd come here for the sole purpose of ensuring no ground was lost in the political battle to subjugate my people and wipe out dissenters—not to waltz or hobnob with political dignitaries.

A hand touched my shoulder, and it was all I could do not to jump.

"Madam Ambassador," said a pleasant male voice.

I turned to see a vaguely familiar face and immediately started flipping through my mental Rolodex to attach a name.

"Secretary Fouchet," I replied, forcing warmth into my voice. "What a pleasure to see you again. Heavens, how long has it been?"

The departmental official from Luxembourg smiled, obviously pleased that I'd remembered him. "Oh, a good year at least," he said. "It was that meeting of the western regional authority in Paris, wasn't it?"

"Yes, I believe you're right," I said, slipping into my role with the ease of long practice, despite the presence of the mass murderer in the room.

"You're looking particularly lovely tonight. May I request the honor of a dance?" Fouchet asked, extending a well-manicured hand to me, palm up.

"Of course," I told him. "It would be my pleasure."

I took his hand and flashed Kam a brief look, meeting his unhappy brown gaze before heading off to play the part of the socially competent diplomat.

Fouchet was a pleasant enough dance partner—prone to the subconscious beta attraction to an omega-in-hiding, but too polite and self-possessed to step outside the bounds of professionalism. He also waltzed well enough that I was in no danger of mashed toes—at least, not until the moment I caught sight of Nikolayev and another official I didn't recognize looming over Kameron. Kam's absolutely straight spine spoke of base terror barely contained.

I nearly stumbled over my own feet, and Fouchet steadied me as we came to an ungainly halt in the middle of the dance floor.

"Forgive me," I managed, in response to Fouchet's solicitous murmur of concern. "I must have slipped on something. I'm not usually such a clumsy dance partner." The words sounded far away to my own ears, and I was barely aware of the details as I extricated myself with enough grace for it not to seem out of place or unusual.

After thanking him for the dance, I walked in something of a daze toward the potential train wreck in progress across the ballroom. *If he can sniff out hidden omegas, he'll also be able to smell fear*, I told myself. *You're a respected UFNA ambassador. Act like it.*

Shoulders squared, chin up, I approached the little cluster of three, aware that others in the immediate vicinity were also turning to look. Kam formed the uneasy vertex of an acute triangle as the other two stood side by side, facing him.

"Ah," he said, in the tones of someone who *wasn't* two seconds away from losing his shit. "Madam Ambassador. I was just telling Chairman Nikolayev and his associate that you would be pleased to discuss the proposed policy changes with them once the summit begins tomorrow."

"Ambassador McCready." The Chairman cut across any opening gambit I might have made, foregoing the proper *'Madam'* honorific as he addressed me. "Is it true that Prime Minister Fairbanks intends to negotiate new restrictions on the current alphomic extradition treaty between the United Federation of North America and the Committee's international tribunal?"

His deep voice seemed to press down on my shoulders, accented with the sharp vowels and growling consonants of his native Russia. I had to physically fight not to bow beneath its weight.

"All of the proposed points of debate are included in the documents outlining the summit agenda, Chairman," I replied pleasantly, no hint of my struggle coming through. "And as Mr. Patel has indicated, I will be happy to discuss them with you once the summit is underway."

Gray eyes a few shades lighter than his utilitarian charcoal suit jacket pinned me, as though trying to peel back the layers of my skull and see inside. I wanted to grab Kam by the hand and flee. I wanted to fall to my knees on the marble floor and roll my head to the side, baring my throat in submission. I wanted to scan the room for our security detail, just to make sure they were there.

That last impulse was the hardest to quell, and while it might not prove quite as disastrous as either of the other two options, it was still an unacceptable show of weakness. I had no doubt Kam was fighting the same urges, and the knowledge that he was strong enough to resist them gave me that same strength. I raised an eyebrow, projecting unconcern.

The nameless sycophant at Nikolayev's side shifted restlessly. "The Committee will not countenance interference in the great work by an upstart administration barely six months into its tenure."

"Then we will have much to discuss, it appears," I told him with false brightness. "I look forward to it. But for now, I'm afraid I must return to a discussion with Secretary Fouchet. It was a pleasure to speak with you."

I gave them both a polished smile and gestured for Kam to precede me toward a larger knot of dignitaries near the buffet table, having glimpsed Fouchet among them.

"Good evening, gentlemen," Kam said politely, before turning and forging a path through the ever-shifting crowd. I followed, feeling the back of my neck prickle almost painfully under Nikolayev's gaze.

TWO

Leona

NOW THAT Nikolayev couldn't see me doing it, I cast my gaze around until I found Chief Beckett standing unobtrusively against the wall, one hand pressing against his earpiece as he spoke into a discreet communications mic pinned to his lapel. His pale blue eyes locked with mine, and he gave me a curt, reassuring nod. A tall, dark-skinned alpha stood nearby, arms crossed. His black tuxedo jacket barely managed to contain the bulging muscle of his massive biceps as he watched over the scene impassively.

The other two members of our security team would be nearby as well, keeping an eye on events. My spine relaxed incrementally, the animal terror of the past couple of minutes fading to manageable levels.

"God in heaven," Kam muttered, like someone who'd narrowly escaped being run over by a bus.

"Hush," I told him, leading him toward Fouchet and the other dignitaries as though nothing at all were wrong. The secretary looked up from his conversation and smiled.

"Luca," I greeted warmly. "I don't believe you've met my attaché, Kameron Patel..."

The rest of the evening passed like dripping molasses, until I began to think it would never be over. We managed to dodge Nikolayev successfully for most of it—omega self-protective instincts coming to the fore. When his presence was unavoidable, there were at least other people present to react to his complaints about the proposed negotiations with greater or lesser degrees of sympathy, deflecting some of that unbearable intensity away from us.

When the party began to break up around eleven p.m., I was more than happy to settle into the middle of a protective phalanx formed by Chief Beckett and our three alpha guards, with Kam at my side—sheltered from the outside world.

Beckett cleared his throat as we entered the elevator that would take us from the ballroom to our suites on the hotel's top floor.

"Madam Ambassador, I'd like to do one more sweep of both of your rooms before you retire."

I glanced at him, surprised. "Weren't they checked earlier?"

"They were," he confirmed. "I'd like to check them again."

"Very well, if you think that's best," I agreed, after only the slightest of hesitations.

Rhys Beckett was one of the most respected security experts in the business, with decades of experience under his belt. This trip was the first time he'd been assigned to us, but if he and his team of alpha underlings wanted to double-check our rooms, they probably had a good reason to do so.

Subjugated alphas had become slightly more common in security roles within the UFNA in recent years, since the expansion of an experimental military program that allowed them to access more specialized training in a carefully controlled environment. And, of course, every unit containing alphas still required oversight by a trusted beta team leader.

Beckett had volunteered to lead such a unit, whereas most betas would have resisted the assignment. Rather than trying to out-alpha the alphas under his command—a task that would have been laughable, given his mild voice, unprepossessing physical frame, and affable demeanor—he seemed almost paternal with them much of the time. I wondered what they really thought of him... these alphas who'd traded their virility for this limited form of freedom.

It was dangerous to think about the alphas, though. Even though they'd been chemically castrated, allegedly to make them more *tractable*, they presented a temptation I didn't need. I didn't even know their names, and I intended to keep it that way. Simply being trapped in an elevator with them like this was nearly overwhelming, with my upcoming heat only days away.

In addition to the dark-skinned giant, there was a sandy-haired male who was all sharp cheekbones and sinewy muscles, along with a statuesque female who moved like some kind of stalking jungle cat.

All three of them smelled *divine*... and that was a perfect example of the kind of thought I couldn't afford to indulge. Beside me, I could practically sense Kam going soft and doe-eyed. I resisted the urge to mash his foot with my stiletto heel, knowing there was no way to make the move anything other than obvious to our stoic protectors.

Deflection was needed—or perhaps distraction, in Kam's case.

"What makes you think our rooms might be compromised?" I asked Beckett. "Should we be worried?"

He gave me a thin smile. "No, I don't believe there's cause for concern. It's merely a matter of logistics. Normally I would have stationed a guard in the hallway to ensure no one entered your rooms while you were absent. However, with Nikolayev and his retinue attending the function downstairs, it seemed more prudent to have the extra manpower stationed in the ballroom — especially given the current political climate in the region."

I nodded in understanding. "Ah. Right. So the rooms weren't watched, meaning someone could have snuck in and planted a listening device while we were at the party."

"Exactly," Beckett confirmed. "Best to be sure."

The elevator dinged, opening onto the lavishly appointed fifth floor. Not all of the summit attendees were staying here, but the Fairbanks administration had spared no expense to ensure that Kam and I would not be forced to commute across Bucharest to a different hotel on the night of the pre-summit soirée. It was yet another manifestation of the unlikely career success we'd carved out, against all odds. Sometimes, I still had to pinch myself.

'Tall, Dark, and Overpowering' stepped into the hallway first, looking in both directions as though he expected assassins to leap out at us wielding AR-15s. The other two alphas fanned out behind him, and Beckett ushered Kam and me out with an economical gesture of one hand.

Kam fished our keycards out of an inner pocket and handed me mine.

Our rooms were next to each other, but didn't share an interior door. I'd noted that fact when we'd first checked in. Now, I mourned it. After facing down a man who would happily see both of us dead if he knew our secrets, I had no desire whatsoever to spend the night alone. I doubted Kam did either.

Over the years, we'd carefully cultivated the impression of a discreet but still mildly scandalous extracurricular affair. Despite the whiff of unprofessionalism, given that Kam was my attaché, it was occasionally useful to portray the picture of a *normal beta relationship* to the outside world.

It wasn't normal, and we weren't betas, but it still helped to deflect suspicion.

However, this wasn't the time or the place to be seen sneaking in and out of each other's rooms during the night. We opened our adjacent doors, sharing a glance.

Beckett's eyes flicked to his female alpha underling. "Alex, take Flynn and check Room 508. Jax and I will take 506."

So much for not knowing their names.

The no-longer-nameless *Alex* gave a brisk nod and disappeared into Kam's room with the dark-skinned alpha—Flynn. Kam tagged along behind them like a love-struck puppy, and I suppressed a sigh. Beckett and the sandy-haired alpha, Jax, entered my room. I followed, staking out a corner away from any lights or electrical outlets, where I wouldn't be in their way.

The space was light and airy, with a huge glass patio door leading onto a balcony. I hated it. Everything about it made me feel exposed and on display, from the walls painted sky-blue to the glow of city streetlights visible through the sheer curtains.

I wanted a nest and I couldn't have one, because having a nest might expose me for what I really was.

The knowledge itched at my insides. Even in my own apartment back in Montreal, it was too dangerous to do anything permanent with the decor that might scream *'omega'* to an observer. I was an ambassador. I entertained. The idea of some random beta bureaucrat stumbling across a dim, red-lit room full of pillows and furs piled on the floor didn't bear thinking about.

I could picture the screaming headlines now—
*'High-Level Unregistered Omega Outed in the Most
Idiotic Way Possible! News at Eleven!'*

So instead, I huddled in the corner of this
horrible, open, sky-colored room and watched the
familiar dance of a security team sweeping for bugs.
So far, no security team assigned to me had ever
found one. To be honest, I was a bit curious at this
point to see what a bug actually looked like.

I crossed my arms and leaned back against the
ugly blue wall, impatient to get off my feet after a
night of dancing and standing around in heels.
Maybe I'd hide away in the bathroom and take a hot
bath with the lights off later, once the others had left.

Despite my best intentions, my eyes locked onto
the blond alpha like steel filings drawn to a magnet
as my thoughts drifted. That was the only reason I
saw his shoulders stiffen as he pulled the cover from
the electrical outlet next to the bed.

"Found one, Chief," he said, and straightened a
moment later with something grasped delicately
between his thumb and forefinger.

Beckett grunted acknowledgement, even as I
pushed away from the wall, shocked.

"Seriously?" I asked. "Can I see?"

The alpha—*Jax*—turned toward me as I
approached, palm extended so I could get a look at
what was resting in it. My first thought was that it
was tiny. The rectangular circuit board had a small
metal cylinder attached to one corner, the top of
which was made of a fine mesh, like a microphone.
That made sense, since that was exactly what it was.

"Wow," I said inadequately.

Beckett looked less than pleased. "Right. That's
unfortunate. Madam Ambassador, I would strongly
suggest moving to a different room rather than
relying on us to find every bug. There may well be

multiple devices hidden in here. For now, let's see if they've found anything next door."

We did, and found Kam watching wide-eyed as two painfully attractive alphas dismantled every electronic device in his room.

"We've turned up two so far," said the one called Alex. Her voice was low and smoky, with a Quebecois accent.

"There was one in the phone handset, and one in an electrical outlet," Flynn added.

Beckett gave them a curt nod. "Well done. These two are going to have to change rooms, and we'll definitely need eyes on the hallway tonight. We'll take guard duty in shifts."

Still somewhat in shock that anyone would go to the effort and risk of breaking into our rooms and planting listening devices, I didn't protest when Beckett asked us to stay here in Kam's room with his alphas while he went down to the lobby to sort out new accommodations for us. He pocketed the three devices the others had uncovered, presumably to use as leverage in case the hotel manager balked.

"Just don't talk about anything you wouldn't want to be overheard," he said dryly.

Jax snorted in poorly veiled amusement.

Except for that single noise of dry humor, the alpha security guards were the picture of stoic professionalism after their team leader left. Kam stood awkwardly next to the TV, arms crossed, trying not to look anywhere that might get him into trouble. I crossed the room and sat in the desk chair, wishing I could toe off my heels without it coming across as too familiar. The idea of being barefoot beneath the alphas' impassive eyes twisted something deep inside me—not entirely unpleasantly.

I quashed the sensation ruthlessly.

The silence was becoming unbearable when Beckett finally returned with a harried-looking hotel employee in tow.

"I'm so terribly sorry about this, Madam Ambassador," the man said in heavily accented English. "I can only apologize on the hotel's behalf. We will, of course, make available all security camera footage from the hallways during the time in question."

"Thank you," I said coolly, rising to my aching feet. "For now, though, what we really need are new rooms. Preferably ones *without* secret listening devices installed."

The man winced. "Yes. About that..."

I raised an eyebrow.

He cleared his throat. "You must understand, with the summit..."

"They're booked solid," Beckett said.

"We do have a double available, thanks to a last-minute cancellation," the hotel employee added quickly, a hopeful tone entering his voice. "I understand it is not ideal, but there are two queen-sized beds, and the view from that side of the building is lovely..."

Beckett gave me a questioning look, since chivalry dictated that a beta woman would be the one to decide whether she wanted to share a room with a beta man who wasn't either a relative or her husband.

I had to swallow back the groan of relief that threatened to escape, burying it beneath a cool facade of indifference. "I imagine we can make it work for one night. Kameron? Are you all right with that?"

"As long as you don't snore, I'll make due," he quipped. "But you should be aware that I hog the bathroom."

The employee nodded enthusiastically, with the air of a man who knew he'd dodged a professional bullet. "Excellent. I'll have someone sent up to move your luggage right away."

I exchanged a final glance with Kam, and went to pack up my toiletries. Twenty minutes later we were installed in a different but equally awful room, designed by someone who apparently thought glass was a reasonable substitute for a wall.

Though the bathroom was quite nice, at least.

Beckett insisted on a sweep of this room as well, but it came up clean. When we were settled, he reminded us that someone would have eyes on the room throughout the night, and that the motorcade would be leaving at seven the next morning. As soon as the security team left, taking their distracting scents of musk, cypress, and sandalwood with them, I slumped onto one of the beds and flopped backward onto the mattress, toeing off my heels, my arms spread wide. Kam perched on the edge next to me.

"I'm still shaking," he said, quietly enough not to reach alpha ears in the hallway outside.

"Yeah," I agreed.

"We must be insane."

I nodded, not lifting my head. "Yeah."

Silence stretched between us, comfortable in its familiarity.

"The rooms in this place are terrible," Kam said at length.

"The worst," I concurred. "I feel like a butterfly pinned in a glass case."

"Do you think, if we're quiet...?" he began, before trailing off.

I knew exactly what he was asking. It was a risk—but this close to my heat, my judgment was apparently becoming suspect. Mostly, though, I needed a decent night's sleep before wading into battle with Nikolayev and his Committee tomorrow.

22

"All right," I said. "We can hang the do-not-disturb sign, and there's a swing latch on the door. We'll have to put everything back well before dawn, though."

"I know," he said. His hand closed around my thigh and squeezed lightly. "Dibs on the bathroom."

"Diva," I told him, without any real heat.

He rose and crossed to the door, opening it just enough to hang the DND notice on the doorknob outside. With that accomplished, he shut it and swung the bar-latch closed for extra security. Together, we dragged a mattress off one of the beds. Being careful not to knock anything over or otherwise make noise, we jammed it into the gap between the two bed frames, where it formed a squashed U-shape on the floor. While he went to take a shower, I pulled the woefully inadequate curtains closed across the offending wall of glass, and gathered all of the available pillows and blankets together.

When it was my turn in the bathroom, I peeled off my velvet evening gown and hung it up carefully. After removing my makeup and brushing out my waist-length red hair, I stepped into the shower, turning my face into the warm spray. I emerged some time later, blow-dried, plaited, and wearing a thigh-length silky nightgown.

In my absence, Kam had finished constructing our makeshift nest by stretching one of the blankets over the gap between the beds, weighting the edges with our suitcases to form a tent-like covering. A single lamp cast a pool of soft yellow light in the darkness of the room. With a heartfelt moan of relief, I lifted the front edge of the hanging blanket far enough that I could crawl inside and wriggle into Kam's arms inside the soft, womblike space.

THREE

Leona

WE SQUIRMED around until we were both comfortable—arms and legs tangled together, pillows jammed around us to stand in for the bodies of other nonexistent packmates. The U-shaped sag of the mattress kept us pressed close, and the blanket overhead reduced the glare from the single lamp to a soft, diffuse glow.

The smell was wrong—laundry detergent and furniture spray rather than *us*. Between my weekly dose of pheromone suppressors, and... what had been done to Kam when he was young, the nest wouldn't take on our scent no matter how long we huddled here. But aside from that, everything else was as close to being *right* as it ever got for people like us.

I burrowed my nose into the place where Kam's neck met his shoulder, taking comfort in the act of scenting him even if there was, in reality, nothing to scent. He gave a tiny shiver, and a heartbeat later, all the tension drained out of him at once. He pressed his cheek against my hair, and the breath flowed out of his lungs in a slow exhale.

"Needed this," he murmured.

Me, too, I thought—but that was another dangerous thing to think.

"Just for a few hours, though," I whispered against his skin. He nodded silently, and I pressed my lips to the skin over his mating gland in apology.

A tremor ran through his body in response, gooseflesh rising in its wake. One of my thighs was pressed between his, and I felt his vestigial omega cock twitch through the thin cotton pajama bottoms he was wearing. Despite the black market testosterone injections he took to stimulate beard growth and make building muscle easier, I knew that it wouldn't harden any further than that.

Kam and I shared every intimacy, and in safer surroundings than this, we gave each other what pleasure we could, when the desire arose. But biology limited us in a number of ways. It wasn't 'sex' in the way that betas defined sex. It wasn't 'mating' in the way that alphas and omegas experienced mating.

It was just… *us*.

Keeping the dark at bay.

Not being totally alone in the night.

"Leo," Kam said, still in a tone so quiet that not even alpha hearing would be able to hear it through the muffling blanket and the hotel room wall. "I am absolutely terrified for you. You shouldn't even be here. Not so close to…"

He trailed off, unwilling to say the word aloud in a building filled with betas, even though none of them would be able to hear. And wasn't that the perfect metaphor for what omega life had become? Here we were, huddled together in a nest that would be more than sufficient cause to have us both hauled off for physical examination and genetic testing if we were caught, yet Kam couldn't bring himself to say *'so close to your heat.'*

"I've got my meds with me," I reminded him, not for the first time. The bottle of aspirin in my suitcase contained five pills that were visually indistinguishable from all of the others—but an omega's nose could sniff them out easily enough. Four were pheromone suppressors that, taken weekly, would keep me from perfuming for up to a month. This, despite the fact that we were only slated to be here for six days before returning to Montreal. The fifth pill was my heat blocker, which I would take three days from now to head off the estrus that would otherwise be on me within the week.

Kam's arms tightened around me. "They're not meds, Leo. They're *poison*."

A lump grew in my throat, but I swallowed it down. "They're tools, Kam. Tools with side effects, yes. But what else am I supposed to do? Drown myself in *Chanel No. 5*? Take a week's vacation every three months like clockwork? How long do you think *that* would fly before someone noticed?"

Kam made a miserable noise against my hair, and shimmied down until he was the one burying his face in the crook of my neck. "I *know*," he said, disconsolate. "But I'm still allowed to hate it, all right?"

"Yes—all right," I soothed, rubbing my fingers through the fine hair at the nape of his neck. I'd always loved his hair—so thick and black, but fine as silk beneath my touch. "I concede that you're allowed to hate it. Could we just... not talk about it right now, though?"

I didn't need Kam to remind me that the toxic cocktail of drugs I required to hide condemned me to some form of cancer in my future—it was a fear that hung over my head in my waking present, and each time I popped one of the pills that were both my salvation and my ultimate demise. And when that day arrived, any attempt to get medical treatment for that cancer would instantly out me as an omega.

I could either live now and die later, or suffer through a half-life of slavery and die anyway, eventually. I'd gone into this with my eyes wide open.

Besides, I'd ridden out one heat cycle on my own—my first one. And I *never* wanted to do that again. Suffering through that days-long, desperately painful craving for sex and closeness when those cravings could never be fulfilled? It was a form of torture—both physical and mental.

Once upon a time, omegas had looked forward to their heats as a time for unparalleled sensual pleasure, the potential for pups, and possible bonding with one or more mates. But that was not my life.

"I'm sorry," Kam said, still holding me tight. "I didn't mean to upset you. I know you've got it under control. You're the strongest person I know."

Then you must not have looked in a mirror lately, I wanted to say. The words stuck in my throat. I couldn't get them out, and he wouldn't have wanted to hear them anyway. I took blockers to short-circuit my heats. Kam, on the other hand, would never have heats at all. And I knew with utter certainty that if he hadn't been mutilated as an adolescent, he would have cheerfully risked exposure and arrest to experience that part of an omega's life as it was meant to be experienced. He would have sought out alphas, no matter the danger... or in the absence of that option, at least a trustworthy beta male. He would have made beautiful pups one day, and whelped them in secret. He would have been the best, most loving and devoted carrier any pup could ever ask for.

"I'm the one who's sorry," I said. "Being here with you like this—it should be perfect, and I'm ruining it."

Kam let out a dissenting noise, and burrowed into me a little further. "You're not ruining it, *odama*," he said, using the ancient word for a co-omega in a mated pack. A pause, and then he added in a teasing tone, "Though it would be even nicer with some alphas to help warm the nest. Three of them, I think. That sounds about right, doesn't it?"

Dangerous, warned the little voice in my head that kept me safe. *Don't go there, even in fantasy.*

Would it really kill me not to be a repressive bitch one hundred percent of the time, though? I might be too scared to go there, but Kam wasn't. Kam still believed in a world where happy endings were possible. Did I seriously want to shoot him down when it came to his harmless daydreams, as well?

I swallowed my misgivings and reached for something, anything that wasn't fatalistic pessimism.

"I'm pretty sure we'd need a bigger nest," I managed, and was rewarded with the pleased curve of his lips against the skin of my throat.

"Oh, yes," he agreed. "We'd need a *huge* nest." A happy sigh. "Just think—all of those lovely muscles. And that female—Alex? Did you *see* the way she moved?"

I couldn't help it—an answering smile tugged at my lips. "Kam. I love you, but you're a terrible clit-slut. You do know that, right?"

He scoffed. "*Excuse you.* I am an equal opportunity slut, at least inside my fantasy world. But yes, that is one clit I'd *definitely* like to tease out of its sheath with my tongue, and ride all night long…"

I settled into the snug nest of pillows and blankets and *friend*, letting Kam narrate all of his increasingly filthy imaginings regarding the trio of alphas assigned to keep us safe in this faraway land. And if some of those fantasies made me squirm against his body a tiny bit, I put it down to my approaching heat.

Nothing more.

By four a.m., we had the nest dismantled and everything returned to its rightful place in the room. Thanks to the happy endorphins still sloshing around in my system, I even managed to get another ninety minutes of sleep before my alarm went off.

By seven, we were settling into the black limo that would take us from Bucharest to the much smaller city of Târgoviște, nestled at the base of the Southern Carpathian Mountains. The summit would take place at an ancient monastery in the foothills. It was, in my opinion, a somewhat odd choice of venue. As far as I'd been able to determine, the place's main claim to fame was that Vlad the Impaler's father was buried in the narthex of the monastery's church. Which was... historically interesting, I supposed?

It was probably meant to be symbolic of the resurgence of the Church in Eastern Europe over the past couple of decades. Or... something. If nothing else, the architecture was apparently well regarded by people who were interested in such things — not that there was likely to be much time or spare energy for playing tourist during the summit.

The motorcade pulled out of the hotel's grand circular drive and into the bustle of the city. Kam and I were in the middle car, with Jax riding shotgun in the front seat, next to a driver I didn't know. The other two alphas, Alex and Flynn, were in the lead car, while Beckett was in the one bringing up the rear, along with some additional support staff from the Foreign Office.

I gazed through the tinted bulletproof window, idly watching the city slide by as I attempted to center myself in preparation for what promised to be a grueling few days of negotiations. Romania's capital was an attractive muddle of old and new, but it was mostly the old that dominated. Even some of the relatively new landmarks, like the massive Palace of the Parliament, had been built to evoke a sense of times past.

It took almost an hour to negotiate the morning traffic and reach the outskirts of the city. For a while, cropland dominated. Before long, however, the landscape turned into parched and dusty scrubland. Even here in Europe, the twenty-year drought had driven agriculture down into the river valleys, where reliable irrigation was simpler to engineer.

Through the front window, I could just begin to make out the Carpathians, shrouded by morning haze. Mountains always made me think of home — not Montreal, but rather, the tiny town in Colorado where I'd been born. Not that the place was really *home* these days — my beta parents lived far away from there, having taken on new identities and moved to the Caribbean, where the Committee held less sway.

They'd had to uproot their lives to protect themselves because *I* existed. In fact, I'd insisted on it, once my career in the diplomatic corps started to take off. They'd given me a chance at a respectable beta life — but the moment my cover was blown, theirs would have been blown, too. They had aided and abetted an unregistered omega throwback, rather than handing me over to the authorities and washing their hands of me as soon as they'd discovered my true sex.

Now, whenever my house of cards inevitably came tumbling down, an investigation would find that both of my parents had been tragically killed in a car crash six years ago. Mr. and Mrs. McCready were no more, and meanwhile, an unremarkable expat couple was living quietly in Jamaica. The guilt of placing them in that position was ever-present in the background of my thoughts, but it was nothing to the guilt I would have felt if they'd come under the magnifying glass of the Committee.

I focused once more on the here-and-now, aware that my mind was wandering—another symptom of approaching heat, though one that I could control well enough as long as I paid attention. Our surroundings out here were downright bleak. It had been more than fifteen minutes since I'd seen a car pass in the other direction. There were likely to be other motorcades using this route, though many of the delegates would have left Bucharest last night and stayed in Târgovişte to avoid the early morning commute.

The car in front of us—the one with Flynn and Alex—slowed.

"What the hell's this?" Jax muttered from the front seat. His hand delved beneath his jacket at the height one might expect to find a shoulder holster, and my pulse quickened. Beside me, Kam straightened in his seat. The driver muttered something in Romanian, slowing as well.

I craned forward, trying to see, and got a confused impression of several off-road vehicles parked some distance away from the roadway ahead of us, nestled among the brownish scrub. Before I could draw breath to ask what was going on, a massive noise deafened me, and the limo went tumbling sideways like a child's toy beneath the force of a fiery explosion.

FOUR

Leona

THE SEATBELT dug into my chest and shoulder, squeezing the breath from my lungs as the car rolled. Metal shrieked around me. The side of my head slammed into the window, my skull predictably proving softer than the bulletproof glass. Pain exploded from the site of impact, my awareness fading to a distant sensation of everything moving around me as my arms and legs lolled, beyond my control.

My vision flared white, then dark. My hearing dulled to a liquid *shush-shush, shush-shush* in time with my heartbeat. When my senses cleared enough to make some kind of sense of my surroundings, I was hanging upside down. Something warm dripped from my temple.

"Leo! *Leo!*" A voice was calling my name from somewhere very close by. I thought maybe it had been calling for a while, and it seemed odd that I hadn't noticed it sooner. Sharp sounds came from somewhere farther away — *rat-a-tat-tat... rat-a-tat-tat.* The combination was loud enough to echo through my aching head and make my ears ring unpleasantly.

A grunt of effort came from next to me, and I turned in time to see a dark shape fall free, landing with a pained yelp on the floor — *roof?* — of the battered metal and glass cage.

The last few minutes gradually reassembled into something that made sense... though my head felt like an overfilled water balloon as gravity dragged too much blood into it. We were in a limo, headed to Târgovişte. The car had flipped over. The noise outside was gunfire. The shape next to me was...

"Kam?" It emerged as a bare rasp.

"*Leo,*" Kam gasped.

Hands tugged at the belt holding me suspended upside down, fighting with the release mechanism to no avail. I blinked, trying to bring my surroundings into focus, but the shapes no longer made sense. Where the driver should have been sitting, there was just twisted metal. I blinked, nauseated by the odd delay between my eyes moving and the change of perspective registering in my brain.

The front passenger side door had been sheared away, leaving it open to the outside. The seat was still there, and a burly form hung from it, upside down as I was. The alpha security guard—Jax, my brain helpfully supplied—groaned and coughed. At least he was still alive. Red liquid dripped from his side, landing on the inside of the limo's roof in a steady *plop, plop, plop.*

"We've got to get you free," Kam said tightly. "Leo, damn it—please *say* something!"

"*Ow,*" I managed faintly, not able to get enough breath past the constriction of the jammed seatbelt for more.

In the front seat, Jax groaned again, the sound trailing off to a low rumble of discontent. His hands scrabbled weakly at his own chest, with no real coordination. Outside, the skull-rattling sound of automatic weapons fire subsided. I could hear car engines pulling up. It sounded like they were right next to us.

"Oh, god," Kam whispered.

Car doors slammed. Voices filtered through the gaps where parts of the car had been ripped away, but I couldn't understand what was being said. The words made no sense. It was a foreign language, but not Romanian. Turkish, maybe?

I blinked stupidly, still hanging from the seat like a landed fish. The muzzle of a gun entered through the missing passenger door, pointed directly at Jax's face.

"Don't shoot," Kam said. "Please. They're injured."

It was the same calm voice he'd been using when I'd returned from dancing at the party last night to find Kostya Nikolayev looming over him—the one that meant he was barely holding it together.

The gunman used the muzzle of the pistol to nudge Jax's cheek roughly. The alpha moaned, but did not stir otherwise. The man withdrew, and a loud, fast-paced conversation ensued. Within seconds, the limo rocked beneath us as hands tugged and yanked at the mostly intact backseat door on Kam's side until it creaked open on protesting hinges.

Kam immediately lifted his hands in surrender, placing his body in front of mine. "They're injured," he said again, and then repeated the words in French. Two men dragged him out through the half-open door. As he disappeared from my field of view, a spike of fear finally managed to penetrate the woolen blanket of shock smothering my emotions.

In the front of the limo, a man sawed away at the seatbelt restraining Jax's body, until he finally fell free with a thump. Another slid into the back seat and started doing the same thing to my seatbelt. I made out several people pulling the alpha out of the car, clearly struggling with his muscular bulk. Then my belt gave way and I tumbled down, the sudden jolt of hitting the roof too much for my wavering consciousness to deal with.

Darkness claimed me, even as a rough hand closed around my ankle and started to drag me out of the door.

The next time I woke, there was a heavy bag tied over my head, and whatever hard surface I was sprawled on was jouncing and jolting. I could hear engine noise, and that sparked a vague memory of off-road vehicles.

Panic slithered through my guts, but a familiar smooth-skinned hand was tangled with mine.

Kam.

I squeezed his fingers, and heard him catch his breath before he squeezed back convulsively. A moment later, the vehicle hit a massive bump. My stomach dipped, and awareness fled once more.

Consciousness came in fits and starts after that. Kam was always there, the clammy sweat of fear slicking our skin where his hand clasped mine. Eventually, the darkness grew complete as my mind apparently gave up the fight for a bit. When I came to, the bag and the engine noise were gone. The hard surface beneath me no longer swayed and bounced.

The air was faintly chilly, damp with humidity and the smell of stone. Kam's fingers were no longer tangled with mine, and that was enough to send me struggling upright, trying to blink my vision into focus despite the sharp, throbbing ache in my temple.

"She's awake." The hoarse voice came from somewhere off to my left. It sounded vaguely familiar, but I couldn't place it.

Footsteps scuffled, and someone crouched next to me, a hand coming to rest on my shoulder. "*Leo.*"

I relaxed. "Kam. Where…?" The rest of the words caught in my dry throat, making me cough.

"Don't try to talk yet," he said softly. "Stay put for a minute—I'll get you some water."

I tried to take in my surroundings as he pushed up from the floor and crossed to the other side of the dimly lit space. Three of the walls appeared to be natural rock, and the floor was packed dirt. The fourth wall looked like plaster... or maybe concrete? It had a heavy-looking metal door set in the middle. A small, barred opening at head height let in the only light—the harsh sodium-yellow glow of a light bulb hanging from the ceiling outside.

Another figure sat slumped against the far wall. Gradually, my omega eyesight sharpened, adjusting to the dimness, and I recognized our alpha escort, Jax. His gaze met mine, impossibly blue, but dulled by a sheen of pain and weakness.

Kam returned, crouching beside me with a bucket and a ladle. I tried to look him over, but he was backlit from the light in the hallway.

"Are you hurt?" I rasped. Everything was hazy, but I had a vague memory of a spectacular car wreck.

"I'm fine," he said. "Just sore and bruised. Drink this, but don't blame me if you get dysentery or something in a few days."

At this point, I would have drunk muddy ditch water if it meant getting some moisture back in my mouth and throat. I steadied the ladle he lifted for me and sipped, covering a grimace. This... might have *been* muddy ditch water, actually. It was stale tasting and unappealingly lukewarm. I swallowed carefully until the desperate edge disappeared from my thirst.

"Where are we?" I asked. My eyes wandered back to the alpha in the room, and I frowned. "Jax? That's your name, right? You're injured. How badly?"

A bunch of half-formed thoughts and memories buzzed around my head like angry flies. I had a feeling that when they finally swarmed me, it would be… *bad*.

"I took metal shrapnel from the limo in my left arm and side, Madam Ambassador," Jax said. "It will be all right once I can dig it out and get the bleeding stopped. Alphas are hard to kill."

"I'll try to help you with that as soon as I make sure Leo's okay," Kam said.

It was matter-of-fact. Jax seemed to accept it, even though he had no way of knowing the horrors that Kam had seen as a youth in the omega breeding pens. All he would see was a pretty, soft-spoken and slightly effeminate beta diplomatic attaché.

"Thank you," said the alpha. "And although you've got no reason to think all that highly of us after what happened this morning, you should both know that no one will hurt either of you while I'm still breathing. The others will come and extract us as soon as they can."

The buzzing memories settled into place. I'd been right — it was bad.

I swallowed convulsively, and focused on pulling my shit together. "Right. I'm sure they will." *If they're even still alive*, I didn't add. Clearing my throat, I continued, "Don't be in such a hurry to throw your life away in the meantime, though. Getting yourself killed won't do anything to keep us safe."

Jax clenched his jaw stubbornly, but he didn't correct me. He had to know I was right, after all.

"My pack will come for us," he repeated, rather than contradicting me.

"Do we know who the kidnappers are, or what they're after?" Kam asked. He tilted my head toward the inadequate light coming from the hallway, and peeled my eyelids back one at a time, staring at the pupils.

"Same size, I hope?" I asked dryly, well aware of the protocol for suspected concussion.

"As far as I can tell," he said.

"They were speaking Turkish earlier," Jax mused. "Separatists, maybe."

"I'm pretty sure at least some of them understand French," Kam said. "Do you speak Turkish?"

"Only a few phrases," Jax replied. "Mostly curse words and insults, if I'm being honest."

"If they speak French, we can communicate if we need to," I told him. "Assuming they decide to listen to us, of course."

"I wouldn't get my hopes up on that front, ma'am," Jax said.

Unfortunately, I suspected he was right about that.

"Do we have any idea where we physically are?" I asked. "This place is underground—I can tell that much."

"I'm afraid I was unconscious during transport," Jax said stiffly, sounding like he blamed himself for not magically overcoming his injuries sooner.

"I wasn't," Kam said. "They tied bags over our heads, so I've got no idea on direction, but this is a cave system in the mountains—possibly a retrofitted mine. It has to be in the Southern Carpathians, I'm pretty sure. The drive only lasted an hour or two."

"Paved roads?" Jax asked. "Or dirt?"

"No roads, at least for a good chunk of it," Kam told him. "Bad roads for the rest. I'm sorry—I couldn't tell if they were paved or not, but there were lots of potholes."

Jax nodded, shifting in place against the rocky wall, only to flinch as he aggravated his wounds. His ambergris and cypress scent soured, and my omega hindbrain helpfully poured stress hormones into my system in response. I tamped down the urge to stumble upright on shaky legs and go try to comfort him.

"Kam," I said instead. "I'm okay. Go help Jax get patched up as best you can, all right?"

I had no doubt Kam was fighting the same urges I was, when it came to the magnetic male sitting on the other side of the cell. He nodded and gave my shoulder a reassuring squeeze before rising stiffly to his feet and heading over to join our resident injured alpha.

"Can you stand?" he asked. "The best light will be right by the door, and we'll need to get a proper look at the situation. It might be better to leave the shrapnel alone if pulling it out would cause too much additional bleeding."

Jax grunted and levered himself upright. Kam helped him out of his torn and filthy suit jacket, easing it off his injured arm. The white button-down shirt followed. It was stained red, and so was the white undershirt beneath it. He'd lost quite a bit of blood—but, as he'd said himself, alphas were hard to kill.

I clung to that knowledge and tore my eyes away when he reached back with his good hand, grasping the torn undershirt and pulling it over his head in a single, smooth movement. Injured or no, a shirtless, muscular alpha was not something I needed to see right now. Not so close to—

My mind blanked out in a moment of perfect, crystal-clear denial.

Not so close to my heat.

Oh, god. My heat was only days away, and I was trapped in a cell with an unfamiliar alpha, at the mercy of kidnappers who might want us as hostages, or for ransom money, or…

Trapped. I was *trapped.*

In a cell.

With my heat coming on.

Cold sweat broke out across my entire body, my heartbeat thundering into triple time. My head pounded in counterpoint to my galloping pulse as sudden panic gripped me. Jax turned to look at me, a frown creasing his sharply chiseled features as though he'd heard my breathing pick up and my heart thumping against my ribcage like a trapped animal.

And… of *course* he'd heard it. He was an alpha, and the cell wasn't that large. Kam looked up from his examination of the bloody tear in Jax's side, following the alpha's gaze to me. Something must have shown in my expression. I'd probably gone pale as a sheet, all the blood draining from my face.

"Leona?" he asked, worry sharpening his tone. "What is it? What's wrong?"

FIVE

Leona

"MY LUGGAGE," I said stupidly. "Is our luggage here?"

Understanding flooded Kam's features, followed by horror. He hid both reactions under a poker face within seconds.

"No," Jax said blankly. "I... don't think our luggage was really top of mind for the terrorists who planted an I.E.D. and snatched us from a diplomatic motorcade on a public highway. Why? I take it there was something important in your suitcase?"

I opened my mouth and paused, stuck for a reply.

Kam looked between us and promptly rescued me. "She... takes medication. For a chronic condition."

"What kind of condition?" Jax asked, because apparently we were going to have this conversation with me staring at his bare chest and the jagged hunk of metal protruding from his sluggishly bleeding side.

"It's personal," I replied weakly. "I don't like to talk about it."

Mainly because talking about it could get me killed, I thought.

"It'll be fine for a few days," Kam said, the tension in his shoulders belying his calm tone. "I'm sure the cavalry will show up before it becomes an issue."

I forced down my panic, grabbing the lifeline he'd just thrown. "Yes," I agreed. "Sorry. It'll be fine. Don't mind me. How bad is that?" I added by way of deflection, gesturing to the ugly wound in Jax's side.

The alpha craned to look at it.

"Better out than in, probably," he said, and reached around with his uninjured arm as though he was going to yank the piece of metal out of his side with no further discussion.

Kam batted his hand away. "Let me. And give me that undershirt—we'll use it to keep pressure on the wound until the bleeding stops."

"You know, that old 'better out than in' thing refers to alcohol," I said weakly. "Not shrapnel."

Jax glanced over at me, his brow furrowing. "Same principal, isn't it?"

"Ugh. *Alphas*," Kam muttered, and tugged the metal free.

The alpha in question didn't even flinch. Kam tossed the piece of shrapnel into the corner, where it bounced against the rocky wall with a light clink before falling to the dirt floor. He pressed the balled-up undershirt against the wound, which was oozing blood but not spurting.

My eyes slid away. Unlike Kam, I'd led a remarkably sheltered life for an omega. I'd always passed as beta... never had to endure the ugliness of subjugated life directly. Before today, the most blood I'd ever seen outside of a movie screen was a bleeding finger after a kitchen knife accident.

My fellow omega had directed his erstwhile patient to keep pressure on the first wound while he twisted Jax's other arm into the weak light, peering at his bulging bicep.

"If the other piece is still in there, it's buried too deep to do anything about," he said.

"It's still in there," Jax said. "But don't worry about it."

"At least it's small," Kam offered.

"Yeah," Jax agreed. "It'll be fine. I can still fight if I have to."

"Nobody's fighting anyone," I said, trying to channel authority into my tone. "We'll talk to them. Negotiate. Find out what they want and try to come to some sort of understanding. I am supposed to be a diplomat, after all."

"The others will find us soon." Jax spoke the words as though they were an unbreakable maxim, and I didn't try to argue.

"Sure," I said. "Until then, we just need to keep it nice and low-key, all right? Let Kam and me do the talking. Everything will be fine."

I wasn't sure who I was trying to reassure—me, Kam, or the injured alpha who seemed to be psyching himself up for a one-sided kamikaze battle against armed terrorists.

<hr>

As it happened, there were no more opportunities for diplomatic discussion than there were for physical fights. Time was difficult to track beneath the unchanging light from the single bulb in the corridor outside, but based on my hunger and the hours I'd slept, I was pretty sure a full day passed before the lock on the door clanked.

It swung open just far enough to reveal a beta man holding an AR-15 pointed at Jax's head. Kam and I froze. Jax just glared at him, unblinking and unimpressed. The man shifted to make enough space for another of our kidnappers to drop a fresh bucket of water inside the door, followed a moment later by a tray.

"Let me talk to you for a moment," I said in French. "Can you understand me?"

The men withdrew and the door slammed shut.

I sighed. "You try next time, Kam."

"Sure," he said listlessly. "I'll give it a shot."

Jax went and wordlessly retrieved the tray of food—bread and dried brown strips of something. Jerky, maybe. My empty stomach churned with nervous worry, but I ate my portion anyway, washing it down with some of the stale water.

The situation was maddening, and it was all I could do to contain my growing panic. We were in a cell perhaps fifteen feet by twenty feet. It was bare, except for a latrine pit. A rough wooden box sat over it, with a hole cut from the top for use as a seat. We had a single threadbare blanket to share between us. Jax had waved it off when I tried to give it to him several hours earlier, so Kam and I had wrapped up in it to sleep when exhaustion overcame us.

My head still ached, though it was getting better quickly. *Too* quickly. I knew I would need to play up the injury for at least another few days, to cover the fact that my pre-heat omega hormones were supercharging the healing process. I'd been knocked unconscious. A beta wouldn't have bounced back from this kind of head wound so easily. I could only hope the grime on my face would distract from the speed at which the bruise was fading.

Jax had fared quite a bit worse than I had in the crash. The shrapnel wound in his side had stopped bleeding after a couple of hours, but the left half of his face was bruised badly enough that even alpha healing would take some time. More worrying, the other piece of shrapnel was still buried in his arm, too deep to pull out without some kind of tweezers or forceps. Infection was almost a certainty—and while Jax hadn't been lying when he said alphas were hard to kill, that didn't mean *impossible* to kill.

Despite his quiet confidence that rescue would be on its way soon, the hours dragged on with no sign of anything going on outside of our little prison, for either good or ill.

The worst part of it was, I desperately needed some kind of a contingency plan, and yet I couldn't say a single word about my heat. Without Jax's presence, Kam and I might at least have tried to brainstorm some kind of damage control. With him here, I didn't dare speak about it, except in the vaguest possible terms regarding my 'lost medication.'

I needed pills that I didn't have. There was no way to get them. If enough time passed without them, it would be *bad*. None of this was helpful in the least. And indeed, as the clock ticked inevitably toward my oncoming heat, rescue still might not be enough to avert my own personal disaster.

One didn't simply run down to the local pharmacy to buy heat suppressors. Getting them without being caught was a complicated and expensive process. If the cavalry showed up and pulled us out of here an hour from now, I still wouldn't be able to get them in time unless my luggage had miraculously survived the crash and someone thought to bring it along during the rescue operation.

My only possible hope would be to disappear into some remote bolthole, where I could hide myself away before I started perfuming. Because once I did, it would advertise my omega-in-heat status to every single person in my vicinity who had a nose.

I *desperately* didn't want to have to ride out a heat cycle alone. And it was probably moot, anyway—I didn't have a clue how I could find a safe hideout in an unfamiliar country during the aftermath of a terrorist kidnapping. Even after we were rescued, I'd be under constant watch. Medical checks. Debriefing. Round the clock guards. There was no way I'd be able to hide what was going on.

Time ticked on, inexorable. I marked it by my companions' periods of sleep… by the guards' infrequent deliveries of bad food and stale water.

By the slow slide of my body toward disaster.

Days passed. The guards wouldn't talk to any of us, in any of the languages we knew. In desperation, I even had Jax curse at them in halting Turkish.

Nothing.

Dark smudges of worry and exhaustion were growing beneath Kam's eyes. He knew exactly what was at stake…exactly how few options I had left. I was certain that the time when I would normally have taken the heat blocker had come and gone, as the hours and days marched slowly by. My pheromone suppressors would be giving up the fight within the next twenty-four hours, at most. And… what then?

Unless Jax succumbed to some kind of blood infection bad enough to render him unconscious, he would figure out what was happening immediately. I knew almost nothing about him beyond the obvious. He was subjugated. Chemically castrated—so at least if someone raped me, it would be our beta captors and not him. He seemed like a pleasant and respectful enough individual—now, at least. But alphas had a reputation. Yes, it was a stereotype… but with the sheltered beta life I'd led, I didn't know enough alphas personally to know how much of that stereotype was bounded in truth.

In fact—sad as it was—my interaction with Jax, Flynn, and Alex was the closest contact I'd ever knowingly had with alphas. Maybe there had been others hiding in plain sight like Kam and I were. If so, they'd been doing a good enough job that I'd been none the wiser.

It hardly mattered, though. Whether or not Jax turned into a caveman at the first whiff of my pheromones, once the guards came in to find me writing on the floor and flooding the cell with heat-scent, it would all be over. They would either kill me—with or without including some combination of torture and gang rape first—or they'd try to use me as some kind of leverage against my government. And I had little doubt the UFNA would cheerfully hand me over to the Committee for trial and execution as an unregistered omega, if it came down to it. Otherwise, the scandal would rock the parliamentary government to its core.

I was pacing, scratching absently at my forearms with my fingernails. I wanted to disappear into the dirt floor... to climb the stone walls and hide in a crevice like a rat. I needed to get away. I needed to be somewhere else. *Anywhere* else.

"Madam Ambassador," Jax said, his manner still perfectly formal and proper despite several days spent huddled on a bare dirt floor nursing untreated wounds. "I know there's something you two aren't telling me, and I think it's time you did. Is it to do with your medical condition, or is there something else?"

Kam's shoulders hunched a little tighter, and he ran a nervous hand through his dark hair. I was spared having to come up with an answer by the sound of the lock on the cell door releasing. Irrational desperation drove me toward it as it opened. I rushed at the two familiar guards, heedless of the semi-automatic rifle in my face. In my peripheral vision, I was dimly aware of Jax hauling himself to his feet... of Kam gasping my name in warning.

"Please," I begged the guards, forgetting to speak in French as my blood buzzed and itched in my veins. "Please, you have to let me out of here! I can't be in this cell—"

The one with the AR-15 used the barrel to shove me roughly backward. I stumbled and hit the ground in a sprawl. The impact jarred my brain loose of its heat-daze in the same instant Jax growled and gathered himself to lunge.

"*No!*" I cried, as the rifle swung around to cover the enraged alpha. "*Shit!* Jax, stand *down!*"

Jax clenched his fists at his sides in frustration, but he planted his feet and did not charge.

"Just… sit down, Jax. Please." Kam spoke in his calmest voice. His body language was open and appeasing—the kind of posture every omega knew how to employ instinctively from early childhood. He switched to French, keeping the same even tone as he spoke to the guards. "We're calm now. There's no need for violence."

"Violence is how we make change." The new voice came from the open doorway, speaking awkward, heavily accented English.

He strode in, unfamiliar, but dressed in the same mix of local clothing style and military surplus gear as the guards. His air of command was obvious.

"Please," I told him. "We need to talk to you. We can come to some kind of arrangement…"

He ignored me, and tossed a battered notebook on the ground in front of us.

"You and you." He pointed first at Kam, then at me. "Learn this speech. Tomorrow we make video."

"If you want money, our government will pay," I tried desperately, knowing it was a lie. Knowing I was throwing away every ounce of dignity I had left by even saying the words. What must Kam think of me right now? What must Jax think?

The leader ignored me. "Learn speech, or we torture you."

He turned and left without a backward glance. The others followed him, the gunman backing out cautiously, with his eyes fixed on Jax the whole time. The door slammed shut. They hadn't left us food or water.

I curled forward, burying my face in my hands.

"What's in the notebook?" Jax asked. "This is bad, but the details might give us a better idea of *how* bad."

I let my hands fall to my lap. Kam must have realized I was too far gone to manage even such a simple action. He slipped past me and picked up the notebook, taking it to the door to make use of the limited light. I watched listlessly as he flipped through the pages from front to back, my skin feeling too tight and too hot.

He flipped back to the beginning and scanned the pages more slowly, his brows drawing together. When he was done, he swallowed and cleared his throat. "It's… uh…"

"Just read it," I said. "Don't try to sugarcoat things."

Kam swallowed again. "First we're supposed to say our names. Then, 'We have been taken prisoner by the glorious forces of the Beta Liberation Front, and will be executed for our government's crimes against beta supremacy.'" My heart sank. "'Even now,'" Kam continued, "'right-thinking beta scientists are perfecting a weapon that will eliminate the alphomic threat once and for all. When it is ready, the whole world will know.' And then there's some BS about how wonderful the terrorists are and how we totally decided to support their cause despite the fact that they're going to cut our heads off."

It was all I could do not to break down weeping on the spot. I could barely think, the entire situation was already poised to go down in flames the moment Jax caught a whiff of my oncoming heat… and now we also had to come up with a way to keep from getting executed, while somehow preventing a terror organization from producing a weapon of mass destruction for use against our people.

50

It was impossible. It *could not be done*, and all thanks to a vicious joke of biology.

This disaster was going to be my fault. My responsibility.

"I can't do this," I murmured, barely audible. "Oh, god — Kam. I'm *so sorry*. I can't stop this."

Our eyes met. He heard the words I wasn't saying, and the same agony shone in his eyes as was doubtless shining in mine.

"Let's not panic," Jax said after an awkward moment — and abrupt, incandescent anger flooded me in all its irrational, hormonal glory.

"We're going to die," I ground out, biting the words off one by one. "A lot of other people are *going to die*. And where the hell is your team? Your *pack*, that was supposed to magically appear and rescue us?"

"*Leo*," Kam warned.

"They'll come," Jax said with a perfect, serene complacency that only fueled my anger. "I have faith in them. But in the meantime, let me take a look at that notebook, Mr. Patel."

Kam handed it over, while my impotent, unreasonable anger twisted around to point firmly inward. I *hated* this. I hated the knowledge that I was losing control of my mind, my emotions… my body. My clothing felt like it was made of nettles. Clammy sweat was breaking out across my back. I was about to plunge into what would be the worst, most horrific day of my tragically short life, and I'd be dragging the others along for the ride before we all died.

My sex began to throb and ache with emptiness. Any moment now, I'd start to manufacture slick. I choked down a moan and crawled to the section of wall where the lone blanket in the cell lay in a crumpled heap, wrapping it around myself to form a pathetic, threadbare cocoon. Kam closed his eyes and bowed his head. Jax shot me a sharp look of concern before visibly recalling himself to the notebook. The faint scent of honey and orange blossom rose around me, and I pulled the blanket tighter.

"There's nothing else written in the book," Jax was saying. "The light's not really good enough to see if there are indentations from writing on other pages that might have been torn out, but…"

He trailed off, nostrils flaring as he scented the air. An instant later, the alpha's eyes landed on me like a physical weight. My entire body tightened. Black market pheromone suppressors gave up the ghost beneath the onslaught, as my scent glands pumped out perfume in fragrant clouds.

My heat had begun.

SIX

Leona

"YOU'RE..." JAX BEGAN, his eyes losing focus as he breathed in deeply. "You're an..."

Kam moved in front of me, blocking my view of the alpha on the far side of the cell. "She's a UFNA ambassador, and you're part of her security team."

He was trying to sound confident. Commanding. To my ears, he mostly just sounded terrified.

"How in the *hell* did you manage to make it to a posting this high?" Jax asked, obviously bewildered.

"By being very good at her job," Kam snapped.

I peered around Kam's legs, succumbing to a deep-seated need to keep the alpha in my line of sight. Blue eyes locked with mine, and he took a step toward us, as though drawn by a string. Kam jerked a hand up — arm straight, palm out. He squared his shoulders, trying to make himself seem bigger.

"No. Stop right there. Take a step back."

Kam put on a good show, but I knew him well enough to hear the faint tremor behind his words. A thread of rational thought pierced the haze of fever and emptiness smothering me. My sweet and gentle omega packmate was planning to stand between me and an alpha who could break him in half like a twig.

"Kam, don't," I begged.

The alpha across from us was breathing heavily, his scent thickening in response to mine. I had to think... I had to push past my body's growing neediness. Every nerve thrummed, attuned to the figure on the other side of the cell. His dark, woodsy aroma flooded my senses, threatening to drown me.

But there was something...

Something important...

"Jax," Kam said carefully. "You can't help her, regardless. Even if she wanted it, you're not in a position to—"

"Yes, I am." The alpha's voice had deepened to a basso rumble. "Step aside. Let her speak for herself."

Subjugated. That was what Kam was trying to say... what my muddled brain had been reaching for. Subjugated alphas were chemically castrated.

Kam shot me a worried look over his shoulder. He must have seen some shred of coherence still in my gaze, because he reluctantly moved a step to the side. Jax stood before me, solid and strong and overwhelmingly *alpha*. My entire body clenched, the muscles of my aching passage cramping painfully. I curled around the agonizing emptiness, still holding eye contact.

The person behind those blue eyes and that irresistible scent was a stranger. And I was a thirty-one-year-old omega virgin who—thanks to years of using heat blockers—had experienced exactly *one* natural heat cycle before now. I was trapped in a cell and facing execution. The thought of his touch—when I would be too weak to resist and too mindless with need to communicate with him—terrified me.

I held his gaze despite my trembling muscles, fighting the urge that made me want to crawl to him on my hands and knees and lick my way up his body an inch at a time.

"Don't touch me," I choked out. "*I do not give you permission.*"

Blue eyes burned. My vision narrowed until they were all I could focus on. After a moment, the alpha firmed his jaw and nodded.

"I understand," he said. "This is going to be a really bad twenty-four hours, Madam Ambassador — but I'll do everything in my power to protect both of you when the guards return in the morning."

A tiny thread of relief cut through my clamoring nerves. I knew I was also supposed to be worrying about tomorrow, but the threat of execution was already growing distant and unimportant compared to the storm raging inside my body.

"*Thank you*," Kam murmured in abject relief, and I didn't think he was only talking about the promise of protection.

"We're still looking at a deeply unpleasant night for everyone involved," Jax said.

"Followed by one hell of an unpleasant day," Kam agreed. "Probably a fatal one. We know. I mean it, though. Thank you."

Jax visibly fought his instincts, and forced himself to step back and reclaim his seat against the far wall. He slid down and rested his forearms on his raised knees.

"Alphas aren't animals," he said. "Despite what you may have heard."

Kam cautiously settled down next to me. "I didn't mean to imply you were. I apologize if it came across that way."

I tried to draw comfort from my packmate's familiar presence at my side, but my body didn't want another omega right now. He kept a careful inch of space between us, and I wasn't sure if his touch would help me or make everything a hundred times worse. Miserably, I huddled deeper into the blanket and shuddered, trying and failing not to shoot darting glances toward the person my body really craved.

Jax looked back at me frankly. "Please tell me you've at least ridden out heats before. Do you understand what you're in for?"

"Yes," I snapped, knowing it was a lie. Being trapped in a confined space with an alpha changed everything—and things had been bad enough the first time, almost fifteen years previously, when I'd had to ride it out on my own. This? This was a whole new level of misery.

"All right," he said, accepting it.

"Leo," Kam said softly. "Do you want me closer? Or should I give you space?"

I don't know, I thought, more than a little desperately. *I want this not to be happening.*

"Just… stay where you are, please?" I managed in a shaking voice. "For now, anyway."

"Okay," he said. "I'll be right here." With a deep breath—one that did nothing to ease the tension rolling off his body in waves—he turned back to Jax. "What about you? Have *you* ridden out an omega's heat before?"

"Oh, yeah," Jax said. "Way too many times. I was a breeder for years in the slave pens. Sometimes the omegas were still too weak from their last litters when the plantation owners threw them back into the whelping rotation. Getting pupped again before they were recovered from their last litter could be fatal, so we'd sit out the heat and get through it as best we could."

"I didn't realize you came from the plantations," Kam replied. "Didn't the overseers punish you for defying them like that?"

Jax gave a humorless laugh. "I imagine it was a bit of a catch-22 from their perspective. Fertility rates plummet if an omega doesn't have privacy and a sense of safety during heat. That privacy gave us enough freedom to wriggle out of breeding when it would have been too dangerous. Mostly, I think the fact that it helped keep the overall mortality rates lower meant they let it slide."

Kam had almost ended up in those same breeding pens, I thought distantly. *If he hadn't been too stubborn... too intractable. If his owners hadn't decided to sterilize him and throw him into the slave auctions instead —*

My lower abdomen cramped again, and I swallowed a moan. I pictured the pups he might have produced... how beautiful they would have been. Unlike him, I'd never wanted to carry. I lacked his innate optimism for the future. How could I justify bringing new lives into a world as broken as ours?

Now, though, my body didn't care about the future, and I hated it for the way it craved breeding, craved pregnancy — craved all the things *that I didn't want, damn it.*

"Sometimes walking can help with the cramps," Jax offered. "For a while, anyway."

I couldn't seem to rally words to reply, and I didn't think my knees would hold me, so I only shook my head and buried my face in the stinking blanket. At least it distracted me from the smell of cypress and ambergris, even if it couldn't block my own sickly-sweet perfume.

There was nothing to do except try to tough it out.

———◆———

I lasted maybe an hour, at most.

"Please," I sobbed, writhing in Kam's arms. I was on fire. Any minute now, it would consume me whole. "I was wrong. I lied! Please, alpha — I need your knot. It hurts! I'm so empty, I can't..."

Jax groaned — a low noise that ricocheted through my body like a shot, raising gooseflesh in its wake. I leaned toward that rough sound of desire, my nipples hardening into painful points.

"Leona," Kam said. "Try to hold on. Just a little longer, all right?"

He'd wrapped me up against his body when I'd first started crying—still cocooned in the ratty blanket. As I'd feared, his touch was both better and worse than no touch at all.

"Alpha, *please*," I begged.

"Heat blockers," Jax muttered. "Damn it."

The words made no sense. I didn't *want* his words. I wanted his *knot*.

"What about them?" Kam asked, still keeping me trapped against him.

"She uses them?" Jax asked. "Well, she'd have to, I guess."

"Obviously," Kam said, a bit sharply. I whimpered in distress, and he shushed me, immediately contrite.

Jax met my eyes. "Madam Ambassador. *Leona*. Heat blockers make your rebound heat stronger."

Kam caught his breath. "She's been on them for years."

Another sob of frustration escaped me. They kept *talking* and *talking*, when all I needed was a knot to fill up the empty void inside me that was sucking me inside out like a black hole. I felt like I was burning, all the moisture in my body boiling itself away in the form of sweat and slick.

"This isn't going to work." Jax dragged a hand over his face. It was shaking. "Her temperature could spike high enough to do permanent damage. We need to do something different."

There was a pause, and Kam's voice sounded horribly uncertain when he spoke. "Were you telling the truth before, about being able to help her? Aren't you on the alpha drug regimen?"

"I was telling the truth, yes—but that's not what I meant." Jax sounded like he was barely holding it together, and I thought maybe, if I could just get my arms and legs free of the damned blanket so I could present for him...? "I've got no problem with an omega changing their mind and stopping a mating during their heat," he went on. "But when a *'no'* becomes a *'yes'* during a cycle this intense, it's not a real *'yes.'* Also, there's the matter of contraceptives. If she's using blockers, I'm guessing she's not on them — and while these aren't great conditions for getting pupped, it's still a possibility."

The words flowed over me without sticking. I couldn't follow the meaning of the exchange, but Kam flinched hard against me.

"No," he said, the whisper barely audible. "No, she's not." I felt him swallow hard. "This could kill her, couldn't it."

Another pause. "It's possible. I know tomorrow's going to bring its own set of problems. But that doesn't mean I want to take that kind of chance tonight."

"Then... what?" Kam demanded. "What exactly are you suggesting?"

The alpha sighed. "She needs a knot. So, the question is, exactly how close are you two?"

SEVEN

Kameron

I BLINKED AT the hulking alpha seated across the room from us. Leo squirmed in my arms, restless and feverish. She was smearing slick against my dress slacks, one of her thighs splayed across my lap.

"I'm… pretty sure I don't have the equipment to do that particular job," I said blankly, my mind shying away from thinking about the scarred wreck that had once been my omegan reproductive system.

"That's not an answer," Jax pointed out, with more patience than I would have expected from an alpha stuck in a cell with an omega in heat, and a perceived male beta who was barely keeping his shit together. "You knew her secret. You were ready to stand up to an alpha twice your size to protect her. Are you together?"

"It's complicated," I said, still feeling like there was a two-second disconnect between my brain and my mouth.

"Here and now, it's really not," Jax shot back, a hint of an alpha bark creeping into his tone. "Have you been intimate with each other, yes or no?"

My spine snapped straight beneath that tone. I had to resist the instinct to roll my head to the side and look away, baring my throat.

"Yes," I hissed. "Which doesn't change the fact that I can't help her with this. I can't get hard, all right? If I could fix this for her, *don't you think I already would have?*"

I could feel the defensive claws coming out, and I cursed myself when Leo whimpered in my arms and began to cry again. I tried to swallow everything down—to project calm support rather than the clammy terror that was choking me like a noose.

"You have hands," Jax said flatly. "So you're going to provide the knot, and I'm going to stay over here and provide the pheromones. It's still not the kind of consent that an omega deserves, but at least it's not getting fucked by a stranger."

Or dying.

The words hung in the air, unspoken.

I fought to settle my churning stomach. After a moment, I managed to shove the fear down far enough to stroke Leo's sweaty hair away from her brow. The bruise on her temple from the car wreck had almost completely faded, I noticed distantly.

"*Odama,*" I whispered. "We're going to try to help you."

"Alpha, please," she whined, rutting mindlessly against my leg. "Need the alpha! Please, *please…*"

I was weeping silently, tears tracking down my cheeks. Fool that I was, I'd always pictured us going out in a blaze of glory when our secret finally came out—making some kind of noble, defiant speech to the television cameras as we were hauled away, swaying hearts and minds everywhere to our cause. Because, of course, that fantasy was so much more comforting than the reality where we were kidnapped by terrorists, and our captors showed up in the morning to find Leo writhing on the floor, begging for sex.

"Mr. Patel. She needs you to be strong right now, okay?"

I had no idea how Jax was keeping it together… how he was managing to speak in a way that made it clear he actually gave a shit about what the two of us were going through.

"Call me Kam," I told him unsteadily. "I think we entered first-name territory a while ago."

"Kam," he said, and in that instant I wanted nothing more than for the alpha to come over here and wrap both of us up in his strong arms, blocking out the world. I set the ridiculous desire aside forcefully.

"Sorry," I said. "You're right, of course. If you think it will work, that's what we need to do. She'll understand. I'm sure she will."

I tried to believe it.

"Sometimes," Jax said, "there are situations where you can only control a very small number of things. Right now, we can try to ease her heat before it endangers her health. We can't do anything about the rest of it at the moment. But we can do this."

"I hear you." I cleared my throat. "Leo, we're going to help you, okay?"

She whined again and mumbled something, but the words didn't make sense. At this point, approaching her first peak, it was apparent she'd lost the power of speech. Instead, she twisted and writhed, struggling to get free of my embrace.

"She's trying to turn over so she can present," Jax said calmly. "Let her go, Kam."

I let her go, my arms feeling empty the moment I did. Sure enough, Leo rolled onto all fours, panting softly as her back arched in an omega's instinctual lordosis. Presenting for sex to the alpha in the room... begging to be filled.

"When you say 'knot,'" I began uncertainly, because this was nothing the two of us had ever done before. There'd been no point in trying. Outside of heat and in the absence of alpha pheromones, penetration wouldn't be pleasurable in the least for her. For me, it wasn't even an option any more.

"Work as many fingers into her as will comfortably fit," Jax said bluntly. "That probably means either three or four. When I say so, and not before, curl them like you're making a fist and keep them like that." He paused. "I'm sincerely hoping that your nails are short."

"They are," I whispered.

The blanket had slipped from Leo's body to land on the dirt floor. She'd shed her suit jacket when the fever started, and her conservative blouse was partially unbuttoned, hanging off one shoulder after her repeated attempts to wriggle out of her clothing. The dove gray pencil skirt—streaked with filth and blood from the car wreck—had hitched up around her hips when she'd climbed half into my lap earlier. Her light green panties were soaked from the river of slick she'd been putting out for the last hour.

She was as beautiful as she always was, but I knew she wouldn't want to be seen like this. Not under these circumstances. My heart ached for her. Hell, my heart ached for both of us. I tossed the blanket over her back, draping it so it hid her lower body from view as I knelt behind her, silently cursing myself, the terrorists, and the world we'd been born into.

"Leo, I'm going to touch you now," I said. "Just my fingers, but Jax says it will feel like a knot. He's here, but he's going to stay a little distance away and lend you his pheromones, all right? I'm going to move your underwear out of the way. If you want me to stop, shake your head, or say no, or even just move away, and I will, I promise."

It was useless. Stupid. She couldn't understand me in her current condition. She wasn't going to resist my touch, because her body was flooded with industrial-strength heat hormones, and she *couldn't* resist. My words were only a salve to myself, not to her.

"You're a good friend to her," Jax said quietly, from his position across the cell.

"No," I replied, my voice shaking. "I'm really not."

I was a coward. Broken. But right now, my cowardice translated into an unbearable fear of losing her before it was absolutely unavoidable. If we were both going to die, then we were both going to die. It was the prospect of losing her and being left alone to face the monsters that truly chilled my blood. I wormed my right hand under the blanket and hooked Leo's panties down to her thighs. She immediately moaned and pushed her ass into the light touch.

"Listen to me, Leona," Jax said, in that low alpha rumble that pierced straight into the deepest part of an omega's soul. "You're doing so well. We're going to fill you up so good, little *odama*. We'll make all of this go away, and then you can rest for a bit."

I placed one hand on Leo's back to steady her and felt around blindly beneath the blanket with the other, following the trail of slick to its source. No sooner had I gotten lined up than Leo reared back, taking two fingers to the hilt with a keening cry. My throat closed up. She was hot and tight, her passage gripping me with the same rippling muscle that would help her squeeze out pups.

"That's it." Jax's encouragement was quiet. The rasp of a zipper reached my ears. "Sorry about this, by the way. It's the only way to sync our pheromones."

"No, I know," I told him. "It's fine."

It wasn't fine. My back was turned, but I could hear the sound of slapping flesh—the low, ragged sound of uneven breathing. Jax was going to bring himself off, timing his release to coincide with me attempting to trick Leo's body into believing she'd been knotted. His scent would change, and with luck that would trigger Leo's first peak to subside, giving her a respite from the torture of out-of-control hormones rushing around with nowhere to go. Of course, it would also leave Jax with his knot waving in the breeze, which was allegedly a miserable experience for an alpha.

Leo fucked herself shamelessly on my fingers, letting out a series of rhythmic, breathy cries. Her sultry-sweet natural perfume was changing... sharpening. I managed to add a third finger, and finally, a fourth, until that slick, velvety heat was enveloping my hand to the crook of my thumb every time she rocked back.

The sound of Jax's hand on his dick behind me sped up. His scent was changing, too, and I had to fight the urge to look over my shoulder and watch him. The two scents coated my tongue and tickled the back of my throat, making me feel faintly lightheaded. My own vestigial cock twitched, growing heavy and sensitive.

Just the pheromones, I told myself, squeezing my eyes shut and cursing omega biology for the hundredth time in the last hour.

"Get ready," Jax said, sounding decidedly strained.

He grunted, and Leo cried out.

"Now," he said hoarsely. "Do it now."

I bit the inside of my cheek and curled my fingers into a loose fist, wincing at the way Leo's body had to stretch to accommodate the movement. Her muscles clenched and pulsed rhythmically, her back going rigid beneath my other hand. The scent in the cell shifted again—honey and orange melding with musk and cypress to form something new. Something thoroughly intoxicating.

"That's it. Now stay like that until her muscles release you. See if you can ease her down to lie on her side so she can rest easier." Jax's tone sounded exhausted, and I was forcibly reminded of his injuries.

Already, Leo was going boneless. With supreme awkwardness, I managed to direct her sprawl so she was lying in front of me with her back to me, my clenched fingers still inside her. This, unfortunately, had the unintended consequence of putting Jax in my line of sight. He was seated against the rocky wall with one leg drawn up and the other stretched out in front of him, his hand clamped around the knot at the base of his very erect dick.

"Dignity is overrated," he told me, with a wry twist of the lips that couldn't really be called a smile. "That's what I always tell myself, anyway." Lines of strain had settled around the corners of his striking blue eyes.

I tore my gaze away from him in favor of checking on Leo.

"She's dozing," I reported. "Her skin's cooling off; she doesn't feel as feverish."

In my peripheral vision, I saw Jax nod.

"Keep the blanket over her," he said. "In less shit-tastic circumstances than this, she'd have one or more alphas sharing body heat with her while she recovered."

The picture those words conjured up felt like a knife between the ribs. *I'm pretty sure we'd need a bigger nest*, Leo had joked in the Bucharest hotel room, the night before everything had fallen apart. I shifted in place, trying not to jostle her. My skin still felt stretched too tight. My cock still throbbed, half-hard and oversensitive.

Jax watched me, and I had to fight not to squirm beneath his frank regard.

"Oh. You're an omega, too," he said, sounding thoughtful rather than surprised.

"What?" I yelped, my heart thundering into overdrive. *How—?*

Jax inhaled deeply, his nostrils flaring. "Your pheromone suppressor couldn't keep up—not surprising with another omega in heat in the same enclosed space. You smell like ginger tea with lemon."

"No, that's not—" I began, before cutting myself off and trying to regroup. "I don't take pheromone suppressors. I don't have any reason to!"

Leo made a discontented humming noise in her sleep, her body clenching tighter around my hand. I looked between her and the alpha in the room, caught out and entirely unsure *why*.

"No," Jax said. "I suppose you wouldn't, in the normal course of things. It's barely detectable, even now. You don't have to worry about the betas noticing. They won't." His expression grew troubled. "I guess they got you when you were young, huh? I'm so sorry, Kam. They're monsters. No one should have to go through that."

Twenty years of unaddressed trauma rose up to lodge itself firmly in my throat. I choked, unable to draw breath.

"Blast. I shouldn't have said anything," Jax murmured. "Damned heat-brain. I'm really sorry, Kameron. Just breathe for a minute, okay?"

"It's fine," I rasped, once I'd managed to drag air past the blockage in my chest. Even to my own ears, I sounded about as far from fine as it was possible to get.

"It's not," Jax said. "And neither are you… but that's okay." He was quiet for a moment before continuing. "You're lucky to have each other. Pack is important."

I looked down at Leo, her fiery mane of red hair draped in sweat-soaked tangles. "Yes," I agreed in a tiny voice. "It's everything."

We lapsed into silence.

Eventually, I cleared my throat. "That knot must ache like hell," I observed, forcing my tone into something a bit more normal.

"You aren't kidding," he agreed. "Though maybe not quite as much as you're hand's going to ache by the time she's done with you."

I couldn't dispute it. I'd already lost feeling in my fingers, and the muscles in my forearm were starting to cramp. More time passed, until finally the strong muscles clamped around my hand began to flutter, and finally eased. I cautiously uncurled my fingers and slid them out of Leo's body. She shifted restlessly at the loss, but didn't wake. Relieved, I wiped my hand on a corner of the blanket and shook it out, feeling the tingle of returning blood.

"You should get some rest while you can," Jax said. "She'll start climbing toward the next peak in a few hours. I'll keep watch until then."

Injured or not, he would be good to his word, I knew. Alphas were hardwired to guard omegas during heat, when they were at their most vulnerable. He'd crash afterward, of course, but until Leo's heat markers faded, Jax's body would consume fat and muscle to sustain a multi-day marathon of no sleep and frequent mating.

He was right, too. I should take advantage of what rest I could get. Feeling shaky—both with reaction to the immediate situation and to other, deeper things—I managed to scoot us both around until I was leaning against the wall with Leo's blanket-wrapped form curled up in my lap. She sighed and nuzzled into me, still smelling of clover honey and orange orchards.

It was so heartbreaking to think of the world depriving itself of the beauty of that scent, forcing her to cover it up to protect herself. I breathed it in deeply, trying to catch a hint of my own perfume intermingled with hers. *Ginger tea with lemon*, Jax had called it. I wasn't sure if I could actually smell it, or if it was mere wishful thinking on my part. Whatever the case, the world at large would never scent me.

That knowledge should have been a relief, since it meant my perfume wouldn't give me away.

It wasn't.

"I'm not really an omega," I blurted, the words bubbling up from the depths of my buried self-loathing. "They took it all away... ripped it out by the roots. I'm not... *anything*. Not anymore."

And after tomorrow, I would probably be dead. I wondered if they'd execute us on camera before sending the video to news outlets around the world. I wondered if anyone would mourn me.

"Kameron Patel. Look at me," Jax said, his tone turning steely. I did, instincts responding to that small flexing of alpha power. He lifted his hand to touch his forehead, his eyes holding mine. "If you're an omega here..." His hand moved to rest on his chest, over his heart. "If you're an omega here... then you're still an omega. No one can take that from you. Do you hear me? *No one.*"

My throat closed up again.

"You can be scarred and still be perfect," he went on, his tone solemn. "You can be injured and still be beautiful. And after seeing what you've both accomplished... seeing how you are with each other—you two are without a doubt the most beautiful omegas I've ever met."

My vision blurred as his words sank into me, settling into place. Unable to answer, I hid my face against Leo's hair and held her tight as my shoulders began to shake.

EIGHT

Leona

EVERYTHING HURT, and someone was crying into my hair. I felt like I was suffering the worst hangover I'd ever had, multiplied tenfold and paired with a vague, generalized sense of impending doom. I was curled in someone's arms—

Kam.

I was curled in *Kam's* arms, and it was his tears slowly soaking my scalp. "*Odama*," I croaked. Lifting uncoordinated hands, I pawed at him ineffectually—weak as a newborn kitten. His embrace tightened, holding onto me as though he feared I might disappear, but his chest only hitched harder beneath my cheek.

"It's all right, Little One." The basso alpha rumble came from some distance away, and my entire body twitched in unconscious reaction. "Just let him hold you. He tried to explain what was happening earlier, but I think you were too out of it to really understand."

"Understand what?" I rasped, still trying to soothe Kam with hands that didn't want to obey my brain's commands. Everything around me was hazy. Dreamlike. There was something important I should be thinking about, but try as I might, I couldn't grab hold of it.

"You've been taking heat blockers for a long time," said that reassuring alpha voice. "That's made this heat way stronger than it normally would be. Trying to tough it out could be medically dangerous for you. I'm lending you my pheromones, and Kam is lending you a hand... so to speak. We're going to need to do that again in a few hours—possibly sooner. It shouldn't be quite as bad this time, since we know not to leave it too long. Until then, you need to rest."

I wasn't at all sure of the meaning of his words. They seemed important, yet I couldn't seem to focus on them. Except for the last part, anyway. How was I supposed to rest when my packmate was upset?

"No," I protested. "*Kam...*"

He gave a harder shudder against me, and his body stiffened as though he were physically dragging his control together. I could smell the faintest whiff of something sharp and lemony rising from his skin, soured by the tang of grief and fear. I'd... never smelled his scent before. How was it possible that I'd never scented him until now?

His chest expanded with an unsteady breath.

"I'm all right, Leo," he whispered. Clearing his throat, he continued in a stronger tone. "Jax said something nice to me, that's all. You know I don't deal with things like that very well."

Again, I had the feeling that I was missing some deeper meaning. I tried once more to lift a hand to his cheek, only to miss and end up pawing at the side of his neck instead. "You're okay?"

He swallowed hard, his throat bobbing. "'Course I am." A slight pause, then, "Is it all right for me to touch you when you need it, since Jax can't?"

I blinked, not sure why the alpha couldn't touch me. He was nearby—I could smell his heavy, comforting scent. But as for the rest of it...

"You're my pack," I told him, and burrowed a bit closer against his body.

He curled around me. "I didn't hurt you, though?"

I tried to take stock, and decided I'd been right before. "*Everything* hurts," I said.

"That's because we left it too long," said the alpha.

Jax.

The alpha's name was Jax, and that should have been important, though I wasn't sure how, exactly.

"Mmph," I said against Kam's collarbone, my hazy thoughts growing cloudier.

"We won't make that mistake next time," Jax assured me. "The next peak won't be so bad."

Again, I wondered why he was staying so far away. It would be much nicer if he were over here, curled up next to Kam and me. Maybe then, Kam wouldn't cry anymore. The fuzzy gray clouds abruptly smothered me, and I slipped into a doze.

I came back to myself—after a fashion, at least—when the aching emptiness inside me yawned wide once more. I *wanted*. My wanting was an endless void that could only be filled by the alpha across the room.

I didn't understand why he wouldn't give me what I needed, no matter how much I begged and cried. Instead, Kam urged me onto my hands and knees as the fever grew, and something filled me that wasn't an alpha's cock. It wasn't what my body yearned for—but it was better than nothing. My pheromones swirled together with the alpha's, eventually triggering a shuddering release of the horrible tension. Again, that faint hint of gingery citrus wafted among the stronger scents choking the room.

Sleep came, followed by something that was almost like wakefulness, but not quite. The alpha said nice things to me in that reassuring, rumbly tone, while Kam held me and stroked my hair. It was pleasant. Time passed. The pattern repeated once more. Afterward, the arms holding me trembled with exhaustion, or maybe something else... something less to do with the physical.

Distantly, I wondered how long this would go on. Something about the thought triggered that same sense of impending doom I'd felt earlier—the one that had been hanging over me for some time now. I mewled, not able to summon words to express my fears.

"Rest, Leona," said the alpha, with a hint of command behind the words. "We'll worry about the next part when it comes."

My body knew what to do with an alpha command, at least. It went boneless, subsiding into sleep.

Some time later, unwelcome scents intruded into my little bubble, setting off alarm bells. *Betas*, my instincts screamed. *Not pack*. At the same instant, the alpha's pheromones spiked with protective aggression.

"Oh, no," Kam said quietly, a world of fear lurking behind the simple words.

The combined signals of *danger, danger* should have snapped me back into something approaching coherence, but I still couldn't seem to control my muscles properly. Adrenaline sloshed around my system with nowhere to go, though it at least expanded my bubble of awareness to encompass the rest of the room I was lying in.

Not a room. A cell.

Parts of the recent past managed to shoehorn their way into my heat-dazed consciousness. Jax had already lunged to his feet, his low growl rolling around the enclosed space as the lock on the heavy cell door clanked open. Kam settled me against the cave wall and knelt in front of me, also facing the door, his arms splayed out to cage my body behind his. He was shaking like a leaf in the wind.

The details were hazy in my memory, but I knew someone was coming for us. When they took us, bad things were going to happen—and I was helpless, barely able to control my own limbs. The door swung open on shrieking hinges, the sound scraping across my nerves like nails on a blackboard. The barrel of a familiar rifle entered first.

Excited voices cut through the air, speaking rapidly with words I couldn't decipher. I peered around Kam's body, my heart thudding. Jax growled again, taking a threatening step toward the guards. The rifle steadied, fixed on him. The other guard pointed a finger toward Kam and me, still talking rapidly. After a moment, both of the men withdrew, and the heavy lock clunked into place, securing the cell door.

"Jax," Kam said, once they'd gone. "Please talk to me. Are you thinking right now, or reacting? Because we're in serious trouble."

The alpha seemed to have grown six inches taller and broader in the space of thirty seconds. My short-circuiting body tingled with need, and if I'd had any kind of muscle control I probably would have stumbled over and tried to climb him like a tree despite the utter inappropriateness of the urge. Meanwhile, in the background, parts of my brain were frantically trying to reboot.

If you try to protect us, they'll just shoot you, I wanted to say, but the words were caught in my throat.

Jax made another low noise of anger. Rather than answer Kam's hesitant question, he turned and strode toward us, moving Kam aside with a gentle hand and scooping me up as though I weighed nothing. He carried me to the wall next to the door, and set me down. The door was designed to open inward, I realized distantly, and it would block me from the immediate view of anyone entering. When I was settled, he herded Kam to huddle next to me. Kam immediately wrapped an arm around my shoulders, holding tight.

Jax crossed the cell, still without a word, and attacked the wooden box that acted as the seat for the latrine, tearing at it with his bare hands. He came up a few moments later with a splintered length of board, wielding it like a club.

"They'll kill you," Kam whispered.

Jax didn't reply. Instead, he returned to the door and positioned himself on the other side from us, makeshift weapon held at the ready.

Heavy footsteps approached—more of them this time.

"Oh, god," Kam said, his fingers clutching the material of my battered blouse.

NINE

Kameron

THE DOOR OPENED again, but only a few inches. It wasn't enough space for Jax to wield his improvised club, or for him to force his way out of the cell. I held Leo close against my side, painfully aware that we had no chance of resisting if the guards got past Jax.

A slender gun barrel poked through the gap—different than the chunky semi-automatic rifle that had greeted us on previous visits. Before I could brace for the inevitable heartbreak to come, the barrel jerked. The retort was strangely quiet, like the sound of a small-caliber pistol with a silencer fitted. Rather than falling down with blood spurting from a gunshot wound, Jax only flinched.

He remained standing, but his hand flew convulsively to his chest, where a fletched dart hung from one bulging pectoral muscle. With a roar, he ripped it free and threw it to the side. Faster than I could follow, he reached out and grabbed the tranquilizer gun, using it to yank the bearer into the door with an ugly clang of flesh against metal.

Dragging the gunman with him, he snarled and staggered through the gap, disappearing into the corridor beyond. I resisted the urge to squeeze my eyes shut as shouts and thumps echoed against the cave walls.

Weak fingers tangled in the material of my shirt.

"Kam," Leo slurred. "Don' resist when they come for me. Let th'm take me. They don' know you're omega. Jus' me."

My stomach churned. She wanted me to hand her over to them...to throw her under the bus in some doomed attempt to save myself.

"Stay here, odama." I removed her hand from my shirt and darted across the cell in search of another usable length of board. The pickings weren't great, but I grabbed a piece that would extend my reach a bit, with the added bonus of a couple of nails sticking out of one end.

Outside, the shouting had subsided in favor of the thumping. I knew better than to hope that meant Jax was winning. They'd tranqed him. As soon as the drugs took him down, we were toast. I hid behind the open door, holding the sad piece of wood like a cricket bat. They might slam the thing open on their way in and squash me against the wall like a bug — but at least they wouldn't see me right away. It was the only chance we had.

The fight in the hallway went ominously quiet. Boots tramped toward the door.

"Kam," Leo said desperately. "*Let them take me.*"

Answering her would have given away my position. Not that there were, y'know, too many places to hide inside this bare cell. For the second time in my life, I stood motionless, barely breathing... convinced I was about to die. The footsteps reached the half-open doorway.

I held my breath, waiting. An instant later — with perfect irony — the heavy door rammed into me beneath the force of a heavy shove, sending me staggering even as I tried to dodge out of the way. I tripped over Leo's legs and hit the ground hard. A boot in the ribs drove the remaining air from my lungs, and gray splotches erupted in my vision.

As though underwater, I heard the men exchange another round of rapid-fire Turkish. I tried to roll over and crawl toward them as two of them hefted Leo up by the arms and dragged her away.

Uselessly, I patted the packed dirt in search of my pathetic piece of broken wood. Aside from the gasp she'd let out when I stumbled over her body on my ignominious way to the ground, Leo was utterly silent as they hauled her from the cell. I wasn't sure if that was better or worse than if she'd been screaming.

The door slammed unceremoniously shut while I was still scrabbling toward it on my hands and knees. I staggered to my feet and half-fell against it, my palms slapping the unyielding metal.

The lock clicked with a terrible sense of finality.

My knees gave up on the job of holding me upright, and I crumpled to the floor, my fingernails scraping against the door on the way down. I stared at the rusty metal with unseeing eyes, a horrible sense of numbness washing over me like frigid, brackish water.

My companions were gone, dragged off to face who-knew-what unimaginable horrors. I had failed them… and now I was alone.

⁂

Somehow, I managed to crawl a few feet away, where I at least wouldn't get slammed by the door again, the next time it opened. I had no illusions that our captors had forgotten about me. As a perceived beta weakling who posed no threat, I had simply become a lower priority than an omega in heat.

I remembered this heavy numbness all too well, although I wished I didn't. The feeling of being caged alone, knowing in the depths of my gut that everyone I cared about was either dead or facing the kind of unimaginable torture that only angry betas could devise.

Committee sympathizers had come for my family in Kolkata when I was twelve. We were purebreds—an ancient family line that had been influential in the Bengal region's silk trade since the fifteen hundreds. For centuries, we'd managed to avoid the cyclical tensions between betas and the old, alphomic bloodlines. Strategic bribery... political influence... even disappearing underground for a generation or two, on occasion—these were the things that had allowed my family to endure. To flourish, even.

Perhaps that long history of overcoming the odds had made us complacent. When the end came, I'd still been a pup to all intents and purposes. Naive, trusting, and far too pretty for my own good. In the months leading up to the pogrom, I'd overheard the adults talking in solemn whispers from time to time, but when the vigilantes arrived with guns and shackles, I hadn't truly understood what was about to happen.

The adults had been rounded up and taken to the courtyard. Two men in black, military-style fatigues had held my littermates and me at gunpoint in the grand hall of the old house. I still remembered the sound of gunfire outside; remembered thinking that it must be fireworks, even though it was daylight and there was no festival.

After the courtyard fell silent, a third man came in and checked us over, one by one, verifying our sex. My three alpha brothers and sisters were taken away. I never saw them again. I learned later that alphas were in low demand for the slave trade at the time, since a single alpha could impregnate many omegas. Of my family, I was the only one with enough potential economic value to make my life worth keeping.

They collared me and dragged me to a truck with a cage in the back. I watched my family home disappear into the distance with almost exactly the same dead feeling that was currently crushing my lungs beneath its weight.

How much time had passed since Leo and Jax had been taken? I wasn't sure. I thought it had only been fifteen minutes or so, but it was entirely possible that my fugue state had distorted my perception of time.

What sort of things could be done to an unconscious alpha and a heat-dazed omega in the space of fifteen minutes? My gorge rose uncontrollably. I staggered onto shaky legs and barely made it to the uncovered latrine hole before losing my stomach contents. Heaving made my bruised ribs feel like they were about to crack in two, but I welcomed the pain. I deserved far worse for not having protected my vulnerable packmate when she needed me.

Muffled gunfire reached me through the walls. My heart stuttered and skipped. I fell back, landing on my ass. Denial raged through me, burning away the comforting numbness.

"No," I whispered... but there was no one left to hear it.

There was... *no one left.*

The gunfire came again—the *rat-a-tat-tat* of a fully automatic rifle answered by the slower retorts of something semi-automatic. I caught my breath, trying to make sense of the sounds. It would only have taken two bullets to finish Leo and Jax. Unless Jax had woken up from the tranquilizer... maybe grabbed a weapon and started fighting back?

But try as I could, I wasn't able to make the scenario fit what I was hearing. He'd been down for the count. Even if he'd regained consciousness, he would have been sluggish and uncoordinated from the drugs.

The weapons fire stopped. I sat frozen on the ground next to the shit pit, the astringent taste of bile coating my throat and tongue.

"*Clear!*" called a distant voice, speaking English.

"*Clear!*" came a different voice, closer this time.

The shuffle of boots moving fast—but with an attempt at stealth—approached my cell door. A face appeared in the small, barred window, silhouetted from behind by the light bulb hanging in the corridor. I still sat unmoving, in plain view. My mouth was hanging open.

"*Target Two located!*" snapped a low, female voice.

A few moments later, the lock clicked and the door swung open. Three figures in dark military garb and balaclavas swarmed into the cell, fanning out to cover every corner of the small space with their weapons. My vision blurred double, images of the day my family was massacred overlaid with images of the present. I still couldn't move—all of my muscles were locked solid with tension.

Cell secured, two of the figures lowered their weapons.

"Shit," said the tallest one. "You can smell that, right?"

The female—the female *alpha*—who'd first peered into the cell gave a sharp nod of confirmation. Then she turned on her heel without a word and went to guard the entrance, weapon held at the ready. Meanwhile, the much shorter and slighter figure on the left lifted his free hand and peeled back his balaclava. I blinked as Rhys Beckett, the beta head of our security team, ran an assessing gaze over me. An ugly, half-healed cut decorated his cheekbone. His expression grew noticeably tight around the eyes as he took in the scene.

"Well," he said, sounding resigned. "This just got a lot more complicated than I'd bargained for."

TEN

Flynn

THE SMELL OF a terrified omega in heat clung to the interior of the cell, making my dick hard at the same time it roused my protective instincts. Beckett wasn't kidding about this mess being a hundred times more complicated than we'd bargained for.

"There are two scents here," Alex threw over her shoulder. "Besides Jax, I mean."

Thoughts of exactly how I'd torture anyone who'd hurt or killed Jax swirled through my head, but I set them aside. I took another breath, letting the fear-tainted perfume in the air settle over the back of my tongue. Alex was right. Not a surprise, since Alex was *always* right about things. That was why she led our pack, after all.

I let my AK-47 drop to hang from its shoulder sling and crossed to Mr. Patel. He didn't look so good. His face was gray and pasty beneath his olive skin, and the sour smell of fresh vomit wafted from the hole in the ground next to him. In that same corner of the cell, someone had torn apart something made of wood. My money was on Jax, trying to arm himself for a fight.

I reached a hand down and hooked Mr. Patel's upper arm, pulling him to his feet. He staggered, half-falling against me, and I took the chance to grab a whiff of the skin at the juncture of his neck and shoulder. He shivered in reaction as I set him back on his feet.

"Omega," I confirmed. "Faint, though."

Beckett shot me a glance. "Flynn, please don't sniff the ambassadorial staff during a rescue mission."

I shrugged. "How else are we supposed to know for sure, boss?"

A haunted look had drawn Mr. Patel's pretty features into haggard lines. That bare hint of lemony perfume told me most of what I needed to know about him. If he'd been on pheromone suppressors that had worn off during his captivity, his perfume would have been at full strength. He must have been one of the ones the betas had caught and mutilated rather than use for breeding. We'd probably only been able to scent him at all because he'd been trapped in a cell with another omega in heat for days on end.

Part of me was impressed, in a distant and detached sort of way. If both he and Ambassador McCready had been hiding in plain sight all this time, they'd done a hell of a good job of it.

"Please," Mr. Patel rasped. "Please… the others. You have to help them."

He was pleading with me directly—not with Beckett. I wondered if he thought we were going to arrest him on the spot for being an unregistered omega. To be fair, that's probably what most people would expect us to do. Or, at least, what they would expect *Beckett* to do.

"That *is* why we're here, Mr. Patel," Beckett said mildly. "To start with, I need you to tell me everything you know. The others' survival could depend on you being completely forthright with me."

Patel blanched further, as though he'd taken Beckett's statement as a thinly veiled threat.

"He didn't mean it that way," I explained. "He just wants you to tell us what happened."

Terrified brown eyes met mine, and that unwanted protective instinct flared. Again, I set it aside. I could see him struggling with himself, every emotion visible on his face. He must have better self-control than this in the normal course of things, I thought, or he would have been found out years ago.

Whatever the case, I saw the moment he decided; saw his last defenses fall. His chin dropped in submission as his eyes slid closed.

"Leona and I are both unregistered omegas," he said hoarsely. "I was sterilized young, but she's still whole. She's been getting by on heat blockers and suppressors. They were hidden in her luggage when we were attacked. She went into heat last night. Jax and I did our best to help her, but she'll be peaking again soon."

"Do you know where she and Jax are being held?" Beckett asked.

Patel shook his head. "Guards tranquilized Jax and dragged both of them away a short time ago."

"How long exactly?" Beckett asked.

Patel squeezed the bridge of his nose with shaking fingers. "I can't be sure. Maybe half an hour?"

Beckett gave a curt nod and motioned for him to continue.

"Yesterday—before Leo's heat came on—they gave us a script to memorize for a video." He glanced around and pointed at a battered notebook lying next to the far wall. "Afterward, they were going to execute us."

I retrieved the notebook and handed it to Beckett, who flipped it open and scanned the contents rapidly. His gaze sharpened.

"What's this about *'a weapon that will eliminate the alphomic threat once and for all'*?" he demanded. "Did they say anything else about this?"

Patel shook his head. "They've barely talked to us. The one who brought us the speech spoke a bit of English. We think they've mostly been speaking Turkish. But you need to go look for the others now. *Please.*"

"Yes," Beckett agreed, stuffing the small notebook into a zippered pocket in his backpack. "We do."

"No signs of life outside," Alex reported, still guarding the door. "Could that really have been all of them?"

We'd only counted eight enemy combatants when we'd stormed in with guns blazing. They were all lying in puddles of their own blood now.

"We'll hope it was, but assume it's not," Beckett said. "Mr. Patel, there's a storage room near the entrance of the cave complex. It will be safer for you to wait for us there than to stay here, on the off chance that there are more terrorists still at large."

The omega's jaw worked. "I should come with—"

"You should stay out of the line of fire and let us do our jobs," Alex interrupted, with the barest hint of an alpha bark behind the words.

Patel's jaw snapped shut, and the muscles in his neck jerked like he had to stop himself from showing throat to us. It should not have been as damned distracting as it was.

"This way. Quickly," Beckett said, and took point. The three of us surrounded our charge and headed for the storage room we'd cleared on the way in.

"There's a scent trail," Alex said. "We may be able to track where they were taken that way."

Beckett gave her a terse nod of acknowledgement. I took Alex's word for it. She had the sharpest nose in the pack, and what was nothing more than a muddle of pheromones to me, might well be more to her.

We left the terrified attaché in the unlocked storage room with orders to stay quiet unless he was discovered, and yell like a banshee if he was. It wasn't ideal, but we'd seen no evidence that any of the terrorists were still here. He would probably be fine, and we couldn't afford to have him unarmed, untrained, and underfoot if we ran into resistance while extracting Jax and the ambassador.

Jax. The annoying bastard had better still be alive. If he was dead, I'd kill him.

"We're following your lead, Alex," Beckett said.

Alex gave a tight nod and led us back to the corridor running in front of the holding cell. We stayed back to avoid further confusing the olfactory landscape, and let her do her thing. Our luck held, in that the place really did seem to be deserted. So far, there'd been no sign of booby traps, either—just rooms full of dusty supplies, makeshift cots, rickety tables with maps piled across them, and lots and lots of rocks.

It was a warren, but it was easy enough to tell which parts were being used and which parts weren't by following the electrical wiring snaking along the walls. We took a couple of wrong turnings and had to backtrack for Alex to pick up the scent again, but eventually even I could smell it like a beacon pointing the way in front of us.

Jax's normal woodsy scent was heavily laden with musk. The omega had gotten to him, and I hoped to hell he'd kept enough of his wits about him to keep from getting dead. Not that I could really blame him too much—that sweet honey and orange blossom perfume was intoxicating as all fuck, and he'd been trapped in an enclosed space with it for god knew how long.

Ahead, the corridor we were traversing ended in a closed door. Like the one on the holding cell, it had a barred window at head height. Beckett stood to one side, poised to open it, and counted us down silently with his fingers.

Three… two… one… *go.*

We swept inside in well-practiced choreography, accommodating the lack of our fourth as effectively as possible. I swung my AK-47 around in a smooth arc, clearing my quadrant of the room. The others did the same, ranging out to check any possible hiding place.

It was empty except for two figures lying unmoving on bare medical tables. In the absence of active threats, I lowered my weapon and let myself look at them properly.

Alex cursed, short and sharp.

Jax was out cold, though a heart monitor on a cart next to him beeped out a slow, steady rhythm. An IV bag hung above the table, dripping fluid through a tube attached to his arm. Alex was at his side in two strides, pulling the needle out. I watched him long enough to confirm the rise and fall of his chest before my gaze was drawn to the second figure like iron filings to a magnet. Leona McCready's heat-scent slammed into me like a freight train, knocking every single thought from my head except one.

Mate.

Her long red hair was sweat-soaked, and her skin was pale except for two feverish spots of color on her cheekbones. *Jesus Christ*—her skirt was stained in front where she'd dripped slick onto it—presumably while she was on her hands and knees, presenting for sex.

The mental image felt like a bomb going off in my brain. In the space between one heartbeat and the next, I knew that both of these omegas were meant to be ours. A figure approached her, and a growl rumbled up from my chest. I took a step toward the medical table without consciously deciding to move.

"*Flynn!*" There was nothing subdued about Alex's alpha bark this time. It slapped my instincts upside the head, and I froze, blinking.

The figure standing near the ambassador resolved into Beckett. He was watching me closely, though without a hint of fear.

"Come help me with her," he said, ignoring the fact that I'd just snarled at him.

I strode to the table and looked down at the battered porcelain doll lying there.

"I'm reasonably sure she's been sedated as well," Beckett said. "Not a bad thing under the circumstances, assuming they used something safe. Take her pulse and count her respirations for me while I help Alex with Jax. Then you're going to need to carry him out of here. Alex can take the ambassador."

I could do that. With a nod of acknowledgement, I took the excuse I'd been given to lift one delicate wrist. My hand dwarfed it. I was only vaguely aware of Beckett stowing the IV bag of whatever they'd been pumping into Jax's veins inside his pack. Then, he and Alex efficiently disconnected the heart monitor leads from Jax's chest.

"Pulse and respiration's depressed, but not dangerously so," I reported, not immediately letting go of Ambassador McCready's wrist.

"Good," Beckett said tersely. He started rummaging through a mini-fridge in the corner of the makeshift lab, checking labels. A few moments later, he straightened with a couple of vials in his hand. The vials and a handful of syringes joined the IV bag already stashed in his pack.

The creamy skin beneath my fingertips felt too warm, making me think the ambassador's body was trying to climb toward its next heat-peak despite her unconscious state. A tiny whimper slipped past her full lips, and in that moment I would have thrown down with Alex for dibs on carrying her, despite Beckett's orders.

That was stupid, though. While Alex could probably lift Jax into a fireman's carry if circumstances required it, his weight would interfere with her ability to move fast and use a weapon much more than it would with mine. My instincts grumbled in discontent, but I lowered the ambassador's arm gently to the table and turned to the others.

"Ready?" I asked.

"Yes," Beckett said, grim-faced. "Let's collect Mr. Patel so we can get the hell out of here. And, please god, let the safehouse our contact arranged for us be as safe as it's cracked up to be."

"This is turning into ten different kinds of clusterfuck," Alex said, equally grim.

She hauled the ambassador's body into a sitting position and ducked under her torso, distributing the omega's negligible weight across her shoulders as she straightened. I had no idea how she managed to avoid sniffing Leona McCready's skin like a cocaine addict snorting a fresh line—but then again, Alex hadn't earned the nickname *'The Ice Queen'* for nothing.

I crossed to Jax and hauled him up the same way, the two cracked ribs I'd sustained in the I.E.D. attack grinding painfully as I steadied the bastard's bulk. Securing him in the fireman's carry with my left arm around his thigh, I grasped my weapon right-handed and brought it into firing position.

Beckett had completed one final sweep of the lab, gathering up a few papers that had been left behind and shoving them into his pack with everything else. "Move out," he ordered. "Stay sharp—I'll take point. Let's get these three to safety, and hope like hell there's a medical lab somewhere around here that's equipped to figure out what they were pumping into Jax."

"Your lips to god's ears," Alex muttered, and fell into step next to me.

ELEVEN

Kameron

THE DARK storage room might have been even worse than the cell. I crouched among a pile of crates in the corner, trying to convince myself that Leo and Jax were still alive… that Beckett wouldn't arrest us and turn us over to the Committee the moment he got his alpha away safely.

Time was still moving oddly. My bruised side ached and throbbed in sync with my heartbeat. I had no idea how long it was likely to take to find the others. And what if they were still being guarded? What if Beckett's team fell to a counterattack in some deep part of the cave complex where I wouldn't hear the gunfire?

A sharp rap sounded against the door, and I nearly jumped out of my skin. I rose on shaky legs, keeping to the shadowed corner as the knob turned and the door creaked open.

"We're leaving," Beckett said.

"The others?" I asked breathlessly.

"We've got them. Move." He jerked his chin toward the corridor, all business.

He would have said something if they were dead, I told myself firmly. He'd be acting more upset. More… *something*.

Outside, the huge, dark-skinned alpha—*Flynn?*—had Jax's limp body slung over his shoulders. The female alpha, Alex, had Leo draped over her shoulders in the same way. The air caught in my lungs.

"Are they—" The words burst free without conscious intent.

"Alive," Alex confirmed. As if to drive home the point, Leo gave a low moan.

"Time isn't really on our side here," Beckett said.

I broke free of my paralysis, following the others out of the cave system. It was cloudy outside, which was probably just as well. Even this dreary gray light was enough to hurt my eyes after days spent trapped in the shadows. How long had it been since I'd seen the sky? I couldn't have said what day of the week it was. More worryingly, I couldn't have said what day it had been when we were first taken.

"It's some distance to our transportation, I'm sorry to say." Beckett kept his voice low. He raked an assessing gaze over me, as though trying to decide if I was going to slow them down. Then his pale eyes scanned the crags and peaks around us.

Did he expect an attack? More terrorists lying in wait for an ambush? The hair on the back of my neck prickled. The skin between my shoulder blades felt tight and vulnerable.

No gunfire erupted as we made our way down a rocky slope toward a wooded canyon. I would scarcely have credited the alphas' ability to negotiate the poor footing with the weight of their unconscious burdens—especially while also holding their bulky automatic weapons at the ready.

After a few minutes without any further drama ensuing, we reached the relative cover of a large pile of boulders. Beckett drew a water bottle and an energy bar out of his pack, handing both items to me wordlessly. I opened the water with relief, rinsing my mouth and spitting before drinking half of it in one go. The energy bar, I stuffed into my trouser pocket—not at all sure my stomach could handle it right now.

"This isn't right," I said, careful to keep my voice low, as Beckett had done. "When they dragged us into the caves, it was only a short distance from where they'd parked the vehicles. They had bags over our heads, but I'm sure there was a road near the cave entrance. Or a track, at least."

Beckett's eyes didn't stray from their careful observation of our surroundings. "I'm willing to bet there's a second exit from the cave system. For one thing, we rescued the other two from some kind of lab, and none of the men we killed on our way in looked like either scientists or medical personnel."

"You think there were other people there, and they got away?" I asked, not liking the potential ramifications of that idea *at all*.

"It seems likely," Beckett said.

We started down a particularly steep slope, scree rolling beneath my feet like jagged marbles, and I had to focus on keeping my rubbery legs steady enough not to fall. Eventually, the landscape evened out into what must have been a dry riverbed. I could see a Range Rover, or some similarly shaped off-road vehicle, parked in the distance.

Somehow, I made it the rest of the way without collapsing or significantly slowing the others down — though my vision was tunneling in, gray fog creeping around the edges by the time we finally arrived.

"Put Jax in the back," Beckett said. "Check his vitals again and make sure he's in the recovery position. Alex, you're driving. Flynn, you're riding shotgun."

After a brief flurry of activity, I found myself in the back seat, propping Leo upright as Beckett climbed in on her other side and slammed the door. The engine rumbled to life. A moment later we were moving — heading, presumably, for civilization, where Leo would still be in heat and our secret would be well and truly out.

Leo squirmed against me, panting. Her eyes had opened to slits, but she didn't seem truly aware of what was happening. Beckett rummaged in the black backpack he'd slung onto the floorboard between his feet and came up with a vial and a syringe.

"What are you doing?" I asked in alarm.

"She was sedated when we found her," he said. "Under the circumstances, I think that's not a bad plan."

Flynn snorted. "Unless you want this pile of bolts to end up wrapped around a tree, it probably is a good plan, yeah."

"Oh, ye of little faith," Alex muttered from the driver's seat.

"It won't work forever," Beckett said. "Not in her current condition. But we're a good couple of hours out from our temporary safehouse, and I'd rather not make that kind of drive with an omega climbing a heat-peak and two alphas in the front seat."

I digested that, steadying Leo against a particularly violent lurch as the vehicle juddered over the uneven terrain.

"All right," I said slowly — not that I was in any position to object. "If you're sure it's safe for her. Next question. Are we under arrest?"

"No," Beckett replied without hesitation.

I wanted to press the issue further. I *should* have pressed it further. There was too much here that wasn't adding up. Why wasn't Jax — allegedly a subjugated alpha — chemically castrated? How had a civilian government security team managed to get resources for a specialist anti-terrorist military extraction mission in a matter of days? And... a *safehouse*? In a foreign country?

The answers to these questions were important. It wasn't an exaggeration to say that our lives might well depend on them. Placing us under immediate arrest before dragging us to the nearest embassy for processing and extradition to the Committee would absolutely have been the correct protocol under these circumstances. The concept of diplomatic immunity in international law was still on the books, but only for betas. It hadn't applied to alphas or omegas for decades now.

And yet, all I could do was cling to Leo's arm, breathing deeply to keep my churning stomach contents in place and hold the swirling gray mist at the edges of my vision at bay. Beckett drew the contents of the tiny glass vial into the syringe with steady hands despite the jouncing of the vehicle. When Leo's perfume thickened, her eyes growing more aware and her movements more purposeful, he called for a halt long enough to sedate her again.

I spared a worried thought for Jax, curled on his side in the back. He was tough. I knew the others were banking on the extreme measures that were usually required to kill an alpha. Realistically, without knowing what had been done to him—and in the absence of medical equipment—there wasn't anything to be done except getting him someplace safe for medical attention.

Before long, Leo lapsed into unconsciousness again, though her perfume still filled the interior of the Rover. After what seemed like forever, Alex pulled onto an honest-to-god road, and the ride smoothed out. I lapsed into a sort of fugue state; my brain having evidently decided that it was throwing in the towel for a bit.

Despite open windows and the sedative's best efforts, the inside of the vehicle was a miasma of pheromones. Spicy cardamom—that was Flynn. Rich jasmine and sandalwood—that had to be Alex. Jax's now-familiar ambergris and cypress was muted, soured by whatever our kidnappers had done to him. Leo's sweet scent overpowered them all. I couldn't get a thing off Beckett except the chemical smell of underarm deodorant—the kind that so many betas seemed to favor.

Just sit back and let the nice alphas take care of everything, my instincts tried to tell me, despite how disastrous that had the potential to be. I couldn't give into omega weakness—I was currently the only thing standing between Leo and whatever was coming next.

My silent internal battle raged. The practical upshot was that I ended up being totally useless, my thoughts locked in an ever-tightening spiral of stress and fear. When the vehicle turned onto what appeared to be a private drive, it came as a complete surprise. I had no idea how long I'd been staring into nothing, clutching Leo's arm like a lifeline.

"This is it," Beckett said dryly, as a cabin came into view through the trees. "Apparently."

"Utilities?" Alex asked. "Food?"

"Allegedly," Beckett replied.

Alex pulled the Range Rover up to the front door and parked it.

"Why have you brought us here?" I asked, fresh dread bubbling up at the realization of how remote this place appeared to be.

"Because no one will think to come looking for you here, while we figure out what the hell's going on with this so-called Beta Liberation Front," Beckett said. "The fact that there's no one else living close enough to smell an omega in heat is a happy bonus. Stay here."

He opened the door and got out, closing it behind him. Pistol in hand, he disappeared around the side of the cabin and returned after a few moments, evidently with a key. The rest of us waited in awkward silence as he went inside. A couple of minutes later, he returned. Flynn stuck his head out of the passenger-side window, and Beckett leaned against the door to speak with him.

"There's water and electricity," he reported, "along with enough shelf-stable food in the pantry to last about a week, which is longer than we'll need. One of you needs to stay here while we get Jax medical attention and start investigating this alleged terrorist weapon. Alex, it's your call who stays and who goes."

The female alpha's catlike green eyes flicked back to meet mine via the medium of the rearview mirror for the barest of instants. Then she turned her attention to Flynn, pinning his gaze.

"You're on omega duty," she said. "And since you're also our resident pervert, I'm hoping you've got something stashed in your luggage that will help her?"

Flynn shrugged. "Yeah, probably."

"Good," Alex said. "Now give me your word you won't cross any boundaries. Whatever the omegas say goes, and it doesn't count if it's not proper consent."

"I know," Flynn replied. "I promise, *alef*. I'll watch over them while you're gone."

"Let's get them inside," Beckett said, backing away from the passenger door to let the huge alpha get out.

Flynn gestured toward the back of the Range Rover. "Someone strip off Jax's shirt and bring it inside. It stinks like him, so it'll help." He opened the door on my side and leaned in. "Can you make it inside on your own, Mr. Patel?"

The rational part of my mind still wasn't sold on the wisdom of going into this remote cabin with my unconscious packmate and an alpha I barely knew. The part that was running on fumes ensured that I nodded wordlessly and climbed out, bracing myself on unsteady legs. Beckett was at the back of the vehicle, fussing over Jax. I wanted to check on the blond alpha… maybe thank him, even though he probably wouldn't be able to hear it.

I didn't move. *Couldn't* move.

Flynn disappeared from my side for a moment and returned to shove a filthy undershirt into my hands. I stared at it cluelessly as Jax's scent floated to my nostrils. The dark-skinned alpha leaned into the back seat and scooped Leo into his arms, pausing for a second to sniff deeply at the base of her neck—just as he'd done to me earlier.

I let myself be herded into the cabin, taking in the smell of dust and neglect. Beckett came inside just long enough to drop a couple of duffel bags by the door.

"I'll send Alex back with the Range Rover as soon as we get Jax the care he needs." He wrapped his fingers around Flynn's massive bicep in a gesture that seemed almost paternal. "You'll be safe here in the meantime, and so will they."

"Course we will, boss." Flynn looked down at the unconscious burden in his arms. "Told you. I'll take care of them."

Beckett gave him a tight smile. "I know you will, Flynn." His pale, sea-foam colored eyes met mine. "Mr. Patel, I know this is asking a lot of your trust— but everything will be all right. No one will harm you here."

All I could manage was a tense nod. Anything else would have given away how badly I was trembling. I wanted so desperately to believe it… but I couldn't ignore the clamoring of my shattered nerves. Right now, it didn't feel like *anything* would be all right—not ever again.

Beckett gave Flynn a final firm pat on the shoulder and left, ready to rush his injured alpha back to civilization. I should have demanded to know where, exactly, we were. Would Alex and Beckett be driving to a hospital in Târgovişte? Were we anyplace *near* Târgovişte anymore? Instead, I stared blankly at Flynn.

He stared back. "You're about to fall over, I think."

Was I?

Oh… right. I totally was.

"Yes," I whispered. "Sorry."

He tilted a massive bicep toward me. "Grab an arm, then. Let's see if we can get you both cleaned up and fed before this one wakes up and needs attention."

I grabbed the arm and held on.

The interior of the cabin was an undifferentiated blur as Flynn led me deeper into the structure. I blinked as an overhead light fixture flared into life, revealing a bathroom. It was basic — almost institutional — with a sink, a toilet, and an area ringed off by a plastic shower curtain. The floor was tile, sloping subtly toward the shower area at the back. A set of plain shelves near the sink held folded towels.

Flynn lowered Leo onto the closed toilet seat and steadied her in a seated position, her chin lolling against her chest. "She's asleep, so you have to tell me what's a boundary and what isn't. Can I bathe her?"

I dragged as many brain cells back into working order as I could. "Uh… no. I'll do it."

"Okay," he said. "I can lift her in for you, though? Maybe keep her underwear on if that would make you feel safer."

I nodded, aware that I'd already made too many compromises on my packmate's behalf — and there would probably be more to come. "All right," I told him.

Flynn nodded and efficiently stripped off the filthy remains of Leo's smart gray skirt-suit, leaving her in her light green bra and panties. He sniffed her again, and I tried not to bristle.

"Don't think we have all that long," he said, lifting her and carrying her across the room to the shower area. He placed her carefully on the floor, back propped in the corner. "Get in there with her. There's soap, and I'll bring you the shampoo I stole from the hotel room in Bucharest."

Numbly, I stripped off my clothes, too wrecked to have any concern for my nakedness. It didn't matter—my scarred and abused body hadn't felt like *me* for a very long time. Flynn's deep brown eyes raked down my length, and I shivered under his gaze.

"Back in a minute with the shampoo," he said.

I stepped into the shower and turned on the water, angling the spray away from Leo's body. It ran rusty for a few seconds before clearing, and warmed up a few seconds after that. A large hand passed a small shampoo bottle around the edge of the plastic curtain, and I took it.

"I'm gonna go get things ready for you," Flynn said, over the sound of spattering water drops. "Don't either of you drown while I'm gone, or I'll be pissed."

I still couldn't seem to muster words. Flynn left to do… whatever the hell he was doing, and I made a concerted attempt to scrub the worst of the last few days off both of us. Leo woke as I was trying to wrestle her around to get her hair rinsed properly.

"Kam?" she slurred. "What's going on?"

"It's all right. We're safe, I think. I'm getting us cleaned up," I answered, aware that my voice sounded flat and distant. "Lean your head back for me."

Her head lolled backward into the spray, and a sensual groan of pleasure cut through the steamy atmosphere. When I was confident I'd managed to rinse most of the soap off of both of us, I turned off the shower and retrieved a couple of towels.

Drying off was hit or miss, and it was fairly apparent the pale bra and panties weren't doing much for Leo's modesty while they were damp. I wrapped the towel around her as best I could, and was contemplating my own filthy clothes when Flynn returned.

He stopped in the doorway, blinking, and I couldn't miss the way his brown eyes darkened. After a beat, he broke himself free of his temporary paralysis. "Damn, but if that isn't a sight," he muttered, seemingly to himself. He shoved a bundle of cloth at me, and I took it. "Here. T-shirt and boxers. Figured you wouldn't be in a hurry to dress in what you've been wearing."

"Thank you," I managed, and shrugged into the comically oversized clothing. It smelled like laundry detergent, with only the faintest clinging scent of spicy musk.

"Brought one for her, too. Just the shirt, though. It's not clean—thought the smell might help her some, later." Flynn hesitated. "Jax's would be better, but it's pretty disgusting with all the blood and stuff on it. I figure we can just put it in the nest for her in case she wants it."

I stared at him, uncomprehending. The... *nest*?

Blinking free of my confusion, I held my hand out for the other shirt. "She's awake—sort of. I'll help her get this on. Thanks."

He handed it over, and I ducked behind the shower curtain, where Leo was still huddled on the floor in her towel.

"Hey, *odama*," I said, trying to keep my tone soothing. "Smell this for me, and let me know if you want to wear it."

I lifted the soft T-shirt to her nose. She breathed in, and her pupils dilated as she let out a decadent moan.

"That's good enough for me, I guess," I said. "You want to lose the bra first?"

"God yes," she murmured, plucking at it ineffectually.

I helped her out of the bra and into the shirt, which hung on her tiny frame, covering her to mid-thigh. Distantly, I was aware that my desire to fuss over her was pretty much the only thing keeping me on my feet. My stomach—settled somewhat now that I wasn't in imminent fear of death—grumbled, demanding food. I had a sneaking suspicion that my blood sugar levels were sloshing down around my ankles somewhere.

Tossing the damp towel aside, I slid the shower curtain back.

"Hi, Madam Ambassador," Flynn said. "Can I pick you up? I'm supposed to ask first whenever you're awake, but it's going to be hard to move you otherwise."

Unfortunately, Leo's eyes went dazed and overwhelmed the moment they settled on the towering alpha in front of her.

"It's fine," I said quickly. "Let's just get her someplace warm and quiet, please."

Flynn nodded and scooped Leo up as though she weighed nothing. He didn't scent her this time— possibly because her perfume was starting to overwhelm the room's atmosphere again. I followed them out, keeping one hand on the wall for balance.

Flynn nudged an interior door open with his hip and disappeared inside. I slipped in after him to find him laying Leo in the center of a huge pile of pillows, couch cushions, and displaced mattresses in the center of what was probably a bedroom. My jaw dropped open as I scanned the dim, red-lit surroundings. The alpha had pushed all of the furniture to the edges of the room, and draped a sheer, red curtain over the single lampshade. I had no doubt that every bed, couch and chair in the place had been ransacked to construct the makeshift nest, which also boasted several blankets.

Leo groaned in relief and burrowed into the softness.

The room smelled partly of alpha and partly of strangers. The woodsy scent from Jax's blood and sweat-stained undershirt was definitely in the mix. There was something else, as well… something that made my stomach rumble. *Tomato soup*?

"Soup and cheesy crackers are on the side table, Mr. Patel," Flynn said, as though it wasn't remotely unusual that he'd whipped up a heat-nest and also made soup for me in the space of barely half an hour. "She won't eat until the heat breaks, but I expect you're probably going to need it."

TWELVE

Leona

I WAS PRETTY sure this was a dream. And if it was? I'd totally take it. Hard-packed bare dirt had given way to soft pillows and cushions. Frightening shadows had been replaced with a warm, comforting red glow. Except for the hint of stranger-smell clinging to the bedding, it was all reassuringly womb-like.

Nest. My instincts sighed in relief.

Unfortunately, while my instincts might be happier now, my body felt like complete crap. Someone had put me through a meat grinder and topped it off by stuffing my mouth with cotton wool... or possibly with a small, furry animal that had died of gangrene.

One or the other.

I'd regained consciousness in a shower, and Kam had been with me. So had an alpha, but a different one. His pumpkin-spice scent clung to the shirt I was wearing, and that part was okay. I wanted Jax to be here, too—but there was only a stale hint of his scent that smelled...off, somehow. Sick, maybe, or hurt.

Something had happened, and I wasn't clear what it was. Kam and the new alpha spoke to me, but the sense of the words drifted in and out. Mostly *out*, if I was being honest. I was feeling feverish and empty again. Restless, I writhed against the cushions and blankets, trying to transfer more of my scent to them.

"She's getting close," said the new alpha. "I brought something to help. What were you using before to knot her?"

Kam knelt next to me, smelling of... tomatoes? Which seemed really random, somehow. Maybe this was a dream after all.

"My fingers," he said.

"Yeah, this'll be better. Here." A pause, as Kam stretched out an arm, reaching for something.

"Do I want to know why you have a knotting dildo in your luggage?" Kam asked.

"Some beta women like 'em," said the other voice. "Especially when the real thing's too big."

I felt Kam take a breath as though to speak, only to let it out again. "You know what? Never mind." A rubbery-looking cylinder with a bulge at the base entered my field of view. It was a pretty, candy cane shade of spiraling red and white. "Leo, this will be better than my fingers. Can I use this on you?"

I didn't want a candy cane. I wanted the alpha. Too bad my words were gone again. I whimpered in frustration.

"She can't answer," said the alpha. "You have to choose for her. What are my boundaries, Mr. Patel? Can I be in the nest with you?"

Another pause.

"Y-yes. I think it might help. But... keep me between the two of you. And keep your clothes on. Well, except when you need to, you know..."

"Get myself off," the alpha finished for him. "Yeah, okay. Can I talk to you while I'm in the nest?"

"Yes, of course you can talk," Kam said quickly. "Look, I know this whole thing is awful. I'm really sorry about all of this."

The cushions shifted as a heavy weight lowered onto them. The spicy smell of horny alpha grew stronger, and I sucked it in like a drowning woman surfacing for air.

"Why are you sorry?" asked the alpha. "Did you cause any of this?"

"No," Kam said. "But I'm still sorry."

I peered past Kam's slender body as the alpha settled his long, muscular form into the softness of the nest. Saliva pooled in my mouth, and I swallowed hard to keep from drooling.

"You shouldn't be, though," the alpha said. "I'm never sorry — not for anything. Simpler that way."

"I imagine it would be, at that," Kam replied.

"So, you two — you're together? Pack?"

Kam's hand smoothed damp hair away from my face. He was shaking. I leaned into the touch, trying to convey reassurance. "Yes," he said softly.

"That's good," said the alpha. "You hear that, Ambassador? Your *odama*'s going to help you out now. You're ready for him, right?"

There was a question in there, along with a promise of something — even if the details were beyond me at the moment. I rubbed my thighs together, feeling a fresh pulse of slick gathering.

"Like I told Jax, I think we're probably into first name territory at this point," Kam said. "Call me Kam, and she's Leona."

"Sure thing, Kam. I'm still Flynn, though. I've only got the one name." The alpha shifted, his lovely dark eyes stroking over me like liquid heat. "You ready to get warmed up, Leona? Kam could make you come a couple of times — get you all nice and ready for this pretty little silicone cock."

Some of that made it through the fuzz surrounding my brain, and he might as well have poured lava on me. I whined and panted, trying to wriggle out of my soaked panties with uncoordinated movements.

"I don't know if that's —" Kam began, trailing off uncertainly.

There was a pause. "Don't know if that's what?" The alpha rolled onto an elbow. "She's okay with you touching her, right? You were already together."

"Well, yes, but..."

"Then here's the thing, Kam. This heat is going to be miserable for her, and the only relief she's going to get is when she's being sexually satisfied. I wish I could do it, but like I said, I'm not allowed."

I reached across Kam's body and managed to get a weak grip on the alpha's wrist, hoping to pull him toward me. He made a low noise of regret before peeling my fingers loose and lifting my knuckles to his lips, pressing a kiss there. Then he gently set my arm back on Kam's other side.

"It just seems wrong when she's like this," Kam said miserably.

"If you were an alpha, though," he began. "If you could help her through this on your own, and you didn't have to worry about pups or any of the rest of it... you wouldn't just put her on her hands and knees and stick it in her, would you? 'Cause you don't really seem like that kind of person."

Kam took in a shuddering breath. "No, of course I wouldn't."

"Well, we're safe here," the alpha said. "And I promised Alex I'd be good, so you don't have to worry about me. You might as well be nice to her and make this as easy for her as it's going to get. I'll just sit here and enjoy the show until you're ready for me to bust a nut and lend her some pheromones."

Kam let out an odd, rusty-gate-hinge noise that might conceivably have been a hysterical bark of laughter. "God, I must be going insane." The words were as shaky as his hand had been. "Leo, my dearest love, I hope this is the right thing. And I wish I *was* that imaginary alpha, so we could be together properly."

His gentle touch traced my cheek, down my neck to play over the inflamed skin covering my mating gland. I arched and moaned breathlessly, drinking in the tingles of pleasure.

"You two are together exactly as you're meant to be," said the alpha. "You're already perfect; you just need a better world to live in. Now, Kam… touch those beautiful breasts for me, since I can't do it. Fuck—if I could, I'd put my mouth all over every square inch of both of you until the pair of you were screaming for me."

Kam let out another shaky noise and lay down, spooning me from behind in the soft warmth of the nest. "*God*," he said again.

A hand cupped my left breast, and I pressed into the contact like a cat. My nipples hardened, a jolt of sensation spreading downward and releasing a fresh trickle of slick. Lips closed over the tendon in my neck, teeth scraping lightly. I rolled my head to the side, exposing my throat and breathing in spicy alpha musk as it grew heavier in the air.

Pleasure rolled along my nerves, everything so different in this cozy place of safety than it had felt in that horrible bare cave. The painful exhaustion and fear that had been plaguing me fell away, subsumed beneath the feeling of loving hands touching all the places that ached to be touched. A low, rumbling voice narrated a never-ending litany of filthy suggestions interspersed with praise.

Kam's hand drifted down to my sex, stroking through the silken slickness there. It *never* felt like this normally—like there was a spring inside me tightening with every pass of fingers over my nub. He dipped inside my passage, my muscles clenching to try and keep him there. After an endless upward spiral that might have lasted minutes or hours, Kam's tongue rasped over my mating gland and I keened, ecstasy crashing over me.

Kam wrapped his slender body around me and held me as I came down, his arms tight around me. A hint of lemon and ginger tickled my nose beneath Flynn's heavier perfume and my own thick sweetness.

"Jesus H. Christ on a popsicle stick, that was hot," said the alpha. He let out a deep breath. "You're about to peak on us, aren't you, sweet thing? That's okay—Kam's gonna fill you up now. He'll fuck you nice and slow for me. Kam, don't let her have the knot until I say so."

I was still lying on my side, but as the word 'knot' registered, I scrambled inelegantly into position, my lower back arching.

"*Fuck me blind,*" Flynn muttered, like a curse. I heard the rasp of a zipper sliding open.

"I'm here, Leo," Kam said hoarsely. "We've got you, *odama.*"

Fingers stroked up and down the length my spine, lighting every nerve through the soft cotton of the pheromone-laden T-shirt. I mewled in approval as something hard and blunt-tipped slid up and down along my labia a few times before entering me.

God, this was so much better than before. It still wasn't exactly what my body wanted, but it was *pleasure, pleasure, pleasure* tingling along my arms and legs, spreading warmth outward from my center. I rocked back and forth shamelessly, trying to get all of it inside me—wallowing in the thickening scent of musk as the alpha chased his own pleasure, barely more than an arm's length away from me.

"Not yet, sweet thing," he said, a low growl lurking beneath the words. "You'll take this knot when I say so, and not before."

"*Good god,*" Kam muttered, sounding like he was in danger of fainting. "Alex wasn't kidding about you being the pervert, was she?"

"At least that didn't sound like a complaint," Flynn pointed out, still in that gravelly voice.

I craned around, omega flexibility allowing me to get a glimpse of him fisting that thick alpha cock of his, in time with the slow thrusts making my toes curl. I dragged my eyes up the length of his body until out gazes locked. With a deep groan, he sped his movements and curled forward. Pearly white pulsed and spilled from his dick, coating his hand and stomach.

"Now," he said. "Give it to her now."

"*Jesus*," Kam said, the word emerging awestruck.

The fake cock pressed all the way into me, my entrance stretching to accommodate the thickened knot near the base and then clamping around it. I let out a shriek and climaxed again, squeezing the unyielding length with rhythmic pulses—perfectly and deliciously filled.

Our mingled perfume drove away the lingering scent of the room's previous nameless occupants. Sugar and spice, citrus and ginger.

"You both did so well," Flynn said. "Time to rest now."

The approval in the alpha's voice washed over me like a salve.

As before, Kam helped me roll onto my side. As before, when he pressed against me, he was shaking. My mind felt a tiny bit clearer than it had before. There was no way I could relax into this relative peace when my packmate was barely holding himself together. I squirmed around in his arms until I could peer over his shoulder and meet Flynn's eyes again, biting my lower lip as the toy shifted inside me.

"Alpha?" I asked.

"What is it, sweet thing?" His voice was dark velvet.

"Kam needs you now, but he's afraid to ask."

Next to me, Kam went very still.

"Is that true, Kam?" Flynn asked. "Do you… need me to look after you for a bit?"

Kam took a tiny, hitching breath, and then another. The silence grew heavy.

"Yes, please, alpha," he whispered, after a long, hesitant pause. Another tremor shuddered through his body. "I just… need… something to make all of this go away for a bit."

A low purr rumbled up from Flynn's chest. His weight shifted among the pillows and cushions. Muscular arms closed around Kam from behind.

"Come here, ginger tea," he said. Still purring, the alpha curled his muscular body around my packmate. I squeezed myself against Kam's front, tucking my head under his chin and wrapping my arms around him, too.

"I love you, *odama*," I murmured against Kam's collarbone. I might've been awash in post-orgasmic hormones, but it was still the truth.

"Hear that?" Flynn asked. "Your packmate loves you. It's all right—you're safe now. You're both safe."

Kam held himself with brittle stillness for long moments, his heart pounding a frantic, staccato rhythm against my cheek. Finally, a silent sob jerked free of his chest, followed by another, and another. Flynn curled tighter against him, his big hand coming to rest on my shoulder as we pressed Kam between us, giving him a safe place to fall apart.

THIRTEEN

Flynn

SOCIAL CUES were complicated, especially in the beta world. That's why I'd always found it easier to trust Alex, or in a pinch, Jax, to make decisions about that kind of stuff, and just do whatever they said. Omegas were easy to understand, though — especially when heat was involved.

Kam was one badly broken omega, partly because beta assholes had apparently gotten hold of him young… but partly because he'd crammed himself into a box that didn't fit. I had a sneaking suspicion that the ambassador — *Leona* — was in pretty much the same spot, though it wouldn't surprise me if she buried the sharp edges a little deeper.

Passing in beta society was hard enough when you were aligned, with your gender matching what they expected of your biological sex. It was even harder if you were unaligned, as everyone in my little pack had ample cause to know. The idea that female alphas and male omegas even existed in the first place seemed to enrage betas. I could only imagine how Kam had twisted himself to fit into the role of *beta male*. Testosterone injections, almost certainly. Brutal gym workouts to maintain the sort of musculature that betas expected, probably.

Meanwhile, Leona would have needed to fight not only the perception that a hyper-feminine woman wasn't suited to a high-stress political post helping to shape international policy, but also the added softness that came with being an omega.

Instead of letting it define her, she'd channeled that soft aura into diplomacy, subtly turning an omega's social influence within the pack against hardened beta diplomats and world leaders. How many of them had found themselves talked around to her point of view with no idea how it had happened, I wondered?

The two of them were pack to each other, but it was clear enough they'd never had anyone to guard their nest so they could let down their defenses every once in a while. Kam was trying to play alpha even though he had no bark or bite to back it up—convinced it was his responsibility to protect Leona when she was at her most vulnerable. No wonder he was shaking apart in the circle of my arms, clinging to his *odama* as he cried out the stress and terror of the past several days.

When it came to emotion, I didn't feel all that much in the normal course of things—and that was the way I liked it. *Numb*. When I did get hit with feelings, it was simple stuff. I was angry at whoever had hurt Jax. If the stuck-up bastard ended up dying on us, I'd be angry at him, too. The emotions of the heat-nest were straightforward, even if I'd only experienced them firsthand on a tiny number of occasions. I hadn't been a breeder on the slave plantation—except once, when a high-value omega was cycling and they didn't have any better options to get her pupped on schedule. Mostly, though, I'd just been muscle. A laborer.

But an alpha still knew what was needed. Protectiveness. Steadiness. That was what we provided, when omegas were vulnerable and coming apart at the seams. It was probably the same thing that made beta women flock to us, whenever they thought they could get away with it without being shamed.

I shifted in the nest of pillows. My dick ached—my knot wishing it was in a nice warm passage where it wanted to be. Of course, my dick ached a lot after sex, since just because beta women thought they could take the alpha knot, it didn't mean splitting them open with *my* knot was something that would end well. Hence the more reasonably sized dildo, among other handy contraband sex toys.

At least it had come in useful here. From her reaction to the modest, beta-sized toy, it was pretty clear Leona was a virgin. I wondered if Kam had ever let an alpha try to work around whatever had been done to his body when they sterilized him. I'd been with two other sterilized omegas sexually since I'd been drafted into the UFNA military program. One had still been able to get off with a bit of patience and creativity. One hadn't.

I vowed to find out which camp Kam fell into the next time Leona went into heat—because, to my mind, there was no question that both of them would be ours by then. I could picture it with total clarity inside my head. Jax would recover from whatever shit the terrorists had pumped into him. Kam and Leona would accept our courting and agree to mate with us. Three months from now, we'd take turns knotting Leona through her peaks. Well… okay. Alex probably wouldn't let herself join in with us, because of what had happened with Irina a few years back. That had been ugly—but it wouldn't happen again. We wouldn't let it.

Maybe Alex would let the 'ice queen' armor thaw a bit for Kam, though, since there was no possibility of pups. I was pretty sure that with enough lube and prep work, Kam could take her up the ass. Alpha clits weren't nearly as girthy as alpha dicks, though the knots more than made up for it, supposedly.

Through all of these rosy visions of our future pack, I held Kam and let the rumbling thrum of contentment in my chest soothe him. Eventually, his quiet weeping subsided into the occasional hitch, until he finally went limp, giving himself over to me. I liked that. I liked it *a lot*. I also liked the way Leona's hand had crept up my arm to fist the material of my shirt, anchoring her body against us.

"Better now?" I asked.

A slight hesitation, and Kam nodded, not speaking.

"All right," I said. "I need to get Leona some water before she falls asleep. I'll be right back."

I climbed out of the makeshift nest a bit stiffly, tugging my shirttails down to cover my dick since there was no question of getting my fly closed until the knot went down. If I'd been inside her, Leona's muscles would still be holding us tied together—there would be a subtle shift in her pheromones whenever she stopped clamping around the toy, and that would convince my knot to deflate.

The water bottles were lined up on the side table where I'd left them. I grabbed two and brought them back. "Here," I told Kam, pressing one into his hand. "Stay hydrated."

He took it, not quite able to meet my eyes with his red-rimmed ones. "After weeping out a bucketful of water, you mean?"

"Well, that and being held hostage in a cave for six days," I said.

He untangled from Leona enough to roll onto an elbow and drink, while I helped her do the same. She definitely seemed more coherent than she had earlier—probably thanks to getting some decent sexual relief for the first time since her heat had started. I supported her head and she drank greedily, finishing three-quarters of the bottle in one go.

"How on earth did you find us?" Kam asked, sounding steadier now, if still a bit sheepish.

"Combination of military satellite intel and doing recon on a shit-ton of cave complexes in the general vicinity of Târgoviște," I said. "Those crazy terrorist bastards weren't nearly as stealthy as they probably thought they were."

I wasn't about to go into detail regarding how we got access to the intel so quickly… or how badly we'd been freaking out as the days slid by with no success. Thank fuck they'd both at least been alive when we found them. We'd been too late in the sense of Leona's heat and Jax's health, but maybe it wouldn't end up being the irrevocable kind of 'too late.'

"Jax said you'd come for us," Leona said quietly. "He never doubted it for a minute."

An emotion that wasn't the simple kind threatened to get tangled up in my chest, so I changed the subject. "You should be enjoying your knot right now, sweet thing," I told her. "But if you wanna talk instead, maybe you can tell us how this setup is working for you. There'll be at least another couple of peaks coming before it eases off."

She blinked huge hazel eyes up at me, and I tried not to melt like a damned snow cone in July.

"This was… better," she said. "Thank you."

Kam watched her with a worried expression. "Was what I did all right? You're sure?"

She blinked at him. "Of course it was, *odama*. Was it… all right for you?"

"I just want to help," he said, a bit desperately. "To… not make it worse."

"You *are* helping," she replied. "Of course you are." Her gaze moved to me. "And… I'm really sorry, Flynn. It's not that I'm scared of you. It's just that I *cannot* end up pregnant. I absolutely refuse to bring children into this world. Not the way it is now."

"Pups," I corrected, trying not to think of Irina… of the way it had taken both Jax and me to hold Alex down and keep her from running off half-cocked when we got news of the arrest. "Pups, not children."

"Leo's parents are betas," Kam said. "So actually, it could go either way."

That made sense. Beta parents were much more likely to be able to sneak alphomic offspring through the system. Though it was hard to imagine how betas could possibly have whelped such a perfect omega female.

"No, I get it," I told her. "It's fine."

Of course, by 'fine,' I meant 'frustrating as hell.' But I could understand where she was coming from, at least.

With a heavy sigh, Kam set aside his empty water bottle and settled in next to Leona, rearranging her in his arms. "You know, once upon a time there would have been easy access to contraceptives for heats. Omegas could buy synthetic alpha pheromones to manage the peaks, or as sexual enhancements outside of the normal estrus cycle."

I grunted and returned to my place on his other side. "Kinda makes me feel surplus to requirements."

Leona gave a sleepy chuckle.

Kam let out a sharp little puff of air. "That's not what I meant. Just that back then, we could have control of our own bodies, and manage our reproductive lives in whatever way we saw fit. "

I thought of the breeding pens. The plantations. "Yeah. I hear you." Breathing in, I sensed the slight shift in the perfume surrounding us. The ache in my cock eased as my body responded to her cues. "Hey, it looks like she's drifting off now," I said. "You want to get the toy out of her? I'll hang out here until you're both asleep, and then clean everything up for the next round."

Kam freed a hand from his embrace of Leona in favor of wrapping it around my forearm as he met my eyes. "Thank you, Flynn. Truly."

And... damn, but these two were going to be the death of me, coming out of nowhere like a fucking wrecking ball.

<hr>

I kept silent watch over the nest as the omegas slept. Hours passed, and Leona's scent was just beginning to thicken again when the sound of a familiar engine rumbled along the private drive. Grabbing my handgun from where I'd stashed it just beyond the pile of cushions and blankets, I rose and went to confirm through the nearest window that it was who I expected it to be.

Alex climbed out of the driver's seat and slammed it behind her, striding toward the front door. She, too, had a hand on her sidearm—just in case. My alpha instincts quieted from their state of high alert. She looked haggard, and I wondered in a distant and detached sort of way if I was going to have to track down and kill some more people after all, to get revenge for Jax.

I stowed my Glock and went to unbolt the front door, letting out a complicated little whistle that anyone else might mistake for a birdcall before I opened it. Her stance relaxed as she took me in, though she did twitch a bit as the scent of heat hit her.

"Is he dead?" I asked, unwilling to beat around the bush.

She entered as I stood back, making way for her. "He was still alive when I left the clinic."

I nodded once, sharply. "Good. Any other news?"

Her face set in hard lines. "The IV bag Beckett snatched from the lab contained a dilute solution of a novel thiophosphonate compound."

"Thiophosphonate." I cast my mind back to our military training. "A nerve agent?"

"Apparently. There are structural similarities to VX agent."

There was a 'but' in there somewhere.

"But...?" I prompted.

She shook her head, frustrated. "But the lab tech seemed confident that this variation wouldn't be dangerous to betas except at very high concentrations."

"The weapon," I said. "The one mentioned in that speech they were supposed to read, that would kill alphas and omegas." It made sense. At least, part of it did. "But you said Jax is still alive."

"Yeah." Alex's mouth twitched into a frown. "Seems like it's not quite ready for prime time yet. Small mercies, I guess."

"They think he'll be okay, though?" I asked.

"They've got him on atropine and pralidoxime at the moment. The IV bag was still mostly full when I ripped the cannula out of him, so he didn't get the dose they intended him to get. The big question is whether there's going to be any permanent nerve damage. It's too soon to tell."

"Shit," I said eloquently.

"How are the civvies doing?" Alex asked, changing the subject.

I shifted mental gears. "About as well as can be expected, I guess."

Alex sniffed the air. "She's getting ready to peak again." Tension lurked behind the statement.

"Yeah," I agreed. "Kam's been doing the heavy lifting. I'm just supplying the pheromones."

Alex raised an eyebrow at me. "You're on a first-name basis, then?"

I shrugged. "He insisted. Can't really argue—once someone's seen your dick waving around, 'Madam Ambassador' and 'Mr. Patel' start to sound kind of silly."

She stared me down, and I tried not to shift uncomfortably beneath that dominant gaze.

"Don't get attached to them, Flynn," she said. "You know that can only end badly."

My jaw tightened. "No, I *don't* know that, *alef*," I retorted. "You haven't spent time with them. They're special. This pack—we could have something with them."

"No," she replied without hesitation. "We really couldn't. They're unregistered omegas hiding in plain sight at the highest levels of beta government. Do you think the ambassador is going to walk into an international summit with a mating bite on her neck?"

"She could wear high-necked clothing," I said mulishly. "We could make it work. I mean, just look at—"

She cut in abruptly. "That's a special situation and you know it. Not to mention, one that's going to go down in spectacular flames one day, probably taking all of us with it."

I growled at her, my heat-induced frustration boiling over. Alex didn't call me on it, since that was the kind of leader she was.

"What she and Patel are doing is important," she said. "We need them as high-level assets in the government more than you need to get your dick wet. Also, there's the small matter that they'd have to be crazy to risk a mating bond with *anyone*... much less us."

I clenched my jaw to keep from saying anything else, since even I could tell I was still sporting a bad case of knot-brain. That didn't stop the thought from whispering through my head.

But what if they did?

FOURTEEN

Leona

THERE WAS a second alpha in the house. The scent of jasmine and sandalwood drifted to me from elsewhere in the cabin. Still, Flynn was alone when he returned to the nest, just as my need began ratcheting up yet again.

"Alex is back," he said. "Jax is still alive, in case you were wondering."

I held onto enough of the sense of the words to feel a swell of relief.

"That's wonderful news," Kam said, sounding equally relieved. "I hope that also means he'll recover completely?"

"Dunno about that part yet." The alpha lowered himself into the nest, still frustratingly separated from me by the barrier of Kam's body. "Let's not worry about that right now. I'd much rather see how many times you can get our girl off before she takes the knot again. You like that idea, sweet thing?"

My heat rose, cutting off all rational thought as I nodded frantic agreement. And so it began again—the seemingly endless cycle of fuck, knot, sleep. It was no longer the nightmarish hallucinatory haze that it had been at first, but even now, the sense of important things happening around me nipped at the edges of my awareness like a stubborn terrier with a cornered rat.

I was growing more and more exhausted, despite the hours spent dozing between peaks. Two cycles... three... four... and then a long period of blankness before I woke in what felt like the middle of the night. My mind was finally clear, though my body felt like I'd gone ten rounds with a professional boxer.

Also, I was *famished*.

"Ugh," I groaned. "Ow. *Fuck.*"

My pillow rose and fell beneath my cheek as someone let out a relieved breath. I lifted my aching head, and found Kam curled beneath me on the mountain of cushions.

"Flynn says your heat has broken," he told me, in that carefully neutral voice he used when he was particularly worried about something. "I won't bother asking how you're feeling."

Memories of the last several days began to filter into my mind, backwards.

"Oh my god," I said. "I... don't currently have enough brain cells functioning to even begin to deal with the burning radioactive fallout from this. Kam, I am *so sorry.*"

His arm was around my shoulders, holding me against him. At that, his fingers clasped my bicep convulsively. "Please don't apologize," he said, a bit desperately. "I don't think I can handle it right now."

I nodded, and tried to focus on something practical. "Okay. I'm starving right now. Is there food?"

In fact, I was having a hard time not grabbing Kam's shirt and shaking him until he gave me a blow-by-blow report on what the *hell* had happened in the days since an I.E.D. had blown up our motorcade. Were we still in Romania? What had happened with the summit? If we'd been rescued by our own security forces, why hadn't we been arrested immediately afterward? I gave my head a sharp shake to clear it, and instantly regretted it when my brain sloshed around like a pickled egg in a jar.

"Alex is getting you something to eat," Kam said. "You haven't had any food in four days. I expect Flynn already found somewhere to crash, now that the pheromones have subsided."

"Right," I said, wincing a bit when my stomach audibly gurgled its displeasure. Rather than focus on it, I moved on to the next important thing that I could potentially do something about. "How are you? And please don't say 'fine.'"

"Fine," he said, way too quickly.

"Kameron Patel, I swear to god—" I began, only to be cut off when a knock sounded at the door.

It opened a moment later, and the female alpha, Alex, entered. She gave a hesitant sniff, visibly steeling herself before entering with a bowl of something held in one hand, and a bottle of water tucked under her arm. I glanced down at my body reflexively, but an oversized black T-shirt covered me from neck to mid-thigh. It smelled of stale sweat and spicy alpha.

Flynn.

I was wearing Flynn's T-shirt.

Jesus Christ.

I shoved the realization aside. "Hello. Is that for me?"

"It is... assuming you can choke down something that's supposedly pork and lentils, based on the picture on the can," Alex said. "Spoiler alert—it bears no actual resemblance to the picture. Welcome to rural Eastern Europe."

"If she tries to give you anything containing either fish meatballs or preserved cod liver, run for the hills," Kam counseled.

At this point, I would have considered cat food if she'd offered it. Which, it turned out, was fortunate. I accepted the bowl of steaming, gelatinous, pinkish-brown mush and started spooning it into my mouth without paying much attention to the taste—pausing at intervals to wash it down with bottled water.

"You'll be wanting a briefing on recent events, Madam Ambassador," Alex said formally. She was standing at parade rest a short distance away—eyes front, not looking at me directly.

"Already?" Kam appeared distinctly uncomfortable. "Maybe you should rest for a day or two first, Leo."

"Will that make me like what I'm about to hear any better?" I asked.

"Doubtful," Alex said.

"Then go ahead and hit me with it now," I told her. "Meanwhile, we'll all pretend that I'm not sitting in an omega nest wearing nothing but a sex-stained T-shirt belonging to an alpha—one who's supposed to be chemically castrated, but isn't. First, though, are there any updates on Jax's condition? I know he was hurt, even though I can't remember the details."

"No, ma'am," Alex said. "We've had no outside contact since I returned here with the vehicle two days ago."

Two days? God, I'd been even more out of it than I'd realized.

"All right," I replied, my heart sinking. "In that case, tell me the rest of it."

In clipped and professional tones, Alex related the details of the roadside attack and kidnapping, painting their subsequent rescue efforts in broad strokes—collecting satellite and spy plane intel, then spending days in a systematic search of the known cave systems in an ever expanding grid. I nearly dropped my spoon when her recitation jarred loose my hazy memories of the videotaped speech the kidnappers had wanted us to make, with its spine-chilling reference to a targeted alphomic weapon.

She went on to describe the early findings related to the modified chemical nerve agent that had been given to Jax, and had almost been given to me. Kam, still curled up beside me, wrapped his arms around his knees, hugging himself.

After freeing us, they'd brought us here, to this isolated cabin in the Carpathians that Beckett had somehow magically conjured for use as a safehouse—another thing that didn't add up. Then she and Beckett had driven Jax to a hospital in Bucharest, before dropping the sample of the chemical at a government lab. Once Jax's condition was stabilized, he'd been transferred to a private clinic with a specialist in alphomic medicine on staff, and Alex had returned here with the vehicle.

"As far as the press is concerned, you're both being held at an undisclosed location due to credible ongoing threats to your safety," Alex concluded.

It was all terribly neat... and parts of it made no sense whatsoever upon closer examination.

"What about the summit?" I asked, since her report had been focused on the nuts and bolts of our kidnapping and subsequent rescue.

"Cancelled," she said. "Or rather, postponed. As far as I'm aware there's been no firm date or location announced for a future meeting."

I placed the spoon in the empty bowl and set them aside, lifting both hands to rub at my temples in hopes of banishing my throbbing headache.

"Okay. Let me think for a minute. We should be able to spin this in the administration's favor somehow. Paint this so-called Beta Liberation Front as a symptom of the wider problem of anti-alphomic extremism. It could shift public sentiment, at least back home." I let my hands fall abruptly. "That is, assuming you're not waiting for me to get my shit together and get cleaned up so you can arrest the two of us. Which... I mean, you seem to have gone to a lot of trouble to avoid that so far, but...?"

"You're not under arrest," Alex said stiffly.

I exchanged a glance with Kam, whose expression clearly said, *could you please not pick at this until she ends up changing her mind?*

"Why not?" I demanded, ignoring his silent plea.

"I have no orders to arrest you." The words were delivered in a wooden monotone.

"And you take your orders from Beckett." I studied her as best I could in the soothing red-tinged light of the makeshift nest, but there was nothing to see. That granite poker face had probably been honed in the military alpha program, and I wouldn't be seeing past it anytime soon. "Does that mean he's a sympathizer?" I prodded.

There wasn't so much as a flicker in response. "You'd have to ask him, ma'am. It's not my place to speculate about my team leader."

Her striking green eyes finally moved to mine, pinning me. So close after heat, the alpha power in that gaze sent a purely physical jolt through me, strong enough that she almost certainly saw it. "That being said, you've both got a decision to make," she continued. "The cave system where you were being held had at least two exits, and we're pretty sure some of the terrorists got away. That means that somewhere out there, someone else knows your secret."

Ah. That probably explained why Kam still looked like he wanted to curl up and sink straight through the floor.

"You'll have to decide whether or not you're going to disappear. Maybe start over somewhere out of the limelight," Alex said. "You know it's possible with the right connections — and there's no way you two got where you are today without help from the underground."

While every word of that was true, I had no intention of scuttling off to Jamaica to huddle in obscurity with my parents—not now, when the next few months would be more important than ever. Not after everything they'd sacrificed to hide my omega status. But… it wasn't just about me any more. There was someone else to consider.

"Kam and I will need to discuss that privately," I told her. "In the meantime, though, I have vague memories of there being a shower in this place. *Please* tell me I wasn't hallucinating that part."

"I'll show you where it is," Kam muttered, uncurling from his miserable hunch.

"Of course," Alex agreed. "I'll be outside if you need me, patrolling the perimeter of the property."

With that, she turned and left. Her stride was purposeful but unhurried—and yet, I couldn't help the impression that she was somehow fleeing the scene. When her footsteps had faded and the muffled sound of the front door opening and closing reached us, I turned to regard my packmate.

"I think she's been really uncomfortable scenting you," Kam said. "She wasn't in here at all, if you're wondering. Not in the nest. Not… *during.*"

My utter and complete mortification at what I could remember of the past few days threatened to rise up and swallow me whole, but I didn't have time for it.

"Okay," I said. "Good to know, I suppose. Now, about that shower?"

But he stopped me from rising with a hand on my arm. "Leo. *Odama.* Please—I need to know. Are we… okay? You kept telling me it was all right… what I was doing. But you weren't yourself, and I still don't know if—"

"Kam." My voice was as soft as I could make it. My heart ached for him, once I pulled my head out of my ass long enough to consider what he must have been going through these past horrible days. I scooted forward and wrapped my arms around him.

"Of course it was all right. You kept me from unraveling... from boiling away until there was nothing left. My dearest heart... of *course* we're okay."

The tension in his shoulders flowed out, on the back of a heavy sigh of relief. His arms wrapped around me in turn, squeezing so tight that I couldn't breathe for a moment. He tucked his face against the crook of my neck, and I felt his lips press a kiss over the sensitive skin covering my mating gland. It was still inflamed after my estrus cycle, and the nerves throbbed with wanting under the light touch.

I thought of what he'd said earlier — that I hadn't been myself during heat. "You're wrong, though," I whispered against the shell of his ear. "I *was* myself. In fact, it's probably the first time in fifteen years that I've been who I was born to be."

"Me, too," he said unsteadily. "Oh, Leo. What are we going to do?"

I stroked his beautiful black hair. "We'll talk about the rest of it later. But right now, *odama*, we're going to take a shower."

FIFTEEN

Leona

IT WASN'T THE Hotel Epoque in Bucharest by any stretch of the imagination, but there was soap, shampoo, and a towel. I wasn't sure if Kam would want to shower with me or not, and in the end, he didn't. It was pretty likely that he'd been glued to my side continuously for the last week or more. I couldn't blame him for needing a bit of space.

Wonder of wonders, Alex had brought our—admittedly slightly battered—luggage along with her when she'd returned from Bucharest. They'd been able to salvage it from the destroyed car, apparently, and the Samsonite suitcases and carry-ons had, in fact, lived up to the promise of toughness from the over-the-top TV commercials. I scrabbled at the zippered interior pocket of my carry-on with shaking fingers and drew out an innocuous looking bottle of painkillers.

The irony wasn't lost on me as I shook them out on the top of the dresser and started sniffing them one by one. The heat-blocker mocked me when I found it about halfway through the bottle's contents… but it would still be useful three months from now, for my next heat. I put it with the normal pills and kept going until I found one of the pheromone suppressors, which I swallowed dry.

It bothered me inordinately that I would have to get used to taking my suppressors on a different day of the week than I'd been doing for the past fifteen years.

Nevertheless, in an hour or two, all trace of my omega perfume would be gone. Back to normal. The thought shouldn't have made me cringe the way it did.

Freshly showered and dressed in something that didn't smell like an alpha in rut, I made my way to the cabin's front room, figuring I could wait there for Kam to get out of the shower. Unfortunately, I hadn't banked on finding Flynn sprawled across the battered sofa, fast asleep.

My scent wasn't suppressed yet, so it was with a sense of inevitability that I watched him blink awake from his post-heat snooze.

"Hey. Good morning, sweet thing," he said, the gravel of sleep roughening his deep voice.

Something low in my belly clenched, and I silently cursed all things hormonal and heat-related. It suddenly seemed deeply unfair that I knew exactly how his cock looked right after he'd come all over himself and popped a knot.

"Good morning," I said, frankly amazed when the words didn't emerge breathless and girly-sounding.

He rolled into a sitting position, muscles rippling beneath dark brown skin. He was wearing a T-shirt identical to the one I'd woken up in, along with black, military-style pants.

His feet were bare.

"Oh, shit," he said. "Sorry. Alex says I'm supposed to start calling you Madam Ambassador again. Blame it on the heat hangover, I guess."

I swallowed, reaching for professionalism and probably falling several miles short. "While I'd appreciate that in public, it does seem a bit ridiculous in private. Maybe we can compromise on Leona."

A smile tugged at his sensuous lips. "Sure thing, Leona. I'd like that." He scrubbed a hand over his close-shorn black hair and stretched, vertebrae popping.

I tried not to stare.

"How are you feeling?" he asked. "Are you hungry?"

My body feels like it's been turned inside out seemed like a bit too much information, so I ignored the first question in favor of the second. "I think my stomach's still processing the canned pork mush Alex brought me earlier, honestly." With a deep breath, I plunged onward. "I wanted to thank you. Not just for agreeing to help me without taking advantage… but also for watching over Kam. I can't imagine what he's been through emotionally since this mess started."

Flynn nodded, not trying to sidestep the subject or make it out to be no big deal. "He's strong, Leona. He'd have to be, to survive what they did to him as a pup. I just let him be an omega for a bit, that's all."

"I know," I told him. "But it still means a lot to me."

Flynn leaned back, resting his arms along the sofa back as he regarded me. He was taking up space—all alpha—and my omega was here for it no matter how hard I tried to push her back inside her box.

"What will you do now?" he asked.

The weight of the world came crashing back, slamming the lid of the box shut.

"I'll need to discuss that with Kam, once we've both had a little more time to recover," I said carefully. "But at a guess, we'll keep doing pretty much what we've been doing—hiding in plain sight, trying to make a difference. Kostya Nikolayev and all the other monsters like him are still out there. So is the Beta Liberation Front, apparently—and at this point, that might almost be worse."

"Back to saving the world, then," he said.

I narrowed my eyes at him, but I couldn't detect any sarcasm in his tone. Still, something about his words rankled. "You disapprove?"

His eyebrows shot up, as though I'd surprised him.

"No—I don't disapprove. I just don't want to see the pair of you get killed. You really think you can go it alone forever? Sooner or later, something bad's going to happen."

"Something bad already happened," I pointed out. "*Lots* of bad things happen, everywhere, all the time. That's the point. But Kam and I managed for years. We'll keep on managing."

Until we can't anymore. The words were unspoken, but they hung in the air.

He leaned forward intently, elbows resting on knees. "All I'm saying is, you two don't have to be alone. You could have a pack."

Warning klaxons sounded in my head. "We already have a pack," I said flatly.

He didn't break eye contact. "You could have *our* pack. Both of you."

Flashing red lights joined the klaxons. *Danger, Will Robinson!*

"That sounds like a good way for all five of us to get killed." I paused. Took a breath. "Besides, I don't get the impression everyone in your pack would be on board with that proposal."

"Alex will get there eventually," he said, with the same utter certainty Jax had said, '*My pack will come for us.*' "It's hard for her because of stuff that's happened in the past. That's all."

I absolutely refused to acknowledge the bitter pang of yearning I felt at the idea of Kam and I being courted… being pursued by a pack of strong, reliable alphas who would pledge to protect and cherish us. Kam loved to talk about the old ways when we were cuddled together, alone in our temporary, makeshift nests—but that part of our culture no longer existed. It had been replaced by breeding pens, involuntary sterilization, and a furtive life spent hiding in the shadows.

"I don't think something like that would be practical, given the circumstances," I said carefully.

He smiled at me, sweet and open. "That's a whole lot of words that don't include 'no,' so I'll take it for now."

I opened my mouth to force out something a little less wishy-washy, but the front door opened abruptly before I could. Alex swept in with a face like a storm cloud.

"*Flynn*," she snapped. "We talked about this."

The whipcrack of her voice had my eyes darting to the side, my head tilting to bare my throat to her submissively without pausing to check in with my brain first. I felt the other two notice my lapse, even as mortification flooded me. Quickly, I jerked my posture straight and my eyes front and center, but it was too late. They'd already seen the supposedly cool-headed ambassador rolling over and exposing her belly at the first hint of an alpha's bark.

Alex's cheeks flooded red with a level of mortification equal to my own, and she straightened to military attention, eyes forward and staring into the middle distance. "My apologies, Madam Ambassador. Flynn wasn't supposed to bother you with that kind of nonsense."

Alpha hearing must have picked up the topic of conversation even through the walls of the cabin. If nothing else, it confirmed what I'd already guessed—Alex had no part in Flynn's crazy offer.

"You know I'm right about this, Alex," Flynn said. "But that's okay. I can be patient."

"I think there have been a lot of pheromones flying around for the past few days," I began, channeling the same omega ego-soothing instincts that had made me a top diplomat. "And before that, a lot of crisis-induced adrenaline. Any omega would be lucky to have a pack like yours… but that's not the world we live in anymore. Kam and I are trying to ensure that world can exist again someday — and unfortunately, that means avoiding any entanglements that might be used against us by those who want to destroy our people. I *am* sorry, Flynn."

He gave me a fond look. "I still didn't hear a 'no' in there — so it's all good, Leona."

Alex shot him a quelling glare before returning her attention to me. "What you're doing is important. Don't let anyone distract you from it. And… let me apologize for barking earlier. You're right that things have been… *intense,* lately."

I tried on a smile for her. "I think you're allowed a free pass for minor infractions after you've helped save our lives."

"I'm just glad we got there in time," she said. "You should rest for a bit more, and once you're ready, we'll head back to Bucharest. I assume you have pheromone suppressors hidden in your luggage?"

"I do," I confirmed. "I should be good to go on that front in another couple of hours. Kam and I need to have a serious talk, and I should probably try to eat something else first — assuming there's something free of both cod liver and fish meatballs. We can leave anytime after that."

"Very good, ma'am," Alex said. "I'll make sure everything's ready to go whenever you are."

I nodded acceptance, and tried not to feel Flynn's eyes on me as I turned and left the room.

I found Kam in the bedroom. The nest had been disassembled — the mattress and bedding back in place on the bed frame; the furniture rearranged. The couch cushions must have been returned to the front room earlier so that Flynn would have something to sleep on other than the bare floor. The lamp, now uncovered, cast harsh yellow light around the room rather than mellow, reassuring red.

Something deep inside me raged at the loss of our ridiculous jury-rigged nest. I shoved that instinct back into its box as well. Respectable beta ambassadors weren't allowed to have nests. Respectable beta ambassadors didn't *need* nests.

Kam sat on the edge of the bed, dressed in slacks and shirtsleeves as he stared at his hands tangled together in his lap. I entered the room and settled next to him, letting my shoulder brush his. He looked up at me from beneath dark lashes—always so beautiful, even with the old sadness shining from his depthless brown eyes.

"Did Flynn talk to you?" he asked.

"Yes," I said simply.

"He asked you if we'd join his pack?"

I nodded. "So… he talked to you, too." For some reason, the idea raised a sense of disquiet inside me.

"Yes. There wasn't a lot to do in the nest except talk—at least when you were resting between peaks." Kam licked his lips and looked down again. "You told him no, I'm assuming."

I'd told Flynn everything *except* no. My unease deepened. "It's impossible. Too dangerous for us. Too dangerous for them. Beckett might be some kind of closet sympathizer—but what do you think would happen when he found out? And he would, sooner or later."

"What if we all left together, though?" Kam asked, and the bottom fell out of my stomach as I realized he was seriously considering it.

"You want to do it," I said faintly. "Oh my god. You want to throw everything away and run."

He looked up at me again, and his dark gaze was pleading. "Leo, it's not safe. People know our secret now. One wrong word, and this entire house of cards could come tumbling down around us."

"It was always going to come tumbling down," I said. "It was only ever a question of how much good we could do before it did! Kam—I can't run away now. *There's still too much to do.* What about the weapon, for god's sake?"

He gathered my hands in his and looked at me, anguished. "I don't want to watch you fall to that weapon, Leo. What if they decide to let it loose at the next summit? We could get out now—go someplace far away, where no one pays attention. Someplace where the Committee's influence is weak. I don't want both of us to die because you were too stubborn to recognize when the game was over!"

I pulled my hands away from his grip, the words cutting like a knife to the gut. "I'm not giving up," I said, barely recognizing my own voice. "Our people need someone to fight for them in the halls of power. Kam, don't make me choose between you and my work."

An ominous silence fell as we sat staring at each other—separated by a handful of inches, along with a gap that suddenly felt as wide as the ocean.

SIXTEEN

Leona

THE FEAR I felt at the idea of Kam leaving me rivaled the fear I'd felt when my heat hit me while we were trapped in the terrorist cave. I closed my eyes, forcing myself to think instead of reacting. God... the dregs of these damned hormones could get lost *any time now*, and that would be *great*.

I was being selfish. I knew that. Kam was one hundred percent right about the added danger to us, and just because I couldn't let it stop me, I had no right to act like he needed to put himself at risk as well. If Flynn had offered Kam the same thing he'd offered me, it probably sounded like a dream come true to him. A pack of alphas to cherish and protect him? A place of safety, away from the influence of the organization that had killed his family, enslaved him, and mutilated him? He'd have to be crazy not to think about accepting.

Opening my eyes, I reached out and grasped his hands again. "Okay. Okay, you're right. Maybe you should consider this. I *do* want you to be safe, *odama*. I want you to be happy. Just... are you sure Flynn can deliver on what he's offering? I don't get the impression Alex is on board with the idea, and we can't know what Jax would think."

"It's two separate issues, Leo," Kam replied in an exhausted tone. "Getting somewhere safe, and joining our packs together. But you're not going to do either one of those things. I already knew that. I'd just hoped..." He shook his head as though chasing the thought away. "Never mind."

"I'm serious," I said, forcing the words past the growing lump in my throat. "Maybe you should go. Find someplace safe. Go to Jamaica. Stay with my—" I cut myself off abruptly, not sure I wanted to let my parents' location slip when we were within range of alpha hearing. "Well, there are people there who could help you settle in, anyway. No one would bother you there."

Now it was his turn to tug his hands free. He scrubbed at his eye sockets with the heels of his palms and kept them there, speaking without looking at me. "I need more time to think about this."

I nodded, even though he couldn't see me. "Okay. I understand. I think we're going to leave for Bucharest soon. I'm not sure yet what happens after that. We're at Beckett's mercy here, and I still have no real idea what his angle is."

"We need to visit Jax and thank him." Kam hesitated, before continuing, "Assuming he's conscious and can understand us, of course."

Christ. I didn't need to wait for public exposure as an omega. Everything felt like it was falling down around my ears right this very minute.

"Yes," I agreed hoarsely. "We sure do."

Could I do this without Kam? I'd have to, if he accepted the offer of safe haven that Flynn seemed to be extending.

The worst part of it was, I couldn't say with utter certainty that these alphas were trustworthy. There were too many holes in their story. They'd saved us, yes. They'd behaved with nothing but honor toward us when we were at our most vulnerable. But they also weren't telling us the whole truth.

Kam wasn't a fool. He'd have realized all of this, just as I had. The difference between us was that he hadn't lost the capacity for faith. Faith in people;

faith in the future. Despite everything he'd experienced, Kam could still look at someone who'd helped him and trust that they were fundamentally a good person. I couldn't. I needed proof first.

And right now, I didn't trust Beckett's motives for not arresting us.

It was a testament to how much danger we were about to face that if Kam decided to place his faith in Flynn and his pack, I wouldn't try to stop him. Either way, Beckett had us on a hook if he ever decided to reel us in.

"Do you want to try and rest some more first, or leave now?" I asked, changing the subject. "The others are ready as soon as we give the word."

"Let's just go." Kam straightened with a final rub of his face and rose. "We can sleep in the Range Rover, assuming no one's going to try to blow us up this time."

I took a steadying breath and rose as well. "If they do, I suppose it won't much matter whether we're asleep or awake when the bomb goes off."

"True," he agreed. "You should eat more before we leave, though. I had a poke around the pantry and found something that looks like normal sardines. It's probably safe."

And so, we were apparently going to employ the 'pretend it's not happening' defense, when it came to the potential unraveling of our years of friendship. In my current state, I was fine with that.

"Sardines," I said. "Awesome. Okay, let's do that, then."

<hr>

Less than an hour later, the four of us were rumbling down a narrow mountain road. My scent had subsided beneath the power of suppression drugs, but Flynn's definitely hadn't, and neither had Alex's.

I stewed in the spicy floral mix, wondering with a sharp pang if I would ever smell the subtle scent of Kam's lemon and ginger again.

Sleep was out of the question as the vehicle rattled down the bumpy, pothole-strewn road. And despite my exhaustion, my brain wasn't about to let me rest when we reached the relative smoothness of the highway, either.

"Will we be going straight to the medical clinic?" I asked, hoping for some snippet of information that might help me figure out Beckett's motives.

"Yes," Alex said. "We need to report in, and that's almost certainly where Beckett will be."

I wasn't sure if there was anything to be read into that or not. On the one hand, I'd noted the man's almost paternal relationship with his underlings shortly after they'd first been assigned to us. It was natural that he'd be worried about Jax, but would a normal team leader really stay with his injured man 24/7? There was the sample of the chemical weapon to worry about, for one thing... though once he'd handed it over to a government lab, it would probably have fallen under someone else's jurisdiction.

Beckett's only official mission had been to keep Kam and me safe at the summit. With his other alphas guarding us, he legitimately might not have much else to do except paperwork and reports for his superiors in the security division.

Eventually, we reentered Bucharest. The city looked as stately and peaceful as ever, which felt wrong somehow. My world had shifted seismically. It seemed unfair that the fresh chaos shouldn't be reflected externally in the city around me.

The private clinic didn't look like much from the outside, though it did have a guarded gate at the entrance. The sentry spoke rapidly to Alex in Romanian. I had no idea if she spoke the language or not, but she handed over a pass. The man examined it and waved us through a moment later as the gate arm rose. The parking lot was small, with only a few other vehicles in it. Alex parked the Range Rover next to a gray Audi sedan, and we got out. Entering the building required another flash of the pass. The inside of the clinic was decidedly nicer than the outside, with soothing, neutral paint colors and tasteful decorating.

I got the distinct impression that the UFNA government would be paying handsomely for Jax's stay here. Alex stopped at the reception window and requested Beckett. Again, she showed the pass, and the woman behind the glass nodded in acknowledgement.

A minute or so later, the door to the waiting room opened, and Beckett stepped through. He ran his pale gaze over us and nodded in satisfaction.

"Oh, good," he said. "Come on back. He's awake."

We followed, though Kam and I hung back at the door to the private suite while Flynn and Alex hurried to their packmate's bedside. Even from across the room, I could see that Jax looked terrible. His complexion was pasty gray, and he had dark circles under his bloodshot blue eyes. His arms rested across his chest, one of them heavily bandaged. His hands twitched and jerked continuously.

Nerve agent, I thought. Uncontrollable muscle contractions would be one of the side effects.

Flynn leaned on the side rail of the hospital bed and stared down. "Wow. You look like hell, asshole."

One corner of Jax's lips twitched. "Good to know I look better than I feel, then. Next time, don't be so late." His deep velvet voice emerged as an exhausted rasp.

Flynn grunted in irritation. "Next time, get kidnapped and held captive somewhere that's easier to find. You *know* I fuckin' hate caves."

"Not a big fan myself, after this," Jax agreed. One of his legs jerked beneath the hospital blanket, and he gritted his teeth.

Alex reached down and clasped his bicep. "We're glad to see you awake, *alef*. Everyone is safe. You did well."

Jax snorted, and immediately winced. "You mean I nearly got everyone killed. What a goddamned shitshow."

Beckett, who'd been standing off to one side with his arms crossed, spoke up. "You did everything you could. The fault lies with the lack of intelligence regarding the attack on the motorcade. It's a mess, true—but as long as everyone's alive, messes can be cleaned up afterward."

"We'd both be dead if it weren't for the four of you," Kam said quietly.

"Dead... or worse," I agreed, not even trying to ignore the omega-shaped elephant in the room.

Jax's eyes tracked to us, and I wondered if he'd even registered our presence before now. "Madam Ambassador. I'm just glad they didn't manage to pump this stuff into you. Thank the others, not me."

"Call me Leona, please," I said. "And you're stuck with our thanks as well—sorry."

"Is it safe to talk in here?" Flynn asked.

"That's part of what we're paying for in this place," Beckett said. He met my eyes, and I noticed that the livid cut on his face from the car crash seemed to be healing well. "Come inside properly and close the door, please."

Distantly, I wondered if this was it—the moment when he'd make some demand in exchange for his unexpected leniency with us. I followed Kam the rest of the way inside and shut the door behind us.

Don't let other people control the conversation. It was Diplomacy 101. Listening was important—but framing the flow of the conversation in the way most beneficial to you was vital.

"Mr. Beckett," I began, "you and your team have gone above and beyond the call of duty. You've been nothing but professional in your dealings with us. And yet, we both know you're off-script. You now possess information about the two of us that would be catastrophic to our lives should it reach the wrong ears."

"She still thinks you're going to turn around and arrest them," Flynn muttered.

I forged ahead. "It seems prudent to point out that we also have information about the status of your team that could be damaging to you. Your alphas shouldn't have been in a position to help me with my… *situation*. And yet, they were."

Flynn's eyebrows shot up, and I could have sworn his scent sharpened with interest. I willed my cheeks not to heat.

"Oooh," he said, with evident relish. "Blackmail. *Ice cold*, Leona. I knew there was a reason I liked you."

Of all possible reactions, I hadn't quite expected that one. Beside me, Kam seemed to be biting his tongue to keep from jumping in with some attempt to defuse the tense situation—omega peacekeeping instincts still on edge after the past few days. Alex appeared utterly impassive. Jax looked like he had a splitting headache—which, to be fair, he probably did.

Beckett showed no signs of either offense or anger. "I don't think threats of mutual blackmail will be necessary under the circumstances, Madam Ambassador. There's absolutely nothing to be gained on my end from ruining the careers of a pair of highly effective government officials. And given your admirable record of working to further the wellbeing of oppressed groups, I'm confident you wouldn't risk bringing harm to my team simply because they haven't been forced to adhere to a barbaric and dehumanizing law."

I felt Kam flinch next to me. He'd been a victim of that same barbaric law — irreparably so.

This still seemed too easy, and things hadn't magically started adding up. But I'd poked and I'd prodded — first at Alex, and now at Beckett — without finding a chink in their assertion that we weren't going to be arrested and turned over to the authorities. There came a point where pushing the issue any further was only asking for trouble.

"In that case, it sounds like we don't have a problem," I told him, even though I was painfully aware that we still *did* have a problem — even though it was an unrelated one.

"I'm pleased to hear it," Beckett said, with the faintest hint of wry amusement hiding in his tone.

"Since that's out of the way, can we have a few minutes alone, boss?" Flynn asked. "Pack business."

I tensed, trying not to show it outwardly.

Alex closed her eyes. "*Flynn*," she said, sounding tired beyond words.

"Fine," Beckett said. "But don't exhaust the invalid, and for god's sake, please don't make my life any more complicated than it already is right now."

I gave him another wary look. It almost sounded like he knew what this private conversation was likely to entail. He patted Alex on the shoulder as he turned to leave. Kam and I moved out of his way, and he gave us a silent nod of acknowledgement as he passed by us on his way to the door. It opened and shut, and we were alone with the alphas — a pack who might well be about to steal my *odama* away from me.

SEVENTEEN

Leona

"SO, I HAD this brilliant idea, Jax," Flynn said.

"It's not actually a brilliant idea." Alex still sounded almost as tired as Jax looked.

"No, it totally is," Flynn continued, oblivious. "We have a pack. They have a pack. We should join packs. It'll be great. We can court them, proper-like. Just like in the old days."

Jax blinked up at him.

"Except, of course, for the part where they're in hiding," Alex said with forced patience, "and haven't expressed any interest whatsoever in doing something so completely and utterly crazy."

"They haven't said no," Flynn argued.

Jax followed the exchange like someone watching a tennis match. "They're also standing right here, and might not appreciate being spoken about in the third person."

I steeled myself. "I'm sorry, but my answer is, in fact, no," I managed, surprised at how difficult it was to force the words out. "Not because of any of you, but because I have to keep fighting for change. I want to live in the kind of world where I could say yes to a proposal like that. But I don't live in that world." The next part was even harder to get out. "However, I can only speak for myself. I don't speak for Kam."

Squaring my shoulders, I tried to brace for having my heart ripped out.

Kam took a deep breath. "I'm afraid I must decline as well, though I wish that weren't the case. Leona is my pack. Where she goes, I go."

I couldn't help the little gulp of relief that broke the silence as I tried to get air in my lungs.

"There's your answer, Flynn," Alex said evenly. "Now leave it be."

Flynn's dark eyes pinned me. "For now I will. But Leona… Kam… I'm going to ask you again in a month or two, and eventually your answer is going to be different. Like I said, I can be patient."

"I'm sorry that you have to decline," Jax said. "I'd have liked the opportunity to get to know you both better, even if I understand why you can't do it."

I risked a quick glance at Kam. He looked distant and detached in a way I really didn't like. Despite his decision to stay, I still couldn't rid myself of the sense of everything falling apart around me.

"What about the three of you, though?" I blurted. "I won't lie—with this weapon on the horizon, the smart thing would be to get out of the line of fire, if you've got the means to do so. I have some contacts—"

"We're not going anywhere, Madam Ambassador," Alex said. "You've got your work. We've got ours."

I gave her a reluctant nod, not truly surprised. "Right. I understand."

"Jax, we should let you rest," Kam said. He still didn't sound like someone who'd given up his fondest dream in favor of risking his life for a very questionable return. He sounded… absent. Like he wasn't really here in the room with me.

"Yes," Alex agreed. "Madam Ambassador, if I might have a private word with you first? Pack leader to pack leader."

Taken by surprise, I hesitated for a moment. "Of course," I said.

She nodded, and her green gaze took in the others with a sweeping glance. "We'll be back in a few minutes."

I followed her outside, and she led me down the hall to an empty patient room not dissimilar to Jax's. She ushered me in and closed the door. I turned to face her, unsure of what to expect.

"You're doing the right thing," she said. "I just wanted to tell you that, because you look like you're not a hundred percent sure."

My breath caught, and I had to swallow twice before I was confident my voice would be steady. "No... I know that. Kam and I — we've worked hard to get positions where we might be able to make a real difference. And with Prime Minister Fairbanks in office now — "

"It feels like change is a real possibility," she finished for me.

"Assuming terrorists don't manage to kill all of us first," I added dryly. "But, yes. That's it exactly. Our generation — we have to give up our own happiness and focus on trying to fix the mess. Maybe that way, the next generation can live and love the way we all deserve to."

Something shifted behind Alex's gaze. For the barest moment, she looked as though she'd been sucker-punched.

I hesitated. "I've said something to upset you. I'm sorry — that wasn't my intention at all."

The hard-as-nails security alpha lowered her muscular frame into one of the padded visitor chairs and ran a shaky hand over her face. "Not you, Madam Ambassador. It's just" — her voice cracked on the word, though it was barely detectable — "*Damn it.*"

I pulled up the other chair and sat in front of her. I wasn't sure exactly how it had happened, but somehow in the hours since I'd emerged from my heat haze, I'd come to think of the standoffish female alpha as a sort of ally to my cause of not getting sucked in by Flynn and Jax's magnetism.

"You went through something that the others didn't," I observed, leaning forward in my seat. "That's why you understand that this could never work. Whatever it was, I'm sorry it happened to you."

She drew herself back to the present with the air of someone who'd had a lot of practice at it. "There was... a female omega, when I was in the military alpha program. She was in the administrative corps—passing as a beta inside the damned army, which tells you everything you need to know about her."

I whistled low. *Talk about some giant titanium balls.*

"Her name was Irina," Alex continued. "We fell in love. Jax and Flynn weren't my pack yet, though we were moving in that direction. It probably wouldn't have mattered—they're both idiots when it comes to this kind of stuff. They wouldn't have tried to talk me out of it even if we had already been pack to each other."

Given what I'd experienced personally, with Flynn in particular, she was probably right about that.

"What happened?" I asked quietly.

Alex met my gaze frankly. "We both managed to get leave for the week around her heat cycle. She'd taken black market contraceptives, so we thought we were safe. Hell, we thought we were invincible—out in the world with our fake freedom and our stupid adolescent belief in our own invincibility. She begged for my mating bite and I gave it to her. Fucking knot-brain that I was."

She took a deep breath and let it flow out.

"Anyway, the contraceptives were either phony or a bad batch. She was pupped after the heat. Since she was at least aligned, we figured she could pass it off as a beta pregnancy and get a discharge from the army, even if it was a dishonorable one."

I winced, having a fair idea of where this was going.

"I never learned the details of what happened, but she was exposed and arrested," Alex said dully. "I never saw her again. They must have extradited her to the Committee, because two weeks later, I woke up in the middle of the night to the agony of the mating bond breaking. They killed her, and they killed our unborn pups."

The bottomless ache in my chest that always came in response to hearing stories like this was way too familiar, and I hated that familiarity with a passion.

"They call *us* animals," I said. "But it's them. They're perverted, sadistic brutes, and we have to stop them."

She nodded. "Yes. That's all that matters—stopping them. But you need to understand. I don't want Jax or Flynn waking up in the night to that kind of horror. That feeling—the sense of the bond stretching and twisting until it's torn out by the roots—I want to make sure they *never* find out what it's like."

My eyes burned in response to the desolation in Alex's tone. I blinked, and two tears spilled over. Moving slowly enough that she'd have plenty of time to pull away, I lifted my hand and stretched forward, cupping her jaw.

"I understand," I said, and her fingers came up to tangle with mine.

She closed her eyes, and nodded. We stayed that way for a handful of heartbeats before she let her hand drop and straightened away from the touch.

"It's in the past," she said. "Let's just try to make sure there's not a repeat in the future."

I hadn't been wrong about her being an ally — but I hadn't understood how determined she was to keep our packs separate. It wasn't only about protecting Kam and me. It was about protecting her own pack as well.

"Agreed," I told her wholeheartedly.

———◆———

Three days later, the specialist at the clinic decreed that Jax was stable enough for air transport back to Montreal. Beckett had spent a good part of that time drilling a coherent story into all three of us, in anticipation of the inevitable debriefing we were about to face. As it turned out, that was a very good thing indeed.

Stepping off the charter plane at Montréal-Mirabel International Airport felt deeply surreal. Jax was still being wheeled off the plane on his medical gurney when Kam and I were whisked away by government security officials dressed in dark suits. I crushed the flutter of irrational panic that threatened to grab me by the throat when we lost sight of Beckett and the alphas.

Two of the security operatives retrieved our luggage for us. We both refused the offer of medical attention. Given a choice, I would have scurried home to my converted loft and hidden under a blanket for a week. Unfortunately, our escorts had other ideas. A black limo delivered us directly to the Foreign Service building, where we spent the next four hours putting Beckett's creatively edited story of the kidnapping to the test in separate interview rooms.

Not for the first time, I wondered if Beckett had actually gotten any kind of official sanction for his rescue operation. On the one hand, if he hadn't, I was at a loss as to how he could have gained access to the kind of intelligence that had allowed him to find us. On the other hand, that simply wasn't how the military chain of command worked. Government security wasn't even *part of* that chain of command.

Whatever the case, I dutifully parroted the story I'd been fed, no matter how many different ways the interviewer framed the questions. At the end, I walked out with an appointment for mandatory trauma counseling and two weeks of leave—both of which I was dreading. The limo dropped Kam at his modest apartment in Little Burgundy, and me a bit farther south in my considerably less modest apartment in Saint-Henri, next to the Lachine Canal. The driver helped me take my luggage up and gave me a polite nod before leaving me alone.

Just like that, it was over.

The silence inside the renovated warehouse loft echoed. There was nothing and no one here to greet me. No roommates, no pets, not so much as a goldfish. I would need to get groceries. I would need to call the cleaning service and let them know I was back.

Instead of doing either of those things, I stood in the entryway with my luggage at my feet and stared into the middle distance for a very long time indeed.

EIGHTEEN

Leona

I'D BROKEN my relationship with Kam. That realization had grown increasingly clear after our return, as the weeks rolled into months. The worst part was, I couldn't quite put my finger on what had changed—only that *something* had.

He was as sweet natured as always. As polite as always. As kind and compassionate as always. And yet, he was no longer *my Kam*. At first, I tried to broach the subject... to find out if there was something I needed to do, or not do, that would make everything all right again. He seemed bewildered by the idea that there was anything wrong in the first place.

It didn't even feel as though he were trying to passive-aggressively punish me for saying no to the alphas. That simply wasn't the way his brain worked. The two of us had just... changed. Something had shifted, and I didn't like it. Not one bit.

Kameron Patel had been through hell while I was still living safely in my parents' house, playing with Barbies and having sleepovers. He'd cut out large pieces of his own psyche in order to function through a childhood and adolescence that had been nothing short of unspeakable. I had the horrible sense that I was watching another piece of him drift away before my eyes, and it terrified me to contemplate how much more he might have left to lose before he would be nothing but an empty shell.

In the depths of night, alone in my ever-so-normal, beta-style bed, I thought maybe I should have said yes to Flynn, if only to make Kam happy. Or maybe Kam had been right and we should have run, with or without the alphas. We could be in Jamaica now, lying on the beach and sipping drinks with little umbrellas in them. We could be hidden safely away with my parents, far from the world that wanted to kill or enslave us.

These were not good thoughts to be having—especially not on the eve of the stripped-down summit that would pit my powers of persuasion against two powerful Committee chairmen, with the future of UFNA alphomic policy on the line. I needed my brain in the game and my *odama* at my back—not the weight of this nagging guilt and uncertainty.

At least we would be on home territory this time. After the shitshow in Romania, these were to be bilateral talks between Prime Minister Fairbanks' progressive administration and the Committee's top two officials—Kostya Nikolayev and the head of the pan-American region, Enoch Sloane. On the table were several relatively minor policy debates, including expanding the roles of alphas in the military. But the centerpiece of the talks would revolve around the current alphomic extradition treaty.

The god-awful agreement—one that allowed accused alphas and omegas to be sent across international borders to face trial and execution by a Committee-led tribunal—was number one on my personal hit list. Challenging that law had been important to me for a long time, but it had soared straight to the top of my priorities after hearing Alex's story.

I had a small arsenal of pre-approved concessions ready to deploy in the pursuit of my—of the *administration's*—goals. Some of them were innocuous. Some of them stuck in my craw. All of them could be valuable in negotiating for the bigger prizes.

If only I weren't still an emotional wreck beneath my brittle veneer of professional competence.

It had been slightly more than two months since the kidnapping. Flynn hadn't made good on his promise to court us further, and I suspected that was down to Alex's influence. I'd quietly kept tabs on Jax's recovery from afar, not trusting myself to visit him in person as he slowly recuperated from exposure to the experimental nerve agent. As of ten days ago, he'd returned to limited duty, though my contact indicated he was still suffering from frequent migraines and intermittent muscle weakness on his left side.

I'd been half-hoping and half-dreading that Beckett's team might be present during the summit—either assigned to us, or to some other UFNA official. But Beckett was out sick at the moment. With Jax on light duty and their beta chief unavailable, there'd been no question of assigning the team to such a high-level function.

The meetings were to take place at the historic St. Paul Hotel in the heart of Old Montreal, not that I expected the grand surroundings to make much of an impression on the dour Committee leaders.

I'd watched Enoch Sloane and Kostya Nikolayev become notorious rivals over the course of the past few years, rising to power in the organization at roughly the same time but on different continents. They were both seriously terrifying bastards, but I was ready and willing to play them against each other if it would help me get what I wanted.

I would do this, no matter that the rest of my life had become a slow-rolling dumpster fire. Despite whatever wrong turn our personal relationship had taken, Kam and I would grasp the opportunity we'd been given, and we would turn it into real change for our people.

------◆------

The morning of the summit dawned chilly and gray. I'd been up since four, and Kam had joined me for final prep work over strong coffee at five-thirty.

"I still don't like these concessions related to genetic testing," he said, frowning at the notes I'd jotted the day before.

"I don't like any of it," I told him, shuffling papers. "But it's like any battle. It's best we have a fall-back position ready in case the enemy gets the upper hand."

"I know," he said, resigned. "I know."

We arrived at the hotel an hour before the official start time and began circulating—getting a feel for the undercurrents swirling beneath the surface. Prime Minister Fairbanks and his wife made their entrance a few minutes before the first round of meetings were called to order. Tall, dark, and charismatic, Fairbanks delivered an opening speech carefully calculated to appeal to the news outlets, replete with easily digestible sound bites that reinforced his coalition government's dedication to improving the lot of all UFNA residents, regardless of sex or gender.

"In conclusion," he said, his deep voice rolling around the cavernous event space, "I hope that these meetings may function as an open exchange of ideas, ushering in a new era of cooperation and respect between the UFNA and the Committee."

Respect, I thought, with heavy irony. *Right. Somehow, I doubt that.*

Polite applause ensued. The Prime Minister was bustled out immediately afterward, no doubt heading off to deal with the next item on his busy itinerary. Enoch Sloane rose to take the speaker's lectern. I wondered if he and Nikolayev had flipped a coin to decide who got to play to the cameras by delivering the opening remarks.

Sloane was a plain-faced man with exceptionally pale blond hair. He had the air of an Alabama fundamentalist preacher, with his drawling Southern accent, his forehead shiny with sweat, and the light of fanaticism in his whiskey-brown eyes. All he needed was a Bible to thump.

I exchanged a glance with Kam, who looked vaguely ill as the man droned on about gender impurity and the importance of rooting out the alphomic cancer at its source.

"They would have been smarter to let the Mad Russian go in front of the cameras," he murmured, too low to reach any ears but mine.

He wasn't wrong. Nikolayev might disdain designer suits and the fancy trappings of elegance, but he had the power of charisma in a way that Sloane decidedly did not. I was already making a mental list of the ways Sloane's lackluster public speaking performance could work in our favor.

He rambled on for a bit longer, ending with a story about an immigration official who'd been exposed as an unregistered alpha, and who'd been secretly facilitating the transfer of alphomic refugees to South America. A familiar scare tactic piece, but I had no doubt that it would play gangbusters with the hard-line conspiracy theory crowd.

I took a moment to mourn the loss of yet another link in the fragile chain of the alphomic underground—that shadowy association of alphas, betas, and omegas who made it possible for some of us to escape what would otherwise be our fate. Members of the underground had helped Kam escape slavery and forge a new identity in a new country. They provided my heat blockers and pheromone suppressors. Their ranks included doctors willing to forge misleading medical reports, and midwives willing to whelp pups from non-aligned omegas in secret.

Without them, we couldn't survive. And yet, the underground always felt like such a tenuous web... one that might unravel the moment the wrong thread was pulled.

The summit inched forward with agenda-setting and last minute scheduling changes, before eventually settling into the real work. The first day consisted of low-level negotiations and workshopping. The second day moved into the nuts and bolts of hammering out changes to existing agreements and feeling out where the sticking points lay.

It was a grind. There were a lot of sticking points.

The third day was make or break. Throughout the meetings, I'd felt the imagined weight of Sloane and Nikolayev's gazes on me, making my skin clammy and the fine hairs on my neck prickle. Beneath the fragile facade of civility, they were predators, while Kam and I were prey. If they sniffed us out, we'd be crushed between their jaws in an instant.

They say Nikolayev can smell an omega at twenty paces, even with suppressors.

That ridiculous piece of fearmongering floated through my mind as the man in question approached the table where I was attempting to discuss the finer points of omega sterilization laws with a Committee aide.

"Ambassador McCready," Nikolayev said, sending the aide scurrying away with an abrupt gesture of one hand. "A word in private, if I may."

Kam looked up sharply.

I steeled myself not to react beyond a raised eyebrow, despite the chill that shivered through me at the idea of being alone with a man who'd murdered his own omega sibling in cold blood.

"Chairman Nikolayev." My tone was admirably cool. "Are you sure you wouldn't care to invite Chairman Sloane into this discussion as well?"

It was a dig, and he probably knew it. His lip curled in distaste, but he only said, "Definitely not. I require clarity and brevity. Not saber-rattling."

I ignored the rigid tension in Kam's shoulders, because inadvertently drawing Nikolayev's attention to it wouldn't be good for either of us. This was the path I'd chosen. If it meant a private tête-à-tête with a monster, then so be it.

"Certainly," I replied, as though my skin weren't crawling at the prospect.

They say his sister's body had been almost unrecognizable after he'd finished with her. They say as a young man, he hunted captured omegas for sport, like animals.

I rose, not daring to meet Kam's eyes for what I might see there. Nikolayev ushered me to a private salon adjacent to the event space with old world courtesy that was bitterly incongruous in a murderer.

He closed the doors behind us, and I willed my heart not to start thundering like a cornered rabbit's. When he turned, it was to regard me with a slight frown furrowing his brow.

"You appear to have recovered well from your tribulations outside Târgoviște," he observed.

Ice rolled through my veins. "Yes, thank you," I replied, willing my voice to remain calm. "You mentioned something about brevity and clarity, Chairman?"

Steel-gray eyes bored into me, and the silence stretched for a painful moment.

"The Committee will not bend when it comes to the renegotiation of the alphomic extradition treaty," he said.

"That's not acceptable," I told him without hesitation, a different kind of tension creeping into my spine. "The Fairbanks administration is determined to gain at least some concessions on the matter, especially relating to extenuating circumstances in individual cases."

"That will not happen," he replied. "And if the UFNA attempts to withdraw from the existing extradition agreement unilaterally, the Committee will ensure that your current Parliamentary coalition falls apart, forcing a new election."

I stared at him, my stomach sinking. "That's blatant manipulation of a foreign power's internal governance."

"Yes," he agreed. One shoulder lifted in a barely perceptible shrug.

Right. Apparently the gloves were off now. I could play that game, too.

"I find it interesting that you are the one delivering this ultimatum, and not your pan-American counterpart. I would have thought UFNA treaties were more in his jurisdiction than yours."

Nikolayev regarded me with steely, reptilian eyes. "In matters of policy, my colleague and I speak with one voice."

"Except for the saber-rattling?" I suggested. A strange sense of detachment washed over me, my fear retreating to a distant point, somewhere out of my reach. "He's a liability, you know. *You* understand how to play the game of public opinion. He doesn't. He can only appeal to the fanatics, but you need to keep more than the fanatical base on your side. You need moderates."

Nikolayev raised an eyebrow. "My dear ambassador, I could not agree more with your assessment. However, it has no relevance to the discussion at hand."

I tilted my head. "You're wrong. It does. You can try to dismantle our Parliamentary coalition. But in return, we can bring our influence to bear in an effort to support Sloane over you—putting the weaker leader in a preeminent position, which will ultimately undermine the Committee in the long term."

The corners of Nikolayev's lips twitched upward, though his face remained cold. "You could do so, yes. And then we would see which of us was ultimately more influential on the world stage. I don't believe you would enjoy the results of that particular experiment."

I focused on not letting my body language falter beneath the force of his overbearing presence. Inside, though, a chill suffused me... because I knew he was right. One nation alone could not bring down the Committee. That was its power. It was a hydra, with its many tentacles twisted and embedded throughout the world.

"Alternately," he continued, in the light tone of one who was about to offer an unsolicited act of kindness, "you could accept that you have lost this battle, and surrender gracefully—in exchange for which, I will ensure that all of the remaining lesser battles on relatively minor issues fall in your favor."

I couldn't help my sharp, indrawn breath of surprise. "*What?*"

"A concession," he said, "from the winning side to the losing one. Your Prime Minister's pet military program... the loosening of restrictions related to permanent omega sterilization, in favor of reversible methods using drugs... a reduction in sentencing guidelines for betas convicted of failure to declare throwback offspring. Surely such a tradeoff would be to your government's benefit."

I hesitated, stuck for words. He was proposing a straight trade — the single large issue in exchange for all of the lesser issues combined. Frustration swelled in my chest like hot lava — not least because in the end, accepting or declining his offer wasn't my decision to make.

"I'll need to discuss it with my superiors," I said, trying not to let any of those feelings come through in my tone. "I should have an answer for you within the hour."

He gave an urbane nod of acceptance, after which I turned and stiffly walked out of the private anteroom.

Kam looked a bit wild-eyed as I returned. "Well?" he demanded.

"I need a secure line to the Secretary of Foreign Affairs," I said. "Apparently, Chairman Nikolayev wants to make a deal."

An hour later, as the Undersecretary was in the process of drafting the finalized agreement for the approval of the Cabinet, I wasn't sure if we'd won, or if we'd lost, or how I should be feeling about any of it. For his part, Chairman Sloane looked positively sour about the list of concessions. Nikolayev's face might as well have been carved from stone.

Alphas and omegas would still be sent to the Committee for sham trial and summary execution, without any form of legal recourse. But, on the other hand, there would now be a path forward toward the abolition of the barbaric surgery perpetrated on every omega who aspired to a life outside the breeding pens.

We listened impassively to the details as the new treaty provisions were read aloud, including the proposed changes to the sterilization laws. I was worried about Kam. Of course, I was *always* worried about Kam these days. His eyes held that same blankness they often had lately — but we couldn't talk here.

And afterward, he *wouldn't* talk.

The summit wound down. My superiors rained professional accolades down on my head for my supposed brilliance in negotiating so many concessions from the Committee at once. The Cabinet approved the new treaty a couple of weeks later, and it was duly signed by the Prime Minister with much pomp and circumstance.

The night after the signing ceremony, Kam showed up drunk on my doorstep with two dildos, a bottle of lube, a vial of contraband alpha sex pheromones, and an aura of almost manic desperation crackling around him.

NINETEEN

Leona

"KAM?" I BEGAN cautiously. "Let's sit down and have a talk, okay?"

My *odama* looked like he was unraveling before my eyes. I sat him down at the breakfast bar and plunked a large glass of water in front of him. He drank it, still wild-eyed and disheveled. The sex aids sat accusingly on the counter nearby, taunting me from my peripheral vision.

"I need to know," he said quietly—and I wasn't sure if it made it better or worse that he did not, in fact, appear to be nearly as drunk as I'd first thought him to be. "Leo, I need to know what I gave up. And... I need to know *exactly* how much was taken from me."

I sat on the stool in front of him and gathered his hands in mine. "*Odama*, I love you. And I will try to give you anything you need, just like you've always tried to give me everything I need. But I'm worried about you. I've been worried about you since Romania, but you wouldn't talk to me. I need you to talk to me now."

He nodded, and let his head fall forward—chin against chest, fingers squeezing mine where they tangled together. "I know, Leo. And I'm sorry. This... *all* of this—it's just that it's starting to feel like we're building a seawall out of sand, and the tide is coming in. We're celebrating the fact that people like us can be sterilized with chemicals now, instead of having our wombs ripped out with hooks. We're *celebrating* that, for god's sake! Why are we acting like this was some kind of victory?"

I ducked my head to meet his eyes. "I'm not celebrating it. But we're claiming it as a kind of victory because chemical castration can at least be undone in the future. It's not permanent."

Not like what happened to you. The words remained unspoken.

He shook his head. "Everything's broken, Leo — and I'm not sure how much longer I can keep pretending it isn't."

Something in my chest clenched, as the simple statement spoke directly to my deepest fears.

"Kam," I began, and had to stop when it came out as a rough croak. I swallowed hard — once, twice. Then I tried again. "I hear exactly what you're saying. But... I don't know what else to do? It's like... okay, we failed miserably with the extradition treaty. But somewhere there's a beta couple who hid their pup from the authorities, and now instead of getting thrown in jail, maybe they'll just get hit with a fine instead. That's good, right?"

"I know it is," he said miserably. "But, Leo — why does it have to be *us*? Can't someone else do the work now? Who knows, maybe they'd be better at it than we've been."

A faint tremor had taken up residence in my hands and arms. He could probably feel it. We were speaking truths that I wasn't ready to speak, because if I thought about them too closely, the entire foundation of my life might slide into the sea on those same shifting sands he'd mentioned earlier.

"Can we... please not talk about this right now?" I begged. "Because it's late, and there are two dildos and a bottle of black market pheromone on my kitchen counter — and I'm not really sure I can deal with all of these things at once."

He leaned forward, and I mirrored him until our foreheads were resting together.

"I'm sorry," he said. "Yes, let's not talk about this now. I need you, *odama*. I need to be with you tonight."

I knew, on some level, that his words were half of a lie. I was not, in fact, what Kam really needed. That's why there were alpha pheromones in my kitchen. But it was also half of a truth. I needed him, too. My packmate. My *odama*. We hadn't slept together or played at nesting since my heat. I'd missed him desperately, and it was pure relief to discover that he'd missed me as well.

"I'm here," I assured him. "You've got me—I'm yours, always. But first, you'd probably better tell me exactly how much you've drunk tonight."

He let out a little huff of reluctant amusement. "Three gin and tonics—the last one about two hours ago. I'd say they didn't help much... but in their defense, they at least gave me enough liquid courage to catch a taxi over here and spill my guts."

"Gin and tonics for the win, in that case," I agreed, and tilted my head forward until our lips met in a chaste, gin-flavored kiss. "I've missed you so much, *odama*."

"I know," he said. "I'm sorry."

"Don't be sorry," I told him. "Get your contraband off my countertop, and come help me gather up the pillows."

Anything that suggested a permanent nest was out of the question in my apartment, where I often hosted work colleagues and parties. But even betas could have a throw pillow obsession—and every spare surface on my furniture was covered with the things.

The converted warehouse was all old wood and high, narrow windows, with the bedroom tucked in the back. Protected. Hidden away. It was about the best an omega could hope for while still looking normal to betas. We dumped the pillows on the stupid beta-style bed in great piles, turning it into something that could half-swallow us in softness. I pulled a red chiffon wrap out of the closet and tossed it over the shade of the bedside lamp, plunging the room into a low, warm glow.

Kam bundled me onto the mass of pillows, where I sat cross-legged, facing him.

"Tell me what you need tonight," I said, taking his hands again.

He licked his lips and glanced away, before dragging his dark gaze back to mine.

"When you were in heat... when Jax and Flynn were there with us, I... felt things," he said. "It had to be the pheromones. I got hard, at least a little bit."

"You perfumed," I said, remembering that teasing hit of lemon and ginger.

"Apparently," he agreed. "I didn't think I could... respond that way. At least, I never have before. Flynn—he and I talked a lot, while you were asleep between peaks. He said sometimes sterilized omegas could still respond. Sexually, that is. That there were other ways to have sex, even with—" He freed one hand to make a vague gesture at his lower abdomen. "Anyway, I want to try. And with the pheromones, it will be good for you, too. Not like heat, but... not like what we usually do, either."

I nodded my understanding.

The two of us were intimate. We had been for years. But where betas were in sexual season constantly, for unbonded omegas, sexual receptivity was tied to the estrus cycle. Without the presence of an aroused alpha—or at least that alpha's bottled pheromones—an omega outside of heat didn't experience sexual pleasure. Not as a beta would understand the phrase, anyway.

Kam and I touched each other because it felt good and reinforced our bond. It wasn't a way to chase orgasms, because in the normal course of things, we'd never catch them. Slow massage. Sensual kisses. An embrace, skin to skin. That was how we bonded. That was how we comforted each other when times were hard.

What Kam was proposing now was something different. It was honestly outside of my experience — though after my heat, I supposed it was no longer outside of Kam's.

"I want to soak both of us in alpha pheromones," he said, not breaking eye contact. "I want to lick your clit and fuck you with one of those dildos, while you suck my cock and fuck me with the other one. I want to drown in you and penetrate you and be penetrated by you."

My lips parted, as shock at hearing my sweet omega talk like that combined with a heavy twisting sensation in my belly. In that moment, I felt hopelessly incompetent to do any of those things without making a hash of it.

"You want the dildo in your…" I trailed off, aware that he must mean exactly that.

He swallowed. "It's how some beta males do it. I, uh, did some research. And I also douched before I came here, so it won't be messy."

"Okay." I pressed a brief kiss to his lips. "You already know I'm clueless here. You'll have to show me how to do it without hurting you."

"I will," he said. "It's all right. I just want to try. Conventional beta wisdom is to use lots of lube and lots of patience. And the lube is for you, too, since I don't know if you'll make slick or not. We'll only do what feels good. I just want both of us to feel good, Leo."

I knelt forward and kissed him again, longer and deeper this time. He returned it—and whatever else did or did not work tonight, at least I had my *odama* back. I fell into his arms with profound relief and held him tight.

"I love you, Leo," he murmured against the shell of my ear.

"Love you, Kam," I told him, and nipped the side of his neck.

He helped me out of my clothes, peeling everything off a piece at a time. I did the same to him, struck by how seldom I'd actually seen him completely naked. Mostly, he kept his boxers on when we were together, or wore a pair of low-slung pajama pants. It occurred to me that he was making himself vulnerable in a way he usually didn't. He would be exposing his scars to me, up close and personal.

I'd seen the scars on his chest many times, where they'd cut out his extra nipples. They'd healed well enough to be relatively unobtrusive. Kam was a purebred omega, though he didn't like to talk about his lost family. I was a throwback, born to two beta parents, my body barely distinguishable from a beta female's without a thorough medical and gynecological examination. If, god forbid, I ever ended up pupped, I'd be unlikely to whelp more than twins, and two nipples would be plenty to get the job done.

But the purebred lines that had avoided beta interbreeding tended to whelp multiples—usually three or four, but sometimes up to six. Purebred omegas almost always had extra nipples. Kam had been born with four, but of course the beta butchers couldn't let that so-called *crime against nature* stand.

There was also a scar at the juncture of his right shoulder and neck where they'd gone for his mating gland. Ironically, they hadn't bothered to check if he was right or left-handed first. If they had, they might have realized he was one of the seven percent of omegas whose mating gland was located on the left side rather than the right.

Small mercy, since it was unclear if a mating bite would take in the absence of the hormones that his body could no longer produce. Unsurprisingly, research into such things was basically nonexistent.

It was the scar he usually hid that was by far the worst. Kam's womb and ovotestes had been pulled out through his birthing passage, which had then been sutured shut. He could never again have normal omegan sexual relations. He could never bear pups.

And now, he wanted to find out if the arousal he'd felt in response to the pheromones of the heat nest had been a fluke — or if he might still have some kind of sexual future after all. He'd come to me for that, and I couldn't express how grateful I was for his trust.

With a final kiss to the corner of my jaw, he stretched across the bed and retrieved the vial of pheromones.

"Please let this supplier not be a fraud," he joked weakly, and opened the stopper.

A scent of gunmetal and sage wafted into the air, backed by a faintly unpleasant chemical tang. It wasn't terribly appealing from an aesthetic standpoint, but within moments, my body began to sit up and take notice.

"It's real," I said, sparing a brief thought to wonder about the alpha who'd produced it.

"Apparently so," Kam said, taking a deeper sniff. "Though it does make you wonder what the price tag would be for an alpha who doesn't smell like a gun battle over Thanksgiving dinner."

He didn't compare the smell to the mouthwatering scents of *our* alphas, for which I was eternally grateful.

"Lie back, *odama*," he told me gently.

TWENTY

Leona

I LAY BACK, reclining into the soft embrace of the pillows. Kam dribbled a bit of the clear pheromone solution into his hand before sliding it palm-down along the centerline of my body from neck to pussy. He returned to dab a bit of it above my upper lip, directly below my nostrils. Carefully setting the remainder aside, he massaged it into my skin with slow strokes. I stretched, arching into his touch.

After the long weeks of uncertainty in both my private and professional life, I was touch-starved to begin with. But it quickly became clear that there was a reason alpha pheromones were considered a sex aid. Rather than only feeling Kam's touch on the surface of my skin, I could feel it deeper, traveling along my nerves and pooling in my belly.

"Oh, that's good," I murmured. "Here, give me the rest, I want to do you."

I rolled upright and took the vial he passed me, pressing his shoulder back until he flopped onto the pillows. He clasped his hands behind his head, looking up at me in the warm light with wide, liquid eyes. I was struck for the thousandth time by how incredibly beautiful he was with his olive skin, finely sculpted features, and sensual lips. His thick black hair was tousled, and his lithe body stretched out beneath me in lines of lean muscle.

I knew exactly how hard he had to work for that beta-like physique, too. Pouring the remaining half of the pheromone suspension into my cupped palm, I set the vial aside and trailed my fingertips through the pool of oily liquid, using it to draw light, ticklish lines along Kam's throat, collarbones, and pectorals, then trailing it down the centerline of his taut abdomen.

His slender cock twitched as I rubbed the remainder into the thatch of dark, wiry hair at the base, and smoothed my palms up the V-shape delineating hips that were a bit wider than an alpha or beta male's would have been. The entire room smelled of oiled metal and herbs now. Touching Kam's lovely body made even more heat pool in my stomach, and I felt the first pulse of slick dampening my folds.

"Looks like you won't have to share the lube," I told him, and he chuckled.

"It's working, then?" he asked.

"Definitely working," I said, and dabbed my finger on the tip of his nose, making him wrinkle it at me.

I settled myself onto his hips, straddling him, and he freed his hands from behind his head in favor of clasping my shoulders as I leaned over him. We kissed, languid and unhurried, my nipples tingling with little darts of unaccustomed pleasure as they brushed against his smooth chest.

He ran his palms up and down my back in broad, sweeping strokes, dipping a bit lower each time until eventually his hands settled on my ass, cupping it.

"I love your body," he whispered against my lips. "I love how soft you are. I love the curve of your waist and the little dimples at the small of your back." His thumbs rubbed over the small depressions on either side of my tailbone.

I moaned and slid down to mouth at his neck. "I love the way you carry yourself, like a dancer," I said against his skin. "I love your eyes, and the curl of hair that always falls across your forehead when you're distracted."

"Will you help me put the toy in?" he asked, lifting a hand to sweep my long hair back from my face.

"Tell me how," I said, peeling myself away from him long enough to retrieve the lube and the dildos. One was fairly narrow—smooth and slightly curved at the tip, with a broad base. The other was a knotting dildo, similar to the one Flynn had loaned us in Romania.

Kam rolled onto his stomach and walked me through the admittedly somewhat awkward process of fingering him open. He'd been good to his word—there was no mess beyond what was caused by the lube. It was an odd sensation to be inside him. His inner walls were hot and tight and velvety soft. His muscles clamped around my fingers the way I imagined my own passage must clamp around a knot, but I didn't get the impression it was in any way a transformative sexual experience for him.

I carefully avoided the twist of silvery scar tissue behind his cock, not sure he'd appreciate having it touched and not wanting to break the mood by asking. Eventually, the well-lubricated toy slid inside his body without much drama, and I paused to look down at him.

"Is that all right?" I asked. "How does it feel?"

He wriggled his hips, frowning a bit. "I'm… not sure yet. Strange. Full." He levered himself onto his side among the pillows and stilled, as though listening to his body. "Let me get used to it for a bit. In the meantime, I want to see you come for me."

My body tightened at his words, and I didn't argue as he laid me on my back and started kissing his way down, pausing to lick and suck at first one nipple, and then the other. A moan escaped me as his teeth grazed the tender flesh, and another pulse of slick dribbled out of me. His hand ghosted across my stomach, and he cupped me between my legs.

The difference with the alpha pheromones was night and day. I *wanted*, but not with the mindless, animal need of heat. Kam's fingers delved through my folds, the sensation jolting along nerves that normally slept undisturbed.

"Oh, god," I breathed, as his thumb circled my clit.

He gave my nipple a final kiss and straightened, looking down at me. "Do you want the cock now?"

I nodded, breathless. "Yes, give it to me, please, *odama*."

I was still on my back, and didn't feel the urge to roll over and present on all fours like I had during heat. Kam gave my folds a final caress and retrieved the dildo, rearranging us so my legs were splayed open and he was kneeling between them. He winced a bit and caught his breath as he settled into place — presumably when the toy shifted inside his ass.

Kam rested his right hand palm-down on my lower abdomen, steadying me. "You're so wet for it, Leo. You're *dripping*."

That sounded right, because when the blunt end of the dildo nudged at my entrance, my whole body felt like it was melting. I whimpered and curled my hips toward the fake dick, feeling it slide inside me without resistance. Kam worked it in and out of me, murmuring endearments and stroking my clit in time with his gentle thrusts.

"So beautiful," he murmured, as my body undulated, chasing the sensations.

I *loved* this feeling, free of the mindlessness and stress of a disastrous heat cycle. "Why —" I cut off with a gasp as the pleasure spiked momentarily. "Why didn't we do this sooner?"

He chuckled, a low, dark sound. "Because it's illegal, probably."

"So's everything—*ah!*—everything else," I managed, past the upward spiraling sensation that was gradually swallowing my thoughts. "When you're us…"

"True," he agreed. "Maybe it's time to stop caring about any of it."

I certainly didn't care about any of it right now. My heart was racing, my nerves tingling. "Give me the knot," I begged. "Please, Kam, I need it…"

Kam thrust in, and my entrance stretched, struggling to accommodate the flare above the base of the dildo. I groaned loudly, writhing, and it slipped inside to the hilt, filling me perfectly. Pleasure crashed over me, and I came hard, clamping around it, the scent of metal and sage in my nose.

"*Fuck*," I wheezed, once the waves receded, leaving me dizzy.

"Wow," Kam said, sounding a bit taken aback. "That looked… good?"

"Good, yeah," I managed. "That was definitely good."

Every breath sent a little buzz of sensation outward from the toy knotting me. With uncoordinated movements, I manhandled Kam around and onto his back so I could get at his body.

I want to lick your clit and fuck you with one of those dildos, while you suck my cock and fuck me with the other one, he'd said. *I want to drown in you and penetrate you and be penetrated by you.*

My inner thighs were soaked. I fumbled my way to his slender, beautiful cock and stroked my fingertips over it before reaching back to tap the base of the dildo in an irregular rhythm. His entire body twitched beneath me. He hooked an arm beneath my thigh and dragged me around until I was straddling his face.

His elegant fingers framed my hips, pulling me down to meet his mouth. At the first stroke of his tongue, my internal muscles rippled around the dildo. I cried out and fell forward, getting a hand around his dick and licking across the head. His answering moan vibrated along my folds.

This was what he'd wanted, and *god*, did he have good ideas. I didn't honestly have any clue what I was doing, when it came to sucking cock. I figured the term was fairly self-explanatory, though, so I wrapped my lips around his tip and hollowed my cheeks. He squirmed and gasped, his length stiffening in my mouth for a moment or two before subsiding again.

We licked and sucked and writhed against each other. Unbidden, it occurred to me that in this position I was basically presenting. A mental image formed of crouching over Kam's face like this while Jax pounded into me from behind, my mouth stuffed with Kam's cock while Flynn took his ass at the same time. In my mind's eye, Alex watched over us from the shadows with a hungry green gaze.

It was too much. With a high-pitched keen rising in the back of my throat, I came again, gushing slick over Kam's face. He made a sound like a sob and shuddered beneath me, still licking into me. An odd sort of mellow, hazy ecstasy settled across my mind. I wrapped an arm around his thigh so I could reach the base of the toy inside him and grasped it, rocking it gently in and out as I continued to suck him lazily.

I don't know how long we stayed like that, but my muscles finally stopped clamping the dildo in place. The scent of strange alpha and chemicals had begun to dissipate, and Kam was still a ball of shuddering tension beneath me. His intermittent, partial erection had faded along with the pheromones, and eventually he tapped my hip.

"Too much," he gasped. "Stop... stop. It's too much."

I shifted off him immediately, and he flopped back against the pillows, looking exhausted. He draped an arm across his eyes and let out a deep sigh. The lower half of his face was soaked with my slick.

He hadn't climaxed.

With the alpha pheromones a fast-fading memory and my higher brain functions returning, the scene quickly lost its luster. We were both sticky and sweaty, stuffed with dildos that were now merely uncomfortable. And Kam hadn't come.

I reached awkwardly between my legs and tugged the toy free, flinching as the fake knot stretched my entrance on its way out. It, too, was soaked with slick. I dropped it on the floor and turned to Kam with growing concern.

"Odama," I began. "Kam? Are you okay?"

It was a ridiculous question. He huffed out a breath of rueful laughter and let his arm drop away from his face. "I'm fine, beloved. It felt... good. You're right, we should have done it sooner."

As I had done a moment ago, he reached back and awkwardly pulled the toy out of his body, grimacing as he tossed it onto the floor next to the other one. I lowered myself to lie next to him, and his arms went around me easily. My back felt cold and exposed, despite his embrace—missing the alpha who should be spooning me from behind. I wondered if he felt the same way. We clung to each other for several minutes, until the sticky unpleasantness became too distracting.

"Shower?" he asked.

"Shower," I agreed.

⁌◆⁍

It was after midnight when Kam finally left—kissing me on the cheek, reassuring me yet again that the sex had been fine, and promising not to close himself off from me in the future. We'd scrubbed ourselves clean, scrubbed the dildos clean, and returned the throw pillows to their native habitat of couches and chairs.

After he left, I slipped on a nightgown and went back to bed, knowing I needed sleep if I didn't want to end up looking like a zombie during the news interview I was scheduled to give later today. Coverage of the new treaty and the laws that would soon result were gaining traction in the news cycle. Alphomic policy was becoming a topic of dinner table conversation in a way that it hadn't been in recent years. I could only hope that was the first step to a real shift in public sentiment. If that happened, then perhaps our lack of progress on the extradition treaty would end up being worthwhile after all.

My mind circled restlessly, caught between worry about the wider world and concern for Kam. I'd enjoyed our flirtation with sex in the moment, but that enjoyment had soured immediately upon realizing Kam's experiment with his own sexual nature had failed. Blind rage wasn't really an omegan trait, but I thought if I ever found myself holding a weapon in the presence of the so-called doctors who'd wielded the scalpels and hooks on his body, I'd kill them.

Of course, that was a deeply unproductive line of thought. Kam would doubtless be the first to tell me so. I thought about what he'd said earlier, that he'd responded sexually during my heat in a way he never had before. It occurred to me that tonight's research hadn't taken all the variables into account. I was back on pheromone suppressors now. While I was in heat, I'd been pumping out omega pheromones by the bucket load. What if Kam's body had been piggybacking off of that? Maybe it wasn't just alpha pheromones that he needed.

Unfortunately, it wasn't as though I could stop taking the suppressors again—not now that I was back in Montreal and back at work. At least, not without some very careful planning. A vacation to somewhere remote, maybe? It wouldn't have to be during my heat. In fact, it would be much better if it wasn't. There was always danger involved in taking time off at regular three-month intervals. People watched for things like that. But a random vacation? It might be doable, even though tongues would wag if Kam took off work at the same time to go with me.

But at least that kind of gossip—beta gossip—didn't have the potential to be deadly. I fell asleep to half-formed plans for a brief lovers' getaway, and awoke at three in the morning to the sound of my front door being kicked in.

TWENTY-ONE

Leona

I FLAILED UPRIGHT in my bed, torn from that deep, middle-of-the-night morass of sleep by an abrupt adrenaline dump. The sound of heavy, rhythmic crashing against the door pierced straight to the ancient part of my hindbrain that governed survival instincts.

Intruders in the den.

No alphas here for defense.

I tried to wrest back a shred of rationality. There were other apartments in the building... other people lived here. Burglars or kidnappers would have made some attempt at stealth. In the normal course of criminal investigation or arrest, the police would be required to identify themselves before breaking in.

When you were an unregistered omega, there was only one reason someone kicked down your door in the middle of the night.

My house of cards had just come tumbling down. My time was up. I could only be grateful that Kam had already left—though for all I knew, other officials were breaking down his door this very moment.

Heavy boots clattered up the metal fire escape outside, blocking any possible exit in that direction. The same high, narrow windows that gave me a false sense of security in my erstwhile den also prevented the possibility of an escape that way. I didn't keep any firearms in my home—there was no loaded revolver hidden in a drawer next to my bed. No shotgun propped in the closet.

With the benefit of hindsight, that had been a mistake. Not because it would have saved me. Rather the opposite, in fact. Waving a gun around when the SWAT team entered would have ensured that I died in a hail of bullets, rather than enduring the fate that almost certainly awaited me otherwise.

Pulse galloping, I hugged my knees beneath the covers and buried my face against them as I awaited the inevitable. The bedroom door slammed open with the sound of wood splintering beneath the force of a heavy bootheel. In a daze, I wondered why they hadn't simply turned the knob to open it. The damn thing wasn't even locked.

Boot steps pounded as several men swarmed in, flashlights waving crazily around the room. Even with my face hidden against my knees, the flashes of light through the darkness were disorienting.

"On the floor! *On the floor!*" shouted an angry male voice.

Betas talked about the fight-or-flight response to trauma. For omegas, it was the flight-or-freeze response, and I'd always tended toward freezing. I didn't move, feeling strangely detached from my body, as though all of this was happening to somebody else, and I was merely hearing the story reported secondhand.

"Get your ass on the floor *now*, bitch!" cried a different voice, replete with barely contained glee at the prospect of violence.

A rough hand grabbed my arm and dragged me bodily off the bed, slamming me face first onto the rug. A boot dug into the back of my neck, pinning me, and all of this was still happening to someone else, someone else. The pain, the choking sensation of not being able to breathe properly—that wasn't me. I was looking down on the scene from a slight remove, at the pathetic form sprawled on the floor with her nightgown riding up to expose one bare ass cheek in the wavering beams of the flashlights. Secondhand embarrassment flooded me on the figure's behalf. How humiliating.

"Cuff the stupid cow," someone said.

Rough hands on skin. Arms pulled behind back. Legs flopping uselessly, trying to gain purchase against the floor. Cold metal trapping wrists.

The overhead lights flipped on. The boot fell away. A hand fisted in red hair, twisting.

"On your feet, bitch."

The sharp, burning pain of hair being yanked out slammed me back into my body, and I gasped, scrambling to get my feet under me.

"Leona McCready, you are under arrest on suspicion of being an unregistered omega. You will be remanded for physical examination and genetic testing prior to extradition to the Committee on Alphomic Suppression for trial and sentencing."

I stood mute, an injured mouse caught beneath the cat's paws. Trapped and as good as dead, once they'd finished playing with me. Men in black military-style fatigues were swarming over my bedroom, yanking open drawers and pawing through the small wastebasket. One of them pulled a tiny glass vial from the trash and sniffed it.

"Smells like alpha pheromones, sir," he reported, wrinkling his nose in distaste.

"Bag it for evidence," said the one who seemed to be in charge.

Had it only been a few hours ago that I was curled naked with Kam, warm and safe in a nest of pillows? It couldn't have been, surely. It felt like another lifetime altogether.

"Grab anything else that looks incriminating. We'll let forensics have the rest. Let's get her in the van. It stinks like a damned slave pen in here."

The hands that had been holding me shoved me forward. I stumbled as they dragged me toward my ruined front door. The other apartments were deathly quiet—my neighbors doubtless huddling inside, thanking their lucky stars that they were upstanding betas with nothing to hide from the authorities.

The officers bundled me into the building's refurbished antique freight elevator. I swayed as it started down toward the ground floor, and my knees nearly buckled when it came to a stop, gravity tugging at me. Ryan, the night security desk attendant, stared at me wide-eyed as I was frog-marched past him in my silky, thigh-length nightgown, hands cuffed and hair askew. I met his gaze as we passed, my eyes pleading silently with him for help.

Ryan's lips parted as though he might say something, but then he pressed them together tightly and looked away. No surprise, really. He'd had no authority to stop the SWAT team when they'd entered the building. It wasn't as though he could stop them from leaving, either.

He would have known that Kam visited me the previous evening. Would the authorities interrogate him? Had they done so already?

The concrete sidewalk was gritty and cool beneath my bare feet. I winced and stumbled as small pebbles dug into my soles. An unmarked white van sat parked at the curb. With horrible clarity, it occurred to me that once I was in that van, it would all be over. That was stupid, though. It was over already. It had been over the moment my front door caved in.

Strong hands wrestled me into the back of the van—not because I was resisting, but because my muscles weren't working right. The van had benches running down both sides of the back, and the area was separated from the driver and passenger seat by a metal wall with a window covered in heavy steel mesh. It reeked of stale urine and vomit.

The man who'd dragged me inside shoved me onto one of the benches. I yelped as my weight landed on my cuffed hands, fingers bending painfully. He wrenched my arms to the side so he could get at the cuffs and clipped a hanging length of rusty chain to them. The chain was attached to a bolt in the frame of the van above my head, and short enough that I had to hunch awkwardly to one side to keep the strain off my shoulders. It occurred to me in a detached sort of way that if the van got in a wreck and I went flying, both of my arms would be wrenched out of their sockets—maybe torn off completely.

My guard settled on the opposite bench, arms crossed and legs spread wide, leering at me. His badge was city police, not federal security—not that it ultimately mattered.

"Where are you taking me?" I asked in a wavering voice. "What precinct?"

"We're taking you straight to hell, bitch," he said. He reached down and cupped his crotch suggestively, his grin widening. "But ask me nice, and maybe I'll take you to heaven first, you little omega slut."

The words slid off, not sticking. There was no point in protesting. I was an unregistered omega. I had no rights. It felt odd to think that I'd been in a meeting room with international dignitaries not so long ago, hammering out policy and treaty details. The fact that these two worlds could coexist on top of each other seemed wrong, somehow.

I didn't respond, and the man's expression twisted into anger. He worked his jaw for a moment and spat, the gob of saliva hitting my bare shin and sliding down.

"Stupid cunt," he said. "Walkin' around like you're something special. You ain't special. You ain't nothin'." He spat again. This time it landed on the floor by my feet.

When I still didn't rise to the bait, he seemed to lose interest. The van rocked and juddered as it sped through the early morning gloom, the chain tugging at my wrists when I swayed. After an eternity, it slowed and turned before backing up and finally coming to a jerky stop. The engine turned off, and I heard doors opening and slamming. A fist rapped on the side, and my guard lumbered to his feet.

"End of the line," he said with a smirk, looming over me as he unhooked the chain and hauled me upright.

The van doors opened. The vehicle had backed up to an institutional-looking rear entrance. Dirty brick walls framed steel double doors that stood open and waiting, like the maw of some great beast. Fluorescent overhead lighting glared from within. I tried to crane around—to get a look at the city and try to identify what part of it we were in—but it was no good. The glare was too bright, the night still too dark, and I was dragged inside before I saw anything of use.

There would be no phone call to a lawyer for me. No chance to tap the brakes on what was about to happen. The SWAT officers handed me over to the precinct's intake officers. I was stripped, cavity-searched, dressed in a scratchy gray smock, and handcuffed again. My blood was drawn from a vein in my arm, and I was finally shuffled off to a freezing cell in an empty part of the station. The door clanged shut, and a few moments later, I was alone with the echo of my own unsteady breathing—once more a prisoner trapped in a cell, but this time without my packmate or an alpha protector for company.

Sometime in the coming hours, representatives from the Committee would come. I would be transferred into their custody and remanded for a sham trial. Not only was my life as good as over, but Enoch Sloane would use my case as fuel for his paranoid conspiracy-mongering. I might well have just brought down Prime Minister Fairbanks' government with my stubborn insistence on staying to fight, rather than running when I'd had the chance.

Did they have Kam in custody, too? Was he even now huddled alone in some other bare cell, somewhere in the city?

Would I ever see him again?

I sank down to sit with my back against the sleeping bench with its thin, plastic-covered mattress. Covering my eyes with my hands, I curled forward against the staggering ache of my own stupidity.

"Oh, Kam," I whispered, a barely audible rasp. "I'm so, *so* sorry."

TWENTY-TWO

Alex

"YOU'RE SURE about this?" I asked, my tone flat. Beside me, Beckett kept his hands on the wheel and his eyes on the road ahead as we pulled up to a stoplight in the murky, early morning gray.

"I am," he said. "We've kept our powder dry long enough. Things are starting to snowball out of control. It's time to make a move."

"You don't usually torture your metaphors this badly, Chief," I observed. "I feel like there's something you're not telling me."

Beckett shot me a sidelong glance, kind but unapologetic. "There are lots of things I don't tell you Alex. Unfortunately, it's part of the job description."

I raised an eyebrow. "You do realize that when things inevitably go tits up, you're not going to be able to protect us, no matter how careful you think you're being. What does *You-Know-Who* think about this current mess?"

Beckett's expression soured at the mention of *the person who shall not be named*. "I'll be sure to ask, next time I talk to them."

I stared at him, unblinking. He ignored the weight of my alpha glare, just like he always did.

"I really hate this, you know," I told him in a monotone.

"I know," he said, not unsympathetically. He turned right, pulling into a modest parking garage. "Here we are. Remember—federal jurisdiction, sensitive political situation, blah, blah, blah. You know the drill."

In my case, 'the drill' was to look stoic and intimidating while mostly keeping my trap shut. I'd had more than a decade of practice to perfect that act, after all.

"Understood. You've got the vehicles organized?" That was my nerves showing through, and I silently cursed myself. Of *course* he had the damned vehicles waiting for us.

"All ready to go," he assured me. "We just need to pick up our passenger."

This day had always been coming—even if I hadn't expected it to happen quite so soon. I squared my shoulders as Beckett pulled the black government-issued sedan into a parking spot and turned the engine off. "Right," I said. "Let's get this done."

We exited the car and marched toward the entrance of the precinct, the picture of official business with our straight spines and dark suits. Once inside, my boss headed directly for the front desk and placed his badge on it.

"Agent Rhys Beckett, federal security," he said in clipped tones. "I need to speak with the duty officer in charge, please."

The female desk sergeant blinked at us, evidently not used to federal agents barging in at six in the morning and demanding things of her. "I'll, uh, tell him you're here, sir. Can I let him know what this is about?"

"Official business," Beckett replied unhelpfully. "We'll wait here while you get him."

Still looking somewhat flummoxed, the sergeant turned and picked up a phone, speaking into it quietly. There was a brief exchange that involved several uncertain glances being thrown in our direction, and in due course, the officer in charge appeared. He was a big man, perhaps in his late fifties, and while he'd let himself go after too much time as a desk jockey, he still dwarfed Beckett in terms of both height and breadth.

Beckett extracted the manila folder that had been tucked under his arm and set it on the desk. "Good morning, Lieutenant...?"

"Dupont," said the man. "And you are?"

"Rhys Beckett, federal security service. There seems to have been some confusion about jurisdiction during a recent arrest. I'm here for a prisoner transfer." He scooted the folder toward Dupont with an air of expectation.

The lieutenant's expression closed off abruptly, leaving no question that he knew exactly which prisoner Beckett was talking about. That, at least, answered the question of whether or not we were in time to get her before the Committee did.

She was still here.

"I wasn't informed of any such transfer." Dupont opened the folder, glancing down at the contents. "This was strictly an MPD operation. We acted on information relayed directly to police detectives from a trusted source."

That *trusted source* was almost certainly a Committee operative. If that was the case, the truly disturbing part was that the information on Leona McCready could only have come from the so-called Beta Liberation Front. The fact that the terrorists and the Committee were apparently in bed together was... not good.

"Indeed," Beckett replied, giving the man a tight smile. "However, you may not be fully aware of the... *delicate political situation* involved in this particular arrest, shall we say. The feds' jurisdiction on this one trumps local jurisdiction. You'll find all of the paperwork in order."

Though it looked convincing, the paperwork in question was not, in fact, in order. It was one hundred percent forged. That little factoid would come back to bite somebody in the ass soon enough. Whether that 'somebody' ended up being us or the lieutenant was an open question at this point.

Dupont frowned over the sheaf of documents. "I'll need to speak to the precinct captain."

"Of course," Beckett said, unperturbed. "We'll wait while you do that."

<hr>

In the end, it took well over an hour for Beckett to politely but firmly bully the station commander into acknowledging federal jurisdiction. I was viscerally aware of the increasing number of hostile looks we garnered from the other officers on duty, as muttered gossip spread through the station. I ignored them. My gender presentation as a female alpha wasn't exactly subtle, so I was used to a certain background level of hostility.

Finally, Beckett turned to me. "Go retrieve our prisoner, please. It looks like we're about ready to leave." He shot an expectant look at Dupont.

The lieutenant gestured toward a burly uniformed officer sitting at a desk nearby. "Owens. Escort this... *agent*... to the cells and transfer the omega to her custody."

As poorly veiled disdain went, I'd heard worse. Owens retrieved a set of keys with a grunt of acknowledgement. I ignored the contemptuous look he raked over me and followed him into the back, passing through a series of security doors. Our footsteps echoed loudly against the cinderblock walls. Cameras tracked our progress with blinking red eyes—more evidence that after today, there would be no coming back for us.

Though honestly, considering Beckett was out front signing his own name to forged federal transfer papers at this very moment, the camera footage of me springing a prisoner from jail without any legal standing to do so was probably superfluous.

Owens eyeballed me with clear distaste. "So, federal security, huh?"

"Yes," I replied tersely, having no interest whatsoever in small talk with this beta meat-brain.

"Wouldn't catch the MPD letting your kind onto the force," he said, not taking the hint.

"Your loss," I told him, as we entered a row of holding cells. "I guess there's no accounting for taste."

"Fuckin' hyena bitch," he muttered, trotting out the old, unimaginative slur for female alphas. I let it slide.

He stopped in front of the last cell on the right. The key clanked in the lock, and he jerked his chin toward the red-haired form huddled in the corner, staring fixedly into the middle distance. "So, is she your little omega girlfriend, or something? Come to get your fuck-toy back?"

That one, I was less inclined to let slide. I loomed over him as he turned to pull the door open, using my slight advantage of height with the full knowledge of how much beta men hated that.

"No," I said sweetly. My lips pulled back, baring teeth in an expression that was only distantly related to a smile. "She's not. Do you know how you can tell?"

"Uh..." He took a half-step back, yielding ground without realizing it.

My voice hardened to steel. "Because *you're still breathing.*"

I brushed past him without giving him another glance, trying with minimal success to soften my stance as I entered and crossed to the figure curled into a miserable ball in the back. The cell was harshly lit by the same fluorescent tube lighting as the rest of the place. Bars formed three walls, open and unprotected. It was devoid of anything soft beyond the one-inch thick plastic pad on the sleeping bench — all sharp edged metal and hard surfaces.

Omega hell, in other words.

"Ms. McCready," I said, aware of how stiff my voice sounded. She was no longer *Madam Ambassador*, and never would be again. Looking down at her dazed face, I was once more amazed by how high she and her sad-eyed *odama* had flown before someone finally clipped their wings.

"*What* — ?" she rasped, blinking huge hazel eyes up at me. "*How?*"

"We're leaving. Transfer of custody." I had the worrisome impression that she didn't really believe I was here. Crouching, I grasped her arms and pulled her to her feet as gently as I could. Bruises in the shape of fingers circled her right bicep, marring the pale, luminous skin. She swayed, my grip the only thing keeping her upright for the first few seconds until she locked her knees.

"You got cuffs?" Owens asked.

I raked a contemptuous gaze over him. "Why? Worried she's going to overpower you?"

He leveled a glare of hatred at me in return. "Prisoners are s'posed to be cuffed."

"Then it's a good thing she's not your prisoner anymore," I said, and led my charge out of the cell on stumbling legs.

Beckett met us at the second to last security door, and ran an assessing eye over the smock-clad form in my grasp. "We're going out the back. I'll bring the car around."

He had the manila folder tucked under his arm once more, but no bag or other sign that Leona McCready's belongings had been returned to her. Of course, it was quite likely they'd dragged her out of her home with only whatever clothing had been on her back—and in the middle of the night, that might not have been much.

Whether she'd realized it yet or not, she'd just lost everything—possessions, money, career... *everything*. To all intents and purposes, Ambassador Leona McCready no longer existed. Idly, I wondered what would rise to take the place of that lost life.

The car backed up to the rear entrance where Beckett had left us waiting. I bundled my omega charge into the back seat, stretching the seatbelt across her body when she seemed disinclined to do it herself. But when I reached to open the passenger-side door, Beckett stopped me with a look.

"*Alex,*" he said, gently reproving. "Get in the back seat. She's in shock, and you're on omega duty."

I swallowed the argument that wanted to rise, aware that my reaction was irrational even as a sick sense of dread settled in my stomach.

"You should have brought one of the others along—not me," I managed.

He didn't reply, because his words hadn't been a suggestion—and Beckett did not engage in debates when it came to orders. Swallowing my misgivings, I circled around the car and got in the back. We drove away, leaving the precinct and the cops behind, along with their slurs and hate-filled gazes.

Leona, barefoot and dressed in a shapeless tunic, stared with unfocused eyes at the back of the seat in front of her. Montreal was waking up around us, traffic growing heavier as the morning crawled sluggishly toward business hours. She didn't speak. Didn't look out the window. Didn't blink. Her face was an ugly shade of gray, her lips tinged bluish.

I couldn't get anything useful from her scent. She was back on suppressors, of course. Instead, I reluctantly lifted a hand and brushed the backs of my fingers against her cheek. Her skin was chilly to the touch, like wax.

"Crank the heater," I said. "She's freezing cold."

Air blasted from the vents, quickly growing warm. Beckett fiddled with the center vents, aiming them through the gap between the front seats. Leona shivered as the hot air hit her skin, curling into herself.

Scent or no scent, the aura of unhappy omega drove a knife through my alpha instincts, bringing back memories I'd worked hard to bury. I was not the right person for this job. Beckett should have brought Jax, or Flynn. I made a not-very-successful attempt to modulate my scent into something reassuring. Scooting close enough for our upper arms to brush, I sat stiffly next to the omega who'd cupped my cheek in her soft hand as she shed tears for the pain of my long-ago loss.

By the time Beckett pulled into a long-term parking lot at Dorval Airport, Leona's waxy chill had given way to shivering and chattering teeth. She still showed no sign of real awareness of her surroundings. I'd covered her with my jacket for extra warmth, and tried to get some water into her from the bottle Beckett handed back to me. I was sure Flynn would have had her wrapped up against his chest by now, soothing her with his body heat and an alpha purr. I... couldn't, and I wasn't sure what kind of monster that made me.

We weren't here to catch a flight. Beckett pulled in next to an unremarkable tan Toyota with Vermont plates, and we transferred to the other car. Within moments, we were back on the road. We crossed first the St. Lawrence River, and then the Canal de Beauharnois, taking Highway 138 southwest into New York, where we once again changed cars. Beckett continued south on NY-30, through the city of Malone and into the wilder areas at the northern edge of the Adirondacks.

We passed Lake Titus and entered the Deer River Primitive Area. Beckett turned onto a private road skirting the edge of Lake Duane. The gravel drive wound through old growth trees and grassy clearings, until eventually a house came into view. It was two stories, built into the side of a hill that overlooked the lake below. The outside gave the impression of someone's extravagant vacation home that had been left to fall into disrepair. The area around it was overgrown, and the cedar siding was weathered.

A white Jeep Cherokee sat parked in the weed-infested circle drive. Beckett pulled up behind it and killed the engine.

"Home sweet home, until we figure out next steps," he said. "Let's get Ms. McCready inside. You'll need to carry her — this gravel would tear up her feet pretty bad."

I firmed my jaw. "Right."

No sooner had I gotten Leona unbuckled and scooped her out of the back seat, holding her bridal-style, than Flynn came rushing out of the front door.

"You got her," he said with obvious relief. Before I quite knew what was happening, he'd lifted her out of my arms and into his own. "How bad off is she? What did they do to her?"

"It's just shock," I said stupidly. "You'll need to treat her for shock."

Flynn nodded and carried her into the house, staring down at her like he could hardly believe she was here. I followed in something of a daze, registering that the inside of the place was a lot nicer than the outside would have suggested. Before Beckett had time to close the front door behind us, a familiar slender, dark-haired omega came hurrying into the entryway, with Jax following behind at a slower pace.

"*Leo!*" Kameron Patel said breathlessly.

Leona let out an ugly, gulping gasp like someone surfacing from drowning, and squirmed in Flynn's hold. He set her on her feet and she stumbled forward, half-falling into her packmate's arms.

"Kam," she said faintly, burying herself in his tight embrace. "*Oh, god.* Is this a dream?"

And, *fuck.* I needed—suddenly and desperately—not to be inside this house.

"I'll check the perimeter," I said hoarsely, before fleeing the scene—leaving behind the two sweet, soft-eyed omegas who'd barely managed to escape the same fate that had claimed Irina.

TWENTY-THREE

Leona

AFTER AN UNKNOWN amount of time spent huddled in the freezing jail cell, I slipped into an odd, dreamlike state that was confusing, but tolerable. Distantly, I was reminded of nature programs I'd watched with my family in childhood, where a gazelle or zebra lay peaceful and blank-eyed on the savanna as the lion ate them alive.

Why don't they scream and fight? I'd asked my father, who'd gone on to explain about adrenaline, endorphin loops, and psychological dissociation. He'd finished by saying that we couldn't really know what went on in an animal's head, but that in the end, nature protected its own by whatever means necessary.

I wondered if the dying gazelles dreamed of an unlikely rescue by a towering gazelle goddess who picked them up and led them to safety with gentle hands, smelling of jasmine and sandalwood and worry.

In my dream, I was in a car, two voices murmuring nonsense in the background. My entire body was numb with cold, but then warm fingers brushed my cheek and hot air blew against my skin, making me shiver as feeling began to return to my limbs. The dream kept changing, the car interior shifting from dark leather to tan vinyl to gray velour. An arm brushed against mine, and I breathed in the illusion of a comforting alpha scent.

Maybe I could just stay like this through all of it—let the trial and the pain and my impending death float unimportantly in the background while I remained in an ever-moving, ever-changing car with a stoic, half-seen alpha at my side, escorting me to the afterlife… if there even was one.

The gray-velour vehicle rattled along a gravel drive, and eventually came to a stop. The voices said things in the background, and I wondered idly if the car was about to change again. Doors opened and closed. Hands released my seat belt and strong arms scooped me out of the seat. I had a vague impression of trees and birds and sky. Then there was an awkward shuffle as new arms reached for me.

Musk and cardamom tickled my nose. I knew that scent, too, and decided that if this dream was to be the last thing I experienced before the lion devoured me, I was okay with that.

"You got her," said a deep voice, the sense of the words beginning to penetrate my awareness for the first time since the hallucination had started. "How bad off is she? What did they do to her?"

"It's just shock," said the other voice, sounding hoarse and strained. "You'll need to treat her for shock."

The world rocked dizzily around me as I was carried through a door, the sky and trees disappearing from sight. I blinked in the low light, gazing up at a handsome, dark-skinned face for a few moments until movement caught my peripheral vision.

"*Leo!*" Kam appeared from an interior hallway, rushing toward me.

I choked, the air suddenly catching in my throat, and began to struggle weakly against the arms holding me. They set me down, and it was all I could do to stay upright long enough to stagger toward that beautiful vision, even if it wasn't real.

Arms caught me.

"Kam," I croaked, burying myself in the tight, illusory embrace. "*Oh, god. Is this a dream?*"

Kam clutched my body to him, his arms shaking around me.

"I'll check the perimeter," muttered a voice from somewhere behind me, and I vaguely registered a door closing.

"Leo," Kam said into my hair. "*Odama*. I don't know exactly what's going on yet, but you're safe. It's not a dream, I promise."

"Feels like a dream," I protested weakly, still clinging to him.

"It kind of does, doesn't it?" he agreed, but the solid, shuddering body pressed against mine didn't waver in its solidity.

A strong hand closed on my shoulder, the smell of fall spices once more wafting over me. Another figure approached behind Kam, ambergris and evergreen joining the mix.

"Alex says you're in shock," said the deep voice from earlier, and my mind tossed up a name to go with it. *Flynn*.

"Warm bath, food, sleep." That was cypress-and-ambergris speaking. Another name bubbled up. *Jax*.

"They're right, *odama*," Kam said. "Come on, let's get you cleaned up and fed. We can talk when you're feeling better."

He disentangled enough to get a shoulder propped beneath mine, my arm draped around his neck for support. Another strong arm wrapped around me from the other side, and I allowed myself to be led away on legs that felt like a newborn colt's. We reached a hallway that was too narrow for three people abreast, and after a brief exchange over my head, Flynn picked me up again, cradling my body against his broad chest.

We ascended a set of stairs to the second story. It was a large house, not at all similar to anywhere I'd ever lived or dreamed of living. That was another tally in the 'not a dream' column I was using to informally keep score. But honestly, at this point, the mental effort began to feel like too much work. It was real, or it wasn't. Either way, it was nice. I gave myself over to it, figuring that in the worst-case scenario, a psychotic break was still preferable to facing my fate at the hands of the Committee while in my right mind.

The landing at the top of the stairs had hallways branching off to the left and right. We turned right and Jax opened the second door leading into a bathroom — large and elegant, dominated by a raised platform leading to a massive sunken tub. Jax crossed to the bath and lowered himself carefully into a crouch to turn on the taps, favoring his left side as he did.

"Shower first, while that monstrosity is filling?" Flynn suggested, putting me down and supporting me until my legs were steady. "You won't run out of hot water. The place has a tankless heater."

After spending hours chilled to the bone in my cell, that sounded like heaven. I nodded wordlessly, not trusting my voice.

Jax straightened. "There's shampoo and conditioner and body wash. I think we covered all of the basics. Kam, will you be all right on your own with her? If so, we'll give you two some privacy."

Flynn grumbled something inaudible. Inside my mind, something flipped — a switch clicking from one position to the other.

"You can both stay," I said. I exchanged a look with Kam. "We want you here."

God, I wanted them here. Besides, it probably *was* a dream, so it's not like it really mattered anymore. If I was going to die out in the real world, didn't I deserve this first? Flynn's brilliant smile in response to my words made it all worthwhile.

"Kam?" Jax asked. "That all right with you?"

A fragile expression that might have been hope lightened Kam's features.

"We want you here," he echoed. "Please."

Jax's worried expression softened. He still looked haggard, and I was sorry that my subconscious hadn't restored him to full health.

"Then consider us your spa staff," he said.

Flynn tugged the hem of my threadbare gray smock. "Want me to burn this?"

"Not until I can watch," I said, and tugged it over my head with the unconcern of someone who knew deep down that this wasn't really happening.

Two sets of eyes landed on me appreciatively. Two scents sharpened. Then Flynn's gaze tracked to my bicep, and he frowned. I looked down and saw the finger-shaped bruises there.

"Do I need to break some necks?" he asked.

My mind shied away from that horrible moment when the police had broken into my bedroom. My arm and the back of my neck began to throb, as though my body had suddenly remembered it was hurt. I swayed in place, and Kam's arm came around me.

"Let's table the plans for bloody revenge until a bit later, all right?" he said.

"Yes, let's," Jax agreed, watching my expression carefully.

"Sorry," Flynn said, looking away. "I didn't mean to upset you, Leona."

"It's okay," I said faintly.

Kam stripped down to his boxers and helped me into the shower. It was spacious and clean, with clear glass-paneled doors. Outside, I could see the two alphas watching us avidly for the first minute or two, until the glass steamed up and obscured them. Was this what it would have been like to have a pack? I blinked at Kam.

"I want this to be real," I told him, the words sounding a bit bereft even to my own ears.

He pulled me into his arms again and held me there for a long moment before easing me back. "Let's get the dregs of this day washed off you, okay?"

I nodded, and let him help me wash my hair and body clean of the stench of the jail cell. When we were done, he turned off the shower and opened the door. One of the alphas had laid a trail of towels on the floor separating the shower from the platform with the sunken tub so it wouldn't be slippery. Flynn took my hand and steadied me from the other side as Kam led me up the low steps and helped me slide into the steaming water.

The alpha gave my knuckles a final rub with his thumb before releasing my hand. Kam lowered himself down next to me in the spacious bath. I sighed with contentment and melted against him, finally free of the bone-deep chill for the first time since I'd been awoken by the sound of men breaking down my door.

Relaxation made my body feel heavy and my mind, slow. I dropped into a half-doze beneath the sensation of Kam's fingers stroking through my wet hair, with two alphas on guard and no need for me to stay alert. Conversation droned around me, but I couldn't spare the energy to focus on it. I registered Kam asking, "*Is Alex okay? She looked upset,*" and Jax replying, "*She's going through some things. Give her time.*"

At one point, Flynn's spicy scent disappeared from the room, and I peeled open an eye.

"It's all right," Kam said. "He's just gone to get you some food."

I nodded and returned to my mindless dozing, nuzzling my face against Kam's neck. Eventually, he nudged me back into full awareness.

"Come on. *Up*. The water's getting cold, and I'm turning into a prune."

I grunted my displeasure at the idea of moving.

"There's food," Jax said, sounding mildly amused.

My stomach rumbled in reaction to the thought of a decent meal.

"You need to eat," Kam told me firmly, and herded me out of the bath. Jax met me with a huge, fuzzy towel. I dried off and wrapped it around me, while Kam rubbed himself down and redressed in his dark jeans and white button-down shirt, minus the wet boxers.

"We'll do something about the clothing situation within the next couple of days," Jax said. "But for now, Leona—Flynn says you don't object to oversized T-shirts as tunics. Hopefully he's telling the truth about that."

He indicated a large gray T-shirt laid out on the vanity. I lifted it to my nose and breathed in a smell like the woods outside.

"Thank you," I told him, and pulled it over my head, letting the towel fall away beneath it. The shirt hung to my thighs.

"Hold still a minute." Kam stepped behind me and eased my damp ringlets of hair free of the collar before braiding them into a loose plait down my back. His movements paused. I watched in the mirror as his gaze landed on the back of my neck and stuck. I thought he must be staring at the bruise blooming there. After a moment, he resumed braiding, and my eyes slipped closed as his fingers brushed my skin.

"Food," Jax said. "Then sleep. When you're recovered, we'll worry about the rest of it."

TWENTY-FOUR

Leona

JAX OPENED a connecting door and led us through to a larger room. I stopped dead in my tracks as our surroundings registered. The room was spacious and windowless, softly lit by lamps shaded with Tiffany-style red and orange glass. Hardwood flooring formed a walkway around the perimeter of the room, but the center was sunken, surrounded on two sides by an overstuffed sectional sofa strewn with mountains of soft pillows.

The floor was piled with thick fur rugs. Other odds and ends of furniture occupied the third side of the pit—a comfortable looking recliner, an oversized beanbag, and a low divan in some unusual modern style of design, with exaggerated, ergonomic curves in the seat. Bookshelves lined the far wall, stuffed with mismatched paperbacks of all colors and sizes.

"What on earth?" I asked blankly.

Another door in the room opened and Flynn entered, balancing a tray in one hand. "Much better than that dump in Romania, right?"

"Omega-friendly safehouses are a bit easier to come by when we're closer to our home territory," Jax put in. "But like I said, the serious talk can wait until you're recovered."

Flynn made his way down into the sunken den and set the tray on a corner table by the sectional. "Speaking of which, Beckett and Alex just headed out to meet with someone about… all of this." He gestured around to encompass the entire situation.

Kam straightened at his words, a thread of tension creeping into his bearing. "And once they've had this meeting, Beckett will explain exactly what's going on?"

"Yeah, he will," Flynn said.

"It's a complicated situation," Jax put in. "Especially after the raid last night. But we won't abuse your patience any more than necessary."

Kam sighed. "No. I get it. I'm taking a lot on faith here—but I'm also painfully aware of what the alternative would have been." His deep brown gaze fell on me, and it was haunted.

"Food," Flynn declared, before the creeping sense of disquiet rising inside of me could gain a solid foothold. "No fish meatballs, I promise."

Jax gave him an odd look. "Fish… *meatballs?*"

"Don't ask," Kam told him, giving a delicate shudder of distaste.

In fact, lunch consisted of chicken soup and buttered hunks of French bread, with a glass of sweet tea on the side. I curled up in the corner of the couch with the bowl on my lap and ate it. When I was done, I set the bowl back on the tray. It was sitting next to a discarded book on the little table—*The Unbearable Lightness of Being* by Milan Kundera. The blue cover had a drawing of a man's bowler hat above a woman's bikini, the wearer of the clothing invisible so it appeared to hover in midair.

I'd been meaning to read that one.

"Want seconds?" The question drew my attention back to Flynn.

I shook my head. "No, thank you. That was delicious, though."

It had been, too. Rich and perfectly seasoned. Filling, without being heavy. Comforting, with all the nostalgia of childhood and loving, familial care.

Flynn smiled, the dazzling openness of it lightening the invisible weight on my shoulders. Jax stretched, twisting his left arm and wrist back and forth as though to ease the muscles.

"Right," he said. "Make this place up however you'll be most comfortable and get some rest. Flynn and I will keep watch — not that there's anyone out here to bother us, but still. You don't need to worry about anything. Sleep as long as you like."

"God, that sounds good," Kam said, sounding exhausted. "Thank you both."

The pile of thick fur rugs that covered the floor of the sunken den called to me, even as distracting thoughts pulled at my awareness. Kam, whose mind often ran on parallel tracks to mine, helped me toss pillows into the cozy space. There was a stack of fuzzy blankets lying folded next to the far end of the sectional. He grabbed a couple off the top, and we curled up together in a soft cocoon, with Kam spooning me from behind.

Jax moved around the room, turning off all but a couple of the lamps. He and Flynn settled in comfortably on the couch, where they spoke in soft murmurs about plans for bringing in fresh supplies and acquiring clothing for Kam and me. Before long, it faded into a comforting background noise, weaving seamlessly with the reassuring scent of alphas on guard.

Despite his clear exhaustion, Kam's breathing didn't deepen into the slow rhythm of sleep. I dozed, but something was nagging at my mind in a way that wouldn't allow it to quiet completely.

It was the book. *The Unbearable Lightness of Being.* The title had stared me in the face, clear as day. But... in dreams, I could never read written text. It wiggled around, refusing to settle long enough for my eyes to make sense of it. Newspapers were pure gibberish. Books might as well be written in Sanskrit.

And then there was the chicken soup. Food in my dreams was always tasteless. The soup should have been a chicken-and-noodle shaped void against my taste buds. Instead it had been rich and delicious, subtly different from the way my mother had always made it.

A soul-deep chill crept through me again, spreading from the inside out. The hazy pall of unreality draped across the events of the last twelve hours began to thin. A faint tremor took up residence in my muscles as the slight remove that had separated me from the rest of the world settled back into place.

"Leo?" Kam's arms tightened around me as my breathing grew ragged.

"Oh, god," I whispered. "It's real. It..." My voice caught, and I swallowed. "It all... really happened?"

Kam pressed his lips against the top of my shoulder, his embrace never wavering. "It really happened. I'm so sorry, *odama*."

I shuddered, curling forward around the pain of understanding. Our old life was gone. Every possession I had ever owned—*gone*. My bank accounts would already be locked. I didn't have a single penny to my name. I would never speak to my friends or colleagues again without risking arrest— both mine, and theirs. Any small chance Kam and I might have had at making things better for alphas and omegas through our positions in government— *gone*.

I—who had never known suffering or deprivation for a single day before that fateful morning when we were kidnapped in Romania—did not possess so much as a single item of clothing. And I'd brought Kam down with me, through my own stubbornness and self-absorption.

My entire body shook with the effort to keep from shattering into a million razor-edged shards. I couldn't breathe.

"Alphas?" Kam's voice was soft. "Leo needs you now, but she won't ask. Not for herself."

Fabric rustled, and Flynn lowered himself to sit in front of me. I could hear Jax settling in behind Kam. The scent of woods and spice surrounded us in a comforting cloud.

"Is that right, Leona?" Flynn asked. His big hand eased the blanket back so he could see my face. "Do want us to look after you both for a while?"

This was happening. The alphas were here, and it wasn't a dream. Any decisions I made would have real, actual consequences for our future. And yet… it still didn't matter—because right now, for me, there was no future. Yesterday's world no longer existed; tomorrow was a blank and impenetrable vista.

I couldn't protect Kam.

I couldn't protect myself.

I was powerless to face this future on my own. The awareness of my own utter helplessness slammed into me like a hurtling boulder. I needed their strength because mine was gone, and it wasn't fair to steal any more of Kam's.

"Please, alphas," I managed around a choked sob. "Oh, god. I don't know what to do now. I don't know what to do—"

Flynn settled onto his side, facing me. His thumb swiped over my cheek, wiping away the tear that had fallen. He scooted forward, one strong arm worming its way beneath me until my head was pillowed on his bicep. The other draped over my waist and settled on Kam's hip, pulling us both snug against his body.

We were jostled lightly as another big body lay down behind Kam. Jax's hand settled on my shoulder. Low rumbles vibrated around the nest—a pair of alpha purrs.

"I love you, *odama*," Kam whispered against the bruised skin of my neck. "I know it feels like the world is ending, but I've done this before. I promise you, it's really not."

His lips pressed against my mating gland, and the last shreds of my control cracked. I huddled between the alphas and my *odama*, my entire body shaking with helpless, wracking sobs. All of the mastery I'd deluded myself into believing I held over my own life had been an illusion—and that realization hurt like knives flaying my skin.

The only shelter left to me lay in the small pack of misfits who'd somehow seen fit to save my sorry ass... and my packmate's.

Kam knew this pain intimately--he'd experienced unimaginable horrors as a child. And yet, he'd managed to survive and grow into the beautiful omega I loved. I owed it to him to survive as well.

"Kam," I choked out. "I'm sorry. I'm so sorry. This is all my fault."

Kam only squeezed me tighter.

It was Jax who spoke. "It's the fault of the world we live in. You were trying to change that world. There's no blame in that. And maybe you can still change things... just in a different way."

"*Jax.*" There was a hint of chiding in Flynn's tone.

"I know, I know," Jax said. "Anyway, that's for tomorrow. Tonight, it's okay to grieve. God knows, we've all got way too many things to mourn."

My remaining strength dissolved like snow in a warm spring rain. With no barriers left to hide behind, I let the tears come, held close and protected by my pack that might have been.

TWENTY-FIVE

Jax

NO QUESTION about it—these two were going to be our kryptonite. I'd thought as much in the cave in Romania, and seeing Flynn with them had confirmed it. The twisted part of it? In some ways, things had become *less* complicated now that their lives had been thrown into chaos.

Leona McCready would never have voluntarily given up her crusade to effect change from her post inside the Foreign Office. And, in my defense, I'd certainly never wanted to see her in this situation, even though something like this had been more or less inevitable. Her secret was already out. Members of the Beta Liberation Front had discovered her omega status, and we hadn't managed to track them down and silence all of them afterward.

We were always going to end up here, or somewhere very like it.

At least Beckett and Alex had managed to extract her before the worst happened. Meanwhile, Flynn and I had whisked Kam away from his apartment before anyone in the MPD had thought to go snooping around Leona's closest colleagues.

From what I gathered, the terrorists still thought Kam was a beta. Even so, it wouldn't be long before the wrong people started making assumptions, especially once they realized he'd disappeared at the same time she had. At least he hadn't been swept up and charged before we got to him.

"I think she's asleep," Kam said quietly.

Adding omegas into our pack wasn't something I'd ever really aspired to. Or at least, it hadn't been something I'd aspired to until Flynn planted the damned idea in my head—and that had only happened recently. Dangerous for them; dangerous for us. Impractical on all fronts, or so I'd always believed. There was, however, no avoiding the fact that having the two of them tucked between us like this felt right.

"She needs the rest," Flynn said. "So do you."

Kam's chest rose and fell heavily within the circle of my embrace. "Yeah."

We stayed where we were until both of them were out cold with the kind of heavy, boneless lassitude that meant they'd sleep for hours. Leona snored softly, congested after crying her eyes out for everything she'd just lost. When I was absolutely certain that the jostling wouldn't wake them, I met Flynn's eyes and gave my head a tiny jerk toward the sofa.

After a reluctant pause, he nodded and eased himself out of the tangle of limbs while I did the same. We tucked the pair snugly into their nest of pillows and blankets, and then flopped onto the sectional nearby. I shook out my left arm as best I could, trying to ignore the shooting nerve pain. That and the damned headaches were the legacy of my stint as an alpha lab rat. It could be worse, obviously… but I chafed at not being at full strength now that the shit was hitting the fan.

"Beckett had better come back with the answer I want to hear," Flynn grumbled.

"I think he will," I told him. "It only makes sense. These two would be wasted hiding away on some remote island. And they'd probably go crazy there with nothing to do."

Flynn shrugged one hard-muscled shoulder. "Wouldn't mind seeing 'em in swimsuits, though."

I stared at him. "Do you ever *not* think with your dick?" I asked, without any real heat.

He grinned at me, a sharply dangerous slash of white teeth in his dark-skinned face. "Well, I mean — sometimes. But just look at them." His avid gaze fell on the pair, still huddled together in sleep. "You're right, though. They'd hate that, I guess."

I sighed, and let my head fall back to rest on the couch. "This is going to mean complete upheaval, and not just for them."

Flynn gave a low grunt. "Alex is barely keeping her shit together."

Our pack leader's hasty retreat earlier hadn't escaped my notice. "She's got reason," I pointed out.

"'Course she does," Flynn agreed. "But I told her we wouldn't let what happened to Irina happen to them, and I was right, wasn't I?"

"It almost did, though," I murmured.

His voice hardened. "Yeah, but it didn't. And it's not going to."

I let him have the last word on the subject, because there was no point in arguing. Flynn had a black and white view of the world that must make the inside of his mind a very straightforward place to be. We all had our pasts, and we'd all been marked in different ways. Alex had built walls of ice around her heart. I'd rebelled against my upbringing in the breeding pens by soaking up every bit of education and culture I could get my hands on, in an attempt to prove that I was more than a dumb animal with a moderately useful dick attached.

Flynn had handed the reins of his conscience to those he trusted, rather than trying to make complicated decisions in a beta-run world that he didn't fully understand. This was, if I were being honest, the first time I'd seen him acting so rebellious about *anything* in a very long time.

"Her next heat is due in nine days," Flynn said.

And… *yeah*. I wasn't exactly unaware of the fact. I hadn't gone out of my way to mark the calendar date or anything like that, but it wasn't as though I could forget it, either.

"You're going to ask them again," I said, with something like resignation.

"You bet I am," Flynn shot back. "Are you sayin' you're not interested?"

I clenched my jaw. "Of course I'm interested, you ass. They're the most amazing pair of omegas I've ever met. Of *course* I am." A frustrated sigh escaped my control. "But unlike you, I'm not willing to spit in Alex's face. She's our pack leader, and this entire situation is driving a knife through her heart— even if she won't show it openly."

Flynn's heavy brow furrowed, the gears visibly turning behind his eyes. "But… that's an old wound, not a new one. You don't get better by stitching something up while the infection's still inside. You have to open it up. Get some sunlight and air on it so it can heal properly."

Fuck. Why was it that every time I discounted Flynn, he came up with something like that? There was a reason I'd thrown my lot in with the giant asshole in the first place, and this was it.

"I'll talk to her," I said. "Actually, we should both talk to her. We need a pack meeting anyway."

"Yeah, no shit," Flynn agreed. "When they get back, all right?"

"Deal," I told him.

He nodded and left me alone on the couch with my thoughts, in favor of easing back into the omega's nest with them. Leona flopped one uncoordinated arm across his stomach and nuzzled into his shoulder without waking. Inside my chest, something clenched with an almost painful tenderness.

Many hours later, the sound of an approaching vehicle tickled the edges of my alpha hearing. Flynn raised his head and met my gaze.

"That's the Jeep," he said. "You go. I'll stay with these two."

Kam drew in a breath and opened his eyes, immediately tensing up. "What's wrong? Is someone here?"

"Just Alex and Beckett," I told him, my body cranking up the reassuring alpha pheromones without any input from my higher brain functions.

What did I say earlier? *Kryptonite.*

"You can go back to sleep if you want," Flynn added. "Jax—bring some food up with you afterward."

"Will do," I agreed. Pausing to collect the Glock I'd stashed next to the couch—just in case—I went to meet the others at the door.

They'd brought groceries. Beckett looked tired and drawn, as well he might after the events of the past day. Alex was inscrutable, though she did lock eyes with me briefly as they entered. I gave her a terse *all-is-well* nod, and she nodded back.

"What's the verdict?" I asked, rather than beating around the bush.

"They're in if they want to be in," Beckett said. "How are they faring?"

"Asleep," I told him. "Flynn's with them. Mr. Patel is holding up well, but Ms. McCready is struggling."

"Not surprising," Beckett said. "No matter how prepared you think you are, when it actually happens, you find out you're really not."

I gave a considering nod. "I'm getting them some food for when they wake up. Later, though, we need to hold a pack meeting if that's okay, boss."

Alex's posture stiffened almost imperceptibly.

Beckett's pale eyes always saw more than they should, but he only nodded. "I can take the food upstairs and relieve Flynn, so you three can have a talk."

"Thanks, boss," I said, heading to the kitchen to put away groceries and make sandwiches.

Beckett joined me there a few minutes later. He'd lost his jacket, rolled his sleeves up to his elbows, and splashed water on his face. I handed him the tray, and he headed upstairs, leaving me alone with Alex.

"Flynn is going to harp on about exactly what you'd expect," I warned her. "But the thing is, I'm not all that sure he's wrong."

"We can't protect them, Jax," she said.

I let out a breath. "Maybe not, *alef*—but we took a pretty good crack at it this morning. Do you really think they'll be *less* safe with an alpha pack around them?"

Of course, she couldn't say no without it being an obvious lie, and Alex hadn't become our leader by lying to us.

"Let's wait for Flynn before we get into it," she said instead.

Our packmate joined us a couple minutes later.

"They're both awake," he said, by way of greeting. "Beckett's gonna talk to them about the offer."

"And you still want to make them a different offer," Alex replied, gesturing the three of us to sit around the battered kitchen table. "You realize their decision on Beckett's proposal will make a big difference here, Flynn. That is, unless you intend to bail on us and run off after them to the South Pacific or something."

"They'll stay," Flynn said with absolute certainty.

"You don't know that," Alex retorted. "They already tried standing and fighting, and look where it got them."

Flynn stared at her. "You have actually *met* Leona McCready, right?"

Alex's lips thinned, and I couldn't get past the haunted look behind her green eyes.

She raised an eyebrow at me. "And where do you stand on this?"

I tapped the tabletop rhythmically with the fingers of my right hand. "The way I see it, there are a couple of options. You and Flynn can throw down, and maybe once you've kicked his ass, he'll reconsider things." Flynn scoffed. I ignored him and continued. "Or we can discuss a compromise."

"I'm listening," she said, not breaking expression.

"Not sure there's much to compromise on," Flynn observed.

"Hear me out," I said. "Leona's heat is coming on in a little over a week. Beckett could probably score a heat blocker for her in that amount of time, but she's already been on that shit for years. Eventually it's going to kill her." This next bit was going to be the tricky part, and I watched Alex's expression carefully. "Or, alternately, he could find her some contraceptives."

Her features froze.

"From a reputable source," I added quickly. "You know Beckett has the right contacts to get the good stuff."

"That's a thought," Flynn said, clearly catching on.

Alex didn't dismiss it out of hand or fly off the handle—and, of course, that was why she led our pack. Well, that and the fact that she could pound both of us into the dirt, if it ever came to that.

"You're talking about a no-strings-attached heat contract. Which, I hasten to point out, is what I thought Irina and I were going to have, before I succumbed to knot-brain in mid-coupling and agreed to give her a mating bite."

"You were alone, and you were both young," I said. "Plus, I hope I don't have to point out that I've been with more omegas than I care to remember, yet I've never been tempted to bite. And Flynn treats sex like it's a recreational sport."

"*Hey*," Flynn protested, sounding mildly insulted. A moment later, he seemed to realize I was on his side in this, and he added, "It's just nice to get close to people, that's all. It doesn't have to be a huge deal."

"We'll all be there to police each other and keep emotions from getting out of hand," I said, hoping to bring my argument home. "This kind of thing wasn't at all unusual in the old days, before the Purge. And isn't that exactly what we're all fighting for? The freedom to be ourselves and manage our lives the way we see fit?"

Alex's jaw tightened, the tendons working with tension for a long moment. "All right." It sounded like the words were being pulled from her. "Counter-proposal. *If* they agree to stay here instead of sneaking out of the country to hide, and *if* they furthermore agree to a heat contract with the two of you — then she uses a cervical cap with spermicide in addition to hormonal contraception, and anyone knotting her wears a condom. I'm present for all of it, and if I see teeth coming anywhere near a mating gland, I will deliver the beat-down of your *fucking life*."

Flynn grinned at her. "Done."

She looked mildly taken aback, either because she'd been geared up for more of a fight, or because she'd just realized that this might really be about to happen. She shot me a sharp look, and I shrugged.

"Works for me," I said, not about to bring up the fact that triple-redundancy in contraception seemed like a bit of overkill, to put it mildly.

She had her reasons. And frankly, I'd expected more resistance, so I wasn't about to make a fuss.

Flynn looked like he could float on air. "Great! It's all settled. Now we just need to wait for Beckett to work his magic."

"Yeah. Great," Alex echoed faintly. "*Fuck.*"

TWENTY-SIX

Leona

I WOKE TO the sound of Flynn talking quietly with someone at the door. Kam stirred beside me and sat up, blinking.

My eyes felt gritty; I had the dregs of a crying headache throbbing in my sinuses. I was sure I looked like hell warmed over—puffy and blotchy red. The events of the past day settled over me with cruel clarity, all of the blessed haziness from earlier gone without a trace.

We were fugitives.

We'd lost everything.

It was my fault.

And after all of that, I'd somehow slept for hours in total peace, wrapped in strong arms and curled against my *odama*.

Flynn and Beckett stood together in the doorway, engaged in a low-voiced conversation. Flynn nodded at something Beckett said, and took the plate that the smaller man had been holding. He crossed the room to us and handed it to Kam. It held two sandwiches, bursting with meat and cheese and tomatoes.

"Chief Beckett needs to talk to both of you," Flynn said. "And I need to talk to Alex at some point. If you want me to stay, I'll stay—but you should know that Beckett's all right. You can trust him."

I hesitated. Beckett had saved our lives on at least two occasions... and yet, I still had absolutely no insight into his true motives or goals. Kam and I exchanged a look. He gave a small nod.

"It's fine, Flynn," I said. "Go check in with your *alef*. Thanks for..." The words stumbled to a halt. *Thanks for letting me soak your shirt with tears? Thanks for bringing Kam here so I didn't shatter completely?*

"Staying," Kam finished for me. "Thanks for staying with us, Flynn."

Flynn smiled his big, brilliant, uncomplicated smile. "Any time, ginger tea. Now, listen to what the boss has to say, okay? I'll be back in a bit."

He rose and left with a nod to Beckett as he passed. The security chief had remained at the door rather than barging into the room we were using as a nest. It was an interesting bit of nuance, coming from a beta.

"May I come in?" he asked politely.

Kam roused himself before I managed to. "Yes, of course." He picked up the plate of sandwiches and set it on the corner table. Then he grabbed one of the blankets and draped it over my shoulders, urging me up to sit on the overstuffed sectional. "Please, come in and make yourself comfortable. We do need to have a talk."

I wrapped the blanket around my body, feeling a bit less self-conscious than if I'd tried to face Beckett in nothing but Jax's borrowed T-shirt. Kam waited until the chief had made his way down to the sunken den and taken a seat on the other side of the sectional before settling next to me.

"Thank you," Beckett said.

I took a moment to study him—this mild-mannered, middle-aged beta with the pale, knowing eyes and kindly manner. He looked drawn, with dark circles under his eyes and new lines etched into his pleasant face. I didn't think I'd ever seen him without a suit jacket and tie before—though to be fair, he probably hadn't stormed the cave in Romania while wearing office attire. I'd just been too out of it to notice.

Now, the top button of his shirt was undone. His sleeves were rolled up, baring slender, sinewy forearms.

"It appears we're in your debt, yet again," Kam said. "Thank you for intervening. Though I do have to wonder what consequences you've brought on yourselves by helping us get away."

Beckett gave him a quick, tight smile. "There are times when the consequences of doing nothing outweigh the risks of taking action."

I still couldn't figure out his angle. "Those consequences would have happened to *us*, though. Not to you or your team," I said carefully, hating how the congested quality of my voice declared my earlier tears to the world.

The chief leaned back against the cushions, regarding me. "Ms. McCready. Mr. Patel. What you've achieved in the Foreign Office is extraordinary by any measure. Believe me when I say, the consequences of losing two omegas in positions such as yours would have been enormous."

Kam leaned forward, perching on the edge of the seat cushion. "But we don't hold those positions anymore. Whatever power we might have had before—it's gone now."

Beckett met our eyes, looking from one to the other of us. "You don't hold *those* positions anymore, no."

I stared at him, a crazy suspicion growing. "You and Alex walked into a police station, and walked out with me in your custody. No *way* was that officially sanctioned. There would have been security cameras. A paper trail. You won't have a position left, either."

"Oh, I assure you, I will," he said with a decidedly wry note coloring his voice.

"But not as a federal security agent," I insisted. "So maybe you'd better tell us who you're really working for."

He gave me a satisfied nod, as though my answer had pleased him. "I've no doubt you've both had contact with us in the past—and in more than one capacity. Unregistered omegas don't rise to public positions without considerable support from behind the scenes."

Kam drew in a sharp breath. "The underground. You're with the *underground*."

Beckett lifted an eyebrow—a tiny flicker of a gesture. "Lost positions or no, the two of you still have contacts in high places, scattered across the world. Some of those contacts will be sympathetic to the alphomic cause. We could use you. Both of you. And—at the risk of being indelicate—under the circumstances, you could use us as well."

I tried not to show outwardly how much I was reeling. "But you're a beta."

That small, secret smile played over his lips again. "You might well think so. And, to be fair, there are many betas in the underground. Not everyone falls prey to the Committee's propaganda machine."

Kam's lips parted. "*Oh*," he said, in the tone of a revelation. "You... you were out sick during the bilateral talks. You were out for a *week*."

"Yes. I'm far too old to rely on blockers for every heat," Beckett said dryly. "Seriously, Ms. McCready—those things will kill you sooner or later."

I caught my breath, realization dawning.

Beckett undid a second button on his shirt and tugged his collar aside, twisting to present his right shoulder to our wide-eyed gazes. A single, perfect bite scar surrounded the place where an omega's mating gland was located—the skin there darkened and raised to indicate that the mating bond had taken.

"Well," I said faintly. "I suppose that explains a number of things."

Kam let out a startled huff, more shock than amusement. "Doesn't it just?"

Beckett's expression turned rueful as he straightened and buttoned his dress shirt. "Indeed. So now, the question once again becomes what you intend to do, going forward. Even in circumstances such as these, with enough lead time, we can still get you out of the country. We could set you up someplace out of the way with new identities. Or... you could join us, with the understanding that you won't be any safer working for the underground than you were while working publicly as unregistered omegas."

My body stilled while my mind processed his words. I stared into Beckett's eyes, searching for any glimmer of insincerity or deceit. I saw only compassion and resolve.

"We'll have to discuss it," I said quickly, even as a faint, burgeoning sense of hope blossomed in my chest.

Maybe this wasn't the end.

I met Kam's soulful brown eyes, and he held my gaze with a look of fond understanding. He'd always wanted a pack — a proper one. And what bigger pack was there than the secret network of alphas, betas, and omegas dedicated to protecting our people from behind the scenes?

"Of course," Beckett said. "Either way, I'm afraid we're going to be stuck here for a couple of weeks at minimum, while more permanent plans can be made. This house is one of hundreds scattered across the country, owned by an utterly unremarkable real estate investment firm with no suspicious ties to anything controversial. We'll stay here and keep our heads down until the scandal of an escaped omega fugitive blows over, and the news outlets start to lose interest."

I couldn't begin to face the reality of my picture being posted all over the front-page news. Not yet. I set that aside for now. There were other things to address, as much as I dreaded doing so.

"I do have another issue," I said.

Kam laid his hand on my blanket-swaddled thigh.

Beckett nodded slowly. "Yes. It's been eleven weeks since Romania. I'm well aware."

I relaxed a bit, still in the process of rearranging my brain around the idea that I was talking to another omega — one quite a bit older than me, who'd had a lifetime of managing heats around the sham of a beta existence.

"It's short notice," Beckett went on, "but barring anything unforeseen, I should be able to acquire whatever drugs are appropriate. However, I'd suggest talking to the alphas first. They're downstairs having a pack meeting as we speak, and you don't have to be a genius to guess what it's about."

I blinked at him. Kam inhaled audibly.

"At any rate," Beckett said, "I should let you eat and talk. There's bottled water in the mini-fridge if you're thirsty. Will you be all right on your own for a bit?"

"Yes," I said, the word so faint it was barely audible. I cleared my throat and added in a stronger tone, "Thank you."

He smiled thinly. "All part of the service. Starting over from nothing is never a pleasant process, but it is survivable."

"And far better than the alternative," Kam replied.

"I've always thought so, yes," Beckett agreed, rising from the couch. "I'll keep the others out of your hair for half an hour, but after that, I'm afraid you're on your own on that front."

With that, he gave us a polite nod and let himself out, closing the door behind him. Silence fell for the space of several breaths, before Kam flopped back against the couch cushions and said, "Holy. Buggering. *Shite*."

I met his eyes, feeling more than a little breathless. "Do you still want to run?"

He gave a single, high-pitched bark of laughter. "*Odama*, I didn't *want* to run before. I just wanted us both to be safe."

"Staying won't be safe," I pointed out.

He sobered. "No. No, of course it won't be. But Leo—I'm not the one whose door was broken down in the middle of the night. Do *you* want to run?"

I thought about it—about everything that starting over would entail. About the fact that there could well be police or Committee operatives pounding down my door again in the near future. I thought about the underground—the shadowy organization that had saved Kam from slavery and provided me with the tools and contacts necessary to maintain my ruse for all these years.

We could be part of that organization. Next time, *we* could be the people who saved some other terrified omega from a lifetime of horror.

"This morning, I thought it was the end," I said. "I thought it was all over for both of us. But, now? Maybe it doesn't have to be."

Kam smiled at me, gentle and understanding. In perfect synchrony, we fell forward into each other's arms.

"Maybe it doesn't have to be," he agreed.

Beckett was good to his word. Thirty minutes after he'd left us, boots sounded on the stairwell at the end of the hall. A few moments later, the first hints of cypress, jasmine, spice, and musk wafted to us.

I'd eaten my sandwich and had a quick wash in the extravagant bathroom. It had left me feeling marginally more human, at least. A knock sounded at the door, and Kam went to open it, shooting me a speculative glance. I had a fair idea of what to expect after Beckett's not-so-subtle hints, but for now, I knew my answer would have to remain the same.

As much as I might long for it—in the depths of my heart, where I feared to look too closely—there was no way that accepting the suit of an alpha pack during a period of so much upheaval was in any way a sane plan. Flynn would ask us, and Alex would look uncomfortable, and I would politely decline. I would ask Beckett to acquire a heat blocker for me. I'd tackle this new phase in my life with a clear head and no distractions.

Kam would support me—because Kam *always* supported me—and we'd revisit the topic when things were less crazy than they were right now.

"Come in," Kam said, acting as gatekeeper to the nest in the old omega tradition.

"Thank you," Alex replied formally. She led the others into the room, and accepted Kam's offer of a seat on the couch. The others settled nearby, giving us space.

I met her eyes. "Thank *you* for getting me out of that place. I didn't get a chance to say it, earlier."

"That was Beckett's doing, not mine," she demurred. "But I'm relieved we were in time."

The pained look in her eyes made me realize she must be remembering the omega she hadn't been able to save. My heart ached for her.

"Nevertheless," Kam said, taking my hand, "we're immensely grateful to all of you."

"So," Flynn said. "You're both going to stay, right? Join the underground?"

I squeezed Kam's fingers. "Yes. If we can't make a difference from inside the government, we'll try to make a difference from outside it."

Flynn's shoulders relaxed. Alex received the news impassively, but she didn't look surprised.

Jax nodded in clear satisfaction. "I'm glad to hear that," he said.

Kam tilted his head, considering. "Beckett's an omega." His eyes fell on Flynn. "A *mated* omega. You certainly kept that quiet."

Flynn shrugged, completely unrepentant.

"It's not the sort of information one lets slip in casual conversation," Alex observed tartly. "Or in *any* kind of conversation, really."

I thought of the old bite mark, ridged and shadowed in the room's warm light. "It's not... one of you three, is it?" For some reason, I found the idea disconcerting.

Jax let out a startled breath of laughter. "God, no."

"I don't think *anyone* knows who his mate is," Flynn said. "But either way, that kind of information is pretty far above our pay grade."

"I've never even heard him use gendered pronouns," Jax added. "It's always 'they' and 'them.' I'd assumed it was someone high enough up the food chain in the underground that it would be dangerous if the information got out."

Alex shot them a quelling look. "It's not our job to speculate."

"No," Kam agreed. "Sorry—I can see how that would be sensitive information."

"And it's not why we're here, anyway," Flynn said. "We've got a proposal for the two of you."

I steeled myself, sending Kam a mental apology. "I'm sorry, Flynn," I began. "I think I know what you're going to ask, and—"

"No, Leona," Jax said, interrupting. "It's not that. Not what you're thinking."

My jaw snapped shut. After a moment, I regrouped. "Oh? Then, what is it?"

Alex took a deep breath. "Jax and Flynn want to propose a no-strings-attached heat contract. You're due soon, and since we'll be staying here anyway, there's technically no reason why you'd have to use a blocker."

My mind went abruptly, explosively blank. Kam glanced at me, taking in my compete loss of brain-to-mouth functionality.

"A heat contract," he echoed. "You mean in the old sense? A one-time agreement unrelated to courting or mating?"

It occurred to me with a distant sort of recognition that Kam had been born to an ancient, purebred family. They'd followed the traditional alphomic ways, right up to the bitter end. He knew about these concepts as something more than hypothetical. He'd grown up around them.

"That's right," Alex confirmed. "No courting. No biting. Careful and considered use of birth control methods to prevent conception."

"Seriously, you should hear what she's insisting on," Flynn put in. "There won't be a single sperm cell surviving the carnage."

Jax threw him an unimpressed look before turning back to us. His bright blue gaze was serious. "Leona, you don't have to take that poison to stop your heat. Not this time, at least." His expression said *not ever, if we can help it.*

My heart began to pound... with fear, or nervousness, or excitement—I wasn't sure.

Kam's fingers were still tangled with mine, and his grip was almost tight enough to hurt.

"Say yes, Leona," Flynn said. "Kam — say yes."

"You don't have to be alone," Jax added quietly. "Our kind are meant to come together. To help each other."

I tore my eyes away from them — dark and fair, brown-eyed and blue — to meet Alex's gaze.

"You can't be all right with this, surely?" I hadn't meant for it to come out sounding like a question.

Alex drew breath, only to hesitate, choosing her words.

"My packmates don't technically need my permission to offer you a heat contract. It's between them and you." She paused. "And as hard as it is for me to really believe it in my heart, the reality is that it harms no one." Her eyes flickered to Jax for an instant. "Irina and I were young. We were alone. We gambled on black market contraceptives and our own self-control, and we lost. On both counts."

"There will be five of us this time," Jax went on. "All looking out for each other. And, as Flynn says, there will also be more birth control products than you can shake a stick at." His eyes went distant. "There are god-knows-how-many pups with my DNA languishing in the slave plantations. I am extremely cognizant of the dangers involved in bringing new lives into this world."

I swallowed hard, picturing blue-eyed youngsters with chiseled jaws and sandy hair.

I turned to Kam with a pleading look, not sure what I was asking of him.

He gave me a smile, but it was strained around the edges. "I think you should do it, *odama*," he said. "What's the harm?"

But I shook my head. "There's no '*me*' here, Kam. There's only '*us*.'"

"You've got that right, sweet thing," Flynn said. "It's both or neither. Ginger tea, you're gonna say yes and let me see if I can rock your world—beta butchers or no."

Kam froze. "I don't think…"

I caught his gaze, squeezing his hand hard. "We've tried it with bottled alpha pheromones, *odama*," I said. "We haven't tried it with the real thing. Not combined with my heat pheromones."

His lips parted as though he might say something, but no words came out.

"Hmm. That sounded an awful lot like a *yes*, Leona," Flynn said, with a hint of smugness.

I paused, holding my breath.

I could have this.

I could give Kam what he wanted—let the alphas see if they could make him feel good in a way that I couldn't. Not on my own, anyway.

I could experience heat as an omega was meant to, without the worries of public discovery or pregnancy.

We could do this. There was nothing left to stop us. And afterward, we could step away, with no long-term consequences.

"Yes," I said, hardly able to believe it, even as the word left my mouth. "Yes… let's do it. Let's spend my heat here in this house. *Together.*"

End of Book 1

Book Two:

Fight or Fly

ONE

Leona

IN RETROSPECT, doing vodka shots with an alpha might not have been the best decision I'd ever made. Though in my defense, there were times when vodka was, without a doubt, the right response to a situation. This was, I felt pretty sure, one of those times.

A copy of *The New York Times* lay on the table between us, the front page dominated by a candid photo of me taken at the bilateral summit a mere couple of weeks ago. I looked harried and exhausted. Probably because I'd been, well... *harried and exhausted.*

"It's not even a good picture," I said, listlessly dragging my refilled shot glass toward me.

HIGH-LEVEL MEMBER OF UFNA FOREIGN OFFICE ARRESTED, the headline screamed. *UNREGISTERED OMEGA ESCAPES POLICE CUSTODY.*

Alex gave me a narrow look as she refilled her own glass with a hand that seemed way steadier than it should be. "Would it improve the situation if they'd used a professional headshot instead?"

I lifted my arm in a sloppy wave. "I'm vain," I told her. "Kam's vain. We're both vain omegas, and if I'm gonna be plastered across every single front page in the country, I'd rather look good doing it, damn it."

On the positive side—if there was one—the article made absolutely no mention of Kam, my fellow omega-in-hiding. Rhys Beckett got about an inch of dedicated column space, since he'd signed his own name to the forged paperwork he'd used to get me out of Montreal police custody. Alex's boss hadn't exactly been subtle when he'd strode in, utterly shameless, and wielded his status as a federal security agent like a bludgeon.

Ex-federal security agent, now. He was a fugitive like the rest of us, though he appeared largely unconcerned by that fact. I got the impression Beckett had cycled through a few different identities over the course of his lifetime. Like me… like Kam… he was an omega hiding in a beta-dominated world. But first and foremost, he was involved in the underground — the shadowy association of alphas, omegas, and beta allies that helped hide and protect our people from persecution in a world ruled by beta supremacists.

He'd helped Kam and me, even if I still wasn't totally sure why. He said he wanted us to join the underground. He said we could still make a difference there. And his alphas… *they* wanted to court us. To join our packs together; maybe to mate. At least, Jax and Flynn did. I got the impression my current drinking companion would rather chop off her right hand than get emotionally tangled up with a pair of fugitive omegas.

She gestured at me with her shot glass and tipped it up, swallowing the contents with a sharp tilt of her head. "Bottoms up," she said, setting the now-empty glass firmly back on the table and reaching for the bottle. "You're not nearly drunk enough yet."

I peered at her through bleary eyes. "How do you know?"

"You haven't asked me the question you want to ask me," she replied.

And… *fair*.

I tipped the vodka down my throat, coughing a bit at the burn. Once I'd recovered, I slid the glass across to her. She filled it and slid it back.

"Right," I said, a bit hoarsely. "Okay, here it is. Am I making a huge mistake here?"

Alex fiddled with her glass, spinning it in her fingers. "About the heat contract? The fact that you're choosing to ask me makes it sound like you want someone to tell you yes."

I threw back the next shot — my fourth — wincing as it went down. "Cut me off after this next one, please," I said, pushing the glass toward her. She nodded and filled it. I sighed, trying to find the right words. "I don't think it's that. I mean, if I ask Jax or Flynn, they'll say they think it's a great idea to spend my heat together. If I ask Kam, he'll give me that sad-eyed smile and tell me it's my choice. At least if I ask you, you'll have an opinion that's not *full-steam-ahead*."

She nodded and knocked back another shot. A small furrow formed between her brows. Alex was dark-haired and sharp-featured — built like a cheetah, and with the same green-gold eyes. All of the fine lines around her eyes and mouth were unhappy ones.

"Would the situation be a lot simpler if my packmates hadn't fallen for you?" she said. "Yeah. It would be, for sure. In fact, if they weren't pining for you and Kameron like a pair of blushing schoolgirls nursing their first crushes, I'd probably tell you to go for it and enjoy the alpha horse cocks. No question about it — heat blockers suck and riding out an unfulfilled heat without blockers sucks even worse."

"But?" I prompted, feeling the alcohol begin to hit properly, loosening my muscles and probably my tongue.

She shrugged. "You already know. They're settling for a heat contract because you would have said no to anything more. That doesn't mean they don't still *want* more. And..." She gestured around, indicating not just the remote safehouse, but the entire situation. "… realistically, how would that even work right now?"

I saluted her with my shot glass and drained it. "That's what I said," I agreed around a cough.

"Here's the thing, though," Alex said. "The fact that my packmates are idiots doesn't change any of the rest of it. I've heard the horror stories. Unaccompanied heats are the worst. And Jax and Flynn may be idiots, but they're honorable idiots with really big dicks, who apparently know how to use them."

I choked on an unattractive snorting laugh, my hand flying to my mouth to cover it.

"If you're trying to argue on the *against* side, no offense, but you might want to brush up your debate skills a bit," I suggested.

She only shook her head and poured herself another shot. "Nah. See, as long as you've got it straight in your head, it's not your responsibility if a pair of alphas are thinking with their little brains instead of their big ones." She hesitated. "At least, as long as no fertile sperm get anywhere near fertile eggs."

I nodded solemnly, aware that I was finally reaching the stage of proper drunkenness. "A-fucking-men to that," I said.

"Honestly," Alex went on, "if you want objectivity, go talk to Beckett. He's been managing this kind of omega shit for longer than either of us have been alive... god alone knows how." The last few words were a low mutter.

"Huh," I said. "Y'know, that's a good idea. I'm shtill... *still* wrapping my brain around him being an omega. And *mated*. Shit."

I'd never had an older omega to help me navigate the minefield of estrus cycles and mate-bonds. My parents were both betas, and while I owed them my life and my freedom after the sacrifices they'd made to protect me from the Committee's tender mercies, they hadn't been much help with the nuts and bolts of my body and its responses. They'd tried, but... knowledge about alphomic biology was tightly regulated. You couldn't just run to the library and check out a book. They'd pretty much all been burned decades ago, back at the beginning of the Purge.

"I'll do that," I decided. "But maybe not till I sober up."

Alex snorted in amusement, her steady parade of downed shots finally starting to outpace alpha alcohol tolerance.

"I'm gonna do this," I told my empty shot glass. "I mean, since you're not dead shet... *set*... against it or anything."

"Not dead set against it, no," she said.

I studied her, taking in her straight spine and tight shoulders, even after eight shots, or nine, or whatever it had been. "Do you ever..." I made vague, waving motions with my fingers. "Like, at all anymore?"

She blinked at me without comprehension.

"Sex," I clarified, confirming that I'd reached the *brain-to-mouth filter failure* stage of drunkenness. "Do you ever have sex, since Irina died?"

"Oh." She poured yet another shot and drank it. "I mean... yeah. Not often, but when the circumstances line up, sure."

I frowned. "With omegas?" I asked, because she'd seemed, like, *really* against that idea after talking about how she'd lost her omega mate and pups.

But she shook her head quickly. "No, with beta men. No uteruses, see? They're safe, and usually okay with one-night stands."

My frown didn't smooth. "Beta men? You enjoy that? Really?"

Alex shrugged a shoulder. "I enjoy the ones who like to take a knot up the ass."

Comprehension dawned, and I made an exaggerated '*oh*' shape with my mouth. "Gotcha." I tapped the side of my nose. "I did that for Kam once, you know. With a…" I trailed off, trying to describe the shape of a dildo in the air. "Thingie. I think he got close—to coming, I mean—but he still couldn't get there."

Suddenly, this seemed like the saddest thing in the world. I met Alex's catlike green eyes, convinced that she would understand. I wasn't sure why, but I felt we'd connected somehow. It was different than the way I'd connected with Jax and Flynn. Less complicated in some ways. More complicated in others.

"He's got a huge crush on you," I confided. "He talked about how he'd like to tease your clit out of its sheath with his tongue and ride it all night long." I paused, remembering the night we'd spent exploring each other's bodies. "You should let him. He's got a really nice tongue."

Silence reigned for an uncomfortable beat.

Wait, had I really just said that out loud? Based on the perfectly blank expression on Alex's face, I had. It was *just* possible I should have stopped after four shots instead of five.

The alpha cleared her throat and gave the vodka bottle a long look—one that said she was thinking about foregoing the shot glass and going straight to the source. But the idea was stuck in my head now, and I couldn't let it go.

"No, listen though. If I'm doing this heat... thing, and you're going to be there to keep an eye on the others, you could, maybe... try to help Kam?" It was perfect. Why hadn't I thought of this before? "He's safe for you. He doesn't have a uterus anymore. And you're both so sad all the time. Maybe you could make each other less sad?"

Alex seemed to be holding her face very still. I couldn't tell what she was thinking, so I gave up and asked. "Well? What do you think?"

She blinked. "I... think we're both pretty drunk. Beckett should be back in a few hours with the contraceptives and other supplies. Maybe you should go sleep it off for a bit."

While I tried to interpret that with a brain that felt like it was slogging through molasses, she rose from the kitchen table and headed deeper into the house, taking the bottle with her. Once she'd disappeared, the ghost of Flynn's voice echoed in my head.

She didn't say no.

TWO

Leona

"BECKETT'S HERE." The clink of a glass being placed on a table accompanied Kam's matter-of-fact declaration.

I pried open gummy eyelids, unsure if I was hung over, still drunk, or some hellacious combination of both. "Great," I rasped, and reached for the water glass.

"I would make some comment about an omega doing vodka shots on an empty stomach..." he began, settling onto the overstuffed sectional couch that delineated two sides of the sunken nest in the safehouse's upstairs den.

"Yeah, don't bother," I told him. "Look at it this way—it's not like maintaining a professional demeanor is really that much of a necessity anymore."

Kam stretched, his rumpled white button-down shirt riding up, exposing a bit of olive skin below the side gusset. "We still don't know what Beckett's got in mind for us," he said. "You never know, maybe we'll have to give up all our vices."

He looked... *tired*. Not exactly a surprise. I was dealing with the shock of having to completely reinvent my life, and not knowing exactly what that would entail. By contrast, he already knew what was coming, at least in broad terms. He'd done this before.

His tousled dark hair, devoid of styling products, curled over his forehead. Bruised circles beneath his soulful brown eyes advertised his need for more uninterrupted sleep than he was currently getting.

We'd been here for a week. My heat was due to start in two days, but it could be a day early or late. Normally, I'd have taken my heat blocker last night, just in case. This time around, I hadn't. That still felt weird.

With luck, Beckett had been successful in getting the contraceptives he'd promised me—because apparently, the five of us were actually going to do this. Three alphas in our borrowed nest. The idea made me feel jittery. Not a bad sort of jittery, necessarily... though I would admit to a certain degree of fear of the unknown. When it came to being knotted by actual alphas, I was a thirty-one-year-old omega virgin.

I finished the glass of water Kam had brought me and set it down.

"Let me freshen up first, and then I'll go talk to him," I said. "Will you come with me?"

"Of course I will," Kam said. He rubbed his hands down his face, stretching the skin. "Tell me, though... how offended are you going to be if I curl up in a corner of the nest and sleep for four days straight while Jax and Flynn take turns fucking you?"

I tossed a pillow at his head. He batted it away with an amused snort.

After splashing cold water on my face in the ridiculous bathroom with its massive sunken tub and separate two-person shower, I gathered my disastrous hair into a bun and secured it with a couple of pencils that I'd liberated from downstairs. While my clothing was no longer limited to oversized T-shirts borrowed from the alphas, my available wardrobe was still painfully basic. The white tank top and black leggings I'd napped in would have to do.

Thankfully, our situation wasn't quite as dire as I'd originally assumed it was. I'd been taken from my loft in a three a.m. raid, and quite literally had nothing left to my name. But Jax and Flynn had managed to scoop Kam up from his apartment before the authorities started snooping around my closest contacts. He'd had time to grab his emergency bag, along with the ten thousand dollars in cash that he'd kept hidden in a wall safe.

I'd had a similar stash prepped and ready to go, for all the good it did me in the end. But—just as I would have shared my resources with Kam, had our positions been reversed—the money he'd hidden away was for both of us. If we were careful, it would be enough to sneak out of the country and make it to Jamaica, where my parents could help us set up new lives.

But now, while that might in fact be the safer option, it appeared we wouldn't be doing it. That was one of the things we needed to talk to Beckett about today, before my oncoming heat stole my higher brain functioning.

I headed back to the den and nudged Kam awake from his doze, trying not to feel guilty about doing so. Together, we trudged downstairs. Interesting smells wafted from the kitchen, making my stomach rumble.

I seemed to be hungry all the time, these last few days. At first, I'd assumed it was stress eating—not helped by the fact that the alphas always seemed to be shoving food at me. Eventually, I realized that it was my body bolstering its reserves for my upcoming heat. For several days, I would survive on only whatever water the others could get me to drink between peaks, burning fat for calories as my body shifted all its resources to my reproductive system.

Led by the nose, I followed the smells and found Jax standing over the electric stove. Flynn sat at the kitchen table, cutting a pile of fruit into pieces and dumping it in a big ceramic bowl. They both looked up as we entered. Flynn's face lit up; Jax flashed us a pleasant smile.

"Hey," Flynn said. "We're just stocking up. No one wants to cook after a good heat, but everyone wants to eat."

I nodded in understanding. "What is that?" I asked Jax, inhaling the scent of meat and browned potatoes.

"Shepherd's pie," he said. "Well, cottage pie, I guess, since it's beef and not lamb. Try some?"

I crossed to him as though drawn to his side by a length of silken cord. The pie itself was in the oven, baking to a lovely golden brown. He scraped the contents of one bowl into another bowl and handed it to me—mashed potatoes sitting on top of a mixture of cooked ground beef and diced vegetables. I took the spoon he offered and devoured it like a starving coyote.

At the table, Flynn chuckled. "Come here for a minute when you're done."

While I was distracted, he'd foisted an apple on Kam, who bit into it with a crunch. I scraped up the last couple of bites of deconstructed cottage pie and offered Jax a tentative smile of thanks before rinsing the bowl and spoon in the sink. I approached Flynn cautiously. He set the knife down and hooked me close to him with a gentle hand at the back of my neck.

My heart rabbited, my body unused to that kind of casual touch from an alpha. When he buried his nose at the base of my neck and shoulder and breathed in, gooseflesh erupted across my entire body. He let me go, holding the breath he'd just taken like a wine connoisseur assessing a rare vintage.

"You're gonna be early," he said. "Go talk to Beckett now and get that out of the way. I want to have plenty of time to play before we need to get down to business."

I couldn't suppress a shiver. Kam's eyes on me were soft when I turned to him.

"Come on," he said. "Let's go make sure everything's in order."

Nodding wordlessly, I followed him with Flynn's call of, "Don't worry—I'm gonna play with you, too, Ginger Tea!" chasing us out.

"Why do I feel like we're on the menu every bit as much as the cottage pie and fruit salad?" I murmured.

"Because we are," Kam said wryly. "Well, you are, anyway. That's basically what you're signing up for, you realize."

I hadn't realized—not properly. Not until just now. My hazy memories from last time involved the alphas holding back, respecting boundaries that I'd needed for my own safety, but hadn't *wanted* in the desperation of the moment. Now, I was extending them carte blanche, at least within the framework of what we'd all agreed to ahead of time.

"I have absolutely no idea what I'm getting into, do I?" I asked.

Kam huffed in what was probably amusement. "You're about to spend four solid days riding a sex-high." He hesitated. "And I'm apparently going to be caught inside the blast zone for most of it. Should be interesting, if nothing else."

I stepped in front of him and turned to face him with my hand on his arm, stopping us in the hallway. "You *are* okay with this, right?" I asked, feeling a wash of guilt over my drunken confession to Alex earlier.

"Yes, *odama*," he said gently. "I'm okay with the nice alphas eating us for breakfast. We're here, we're safe—for a given definition of the word—and it makes no sense for you to take that toxic poison you call a heat blocker when you can have a natural heat shared with alphas you genuinely like. I like them, too, by the way. In case that wasn't obvious."

I knew he was telling the truth. I also knew he didn't really think he'd be able to get anything out of it beyond that—not after the mutilation he'd undergone as an adolescent. That was clear in his tone, even if he hadn't meant for it to come through.

"I… might have confessed to Alex that you have a crush on her while I was drunk," I blurted, wincing before adding, "and asked her to have sex with you."

Kam's face went utterly still. Sheepishly, I let my hand drop from his arm.

"At which point she freaked out and ran for the hills, I assume?" he asked slowly.

I sighed. "Not exactly. She, uh, changed the subject." *And then ran for the hills with a bottle of vodka in tow*, I didn't add.

He sighed, too. "You probably shouldn't have done that."

"I know," I told him. "And I'm sorry. But she's sad, and miserable, and she's going to try to wall herself off from what's happening for four straight days while the house is choked with heat pheromones. And you're also sad, and miserable, and you're going to try to wall yourself off from what's happening the minute I'm too out of things to stop you. I just want you to be happy, Kam." I studied his tired, beautiful face. "If she offered, would you turn her down?"

"No," he said. "I wouldn't. That's what scares me."

I cupped his cheek in my palm. "Promise me you'll try to enjoy yourself, whether it's with her, or with Flynn, or even Jax. Maybe it will be different with my heat pheromones and the alpha pheromones together."

I could see in his eyes that he still thought it was hopeless. His beta owners had considered him too difficult to deal with; too stubborn for use in the breeding pens despite his impeccable purebred bloodlines. They'd sterilized him before tossing him into the slave market—ripping out his ovotestes and his womb, suturing his birthing passage closed. We'd tried before, but in the end, we hadn't been able to work around what had been done to his body.

Despite his obvious discomfort with the subject, he covered my hand with his and slid it forward so he could press a kiss to my palm. "If it makes you feel better, I don't think I'm going to have much say in the matter if Flynn gets his way. I'm sure I'll enjoy myself to whatever degree I still can."

I had the feeling he was humoring me, the same way he'd been humoring me when he swore that our failed sex experiment the night before my capture had been *'fine.'* But it would be churlish to press the issue any further.

"Okay," I said. "I'm holding you to that."

He found a smile for me. We continued to the living room, where Beckett had set up his makeshift office. He was waiting for us there, a brown paper bag sitting on one corner of the coffee table.

"Hello," he greeted. "It's last minute, but I was able to acquire everything you need. Still comfortable with your choice, I hope?"

"Committed, anyway," I replied. "I've got a bit too much of a crawling-out-of-my-own-skin thing going on for the word comfortable to feel appropriate."

He nodded, unperturbed. "You're getting close, it seems. If you're ready, I can administer the contraceptive shot for you now. There's probably no point in putting it off."

I swallowed and nodded agreement, watching as he drew a sealed syringe and an unlabeled vial from the bag. He tore open the syringe's plastic packaging and plunged the needle through the vial's rubber seal, drawing up its contents. After flicking the syringe to loosen the air bubbles, he pressed the plunger until a bead of liquid dripped from the needle tip. Then, he turned to me.

"This will prevent ovulation," he said. "Normally you'd release an egg with every peak. With this stuff in your system, you won't. There's also a selection of condoms, along with three sizes of cervical caps. You'll need to try them ahead of time to see which size is most comfortable and secure, but as an omega who's never been pregnant, I would guess the medium size is your best bet."

Kam had been standing nearby, watching the exchange. "You know," he said with a hint of wry humor, "it's a bit surreal watching you dispense information on cervical caps when I've also seen you wearing a balaclava and waving an Uzi around."

"It was an AK-47," Beckett said placidly, and Kam gave a little snort.

"Well, I for one am grateful for both of your skill sets," I told him. With a gesture, I indicated the syringe. "Is that going in my shoulder?"

"It's intramuscular, yes," he said. "Your shoulder will be fine. Left arm?"

I nodded and offered him my left shoulder, bared by the tank top. He steadied my arm and a moment later I felt the pinch of the needle entering. A few seconds later, it was done. Maybe I should have had more misgivings about letting this person I barely knew inject drugs into my body... but he'd saved us twice. He was the one and only reason I wasn't currently awaiting a show trial followed by a messy execution at the hands of Enoch Sloane.

Also, there was the small matter that I'd been using drugs provided by people I barely knew to control my omega biology since I was sixteen.

"Thank you," I told him. "And not just for the shot."

Beckett gave me the same small, tight smile that I'd seen several times before. It was a smile that said he appreciated the sentiment, while also hating the reasons behind it. I wondered how long he'd been fighting as part of the underground, and how he dealt with the frustration of things never changing, except for the worse.

"Don't mention it," he said.

I'd been poised to ask him the same question I'd asked Alex — *am I making a mistake?* But somehow, that wasn't the question I needed answered anymore.

"Is there anything you think I should know, going into this?" I asked instead. "My parents were betas, and I've been suppressing my heats for fifteen years. I'm going in blind; I have no idea what I'm doing."

Kam's hand found mine, our fingers tangling as he gave me a supportive squeeze. I squeezed back.

Beckett leaned back on the couch. "The first rule of a heat contract is to choose your alphas wisely. You've done that already. As much as I hate to say it, beyond that, hormones will pretty much dictate that you'll take whatever they dish out, and probably beg for more. Hence the importance of rule number one."

I thought back to my vague memories of Romania — of begging for sex barely an hour after I'd explicitly refused it, a slave to my own desperation.

"Point taken," I said.

But he shook his head. "Don't take that the wrong way. You've chosen three honorable alphas, one of whom will be on guard the whole time to make sure no one gets carried away. Your heat should be a time of joyful connection. Sharing it with packmates and friends is a blessing. Cherish it."

My throat tightened, and I had to swallow against the thickness there. I gave him a nod of understanding in lieu of words. In a perfect world, I would be the sort of omega who wanted pups, living in a world where that dream posed no danger. Kam and I would be mated to a pack of alphas, sharing my heat joyously and without reservations.

Failing that—living in the world we inhabited now—this heat contract might be the only taste of that kind of happiness I would ever get.

Kam shifted beside me. "I understand that this is a sensitive question you may not be able to answer, but do you ever get to share heats with your mate?"

Beckett's answering smile was achingly sad. "Not nearly as often as we'd like," he said. "That's how I learned to cherish the times we do have."

THREE

Leona

THAT EVENING, I explored the wonderful world of cervical caps and confirmed that I was, in fact, a size medium. I also confirmed that the things were awkward as hell to put in and take out.

"Stop laughing," I growled at Kam. "If I'm too heat-drunk to deal with getting it in and out, you're going to be first up to pinch hit."

That at least shut him up.

I was growing restless, the same feeling of my skin being too tight and hot that I remembered from my last heat. Flynn had been right. I wasn't going to last two days. This was happening tomorrow, and there was no stopping it now.

The nest wasn't right. I rearranged it, then rearranged it again half an hour later. Finally, Kam coaxed me into the comically large sunken bathtub, with its endless supply of on-demand hot water. I fidgeted in his arms, both wanting the feel of skin on skin and finding myself frustrated by it.

A knock sounded at the door of the den, muffled through the closed connecting door to the bathroom. "I'll take care of it," Kam said, hoisting his lean body out of the bath and wrapping a towel around his hips.

A couple of minutes later he returned, poking his head in. "Jax brought food."

I wrinkled my nose, unsure if I wanted it or not.

"There's chocolate cake," he added.

My stomach growled like a horny alpha in response to those three magic words, the fickle little bitch. "Coming," I said, and hauled my traitorous body out of the warm water.

Clad in one of Flynn's black T-shirts, I padded in and found a plate waiting for me with a slice of the cottage pie sending up curls of steam—presumably reheated, unless Jax had whipped up a second one after we left. A wedge salad joined it on one corner of the plate. The promised slab of chocolate cake sat in a separate, smaller dessert dish, with a scoop of vanilla ice cream melting over it.

Kam was already tucking into his food, still wearing nothing but the towel because why the hell not? I settled in diagonally across from him on the overstuffed sectional and dove in.

Yes, I started with the cake. *So sue me.*

"Jax asked if they could come to the nest around ten tomorrow morning," Kam said, once the initial round of face stuffing had eased. "I told him it was fine. Is that all right?"

I hesitated, then nodded. "I think that'll be about right, to be honest."

"He also said Beckett will be heading out to meet with some other people about what comes afterward. Even though he's on pheromone suppressors, he didn't think you'd appreciate a strange omega rattling around the place while you're in heat."

I gave a humorless little laugh. "He'd know better than me—I've got no clue. And *crap*. I totally intended to grill him about the what-comes-next part when we saw him earlier."

"He may not know yet, if he's still hashing things out with other members of the underground," Kam said. "I'm willing to bet the whole thing's organized in cells. Good for security, in case someone important gets captured. Not so good for quick communication with the higher-ups."

I grunted. "You're probably right. Not like I'll be in a position to fret about it for the next few days."

"I expect you'll be in a bunch of different positions, but probably not that one, true. Don't worry. I can fret for both of us," Kam replied wryly.

I wrinkled my nose at him. After eating a bit of my salad and maybe three-quarters of the cottage pie, I pushed the rest away. Kam divided his cake in half with his fork and pushed one of the pieces into my dessert dish.

"I love you," I told him.

"I know," he said, and reached for my unfinished salad and entrée.

When everything was gone, he took the plates and silverware downstairs to wash. I let him, figuring I wasn't really fit for company tonight. At least, not for company that wasn't him. Since there was really nothing else that needed to be done, I grabbed *The Unbearable Lightness of Being* from the corner table and dragged it down into the nest with me to read. Cocooned in two fuzzy blankets and propped on a small mountain of pillows, I made it through about nine pages before I fell asleep.

⸎

When I woke up, my skin felt hot and prickly. I remembered this feeling from before, and the bad associations made my heart speed up until it was thudding wildly against my chest.

"Good morning," Kam said. "It's almost nine-thirty. The alphas will be here in about half an hour. How are you feeling?"

I blinked gritty eyelids open, revealing our cozy nest lit by soft red bulbs. I couldn't help but compare my surroundings to my untimely heat where we'd been held captive in the cave and at risk of discovery at any moment. Aside from the obvious upgrade in comfort and luxury, this felt *safe*.

I was grateful to be in a remote house where no one would be able to find us. My packmate extended a glass of orange juice in my direction, and the earlier adrenaline spike subsided to a generalized feeling of shakiness. I wriggled out of soft blankets that suddenly felt as irritating as burlap and took the glass from him.

"Umm," I rasped. "Not great? It's definitely coming on soon."

The orange juice tasted off, like my taste buds were screwed up or something. I drank it anyway.

Kam gave me a sympathetic nod. "Your scent's starting to change. If you want a shower, you should probably have it now. I've already had one. I even left you some hot water."

"It's a tankless heater," I pointed out.

"Like I said, I left you some," Kam said, and took the half-finished glass of juice when I handed it back.

I stuck my tongue out at him, but I did stagger upright and shuffle off to the bathroom. In the end, I settled on a lukewarm shower as being the least irritating option. Hot water made my already feverish head swim. Cool water made my nerves feel like someone was running sandpaper over them. I gave myself a cursory wash and kept my hair as dry as I could. The idea that someone might wash it for me later sent an unexpected jolt through my belly, and a pulse of slick dribbled down my leg.

O-kay, then.

I turned off the water and dried myself with one of the fluffy towels from the rack. Kam had left a fresh oversized T-shirt on the vanity for me. Well... maybe *fresh* wasn't the word. It was worn to gossamer softness from repeated use, almost translucent in places, and it smelled like sitting in the woods with a steaming cup of mulled cider. With a jolt, I realized that Flynn and Jax had taken turns wearing this shirt without washing it in between.

Holy. Shit.

I buried my nose in the fabric and breathed in. I might as well have been snorting a line of coke. Eventually, I emerged from my pheromone high enough to pull it over my head. Even the well-worn cotton irritated me, but the scent made up for it. And while it might have been perfectly acceptable etiquette to welcome your heat partners into the nest while buck naked for all I knew, I wasn't *quite* there yet.

My hands trembled a bit as I filled the cervical cap with spermicide and put it in, cursing under my breath the whole time. When it was finally in place, I straightened and moved to stand in front of the mirror, looking at my reflection as though it belonged to a stranger.

Flushed cheeks. Parted lips. Dilated pupils. Nipples threatening to drill holes through the ancient T-shirt. A cloud of *eau de desperation* forming an almost tangible aura around me as my body pumped out its honey-flavored perfume.

Welp. As Kam had said, this was going to be... interesting.

I let myself out of the bathroom and immediately walked into a wall of alpha pheromones. They were already here. Three sets of eyes fell on me as though drawn by a magnet.

"Hi," I said nervously, trying to ignore the fact that I wasn't wearing underwear and I'd just dribbled out another pulse of slick. Flynn's nostrils flared.

"Hello," Jax said, his gaze dipping to the hem of the borrowed shirt.

Alex was the first to tear her eyes away. "We're just getting everything in place. But I can finish up with that. Make yourself comfortable, and you can hash out any final details. Beckett's gone, by the way. We've got the place to ourselves."

The melding of delicious alpha scents in the air was threatening to steal my higher brain functions right there and then. I unstuck my feet from the floor and descended into the sunken nest area, wading through fur and cushions. Wanting the feel of all of that softness around me, I sunk down next to where Kam was sitting primly on the sectional, pressing my shoulder against his knee.

He rested a hand on the back of my neck to soothe me. His thumb rubbed gently across the sensitive skin as I drank in his reassuring presence.

Jax and Flynn entered the nest and sank down across from me—Flynn lowering himself smoothly into a cross-legged position. Jax moved more slowly, still favoring his left side after the muscle damage he'd suffered from an experimental nerve agent.

"We're gonna take care of you," Flynn said, his voice a low basso rumble. "Both of you. But Jax wants to ask you first if there's stuff you particularly like or don't like."

I raised an eyebrow, struggling to hold onto rational thought beneath the onslaught of pheromones. "Just Jax? Not you?" I asked.

Flynn grinned at me. "Nah. I've got a pretty good idea already. I was doing more than sitting in the corner jacking off last time, you know."

A full-body shiver took me, as hazy memories of Flynn's rough voice narrating filthy suggestions as Kam fucked me with a dildo flitted across my mind. He'd been watching us the whole time, cataloguing my responses. Probably Kam's as well, now that I thought about it.

"Oh," I managed.

Jax shot Flynn a flat stare before turning his attention back to me. "Unlike my packmate, I'm not a mind reader. I'd love to hear about your likes and dislikes, so we can make sure this is as good for you as it can possibly be."

I looked at him blankly for long moments, trying not to get swept up in the way his full lips moved as he spoke, or how incredibly blue his eyes were.

"Uhh…" Outside of my last heat, the sum total of my experience consisted of the times Kam and I had fooled around. "I like… oral?"

"Giving and receiving?" Jax asked. "Or just receiving?"

"Both," I said, aware that an alpha cock was likely to be a much different proposition than Kam's slender, half-hard shaft. The idea still made my mouth water. I swallowed and licked my lips, both alphas' gazes dipping to my mouth as I did.

I thought about the stories betas told about alphas, and added reluctantly, "I don't think I want it rough. I wouldn't want to be held down or… forced."

Kam's fingers stilled against the skin of my neck. I glanced up at him, but his face was a mask.

"Our sweet girl wants to be worshipped," Flynn said. "I could've told you that. It's our Ginger Tea here who wants to be pinned down by the throat and used over and over until he breaks."

The faintest sound of an inhaled breath came from above me, and my eyes flew to Kam's face again. He was still holding his expression carefully neutral, but his eyes had darkened, and there was a fine tremor in his hand.

Jax looked between his packmate and mine before addressing Kam in a wry tone. "I think we'll start out concentrating on Leona. If this asshole is wrong about things, just stay near Alex and she'll make sure he minds his manners. And if he's right, well… we'll have plenty of time to play with that, once the initial edge is off."

"I'll take that under consideration," Kam replied, a bit hoarsely.

Flynn let out a rumble of laughter.

I frowned up at my packmate, placing a hand on his knee and giving it a squeeze. "Are you all right, *odama*?"

The atmosphere had grown a bit... *odd*, and I couldn't quite pin it down. I felt like Flynn's words should have upset me, rather than sending a trickle of heat down my spine. There was nothing threatening in his scent or demeanor. If anything, it felt *fond*. And Kam didn't seem upset, as such... only disconcerted.

"Of course I am, Leo," he said. "Let's just keep the focus on you, where it belongs."

"I'm good at multitasking," Flynn said serenely. "But that's enough talk. As much as I like seeing you in my shirt, I'd much rather see you out of it. Easier to give you a massage that way."

My breath caught at the idea of Flynn's big hands running over my body. I felt a flush heat my cheeks. "I'm not sure that's..." I trailed off, unsure how to finish the sentence.

"Do as he says," Jax ordered. There was nothing unkind in his tone, but the hint of alpha power beneath it went straight to my core. "Alex is watching over things. Your *odama* is watching over things. It's time to let go and let the rest of us take care of you."

I couldn't breathe for a moment, as a lifetime of struggle not to succumb to omega weakness battled my body's need for surrender to the alphas who would knot me through my heat. My gaze flew to Kam's. He took my chin in his slender fingers and leaned down, pressing a kiss to my lips.

"I'm right here, beloved," he murmured into our shared air. "But it's them you need right now."

Liquid warmth rolled through my body. The nest was awash in the scents of cypress and musk, cardamom and sandalwood. It felt like a drug… like an answer to a question I hadn't thought to ask yet.

"Come to us, Leona," Flynn rumbled.

Without conscious thought, my arms and legs moved, pulled by that tone of casual command. I crawled toward the alphas who'd shepherded me through a heat once before, the softness of the nest cushioning my hands and knees. When I reached them, I knelt, not able to look either of them in the eye.

A dark-skinned hand entered my field of vision. Fingers cupped my jaw, and Flynn's thumb brushed over my lower lip, lighting every nerve in my body. My nipples tightened into painful points. He lifted my chin until I had to look at him.

"Shirt off, little omega," he said. The merest hint of an alpha bark had me scrambling to pull the oversized tee over my head and toss it away. I crossed my arms over my chest to cover it, not even sure where the impulse had come from. My sex was throbbing.

"None of that," Jax said gently. "Let go, Leona. We've got you now."

A touch on the side of my neck guided me to bare my throat for them, and my whole body followed a moment later. I rolled onto my back among the soft furs and cushions, all of the tension flowing out of me as I showed the alphas my belly, and nothing horrible happened.

"So beautiful," Flynn said, running a single fingertip from my chin, down my throat, between my breasts, and along my stomach to my navel.

I shivered, feeling more slick gathering between my legs, and let the alphas take control.

FOUR

Leona

I COULD HAVE everything I wanted this time, I thought distantly. *This was allowed.* There would be no holding back, no poor substitutes for what I really needed.

"Lie on your front," Flynn said, urging me to roll over with a touch. "Not that I wasn't enjoying the view."

I did as I was bid, humming a bit as I nestled into all the softness. Jax shifted position to settle next to my head, which lay cradled on my arms. A moment later, callused fingers threaded through my hair, dragging across my scalp over and over in a soothing, rhythmic motion.

"That's more like it," Flynn said.

Something clicked above me, and I shivered as cool wetness dribbled down my spine. The click came again—the opening and closing of a bottle cap. Strong hands slid up and down the length of my back, spreading the massage oil over the feverish flesh. I groaned as thumbs pressed into the tight muscles between my shoulder blades, knotted by months… *years*… of unrelenting tension.

One by one, the knots gave way, as though they were as powerless beneath an alpha's hands as the rest of me was. Bliss and need grew in equal measure as Flynn dug into my muscles while Jax's fingers stroked and tugged at my scalp.

"You like that?" Flynn asked, a purr rumbling up in his chest.

"Yes, alphas," I replied breathlessly. "Please don't stop."

"We're not gonna stop, sweet thing," Flynn said.

This wasn't full heat yet—not even close. But the promise behind the words still made my empty passage clench.

Flynn's strong hands moved lower, kneading my ass. I squirmed, my legs falling open invitingly as I proceeded at maximum velocity toward full-on omega slut mode. Instead of taking the invitation, though, he chuckled and continued down my legs, kneading my hamstrings and calves, and finally my bare feet. A tiny squeak escaped me as his thumbs dug into my arches—the kind of noise prey makes when it's been caught.

When he worked his way back up my legs, his big hands roamed the insides of my thighs. Anticipation froze my breath in my lungs. He paused, chuckling again.

"Might want to keep breathing, sweet girl," he said. "It's kind of important, after all."

His fingertips teased the final inch separating him from where I wanted him. My lungs burned, lightheadedness making me dizzy until the air finally exploded free in a gush, and I dragged in panting breaths.

"There you go," Flynn said, and slid several thick fingers inside of me.

I keened at the perfect, burning stretch of it, and tried to fuck back against him, driving them deeper.

"Shh," Jax murmured. His fingers tangled in my thick hair, wrapping it around and around his hand until the strands tugged against my scalp, holding me in place. "Stay still, Leona. Just let it happen."

I trembled, desperate for more, more, *more* as Flynn slowly thrust his fingers in and out of my body.

"So wet already," Flynn said, "and you're not even near your first peak yet."

His fingers trailed farther forward to circle my clit. I grabbed fistfuls of the fur beneath me, feeling my release building. Flynn alternated fucking my passage and teasing my clit, driving me a little bit higher each time, until the pressure finally became too much and escaped its confines in a series of wrenching spasms.

I moaned, going completely limp as my muscles unclenched. The hand in my hair eased. I peeled my eyes open in time to see Jax pulling his shirt over his head. He tugged the waistband of his dark track pants down far enough to free his cock. It was hard, and seemed very, *very* large all of the sudden.

"Bet you're glad that shit they pumped into you in Romania didn't break your dick, huh?" Flynn asked.

Jax shot him an unamused look. "Yes, thank you. I'm glad it didn't break my dick, asshole."

Personally, I was having trouble focusing on anything but the alpha horse cock on display. Despite the orgasm that had just floored me—*literally*—fresh hunger was already coiling in my gut. I wanted that cock, and this time, I was going to have it, damn it. I elbow-crawled halfway onto Jax's lap, looking up at him from under my lashes.

"Hello, beautiful," he said, gathering my hair back again. "See something you want, I take it?"

I smiled at him, giddy with how different this was from last time. With how *perfect* it was. "Yes, alpha," I said breathlessly, and reveled in the feel of his big hand guiding my lips to him.

I'd been right. It was nothing like taking Kam in my mouth. I licked the salty head, dragging my lips around and over the blunt tip until the hand in my hair pressed me down. I had to stretch my lips wide around Jax's girth, and a moan vibrated up from my throat.

"Ooh. That looks awfully good, sweet thing," Flynn said from behind me. Without warning, his fingers breached me again. "Think she'll bite you if I make her come again while you're fucking her mouth, Jax?"

I whined as his fingers curled, stretching me from the inside with every slow stroke in and out. More slick dribbled out of me, the wetness making tiny, obscene sucking noises as he moved.

"No," Jax said dismissively. "Of course she won't. She's a good girl." His hand urged me to take him deeper, even as Flynn twisted his wrist and teased my clit with the barest brushes of his thumb.

I rocked between them. Getting away from one only meant pushing the other deeper. My muscles trembled with the desire to *take, take, take.* I wanted to take everything they had, over and over—until the growing void inside me was full to overflowing, and they were empty and sated, tied to me irrevocably.

The teasing brushes against my clit gained purpose, demanding that my body respond. And it did—helpless before the power of pheromones and my own need. My second climax swallowed me like a bottomless pit opening up beneath me, and I cried out around the cock in my mouth. Neither alpha let up, Flynn's fingers drawing more and more from me until I couldn't tell down from up, and my vision dimmed to gray.

When awareness returned, it was clear that some time had passed. I'd been moved, and was lying sprawled on the weird, curvy divan thing with my head and shoulders supported on a familiar lap, and a blond head buried between my thighs.

"*Mmph,*" I whimpered, as Jax's tongue lapped lazily along my slit. Tingles of sensation darted along my spine like champagne bubbles.

"Always knew she'd be responsive as hell," Flynn observed from somewhere nearby. Callused fingers tweaked my left nipple, tugging it up until it slid free, my breast bouncing.

"Hello. You all right, *odama*?" Kam asked.

His slender fingers stroked the hair back from my face, and I hummed, my body thrumming with a strange combination of need and relaxation.

"Mm-hmm," I managed, licking my lips and craning to look up at him with hazy eyes. "You were right. This weird sex-couch thing makes more sense with two people."

I was slurring my words a bit.

I didn't care.

This was awesome.

The thing I was lying on looked like some crazy piece of modern art. I'd tried it out shortly after we'd arrived and declared it not remotely comfortable for reading, at which point Kam had chuckled at me and explained that it was sex furniture. Now, with my ass supported on one curved end at exactly the right height for Jax to kneel between my legs, I was a convert.

"It's great. Exactly the right shape to support a sexually exhausted omega so we can sexually exhaust her some more," Flynn agreed. "So, is it working?"

He tweaked my nipple again at the same moment Jax's tongue dragged over my clit. My eyes rolled back. "*Nngh*," I told him.

"I think it's working," Kam said, sounding a bit breathless.

I made uncoordinated grabby-hands motions toward Flynn. He leaned down until I could bury my nose against the base of his throat and inhale his thick, spicy scent. A purr rose in his chest. He let me nuzzle at him for a bit while Jax continued to lick me toward another peak, but eventually he tilted my head back and brushed his lips over mine in a teasing kiss that grew gradually more heated until I was desperate for air... but not quite desperate enough to pull away.

It went on and on—lips and tongues and nipping teeth, until Jax closed his lips around my clit and sucked. I arched and came silently, pinned between two mouths. Something inside me felt like it had broken open, spilling out fresh need at the same time my body gushed a new pulse of slick onto Jax's face. He lapped it up with a pleased rumble that vibrated against my oversensitive flesh, and I shuddered in Kam's arms.

Flynn ended the kiss with a final sharp nip to my lower lip. I panted, staring at Kam's upside down face above me. Flynn took Kam's jaw in his large hand and tilted his face up.

"You're perfuming," he said, shifting his grip to cup Kam's nape and roll his head to the side, baring his throat.

"Yes," Kam replied faintly, as Flynn lowered his nose to the bare skin of Kam's neck and breathed in deeply.

"Mmm," said Flynn. "There's my ginger tea and lemon. We're gonna have such fun with you later..."

Kam shivered, and I felt a twitch beneath me as his omega cock tried to harden. I writhed my upper body sinuously in his lap, and his arms tightened around me convulsively.

"Yes, alpha," he whispered.

The emptiness inside me was growing again, despite the orgasms. It was becoming unpleasant now—all the touching and licking and kissing more of a tease than a relief. I whimpered, feeling the urge to turn over and present.

"It's time, Leona," Jax said, pressing a lingering kiss to my mons.

Kam gave me a final squeeze and let me go. Jax helped me slither down to the soft interior of the nest, where I rolled over onto my elbows and knees. My lower back arched in response to the rough fingertips sliding along the length of my spine. The room felt hot and close.

"Please, alphas," I begged, knowing that this time, I could have what I wanted. "Please fill me up—I'm so empty..."

"We've got you, sweet thing," Flynn said from somewhere behind me. I heard the rustle of fabric and craned around, needing to see. I was rewarded with the sight of a hot, naked alpha, his rich brown skin gleaming in the warm light of the nest. He ripped open a small packet and rolled the latex sheath over his straining cock.

Jax settled in front of me, and I turned to look at him. He was bare from the waist up, but still wore his loose track pants. Kam had retreated to the sectional. His eyes met mine and held for a long moment, until the third alpha in the room drew my attention. Alex sat on the other side of the couch, watching me with a gaze sharp as a hawk's.

I was still looking at her when big hands clasped my hips from behind. I closed my eyes, imagining how Flynn's dark skin would look pressed against my pale body, and let out a shaky breath.

"Gonna fill you up so good, sweet thing," Flynn rumbled.

Another whimper escaped as something impossibly large and unyielding slid against my soaked folds, lining up with my passage and pressing in with steady insistence. My body stretched to accommodate Flynn's girth with a delicious burn unlike anything I'd ever felt before.

I cried out, tears gathering in my eyes, and Jax's thumb swiped them away when they overflowed.

"You're doing so well for us," he said. "Such a good omega, taking Flynn's cock. We're going to make you feel so good."

More tears spilled over, and a sob caught in my throat as Flynn's huge erection filled me. I felt as though I had been made entirely for this moment, and it had taken me thirty-one years to get here.

"Please," I whispered. "Please, please, *please*—"

He began to move, and I was lost. Thought fled, leaving only instinct behind. It was too much, and not enough. It was *everything*. The world beyond the place where our bodies joined faded to unimportance. It could have lasted minutes or hours—I had no idea. I was drowning in scent, awash in emotion and touch and sensation.

Jax's thumb brushed my lower lip and pressed inside, sliding past my teeth, over my tongue. Flynn's hips snapped against mine, jolting my body with every thrust, a low growl rumbling in his throat. One of his big hands released his grip on my waist, sliding up my back to close possessively over the mating gland at the juncture of my neck and shoulder.

I screamed, my body clamping around Flynn's cock. He went still for an endless moment, then jerked through his release with a deep groan. I felt him panting behind me, even as the knot at the base of his cock swelled, locking us together and stretching me even further.

"God, Leona," he said hoarsely.

"Look at you two," Jax murmured, stroking my tearstained face with the backs of his fingers. "Come on, love. Let's get you curled up on your side so you can rest and enjoy your knot. Alex and I will watch the nest for you."

"Kam?" I rasped, as Jax helped Flynn maneuver us onto our sides with as little jostling as possible.

Even so, Flynn's knot shifted inside me, and I shuddered in fresh ecstasy.

A slender figure knelt in front of me as I settled in, spooned from behind by Flynn's bulk. "I'm here, *odama*."

I reached for him and he came to me, bracketing me from the front. Now that the peak had broken, the sweat cooling on my skin lent a faint chill to my body — but Jax laid a blanket over us, and with an alpha at my back and my *odama* at my front, there was enough heat to chase it away. I floated in a blissful, trancelike state while Flynn stroked my hair and murmured endearments in my ear, until eventually my body released its hold on him.

Flynn eased out of me as gently as he could, and he and Kam held me pressed between them. Temporarily sated, I drifted into sleep.

FIVE

Kameron

FLYNN GOT UP and disposed of the condom once he was sure Leo was down for the count, but as soon as he and Jax had cleaned her up to their satisfaction, he returned to his place curled around her back.

She was totally out of it by that point, not even stirring when I carefully extricated myself from her arms and returned to my perch on one end of the sectional couch. I was a wreck, and I didn't know what to do about it—my phantom nipples aching, my cock pulsing and oversensitive against the seam of my jeans.

This time around, even I could smell the faint perfume my body was putting out in response to all the heat pheromones choking the room. Jax came and crouched in front of me. Part of me wanted to cringe back from him, and the other part wanted to fall forward into his arms and beg him to take care of me. I did neither.

"You don't look like an omega who's enjoying himself in the heat-nest," Jax said without judgment. "What can I do to help?"

"I'm fine," I said. "Everything's fine. I'm not the focus here."

If I became the focus, then I risked finding out once and for all that there was no hope for me. Right now, the possibility existed that I could still experience some sort of connection with these alphas, however stunted. But if I let them try and I still couldn't perform as an omega in the heat-nest should... it was over. How ironic that between Leo and myself, I'd always been the one with the big talk when it came to sex with alphas... but now that it was actually on offer, I was terrified.

"You're lying," Jax said, "but that's your prerogative. I respect your choice."

A new voice intruded. "I don't."

My eyes flew to Alex, curled on the other section of the couch like a jungle cat lounging on a rock.

"I won't have an omega huddled at the edge of the nest, looking like he wants to sink through the floor and disappear," she continued, tone steely. Her forest-colored alpha gaze fell on me with a weight so heavy it threatened to bow my shoulders. "Not on *my* pack's watch. Come here."

I swallowed convulsively, my heart rising in my throat.

"You tell 'im, Alex," Flynn said, not moving from his spot in the nest. "Soften him up a bit, and I'll be along to help in a few hours, after Leona wakes up."

Alex didn't even spare him a glance. That heavy gaze was still resting squarely on me. "You're not listening to your alpha," she said, in a deceptively soft voice. "Why is that?"

Her summons had been a command... but it was also a promise of protection. These alphas had protected us, even at the risk of their own lives. And god, how I wanted someone to protect me—even if it was from myself.

I bowed my head and slid to the cushion-covered floor. "I'm sorry, alpha."

"Don't be sorry," Alex said. "Just get your omega ass over here."

Jax looked between us, his blue eyes assessing my defeated posture. "Be careful with him, *alef*."

"He doesn't want careful," Alex replied, still not looking at her packmate. "He wants someone to remind him of his value here. Of his place."

"What *is* my place here?" I whispered, my gaze wandering past Jax to fall on my *odama*, held securely in Flynn's arms as she slept off the aftermath of her first peak.

"Your place is to be given whatever you need while you're under our care," Alex said. "No matter what that might be."

My throat closed up and I crawled to her. She reached out a hand, and I followed the touch on my jaw as she positioned me on a pile of cushions heaped in front of her on the floor next to the couch.

"Right now, I'm pretty sure you need to stop thinking," she told me. Her voice turned wry. "Believe it or not, I'm familiar with that particular problem."

I gazed up at her, wondering what would be left of me if I let go of all the thoughts and worries swirling around the inside of my brain like angry dust devils. Those worries seemed to define me these days.

Alex was tall and strong and sharply beautiful — dark-haired and green-eyed and leanly muscled beneath the black tank top and gray sweatpants she wore. Her feet were bare.

She didn't crack a smile. Her expression might as well have belonged to a statue of Lady Justice, or maybe the Huntress Diana. I thought about the hotel in Bucharest, before everything had fallen apart — when I had waxed lyrical to Leo about teasing the enigmatic female alpha's clit from inside its folds with my tongue.

And... *god*. She knew about that little fantasy now, didn't she? Leo had blurted it out during a drunken confession. I should probably be angry about that, or maybe mortified. Shouldn't I?

Alex's long fingers tangled in my hair and tugged, the pull on my scalp landing just a hairsbreadth on the wrong side of pain. I gasped and arched my head back, my throat bare to her gaze as my cock throbbed and jerked weakly against my fly. Why the hell had I decided to wear jeans today?

"You're still thinking too loudly," she said. "Believe me when I say, I can come up with ways to make sure you stop."

The grip on my hair pulled my head back another inch. A high sound that I refused to describe as a whimper was born and died in the back of my throat. It... wasn't a protest, exactly. With a small jolt, I realized that for that moment in time, every single thought had fallen out of my head like Scrabble tiles dumped from the box. They lay in a jumble somewhere beneath me—unreadable nonsense waiting for someone else to pick them up and make sense of them.

Some of the long-held tension slid out of my spine.

"There now," Alex said, gentling her grip in favor of guiding me to rest my head on the edge of the couch cushion next to her thigh.

I breathed in her smell—clean sandalwood and the complex sweetness of night jasmine. Her fingers that had been harsh and unyielding before grew soft, stroking through my hair and making me shiver. A wavering sigh emptied my lungs, and I tried to resist the sudden, irrational urge to weep.

Fucking heat pheromones. They weren't even *mine*.

"We can stay like this for a bit," she said. "There's nothing else you need to do except feel whatever you're feeling. Sometimes feeling shit like that sucks, but locking it away sucks worse in the long run. Ask me how I know." The last few words were an exhausted sigh.

I reached my hand out and covered her knee, my body moving before my mind could come up with a dozen reasons why it was a bad idea. Her fingers stilled in my hair for a moment, but then she resumed the soothing rhythm.

Time passed. Whenever my shoulders started to tense up, Alex's hand tightened in my hair, the shivery almost-pain abruptly clearing my thoughts again, and only relenting when I went limp and compliant in her grip.

It shouldn't have meant anything. It was... nothing, really. A fist in my hair, or a light stroking over my scalp. Punishment and reward. And yet, the minutes ticked by, becoming hours, and somehow I ended up lying on the couch instead of kneeling on the floor. More time passed, and I found my head pillowed on the alpha's thigh.

How had that happened?

Eventually, the achy oversensitivity in my cock eased as the air cleared a bit, Leo's pheromone production waning during the valley between heat peaks.

Even so, I was *aware* of my body in a way I usually tried to avoid — probably because there was nothing else for me to think about right now. Or at least, nothing that didn't immediately result in my hair getting pulled until I stopped.

My body was such an odd thing. I hated it, while knowing objectively that it wasn't fair of me to feel that way. It wasn't my body's fault that its insides had been raped and scarred by monsters who thought they owned me and could rip out whatever parts of me didn't meet with their approval. It wasn't my body's fault that I injected it with testosterone and worked it to exhaustion in the gym, so I would look more like a beta.

My physical form had always done its best for me. Hell, it had even saved my mating gland by being left-handed — hiding that part of me on my left shoulder rather than my right one, where the butchers had assumed it would be. That little gland was still gamely churning out weak omega perfume, despite everything it had endured and continued to endure.

For the first time in what felt like a very long time, I listened to my body instead of trying to tune it out. It was oddly peaceful; my physicality settling around me like a familiar cloak in this warm, soft room full of alphas who had promised to watch over us.

Was this strange interlude helping Alex find a sense of peace with her ghosts as well? It was clear she had quite a collection of things haunting her, even if I didn't know the details. I wasn't sure if it was helping her or not. She wasn't purring — but she was at least focused enough on me that she'd sensed every single time my mind started to wander back to my worries. Surely that couldn't leave room for much else, could it?

Right on cue, her hand tightened, sending shivery tingles from my scalp down the length of my spine. I released a breathless moan and went limp again, making a point of nuzzling into her thigh as she returned to stroking me.

At some point, relaxation morphed into dozing. I awoke to the feeling of slender fingers playing over my mating gland, raising gooseflesh across my chest and arms. Weak perfume or no, the gland was a fairly useless appendage at this point. Without enough omega hormones circulating to regulate it, there was no way it could perform its intended function of bonding me to one or more alphas. It was still sensitive, though — and Alex's light touch drew a low whine from my throat.

"I sure do like the sound of that," Flynn said.

"It did sound like a good noise," Jax agreed.

Flynn stretched in the nest, scenting the base of Leo's neck as he did. "She's waking up," he said. "She'll be ready for the next round pretty soon, I'll wager."

Leo stretched as well, unconsciously mirroring the alpha behind her. "M'awake," she murmured, sounding anything but. Her bleary hazel eyes ran around the room, falling on me in my alpha-drugged haze. She smiled, an expression like the sun coming out. As it always did, it made me want to kiss her or collapse into tears, or maybe both at the same time.

"*Odama*," she said softly.

I swallowed, my throat clicking.

Jax approached, giving Alex a questioning look that asked her permission before he settled down across from us.

"Hey, Kam. Are you ready to talk to us yet?" he asked.

I licked my lips. "I hate what was done to my body. I don't think I can enjoy sex. And part of me wants to know for sure, but I'm also afraid to find out." The words poured out like water from a broken jar.

Jax nodded. "You've tried before?"

Leo crawled over to me and climbed onto the couch, squeezing in behind me and laying her head on my hip. "With me," she said. "But not with alphas." Her honey and orange blossom scent wrapped around me, further sensitizing my skin.

"We used black market alpha pheromones," I said.

Flynn made a disgusted noise, joining the rest of us and flopping down next to Jax. "Coulda just asked and had the real thing, Ginger Tea."

Jax elbowed him, and Flynn responded with a warning growl.

Flynn gestured between himself, Jax, and Leo. "Did any of this do it for you? Get you going earlier?"

"Yes," I said, "but getting aroused and getting off are two different things."

It felt surprisingly cathartic to just blurt it all out; throw the ugly, bleeding stump of my omega reproductive system on the ground so the others could stare at it.

Flynn shrugged. "Yeah. Like I told you in Romania, I've been with a couple of sterilized omegas. One could still get off and the other couldn't." He tapped the side of his head. "I get the impression that a lot of it has to do with what's going on up here. And no offense, Ginger Tea, but your brain is one big tangle most of the time. This is only the second time I can think of when I've seen you let go."

I flushed, glad my olive complexion would hide the blood rushing to my cheeks. The other time had been when I'd lost my shit and sobbed in Flynn's arms after Beckett and his pack had rescued us in Romania and whisked us away to safety.

"Uhh," I said.

"Leo's gonna start climbing toward her next peak soon," Flynn said. "And the pheromones will be flying again. Jax'll take care of her this time. While he's doing that, I want to see if Alex and me can get you off between us. So, Alex? You up for that? Because you can't get him pregnant and you can't accidentally mate him, so your usual excuses won't cut it."

It was blunt to the point of cruelty — explicitly defining the things that made me feel broken — but the obvious lack of any intent to hurt allowed Flynn's words to slide off me without sticking. These were facts. Everyone here knew them. The truth of them existed whether anyone said them aloud or not.

I wasn't sure how Alex would respond, though. A touch on my chin turned my head until I was looking up at her.

"Is that what you want?" she asked, her green gaze holding mine.

I blinked. Was it what I wanted?

Leo poked me in the hip, and I flinched in surprise. "It's eating you up not knowing," she said.

I frowned at her. "Aren't you supposed to have heat-brain right now?"

She shrugged, unapologetic. "It feels different this time."

"She's not coming off blockers," Jax said. "This is a normal heat, not a crazy rebound heat spent imprisoned in a terrorist cell with an alpha she doesn't know."

"What he said," she agreed. "Now answer the question before my brain *does* get stupid again."

"Y-yes?" I said, sounding like the wishy-washiest omega on the planet.

"Cool," Flynn said. "Now take your damned clothes off. Why are there still so many fucking clothes on in this room?"

He was naked. So was Leo, though I wasn't entirely sure whether she was aware of the fact. The rest of us were still fully clothed—Jax had even put a shirt back on after the first round.

There was something important left to address, though. I looked up at Alex again. "You haven't said yes."

The alpha seemed to shake herself free of some sort of reverie. "Told you earlier," she said. "We're here to give you both everything you need." There was a careful sort of distance in her expression, but no hesitation in her tone.

Flynn clapped his hands and rubbed them together. "Right. First, I want to see you and Leona together. I already know what you can do for her when she's horny and craving a knot, and it's hot as fuck. But I wanna see what she does for you, too."

I rolled onto my back to better see Leo. She crawled up my body and took my face between her hands. "I love you, Kameron Patel," she said. "You know that, right?"

I mirrored her, capturing her face in my palms. "Of course I do. I love you, too, *odama*."

She pressed forward and kissed me, like we'd kissed so many times before. For a moment, I could almost forget that my head was lying on an alpha's thigh and Leo was leaking slick onto my jeans. But I was still in that surreal place of being fully connected to my body, and she was pumping out heat pheromones with ever-increasing intensity. In no time, the tight, achy feeling began to slide over me again.

"You'll feel better with your clothes off," she murmured against my lips, as though she could read my mind. "Trust me on this one."

I sighed. "Right. Let me up, then."

Leona rolled off me, and I sat up, feeling hopelessly self-conscious and awkward as I reached for the buttons of my shirt. I tried to take in the others with glances quick enough not to count as real eye contact. Jax was frowning. So was Leo. Flynn looked thoughtful. Alex, by contrast, was drilling holes through me with her green eyes. I flushed again beneath the weight of that heavy alpha gaze, not liking this feeling of being hot and bothered while knowing it was likely to lead nowhere except frustration.

I hated the fact that I felt like this, having to make decisions about every little thing. Getting undressed… deciding what Leona and I should try to do together… deciding what I did or didn't want the alphas to do.

I *hated* it.

"Stop," Alex said, a full-on alpha bark.

My spine snapped straight, my hands freezing on my half-open shirt, even as a humiliating sense of relief swept through me.

"Yes, alpha," I breathed.

She stood up, straightening to her full height and looming over me. "This isn't what you want. Enough dissembling. Tell me—*right now*—exactly what you need."

The alpha power in her voice took the choice of whether or not to answer away from me. I was an omega, and broken or not, I *would* obey an alpha's command.

"I don't want to have to make these choices," I said with a gasp. "I want someone else to make them for me. I just want to be..."

I trailed off, thinking of Flynn's words. *It's our Ginger Tea here who wants to be pinned down by the throat and used over and over until he breaks.* A shiver trickled down my spine.

"*Used*," I finished miserably.

SIX

Kameron

"OH, *KAM*," Leo murmured. I wondered if she was thinking of how gently she'd always treated me when we were intimate, and a fresh surge of guilt hit me.

"Told ya," Flynn said under his breath.

Alex shot him a quelling look.

"You want it not to be about you at all," she offered, her voice losing its bark.

"Yes," I said, with utter relief at the understanding in her tone. My shoulders slumped, my chin dropping to rest on my chest. "Please, just… do it to me? Make me take it. I don't want to have responsibility for what happens to me."

Alex and Jax exchanged a long look, an entire wordless conversation taking place between them.

"He's perfuming, even if it's faint," Jax said. "If he's in genuine distress at any point, we'll be able to smell it."

Alex hesitated for only a moment. Then she gave a single nod.

I should have been irritated that they were discussing me in the third person. Instead, my anxiety faded, replaced by a shaky sense of calm because the alphas were taking control. My hands fell to lie limply in my lap, the buttons of my shirt forgotten.

"Leona." Jax's voice radiated alpha reassurance. "Give your *odama* a hug, and then let's give the others some space for a bit. Can you scent him?"

"Yes," Leo said, her hazel eyes very wide.

"Then we'll know if anything's upsetting him," he said firmly. "Otherwise, he needs his alphas right now, not us."

Leo chewed her lower lip for a moment before nodding reluctant agreement. She wavered to her feet, the next peak already coming up on her. When her arms came around me, I hugged her back tightly.

"They're going to take care of you," she murmured, and pressed her lips to my mating gland in a gentle kiss.

I couldn't speak, so I buried my face in her fiery hair for a moment before letting her go. Jax extended a hand to her, and after a final long glance at me, she took it.

"So, can I play with him now, Alex?" Flynn asked, once the pair had crossed to the far side of the nest and claimed a spot.

My heart beat faster. Prickly sweat broke out across my back.

"Go ahead," Alex said, taking a seat on the other side of the sectional and crossing one leg over the other like a queen on her throne. "Let's see what we've got to work with here."

"About damn time," Flynn said.

Before I could draw breath, he was in front of me—his big hands grasping the material of my shirt and yanking it open. Buttons popped loose as he manhandled me around and pulled the shirt down below my elbows. My cuffs were still fastened, the fabric trapping my arms behind me by the wrists. Flynn wrapped the material around and around, tangling me further, and my body went hot all over.

Trapped.

A high-pitched noise escaped my throat and I tried to squirm away, only to end up on my back on the couch barely a heartbeat later. I jerked my shoulders, attempting to free my arms to no avail.

"Nuh-uh," Flynn said. His hand closed loosely over my throat. "None of that now, little omega."

Pinned.

"Let me up," I whispered, desperate to make sure he was really in charge... that my choices really didn't matter to him.

"No," he said, his free hand tugging at the fastenings of my jeans. He pulled them down roughly, heedless of my half-hard and painfully oversensitive cock. His scent of musk and cardamom was nearly overpowering, twining with the other alphas' scents and Leo's heat perfume. From the other side of the nest, I could hear her breathy gasps as Jax did... *something*... to her.

My nipples hardened to aching points.

"Hmm. Seems like we should be able to do some good with this," Flynn mused, and closed a meaty hand around my shaft.

It was too much, *too much*. I keened, trying to scrabble backward on the sectional with my legs trapped by my jeans and my arms trapped by my shirt. The hand on my throat tightened in warning.

"*Stay*," Flynn ordered, like someone might command a dog.

I shuddered, compelled by the alpha's command... forced to lie there and feel what he was doing to my body, whether I wanted to or not. On the other side of the room, Leo whimpered and cried out, the unmistakable sound of an omega having an earth-shattering orgasm administered by an alpha. My body thrummed with overstimulation as Flynn's callused hand squeezed and kneaded my cock, forcing it momentarily to full hardness.

He paused long enough to spit on his palm before wrapping his hand around me again and pumping... not gently. I knew how this would go, even if I couldn't do anything about it under the circumstances. It would be overwhelming at first, before becoming tolerable and even pleasant for a time, after which it would grow uncomfortable, then painful, and eventually unbearably excruciating.

I lay tense beneath Flynn's grip, my pulse fluttering against his fingers on my throat. Liquid heat slowly began to build in my gut, distracting me from the overstimulation and eventually replacing it. A moan wrenched free of my lips, and as though that had been some kind of a signal, Flynn let go of my cock. It wilted almost immediately in the absence of direct stimulation, but the heavy, warm feeling in my stomach lingered.

"Think that's enough of that for a bit, huh, Ginger Tea?" he said, not waiting for a reply. "Let's see about those pretty brown tits of yours next. They're awfully hard, considering how warm it is in here."

He thumbed my left nipple. A sharp tingle zinged along my nerves. Gooseflesh erupted across my chest as I swallowed a gasp. His fingers closed over the pebbled point, pinching and tugging sharply. I arched off the couch cushion with a strangled yelp.

He chuckled. "Bet you felt that in all four of them, didn't ya?"

"They cut out two," I whispered, knowing he would be able to see the small, jagged scars.

Flynn grunted and pinched the other nipple. I jerked at the phantom sensation.

"Maybe. But if I can still make you feel 'em, are they really gone?" he asked.

I might have answered, except it was too hard to focus on words with Flynn torturing my chest, alternating pinches with scrapes of his blunt fingernails until I was a breathless, squirming mess.

"Well, that was fun," he said. "We'll have to do some more of that later."

I managed a strangled '*hngh*' noise, too wrecked to move even when the hand around my throat disappeared. A muffled, high-pitched cry came from Leo's corner, and I turned my blurry gaze to find her draped over Jax in a sixty-nine position with his head buried between her thighs and his giant cock down her throat. As though she sensed me looking, she opened her eyes and met mine with a look equally as glassy.

Flynn pulled my jeans down and off, leaving me naked except for the shirt still tangled around my arms. "You ready for him now, Alex?" he called.

"Bring him over," she said.

I blinked, having completely missed it whenever she'd risen from the couch and removed her clothing. She reclined in the dip of the ridiculous sex divan—upper body resting against the taller end that acted as a backrest; legs straddling the seat to expose the folds between her legs, feet braced flat on the floor.

God, she was… magnificent. The polar opposite of Leo's omega softness, with her small, vestigial breasts over ripped pecs, and a sinuous, lean-muscled body that belonged on ancient statuary somewhere.

Flynn—equally impressive, but in an entirely male and overpowering way—watched me ogling his pack alpha with an amused huff. "Come on, Ginger Tea. Time to make yourself useful."

He leaned down and hoisted me over his shoulder before I even knew what was happening, clamping a hand over my bare ass to steady me. Flynn rose as though I weighed nothing and carted me over to the sex couch. He deposited me on my knees at the foot of the thing—worshipping at Alex's altar, so to speak.

Flynn gestured at her. "Go on," he said. "Get her ready while I get you ready. Use your mouth, in case that's not obvious."

Since no one had bothered to untangle my arms from behind me, it was, in fact, pretty obvious. I blinked up at Alex, reclining in front of me.

"Come here, omega," she said.

There was no way to comply except to slither onto the end of the sex couch on my belly, and neither of the alphas seemed to care how awkward and ridiculous that looked.

Because this wasn't about me.

This was about an omega giving an alpha pleasure in the heat-nest. It didn't matter if my womb was gone and my passage was sewn shut, because my mouth still worked and that was what Alex wanted to use right now. The realization shook something loose inside me.

I managed to get my hips draped over the swell at the low end of the divan, but without the use of my arms, I was stymied when it came to getting my mouth where it needed to be. God, I could smell her — *right there*, but just out of reach. I'd never been this close to a female alpha's sex. I wanted to be even closer.

There was a mystique around female alphas, even among purebreds. Before things had gone to hell, I'd been just old enough to join the secretive cliques of prepubescent omegas who passed around naughty photos of naked female alphas, along with faded copies of diagrams from biology textbooks that had been banned decades earlier.

Hyenas, the betas called them, for the superficial resemblance to a species whose females had pseudo-phalluses visually indistinguishable from the males' penises. Female alphas' clits resided inside a sheath until they were stimulated, at which point they emerged as they grew erect. They were about the same length as a male beta's cock, but lacked the girth. If the schoolyard whispers were to be believed, the knots made up for it.

I had a pretty good idea where that knot was going to end up today, and the thought tightened something low in my gut. It might have been trepidation. It might have been something else.

Alex took pity on me and grasped my hair, dragging my head up until my mouth was where she wanted it. "Lick," she ordered.

I did, drowning in the scent of sweet sandalwood as Leo whimpered out another orgasm somewhere behind me. My cock throbbed, trapped against the buttery leather of the divan.

The tip of Alex's clit was already poking out from its hood. I traced the shape with my tongue, tasting salt and musk and the aromatic forests from around my native Kolkata. Had watching Flynn touch me excited her? Had she been watching Jax take Leo apart as well? The idea that we both might have had this effect on her sent a flutter of omega pride through my chest.

Behind me, the unmistakable sound of a plastic bottle cap being popped open made me freeze for a moment. Alex tugged on my hair, redirecting me to my purpose, and I gamely went back to licking and sucking her emerging length to hardness.

Cool liquid dribbled into the valley between my buttocks. I shivered and whined around my growing mouthful of alpha clit. Flynn, being Flynn, wasted no time in swirling a thick finger around the rim of my ass a couple of times and shoving it unceremoniously inside. I gasped at the burn and jerked my head back from Alex's sex.

She tightened her grip on my hair and put me right back where she wanted me, sucking on the slender, erect shaft that was already growing long enough to tickle the back of my throat as she thrust slowly in and out of my mouth.

Flynn's other hand landed on my left buttock with a sharp slap. I jerked and grunted, my ass clenching hard around his finger.

"Did anyone say you could stop, little omega?" he asked cheerfully. "Keep your mind on your job."

How I could be expected to keep my mind on anything under these circumstances was something of an open question—but of course, that was the entire point. The finger in my ass ached and burned unpleasantly, and *no one cared*. At least, not unless it genuinely hurt me to the point that it soured my scent.

The sounds and smells of sex were all around me. Normally, it would have been a reminder of what I couldn't have... of what I couldn't *provide*, as a ruined omega. But I was already a part of this. Alex was going to fuck me and knot me and come inside of me. She was fully hard in my mouth, even now.

Flynn was poking around in my ass like someone fumbling for a light switch in the dark, and I was still not *remotely* sold on gay betas' answer to penetrative sex. He hummed in consideration and pulled out, manhandling my hips higher and jamming one of the countless cushions beneath me to change the angle of my hips.

More lube, and two fingers pushed inside me. By rights, this should not have been an improvement—only, it kind of *was*. Alex pulled my mouth off her clit.

"Can't find it?" she asked cryptically.

"Gimme a minute," Flynn grumbled. "I think maybe it's... *ah*."

He twisted his fingers and stars exploded across my vision, stealing my breath.

"It's way up in there, all right," Flynn said, rubbing his fingertips over the same place again, with the same result. "Could be a purebred thing, I guess."

I writhed, unable to draw breath as he worked the magic spot with a steady rhythm. The sensation was difficult to describe — like I needed to come and piss and empty my bowels at the same time, despite the fact that I'd been perfectly fine a moment before. Mostly, though, I needed him *not to ever stop.*

"Oh, god," I choked out, my voice joining the chorus of Leo's moans.

"I think this'll work," Flynn was saying, addressing Alex as though I wasn't even present. "We'll just need to hit him with everything at once and not let up."

A third finger stretched my entrance, and although Flynn was no longer sliding his fingertips over that spot, my body still vibrated like a struck gong. I breathed rapidly through my nose, feeling as though I was losing control of my muscles and my thoughts in equal measure.

"Our girl over here is just about ready for another knot," Jax called. "Can we help at all?"

"Yeah, come on over and join the party," Flynn replied, twisting his wrist again and dragging a gasp from me. "Grab one of the small condoms for Alex while you're at it. It'll make cleanup easier."

I heard Jax murmur something sweet and encouraging to Leo, who moaned. A moment later, something shiny arced through the air and Alex caught it one-handed. I watched with parted lips as she tore the foil packet open and sheathed her slender shaft. She reached for the lube Flynn passed her and slicked up the condom before closing the cap and tossing the bottle aside.

"Get him up here," she said.

Flynn's thick fingers slid out of me, leaving me aching and empty. Before I had enough time to properly register the feeling, strong hands lifted and turned me to straddle Alex's lap, my back to her front. She gripped my hips, positioning me where she wanted me — and *dear god*, was she strong.

I only had a moment to think, *this is it, an alpha is going to take me*, when the tip of her hard clit nudged my entrance. My own bodyweight pressed her inside, past the tight ring of my body's defenses. After Flynn's preparation, it should have been easy to take her — but she felt huge.

Overwhelmed, I tried to buck, to squirm away — but her hand tangled in the sweat-soaked shirt still binding my arms, and her knees hooked inside of mine spread me wide, splaying me open and helpless, with no leverage to lift myself.

"I've got you now, little omega," she said. The words sounded like a threat, but the tone was a promise.

My body clamored — for more, or for less — I wasn't sure. My breath came in shallow gulps. I tried to imagine what I must look like… hair disheveled, mouth swollen and red from the slide of Alex's shaft, legs forced wide, omega cock on display.

Trembling muscles gave up the fight one by one. Alex took my weight effortlessly, easing me back until I lay fully against her, my arms trapped against her six-pack abs, her small breasts pressing against my back. Her clit, buried deep inside me, brushed against that place Flynn had found earlier. A tremor rattled through my body, and I choked on air.

Jax deposited Leo in more or less the same position I'd been in before, except her arms weren't pinioned. I didn't know what my eyes looked like, but hers were dark and wanting, the pupils blown wide. With her hips supported on the curved end of the divan, she was basically presenting for the alpha behind her.

"Leo," I rasped, caught by how beautiful she looked like this — naked and debauched, ready to be filled by the blond god kneeling at her entrance. Jax slid into her, slow and deep, drawing a decadent moan from her bee-stung lips.

"Go on, sweet thing," Flynn rumbled. "Help us out, here. You know you want to taste him."

My heart kicked hard against my ribcage, but Leo's hands were already grabbing my thighs. Her skin was hot... feverish... but it was nothing to the heat of her mouth when her lips closed around my cock. I was hard, I realized. *Really* hard. Fully erect, and achingly sensitive.

The familiar feeling of *too much, too much* scorched its way up my spine. But again—no one here cared. They'd *promised* me they wouldn't care, wouldn't stop, wouldn't let me get away from them. I whimpered. Leona's fiery heat was somehow pouring out of her body and into mine. My nipples ached... all four of them... even though no one had touched them yet.

"Now there's a sight," Flynn said, standing next to the divan. "Guess I'll have his mouth, since everything else is already in use."

"Oh, fuck," I yelped, as Flynn fisted his cock with one hand and tangled his other hand in my hair, pulling me to him.

Alex rolled her hips, dragging the tip of her clit over the place inside me that sent stars across my vision. My mouth fell open, and Flynn pushed the head of his cock past my lips. I grunted a token protest, jerking against the restraint of my shirt, only to have my struggles ignored. Both Jax and Alex started moving, and the banked embers in my belly burst into flame.

Every deep thrust from Jax pushed Leo forward, shoving my cock down her throat. Every roll of Alex's hips set off fresh fireworks behind my watering eyes. Flynn's ridiculously huge cock stretched my lips wide. It was hard to breathe around him, which added to my growing lightheadedness and loss of control. My body was barreling toward a precipice that had nothing to do with my brain, and all I could do was come along for the ride.

A sharp tingling sensation began at the base of my spine, shivering along my nerves until my scalp started to prickle. Unfamiliar muscles within the cradle of my pelvis coiled, tensing. When I could get air at all, the smell of alpha and omega heat pheromones was choking—sweet and spicy, woodsy and pungent. My spine arched, my body going rigid as I tried to chase that elusive feeling coiling and writhing inside me.

Leo keened around my cock, reaching her peak as Jax pounded into her from behind. Her fingers curled convulsively around my thighs. I teetered on the edge of something, my body trying to follow her but not quite getting there as I struggled toward the apex.

Alex wrapped an arm around me, her fingers finding one of my remaining nipples and pinching hard. "Let go," she said simply.

The jolt of sensation from my nipple rocketed straight to my cock, and from there to the place where her clit was grinding inside me. Every muscle in my body locked solid, even as euphoria drenched me as though someone had poured it over my head from a bucket. I was seamlessly connected to all of the others caught in the throes of pleasure within the heat-nest, and for an endless moment, nothing else existed except that incomprehensible ecstasy.

My body jerked like a puppet on a string. Alex shuddered beneath me with a low groan. Her clit throbbed inside of me, and a new pressure grew as her knot swelled. Flynn slid out of my mouth, thumbing the trail of saliva from my lower lip with a gentle caress.

"Knew you could do it, Ginger Tea," he said, sounding pleased.

I huffed out a breath that was half a laugh and half a sob as my muscles went lax, a sense of indescribable well-being washing over me. Leo released my softening cock in favor of pressing messy, uncoordinated kisses on my inner thighs.

For some reason, tears were streaming down my cheeks in rivulets. I let Alex take my weight, my body stretching around the place where she was knotting me. She was so tall that the back of my head slotted neatly against the crook of her neck when I leaned against her. Her hand, still wrapped around me, settled over my heart.

"Rest now," she said, like it was an order.

I turned my tear-stained face toward her, letting her tuck my head beneath her chin, and did as my alpha told me.

SEVEN

Alex

I'D FORGOTTEN, damn it. I'd forgotten what it was like to be knot-deep in an omega, holding them as they came down from a crashing peak. Not that Irina had been carrying anything like the kind of baggage that Kameron Patel was carting around—but the emotions of the heat-nest were still the same.

It wasn't remotely like knotting an obliging beta male. I was drunk on Leona's heat pheromones, my own alpha hormones sloshing around my brain in a heady cocktail of *protect* and *mark* and *dominate* as Kameron's body fluttered and clenched around the swollen base of my clit. My mouth watered with the need to bite, for Christ's sake—and only the knowledge that doing so wouldn't accidentally initiate a bond kept me from freaking the fuck out.

Was I broken? Defective somehow? Did all of the self-control I exercised in *every other aspect of my life* mean nothing the moment I was around an omega in heat?

I'd been watching the others like a hawk, and there'd been no indication so far that biting had even entered their minds. *I've never been tempted to bite,* Jax had said, and maybe he'd been telling the truth. Maybe it was just me.

I swallowed saliva, smelling the faint hint of ginger and lemon through the heavier miasma of sweetness. The omega in my lap made a humming noise and nuzzled against my throat. His cheeks were wet. Something clenched painfully in my chest.

Flynn crouched beside the divan where the rest of us were piled in a messy tangle. He reached out one big hand and ran it through Leona's sweat-soaked hair. Her head was still resting on Kameron's thigh. Her body, limp as a dishrag, was draped over the lower end of the couch. Jax knelt behind her, apparently intending to let her ride out his knot right where she was. He murmured soothing nonsense to her, stroking his fingers up and down her spine. His focus was on her, just as it should be.

Flynn's focus, on the other hand, was on me. He gestured in a clear request for permission to touch Kameron while I was knotting him. I gave him a weary nod, stomping down on the ridiculous warning growl that wanted to rumble up from my chest.

My packmate laid his palm flat over Kameron's belly, fingers spread. The omega's breath puffed out in a sigh against the side of my neck.

"Did that feel good, Kam?" Flynn asked. "Did you like it when we made you come?"

Kameron nodded, not lifting his head from the crook of my neck. "Mm-hmm. 'S good. Thank you, alphas."

Flynn nodded as well. "You want it again, you just ask. We'll pin you down and make you come whenever you want. Lots of time to make up for, right?"

I tried not to tense up, not wanting to upset the omega still trapped on my knot. That hadn't sounded like Flynn was only talking about the period of the heat contract. In lieu of saying anything aloud, I directed a glare in his direction.

It bounced right off him.

"What about you, *alef*?" he asked me. "You doin' okay?"

And how the *hell* was I supposed to answer that?

"Fine," I managed.

And now Jax was shooting me worried glances as well. *Brilliant.*

"*Fine*," I repeated more forcefully. Kameron let out a happy little gasp in response to the hint of a bark in my tone. He rolled his head to the side to bare his throat to me, which was *not* helping the situation, damn it. Leona didn't react at all—already down for the count, it seemed. The others had the good sense to back off.

I shoved everything out of my head as best I could, letting myself sink into the raw physicality of the joining instead, as I waited for my knot to go down.

Later, as Leona dozed under Jax and Flynn's watchful gazes, I sat once more on the end of the sectional. I'd snatched a quick shower and put some clothes on. So had Kameron. He sat on the cushion-covered floor at my feet, with his back propped against the front of the couch, loosely hugging his knees.

The unrelenting aura of tension that usually hung over his head like a cloud was gone—it was amazing what a good fuck could do. Now, he merely appeared thoughtful.

"You're still thinking too loudly," I told him, somewhat against my better judgment.

He glanced up at me, surprised. "Really? I thought I was being admirably quiet about it this time."

I raised an eyebrow, and he huffed. "All right. Yes. I'm trying to decide if it's appropriate to ask a personal question. I've been leaning toward *no*."

I had a pretty good idea of what that question would be. "No, go ahead. You've had my clit up your ass. You might as well ask."

Honestly, I was kind of surprised Leona hadn't given him the complete rundown on my messy past already.

"Irina," he said quietly. "Who was she?"

I waited for the familiar tide of old pain to rise, crest, and slowly ebb. "Irina Pasternak was the omega I couldn't save. She was carrying our pups... and also my mating bite."

"Ah," Kameron said. Nothing else—no hollow sympathy, no request for further details.

"What about you?" I asked. I told myself it was just a way to redirect the conversation away from me, but the truth was, I was curious. These two must have had the devil's own luck to get as far as they had.

His shoulders rose and fell on a silent sigh. "I was born in Kolkata. The locals got tired of our purebred family being too prosperous and too comfortable with our own position. Committee sympathizers came for us when I was twelve, and I was the only one considered economically valuable enough to keep for the breeding pens. When I turned out not to be pliable enough for their tastes, they sterilized me and threw me into the slave market."

I waited while he gazed off into the distance. He'd summarized his past in a bland monologue, much as I had. I understood the need to tamp those emotions down. He turned and glanced at me before continuing in a more normal tone.

"The person who bought me was secretly working with the underground. She shipped me off to North America and arranged a beta identity for me."

"Lucky," I said.

"Yes, I suppose so," he agreed.

An oddly comfortable silence fell between us. I was aware of Jax and Flynn listening in on the conversation from across the room, but they didn't try to interrupt.

Kameron's story wasn't miles different from Irina's—though I wasn't about to say so aloud, given how hers had ended. Irina had at least escaped sterilization, but she, too, had been purchased by one of the underground operatives we called the *catch-and-releasers*. It had always enraged me that the best we could seem to come up with was this patchwork method of freeing individual alphas and omegas from slavery. What I really wanted was to put a torch to the entire damned institution and burn it to the ground.

This, clearly, was one of several reasons I was only a lowly foot soldier in the resistance, rather than a four-star general.

"Would you do something for me, please?" Kameron asked, some minutes later.

Tension coiled in my shoulders, but I'd been the one to insist that any omega in my pack's nest would get exactly what they needed, no matter what that was.

"Yes?" I said.

He released his grip around his knees, his posture going loose-limbed and exhausted. "As, er, *enlightening* as the experience was, I don't think I'm going to be in any kind of shape to play host to a knot for the next day or two."

Flynn snorted, but—somewhat surprisingly— kept any off-color commentary about female alpha knots to himself.

Kameron wisely ignored him. "That being said, I am so tired right now I can barely see straight. I, uh… I haven't been sleeping well lately."

That was obvious enough from the dark bags under his eyes. "Tell me what you need," I said.

He hesitated. "Would you watch over things while I rest? I mean—I know you were doing that already," he hurried to add. "What I'm asking is..." He trailed off.

"He wants you to watch over *him*," Flynn said. "Ginger Tea, no offense, but you're still really bad at asking for things."

Kameron ducked his head, not denying the allegation. An unpleasant mix of dread and longing tugged at me, but there was no avoiding the promise I'd made to look after his needs. I scooted forward, lowering myself off the couch and into the nest— trying not to feel awkward about it.

"Come on, then," I said, cringing inwardly at how painfully useless I was at things like this.

Flynn rolled his eyes at me. Jax lifted an eyebrow. "Will wonders never cease," he muttered. I mentally planned the kind of sparring sessions for them that would leave both of them bruised and aching for a week.

Kameron, blushing hard enough that it was visible even with his rich olive skin tone, curled up next to me in the soft nest and rested his head on my thigh. My hand lifted to stroke through his thick, silky hair, seemingly of its own volition. He drew in a slow, careful breath, and when he let it out, I felt his muscles grow slack with relief.

"Thank you alpha," he murmured.

I didn't reply—but I did keep stroking his hair... while trying my best to ignore the knowing looks that my packmates were giving me.

Jax and Flynn took turns knotting Leona through the rest of her heat. I maintained a martial eye on the birth control situation, ensuring that her cervical cap was removed and replaced at the appropriate intervals.

No one could have slept through her increasingly wild peaks, but Kameron still slept *a lot*. He probably needed it, especially since Flynn talked him into a second round of sex after he'd had a couple of days to recover from the first one. Well, I say *talked*. The others had grown increasingly feral and growly as the heat progressed, so it was more a case of Flynn having pinned Kameron on his back and straddled his hips to keep him there, before informing the omega that he was going to come this time with my clit up his ass and Leona sitting on his face, drowning him in slick.

As I thrust into his pliant body some time later, angling my hips to give Jax room to administer a fiendishly thorough handjob at the same time, it occurred to me that I might have seriously underestimated the depths of my packmates' sexual depravity. That was right before Leona—straddling Kameron's face as promised—keened out an orgasm, her huge hazel eyes going distant and hazy. The fresh flood of pheromones triggered Kam, and his thrashing and clenching triggered me. I was only distantly aware of the snarls and moans as Flynn dragged Leona off of Kameron's face, fucking into her from behind while Jax knelt in front of her and fed her his cock.

Eventually, inevitably, Leona's heat subsided. I let the others pamper the two omegas with baths and blankets and an endless supply of food. At one point, Kameron flopped down next to me on the sectional and handed me a plate with a sandwich on it.

"Well," he said. "That was certainly..." He trailed off, looking more than a little dazed.

"Yeah," I agreed, and bit into the sandwich.

Though clearly exhausted, Leona McCready was *glowing*. There really wasn't another word for it. We both watched her with something like fascination.

Kameron sighed. "So, is it too soon to start talking about what comes next?"

I shrugged. "I'd be more than happy to, except I won't know the answer to that question until Beckett gets back from his meetings with the higher-ups. He should be here tomorrow."

But *tomorrow* came and went with no sign of the man. So did the following day. The morning after that, there was no denying the obvious conclusion. Something had happened to our team leader, and the five of us were potentially screwed beyond belief.

EIGHT

Leona

I WAS GOING to be sore for days, and I couldn't even be mad about it. My heat spent with Kam and our three alphas had been blissful, right up until the horrors of the outside world intruded on our cozy nest—as had always been inevitable.

The morning after I managed to recover from my heat-high and subsequent crash, Flynn had looked at me over breakfast and said, "You know it could be like this all the time, sweet thing. All you and your *odama* need to do is say yes."

And I'd wanted it. Oh, how I'd wanted it. In fact, I'd wanted it badly enough that instead of saying no like a rational person, I'd met Kam's eyes for a moment's silent conversation before turning back to Flynn and replying, "Ask us again after we've made things better in the world."

Then, as if I'd singlehandedly manifested disaster by daring to dream of a better future, Beckett failed to return. Two days passed beyond the deadline when he should have been back, and the alphas were in crisis mode. Meanwhile, Kam and I were in the maddening position of being worse than useless. Not only were we no help when it came to tracking Beckett down, but our status as fugitive omegas meant we needed protecting.

At the sound of a vehicle crunching up the winding gravel drive, Jax and Flynn were up and heading for the front door in near-unison. Alex had gone to check in with a contact—a man Beckett supposedly would have left a message with, if he'd been unavoidably detained but was otherwise okay.

The familiar white Jeep pulled up and parked. Alex slid out and slammed the driver's door behind her, looking focused and deadly as she marched up to the house. Jax let her in.

"Well?" he asked.

"Nothing," she bit out. "Beckett didn't contact the guy. So the next step is to decide if we're going to bug out and try to join some other cell in the underground, or follow Beckett's tracks and try to figure out what happened to him."

"We go after Beckett," Flynn said without hesitation. "Obviously."

"It's not that simple," Alex shot back. "Not now."

"Because of us," I hazarded, gesturing between Kam and me. "Don't let us get in your way. We can fend for ourselves if we have to."

It wasn't a lie, although there was no question we'd be a lot more vulnerable without this pack of alphas protecting us. I'd been dragged from my apartment at three a.m. with nothing but the flimsy nightgown I'd been wearing, but Kam had ten thousand dollars in cash, along with a few personal belongings. That money would help pay for my escape as well as his—even if the idea of fleeing the country and leaving the others behind made me queasy.

But Alex shook her head. "It's partly that, yes; but there's also another consideration."

The muscles in Jax's square jaw twitched. "You need to leave me behind, too. I'm still not in fighting shape. I'd only slow you down."

I covered a wince. Though he was much better now, Jax was still recovering from muscle weakness and nerve damage on his left side. I still seethed thinking of those bastards in Romania who'd held us prisoner, injecting Jax with their poisonous experimental weapon designed to kill alphas and omegas while leaving betas unharmed.

Kam cleared his throat. My packmate had been uncharacteristically subdued since my heat ended—still processing things, I suspected. Now, though, he spoke up.

"Then Jax should stay here and guard us while Flynn goes with you, Alex," he said. "It's the most logical use of resources. From what I gather, it would be dangerous for Beckett to end up in the Committee's hands. He knows too much."

Flynn tapped his fingers against the wall. "He's right. There's the identity of Beckett's mate to worry about, for one thing."

Beckett was the only mated omega I'd ever met. The secrecy surrounding the identity of his partner was absolute, and the others had speculated that he or she must be someone high up in the organizational structure of the underground. If whoever had captured Beckett managed to pry that information out of him, it could potentially cause untold damage to the alphomic resistance.

"Is there any reason to think the location of this place has been compromised?" I asked.

"That depends entirely on who has Beckett right now, and how good they are at torturing people for information," Alex said tightly.

A chill skittered down my spine, but I squared my shoulders. "Any *concrete* reason?" I pressed.

"No," she admitted, before adding, "There's also no concrete reason to think it hasn't been compromised."

"I'm willing to take the risk," Kam said quietly. "Jax?"

Jax's tense posture said he wasn't happy at being left behind while his pack went into danger. Nevertheless, he gave a single, terse nod. "It makes sense. We'll need a second vehicle, though, in case we need to make a run for it. This place is in the middle of fucking nowhere."

"I think that's kind of the point," Flynn said. "Still, he's right."

Kam exchanged a glance with me. "We have ten thousand in cash. You should be able to pick up something cheap with a salvage title, and not have to dig too far into that amount."

"That'll work," Flynn said. "There ought to be some counterfeit or expired license plates hidden somewhere in this place. That's pretty standard for this kind of safehouse."

"What about you two?" I asked. "Do you have access to enough money for what you need to do? Gasoline, food, that kind of stuff?"

If they didn't, Kam and I would have to decide how much of our limited funds we were willing to throw at this mission. Ten thousand dollars was enough to smuggle two people out of the country, but it wasn't an extravagant amount. We could only afford to lose so much of it before one or both of us would be stuck here. And as omega fugitives, it wasn't as though we could easily get more money. We owed Beckett, though—we'd probably both be in the Committee's hands right now if not for his intervention.

"Let us worry about that," Alex said.

I had no idea if she meant they already had access to money, or if she planned to rob a bank, or what. But I was in no position to question the alphas—not when they had their shit together, and I totally didn't. I was still trapped in a strange limbo. My past life had been ripped away irretrievably, and I didn't know yet what the future would look like.

For a while, it had seemed like our future would be in the underground. With Beckett gone, that option might be lost to us. The uncertainty ate at me, now that the mindlessness of my heat had loosened its grip.

"Is this the plan we're going with?" Jax asked.

Alex hesitated before offering a sharp, affirmative nod. "It is. We'll acquire a second car before we leave. Flynn and I will track down the people Beckett went to meet with. We can at least find out if he made it to those meetings or not. We'll be back in four days. If we're delayed, or if we find a lead worth following, we'll leave a message with Beckett's contact—the one I spoke to today. If you have to leave this place before we get back, you do the same."

It concerned me that this was essentially an identical plan to the one Beckett had used, and that hadn't worked out very well for him. Unfortunately, I didn't have anything better to offer as an alternative.

"Right," Flynn said. "It's no good standing around here with our thumbs up our asses, in that case. Let's get moving."

It took the rest of the day and half of the following one to get everything set up. Kam and I mostly stayed out of the way. With my photograph plastered all over the newspapers, it wasn't as though I could run to the nearest grocery store to pick up supplies.

In a role reversal from the past several days, Kam and I committed to ensuring that the others were fed and actually got some sleep. Flynn and Jax in particular were still recovering from four solid days of mating and guarding the nest during my heat. Alphas were tough, but that kind of thing took a toll. I figured the least we could do was pamper them a little.

Flynn acquired a sketchy looking Chrysler LeBaron, its hood and left front fender an entirely different color from the rest of the car.

"Frame's a bit twisted," he said. "It pulls to the right a little at highway speeds."

"So do I these days," Jax grumbled, accepting the keys.

Kam had unearthed the promised collection of license plates from a closet upstairs. He went outside to mount them on the Franken-Chrysler, lending the car a tissue-thin facade of legality.

With fresh supplies laid in and the transportation issue solved, Alex and Flynn wasted no time in packing their clothing and weapons—eager to depart before the trail grew any colder than it already was.

I stood in the entryway of the house, my arms crossed tightly, trying not to succumb to the sense of impending doom that threatened to swallow me whole. For a few short days, everything had been perfect. I'd known going in that it wasn't the kind of perfection that could last—not for people like us. And I'd *still* been suckered in.

A new purpose in life.

A pack of misfit alphas devoted to my pleasure, and to Kam's.

It was too perfect—not the way real life worked.

"C'mere," Flynn said, and reeled me in. He had his travel bag slung over one broad shoulder. I let myself be reeled, desperate for a final taste of his overpowering *alphaness*. He held me against his hard-muscled chest and kissed the top of my head.

"Be nice to Jax while we're gone," he rumbled against my temple. "He's gonna be climbing the walls. Guess you probably will be, too."

"Probably," I agreed.

"You know, fucking is really good for stress relief," he said conversationally. "Just throwing that out there."

I felt a flush rise to my cheeks—a ridiculous reaction, given the events of the past week.

"For god's *sake*, Flynn," Alex said, saving me the necessity of a reply.

Flynn shrugged, and let me go when I regained enough self-control to pull away. He reached for Kam next, taking him by the chin and rubbing a thumb possessively across his full lower lip. Kam drew in a sharp little breath.

"Be good until we get back, Ginger Tea," Flynn said. "Or don't—it's usually more fun that way. See you in a few days."

"Stay out of trouble, asshole," Jax said. "Good hunting, Alex."

Alex gave him a short nod, clearly not one for lengthy goodbyes. Her catlike green eyes played over us, her gaze catching momentarily on Kam before she jerked it away.

"*Au revoir*," she said, and led Flynn out the front door.

We watched as the pair climbed into the Jeep. The engine turned over, and the vehicle headed away, leaving the Chrysler sitting alone and looking vaguely forlorn in the overgrown circle drive.

NINE

Leona

JAX SPENT the first day after Flynn and Alex departed stringing booby traps across all of the trails and tracks leading to the house. Fishing line—attached to every can, jug, and piece of metal trash we could find—now crisscrossed any trail large enough to accommodate people, strung inconspicuously at ankle height. Any intruder would trip the line and set off a cacophony of noise from the items secreted in the underbrush.

Despite the brisk nights, windows stood open on all sides of the house, letting in the sounds from outside so sensitive alpha and omega hearing could more easily pick up the noise of a trap being sprung. Jax set up a rotation schedule for guarding the house—eight hours on and sixteen hours off for each of us, during which we kept constant watch on the driveway and listened for disturbances coming from any other direction.

Jax was, of course, armed. But neither Kam nor I had any familiarity with firearms, and the noise involved in trying to learn on the fly would have drawn too much attention to our secret hideout. So as far as I could tell, our grand strategic plan in case of emergency was to run and get the alpha so he could shoot at whoever was trying to capture us. As battle strategy went, it didn't sound all that promising.

In fact, the current situation was eerily reminiscent of the way Kam and I had lived for years. We'd thrown together an iffy escape plan for when the worst inevitably happened, then sat back and waited for things to implode—because there was really no other option.

This felt very much like that, only dialed up to eleven.

As unregistered omegas, Kam and I had largely managed to ignore the potential for disaster as we lived our day-to-day lives. We'd have gone crazy otherwise. Maybe it was the difference in alpha versus omega psychology, because by contrast, Jax seemed hyper-focused on the danger twenty-four hours a day. I appreciated his dedication, but it was also exhausting.

With our assigned eight-hour shifts, it meant whichever two of us weren't watching for danger were pretty much left to our own devices the rest of the time. It didn't take long for me to start pondering Flynn's parting words to me.

You know, fucking is really good for stress relief. Just throwing that out there.

Jax had taken the three a.m. to eleven a.m. shift, since that was the roughest one. Kam had claimed seven p.m. to three a.m. since he was prone to insomnia anyway, leaving me with the cushy eleven-to-seven daytime shift.

When Kam showed up on the second evening to relieve me, he wrapped me up in his arms and pressed a kiss to my temple before pulling back to meet my eyes.

"How do you feel about using omega wiles to manipulate a stubborn alpha?" he asked.

I blinked at him. "I think I'm fresh out of wiles," I said uncertainly.

"Uh, no. Trust me, you're *really* not," he shot back. "Would you please do me a favor and turn Jax's brain off for a few hours before his skull bursts into flame or something? He's lovely, and I'm glad he's here, but he's also slowly driving me mad."

"I think he's just stressing out over the fact that he couldn't go after Beckett with the others," I said. "That's got to be rough on him. He's overcompensating, trying to keep us safe."

Kam patted my arm. "Yes. Which is why I'm siccing you on him. You have compassion for his situation. Whereas I mostly want to throw something at his head, and tell him that cleaning the same guns over and over won't magically make them more effective if someone sends a SWAT team after us."

I let out a startled laugh, even though nothing about it was remotely funny.

"Right," I told him. "Fair enough—I'm on it. But just so you know, you're starting to think like Flynn. I want you to really stop and ponder that while you're busy staring fixedly at an empty driveway for the next eight hours."

He patted my arm again and took up my post. "I love you, but I also reject your hypothesis in the strongest possible terms, *odama*. Go be wily, and I'll come find you in the nest when I get off-shift later. There's food in the fridge if you're hungry."

"Thanks," I said, and then added, "I think."

I left him to it. After a meal of cold leftovers, I headed upstairs and tracked down our wayward alpha in one of the spare bedrooms. Kam had been one hundred percent serious—Jax was seated at an old desk with one gun in his shoulder holster and the other in pieces in front of him, polishing one of the disassembled bits with a black-smudged rag.

"Hi," I said. "Rammed any good holes lately?"

He did a comical double take in my direction. I smiled sweetly and indicated the pistol on the desk. Understanding dawned, and he did at least have the good grace to look sheepish.

"It helps me relax," he explained.

I raised an eyebrow. "Good god—in that case, I'd hate to see you when you *haven't* been obsessively cleaning and oiling your guns."

He set the oddly shaped piece of metal aside. "Kam sent you, I take it?"

I nodded. "Mm-hmm. You're slowly driving him insane with your hyper-preparedness, apparently."

"Ah," he said. "Sorry."

I shrugged. "Don't take it personally. I think it's just that we're used to trying our best to ignore the guillotine hanging over our heads when it's not actively falling on us. Less stressful that way."

He shot me a wry look. "Maybe for you."

"Tell you what," I offered. "Let's keep each other company instead. Put that thing back together while I go take care of something. Back in a bit." I felt his eyes on me as I left the room and went down the hall to the nest, and the bathroom beyond it.

Something had changed in me over the past couple of weeks—besides the inevitable change that comes from having your life upended and the resulting debris set on fire. Or maybe that was part of it, too; it was hard to tell. Whatever the case, my usual sense of living on borrowed time had shifted in some indefinable way. I'd come to realize that, in many ways, I *hadn't* been living before. Not really. I'd only been existing, which was a very different thing.

I let myself into the extravagant bathroom and crossed to the sunken tub, where I crouched to plug the drain and turn on the tap. While it was filling, I stripped off and took a very quick shower in the separate stall, shampooing my mass of red hair and massaging conditioner into it. When I was done, I toweled off, leaving it hanging down in wet ringlets.

With a towel wrapped around my naked body, I adjusted the temperature of the bath a bit warmer and let it finish filling before turning off the taps.

Then, I went to employ wiles against an alpha for probably the first time in my life.

———◆———

Jax's piercing blue eyes darkened as he took me in, a hint of the feral alpha who'd knotted me so possessively during my heat peeking through the veneer of an otherwise thoroughly civilized man. I stood dripping on the threshold, my chin tilted to show him a hint of throat as I looked at him through heavy lashes.

"Come with me, alpha," I said without artifice. "We need to relax for an hour or so, and then we need to sleep."

I saw him wrest back control of his libido; saw the regret coloring his gaze.

"I need to be ready in case anything happens," he said. "I'm sorry, Leona."

But I wasn't having it. "Does being naked and wet make your aim with those things worse?" I asked, indicating the pair of guns.

He frowned. "That's not—"

"Will being fully clothed make the odds any better if a Committee SWAT team shows up to surround the house?" I pressed.

He let out a sigh. "Probably not, but waving my dick at them as I'm hauled off wouldn't be a very dignified way to go out."

"Neither was being dragged out of bed in the middle of the night wearing a silk nightgown and no underwear," I said dryly. "And yet, here we both are."

I saw reluctant agreement soften the line of his shoulders.

"You want me to come take a bath with you?" he said, as though trying the words on for size.

I nodded. "Kam said I should use my omega wiles to get you to unwind for a bit before you drive him completely around the bend." I batted my eyelashes at him ridiculously. "Is it working?"

He laughed despite himself. "So, this must be how you negotiate international treaties, huh?"

I glanced down at my towel. "Well, I mean, I usually negotiated while wearing a few more clothes than this."

"Then you missed a trick. They wouldn't have known what hit them." He hauled himself to his feet and scooped up the now-reassembled gun. "Come on then, you wily little omega. But if I end up naked during a shootout, I reserve the right to say I told you so."

I smiled at him, unrepentant, and hoped desperately that things wouldn't come to that—because I would, in fact, feel pretty damned guilty if they did.

His slight limp was noticeable as he followed me back to the bathroom. I wondered if he would ever recover fully... and there was yet another thing for the guilt pile. That pile was in danger of growing out of control. However, it was also part of the past, not the present. None of it could be changed now.

I let my towel slip to the floor as I stepped through the doorway, not looking back at him as I crossed the bathroom and climbed onto the platform housing the huge sunken tub. Jax's gaze burned the back of my neck as I carefully stepped into the hot water and lowered myself down to lean against the edge with a happy sigh.

It was odd—I'd spent more time naked in the presence of other people in the last month than I had in the previous fifteen years combined. As an aligned omega with beta bloodlines, my body could pass a certain amount of scrutiny. But unregistered omegas did *not* seek out beta doctors, or otherwise put themselves in a position to be seen naked, if it was at all avoidable.

In the last few weeks, though, I'd been naked with Kam. I'd been naked with Jax, and with Flynn, and even with Alex — though I was pretty sure Alex would have run for the hills if she hadn't felt obligated to watch over her pack during the heat.

And I'd *liked* it.

I'd liked being seen. I'd liked being appreciated for my physical form. It was probably shallow of me... or maybe not. In a world that hated me because I was an omega, perhaps it was natural to crave that kind of acceptance from people who thought my hidden nature made me beautiful, rather than a freak.

Jax limped over to the tub and looked down at me, sending a frisson across my exposed skin.

"You really are stunning, Leona McCready," he said. "I hope you realize that."

I couldn't help the shy smile that tugged at my lips. "Well, you know, you're not so bad yourself." I raised my eyebrows. "From what I remember, at least. Maybe you'd better give me another look, just to be sure, though."

He snorted. "I'm a scarred reject from the breeding pens."

"You're a blond-haired, blue-eyed alpha Viking with bone structure that could cut glass," I corrected. "Not to mention, one of only three people I trust to protect my *odama* and my nest."

Jax exhaled a breath like it had been startled out of him. "Good god, woman — stop talking like that."

It did the trick, though. He started pulling off clothing, after setting the pair of holstered guns within easy reach. I ached in sympathy at the way he favored his left side, shrugging his shirt awkwardly over that shoulder.

And yet, it could have been so much worse. It still might be, once the Beta Liberation Front perfected their nerve agent into a targeted alphomic weapon. But they hadn't succeeded yet. I had to focus on that. They'd used Jax as a lab rat, but he was still alive. He hadn't died.

"Come here," I said, extending my hand to the scarred classical statue standing over me.

He gave me a long look and took it, allowing me to steady him as he lowered himself to sit on the edge of the tub. He paused a moment, then eased into the water with a long sigh.

"Good?" I asked.

"Yeah," he agreed.

I waited until he was settled before sliding across to straddle his lap. He was half-hard under the water. I leaned against him, and his arms immediately came around me as I buried my nose in the crook of his neck and breathed in his clean forest scent.

My heat cycle was well and truly over, but alpha arousal pheromones were still an aphrodisiac for omegas. My body grew warm and heavy against his. I could happily have sunk down on his cock and ridden him into mutual oblivion, now that I was no longer fertile and pregnancy wasn't a concern.

He made a noise of regret. "You're getting ideas. And while I like those ideas a lot, I'm gonna have to draw the line at knotting you when I'm supposed to be guarding you."

"I know," I said, not moving from my comfortable sprawl. "Tell me something, though. I understand that it's unpleasant popping a knot outside of actually mating. But I sucked you while Flynn was knotting me, and vice versa. Isn't that frustrating? Having sex but not coming?"

File this under '*things I never thought I'd be having a conversation about, especially while naked.*' But it wasn't awkward — not with Jax. It probably wouldn't have been with Flynn, either… though I was fairly sure trying to have this conversation with him would devolve into actual sex in an astonishingly short period of time.

"Not always," Jax said. "In the heat-nest, it's just a normal part of foreplay. We were taking turns with you, so it was a warm-up for the next round, if that makes sense."

"It does," I assured him.

"And it can be nice to get teased for a bit without it necessarily going further," he went on. "It kind of depends on the mood. There's nothing wrong with fooling around for fooling around's sake."

I pulled away enough to smile up at him. "Is that so?"

He stroked my wet hair back, giving me a wry look. "Why do I feel like you're asking me leading questions?"

Reaching a hand between our bodies, I wrapped my fingers around his heavy girth and gave him an experimental stroke. "Damn," I said. "There goes my clever subterfuge."

His summer-sky gaze went heavy lidded. A moment later, I was on my back in the tub with six-foot-plus of horny alpha on top of me, and no real awareness of how I'd gotten there. Warm water sloshed around my chin. I gasped, straining up, and was met by a pair of faintly chapped lips covering mine in a kiss that quickly turned filthy.

By the time he let me up for air, I was breathless.

The smell of cypress and musk filled my senses. One large hand rested between my shoulder blades, preventing me from sliding underwater. His touch guided me to arch my spine until the tips of my breasts broke the surface. His teeth closed around my right nipple, drawing an undignified whine from my throat. A pulse of hot slick turned my inner thighs slippery beneath the water.

It was possible I hadn't thought this plan all the way through.

"I miss your perfume," Jax said, and bit the other nipple.

I yelped, arching helplessly into the stimulation. "C-couldn't risk it in case we need to run," I managed.

He licked over the abused flesh, drawing a shudder and a fresh pulse of slick. "I know."

Twisting in the tub, he rearranged us so that he was sitting with his back propped against the side, and I was once more straddling him—facing away this time. His hand cupped my chin, drawing me back to rest against his chest with my throat bared and his hard cock nestled between my ass cheeks. His right hand moved confidently downward to cup my pussy, where I was slippery with arousal despite the water.

"I'm going to make you come," he said. "Twice. And then we're going to dry off and go into the nest, where I'm going to lay you out on a pile of pillows and fuck those beautiful breasts for a bit. When Kam comes back after his watch, he's going to find you naked and wrecked."

"Okay," I agreed breathlessly, my throat working against his light grip.

"Mmm," he said, and tipped my head, exposing the side of my neck opposite from my mating gland. I moaned as he kissed his way along it, and gasped when his teeth closed on the juncture of my neck and shoulder.

Something dark and primal rose within me, even though he was only playacting at a mating bite. Nevertheless, my body *knew*. His fingers slid the final inch, parting my folds, and we were off to the races.

TEN

Flynn

"SO, ARE WE gonna talk about this at some point, or what?" I asked, not taking my eyes off the highway unspooling beneath the Jeep's tires. Beside me in the passenger seat, Alex shifted restlessly.

"There's nothing to talk about," she said.

"Bullshit." I shot her a sidelong glance. Her profile could have been carved from granite.

She blew out a frustrated breath through her nose. "What is there to say, *alef*? You and Jax negotiated a heat contract. Somehow you dragged me into it as well, because apparently I'm an idiot. It was a nice few days. And then everything went to shit again, because that's what always happens."

"'*Nice*'?" I echoed skeptically. "That's the word you're going with?"

"Yes. It is. They're nice omegas. Having sex was nice. Everything was fucking *nice*, and now Beckett's gone and we're screwed."

I could feel her icy green glare on me without turning to look. She was trying to derail me... to get me thinking about Beckett instead of her issues. But the thing was, we couldn't do anything about Beckett until we got where we were going and talked to his contacts. Which meant there was no reason not to hash this out now, while we had the chance.

"Here's what I don't get," I said. "Leave Leona out of it for a minute, because I know that's a whole different can of worms as far as you're concerned. Let's talk about Kam instead. You can't mate him.

You can't get him pregnant. You obviously like him. And you're still acting like it's Irina all over again. Why?"

There was a heavy pause.

I waited it out.

"You don't understand what it's like," she said eventually. "You have no conception of how it feels to lose an omega under your protection... to know that you've failed them, and to have their death on your conscience. I don't ever want you to learn what that feels like, *alef*. Either of you."

I thought about that for a few minutes.

"Okay. But what does you denying yourself have to do with that?" I asked. "Because watching you be miserable and alone isn't exactly convincing me and Jax not to go after those two while we have the chance."

Another pause.

"I—" Alex began, only to cut herself off. "I don't wish to discuss this now."

I snorted. "Yeah, I kind of got that part already."

"It's a distraction, and we can't afford distractions." Alex turned her head away, looking out the window. "Beckett's disappearance feels like an endgame scenario. For us, at least. Maybe even for the underground as a whole."

Personally, I would have been more than happy to focus on that distraction until we reached Montreal. Idly, I wondered if Jax was getting in some good *distractions*, alone in the remote safehouse with a pair of tempting omegas all to himself.

Lucky bastard.

Still, Alex had a point. Bravado aside, I understood that there was a good chance we weren't going to come out of this unscathed.

"You've really got no idea who Beckett's mate is, huh?" I asked. That was the part I kept coming back to—how much damage might be done if the wrong person managed to get their hands on that information.

"I really don't," Alex replied with a sigh. "And right now, I almost wish I did, just so I'd know how badly to panic."

We lapsed into silence as the outskirts of Montreal came into view.

<hr>

After some discussion, we'd decided to approach Beckett's contacts in the same order he'd intended to meet with them. He'd had three meetings planned, and we figured that if he hadn't made the first meeting, it was pretty much a given that he wouldn't have made it to the other two, either.

If he'd disappeared between one meeting and the next, it might at least give us some kind of a starting point in order to trace him. There'd been nothing in the newspapers so far indicating he'd been arrested. That could be good, or it could be bad. On the one hand, if he'd been scooped up and dumped into the legal system that would ultimately funnel him to the Committee's brutal parody of 'justice,' he was out of our reach and as good as dead. The underground didn't have the resources to go up against the Committee head-to-head—not even close. They'd crush us like bugs the moment we tried to crawl out of the woodwork.

On the other hand, it could be just as bad if Enoch Sloane had snatched Beckett in secret and was keeping him off the books for some reason—most likely so he and his lackeys would have time to extract every last bit of information from him without the pressures of having to give him a sham trial. We also had the Beta Liberation Front assholes to consider. They might or might not be secretly working with the Committee. They also might or might not have their own reasons for wanting to take out the guy who'd singlehandedly busted up their operation in Romania.

Fuck, what a mess.

Beckett's first scheduled meeting had been with the go-between for another cell that was adjacent to ours. The guy was a beta, and he owned, of all things, a hair salon. We arrived to find the place empty and boarded up, the faded sign hanging off-kilter from a single chain above the locked door. That was our first hint that things might be even more serious than we'd thought.

"Keep driving," Alex said tightly. "Don't slow down."

I did, well aware that if the authorities had shut the shop down because of its ties with the underground, they might have surveillance in place to identify anyone who came poking around in search of the proprietor.

I continued for several miles before pulling into the parking lot of a run-down diner.

"It could be a coincidence," I said, though it almost certainly wasn't.

"I don't believe in coincidences," Alex replied. "But we don't have any way of knowing if the place was raided before or after Beckett showed up. Or even *if* he showed up."

"On to the next one?" I asked.

"On to the next one," she agreed.

The next meeting Beckett had scheduled was a step up the food chain, and as such, neither Alex nor I had contact details for a specific person. All we had was a location and a code phrase that would only be good for another day or two before it changed. The location was a large, well-known casino. Alex sent me in alone, since I was less conspicuous than a six-foot-tall butch female alpha would have been.

I double-checked my fake ID, tugged my suit jacket straight, and went inside. Once I got to the gaming floor, I searched out the pit boss and flagged her down. She was a beta woman with really big hair and a plastic smile.

"Can I help you?" she asked.

"Yeah, can you recommend a restaurant around here that does Ukranian food?" I asked.

She blinked at me. "Uh, that's... oddly specific. I think there's one downtown run by a family of Bulgarians. That's about the closest thing I know of." With that, she gave me another vacant smile and walked off.

It hadn't been the code response.

I found an empty blackjack table manned by a bored looking dealer and sat down to play. After I'd lost a bit of money, I jerked my chin toward the woman as she made the rounds through the various tables.

"New pit boss?" I asked. "I haven't seen her here before."

The dealer's uninterested eyes followed the gesture. "Oh, yeah. Not just her, either. New ownership came in last week and took a broom to the entire management team—swept 'em right out the door."

"Huh," I said. "That's pretty crazy. Hit me again, please."

He dealt me a six, for a total of eighteen.

"Stand," I said.

The dealer flipped over the hole card, revealing two tens.

After a couple more games, I tipped the guy and headed out.

"Well?" Alex asked, when I climbed into the Jeep and slammed the door shut.

"We're in the shit," I said without preamble. "Someone's taking out the underground in Montreal a piece at a time. They're cutting deep and fast. My guess is they must have inside knowledge."

***

Beckett's third meeting was always going to be more of a challenge to deal with — another reason we'd put it off till last. This was the high-level stuff, where we assumed he'd been planning to discuss what Leo and Kam might be able to offer the underground thanks to the international diplomatic contacts they'd made over the years.

We didn't have a name. We didn't even have a location. Ironically, we might have been able to get that information from the person he'd intended to contact through the casino, but that approach was fucked, now.

"We need to go lower down the ladder, not higher," Alex said. "Find out what the foot soldiers know about the sweeps that are taking out the higher-ups."

I grunted acknowledgement. "Try The Jackal first?"

"Might as well start there," she agreed.

The Jackal was a dive bar at the edge of La Petite-Patrie, an unassuming working-class neighborhood situated south of Avenue Papineau and north of the railroad tracks. The owner wasn't a member of the underground as far as I knew, but she'd raised *not giving a shit about what her patrons got up to in her bar* to an art form. That made it a popular place for sympathizers to gather and discuss low-level business, and it meant we were likely to find a familiar face or two there.

The place was a squat brick building on the corner of two unremarkable streets, clinging like a grungy barnacle to a much larger building next to it. The neighborhood was a dump with cracks and potholes in the roads, not to mention a pervasive air of sketchiness. The view from the row of tiny, flyspecked windows along the side of the bar wall overlooked the loading dock at the back of a grocery store on the next block.

"You take me to all the nicest places," I told Alex. "Have I mentioned that lately?"

She shot me a glare and didn't reply.

Our entrance hadn't garnered much in the way of interest from the other patrons. The place was busy enough, with people getting off from their nine-to-five jobs and stopping by for a drink on their way home. I scanned the crowd, aware of Alex doing the same beside me. She touched my arm and jerked her chin toward a rat-faced man nursing a beer at the end of the bar.

His gaze flew up to us as we approached, his expression startled and wary. He looked vaguely familiar, but it wasn't anyone I knew personally. Alex apparently did, though.

"Étienne," she greeted.

The man's eyes grew wide. "Alex — what the *hell* are you doing here?"

"Good to see you, too," she said, deadpan. "I need information. Something big is going down, and we're out of the loop. We need to get back in the loop fast so we can figure out what's happening."

The guy looked like he was about to have an aneurysm. "What you need is to get the *fuck* out of *Montreal*. Are you crazy? Beckett got his name plastered all over the newspapers for breaking an unregistered omega out of police custody last month, and you're one of his alpha lapdogs. Think they're not after you, too?"

"Beckett's missing," Alex said flatly. "That's why we're here."

"Oh, *shit*." Étienne pushed his beer away. "How long has he been gone for?"

"A few days. He came to Montreal for a series of meetings and didn't come back when he was supposed to. Didn't leave a message with the usual go-between, either." Alex leaned closer. "We've been following a trail of busted businesses and casinos. What the hell is going on in this city?"

Étienne's eyes darted from side to side as though worried someone might be listening in, despite the loud buzz of conversation surrounding us. "It's been crazy for the last couple of weeks. Like, *batshit*. Every mid-level meeting place in the damned city has been hit with raids, and a lot of the higher ones, too. I almost stopped coming here to The Jackal in case they start dropping the hammer on the low-level joints, too — but it's the only way to get any news."

Alex exchanged a look with me before returning her attention to Étienne. "Is it just Montreal? Do you know? Or is this happening in other cities, too?"

He raised his hands in a helpless gesture. "No clue. The lines of communication have been cut. It's like we're under siege, and the longer it goes on the less information there is about what's happening."

There were wider implications, but only one that I was focused on right now. I tugged Alex to the side and lowered my voice, speaking close to her ear. "We're not gonna get anything useful about Beckett if everyone who might know something has already either been busted or made a run for it."

Alex was as tense as a drawn bowstring. Étienne gave a final nervous glance around the bar and rose to leave, looking like a man who would prefer to be pretty much anywhere else. Neither of us made a move to stop him.

"We need to get back to the others and reassess whether or not to cut our losses and find a different cell," Alex said. "If someone's got access to this level of information about the underground, it won't take long before the safehouse network is compromised, too."

The instinctual need to make sure Jax and the omegas were safe warred with my need to go after Beckett. I shoved the emotional turmoil aside, unwilling to deal with it.

"Okay," I said. "I'm not giving up on Beckett yet, though. Not until I know for sure that he's either dead or out of our reach for good."

Alex opened her mouth to say something, but the ambient hubbub of conversation in the bar rose abruptly in alarm. Several patrons surged to their feet, and others were crowding toward the line of grimy windows. The back of my neck prickled ominously.

"Trouble," I said unnecessarily.

Alex was already elbowing her way to one of the windows. I followed, shoving patrons out of the way until I could catch a glimpse outside, where half a dozen unmarked vans were parked across the street. Armed, black-clad figures spilled out of them in numbers that seemed ridiculous for a simple bar raid.

"*Fuck*," Alex cursed.

People were already scrambling for the exits—front and back. They were going to be met by a wall of armed police, though... assuming these were actually police and not something even more sinister.

Alex and I were both armed, but not with anything that would stand up to the kind of firepower on display outside.

"We fighting or what?" I asked, having to raise my voice over the increasing pandemonium of panicking patrons inside the bar.

"If anyone in here pulls a gun, they'll take it as an excuse to mow these people down," Alex shouted back. "Let's try to make for a back room, see if we can get behind their lines somehow and sneak out."

Assuming even a basic level of competence from the grunts outside, it wasn't a plan with a high likelihood of success—and she knew that as well as I did. Still, I scanned the interior looking for an employees-only door. Alex saw it first and pointed me in the right direction, just as the front door burst open and several small objects arced into the building.

Alex's hand closed convulsively on my arm, yanking me in the opposite direction.

"Stun grenades!" she cried, a moment before a wall of blinding light and deafening sound slammed into the crowd. I staggered and fell, the screaming that had started when the door opened cut off abruptly as my hearing went away.

ELEVEN

Jax

FLYNN AND ALEX hadn't returned, and the sense of watching a bad plan careening off the rails was becoming inescapable. There was still one more step to take before I transitioned into full-on panic mode. I'd need to check with Beckett's guy and make sure there wasn't a message waiting to explain why they were late. Then, if there wasn't one, I'd have to ask myself if I was going to abandon my pack, or if I was going to abandon the two omegas I was duty bound to protect—because it wouldn't be fair to drag Leona and Kam deeper into danger if I went after Alex and Flynn.

Kam and I were seated at the kitchen table. We had a clear line of sight to Leona, who was in the front room watching the driveway. This way, she could follow the conversation and keep an eye on things outside at the same time.

"Don't make your decision based on us," Kam was saying. "I know we'd be worse than useless in any kind of covert mission, especially with Leo's face plastered all over the news. We can stay in hiding while you do what you need to do—and if worse comes to worst, we could still buy our way out of the country if we had to."

He was trying to give me an out, and the scary part was, I might end up taking him up on it if there turned out to be no other option.

"What he said," Leona called from the other room. "My parents are hiding out under assumed identities in Jamaica. They'll help us, and if you and the others can make it there, I guarantee they'll help you and your pack, too. We could regroup and figure out what to do from there, where it's safer."

"We'll keep that option on the table," I said.

I'd wondered about her parents—she'd mentioned previously that she'd convinced them to leave the country for their own safety. They'd concealed their throwback child instead of turning her over to the Committee as they'd been legally bound to do, when she'd presented as an omega. Once her rise through the diplomatic corps had become meteoric, the danger to them became too great.

Ironically, one of the last things Leona and Kam had achieved in the diplomatic corps before Leo's arrest was the successful negotiation of a new treaty lessening the legal penalties for the so-called crime her parents had committed.

Whatever the case, I was glad to learn that they were well and evidently in a position to help her and Kam if things got really bad. I wasn't at all sure that getting out of the country would be as straightforward as Leona seemed to think, though. I guess it would depend on what kind of contacts they had access to in the underground. No unregistered omega got as far as they had without *some* kind of help, even if it was low-level stuff like acquiring pheromone suppressors.

Kam's fingers tapped against the tabletop in a nervous rhythm. "She's right that you should get out, too. And… the others."

There was a slight hesitation in the final words. I looked closer, and saw the hidden fear behind Kam's deep brown eyes. Like me, he expected the worst. He'd already written Beckett off, and he was bracing himself to do the same for the two alphas who hadn't returned to us when they said they would.

"I'm sure they just got held up and left a message with Beckett's contact," Leona said from the window. "It doesn't automatically mean something's gone wrong—it could mean they've found a lead."

There it was in a nutshell—her light to Kam's darkness. Yang to his yin. I wasn't sure if she really believed her own words, or if she was only trying to lighten the atmosphere of dread hanging over the room. To be fair, she might be absolutely right. Once upon a time, I probably would have assumed the best instead of the worst, too.

When the *hell* had that changed, anyway?

"Hopefully you're right," I said. "Whatever the case, I think we should find a new place to hide out. We've been here too long. We can leave a message for the others at the same time we're checking to see if they left one for us."

Kam shot Leona a speculative look. "Hmm. How do you feel about dyeing your hair, *odama*?"

She shot him a sour look. "Probably about the same as you'll feel about shaving off your beard, baby face."

He ran a hand over his short, anchor-style fringe of dark facial hair. "*Excuse me.* Do you have any idea how hard it is for an omega to grow a beard?"

"Sure," she called back. "I mean, I've heard you bitching about it often enough, right?"

They were trying to take my mind off things. Omega instinct, to comfort an upset alpha and defuse a tense situation. I wish I could say it was working.

God. Why could we not have met these two in a different world, where we could have courted them and mated them and had a *life*, instead of this constant barrage of slow-rolling crises?

"It's not the worst idea," I said, because honestly, that flaming red hair of hers *was* kind of hard to miss.

"So, we'll leave in the morning to meet with this message guy in Montreal?" Kam asked. "And buy hair dye."

"Right," I said, having no better plan. "Assuming the car's up to it, we can try for Burlington afterward and hide out there for a bit. It's only a couple of hours' drive from Montreal, and there's a fair amount of anti-Committee sentiment brewing in Vermont. Might be safer."

Kam nodded.

"Sounds good," Leona agreed. "You know, as strange as it sounds, I'm going to miss this house."

It didn't sound strange at all. This was almost certainly the first place she'd ever stayed that had a proper omega nest, for one thing.

"If I were Flynn, I'd have some kind of crass joke at the ready regarding how memorable alpha dick is," I said, trying hard not to picture Flynn captured or dead, somewhere far out of my reach.

Kam gave a soft snort. "Well, to be fair, it *is* pretty memorable."

"There's certainly a decent amount of alpha dick tied up in my growing nostalgia for the place," Leona agreed solemnly.

I couldn't help a short laugh, despite the darkness surrounding us. For a few shining days, things had been idyllic. A pack house—though admittedly, a borrowed one—shared with people I'd happily spend the rest of my life with. Now, the question had once again become how short the rest of my life was likely to be.

"I'm honored that you chose to let us share your heat," I said. "And I know the others feel the same way."

Kam's eyebrows twitched upward a fraction. "What, even Alex?"

I gave him a sad smile. "You're the first omega she's been with since she lost her mate and pups years ago. That should tell you everything you need to know." I cleared my throat. "Anyway, take some time today and gather up everything you intend to take with us, but pack light. I'm going to see about dinner."

I got up to wrangle a decent meal for the three of us, hoping to make up for the fact that I'd left the bulk of the cooking to them over the past few days while I obsessed about the untenable security situation on the property. After making sure they were fed and set for the evening, I did a last circuit of the property line before dark, ensuring that all of the booby traps were still in place. Then I packed up my belongings and went to bed, determined to get a few hours of sleep before relieving Kam from his watch at three a.m.

I was somewhat successful in that endeavor, though my dreams were, to put it mildly, not the best. When I strapped on my shoulder and hip holsters and made my way quietly through the darkened house to the downstairs living room, it was to find that the two omegas had dragged the old sofa to a position in front of the window. Kam was seated near one end, dutifully keeping the watch, while Leona lay curled up against his side, wrapped in an afghan and fast asleep.

Kam glanced up at me as I approached, pausing in his rhythmic stroking of her fiery hair. I stopped, looking down at them—struck for the hundredth time by the picture they made together.

"Hi," Kam said softly. "I think we're both a bit on edge. Is it okay if we curl up here and help you stay awake by snoring at you?"

My heart clenched, falling victim yet again to the kryptonite these two seemed to possess.

"Always," I said.

"Thanks." Kam yawned, lifting the hand that wasn't cradling Leona to cover his mouth as he did.

"Nothing to report, except a confused looking deer that wandered up a few hours ago and then bounded off in a huff. What time did you want to leave in the morning?"

"Let's say eight o'clock," I decided. "We can grab some breakfast first, and it should still give us plenty of time to get to Montreal, check in with Beckett's contact, and drive down to Burlington before dark."

"Assuming the Franken-Chrysler doesn't break down along the way," Kam said.

"I'm sure it will be fine," I told him, since I suspected that the car was going to be the least of our worries.

I was ridiculously and irrationally charmed by the fact that our quiet conversation hadn't caused Leona to so much as stir — though she did mumble a sleepy protest when Kam shuffled them around so he was lying full length on the couch with her body sprawled half on top of his. Giving into temptation, I settled into the small space left between the throw pillow Kam was using to support his head, and the sofa arm.

It provided a perfectly good view of the driveway, and had the added benefit of leaving both of them within easy reach. As I alternated stroking my right hand through first Leona's hair and then Kam's, the sweet aura of drowsy omegas leant me a fragile sense of peace as I contemplated what we might find tomorrow. Maybe Leona was right, and the others had found a promising lead on Beckett. Maybe we could still get him back and find a safe harbor somewhere. *Together.*

My thin veneer of serenity lasted for an hour or so, until the distant clatter of metal cans and plastic jugs on the far side of the house jerked my head around. Adrenaline flooded my system like an electric shock.

TWELVE

Jax

THE TWO omegas at my side were instantly awake, instinct pulling them from sleep in response to my sudden tension.

"What is it?" Leona asked, terror underlying her hoarse whisper.

It occurred to me what had happened to her the last time she'd been abruptly awoken from a sound sleep in the middle of the night. Unfortunately, I couldn't guarantee it wasn't about to happen again, even though whoever was outside would have to get past me to get to either of them.

"Something tripped one of the alarms," I said, rising to my feet. "Could be another wandering deer. Could be something worse."

Her eyes were very wide, luminous in the weak moonlight filtering through the trees outside.

"What should we do?" Kam asked quietly. He sounded more resigned than panicked.

"I need you to get the box of Molotov cocktails out of the storage room and soak the wicks with vodka." I pulled a lighter out of my pocket and handed it to him. "Leona, watch the driveway while I get to the other side of the house and check on the disturbance. Give a yell if you see anyone approaching from the front."

They both nodded their understanding. With a deep breath, I hurried off to see how much shit we were in, leaving them to get things prepped at the front of the house. Using the Molotovs in a wooded area like this was a gamble, but we were seriously low on options. There was no wind to speak of tonight, and I was banking on the surrounding forest being too damp to sustain the kind of fire that might blow back on us and burn down the house.

At best, the homemade firebombs might give anyone approaching second thoughts, while also illuminating the scene outside to give me a better view of my targets. At worst, they'd cause a bit more chaos than I could manage alone with just a pair of semiautomatic handguns.

I jogged through the house, my nerve-damaged left side complaining with every step. My head ached a bit more than usual tonight, not helped by the current adrenaline dump.

Suck it up, buttercup. I could almost hear Flynn's voice in my ear. As long as my vision didn't start swimming badly enough to affect my aim, I'd deal with it.

The safehouse had security lights on each of the outside walls, but we'd kept them off to avoid attention from anyone who might have a clear line of sight to the house at night. No point in advertising our presence here, after all.

Now, however, I charged into the dining room on the side of the house where the noise had come from and switched on the exterior floodlight. It illuminated the woods beyond the grassy side yard, throwing crazy shadows among the branches and tree trunks.

Some of those shadows were moving.

"*Fuck*," I breathed.

We'd left the window open, to make listening for noise coming from outside easier. Standing to one side, out of the line of fire, I pulled the gun from my shoulder holster, checked the clip, and loosed a shot in the direction of the movement among the trees. I held out very little hope of hitting anything through the confusion of trees and underbrush, but getting confirmation that we were armed and aware of their approach might at least slow our attackers down and make them rethink their strategy.

I ducked behind the cover of the wall again, waiting to see if there'd be any immediate return fire. There wasn't.

Leona slipped into the room a few moments later. I waved at her to stay out of any potential line of sight from outside. She crouched low and skirted the wall to approach me.

"There are people moving around in front, and also on the west side of the house," she said. Her voice was shaking. "The east side is so overgrown that it's difficult to tell, but there may be some there, too. It's hard to see how many there are, exactly, but... well... it's a lot."

We were in trouble, and she knew it.

"The moment anyone leaves the tree line, you lob a Molotov at them," I said, just as another clatter of tin cans came from the woods to the west. "I'll try to keep them busy here and on the east side. They haven't fired on us yet, but there's no question they'll be armed. Stay away from the windows except to hurl bottles at them."

"Jax," she said quietly. "There are too many. The three of us won't be able to fight them off by ourselves."

"If they get in, you and Kam run upstairs to the nest," I said, not answering her directly. "I'll try to hold them at the bottom of the stairs."

She gave me a heartbroken look, and it was fucking Romania all over again—knowing that all I could do was die for them, and it still wouldn't be enough. I could tell she wanted to argue with me. Instead, she reached up and grasped the back of my neck, pulling me down for a brief kiss.

"All right," she whispered, her voice husky with emotion. "Thank you, Jax."

My throat tried to close up, but we didn't have time for that kind of shit.

"Go," I managed. "Throw a few bottles at them and make them think twice about leaving the trees."

With a hesitant nod, she retraced her steps along the wall and ducked out, returning to her *odama* at the front of the house. I shoved every emotion except cold anger down into the deep, dark pit behind my ribs, and snuck another look out of the corner of the window. The shadows seemed closer, so I let off another shot—painfully aware that my supply of ammunition was far from bottomless.

It was barely two minutes later when several things happened at once. I smelled burning cloth, and heard Kam's grunt of effort as he presumably hurled the first Molotov cocktail out of the window. The muted crash of breaking glass and a distant roar of flames outside coincided with a high-intensity spotlight flaring into life at the edge of the tree line, directed right into the window I was peering out of.

The dazzling light blinded me, obscuring what was going on behind it. I cursed sharply and lifted my gun, trying to aim for the source and take it out. It took four shots before I heard the crash of something shattering and the spotlight went dark, leaving me blinking away afterimages. Before I could clear my vision, a second, identical light came on, every bit as powerful as the first. My headache pounded with renewed viciousness in response. I clenched my jaw against the pain and sent half a dozen more shots out the window—all without obvious effect.

Staggering away, I kept a hand on the wall in an effort not to run into anything, and headed for the east side of the house to try and discourage the ones on that side from getting too cocky. I arrived to find the same thing there — multiple high-intensity lights playing over the house in a blinding onslaught that made it impossible to get a bead on the approaching forces. I shot a few rounds at them anyway and succeeded in taking out one light — but it didn't make much difference with others still drilling holes through my skull.

From the sounds of it, Kam and Leo were still lobbing Molotovs — though I had little doubt they were facing similar conditions. I headed to the living room to grab a few of the gasoline-filled bottles for myself, figuring they might end up being a more effective weapon at this point.

A metallic clanking noise came from elsewhere in the house, like something had hit the floor and rolled. It sounded as though it had come from the dining room, and all the tiny hairs on the back of my neck stood up in unison. A low hissing noise followed a second later.

"Fuck!" I charged back to the room. I could barely fucking see with the brutal light coming from outside, but the sound of escaping gas was enough to guide me to a small canister on the floor. Holding my breath, I scooped it up and hurled it out the same window it had just come through.

Around the house, more clunks sounded, followed by more hissing. A second canister arced through the dining room window and skittered against the wall. I scrambled for it, getting a face full of pale, odorless gas as it hissed into life before I could toss it outside with the other one.

Rather than wait around, I stumbled toward the front room in search of Leona and Kam, uncomfortably aware of the faint numbness settling over my extremities after even such a brief exposure to whatever the fuck was in those devices. I absolutely refused to think about the VX nerve agent derivative the terrorists had been working on. Right now, all that mattered was making sure the omegas got away from it.

I slid to a halt in the doorway to find Kam slamming an upside down wastebasket over one canister, while Leona lunged for one sitting in the corner and threw it outside. There were more of them in the other rooms, too—the crazy beams of blinding light from outside illuminated wisps of white vapor rolling along the floor like someone had switched on a Hollywood fog machine inside the house.

Another canister clattered into the living room and ricocheted off the wall, sliding under the sofa and bursting into hissing life.

"Get upstairs!" I ordered, appalled to find that my words were slurring. "Keep th' windows closed so they can't throw any into the second floor. I'll clear these out!"

Vapor streamed from beneath the upended trashcan. Leona—who'd been tugging fruitlessly at one corner of the sofa in an attempt to get to the other one—fell to one knee, coughing. Kam and I lunged for her in unison.

"Get her out!" I ordered, pressing her into Kam's arms and grabbing the sofa myself. He staggered in the direction of the staircase as I shoved the offending furniture away and tried to feel around through the growing cloud of gas for the source of the hissing. The air in the room was growing hazy, and I could barely make out the pair going down in a tangle of limbs just before they reached the doorway.

"*Jax!*" Kam's hoarse cry dissolved into coughing.

He sounded like he was shouting down a long tunnel, even though he was barely fifteen feet away. My clumsy fingers bumped against a metallic casing. When I tried to pick it up so I could throw it away, the whole floor came along with it and slammed me unceremoniously in the face.

I lay on the hardwood, disoriented—trying to remember which way was up so I could get my damned face out of the gas. Despite my efforts to push my body upright with my arms, nothing happened. Distantly, I heard the sound of men shouting orders outside. Boots pounded across gravel, but it might as well have been happening on a different planet as far as my brain was concerned.

Maybe if I just close my eyes for a second, I thought. *Just to regroup...*

I didn't open them again.

THIRTEEN

Leona

I WOKE UP with a pounding headache and my tongue stuck to the roof of my mouth. An unpleasantly hazy blank space separated my memories of the recent past—searchlights blinding me as hissing metal canisters flew through the windows—from wherever the hell I was now.

There was a kind of strange hissing background noise here, too—but it was different than before. More of a low drone. *Airplane,* my brain identified helpfully. I pried sticky eyelids open. It felt like dragging sandpaper across my eyeballs, and I could only see blurry shapes without detail. To make matters even more unpleasant, I desperately needed to use the restroom.

A soft groan of distress escaped my lips. I would have committed murder for a glass of water.

"Leo?" Kam's soft rasp cut through my confusion like a razor blade. It sliced through my numbness to release the cold terror that I'd forgotten about in my drugged haze.

I made another wordless noise and reached in the direction his voice had come from. My arm jerked to a halt, unyielding metal digging into my wrist. I pulled fitfully against the restraint. Metal clinked against metal.

"You're handcuffed to the seat," Kam said hoarsely. "We both are. We're on a plane—flying south, I think. Are you all right?"

More memories crowded in. Dear god — *the gas canisters*. I'd thought they'd used the nerve agent on us… that we were all as good as dead.

"We're alive?" I croaked. It came out sounding like a question. I tried to reach for him again, only to remember the handcuff when it pulled me up short. I lifted the other arm instead, reaching awkwardly across my body. Chilly fingers tangled with mine and squeezed.

"For the moment, we are," Kam replied.

I blinked rapidly, desperate to get some moisture in my eyes. "Jax?" I asked, dreading the answer.

"Here," came the tight reply.

Tears of relief at the proof that all three of us had survived finally allowed me to lubricate my eyeballs, and blink my surroundings into some kind of focus. We were on a mid-sized turboprop plane, based on the engine noise. It was daytime. Kam and I were each handcuffed to our metal seat frames by our right wrists, with our left arms free. Jax, by contrast, was shackled hand and foot, his muscles bulging as he strained against his bondage.

We were at the front of the plane — Kam next to me in the window seat, with Jax across the aisle from us. I craned to look behind me and found a good two dozen stony-faced military or paramilitary types watching us fixedly. My stomach dropped.

One of them unbuckled his seatbelt and rose, approaching us. He stopped and looked down at me for a moment before extending a canteen toward me. An angry red burn mark covered his right cheekbone — a few blisters decorating the center, and the eyebrow on that side half singed away.

"Drink," he said, in a heavily accented voice.

Russian? From the heavy vowel and the way he swallowed the 'k,' I thought it must be.

I let go of my grip on Kam and took the canteen cautiously, holding it with my free hand so I could unscrew the top with my cuffed hand. The water was lukewarm but seemed fresh, so I drank cautiously — cognizant of the current state of my bladder.

The fear was going to hit me properly any time now. There was only one thing this could mean — we'd been captured by the Committee. And yet... aspects of the situation felt *off*, somehow.

I offered the canteen to Kam. He shook his head, so I capped it again and handed it back to the soldier.

"Thank you," I told him, trying to feel out the situation a bit more. "May I ask whose custody we're in?"

The part of me that remembered being dragged out of my apartment in the middle of the night wanted to cringe back in fear, expecting a blow in retaliation for my question. But my higher brain functions were still rebooting — not quite on board with the program yet. It allowed me to pretend this wasn't what it realistically had to be, and let me act with a level of courage and detachment I probably wouldn't have been capable of displaying otherwise.

"You are prisoners of the Euro-Soviet branch of the Committee on Alphomic Suppression, *malyshka*," he said. I'd been right — there was no mistaking his Russian accent. "Be glad you did not succeed in killing any of my men, or this flight might have been much less pleasant for everyone involved."

Jax jerked sharply against one of his wrist shackles, the seat frame creaking with strain. It was pretty clear he'd have been happy to take his chances with that.

"Where are you taking us?" Kam asked, trying his luck since the soldier seemed willing to talk.

"That is not your concern," the man said.

"Why the Euro-Soviet branch, though?" I pressed, desperately attempting to get some more brain cells firing. "Why not the North American branch? Aren't we outside your jurisdiction?"

The man gave a thin smile that twisted with discomfort when it pulled at his burn injury. I wondered which of our Molotov cocktails had been the one to get him.

"Not for much longer," he said.

That was unhelpfully cryptic. Practicality raised its head before I ended up making him angry or driving him back to his seat.

"I really need to use the bathroom. Is that allowed?" I asked, doing my best to look unthreatening. Not a stretch, really.

He beckoned to another of the soldiers, who came and joined him in the aisle. The second man removed a small keychain from his pocket and leaned down, unlatching my cuffs.

I rubbed at my wrist, rising on wobbly legs as the new soldier stepped back to give me space. He gestured toward the rear of the plane.

Jax rattled his cuffs again. "Touch her, and I'll see you dead, even if I have to crash this plane to do it," he said, his tone murderous.

It hit me rather abruptly that Jax was… *not okay*. Which, I mean, *fair enough*. None of us were okay. I was still functioning because the situation hadn't hit me properly yet. And Kam only went to pieces *after* a crisis; never *during* a crisis.

"It's all right," I told Jax softly, begging him with my eyes not to provoke our captors. "If they wanted to hurt us, they'd have done it already."

This was the Committee, after all. The torture and death would come later.

The thought sent my balance slewing sideways for a second. I grasped the chair back and steadied myself, allowing the soldier who'd uncuffed me to usher me past the rows of uniformed beta males. Their eyes were a heavy weight on me, but none of them raised a hand or spoke a word as I squeezed past them in the narrow aisle.

The bathroom was barely big enough to sit down, and my guard didn't blink an eye when I closed the door and engaged the privacy lock. When I was done, I washed my hands and splashed water on my face from the tiny sink, then straightened my shoulders and exited. The guard led me back to my seat, where the man with the burned face still stood watch over Jax and Kam. Once I was handcuffed again, they both left, returning to their seats without a word.

"This doesn't make sense," Kam said in a low voice.

There was little doubt that the closest soldiers would be able to hear us, but they didn't show any indication that they cared whether we talked to each other or not.

"No," I agreed. "It should have been Enoch Sloane's operation. Why is the Euro-Soviet branch poaching on UFNA territory?"

"Turf wars," Jax muttered, still looking like he'd enjoy nothing better than getting free and ripping out some spines.

I traded a considering glance with Kam. It was an open secret that Kostya Nikolayev, the head of the Euro-Soviet branch, was locked in a power struggle with Enoch Sloane.

"Maybe," I allowed.

"Too bad that doesn't really help us," Kam said.

Unfortunately, I had to agree with him.

<hr>

When the plane finally banked some time later, making a final approach for landing, Kam peered through the window, craning to look down. "That's

Cuba, I'm pretty sure," he said, his brow furrowing. "We passed over the Florida Keys not long ago."

I stretched, crowding against him to get a look as well. Based on the long, narrow shape of the island, he was right. We were heading for the one of the southeastern provinces—a green and mountainous stretch of land. With a sudden ache in my heart, I realized that I was, at this moment, only five hundred miles or so away from my parents in Kingston—separated by nothing but a tiny expanse of salt water.

Hi, Mom and Dad.

Bye, Mom and Dad.

"Cuba has strong Russian ties," Jax said.

"Makes sense," I replied. The island nation had so far managed to avoid being snapped up by the United Federation of North America as either a territory or a protectorate. They'd done that by playing footsie with the Soviets, who were more than happy to have an ally located a scant hundred miles off the coastline of their rival on the world stage.

My insides rose unpleasantly as the plane shed altitude. The runway where we eventually touched down was a bit bumpy, but serviceable—obviously a private airfield, though an expensive one based on the size. Mountain slopes draped in vibrant green tropical forest vegetation surrounded the narrow valley containing the airstrip. The plane taxied to a stop in front of a hangar with corrugated metal siding, where several black, official looking vehicles waited next to an army truck with canvas covering the back.

The sound of the men behind us unlatching their seatbelts dragged my attention away from the window. Four of them approached us, including the two who'd been up here earlier to give me water and take me to the bathroom.

"This is what will happen next," said the one who seemed to be in charge. His eyes settled on Jax. "You will all be taken to a vehicle and transferred to a holding facility for processing. Two guards will escort your omega companions, with guns trained on them the whole time. If you attempt to resist or escape, they will shoot. Do you understand?"

"Yes," Jax said, his eyes promising bloody vengeance at some unspecified future date.

My heart sped up, tripping over itself at the thought that we would soon be separated. And then, the real horrors would begin. The panic that had been lurking beneath the surface of my thoughts rippled, threatening to surge up and swallow me.

Would it be better to end it here? To fight back, and provoke them into shooting all three of us? But... I couldn't watch as Kam and Jax were shot down, their lives bleeding onto the ground in front of me. I *couldn't.*

And there was also the mystery behind the Euro-Soviets' interference. Why them, and not Sloane's men? Why *Cuba*? It didn't make any sense, and part of me was desperate to solve the puzzle. As horrified as I was at the thought of being separated from the others, at least then I wouldn't have to watch them suffer... or die. Just like they wouldn't have to watch me suffer and die.

We had a little more time until I had to let them go. We had the vehicle ride to this *holding facility*.

Two guards unhooked Jax's shackles and urged him to his feet at gunpoint. I stood up when my guard indicated I should, trying to control my trembling as a gun barrel pressed lightly against my back. Behind me, I heard Kam rise as well. We trooped out of the cabin, and descended a portable staircase that had been rolled into place at the plane's entrance.

The sun was dazzling. It was a perfectly warm, balmy tropical day. A faint breeze rustled my hair. The air smelled of damp earth and growing things, marred slightly by the exhaust from the plane and the parked vehicles.

Our guards directed us toward the back of the military truck.

"Get in," said Kam's guard.

Kam found a hand and foothold and clambered into the covered truck bed, his guard following right behind.

"You, too," said the man behind me, nudging me with the gun.

I was still shaky with emotional reaction—not to mention the dregs of the tranquilizing gas—but I managed to climb in after a couple of clumsy false starts. There was a space on the bench next to Kam, and neither of the guards protested when I took it, my thigh pressing against my *odama*'s. They didn't protest when I took his hand, either, curling our fingers together for comfort. The second guard merely sat down on my other side, the pair of them hemming us in, guns still trained on us.

Jax entered, favoring his left side heavily.

"Sit there," said one of the guards, indicating the bench against the opposite side of the truck bed from us. The alpha complied, warily assessing our situation, and was promptly flanked by his two armed guards.

The vehicle jerked into motion, jouncing and swaying. I considered trying to engage the soldiers in conversation in an attempt to get more information, but the engine rumbled loudly and the air in the covered bed stank of diesel exhaust. Besides, what did I truly expect to accomplish? These men were hired muscle, nothing more—even if they'd showed more restraint in their dealings with us than I might have expected.

I squeezed Kam's hand tighter and leaned against him, staying silent.

The weight of Jax's bloodshot blue gaze rested on me heavily. I met his eyes, even though doing so was painful. He glanced away, but not before I saw the fear lurking in his expression. A moment later, our gazes connected again, and he let me see his silent apology for not somehow magically having prevented all of this.

He was alone, separated from his pack and sick with worry over their safety. For the second time in only a handful of months, he'd been thrust into the role of sole protector to two omegas, pitted against overwhelming odds. This time, his failure would certainly mean his death... but that wasn't the part that was eating him up.

It was us. Kam and me.

We wouldn't have wanted anyone else as a protector, I tried to convey wordlessly. Maybe I should have gathered my courage and said it aloud, but the idea of giving these beta Committee soldiers a glimpse into something so personal was unbearable.

The journey dragged, though it probably didn't last more than twenty minutes in reality. I spent it pressing my body as closely as I could against Kam's—trying to ignore the guns pointed at us. Instead, I watched the thoughts and regrets scull behind Jax's eyes like clouds against a brilliant summer sky.

The unpleasant judder of bad roads and worn suspension eased to something smoother. Paved, I was fairly sure. We couldn't see anything with the canvas pulled across the opening in the back, but I sensed we were close to our destination. I soaked in the presence of the others, not knowing when I might need these final memories of closeness to hold a worse reality at bay.

The truck rolled to a stop with a high-pitched squeal of brakes, and a fresh puff of diesel exhaust made my nose wrinkle. One of Jax's guards pulled the canvas flap covering the opening aside.

As perfunctorily as they'd ordered us into the truck, the soldiers ushered us down from the bed. I swayed, my knees threatening to give way, but the man guarding me steadied me with one hand.

I looked around, taking in our surroundings. We were on some kind of private estate. The area was every bit as secluded as the airstrip had been. There was a massive house in the Colonial style of architecture standing nearby, its exterior white and gleaming in the afternoon light. Our escorts herded us toward a large outbuilding. While not nearly as ornate, it appeared to be of the same solid brick and stone construction as the house.

Holding facility, the lead guard had said.

This wasn't what I'd pictured, but it would be every bit as inescapable as a prison. For one thing, there was nowhere to run except into the endless mountain forests. And even that much would be a stretch—dozens of uniformed guards patrolled the property with high-powered rifles slung over their shoulders.

It was likely the Committee had properties like this one scattered across the world. With a chill, I wondered what horrors lay within the square outbuilding with its small, high windows and plain white facade.

We found out soon enough. The main entrance opened onto a guard station, which wasn't unexpected. There, we were handed off to new guards led by a slender woman with a military cap pulled low on her forehead, the bill throwing her face into shadow. She and her underlings were armed, and every bit as no-nonsense as the soldiers on the plane had been.

I noticed Jax giving the woman an odd look—perhaps surprised to find a female in a position of power within the reactionary ranks of the Committee. The male guards prodded us into motion, ushering us down a hallway and through an electronic security door. Beyond lay a second doorway. It was vaguely reminiscent of the thick metal cell door in the terrorist cave in Romania, and I couldn't suppress a shiver.

When the woman opened it, however, the room beyond appeared to be a basic but pleasant living space with a decently sized bed, table, chairs, sink, toilet, and even a homey rug covering the concrete floor. I blinked in confusion.

"In," said the woman in a light Russian accent, and Jax pierced her with another long stare.

"All three of us?" Kam asked hesitantly.

"Yes," she said. "Move."

We entered, having little choice since the security door behind us was already closed. The woman drew her sidearm but kept it pointed at the ground.

She jerked her head toward the table and chairs. "Sit."

Cautiously, we crossed and did as we were told. I locked eyes with Kam—his left shoulder lifted in a bewildered shrug. Once we were seated, she turned to her subordinates.

"Close the door and wait outside," she ordered in a clear tone of command.

The men left without question, closing the door behind them and leaving us alone with the woman. She regarded us from beneath her cap, face still in shadow.

"Be aware that if you were to succeed in overpowering me—which is doubtful—it would not help you escape this room." She stepped back to lean her shoulders against the wall. "And now, we will talk."

"Show us your face," Jax rasped. "*Show me your face*, damn it."

Full, red lips twitched beneath the cap's shadow. The woman lifted a hand to tug it free, the gun in her other hand never wavering. Honey blonde hair swept up in a practical chignon topped a pixie-like face with large gray eyes. I heard Jax draw in a sharp breath. Kam and I traded a brief, mystified look.

"*Irina*," Jax breathed, barely the shape of a word.

Irina smiled, sharp and sibylline. "Hello, Jax. Fancy meeting you here."

FOURTEEN

Leona

KAM AND I gaped at them. *Irina*? As in, *Alex's* Irina? What the actual... *what*? Of course, Jax looked every bit as gobsmacked as I felt. Maybe even more so.

"You... you're... not dead?" he choked out, at more of a loss than I'd ever seen him before. In the next instant, anger slid over his pleasant features. "And you're working for *them*?"

Not just anger. Rage. It dripped from every pore.

Irina raised an eyebrow. "No, Jax—I've cunningly infiltrated their operation over the course of several years, and now I've randomly decided to blow my own cover by talking to someone who can identify me. I know you've had a rough day, but do at least *try* to use your fucking brain."

A low, menacing growl rumbled through Jax's chest.

"Excuse me," I said, rising from the table and stepping in front of Jax before alpha rage could get the better of him. Kam mirrored me, and between us we cut the woman off from his line of sight. "It's pretty clear there are some undercurrents here I don't understand, but for now, maybe you can tell me why we're in Euro-Soviet custody after an operation that took place inside UFNA territory."

"Oh good," Irina said. "Someone's still using their brain, at least."

"Chairman Nikolayev and Chairman Sloane have a very public feud," Kam suggested. "And Leona McCready is a high-profile fugitive. Catching her seems like it would be something of a coup in PR terms."

"*Two* people using their brains," Irina said. "Even better! But no, that's not it."

"Then what?" Jax snarled. I glanced back to find him gripping the edge of the table with an intensity that might splinter the wood at any moment.

"Enoch Sloane has Rhys Beckett," Irina said simply. "And *that* is a serious problem for everyone."

My heart sank, even though Beckett's capture by the Committee had always been the most likely scenario to explain his disappearance.

"Why is it a problem?" Kam asked cautiously. "Again, it seems as though it would be a cause for celebration among the Committee higher-ups."

"You might think so," Irina agreed, grim-faced. "But here's the thing—Sloane isn't running him through the usual channels. He's keeping Beckett off the books. And now, we have reason to think Sloane has also acquired effective leverage to use against him."

"Leverage," I echoed, my stomach joining my heart in free fall. "What does that mean, exactly?"

"It means Sloane's got Alex and Flynn as well," Jax grated. "And he thinks he can use them to crack Beckett wide open. *Fuck.*"

Irina met my eyes. "Sloane wants the identity of Beckett's mate. It's absolutely vital that he doesn't get it."

A fresh jolt of disquiet tightened my shoulders at the casual way Irina had thrown that little-known fact at our feet. The idea that Beckett's omega status was apparently common knowledge inside the Committee was bad enough. That they also knew about the existence of his secret mate seemed inconceivable.

"So Nikolayev wants the information instead?" I asked, still trying to arrange these puzzle pieces into something that made sense, when all I really wanted to do was crawl into a corner and rock mindlessly back and forth for a bit.

"Sloane will use the information like a wrecking ball, not caring what's destroyed in the course of his jihad," Irina replied. "Nikolayev moved to ensure that Sloane didn't get hold of you, too. Not that it will matter in the end, if Sloane is able to achieve what he wants using the tools he already has."

"And by tools—"

Jax grunted and cut me off. "She means Flynn and Alex." I glanced over my shoulder in time to see him shoot Irina a look of pure hatred.

There was a faint pause, and then Kam asked, "How did Nikolayev discover the location of the safehouse where we were staying?"

It was a good point. If Sloane had tortured the information out of Beckett, that would at least have made sense. But how would *Nikolayev* have gained access to that kind of closely guarded knowledge?

"He knows all sorts of things you might not expect him to," Irina said. "It's kind of his thing."

"I want to talk to him," I said impulsively. It was half a lie—I did not, in fact, want to face the terrifying Committee chairman, especially as his prisoner.

His… strangely well-treated prisoner.

But Nikolayev was a reptile, whereas Sloane was a rabid dog. My rational mind screamed that they were equally dangerous—just in different ways. But my instincts remembered the cold-blooded concessions Nikolayev had made to me at the summit. He understood the necessity of give-and-take when larger things were at stake. He was *rational.*

At least, he was rational if you ignored the stories about what he'd done to his throwback sister, and the fact that he'd allegedly enjoyed hunting omegas like animals for sport when he was younger. Gooseflesh prickled over my body, despite the fact that the cell was pleasantly warm.

"The chairman is already on his way here," Irina said. "I've no doubt he'll want to talk to you, too."

Great. *There* was a conversation to look forward to. Be careful what you ask for…

"Tell me something, traitor," Jax said, in a low, dangerous tone. "Since you're still alive, what about the pups? Alex's pups?"

Irina went very still for a moment. Her voice grew thin and distant as she said, "They're dead and burned to ash, torn from my body… just like our mating bond." Then she blinked free of her momentary reverie. "I will leave you now. Food and drink will arrive shortly. After that, you have my word that you will not be disturbed until morning."

With that, she turned her back on us and left the cell. The sound of the lock clicking into place echoed behind her.

✦

The food came as promised. We ate it, because that seemed like a better decision than not eating it and being hungry. It wasn't drugged. It wasn't even disgusting slop. Large parts of the current situation still didn't make sense.

Additionally, Jax was losing it. With his boss and packmates captured and quite possibly undergoing torture at Enoch Sloane's hands, the three of us in Committee custody, and a ghost from the past haunting him, our kindhearted alpha had finally reached capacity.

"It's crazy," he said, pacing back and forth across the cell with hitching, uneven strides. He scrubbed a hand through his close-cropped blond hair, ruffling it. "This is *crazy*. Why would she work for them after what they did to her?"

"How certain are you that she's telling the truth about the pups?" I asked, hating that there was even a question about it.

It was Kam who answered. He was sprawled on the bed, rumpled and obviously exhausted. "If Alex felt the bond break, the only possibility I can see is that they cut out Irina's mating gland. And if that's the case, it's unlikely the pregnancy could have continued to term, even if they didn't sterilize her at the same time. The hormonal disruption would have been too much."

Jax growled, and didn't pause in his restless pacing. "Right. So they mutilated her, killed her pups, and now she's acting like Nikolayev's pet lapdog? That's even worse."

I tapped a fingernail against the table. "Why is she alive at all? She was an unregistered omega openly infiltrating the beta military. She should be dead."

"Another good point," Kam agreed.

"And once again, she was captured in the UFNA, but here she is with the Euro-Soviets." I sighed. "If we were free and we still had our positions at the Foreign Office, we could at least dig into the court records. Find out what her official fate was supposed to be."

"If we were free, we could do a lot of things," Jax said, frustration rolling off him in waves.

"As much as we might wonder what's going through Irina's head, there's another angle I don't get," I mused. "What's the value in keeping her? From Nikolayev's perspective, I mean? She's an omega. Yes, she was in the beta military, but only on the admin side, right?"

"Yeah," Jax confirmed.

"So what makes a brainwashed omega valuable enough for him to not only keep her alive, but put her in a position of authority over beta soldiers?" I glanced between my two companions. "Why not use a brainwashed alpha instead? Or, for that matter, just use betas since the entire point of the organization is to get rid of alphas and omegas?"

"Omegas can be fighters, too," Kam said quietly. "It's a different skill set—speed and flexibility rather than brute strength. Just look at Beckett. But you're right, in the context of the Committee, it doesn't make a lot of sense."

Jax came to an abrupt halt in the center of the room. His eyes bored into me. "I don't want you alone with Nikolayev." His blue gaze played over Kam as well. "Either of you."

I didn't want to be alone with Nikolayev either, but my wants—and Jax's—didn't really come into it at this point.

"Jax," I said, as calmly as I could manage. "We're prisoners. As much as I appreciate having you here, you can't protect us now."

That was probably a harsh thing to say to an alpha—confirmed when Jax snapped, *"You think I don't know that?"* with a whipcrack of alpha bark in the words.

Kam and I flinched in unison. Jax froze, his shoulders a rigid line of tension.

"I'm sorry," he breathed. "Shit—I'm sorry. I didn't mean to bark."

I forced myself to relax, unclenching my muscles one by one. "We know. It's okay. We're all on edge."

He seemed to deflate, pulling out the chair across from me and sinking into it. He put his elbows on the table and scrubbed the heels of his hands against his eye sockets before looking up with a sigh.

"You know what I can't stop thinking about?" he asked.

"What?" I said.

He blew out a sharp breath. "If we were all mated, I'd at least be able to tell if Alex and Flynn are okay. If they're in pain, or..." He trailed off and shook his head.

"They're almost certainly not *okay*," Kam said, quietly brutal. "Knowing what Alex went through with Irina, would you really want a front-row seat for whatever's happening to them?"

Jax was silent for a long moment.

"Yes," he said hoarsely, and just like that, the fragile bravado that had sustained me up to this point fled. I wanted to cling to him and cry.

"We're in a cell inside a remote compound in rural Cuba," Kam went on. "We've been given assurances that no one will disturb us until morning. That might be true or it might be false, but in the end, I'm not sure it really matters. There is quite literally nothing productive we can do until Nikolayev or someone else in power shows up to talk with us. I, for one, have no desire to huddle on this bed alone while you two stay up all night exhausting yourselves with what-ifs. So would both of you please come over here and ensure I don't have to do that?"

I wiped away a stray tear that escaped my shaky control. We'd been given the gift of one more night together, even if we were missing some of the people who should have been here with us. Tomorrow was shrouded in a fog of uncertainty. Tonight might be all we had left.

Rising from the table, I held my hand out to Jax. After the smallest of hesitations, he took it.

"We're making a habit of this," I told him, leading him toward the bed. "The three of us stuck in a cell together."

"At least this time you can hold us properly, instead of sitting against the far wall with your dick out," Kam put in. "The lack of untreated shrapnel wounds is a nice touch, too."

I dropped Jax's hand and toed off my shoes. The alpha pinched the bridge of his nose and let out a pained huff that might have been distantly related to a self-deprecating laugh.

"And I still can't do a damned thing to keep you safe," he said. "It's like déjà vu all over again."

Kam shrugged. "If it makes you feel better, we can't do a damned thing to keep you safe, either. Life sucks."

And then you die, I finished silently.

Jax raised an eyebrow at Kam. "You're a real barrel of sunshine, you know."

"That's me," he agreed.

"He's loads of fun at parties," I said, trying to lighten the mood. "You know, he once accidentally-on-purpose spilled a gin and tonic down my cleavage at a Foreign Office Christmas party, when we were competing for the same internship."

Kam scowled at me. "That's a gross mischaracterization and you know it."

I shoved Jax into the center of the bed, pleased that he was distracted enough to allow it.

"All right, fine," I said, squeezing in on Jax's other side. "You only did it because my pheromone suppressor gave out early and you were trying to hide my scent before any of the betas noticed. Details, details."

"I didn't even want that internship!" Kam protested. "They were trying to foist it on me. I was *more* than happy to let you have it."

"'*Let*'?" I echoed, leaning into the banter even as I leaned into Jax's side, curling a leg over his and reaching across his chest to tangle my hand with Kam's. "You '*let*' me have it?"

"Yes," Kam said emphatically, mirroring my position on Jax's other side. "I *let* you have it. You're fabulous, Leo—but you had no idea how to employ omega wiles back then. Seriously—*none*."

Jax's arms came around our shoulders and tightened. "You're both using them now. On me."

I gazed up at him from beneath lowered lashes. "Is it working?"

He tugged me up far enough that he could press a kiss to my temple, and then my lips. Warmth crept through me from the point of contact, banishing some of the chill of fear that had been clinging to me. I watched as he pulled away and repeated the action with Kam, his movements tentative.

It occurred to me that this might well be the first time they'd kissed. Some of my memories were hazy, but I was pretty sure Flynn and Alex had been the ones to monopolize Kam during my heat.

Kam's eyes fluttered closed, and his free hand came up to brush Jax's cheek lightly. The stress-soured scent of Jax's woodsy pheromones sweetened into musky arousal between us, and I felt an answering sensation of liquid heaviness growing within the cradle of my pelvis.

Maybe it was reckless since we had no real assurance that Irina had been telling the truth, but if this was to be our last night of privacy and togetherness, my body knew *exactly* how I wanted to spend it.

FIFTEEN

Kam

IN THE END, my life had ended up far better than I could ever have expected. Mere hours ago, I'd thought I was about to join Leo and Jax as the first official victims of an experimental nerve gas. Even after waking up, the most likely scenario had seemed to involve a fate far less pleasant than being locked in a comfortable room with my packmate and a friendly alpha.

Jax was in some ways a very straightforward man, and in others, a difficult one to read. He'd kept his distance with me, at least compared to Alex and Flynn. I wasn't at all sure how our edges were supposed to fit together in the complicated puzzle of this pack-that-might-have-been.

Right now, I was desperately glad for his chapped lips sliding over mine, and his heavy-muscled arm pulling me against him almost painfully hard. As far as I was concerned, *not thinking* was the name of the game—for tonight, at least. I hadn't been exaggerating earlier. The other two would have spent a sleepless night treading and retreading the same limited set of facts in hopes of feeling more in control of events, and I would have spent a sleepless night watching them do it.

We'd have more answers tomorrow, even if they weren't answers we liked. Tonight, comfort and oblivion sounded like much more appealing options.

If nothing else, this was shaping up to be a much more civilized exit from life than the cave in Romania... so far, at least.

Jax let me up for air, and I took the chance to lean across his broad chest and catch Leo in a kiss. Her normally silky lips were chapped as well—the victim of hours of unconsciousness and the dry, recycled atmosphere in the airplane cabin. After a few moments, she pulled away and met my gaze with dark, dilated eyes.

"I want him to knot me," she said. "On a scale of one to ten, how crazy is that?"

I considered it for a moment. "It's a risk—but only if Irina lied. Though there could be hidden cameras or microphones for surveillance, I suppose."

Jax was looking between us like we were *both* crazy, which at least meant he'd stopped obsessing about Irina and Nikolayev for the moment. "If they came for us, we'd be totally vulnerable."

A stubborn gleam entered Leo's hazel eyes. "It'd be worth it to see the shock on their faces. If they hate us so damned much, they can get an eyeful of exactly what offends their fragile beta sensibilities. Fuck them all."

Maybe it was an odd thing for me to be proud about, but in that moment, I was proud of my freshly liberated *odama*. Jax let out a sharp breath and pressed his forehead against her temple for a long moment.

"Kam?" he asked. "Are you all right with this? What do you need from us?"

I tucked a strand of Leo's wild hair behind her ear. "Just let me kiss you both. That's all I want tonight."

It was the simple truth. Maybe it was the fact that I finally knew what lay on the other side of my body's capricious sexual arousal. Or maybe it was that I now knew exactly how much work was involved in getting to climax, given my body's particular… *limitations*. Whatever the case, it felt easier now to simply dwell in a low level of arousal and appreciate the feeling on its own merits. It was reminiscent of the way Leo and I used to share gentle intimacy, before this pack of alphas had come into our lives. Only, it was *more* somehow.

I could be part of this without needing to perform. My presence, accepted and desired by both of my bedmates, was enough.

Leo kissed me again, and then broke away to kiss Jax. He made a low noise and tangled his hand in her hair, taking control of her mouth while she took control of the fastenings of his trousers. I settled back to watch for a bit, breathing in the scent of aroused alpha while missing Leo's honey and orange blossom perfume—still masked beneath the pheromone suppressors Beckett had acquired for her.

She broke away with a gasp, whispering, "I love you both."

"We love you, too," I answered without hesitation.

God, how I loved her. Fiery and sweet, determined to make our fucked-up world bend to her will—even if that meant the petty defiance of taking a knot from our alpha lover in a Committee cell on the eve of our ultimate fate.

I wanted to live in the world she envisioned, where we could mate a pack of noble, adoring alphas and live together in a giant house with a cozy nest, our pups running and playing in the hallways, shrieking with happiness.

"Love you," Jax echoed quietly. "I'm sorry things couldn't be different."

"We made a difference," Leo said fiercely. "We might not have won the war, but we *did* make a difference. And we'll keep trying to make a difference until we can't anymore."

She untangled from us, but only long enough to slip off the simple sweater and leggings she'd been wearing when Nikolayev's men had taken us. Her underwear followed, exposing her petite, softly curved frame to our appreciative gazes.

Jax made a low noise, deep in his chest—and it was clear that a few days spent in Leo's heat nest had trained my body to respond to that noise. Something inside me grew soft and pliant, uncoiling from its usual tense knot.

Leo didn't waste time on foreplay. She freed Jax's cock and straddled him, sinking down on his length. He growled, the sound mellowing a moment later to a rumbling alpha purr. A whimper of pleasure escaped her in response.

"So gorgeous," Jax said. "The both of you. Kam… lose the shirt, please. I want to see more of you."

I unbuttoned the offending article of clothing in a pleasantly drugged haze, slipping out of it and pulling my white undershirt over my head as well.

"Better," Jax said, and tangled his fingers in my hair, tugging until it drew a gasp from me.

Jax had apparently been paying attention before. *Fuck.*

I melted into the pressure, but instead of dragging me to his mouth, he presented me for Leo to kiss. She attacked my lips with a ferocity I'd never felt from her before. Her fingers came up to grip my jaw, holding me where she wanted me, and I was lost.

Leo rode Jax hard, his alpha strength meeting her thrust for thrust as they passed me back and forth between them. I stopped thinking and simply felt, letting everything else go. Committee guards could have stormed the cell, and I still wouldn't have pulled away from the lips and teeth marking and sucking at my mouth, my jaw, my neck.

Jax nipped his way down the left side of my throat, his breath coming harsh. Leo's rhythmic, breathy cries rose in pitch as she careened toward her release, dragging Jax with her. With a final rough gasp, her muscles went rigid, and she jerked through her climax.

Jax groaned and spasmed as well. His teeth clamped over the juncture of my neck and shoulder—right over my mating gland. I cried out in a shocked combination of pleasure and pain as the skin broke, my blood and his saliva mixing. My entire body shook, gooseflesh erupting all over. My heart felt like it might explode, it was racing so fast.

The three of us remained suspended in that tableau for what seemed like a lifetime but was probably only seconds. Then Leo collapsed against Jax's chest, panting. I could feel the humid warmth of Jax's breath against my neck. He pulled back slowly, with the air of someone who'd just come back to himself and realized what he'd done.

The skin over my mating gland throbbed as the cooler air hit it. Blood beaded on Jax's lips.

"Oh fuck," he said. "*Fuck.* Kam, I'm sorry. I didn't mean—"

Dazed and knot-drunk, Leo came back to herself enough to peer at me with growing shock. I opened my mouth to say… something. Nothing came out.

"I didn't mean to…" Jax tried again. He trailed off and scrubbed at his mouth with the back of his hand. "I'm *so* sorry. I saw the scar where they took your gland. I didn't mean to bring back bad associations."

"Kam's left-glanded," Leo whispered, still watching me with wide eyes.

Jax blinked. "You're—"

I lifted a hand to the throbbing flesh. My fingers felt numb.

"Left-glanded," I repeated slowly. "They didn't get my mating gland because it's on my left shoulder, not my right. That's rare—they didn't bother to check first."

A look of blank shock washed over Jax's features. His gaze dropped to my hand covering the bite mark.

I let out a little laugh. It sounded wrong—not like a laugh at all. "Don't worry. It's as broken as the rest of me. It doesn't work anymore." I swayed a bit. "I feel strange."

"*Odama.* Come here," Leo said. She sounded like she was on the verge of tears.

I half-fell into their arms.

"Kameron," Jax said against my temple, holding me against him. "I would mate you both without a second thought. "But not like this—never like this, without asking you first."

"Don't feel too bad," I managed in a faint tone. "The joke's on you. I might be a purebred, but at this point, my dowry is an embarrassment."

Leo's arm tightened around me, pressing me closer between them. "Downright nonexistent," she agreed. "So's mine, by the way. You should have warned me I was supposed to have a dowry, Mr. Purebred. Is that seriously a thing?"

Jax had gone very still, as though he couldn't believe we were joking about it.

"I wouldn't worry about it," I told her. "Probably a bit moot under the circumstances." I shifted in their arms, a bit uncomfortably. "Though, if you could get your mouth back on that and stop the bleeding, it would be much appreciated, alpha."

Jax hesitated, but after a moment he scooted me a bit farther up his body and lowered his lips to my shoulder, pressing an achingly soft kiss there before covering the bite wound and rasping his tongue across the ragged skin. I closed my eyes against the fresh flood of full-body tingles — mated in the eyes of a legal system that no longer existed… and in none of the ways that actually mattered. *Oh, the irony.*

SIXTEEN

Leo

JAX AND I held Kam between us. Shock at what had just happened swirled with the pleasure pulsing through my core from the knot tying us together.

I didn't think Kam was angry or even upset at Jax's lapse of control. Of our three alphas, I would have pegged Jax as by far the least likely to slip like that—but I'd also been painfully aware that he was struggling emotionally, reeling from both the loss of his pack and our capture, followed by Irina's revelation. Of course, he'd had no way of knowing that the ugly scar on Kam's right shoulder hadn't succeeded in its aim of destroying his mating gland. In the absence of the swelling and redness that came with an omega's heat cycle, his left shoulder just looked like any other normal stretch of skin.

Rather than talk the situation to death, we just clung. Jax's woodsy scent tickled my nostrils, and his big hands wrapped around us both, holding tight. Eventually, the lingering pleasure eased, my body relaxing its grip and allowing Jax's knot to go down. I eased off him, kissing his lips and Kam's temple.

"Stay here," I told them. "I want to clean up a bit, and then I'll be right back."

Jax nodded. Kam made a half-aware, sleepy noise.

The facilities were basic—a sink and a toilet—but still miles better than the terrorist cave. There was toilet paper available, along with disposable hand towels, so I took care of business and managed a quick wash. Wetting a couple of the paper towels with warm water, I returned and handed one to Jax. The other, I used to dab at the bite mark on Kam's shoulder. It was inflamed but no longer bleeding... alpha saliva having done its job to begin the healing process.

Everything I knew about mating, I knew from Kam. Just as the removal of Irina's mating gland would have disrupted her pregnancy, in the absence of the rest of Kam's reproductive system, his mating gland would no longer function properly. There would be no genetic pairing, no psychic bond.

At least, that was the theory.

"Any side effects, either of you?" I asked cautiously.

Kam shook his head wordlessly, not lifting it from Jax's chest. Jax had finished cleaning himself up and refastened his pants one-handed, still holding Kam against his side.

"No," he said softly. "I don't feel anything."

I retrieved my clothing from the floor and pulled it on except for my bra, turning my panties inside out in the absence of clean underwear. I took a certain vicious satisfaction in the knowledge that this room would reek of sex when our captors arrived in the morning. But I was not, in fact, in any hurry to have the guards burst in on us while I was naked.

After throwing the used paper towels away, I rejoined the pair on the bed and pulled the blanket up to cover all three of us. The mattress was honestly too small for this, but I couldn't imagine sleeping anywhere else.

***

The presence of warm bodies next to me combined with my post-orgasmic haze meant that I slept better than I might have expected. Kam was subdued when we finally awoke. Jax was already back to restless frustration, up before us and pacing the room.

"All right?" I asked Kam, stretching cautiously.

"Sore shoulder," he said. "That's all."

I wondered if he would have preferred the mating to take root, even though it had been unplanned. Somehow, it seemed like a really bad idea to ask.

Breakfast arrived—some kind of porridge with paper cartons of orange juice. Scarcely had we finished it when the lock clanked and the door swung open again. Two armed guards entered, weapons raised and pointed at Jax, who rose slowly from his chair.

The fine hair on the back of my neck prickled as a third figure entered.

Kostya Nikolayev looked like a man exercising iron control to hide the fact that he was coming apart at the seams. Frustrated energy crackled around him, and his steel-gray eyes snapped fire. But even in the wilderness of southern Cuba, his charcoal two-piece suit was impeccable.

"Leona McCready," he said, in his rich Russian accent. "Come with me. We must speak now."

Jax tensed, and I had the horrible feeling he was doing the mental math to decide if he could lunge forward and break Nikolayev's neck before falling over dead beneath a hail of gunfire from the guards. My own heart pounded uncontrollably, but I threw up a hand toward him, palm out, and said, "Jax. *Don't.*"

This was what I'd asked for, after all. I didn't want to have to worry about Jax erupting into violence while I was trying to decipher the finer details of this situation. I also didn't want Kam present, where he might be used against me. Of course, I was deluding myself—he and Jax could be used against me just as easily while they were trapped in this cell. It still made me feel better not to have them directly under Nikolayev's angry gaze, though.

"*Don't*," I repeated. "It's all right. I'll be back in a bit… or possibly, I won't be. Either way, I love you both. Never forget that."

Jax looked like he was holding onto his control by a thread. Kam had the expression of someone who knew exactly what it was like to watch a loved one walk out of a room for the last time. I wrenched my eyes away from them and turned to the Committee chairman.

"Lead on, then," I said.

The guards escorted me out. A moment later, the door to the cell snicked shut and locked behind me, cutting me off from my fracturing alpha and my sad-eyed *odama*. The security door in the hallway opened for us, and then it too, slammed closed behind us. Nikolayev led the way deeper into the building, the two armed guards flanking me in clear threat.

We ended up in a conference room. It wasn't large, but it was oddly normal looking—like any such room you might find inside an average office building. Nikolayev gestured me curtly to a seat and dismissed the guards, who left without a word.

"Not worried I'll try to shiv you with the plastic spoon from breakfast?" I asked, fighting the damned omega compulsion to bare my throat to this overpowering terror of a man.

"I have neither the time nor the patience for banter," Nikolayev said. "No more than I have time for your alpha's dramatics. Give me all the information you have on Rhys Beckett's disappearance."

"To what end?" I asked. "You'll forgive me if I'm not in a hurry to answer, when you want to see him dead as much or more than Sloane does."

It was a risky opening gambit, and indeed, Nikolayev's eyes flared with murder for a split second before he hid the expression behind a granite mask. Nevertheless, I needed to understand what was happening here before I started handing out information that might come back to bite the entire alphomic underground in the ass.

"I intend to retrieve Beckett from Sloane's custody," Nikolayev said, biting the words off. "By force, if necessary."

"Okay," I replied. "Let's dig into that a bit further, please. Why should I consider it preferable for Beckett to be in your custody rather than Sloane's? What are you offering that would make it a good deal for me? Because it sounds an awful lot like exchanging the frying pan for the fire."

Nikolayev stared at me. It felt like he was staring *through* me. I valiantly tried to hide the shudder that wanted to break free.

"You know better than that, *Ambassador McCready*." His voice lowered to a lethal purr, and he placed heavy irony on the title. "Or have you so quickly forgotten our mutually beneficial exchange in Montreal?"

His presence felt like a physical pressure in the atmosphere, weighing down my shoulders—trying to make me bend beneath it. It was all I could do to hold his gaze, unblinking.

"Are you implying the possibility of concessions in exchange for getting what you want?" I asked. "Because I feel I must point out that when you had dealings with me before in Montreal, you thought I was a beta."

He raised an eyebrow—though I got the impression he was working hard to convey that level of insouciance. "Did I indeed? You are aware of my reputation, are you not?"

That stopped me in my mental tracks.

They say he can sniff out an omega at twenty paces, even with pheromone suppressors.

Had he known, even back then? That was what he was implying, and not very subtly. It might be the truth, or it might be a lie. But if it was true, it meant that Nikolayev was not, in fact, hell-bent on mindlessly catching and killing every hidden omega in existence. Which made him more strategic than I'd given him credit for. And, if possible, even more dangerous.

"Do you want Beckett dead?" I asked bluntly, focusing every omega sense I had on his body language—searching for deception.

"No," he replied blandly.

"Do you want him alive so you can torture the same information out of him that Sloane's after?" I pressed.

"I don't need his information," Nikolayev ground out. "I only need to ensure Sloane doesn't get it."

Every instinct I possessed screamed that I shouldn't be able to get under Kostya Nikolayev's skin this easily. I shouldn't be able to interrogate him like this. I was a known omega fugitive—his prisoner. This was wrong, wrong, *wrong*... but I couldn't see the lie. I couldn't see the shape of the gap where the puzzle pieces were missing.

"I require that you exercise whatever persuasion is necessary to tame your angry alpha so I can use him in the retrieval mission," he said. "Do you have an active mate-bond with the two alphas Sloane captured to use as leverage?"

"*What*? Why?" I demanded, completely derailed yet again.

"*Answer the question.*"

It was a bark worthy of an alpha, and my spine snapped straight beneath it. "No!" I gasped, before clawing back a shred of control. "No, we're not mated."

He made a hissing noise that brought to mind the reptile I'd accused him of being.

"What does that have to do with any of this?" I asked.

"Tactical advantage," he snapped.

Had he wanted to use the psychic connection between mated pack members as some sort of... *location tracking*? Did it even work that way?

It was a gamble, but I was about to concede on the basis that being physically reunited with Beckett and the others was better than being separated. Together we were stronger, surely. I pushed my reservations aside.

"I'll get Jax on board, but only with conditions. You also retrieve the two alphas Sloane is holding as leverage against Beckett."

Nikolayev sneered at me. "I'm hardly likely to leave Sloane with that kind of *leverage*, as you put it."

Making sure that Sloane didn't keep Flynn and Alex *could* mean rescuing them along with Beckett. It could also mean killing them as a means of removing them from the chessboard.

"And Irina leads the rescue mission," I went on, banking on the omega being more inclined to retrieve her former mate than put a bullet in her head. *Please, let that be a reasonable assumption on my part.*

"Relying on sentiment?" Nikolayev mocked, confirming that he knew very well of the connection between his soldier and one of Sloane's prisoners. "Very well. I concede to your demands. Now tell me what you know."

Hoping I wasn't making a horrible mistake with all of this, I recounted the events surrounding Beckett's disappearance, as I knew them.

When I was done, he nodded. "You will be returned to your cell now. You have thirty minutes to convince your guard dog to do as he's told."

"Wait," I said quickly, before he could turn around and stalk out. "Irina. You know very well who and what she is. Why is she working for you? Why isn't she dead?"

"Only a fool wastes a valuable asset," he replied, his mind clearly focused on organizing the retrieval mission. He paused, pinning me with those piercing gray eyes again before adding, "And you should know that Enoch Sloane is most *definitely* a fool of the first order."

With that, he did leave, and was replaced immediately by the two guards. They marched me back to my cell—and the alpha I was about to try and convince to join a paramilitary operation under the command of a man we all hated.

SEVENTEEN

Jax

MY RELIEF AT Leona's safe return did nothing to make me like what I was hearing any better.

"And the bastard wants me to come along on this so-called 'retrieval mission' *because*...?" I asked.

Leona sighed. "To begin with, he apparently thought we were all mated. I think he wanted to use the bond as some sort of tracking aid, or... something. Now that he knows we're not, I'm pretty sure he wants you there so Alex, Flynn, and Beckett won't fight back against his people while they're trying to extract them."

"I'm supposed to be the fucking Judas goat?" I said. "No, thank you."

Kam had been watching the exchange. At that, he spoke up. "Leo. You agreed to this. What are you seeing here that we're not?"

"Or did he force you to agree by threatening us if you didn't?" I added, since that seemed like an obvious possibility.

"Oddly enough, he didn't," she replied. "Here's the way I'm looking at it. If we're all together, we have a slightly better chance than if we're separated. And while I don't claim to know what game Nikolayev is playing, I *absolutely* know what game Sloane's playing. If Sloane gets the name of Beckett's mate, it sounds like that's going to be a disaster for everyone."

"And if Nikolayev gets it instead?" I asked.

She pulled out a chair and sat down. "I'm not sure. Sloane wants to burn down the world and rebuild it in his own image. I get the impression Nikolayev would prefer there to still be a functioning global society at the end of the day, because he knows that being the king of a smoldering wasteland isn't much of an accomplishment."

Kam, who'd been sitting on the bed, nodded thoughtfully. His hand lifted to rub absently at his left shoulder, where I'd bitten him. I wasn't sure he was even aware he was doing it.

"The Committee only exists as long as it has an enemy to rally people against," he said slowly. "As long as there's a credible threat of alphomic rebellion bubbling beneath the surface, Nikolayev has a job, not to mention an infrastructure funneling money and influence in his direction. But if alphas and omegas no longer pose any sort of threat in the minds of his followers..." He trailed off and shrugged.

"He's under pressure." Leona met my eyes frankly. "I don't know if the threat of losing his position would be enough to account for it, but I'll stake my life that he's fraying at the edges right now. It makes me wonder if there's more to Beckett and his secrets than we know about."

"So you want to try and get the others into the custody of the slightly less insane Committee chairman," I said. "What if you're wrong about this, and the fact that Nikolayev isn't as much of a nutjob as Sloane means that he's actually *more* dangerous?"

"It's possible," she said. "Here's the thing, though. Nothing's stopping Nikolayev from having Kam and me hauled out of this cell under threat of immediate death if you don't do exactly what he tells you to. I'm wondering why he didn't lead with that, personally."

My lips twisted, old bitterness getting the best of me. "Easy. A willing slave is always better than an unwilling one."

"There's also Irina," Kam said. "There was nothing stopping him from sending her to the executioner after she was arrested and tried. But he didn't."

I could feel my blood pressure spike at the mention of Alex's traitorous mate. "Maybe that says more about her than it does about him," I bit out.

"No," Leo said flatly. "It *really* doesn't."

"She wasn't the one with the power," Kam said. "Unless she had some kind of information valuable enough to use as blackmail against Nikolayev, he had all the leverage, and she had none."

"Even if she did have something to use against him," Leo added, "killing the blackmailer usually solves those kinds of problems. Also, if she were being kept alive because she's got dirt on Nikolayev, it would make a lot more sense to pay her off and hide her away someplace safe and obscure, rather than putting her in a position of power within a private paramilitary force."

My instincts clamored against collaborating with these assholes who were holding us prisoner, but Leona had a point that if Nikolayev decided to force my hand, he had two very good ways to do so.

"You both want me to do this?" I asked.

They exchanged one of those looks that contained an entire wordless conversation.

Leo was the one to answer. "We know the others are in a horrific situation right now—probably undergoing torture. No matter how strong Beckett is, you know he loves the three of you like his own pups. He won't last forever before he breaks."

The words were like a knife in the gut, twisting and tearing. I had to physically stop myself from hunching over beneath their force.

"If they're here with us, it might end up being better and it might end up being worse," Leo said softly. "But at least we'll be together, and we can go from there."

There was a painful pause.

"All right," I managed eventually, well aware that I was a nerve-damaged emotional wreck who probably had no business getting within ten miles of a covert ops mission.

Leo nodded. "I insisted Irina be the one to command the mission. With luck, that will ensure Flynn and Alex get out alive, along with Beckett. Nikolayev won't let Sloane keep them, but I'm not entirely convinced he cares all that much how they're taken off the board."

"Either we'll all get out or none of us will," I vowed, aware that might not have sounded terribly reassuring.

"We know," Kam said. "Go and bring them back to us, okay?"

<hr>

Nikolayev didn't keep us in suspense long. Irina arrived roughly half an hour after Leona had been returned to our cell.

"Are we good, then?" she asked, her hand resting not-so-casually on the grip of her sidearm.

"Yeah," I said, my hands clenching into fists beneath the cover of the table. "Fucking *stellar*."

She cocked an eyebrow at me. "Glad to hear it. Say goodbye to your omegas and shift your ass, in that case. The clock's ticking."

The idea of leaving Leona and Kameron defenseless in Nikolayev's custody went against every alpha instinct I possessed. All at once, I wanted to grab Irina by the shoulders and shake her until her teeth rattled and answers fell out. I swallowed the impulse down — bitter and acidic in my throat.

Leo touched my shoulder. "Try to get them back for us, Jax. We'll be here waiting."

I reached out and clasped my hand around the back of her neck, pulling her in for a fierce kiss. She kissed back with equal fierceness, easing away with a final sharp nip to my lower lip. I'd be feeling the tingle for hours.

Kam had been hanging back, his arms crossed defensively in front of him. "You should be aware that it's considered awfully bad form to get yourself killed in order to wiggle out of an accidental mating," he said in a mild tone.

I pushed away from the table and rose, crossing to him and cupping his face in my hands. The left one shook, damaged nerves fighting against my brain's control.

"Wouldn't dream of it, Ginger Tea," I told him, borrowing Flynn's nickname. I pressed a chaste kiss to his forehead. Pulling back, I handed him off to Leo, who wrapped an arm around his shoulders. "Try not to scandalize the beta bigots too much while I'm gone, okay?"

"*Hmph*. Where's the fun in that?" Leo asked, playing at bravado. "Go on, now — but hurry back. We'll miss you."

I closed my eyes, took a slow breath, then nodded and turned away to follow Irina out of the cell.

———◆———

"Give me a rundown of your physical limitations," Irina said as we marched down the endless corridors that seemed to define this place. "Something fucked you up bad. What was it, and how serious is the damage?"

"Intravenous dose of an experimental VX nerve agent variant," I replied, aware that since I was doing this, I would have to play by the rules set for me by my traitorous shit of a temporary commanding officer. "I have headaches and intermittent muscle weakness on the left side."

"How's your head right now?" she asked, as though she didn't actually give a fuck.

"Pounding like a drum," I informed her in the same tone.

She shot me a sidelong glance. "Can you see straight enough to hit a target?"

My lip curled. "Ask the grunts you sent to take us down in New York."

"The fact that they're all still alive isn't exactly a ringing endorsement," she said tartly.

"Wasn't aiming for them," I lied. "I was aiming for the goddamn floodlights they were using to blind us."

"Sure you were," she replied, in a tone that said she was humoring me. "Fine—as long as you're clear on which direction to point the end that goes *boom*."

"Don't fucking tempt me," I muttered, and stopped abruptly. The guards behind us gripped their weapons warily, but Irina halted and turned to face me.

"What is it?" she asked.

I stared down at her tiny frame. "You want this mission to go smoothly? Do *not* reveal yourself to Alex until after we're safely out. Let's just say, she isn't going to take any of this well."

Irina let out an indelicate snort and started walking again. "You think? Yes, your tactical advice is noted. Thank you *so* much."

I clenched my jaw against the throbbing pain in my skull and started after her. We ended up in a quartermaster's supply room, where I was kitted out in state-of-the-art black tactical gear.

"Weapons?" I asked.

"Sure," she said. "When we're ready to go in, and I can be relatively certain you'll have other things to worry about besides putting a slug in me or one of my men."

The next stop on the itinerary was the briefing. Apparently, Nikolayev was in a big hurry when it came to implementing his plan, because he certainly wasn't waiting around on things. I thought back to what Leona had said earlier.

I'll stake my life that he's fraying at the edges right now.

According to the briefing, Beckett and the others were being held at a secure facility near the Alabama coast—a six hundred mile flight that we would be making in a convoy of three Black Hawk helicopters, each one outfitted with an ERFS long-range fuel system. Since the choppers would be broadcasting legitimate Committee identification codes, the plan was to land inside the compound and swarm the facility's security forces, using the element of surprise to power our way in, secure the three targets, and get out the same way before backup could arrive.

It was the kind of brute-force attack that appealed to me, both for its simplicity and for the opportunity it was likely to provide to bash some heads. It wasn't, however, the kind of plan I would have pictured Nikolayev coming up with. Of course, his normal job involved bullying politicians and arranging firing squads. Nothing I'd ever heard about him mentioned anything about a military background. He probably had other people to strategize helicopter raids for him.

There were schematics showing a basic layout of the target facility—possibly gleaned from satellite intel—but they were light on detail. In many ways, we would be going in blind—and apparently in broad daylight as well.

Irina's eyes landed on me heavily. "At no time during our mission will anyone here identify yourselves to the three targets as being associated with either the Committee or Chairman Nikolayev. Is that clear?"

"Crystal," I said, as the others in the room muttered acknowledgement. And wasn't *that* going to make the conversation I had with Alex and Flynn afterward a real treat? Assuming we survived long enough to have it, of course.

Hi, guys—sorry I failed to mention that I helped drag you out of Sloane's hands so I could dump you into Nikolayev's, instead… because apparently I'm working for the Euro-Soviet Committee now. Leona asked me to do it, you see—and, well, it seemed like a good idea at the time.

On second thought, maybe I should leave the explanations to her and Kam, assuming the six of us weren't chained up in separate dungeons by that point. Christ, what a goddamned mess.

After a few more minutes of tactical briefing, Irina ran her cool gray gaze over the assemblage. "That's it, soldiers. Let's go steal some prisoners. Departure is scheduled in fifteen minutes."

EIGHTEEN

Jax

EACH CHOPPER had a pilot, a copilot, two crew chiefs, six soldiers, and two stretchers aboard. As soon as I was strapped in, Irina handed me a bottle of water and two pills.

"Aspirin," she said. "For your head."

"Thanks." I palmed the pills rather than swallowing them, since I had no way of knowing what the hell they actually were. When I was sure no one was looking, I stuck them in a convenient pocket in my tactical vest. Maybe there was no obvious reason why she'd want me incapacitated before the mission, but I wasn't about to take a chance she might slip me something to make me more compliant or biddable.

The seal on the plastic bottle cap was intact, so I did at least drink the water.

It had been a while since I'd flown any appreciable distance in a helicopter. Ignoring the pounding pain in my skull, I donned my headset and tested the push-to-talk button on the cord, familiarizing myself with the unit.

Within minutes, the engine roared to life. The rotor spun up, and we were off. This would be a twelve hundred mile round trip, mostly over water, with enough fuel for thirteen hundred eighty miles on a good day. There wasn't a huge margin for error, especially if someone in Sloane's compound knocked a few brain cells together and managed to shoot out one of the chopper's external fuel tanks.

It was a calculated risk, since a refueling stop was impractical. Get in, get out, get back to Cuba. That was the long and the short of the mission.

The three-and-a-half hour flight dragged, but the closer we got to our destination, the more my damned alpha instincts took over. My pack was in trouble, and I was coming to get them out. The rightness of that part of things threatened to overwhelm the very real fact that I was following the orders of *Kostya fucking Nikolayev*, and I'd basically just sold my soul to the Committee on the basis of Leona McCready's hunch.

Get them out safe, and worry about the rest of it later, I told myself firmly. It wasn't as though I could change my mind now, with the Alabama coastline a brown and green smear in front of us.

Irina was strapped in directly across from me. Her gray eyes had barely left me during the long flight, but she'd wisely refrained from trying to make conversation over the headset. I got the impression that she was a focused and no-nonsense commander in the field — not surprising, given what I'd known of her from the time before the mess with Alex.

Now, she pulled out a semi-automatic pistol and checked the clip before handing it across to me. It was a SIG P210, stamped with the Swiss army designation in the serial number. I checked the safety and pulled back the slide, chambering a round before stowing the gun into my shoulder holster, cocked and locked. Irina passed over four extra magazines. Forty rounds. I supposed if I ended up needing more than that, it would mean we had bigger worries to contend with.

I offered her a wary nod of acknowledgement.

We were approaching land. In the cockpit, the pilot hailed someone, speaking in a bland UFNA Midwest accent at odds with the Eastern European drawl I'd heard in my headset earlier.

I supposed that if you were going to try and infiltrate a Committee facility by air, actually being part of the Committee was a big help. The mic from the cockpit cut out. Presumably, the pilot and whoever he was talking to had started exchanging sensitive security codes.

If clearance wasn't granted, we'd bluster our way in regardless. Sloane's compound was unlikely to have robust ground-to-air defenses... *supposedly*. It was a prison facility, not a military installation. Besides, the list of organizations that would dare attack the Committee openly like this was, shall we say, somewhat limited.

Long minutes passed before the mic crackled into life again.

"Landing clearance granted," the pilot said in his native accent. "ETA in eighteen minutes."

"Prep for action, boys," Irina said crisply. "We only get one shot at this."

⸻◆⸻

Sloane's compound screamed 'prison' in a way that Nikolayev's property in Cuba didn't. It was likely that it had, in fact, been a federal or state correctional facility in its former life. Chain link fencing and razor wire surrounded the stark rectangular concrete building, while guard towers dotted the perimeter.

Those towers would be the first order of business, but they weren't my problem. I was part of the tactical group tasked with retrieving Flynn and Alex. Meanwhile, Irina would be leading the group going after Beckett, on the assumption that he was likely being held in high-security solitary confinement.

All of Nikolayev's forces would be wearing balaclavas to hide their faces—all except me. My Judas goat role relied on letting my packmates see me and be reassured enough to let a bunch of armed troops drag them onto a helicopter.

The political fallout of our smash-and-grab operation was outside of my purview, and I wasn't sure I really gave a shit about it anyway. I wondered, though, if Nikolayev would plead complete innocence when Sloane came screaming to him afterward, blaming the breach on lax security in Sloane's own operation and using any security footage of my face as supporting evidence of an alphomic operation, perhaps by the underground Sloane was so set on dismantling.

Again—not my problem. I'd have plenty of fallout of my own to deal with, once the others realized what I'd done.

The chopper settled onto the helipad on the building's roof. Around us, the other two would have done the same, landing in a triangular nose-to-tail configuration that gave the door-mounted machine guns on the outer sides complete three hundred and sixty degree access to our surroundings.

We waited—unstrapped from our seatbelts and ready to move fast when the order came.

Within minutes the roof access door opened, and a delegation in blue uniforms approached. I had a perfect view through the open side door of the helicopter as the machine guns opened fire and mowed them down before turning their collective firepower on the guard turrets.

Glass shattered, ensuring that the chaos inside the towers would delay any return fire, on the off chance that any of the guards inside had survived. We poured out of the choppers, guns drawn. Those of us assigned to the two retrieval teams made straight for the roof entrance, while the remaining troops dug in around the helicopters, ready to protect our only transportation out of here.

The door was locked—proof that the people who'd come out to meet us weren't complete idiots, at least. Irina stuck a directed explosive charge over the mechanism, and we fell back as it deployed with a dull *crump*. The door swung open, the metal warped and glowing red where the lock had been blown out. Around us, klaxons began to wail.

We swarmed inside. Those in the lead shot down the handful of guards rushing up the stairwell to meet us. I hopped over the slumped bodies as we hurried downward into the guts of the building, cursing the weakness on my left side as my leg threatened to waver beneath the extra strain.

Those damned klaxons weren't doing a thing for my aching head, either.

The helipad stairwell led down to the admin wing, as we'd anticipated. Security wasn't as tight here as it would be in the prisoner areas, and we only had to blow one more door to gain access to the main administration area. Terrified desk jockeys huddled inside offices with inadequate wooden doors—easy to kick down.

"Who in here knows where the high-value prisoners are being kept?" my team leader—a beta male named Kowalczyk—bellowed in a passable UFNA accent. "Point them out or we mow down everyone in this room!"

Several tentative fingers pointed toward a harried looking man in a tan suit, whose face paled when he realized his colleagues had just given him up for slaughter like a Christmas turkey.

"The rest of you lie face down on the ground!" Kowalczyk ordered, while two other soldiers grabbed the guy in the suit. One of them jammed a gun in his ribs, and a high-pitched whimper of fear escaped him.

"Out," the trooper with the gun ordered, managing a less convincing attempt at a local accent.

We left the other admin workers cowering on the ground, waiting until we were back outside before Kowalczyk grabbed the man's jaw in one meaty hand and said, "Lead us to the omega named Rhys Beckett and the alphas designated Alex and Flynn, or I shoot out both your kneecaps."

The man was practically gibbering in fear. "B-b-but you won't be able to get to them! The security—"

"Is our concern," Kowalczyk cut in. "Your concern is the unbearable pain and permanent disability that will result if you provoke me into shooting you. I can always find another office drudge to tell me what I want to know."

I had to give it to the man… he had 'dead-eyed and terrifying' down to an art form. Not normally a compliment, true—but it was useful under the circumstances. My sensitive alpha nose detected the smell of urine a couple of seconds before the dark stain appeared on the office guy's trousers. *Classy.*

Kowalczyk released the man's jaw with a look of disgust.

"I c-can take you, but I don't have keys for the checkpoints," the guy stammered.

"We don't need keys," Kowalczyk said, and stepped back, gesturing with his gun. "*Move.*"

One of the soldiers shoved him, and the man stumbled forward.

"Th-this way," he said, gesturing toward a set of double doors.

Both teams made their way into the prisoner wing at the guy's direction. Irina was staying inconspicuous, I couldn't help noticing. It made sense. Even if she could pull off the accent, the presence of a small woman in a paramilitary operation was too memorable. From what I understood during the briefing, they wanted any surviving witnesses to remember only a bunch of masked, black-clad goons with guns… except for me, with my face bare for the world to see.

Judas goat and sacrificial lamb all rolled up in one neat package, I thought. *Just tie a fuckin' bell to my neck next time.*

We ran into guards in twos and threes, reinforcing the idea that places like this were geared toward preventing the people inside from getting out, not preventing people outside from getting in. At least, not if those people were armed, trained, and possessed explosives.

The first few prison guards fell before they could even get a shot off. When we had to stop and blow the lock on yet another security door, it gave the guards inside enough time to set up an ambush. Bullets flew as soon as the door swung open. We were hugging the walls in anticipation of such an attack, but one of Nikolayev's men went down with half of his neck blown away.

Irina pulled a flash-bang grenade from her belt and tossed it through the door. I turned away and covered my ears. After the blinding light stopped spearing through my tightly closed eyelids, I stormed into the newly opened section with the others and gunned down two guards who were struggling to regain their feet.

The others took care of the rest. Kowalczyk confronted the admin guy, who was clutching at his right ear, tears streaking down his bloodless face.

"I can't hear!" he said, too loudly. "*I've gone deaf!*"

Kowalczyk stared him down, muttering, "*Fuck's sake.*" He lowered the muzzle of his gun meaningfully toward the man's knees.

"It's th-this way," office guy said, pointing with the hand that wasn't still cradling his ear. "S-sorry. Left at the next junction! That's the high security wing!"

We waded through the carnage in the corridor, toward the next T-junction. Four more of Sloane's guards shuffled off this mortal coil beneath a hail of our gunfire, and eventually we reached a door marked *MAXIMUM SECURITY* in bold, blocky lettering.

Thankfully, the door itself was no different to any of the others we'd blown open. The corridor beyond was oddly deserted. The lack of an active defense prickled the hair on the back of my neck. Cameras whirred, their red eyes watching us from the ceiling.

"The omega will be in interrogation room one," office guy babbled. "The alphas will be in interrogation room t-two! Now please let me go, *please*! I did what you asked!"

Kowalczyk nodded to the man's guards. The one who'd held a gun on him lifted it and shot him through the head without comment. Office guy slumped to the floor, twitching.

Irina exchanged a glance with Kowalczyk and made the hand signal for 'split up.' The two teams would peel off to retrieve our separate targets, and then try to get the hell out before anyone in the facility managed to get outside backup involved.

Each team had started out with six soldiers. Ours was down to five, and one of Irina's was bleeding from the shoulder. It didn't matter—we were close enough to Beckett and my packmates that I could practically smell them. The pounding agony in my skull had faded to something distant and unimportant. The weakness in my ravaged body wouldn't slow me down because I wouldn't let it. My senses thrummed, wondering where the trap was.

Interrogation Room One was at the end of the corridor. It killed me inside not to hang back and watch as Irina and her team prepared to force their way in, but that wasn't my part of the mission. Interrogation Room Two was around the corner. My heart pounded, driving blood through my veins and strength to my muscles as Kowalczyk set the directed charge above the lock. The five of us pressed our backs to the wall on either side of the door.

Crump, and the door swung open a few inches, off-kilter on its hinges. Kowalczyk kicked it open and promptly went down with a cry, blood spurting from an artery in his thigh. Through the open door, I got a confused impression of a man in a guard uniform, a second man in a white lab coat cowering behind a table… and Flynn chained naked to the wall with a pair of battery leads clamped to his chest.

With a roar, I put my head down and charged the man with the gun.

NINETEEN

Flynn

MY HEAD MIGHT have been fuzzing in and out like a television with poor reception, but when one of the torturers *du jour* stepped away to answer the phone hanging on the wall by the door, I knew something was up.

Alex was either down for the count or faking unconsciousness after Goon Number Two had finished breaking the last two fingers on her left hand—I wasn't sure which. We'd both been giving these fuckers false information for the past day and a half, singing like canaries without letting anything important slip. Problem was, they weren't torturing us because they wanted us to talk. They were torturing us because they wanted *Beckett* to talk.

It didn't take a rocket scientist to guess why there were enough cameras pointed at us to film a big budget Hollywood movie. We might not have seen Beckett ourselves, but he was here. I was sure of it. When the phone call came through and the goons started acting nervous, you can bet I was listening with both ears—even if I didn't lift my head from where it lolled against my chest.

The words *'security breach'* and *'armed intruders approaching'* were sweet music to my ears. Yeah, it could have been completely unrelated to us... but I was betting it wasn't. I was betting it was Jax. I didn't claim to have a clue how he might have gathered the kind of assault force that could break into a Committee holding facility. Maybe the underground had military assets Alex and I didn't know about. Maybe Beckett was an important enough cog in the wheel to inspire them to use those assets.

Didn't matter.

What *did* matter was that I was still naked and chained to the back wall like a goddamned bull's eye target, though they'd at least stopped shocking me in favor of losing their shit over whatever was happening outside. I was about to be an eyewitness to whatever went down next—though not a very good one, since one of my eyes was already swollen shut and the other one was well on the way.

I couldn't get loose on my own. Best-case scenario, I'd get a front-row seat to someone putting bullets in these assholes. Worst case, I'd be in the line of fire as well, and end up bleeding out before I got the satisfaction of seeing them all die.

Goon Number One hung up the phone. "Take cover and be ready. Grab that one and get out of sight behind the door," he snapped to Goon Number Two, pointing at Alex's crumpled form. Then he drew his gun and positioned himself in a classic firing stance several feet back from the doorway.

The second goon dragged Alex to the wall on the far side of the door, where it would block them from view if it opened. She didn't stir as he crouched behind her and hauled her upper body against his so he could jam the muzzle of his gun against her temple. Meanwhile, the mealy-mouthed lab tech in his white coat ducked behind the table that held the voltage regulator and various other torture devices, as though he thought that was what 'taking cover' meant.

The walls were thick in this place, but I thought I could make out muffled boot steps pounding in the corridor outside. *Show time.*

The sound of a directed explosive charge was shockingly loud as it echoed off the concrete walls of the room. Smoke and dust obscured the view for a moment, but I heard the creak of tortured hinges that meant the door had given way.

Metal shrieked as it swung wider, possibly beneath the force of a kick. A man stood silhouetted in the gap for a bare second before Goon Number One squeezed off a round. The silhouette crumpled to the ground with a hoarse cry.

A second figure appeared in the gap with a roar of rage and charged, leading with his right shoulder. I caught a flash of blond hair, and I *knew*. It was Jax. I still had no clue how the fucking bastard had managed to organize this, but somehow he had.

Goon Number One fired off another wild shot, though he must have known that nothing short of a bullet through the heart or the brain was going to stop an enraged alpha mid-charge. Jax plowed into him like a rugby player and they both went down. My packmate drew back the hand that held his weapon and landed a savage blow with the butt of the pistol. The goon went limp.

Jax staggered to his feet, his blue eyes feral with rage as he took me in.

"Check your five," I rasped.

He whirled, raising his sidearm—his gaze swinging to the five o'clock position where Goon Number Two still had a gun pressed to Alex's head. Three other soldiers kitted out in black gear and balaclavas charged in, following Jax's line of sight to the pair huddled on the floor. Two of them aimed handguns at Alex and the goon, while the third covered Lab Boy, still cowering behind the table with his clipboard.

"Drop it," Jax ground out.

"Fuck off," said the goon. "You gonna shoot through her to get to me?"

"Why not?" asked one of the other men. Something about his accent sounded odd. I couldn't quite place it. "What do we care about some hyena bitch?"

A muscle in Jax's jaw twitched. I started planning ways to use the torture instruments lying conveniently on the table if anyone shot Alex. What the hell kind of mercenaries was Jax using for this operation, anyway?

"Hey, fucker," I snarled. "Try it, and see what happens."

Alex chose that moment to explode into life. She wrenched her upper body forward and drove her elbow back, twisting like a snake to get her unbroken right hand around Goon Number Two's wrist, jerking his gun hand up. The pistol went off, the bullet embedding itself in the ceiling and sending chips of concrete shrapnel raining down. A heartbeat later, the weapon was in Alex's hand and pointed at her captor's head. Another explosion of sound, and Goon Number Two's brains splattered against the wall behind him.

I gave her a quick onceover. Then I gave Jax a quick onceover, taking in the wet patch on his left thigh. "You're bleeding, asshole," I said, jerking my chin at the shiny stain.

He glanced down. "Mother *fucker*," he said, and shot the unconscious goon he'd tackled to the ground earlier. The gun swung toward Lab Boy, who was hunched against the wall now, holding his clipboard in front of his chest like he could use it to stop a bullet.

"You," Jax said. "Get him out of those chains."

Lab Boy froze for a second, his eyes as wide as dinner plates. Then he pointed at the man Alex had killed. "That guard had the keys."

"Then I expect he still does," Jax snapped. "So fucking *get them*."

The tech scurried into motion, every gun in the room trained on him as he fumbled through Goon

Number Two's pockets and came up with the keys. His already pale face whitened further as he cautiously approached me and reached for the first wrist shackle. I grinned down at him, showing teeth, and his pale eyes darted away nervously. The second wrist shackle followed the first. I stood still and docile as he crouched down to get the ankle shackles.

When I was finally free, I pulled the electrical leads off my nipples and tossed them aside. Next, I reached down and grabbed Lab Boy by the neck, spinning him to face away from me. I ignored the pain of abused muscle and bone as I got a grip on his chin with my other hand and twisted. His startled yelp cut off in a crunch of bone and cartilage. I let the body slump to the ground and stepped around it, since I hurt too fucking much to step over it if I didn't have to.

Crouching down to pick up Goon Number One's gun was agony, but damned if I was walking out of this room unarmed. I managed to regain my feet without falling over and turned a scowl on the soldier who'd threatened to shoot through Alex to get to his target.

"Are you and me gonna have a problem?" I asked.

"Stow it," Alex croaked, cutting me off. "Exit plan?"

"Choppers on the roof," Jax said. "We need to move."

He didn't ask if we could make it under our own power. Bastard knew us too well for that. One of the other soldiers knelt to check the pulse of the guy who'd been shot in the doorway and shook his head.

"Leave him," said the guy who'd called Alex a hyena. Apparently, he was a cold-hearted bastard all around, then—not that I was about to argue the call. Last thing we needed was to have to haul a corpse through a battle zone.

The others cleared the corridor and set a rapid pace. Jax hung back to make sure Alex and I were keeping up. I wondered when that bullet wound was going to catch up to him, and hoped it happened after we reached the promised choppers rather than before.

Alex was gray-faced and stoic as she stalked along next to me, gun held steady in the hand that wasn't a twisted mess of broken bones. I was mildly jealous that she at least had a prisoner's uniform to wear. Breaking out of a Committee torture facility buck-ass naked might make for a good drinking story someday, but the actual reality kind of sucked. For one thing, it was goddamned cold in here. Or possibly I was going into shock. Hard to tell which.

We met a few guards along the way, alone or in pairs, but there wasn't nearly as much of an organized defense as I might have expected. It made me wonder how many Jax and the others had killed on the way in. I also wondered how long it would take Sloane to call for outside assistance. I didn't know enough about the distribution of Committee assets in this part of the country to even hazard a guess.

After a more intense shootout that winged the hyena guy on the right arm, we broke through and entered what looked like an administrative area. It seemed to be deserted — at least until we came to the open door of a stairwell and saw the bodies piled inside. All but one was wearing the blue uniform of prison staff. The other was dressed in black.

One of the soldiers who hadn't spoken before cursed sharply in a foreign language, and I guessed it was someone he knew.

Above us, the way appeared to be clear. We just had to climb god knew how many flights of stairs to get where we were going. I was already operating in that physically detached sort of way where your muscles did their own thing, despite whatever injuries your brain was ignoring in the heat of the moment.

There were limits, though—and after we'd made it up three flights and part of a fourth, Alex gasped. She was behind me and in front of Jax, who was bringing up the rear. By the time I whirled to see what was happening, Jax had already caught her around the waist and was hauling her right arm across his shoulders to support her.

"Go," he growled, dragging her up the stairs with no regard to the bullet hole in his thigh or the nerve damage that had weakened his left side.

I went, ignoring the gray fog edging into the corners of my vision. The bruises on my face throbbed, and my legs were getting the numb, rubbery feeling that meant they weren't going to keep working forever.

After what felt like an eternity, we burst through a twisted metal security door and into daylight. The sudden brightness brought tears to my one functioning eye. While I tried to blink the blurriness away, a familiar hand clamped around my shoulder and propelled me in the right direction, toward one of the looming dark blurs. The engine noise was deafening, and the rotors had already spun up, generating a powerful downdraft as we crossed the final few yards.

More hands grabbed me and pulled me inside. I twisted to make sure Alex and Jax were aboard as well.

"Where's Beckett?" Jax shouted, pitching his voice to be heard above the racket.

"On one of the other choppers!" someone shouted back.

"These two need stretchers!" Jax said.

After the confirmation that Beckett was safe, I'd already heard everything I needed to hear. With a sense of exhausted relief, I let my knees buckle. My surroundings went black before my body had a chance to hit the metal deck.

TWENTY

Jax

THE PAIN OF the bullet wound in my thigh hit me once Alex and Flynn were safely strapped into their stretchers and having their injuries assessed. Blood was oozing from my wound but not pulsing, despite the strain of half-carrying Alex up the final couple of flights in the stairwell. That alone told me it hadn't hit anything vital.

One of the soldiers cut a slit through the heavy fabric of my trousers to check it, and confirmed it was barely more than a graze. The man slapped a gauze pad over it and gave it a perfunctory bandaging job, after which I put it out of my mind as unimportant.

We'd gotten them out. All three of them. Now that the rush of battle was fading, I had no choice but to start thinking about what came next. What would I be delivering them into?

My headset crackled to life with the tinny sound of the pilot's voice. "We've got enemy choppers incoming. Strap in and get ready for an interesting ride."

Right. Maybe I'd spoken too soon. Apparently, Sloane's cavalry was about to arrive.

The Black Hawk lifted into the air, spraying a final hail of machine gun fire over the section of the compound on our port side. No doubt the other two helicopters were doing the same. Within moments, we were gaining altitude and angling toward the coast, with the Gulf of Mexico beyond.

"Are they armed with missiles?" asked a voice I didn't recognize—probably whoever was in charge in the absence of Irina and Kowalczyk.

"Can't tell," the pilot replied over the comms. "I expect we'll find out soon enough."

This had always been a possibility. To be fair, it could have been worse; if they'd managed to scramble military jets instead of helicopters, we'd be screwed. As it was, it would be a straight-up horse race. If we had more fuel than they did... if they weren't armed with weapons that could be used at long range... if we weren't appreciably slower than they were... if all of those things were true, we might get out unscathed.

"Range is an estimated forty-five nautical miles," said a voice that I tentatively identified as the copilot. "Calculating the pursuing choppers' flight speed now..."

I waited with everyone else, trying not to hold my breath.

"Pursuing aircraft are traveling at one hundred sixty knots," said the copilot.

I wracked my brain for the Black Hawk's specs, but the pilot saved me the trouble.

"Our top sustained cruising speed is one hundred fifty-two knots. I can punch it up to one hundred fifty-nine knots if you don't mind guzzling fuel. Orders?"

There was a brief pause, and then the soldier who appeared to be nominally in charge now said, "Punch it. If they get close enough to shoot us down, fuel won't matter."

It was the right call... unless we ended up having to ditch this bird in the ocean after running out of gas. I felt the slight increase in g-force as the chopper sped up.

"Choppers Two and Three are accelerating to match us," the pilot said. "The hostiles can still catch us, but it will take them a while at this speed."

My headset went silent as everyone in the helicopter shut up and strapped in, waiting to see how things would play out. I'd taken a seat near the two stretchers laid out on the deck, and I passed the time watching the slow rise and fall of my packmates' chests.

Slightly less than an hour later, the copilot's voice came over the headsets again. "Enemy choppers are within firing range. Repeat, enemy choppers are within firing range. No missiles detected, but we're taking machine gun fire. Do we engage?"

"Negative," said the de facto commander. "We don't have the fuel for a battle. Attempt evasive maneuvers, but keep heading for the base at top speed."

I wasn't sure what evasive maneuvers he thought the pilot would be able to manage without significantly altering course. Then again, no one had asked me. The helicopter dipped and swerved, my stomach struggling to play catch-up.

"Chopper Three is hit!" the pilot reported. "Smoke from the main rotor assembly! Taking evasive action to give them space to maneuver!"

The pilot banked into a steep turn to the port side, and we all scrambled for purchase.

"It's no good!" he called. "They're in a spin. They're going down!"

Through the windows on the opposite side of the fuselage, I saw the horrible sight of a helicopter spiraling crazily, smoke pouring from the main engine, its trajectory headed for the unforgiving sea below. My heart jumped into my throat.

"God*damn* it!" the commander cursed. "Status of the pursuing choppers?"

There was a painful pause. Then, "Pursuing craft are changing course. They're… they're turning back, sir. Must have hit the edge of their range."

Depending on where they'd started from, they could easily have utilized half of their fuel supply by now if they weren't outfitted for long-range service. They would have to head back or risk the same watery fate that had just befallen Chopper Three. And right now, I didn't give a flying fuck about any of that.

"Which helicopter was Beckett on?" I asked hoarsely, barely recognizing my own voice.

"Chopper Two," the commander replied grimly.

The steel band around my chest snapped, and I sucked in a wheezing breath of air.

Respectful silence reigned for the rest of the trip, broken only by necessary communication between the pilot and copilot. It felt like an age before the sandy browns and vibrant greens of Cuba appeared before us, more welcome than I ever would have guessed they'd be.

Please, just let us get down safe, I thought. *Get us back to Leona and Kam, and let all six of us survive this nightmare for another day. We'll deal with the rest when it comes.*

Numbly, I watched the ground get closer and closer, until the Black Hawk touched down with a dull thump. Through the windows, I saw Chopper Two land safely nearby, and breathed a sigh of relief. Both helicopters' engines powered down with a low whine, leaving us once more inside Kostya Nikolayev's territory.

I tried to take stock. I was still armed, but with Flynn and Alex unconscious, all I'd be able to accomplish with a single handgun was getting myself—and possibly them—killed. We were still trapped. I needed to make sure the others got medical treatment for whatever was wrong with them. I'd seen Alex's left hand before one of the soldiers had bandaged it to immobilize the broken fingers. The memory made me long for a neck to break, the same way Flynn had broken the lab tech's.

Once I was sure the others were being cared for, I needed to find Leona and Kameron, to confirm they were safe and let them know what was happening. My hand shook with adrenaline fatigue as I reached for the clasp of my safety harness and unlatched it. Both side doors on the fuselage slid open, revealing several figures hurrying toward us. Neither Alex nor Flynn stirred in response to the commotion; no more than they'd stirred when we were being shot at earlier. I positioned myself in front of them. Anyone coming for them would have to answer my questions first.

Before long, the soldiers had cleared out and two men wearing the uniforms of Nikolayev's prison guards stepped in. Interestingly, they were unarmed.

"Stop," I said. "These two need urgent medical attention. Are they going to get it?"

The one on the left looked at me like I was an imbecile. "Of course they are," he said in a pronounced German accent. "There are alphomic specialists waiting outside. Now if you would please move so we can get them off the helicopter?" He glanced at my leg. "And have someone direct you to the medical building to get that seen to once you've been debriefed."

I moved aside reluctantly, watching with an eagle eye as the broad-shouldered pair lifted Flynn's stretcher and carried him outside. A second pair came in immediately afterward and did the same with Alex. I followed them out, favoring my left leg heavily and silently cursing the asshole who'd shot me.

Flynn was already being transferred to a gurney, with Alex close behind. We were losing the light.

Nearly a whole day had passed since Leo had been taken away after breakfast for her private meeting with Nikolayev, and then come back afterward to talk me into helping with this mission.

Had it been a mistake? I still didn't know the answer, but after seeing what had been done to my packmates in the handful of days since they'd been captured, it was hard to think so.

Medical staff in white coats leaned over Alex and Flynn, pressing stethoscopes to their chests and carefully palpating their ribs. Marginally reassured that they weren't going to immediately be hauled off for more torture, I turned my attention to the second helicopter. Something occurred to me, and I stopped a passing soldier.

"Was Irina on that chopper? Or was she on the one that went down?" I asked.

"She was on that one," the soldier replied. "She's gone to make a report."

"Thanks," I said, not particularly caring if she were dead or alive on my own behalf. Still, I could only imagine that the fallout from Alex learning about all of this would be even worse if I had to tell her that her former mate had miraculously survived execution, only to fall into the ocean in a burning chopper after helping to rescue her. At least I could spare her that much.

The next order of business was Beckett. It seemed to be taking a long time for them to bring him outside, and my worry spiked as I approached the helicopter and heard the sound of animal snarling coming from within.

It was the sound of a cornered omega.

I didn't think—I just charged inside, grabbing at the edge of the doorway for support when my leg threatened to give out.

"Get away from him," I growled at the two betas trying to approach the stretcher. When they didn't respond immediately, I pulled out my gun and pointed it at them. "I said back away *now!*"

They backed away, hands raised. At the same instant, the scent hit me.

Lavender and peppermint. I'd never smelled it before, and yet I felt like I knew it intimately. It was the scent of the carrier-figure I'd never had until I was already a grown man… a scent that said *family.* And it was pungent with heat markers.

"We think he's been drugged with sodium thiopental," said one of the betas, still holding his hands up. "Sloane's been known to use it to loosen prisoners' tongues, but he's reacted badly to it."

Maybe they couldn't smell it yet. *Fuck*—Beckett wasn't anywhere near due for a heat right now. But he also wasn't young anymore. He was approaching estropause, and omegas' systems could get a little crazy as they started to shut down. Could the drug have sent him into an off-cycle heat?

I holstered the gun, since the two men didn't seem like a threat. "Seriously, just back off. I know him; we're like family. I'll try to calm him down and get him outside, but he needs a *specialist*, you hear me? A specialist in omega medicine."

Again, I received that look—like I was a few screws short of a full set.

"Yes, the doctors are waiting outside for him," said the one on the right.

I nodded and gave them a jerk of my chin that clearly said *'please fuck off now.'* They fucked off, somewhat to my surprise. When Beckett and I were alone in the cabin, I scooted carefully down the wall into a sitting position with my injured leg held straight out in front of me, so I wouldn't be looming over him.

"Hey, Boss," I said quietly. "Sorry I was late."

God, he looked horrible—like a man who'd seen into the mouth of hell and barely lived to tell the tale.

His heat-scent was sour with stress and fear. It wouldn't have affected me regardless — we might not have been blood-related, but we'd become family long ago. I tried to regulate my emotions into something reassuring, despite the fact that the only thing I could think of worse than placing him in Nikolayev's hands in the first place, was doing so when he was helpless in heat.

Pale, bloodshot eyes the color of a stormy sea met mine, the barest hint of recognition lighting them. Relief eased the tension in my shoulders.

"There you are, Boss. Come on — aren't you just dying to read me the riot act for taking so long to come and get you? Flynn and Alex are here, too... in case no one told you yet. They're getting checked over by the doctors, and you need to do the same."

I thought I could see a flicker of understanding behind that stormy gaze, but then a commotion outside interrupted. Beckett's eyes went wild again, and he jerked violently at the velcro cuffs restraining his wrists to the rails of the stretcher.

"Easy now —" I began, only to be cut off by shouts from outside.

"*Sir! Sir! You mustn't go in there yet... there's an alpha inside — !*"

The clang of rapid footsteps on metal decking echoed through the fuselage. An aura of promised violence reached me the instant before Kostya Nikolayev appeared at the far end of the cabin, his hair disheveled and his lips curled back in a wordless snarl.

Every instinct I possessed had me upright in a heartbeat despite the bullet wound in my leg and the weakness in my muscles. In a flash, I was standing protectively in front of Rhys Beckett, drawn up to my full height... my muscles bulging with threat.

"*Get. Out,*" Nikolayev hissed. His voice didn't even sound human.

"You child-murdering *fucker*," I growled. "Take one more step, and we'll see if I can rip your head clean off your spine before any of your lackeys can put a bullet through my skull."

Gray eyes glowing with rage, Nikolayev stalked forward.

TWENTY-ONE

Leo

I RAN AFTER Irina and Kam, huffing and puffing as I tried not to fall too far behind. Irina had retrieved us from our cell only moments ago. She hadn't told us anything beyond the fact that they had *'successfully retrieved the targets.'*

Two huge black helicopters sat on the pavement that apparently served as the compound's helipad. Dozens of people milled around them. Several were gesturing and shouting in Russian. Confusion and chaos reigned.

Irina collared a man in a white coat who was standing next to an empty gurney. "What's happening?" she demanded.

"He went charging in there after Beckett, but one of the alphas was already inside," the man replied in clipped tones, gesturing toward the nearest helicopter.

"Who went in? Nikolayev?" Irina said in a tone of foreboding, and the man nodded.

"*Fuck!*" she cursed, and charged toward the helicopter.

My stomach dropped. Kam and I exchanged a wide-eyed look and followed her up the metal ramp that had been placed beside the chopper's open side door. Our footsteps clanged loudly.

An idea so improbable that I could scarcely credit it had been percolating through my mind during the course of this endless day of waiting. I hadn't said anything to Kam, since I had no proof—

and more than a hint of suspicion that the stress was finally getting to me, making me see patterns that weren't there.

But when we skidded to a stop behind Irina and got a look inside the cabin, I knew with utter certainty that I was right.

"Sir!" Irina said, lunging forward and wrapping her fingers around Kostya Nikolayev's arm. "Sir, please! Just stop for a minute! He's only trying to protect—"

Nikolayev *growled*.

At the far end of the cabin, Jax stood poised in front of a struggling figure on a stretcher. The alpha's fists were clenched, and blatant desire for murder lit his blue eyes. A faint hint of mint and lavender wafted to my nose, the pleasant scent overlaid with the sourness of fear and desperation.

"Oh my god," Kam breathed.

"Jax!" I cried. "Step away from him—you don't understand!"

Screwing up my courage, I held my breath and squeezed past Irina and Nikolayev toward the front of the cabin. I clamped a hand around Jax's arm the same way Irina had grabbed the Russian's.

Jax bared his teeth and tried to shove me behind him, but I set my feet, refusing to budge.

"I'll kill him before I let him lay one hand on Beckett," he snarled, his eyes never leaving Nikolayev's. "I should fucking kill him anyway."

I grabbed the front of his shirt and pulled on it until he looked down at me. "No! Look at him, Jax! Don't you see? He's Beckett's mate!" I said. "Nikolayev is an alpha—he's the one Beckett's been protecting all this time!"

Jax blinked down at me, a hint of shock breaking through mindless alpha rage.

"Please, Jax," I begged softly. "Get out of his way before he decides to go through both of us."

I could feel the tremor of exhaustion in Jax's muscles, and I hadn't missed the red-stained bandage wrapped around his thigh, either.

"Do as your omega says," Nikolayev ground out, his Russian accent thicker than I'd ever heard it before. "*Now.*"

Kam darted past Irina to join us, taking Jax's other arm. "Let's step into the cockpit for a moment, yes? Unless my nose deceives me, those are heat markers — and while you might be willing to stand between an omega in heat and his mate, I'm *really* not."

Between us, we dragged Jax step by hitching step around the stretcher and into the pilot's area at the front of the aircraft. Kam steadied Jax as he swayed, his left leg threatening to buckle. We pressed him to one side of the small area and caged him in with our bodies. His ragged breathing filled the cockpit as he struggled to take this new twist on board.

Nikolayev yanked his arm out of Irina's grip and was at Beckett's side in three long strides, kneeling next to the stretcher and tearing away the velcro cuffs binding Beckett's wrists to the metal side rails. Beckett let out a tortured noise and dove forward into Nikolayev's arms, burying his face in the Russian's neck and shaking uncontrollably.

Nikolayev held him fiercely and rocked him back and forth, murmuring, "*Solnishko*, my heart — I have you now… it's over. It's over, I promise — your alphas are safe. I have you."

Beckett made another terrible sound and clawed weakly at the back of Nikolayev's suit jacket, grabbing handfuls of the material and holding tight.

My throat closed up, and I had to look away, turning toward Jax's chest. I was peripherally aware of Nikolayev scooping Beckett up as though the smaller man weighed nothing and whisking him away, out of the helicopter.

Jax drew in another shaky breath, his arms coming up to pull Kam and me against him. I hugged back hard.

"He'll be all right now," I said. I *had* to believe that was true. My entire world had just been turned upside down with the confirmation of my crazy theory—but Nikolayev wouldn't allow any harm to come to the man he'd just carried away like he was handling the most expensive and breakable glass.

"When did you realize, *odama*?" Kam asked, pulling back a bit from the three-way embrace.

"I didn't," I said. "I mean, there were some things that weren't adding up, but I wasn't sure until just now." I looked up to meet Jax's dazed expression, hoping desperately that Nikolayev hadn't been lying about the others. "Flynn and Alex—are they okay?"

"No," Jax said hoarsely. "No, they're not. But they're here, and they're alive."

"Then we'll deal with the rest of it as it comes," Kam said. "And speaking of people who obviously aren't okay—you're about to collapse. We saw a man outside who looked like medical personnel. Come on."

By the time we helped Jax hobble outside, there was no sign of the man in the white coat—or of Irina, Nikolayev, or Beckett. We got directions to the medical building from one of the people working on the other helicopter and began the slow trek in that direction.

"So apparently we're not prisoners anymore?" I asked, still trying to rearrange this new revelation into my worldview.

"I think the guy in charge was a bit too distracted to worry about details like that," Kam muttered. As the taller and stronger of the two of us, he was doing the lion's share of the work in keeping Jax upright and moving forward.

"Irina was the one who let us out of the cell," I mused, remembering the way she'd grabbed Nikolayev in the helicopter cabin, holding him back from an alpha killing rage. "She's high up in this secret hierarchy, I'm sure of it."

Jax shot me an alarmed look. "Alex didn't see her when she brought you out to the choppers, did she?"

"No," I told him. "We didn't see Alex or Flynn when we came out."

He relaxed. "They must have already been wheeled off to this medical unit. Good."

"So Alex doesn't know about Irina being alive yet?" Kam asked.

Jax shook his head. "Irina was with the team going after Beckett, and she was in the other chopper on the way back. Alex lost consciousness before we lifted off, and she hasn't woken up since."

Worry for all three of our alphas pricked at me. I hoped we'd get some answers once we delivered Jax to the doctors.

"That's not going to be a fun conversation for anyone when she wakes up," Kam pointed out.

"No," Jax agreed. "It's not. No more than the *'hey, I've delivered you into Nikolayev's hands, and it turns out he's the one Beckett's been protecting… but I didn't know it at the time'* conversation."

Every few seconds, some new piece of fallout from that particular revelation popped into my head to throw me for a loop again—but right now, Jax, Flynn, and Alex were at the top of my worry list. The rest of it would have to wait, even if waiting felt like standing at the bottom of a snowy pass and expecting an avalanche to fall on my head.

"One thing at a time," I said.

We made it to the squat, unremarkable building beyond the main house that allegedly contained the medical facilities. The armed and uniformed guard stationed in front took one look at Jax and waved us inside.

The interior was basic, but clean and well lit. Darkness had nearly fallen outside, and I blinked a few times to accustom my eyes to the glare of overhead fluorescent lights. Jax waved away the offer of a gurney and instead let the two orderlies take his weight from Kam and me.

"We're staying with him," I said quickly.

"You can come into the ward as long as you keep out of the way," said one of the orderlies.

"That's fine," Kam told him.

We followed them down a hallway that opened into a large area containing perhaps two dozen medical cots, several of which were occupied.

Jax glanced back at us and saw me looking at the carnage. "Sloane's people fought back," he said grimly. "They shot down one of the choppers, too. It was just blind luck that it wasn't one of the ones we were on."

I couldn't afford to think about that too closely — not if I wanted to keep my composure. "You made it, though," I said. "We all made it."

As the orderlies helped Jax to an empty cot, I scanned the room, aware that Jax and Kam were doing the same. My gaze caught on a large, dark-skinned man lying unmoving on a bed in the corner, and my breath hitched.

"It's Flynn," Kam said. "I don't see Alex."

Jax grabbed one of the orderlies by the forearm. "The female alpha with the broken fingers. Where is she?" His tone said they'd better have a goddamned good answer.

"Being prepped for surgery," the man said matter-of-factly. "Her hand is badly injured. It'll need rods and pins."

My gut churned. I tried to tell myself she'd broken it punching some asshole in the jaw… and didn't believe it for a minute.

"Can we see the other alpha who came in?" I pointed at Flynn, who was currently untended.

The orderly's gaze flicked up, following my gesture. "Yeah, go ahead. If he wakes up, call someone over and then try to see how aware he is. There's a possibility of concussion."

"His skull is the hardest part of his body," Jax muttered. "Go on, you two. Go sit with him. I'll be right here for a bit, I'm guessing."

"We'll watch over him," Kam promised.

I wanted to dart forward and kiss Jax first, bless his giant, uncomplicated heart—but I was cognizant of the orderlies' warning not to get in their way while they were working. They were already leaning over him, efficiently removing the makeshift bandage around his leg.

There were no handy chairs nearby, so actually *sitting* with Flynn wasn't really an option. My heart ached as I stood over him, taking in the black and blue of his bruised and swollen face… the small burn marks littering his bare chest. I knelt on the floor and rested an elbow on the edge of the thin mattress, while Kam perched on the edge of the cot on Flynn's other side.

Needing to touch, I reached out and trailed gentle fingers over Flynn's collarbone. "Hey," I whispered.

For a long moment, there was no response… but then Flynn's chest rose and fell on a deep breath.

"Honey and orchard blossoms," he rasped. His right eye blinked open—the left was swollen shut. He gazed blearily between us, and a slow smile tugged at the corners of his split lips. "Now there's a nice way to wake up."

TWENTY-TWO

Leo

"FLYNN," I SAID in relief. My hands hovered, unsure where to land. "I don't know where it's safe to touch you."

He gave a hoarse chuckle and wrapped an arm around my shoulder, tugging me against his chest. I was still worried I'd hurt him if I squeezed back, so I tried to keep my weight as light as possible against him as I soaked up the contact. Spicy musk tickled my nose, soured by stale sweat. I breathed it in deeply anyway.

Kam patted his shoulder, then stood up. "I'll find a doctor."

"Alex and Beckett?" Flynn asked. "They okay?"

"They're here," I hedged, not moving from his embrace. "Alex is in surgery for her hand. Beckett is… a bit more complicated, but I'm pretty sure he'll be okay now. Jax has a hole in his leg, but he seems all right otherwise. He's just across the ward."

Silence fell for a moment, too heavily.

"There's something you're not telling me, sweet thing," Flynn said, proving that his hard skull had apparently done its job of protecting his brain after all. "Is it something I need to know about?"

I pulled back so I could meet his single, bloodshot eye. "It is, but the doctors want to assess you for concussion first. Promise I'll tell you right afterward, okay?"

He gazed up at me with an easy sort of trust that broke my heart. "If you say so, Leona. Just hope they're not planning on asking me any hard questions—I forgot to study for the test."

"If you know what year it is and who the current prime minister is, I think you're probably fine," I told him.

Kam returned with a doctor in tow, and the woman ran through the usual protocol of checking pupillary reaction while asking a few basic questions. When she moved on to ask him if he remembered what had been done to him, my stomach dipped unpleasantly.

"Mostly beatings and electrical torture," he said, as though it wasn't completely horrific. "Got a couple of teeth loose on the right side, and I'm fucking pissed because I'm pretty sure nipple clamps are ruined forever for me now."

"We'll schedule you for dental assessment as soon as you've had a bit more time to rest," the doctor replied, equally matter-of-fact. "And I'm all too familiar with alpha bravado, so I'll see if we can get a trauma specialist in for counseling."

"*Trauma counseling*? Seriously? You've really got all the bells and whistles here, don't you?" Flynn mused. "Does kind of make me wonder where the hell we actually are, though."

The doctor gave a bland smile and left without answering.

"About that," I said, when the three of us were alone again.

"Yeah," he agreed. "About that."

"We found out who Beckett's mate is," Kam said. "And… it's a bit complicated, to put it mildly."

"Also, Irina's alive," I blurted. "Alex doesn't know yet."

Flynn stared at us for a long moment. "Maybe you'd better start from the beginning."

"Right." Kam exchanged a glance with me and cleared his throat. "Shortly after you failed to check in, paramilitary troops stormed the safehouse in the middle of the night and captured us. They flew us to this compound, which is in Cuba, by the way."

We ran through the unlikely sounding story, interrupting each other with various salient points until I finally finished, "And by that point, Beckett was in heat. Nikolayev stormed into the helicopter to get him, which is when we realized that he's the mate Beckett's been protecting all this time."

Flynn continued to stare at us for so long that my eyes watered with the need to blink on his behalf.

"Bullshit," he said eventually.

"Apparently not," Kam told him. "It... mostly adds up, though there are a few questions I'd like the answers to, before we pulled get much deeper into this situation."

There were questions I needed answered, as well. Questions about Nikolayev's dead sister, and the unregistered omegas he'd so famously hunted down for sport on his family's estate in Russia. Questions about how Beckett had ended up mated to the chairman of the Euro-Soviet Committee.

Flynn gave a slow, one-eyed blink. "You said Irina's alive. You absolutely sure about that?"

"Jax is sure," I said. "He knew her before, right?"

"Yeah," Flynn replied after a faint pause. "He did. Shit, that's gonna be Armageddon all on its own, if it's true."

"She's close with Nikolayev, from what we've seen so far," I said. "She also organized the mission to retrieve you."

"Fuck me sideways," Flynn muttered. "Gotta say, this isn't what I expected when I woke up to find you two looking down at me."

"I think I can safely say that none of us expected this," Kam said.

"With the possible exception of Beckett," I couldn't help adding. While I could certainly understand the need for secrecy, Flynn's boss still had some serious explaining to do.

"If Beckett's in an off-cycle heat, it'll be a few days till we get any answers worth a damn," Flynn said. "Can't say I'm real happy about that situation, given that I still don't trust Nikolayev as far as I could throw him. And I don't think I could throw him very far at the moment."

I closed my eyes, remembering the way Beckett had fallen into his mate's embrace in abject relief. "You didn't see them together. Honestly? I think that part of it's just fine."

Flynn let out a wordless grunt, neither agreement nor disagreement.

Alex was in surgery for several hours, which was worrying. When she was finally wheeled out, still unconscious, Jax bullied the staff into placing her in a cot next to Flynn's. He also ignored his own medical orders by getting out of bed to sit with her—but at least that inspired the orderlies to locate a few chairs for us.

Kam offered to take hand-holding duty so Jax could rest, but Jax refused.

"Only because I don't want to risk you ending up with a busted hand, too," he said. "Once I'm sure she's not going to try and murder the nearest person when she wakes up, she's all yours."

Flynn was dozing, his body recovering from the abuse it had taken. The doctors had x-rayed his jawbone earlier, and they at least seemed to think he wouldn't lose the teeth. He was slated for a procedure in the morning to stabilize them, so the stretched ligaments anchoring them to his jaw could have a chance to heal.

In addition to her broken left hand, Alex had been flogged. The slow burn of rage that had kindled in my stomach as the doctor described the damage to her back still hadn't subsided. Flynn had apparently sensed my very un-omegalike fury, because he'd said, "For what it's worth, she shot the guy in the head afterward. *Boom* — exploding skull fragments, brain splatter, the whole nine yards."

That did, in fact, make me feel better… which was objectively a bit worrying. I was supposed to be a diplomat, and diplomats weren't supposed to fantasize about people being killed in horrible ways.

We waited, watching over Flynn and Alex as they slept. I had Flynn's large hand clasped in mine, simply because I couldn't bear not to have physical contact with him after the terrible days of uncertainty.

By unspoken mutual agreement, we didn't discuss any of the recent cataclysmic revelations — or the resulting unimaginable consequences for the underground. Silence reigned in the echoing infirmary, broken only by the occasional snore or cough from one of the injured soldiers sharing the space with us. The lights had been lowered to make resting easier, but there was still enough illumination to allow the nurses to see what they were doing when they came through at regular intervals to check on their patients.

The clock on the wall read two forty-five a.m. when Alex gave a low whine of distress, moving restlessly in her sleep. She'd been placed on her right side to keep the pressure off her injured back, with her left hand in its complicated frame of splints and wires strapped to her chest in a tight sling.

Flynn woke instantly, wincing as he rolled into a sitting position on the edge of the cot. We all turned toward her, watching closely.

"*Alef*?" Jax asked quietly. "It's all right. We're all safe. Beckett, too. Can you open your eyes for us?"

It was so typical of this pack. Alex wouldn't care whether or not *she* was safe unless her packmates were as well—and Jax knew that. Her back was to me, but I heard her sharply indrawn breath; saw her shoulders tense as she became more aware of her surroundings. Kam, who'd been seated at the foot of her cot, rose and came to stand behind Jax's shoulder.

"Hello, alpha," he said. "Jax tried to mate me while you and Flynn were gone. Please don't break his fingers, though. There's enough of that going around as it is."

That seemed to do the trick, as far as snapping her out of her instinctual panic. Her head shot up.

"Jax did *what*?" she demanded, her voice a bare rasp.

I gave Flynn's hand a final squeeze and grabbed the cup of water sitting on the tray table between the cots, going to join the others.

Jax shot Kam a confounded look. "Not exactly the most pressing issue, I'd've thought."

"It was a misunderstanding, anyway," Kam said magnanimously. "No harm done." He took the cup from me. "Here. Mind your hand, though. And your back. And anything else that hurts, for that matter."

Alex gave both him and Jax wary looks as she let Kam slip the straw between her lips. She drank a few sips and pulled back, craning down to look at the hardware strapped around her damaged hand.

"How do you feel?" Jax asked.

Alex's green gaze turned inward for a moment. "Like shit," she replied succinctly. "Flynn?"

"Right here," Flynn said. "Nice one earlier, with the 'playing possum' thing. Gonna have to remember that for next time."

Alex craned around, reassuring herself that Flynn really was all right. "Beckett?" she asked.

"He's being looked after," I said.

Her eyes narrowed. "I don't like that phrasing."

"We found out the complicated way who his mate is," Jax said. "It's Kostya fucking Nikolayev, Alex. He's a *goddamned alpha*, hiding right at the top of the Committee."

And…wow. No coddling happening here, was there?

There was a longish pause. "I'm still drugged," Alex said uncertainly.

"Yeah, you are," Jax agreed. "But you heard that right, all the same." He hesitated. "And there's something else."

"Jax, *no*," I burst out. This was *not* the right time, hard on the heels of dropping the Nikolayev bomb on her. She looked awful—gray-faced and dazed.

It had been the wrong thing to say. Her hazy gaze sharpened—a hound hot on the scent trail.

"What is it?" she demanded. "Tell me."

Jax took a slow breath. "It's Irina, Alex. She's here. She's alive."

TWENTY-THREE

Leo

ALEX SHOOK HER head slowly back and forth. "No. No, she's dead. I felt her die." Blank incomprehension morphed into flat denial behind her unfocused green gaze.

"You felt the bond break," Kam said softly. "They took her mating gland, Alex—just like they tried to take mine. That was why the bond snapped."

"I—" She cut herself off. Shook her head again, though there was no conviction behind the gesture this time. "But, we didn't... she wasn't..." Again, she trailed off. A painful silence stretched for the span of several heartbeats, before she asked in a wavering voice, "The pups?"

Jax sighed heavily. "I'm sorry, *alef*. They're gone."

I wanted to cry the tears Alex couldn't, like I'd done for her back in Romania. They burned at the backs of my eyes, but I didn't let them spill. This time, I didn't think they'd help.

"I have to see her," Alex whispered. "If she's here, I need to see for myself."

"She led the retrieval mission to get you, Flynn, and Beckett back," Jax said. "But she's been avoiding you so far. During the mission, it was because that kind of distraction could easily have turned deadly. Now, I'm not sure why she still hasn't come. She could still be in debriefings. It's the middle of the night, though... and none of us know where her quarters are located. Or even if we're still supposed to be prisoners, for that matter."

Alex's breathing had grown uneven as she struggled with whatever emotions she was experiencing in reaction to the blunt revelation.

"Then leave me alone, all of you." The words emerged as an angry snarl, but the unsteadiness behind them was unmistakable.

"We're not leaving you alone, *alef*," Jax said.

A dangerous edge sharpened Alex's glare. Flynn had no way to see it from his position behind her, but he must have sensed it somehow.

"Oh, just fuck off back to your cot, Jax. Not all of us want to dissect every little goddamned thing. Let the woman have some privacy if she wants it."

Jax shot him a frustrated look, but he must have decided it wasn't an argument worth having tonight. We were all exhausted—and if Kam and I were exhausted, I could only imagine how much worse it must be for the alphas.

"Fine," Jax said. "We'll deal with things tomorrow. Like you said, it's not like we're going to get any useful answers for another few days. I'm sorry I pushed, Alex. Try to get some rest."

Alex didn't reply. She looked like a trapped animal, ready to gnaw off an injured limb if it meant she could escape. Part of me wanted to venture outside and search for Irina, just so Alex would stop looking like that—but it was three in the morning, and the compound was teeming with armed guards who might or might not assume I was still supposed to be in a cell.

"I'll ask one of the nurses if there's a way to get a message to Irina," I told her.

Alex gave a single, tight nod, meeting my gaze with something like gratitude for the barest instant before she squeezed her eyes shut and turned her face into the cot's thin pillow.

Jax still looked like he wanted to stay at her side. I nudged his shoulder until he rose with a grumble and hobbled back toward his cot. As promised, I found a nurse and asked for the message to be delivered, requesting Irina's presence in the infirmary at her earliest convenience.

Reluctant as I was to be separated from the alphas by even such a small distance as a different cot, the reality was that the blasted things were *not* built with two people in mind—particularly when one of those people was over six feet tall and built like a tank. Two smallish omegas were a different story, though. When Kam gestured me toward the empty cot he'd claimed next to Jax, I went along willingly. And if I had to climb half on top of him to keep from falling off? Well, neither of us was complaining.

———◆———

I woke a few hours later feeling as though I'd been up until three in the morning and then slept double with someone on a narrow shelf—not surprising, under the circumstances. I desperately wanted a shower. Actually, I desperately wanted a shower, an appointment with my hair stylist in Montreal, a new wardrobe, makeup, and a manicure.

Somehow, none of those things seemed terribly likely.

Kam, who was very nearly as high-maintenance as I was, hadn't fared much better. His hair stuck out at ridiculous angles, and he had dark circles under his dark circles. I considered commiserating with him about the lack of amenities, but that thought was completely derailed when a slender figure wearing the uniform of Nikolayev's private guard entered.

Irina's gray eyes swept around the bustle of the medical ward. They caught on Alex's back for a long moment. Alex didn't stir — proof, if any were needed, that their bond was truly destroyed. If it hadn't been, her mate's arrival would have woken her from the soundest sleep.

Eventually, Irina wrenched her gaze free and approached Kam and me.

"Good morning," she said in a cool tone. "I've arranged for more suitable accommodations where you and your alphas can recover, once they've undergone any additional treatment they may need for their injuries."

At the sound of her voice, Alex did wake. She stiffened on her cot, drawing in an audible breath.

"Thank you," I replied uncertainly. "And thank you for coming here. Alex wants to speak with you."

"I'll just bet she does," Irina murmured. Then, more conversationally, "Someone will be along shortly to show you to your suite. Until then, there's a continental breakfast set up in the nurses' staff room, I believe."

With that, she turned with military precision and moved to Alex's cot. Kam and I watched with trepidation. Meanwhile, Jax and Flynn were both still out cold thanks to a combination of physical and mental exhaustion topped with painkillers.

"Is this going to be all right, do you think?" Kam asked.

"I have absolutely no idea," I told him truthfully.

TWENTY-FOUR

Alex

THAT VOICE. I knew that voice. It had been a part of me once—the other half of my whole. And it was here, in this place that should have been a house of horrors, but that we were now supposed to believe was a haven.

Irina Pasternak. The omega I'd mated, pupped, and then lost to the Committee. She was speaking to Leona McCready, mere yards away. Discussing accommodations, her voice as cool and unaffected as though she were nothing more than Nikolayev's pet soldier. As though she hadn't once been... *mine.*

I could hardly breathe for the pain of it.

Leona was thanking her for coming... because I'd demanded to see her. Because I hadn't really believed it was true. I wasn't entirely sure I believed it now. What were the odds I was still in Sloane's interrogation room, unconscious and delirious from my injuries? Perhaps the rest of this had all been a dream?

More low voices, and then footsteps approached. I would have to open my eyes and look soon. Any second. Any second now...

The boots stopped beside my cot. I couldn't scent her. They'd taken everything that had made her an omega. That had made her *my* omega. They'd taken our *pups.* I tensed the muscles in my broken hand, pulling against the pins and stitches holding bones and ligaments together—using the pain in an attempt to ground myself.

"Alex," she said.

I opened my eyes. My former mate stood before me. She looked much as she always had—serious gray eyes too large for her elfin face, honey-blonde hair done up in a regulation twist. But there were new lines around her eyes and at the corners of her lips, just as there were around mine.

"Well, this is awkward," she said.

There was a heavy beat of silence.

"How can you be here?" I asked. "How is any of this real?"

"I imagine it's all a bit of a shock," she agreed. With a quick frown, she glanced over her shoulder. "Let's have this conversation somewhere more private. I assume you can walk?"

My hand itched like termites were crawling beneath the skin. My back was a blank canvas of drugged numbness that whispered *bad*. But my legs seemed fine. I heaved myself into a sitting position on the edge of the cot, finding my balance slightly off thanks to one arm being strapped against my chest.

Irina stepped back, giving me space as I rose on unsteady legs. The room stopped spinning after a few seconds, so I gave her a cautious nod.

"This way," she said, and headed toward a door in the back of the infirmary.

I followed, being careful of my body in a way I'd never needed to before. I'd been injured from time to time, of course—but never like this. I'd never had to be stitched and patched back together with steel pins and thread.

I really wasn't enjoying it so far.

Irina led the way to what seemed to be an examination room. It was unoccupied and had a lock on the door, which she engaged. I sat down in the single chair, mostly because trying to stand held the possibility of a humiliating collapse at some point.

Irina leaned hipshot against the functional row of cabinets that held a sink and several drawers.

"You have questions," she said. "I can't answer all of them, but I'll answer what I'm able to."

I couldn't read her face or body language, and that was new. No unregistered omega managed to sneak into the armed services without being an exceptional actor, but she'd never hidden herself from *me*. Fresh disquiet rose in my chest.

Questions. Where to even start?

"How?" I asked, the single word encompassing most of what I was so desperate—and terrified—to hear.

Her chest rose and fell on a deep breath. "How did I survive?"

I nodded.

"Nikolayev was not yet the Chairman when I was arrested, but he was an up-and-comer with a reputation for viciousness," she said. "I assume the others have already told you that he's a plant. The underground's most valuable mole, hiding in plain sight."

"He's a monster," I said, because I hadn't even *begun* to process the idea of Nikolayev being Beckett's mate yet.

"He has spent a lifetime cultivating the persona of a monster," she replied carefully. "There's much more you still don't know, but everything he's done has been in service to the cause of alphomic resistance."

"At what cost, though?" I muttered, thinking of all the dead alphas and omegas.

"Less than you think, and more than many would be willing to pay," she shot back. "Anyway, my family and I were immigrants. You already know this."

I nodded. They'd come from the Ukraine when Irina was nine. She'd lost much of her accent, but not all of it. Now, it was more pronounced than I remembered.

"What you don't know is that my mother was friendly with Sofia Nikolayev, Kostya's sister, when they were at university together."

"Nikolayev's sister... the one he killed when she presented as an omega in adolescence?" I asked skeptically. "That doesn't add up."

"Yes." Irina let out a little huff of dark amusement. "Such a shocking act of violence, wasn't it? They say the body was *practically unrecognizable* when he was finished with her."

The words clicked into place, and I blinked. "You're telling me he faked a murder? Of his own *sister*?"

"The family did, yes. Sofia Nikolayev is now Sofia Shevchenko, married to a beta soviet chancellor in the Ukraine. Together, they are the nominal leadership of the underground in that area—and congratulations, because you now possess information that could bring down a sizable chunk of the resistance. Not to mention a sizable part of the Ukranian government."

I shook my head, trying to settle everything into place through the haze of pain, exhaustion, and drugs. "But your arrest. That doesn't explain—"

"I told you my mother had a connection to the Nikolayev family," Irina said. "When I disappeared, she used it. The Committee's extradition laws are draconian. The fact that I was born in the Ukraine was grounds for the Euro-Soviet Committee to have me hauled back there. I was a special case, you see. I'd infiltrated the beta military. Such an egregious offense brought me to Kostya's personal attention, and we all know what he does to omegas on his family's private estate." Her voice dripped with irony.

"Your trial and execution records were sealed," I said hoarsely.

She shrugged. "Of course they were. Stories of hunting down prisoners in the forest like animals play well with the zealots, but it makes for messy paperwork. Especially when those prisoners are actually disappearing rather than dying."

"But our pups." My throat felt tight around the words. "He *mutilated* you! Our bond..."

Real anger flared in her eyes. "He did no such thing!" she snapped. "He was just... a bit too slow."

She looked away, her hand lifting to brush fingertips over her lower abdomen. It was the first unintentional body language I'd seen from her. "I've no doubt the bastards who violated me assumed I'd die of shock and blood loss on the flight across the Atlantic. That's probably why they didn't fight the extradition harder."

My good hand clenched into a fist against my thigh as I pictured it—my nails digging crescents into the flesh.

"Kostya hid me away on his estate," Irina continued in a detached tone. "He got me medical care, and when I'd recovered to the extent it was possible to do, he asked me if I wanted to fight for him from inside the very organization that is trying to destroy us. I said yes."

"You let me think you were dead," I whispered.

She looked suddenly very tired. "Of course I let you think I was dead. What did you expect me to do? Mail you a letter explaining that a high-ranking member of the Committee is also a high-ranking member of the underground, and that he'd saved me so I could work for him? That was never going to happen."

My head was spinning with more than the painkillers now. "But Beckett—"

"Is Nikolayev's mate," she said sharply. "And you were not in his confidence when it came to that fact."

That was a knife straight to the gut—a brutal reminder that Beckett hadn't trusted us enough to tell us more than the bare minimum we needed for any given mission.

Irina must have seen something of this in my expression, because she continued in a gentler tone. "He did it to protect you."

A rusty sound emerged from my throat—the opposite of a laugh. "Yes. And look how well that's worked out for everyone involved."

Irina's expression closed off again. "You're all here. You're alive. There are worse outcomes."

"So what does this mean for us?" I demanded, needing to know what she expected of me now that this years-long charade was finally ending.

Her faunlike brows drew together. "It means nothing for us, Alex. I'm sorry—but we were adolescents and we didn't have the faintest idea what we were doing. I was in heat and I begged you to bite me, and in the heat of the moment, you did. You didn't want a mate-bond any more than I did, once the hormones wore off."

I stared at her, stunned.

She stared back, unblinking. "Look me in the eye and tell me you wanted me to get pregnant any more than I wanted to *be* pregnant. For god's sake, Alex, that's why we used contraceptives in the first place."

"I would have protected those pups with my life!" I told her, appalled at her implication.

"That's not the question I asked," she replied evenly.

My mouth worked for a few seconds before words formed.

"I still don't know what you expect to happen now," I said, trying to drag the conversation onto some sort of footing I could control. If she would only tell me what I was supposed to do with this mate-bond that wasn't... I could do it. I could take *action,* instead of this terrible uncertainty and guilt.

The look she gave me was very nearly pitying. "Alex, I don't expect anything to happen now, except that you'll be grieving for someone who's alive rather than someone who's dead."

"Irina. I don't understand what you're saying." Even I could hear the hint of desperation creeping into my voice.

"I'm with someone," she said. "I'm in a relationship that makes me happy. He doesn't make me feel as though my lack of a mating gland or a womb makes me somehow incomplete as a person. And..." She paused and glanced away, unable to meet my eyes. "... he isn't a constant reminder of a past I would rather forget."

I blinked at her, trying to force the sense of the words through a blank wall of incomprehension.

She wasn't finished, though. "Don't live in the past, Alex. You have a future waiting, too. You just have to reach out and take it."

I tried to say something. *Anything.* I couldn't. There was a great upswell of something ugly and putrid growing inside me, and I knew I couldn't be in this room when it burst free. I rose from the chair without a word, unlocked the door, and left—ignoring the call of "*Alex, wait*—!" from behind me.

TWENTY-FIVE

Leo

WHEN IRINA HAD said *'more suitable accommodations,'* I'd mostly been hoping for something that didn't involve heavy locks and security doors. I hadn't expected the entire ground floor of the east wing in the spectacular main house.

We were shown to the rooms by someone I could only describe as a butler — a tall, stooped older man missing one arm and an eye. He gave us the guided tour, announcing the purpose of each room in a precise German accent. When we'd completed the trek through bedrooms, bathrooms, fully stocked kitchen, dining room, living room, and yes, a nest, he turned to face us, his tone and expression grave.

"I must ask you not to venture into the west wing. Chairman Nikolayev is currently sequestered there with his mate, and he does not wish to be disturbed."

"We understand," I said, equally gravely. "We have no wish to interrupt our host and his mate during this private time."

I wasn't entirely sure the two alphas behind me agreed with the sentiment, but they'd be bothering Beckett during his heat over my dead body. We might not have all the answers we wanted, but if there was one thing I had faith in right now, it was the devotion I'd seen between Beckett and his unlikely, impossible mate.

"Then I will leave you to rest," said the probably-a-butler. "If you need assistance with anything, the bell pulls in the rooms are all functional. Use them and someone will come immediately."

"Thank you," I told him. "You've been a great help."

The man bowed formally and departed, leaving us in the lavishly appointed wing of a fully staffed colonial-era mansion in the middle of the Cuban rainforest.

"This is nuts," Flynn said. The words were a bit slurred after the dental surgery he'd just undergone to stabilize his loose teeth, but the meaning was clear enough.

On the one hand, I sympathized with the sentiment. But on the other hand, it made sense, given what we now knew. "Beckett is Nikolayev's mate, and you're practically Beckett's pups," I said. "It's not really that surprising that he'd roll out the red carpet."

"Didn't stop him from tossing us in a cell when we first got here," Jax muttered. He lowered himself onto the sofa of the living room where we'd fetched up at the end of the tour, leaning the cane he was grudgingly using against the armrest.

Kam sat on the other end, his head falling to rest against the back of the couch. "I get the impression that if Beckett hadn't been in heat, Nikolayev wouldn't have let their status as mates slip like he did." He stared up at the pristine white plaster of the ceiling and the intricate gold-painted cornices for a long moment before adding, "And to be fair, it was a very pleasant cell, as cells go."

"I'm amazed he was able to maintain the facade as long as he did," I said. "He must have felt every moment of Beckett's interrogation and torture through the bond." To be able to pretend disinterest while experiencing the pain of the one closest to you in all the world...

I shivered.

Flynn flopped down in an armchair, wincing a bit. Thanks to alpha healing, the swelling on his face was already starting to go down, but he'd still been through the wringer.

Speaking of which—

"I don't like the fact that Alex insisted on separate accommodations," I said.

"No," Kam agreed darkly. "The two of you don't find that worrying at all?"

"Figured she was probably getting reacquainted with Irina," Flynn said.

"Seems likely," Jax agreed.

I turned to him. "I still can't believe you dumped all of that on her with no warning." There was censure in my tone, and I couldn't help it. This had been eating at me ever since Alex woke up.

Jax met my eyes and held them. "Leo, the thing you don't understand about Alex is that she won't accept coddling, and she hates prevarication. Period. If she wanted to be here with the rest of the pack, she'd be here. She was pretty damned clear that she wanted space from us."

"What we want and what we need are often two very different things," Kam said philosophically. He rolled his head up from his perusal of the ceiling. "You could have at least tried to talk to her afterward."

Flynn scoffed.

"Sure," Jax said. "And I could have gotten my ass verbally reamed if she was in a good mood, or punched in the face if she was in a bad mood. She's still got one good hand, you know."

He must have noticed my answering scowl, because he softened a bit. "Alex doesn't do feelings, Leo. Trying to *make* her do them doesn't end well for anyone involved. That's just the way she is. It's not our place to try and change her—not that we'd want to in the first place. She's Alex. She's our *alef*, and she's also an emotionally constipated hardass. A fact that's saved our lives on more than a few occasions."

"I'm gonna tell her you said that," Flynn said, sounding half asleep. His eyes were sliding closed, exhaustion catching up to him again.

"Which part?" Jax asked, frowning with what appeared to be genuine alarm. The only answer he got was a snore.

"You should both get some more rest," I said, resigned to losing the argument for now. If she didn't resurface tomorrow, I'd go track Alex down myself. Maybe I was in the wrong here, and she was shacked up in Irina's quarters making up for lost time like the others assumed. I hoped that was the case, even if the idea brought an odd little pang of loss with it.

Perhaps the feeling was on Kam's behalf. That was probably it.

"I want a shower," the omega in question declared. "In fact, I want *all* the showers. God, I feel grungy."

"Ditto," I agreed, not wanting to be alone with my dark thoughts. "Share with me?"

"Always," Kam agreed. "Jax? Why don't you see if you can get Flynn to the nest? He's going to need spinal readjustment if he sleeps for too long in that chair."

Jax grunted acknowledgement and levered himself to his feet. I got up as well and crossed to kiss him. His lips were soft against mine, and he wrapped an arm around me, pressing my body to his.

"How big is this shower anyway?" he asked, after I broke the kiss.

I raised an eyebrow at him. "Not *that* big. Also, you're not supposed to get the bandages wet."

"Sponge bath later?" he asked.

Kam snorted, and I couldn't help the huff of laughter that escaped.

"Deal," I promised him.

I stepped out of his embrace and went to press a kiss to the less-bruised side of Flynn's face. He hummed and nuzzled sleepily into the contact.

"Go sleep in the nest," I told him. "We'll be along soon."

"'Kay," he mumbled, not truly awake.

Kam and I headed for the hallway with the row of bedrooms. Among other shocks of the day had been the discovery that Nikolayev's soldiers had rescued our packed bags from the safehouse in New York and brought them along when they captured us. Kam's remaining cash after the purchase of the old car was untouched, and the Kali mask I'd bought him shortly after we first met was undamaged.

More importantly, it meant we had clean clothes. When a rummage around the master bathroom unearthed a decent selection of soap, body wash, shampoo, conditioner, and moisturizer, Kam let out an almost orgasmic groan of pleasure and fell forward onto the treasure trove, gathering the bottles to his chest in the parody of an embrace.

"Oh, thank god," he said.

We stripped and squeezed into the shower stall — which would not, in fact, have accommodated an alpha along with us — and washed each other with the sort of relief that only grimy, high-maintenance omegas could appreciate. When I reached the half-healed bite mark at the base of Kam's neck, I paused.

"How are you doing, really?" I asked, brushing soapy fingertips lightly across the raised flesh. "Are you okay with this?"

He slumped forward into my arms, and I leaned into his embrace in turn.

"Yeah," he said. "I am. Really, it's fine. I... kind of like having it there, if I'm honest."

I pressed my lips to his mating gland as I'd done so many times before. It tasted slightly different than

I was accustomed to, and the texture of Jax's tooth marks was unfamiliar beneath my tongue. Kam's shudder of pleasure was the same as it always had been, though.

He pressed his face to the base of my neck and breathed in. Even in the shower, I knew he was scenting me.

"I love that you're off the suppressors," he said against my skin. "Please don't go back on them unless there's a good reason."

It was odd, walking around in the sweet haze of my own perfume—but also freeing, somehow. "Okay," I said, and felt his lips curve into a smile where they pressed against me.

We finished washing each other and rinsed off, stepping out of the now steamy shower stall to dry off with thick towels and rub lotion over everyplace that needed it.

"Are you coming to sleep?" I asked, even though it was only mid-afternoon.

Kam took a deep breath and let it out, considering. "I think I need to burn off some nervous energy first. Since we seem to be guests instead of prisoners now, I might go make use of that gym we saw in the rehab wing of the medical building."

I smiled at him, hopelessly fond. "You've turned into one of those people who's addicted to working out and misses it when they can't, haven't you?" I teased.

"Apparently," he said, with a short laugh. "Admit it, though—you love reaping the benefits."

He flexed his left and right pectorals alternately, showing off the sleek dancer's build I loved so much in the most ridiculous way possible. I dissolved into undignified snort-laughter and leaned over to kiss his shoulder.

"Busted," I admitted. "And here I thought I was being so discreet about ogling you."

He kissed my neck. "I'm onto you. I've got a sixth sense like that. Go keep our alphas warm. I'll be back after I've worn myself out and had another shower."

"Have fun," I told him. "Try not to intimidate any of the soldiers with your awesome gym bod."

I threw on an oversized T-shirt that I'd shamelessly stolen from Jax's bag of belongings and went to rejoin the others. They were in the nest as promised, already asleep again—but they'd left a me-shaped gap between them in the massive pile of pillows and blankets on the floor.

I dragged a beanbag over and wriggled into that space, reclining with their heads resting on either side of my thighs. That made it convenient to run the fingers of my right hand through Jax's short blond hair, massaging his scalp. Meanwhile, the fingers of my left hand stroked lightly over Flynn's temple, avoiding the worst of the bruising.

Flynn mumbled something unintelligible and threw a possessive arm over my legs. Jax shifted position until his head rested on my thigh rather than next to it. With that, I settled back and closed my eyes, relieved to let the cares of the day fall away.

TWENTY-SIX

Kameron

MY BODY WAS only partly my own, most of the time — but Leo had been right that when I was exercising it, I found a sort of freedom that was hard to come by in other circumstances. It was not the body I'd been born with, but in the gym, it did my bidding and I settled into my skin in a way that was often difficult to achieve otherwise.

I thought maybe sex would eventually become another such conduit to self-acceptance — at least, the kind of sex I'd had during those intense days of Leo's last heat. I prodded at the idea of Alex, who'd understood so much about me without being told, reuniting with the mate she'd thought lost for so long.

I was happy for her, truly. And also honest enough to grieve a bit on my own behalf, in case this meant she wouldn't want anyone else besides Irina. We wouldn't know that until we all had a chance to talk — and unfortunately, talking didn't seem to be Alex's forte. I hoped Irina balanced her in that regard, but the omega woman's cool demeanor when she'd come to us in the infirmary didn't bode well. Honestly, I was worried for Alex... though I doubted she'd appreciate the sentiment.

For now, though, I intended to put everything out of my mind for a bit in favor of exhausting myself.

The gym in the medical building was geared toward patient rehabilitation, but it would work just fine for my purposes with its weights, treadmills, and elliptical machines. The guard at the door waved me in, and one of the nurses I recognized from the overnight vigil with our alphas gave me a pleasant nod of greeting.

No one questioned my presence as I headed deeper into the building. The gym was exactly as I remembered it from our brief visit, when one of the doctors showed it to us and suggested Jax make use of the facility once his wound was a bit more stable.

I entered with my towel thrown over one shoulder and let my eyes wander over the handful of other people present, all of whom seemed to be looking in one direction rather than using the exercise machines. Following their gazes, I froze in place at the sight of a tall, sleek-muscled figure pummeling the ever loving shit out of a punching bag — *one-handed*.

"Oh, no," I whispered, my heart sinking.

Alex's shoulders were hunched, her weight balanced lightly on the balls of her feet. Her hair was loose, hanging in lank, sweaty strands. Blood streaked the back of the simple hospital clothing she wore as the unhealed whip marks on her back bled through the bandages — the wounds no doubt reopened thanks to the violent punches she was throwing right-handed. Her left arm still appeared to be in its sling, thank god, but there was no way the doctors had cleared her for this kind of activity. The sound of the heavy, thumping blows echoed through the gymnasium.

"Alex," I said, appalled. And then, louder. "*Alex!*"

She didn't hear me, or she was ignoring me. With a feral cry of frustration, she redoubled her efforts to reduce the punching bag to a torn mass of leather and stuffing. *Christ* — her knuckles weren't even wrapped. I dragged my eyes away long enough to look at the others in the gym. They seemed at as much of a loss as I was.

"You know her, right? Should we try to stop her?" asked a beta man with a bandaged shoulder.

A sudden, crushing sense of my inability to deal with this situation on my own assaulted me. But I could only imagine what would happen to any beta stranger who dared to get between Alex's fist and that punching bag.

"No," I said. "Just, uh… give her some space and keep an eye on things, please? I'll be back as fast as I can with help."

The guy shot me an *'are you kidding'* look as I turned to leave. I couldn't really blame him, but I was already jogging rapidly through the medical building, toward the front entrance. Maybe I should have flagged down some doctors, but the vision of half a dozen orderlies tackling Alex to the ground and holding her down while someone injected her with a sedative made me want to vomit.

I ignored the startled questions directed at me by the staff as I charged outside and hared back to the main house. I was breathless when I barged into the nest and skidded to a halt just inside the door. Leo jerked awake from a light doze, her gaze turning frightened when she saw the state I was in. Jax and Flynn, fast asleep on either side of her, didn't stir.

I thanked the universe for heavy-duty painkillers, because my instincts said the alphas' presence would only escalate things further. They seemed to have a very rigid idea about who Alex was and what she needed — one that I suspected was no longer accurate.

I lifted a finger to my lips, urging quiet. "I need you at the gym, *odama*. It's Alex — she's there alone, melting down."

Leo's expression immediately morphed from startled fear to empathy and terrible sadness. "Let me find some pants," she whispered. "Write the others a note, will you? I don't want them to wake up and find both of us gone with no explanation."

I nodded, hurrying to the kitchen for paper, a pen, and a bit of scotch tape as she carefully extricated herself from the nest.

Alex alone and having a meltdown at the gym, I scribbled. *Leo and I have gone to calm her down. Will bring her back here afterward. Please don't follow — leave it to us. Kam.*

I took the note back to the nest and taped it to the beanbag positioned between the two men, so it would be right in front of their faces if they woke up. Leo was waiting for me in the hallway, wearing leggings and sneakers beneath an oversized shirt. Her hair was pulled back in a messy ponytail.

We jogged toward the medical building, and that alone told me how worried Leo was, since she *despised* running for any reason. The guard lifted a hand to stop us this time, staring at us with a frown.

"Problem?" he asked.

"I hope not," I said. "We've got a friend inside who just received some bad news. She's upset."

He gave us a skeptical look up and down, but let us in. We hurried through the building to the gym, where the situation hadn't improved in the interim. Blood smeared the leather of the punching bag now, proof of the damage to Alex's unwrapped knuckles.

"Oh, Alex," Leo murmured, pushing past me to move farther inside. She looked around at the uncomfortable expressions on the other people's faces, and let out a sigh. "I'm so sorry," she said. "But could you all give us some privacy for a bit?"

"Not so sure you two should be in here alone with her, ma'am," said the bandaged beta. "She could be dangerous."

"Not to us," Leo replied, with the same air of utter certainty that had turned contentious diplomatic negotiations in her favor and convinced world leaders to change longstanding views to suit her.

The others exchanged uncertain glances, but then the bandaged man shrugged his good shoulder. "If you say so. Yell if you need help."

"Thank you," Leo told him.

I stood out of the way as the others trooped out of the room, leaving us alone with the sound of rapid, heavy blows and ragged breathing. We flanked Alex's sweat-soaked form, giving her a wide berth as we entered her field of vision.

"Go away," she grated past a clenched jaw. Blood spattered in fine droplets from her split knuckles with every devastating impact.

"No," Leo said softly.

Her teeth bared in an audible growl. "Fuck off with your tears and your diplomacy and your goddamned feelings bleeding all over the place. *Leave me alone!*" The last three words were punctuated with three rapid-fire blows. A small split opened in the leather, white wool stuffing peeking through it.

"Shan't," I said, my heart breaking for her. I met Leo's eyes, silently telegraphing the foolhardy thing I was about to do. She nodded agreement.

As one, we stepped forward. I grabbed Alex's bleeding fist in mid-blow, grunting under the impact against my palm and thanking my lucky stars she was already exhausted. At the same moment, Leo slipped between the alpha and the abused punching bag. Alex jerked her hand free with a gasp and stumbled backward, landing flat on her ass. We knelt in front of her, forming three corners of a sweaty and breathless triangle.

She looked terrible. Her face was bloodless and gray, dripping with clammy sweat. Her hair was matted and tangled, hanging loose since she couldn't do anything practical with it one-handed. Her left hand lay against her chest, fingers curled like the legs of a dead spider, caged inside the frame of wires and pins. The smell of night jasmine and sandalwood languished beneath the stench of sweat and festering grief.

"What did Irina do to you?" Leo asked, her voice hard with anger.

Alex stared at her like she was some sort of exotic alien life form. "Nothing," she snarled. "She did *nothing*."

"The hell she didn't," Leo shot back.

"Something obviously happened," I said in a softer tone. "Please tell us."

Flat green eyes speared me. "She did nothing. She... *wants*... nothing." Her voice cracked on the last word.

"Oh," Leo breathed. "You wanted her back, and she... what? Rejected you?"

Alex made an angry, dismissive gesture with her free hand—her fingers bruised and tinged ruby with blood. "Why would she not? It's been years. The bond is broken. She's found another person and no longer wants me."

"I'm so sorry, Alex," Leo said. "I can't imagine how that must—"

"That's not why I'm angry," Alex said, cutting her off with a sharp jerk of the head. "It's as she told me. We were barely more than pups when I mated her. We were a pair of *idiots*."

"Then, what?" I asked carefully.

"You don't understand!" she flared. "You can't understand—no one can!"

"Explain it to us," Leo insisted, in a tone that brooked no argument. "*Tell us*, Alex."

"She was alive!" Alex cried. "My mate was alive, and I didn't come for her!"

"You couldn't have known," I said, taken aback by the pain in that simple declaration.

"But you still blame yourself," Leo said slowly. "If she was dead, then you'd already failed. There was nothing more to be done. But instead..." She trailed off.

"They killed our pups and ripped her body to pieces," Alex said jaggedly. "She was broken and frightened and alone, and I didn't lift a *fucking finger* to find her and save her."

"Does she blame you for that?" I demanded, ready to go give a certain omega a piece of my mind if she'd said any such thing.

"Of course she fucking doesn't," Alex snapped. "She's moved on. She doesn't love me. She never—" The words choked into silence.

Do you love her? I wanted to ask—but Leona was giving me a warning look.

"I would have loved those pups with my last breath," Alex whispered, and perhaps that was an answer, of sorts. "*God.* We were almost—"

A family, my mind supplied, into the blank space. And oh, how intimately I knew that pain. Pups that might have been. A family that might have been.

I lifted a hand toward her, inching forward on my knees, clearly communicating my intention. When my arm came around her shoulders, high enough to avoid the fresh blood seeping through the bandages, she stiffened.

"Don't touch me," she said hoarsely.

I stilled. "Tell me that again like you mean it, and I promise I'll let go," I said, hoping it wasn't a terrible mistake.

Silence fell, broken only by the awful, labored sound of breathing that wanted to be sobs. One heartbeat, two, three—and Alex slumped against me, shuddering. Leo scooted up on her other side and wrapped her between us, being as careful of her broken hand as a mother bird with a newly hatched chick.

"You have a family," Leo said. "You have a *pack*, Alex. Please, let us take you back to them. They need to know that you're hurting."

Alex let out a low moan of pain and leaned into us, trusting us with her weight. We stayed like that for several long moments, just supporting her between us.

"Do you need to see one of the doctors first?" I asked—worried about the damage she might have done to herself.

Alex uncurled enough to glance down at her bruised right hand as though it belonged to someone else, before shaking her head slowly. "It's fine," she rasped.

She let us heft her to her feet on rubbery legs. After a moment, she nodded, and the three of us began the awkward shuffle toward the front door and the huge house across the compound.

It was more or less the mirror image of when we'd dragged Jax to the infirmary, though Alex gained steadiness as we walked, rather than growing weaker. It felt like the short journey took forever, but eventually we entered the east wing to find Flynn pacing restlessly in the foyer while Jax leaned against the wall, looking pale and haggard.

"Shoulda woke us up," Flynn growled. His eyes were for Alex, though. He looked like someone had taken his compass away and handed it back with the needle pointing south instead of north.

"What happened?" Jax asked quietly.

"Rough day all around," Leo said shortly.

"Is it Irina?" Flynn asked.

"Not here," Leo shot back. "Let's go to the nest."

"Bathroom first," I said. "I want to clean up those split knuckles, if nothing else."

"I'm not an invalid," Alex snapped.

"Take a look in the bathroom mirror and tell me that," I retorted.

Jax and Flynn looked like they thought they should be doing something, or saying something, but they had no idea what it was. I hadn't been wrong about them having an unshakable idea of Alex that didn't really match up with the current reality. Leo and I swept Alex toward the bathroom, where we cleaned her up as best we could over her half-hearted protestations.

I still wasn't happy about the fresh bleeding on her back, but removing and rewrapping the bandages would probably make things worse by pulling open the places where the gauze had scabbed to the skin with dried blood. I resolved to drag her back to a doctor in the morning, or perhaps see if one of them would come here for a house call.

We led Alex to the nest when we were finished, where Jax and Flynn were waiting awkwardly. They'd cleaned up as well at some point, their hair damp and most of the day's grime wiped away.

"Will you tell us what happened?" Jax asked again.

Alex shook her head, but Leo plowed right over her. "Irina's moved on. She's with someone else. Alex blames herself for not having known she was still alive and going after her. And she's grieving her pups."

"Oh," Jax said blankly.

"*Fuck*, Alex," Flynn said, running a hand over his close-shorn black hair. "That's some rough shit. You should've said."

"We're sleeping pack-style tonight," I decided. "Alex, lie down."

"I'm not tired," she muttered.

"You're exhausted," I said, kicking off my shoes and leading by example. "Now lie *down*."

I didn't really expect her to give in without a fight. But she slumped to the cushion-strewn floor, as though hearing me say how tired she was made it real for her.

"Get the lights," Leo said, as she lay down on Alex's other side, mindful of her sling.

After the tiniest of hesitations, Flynn crossed to the door and flicked off the lights. A couple of small nightlights came on, casting a soft reddish glow over the room. Flynn came and lay down behind Leo, slinging an arm across her. Meanwhile, Jax lowered himself carefully to the floor on his bad leg, settling in behind me.

Silence settled over the room, broken only by the sound of our breathing—but it wasn't an easy quiet. Eventually, Jax broke it.

"You had no way of knowing she was alive, *alef*," he said, echoing what I'd told Alex in the gym.

I felt Alex swallow. "We're supposed to come after the ones who are lost," she said, barely more than a whisper. "We're always supposed to come for them. *Always*."

I thought of Beckett, Flynn, and Alex coming after us in the terrorist cave in Romania… of all four of them coming to save us when Leo was arrested. Of Jax rescuing Flynn and Alex from Sloane's torture cell.

"Doesn't sound like Irina was lost, though," Flynn said. "Someone *did* come for her. It just wasn't you."

Unexpectedly, a choked sob emerged from next to me. I put my hand on Alex's shoulder. It was shaking.

"It's all right to grieve," Jax said, sounding a bit choked up himself. "I'm sorry we didn't know you were hurting. I wish you'd told us, *alef*."

"There's been no time to grieve," Alex said in a strangled tone.

"There's time now," I said, squeezing gently.

"They killed my pups," she said around tears. "They killed my *pups*."

And then she was crying in earnest, wracked with ugly sobs as she turned blindly toward me. There was nothing to do except hold her—this hard-as-nails alpha who'd carried all her pain inside for years... for a lifetim*e*. Leo curled around her and stroked her hair, murmuring soothing nonsense as Jax and Flynn reached across us to rest their hands on their *alef*'s shoulder and hip.

"This is pack pain," I said, remembering the way my family would gather to mourn a loss when I was small, in the time *before*. "In a pack, you never have to bear such grief alone."

"Never," Jax agreed.

"Never," Flynn echoed.

"Never," Leo whispered.

Alex only sobbed harder, her tears soaking into my shoulder.

TWENTY-SEVEN

Leo

WE SPENT THE next four days with the world locked outside the doors and did nothing but rest, eat, and connect. Alpha healing meant that Flynn's bruising subsided to slowly fading greens and yellows, and the ugly furrow left in Jax's thigh by the passage of a bullet scabbed over.

The doctors tutted over Alex's back and hand when Kam put his foot down and insisted she let them look at her. He'd barely left her side, and I was pretty sure Jax and Flynn's newly solicitous behavior toward their pack leader was slowly driving her insane. I liked to think the pendulum would swing back to more of a happy medium that everyone could live with, given enough time.

I didn't think I'd ever been so lazy in my life. I slept nearly as much as the people who'd been injured—sometimes in the nest, sometimes in the bedroom I'd claimed as mine. I wasn't willing to flaunt it in front of Alex while she was grieving her own loss so sharply—but privately, the sponge baths I'd promised Jax and Flynn had turned into slow, gentle sex on three occasions, twice separately, and once together.

It was a different experience, having the alphas sleepy and passive beneath me as I took my time, caressing skin with slow strokes and taking them inside me with tender care, riding them until they groaned and spilled, knots locking me in place— exactly where I wanted to be.

It was too late to protest that I couldn't mate them, and we all knew it. There was still one thing holding me back, though.

"I'm asking again," Flynn said at one point, when I was draped boneless across his torso. "I warned you I would."

His knot sent shivers of pleasure up and down my spine with each slow breath I took. I pushed up on my elbows so I could look at him, being careful to avoid the raw electrical burns still littering his chest.

"That's playing dirty," I told him, as liquid pleasure shifted and sparkled inside me.

A half-smile tugged at one corner of his lips. "Only way I know how to play, sweet thing."

I sighed, swallowing a moan as the small movement shifted him inside of me. "You already know I'm going to say yes eventually."

The smile widened. "I knew that a long time ago, Leo."

"But I won't break up your pack by only mating you and Jax, leaving Alex out in the cold," I went on, before he could get too smug about it. "For one thing, I'm pretty sure Kam's in love with her, even if he hasn't quite realized it yet. And I... care for her a great deal," I finished, thinking of the noble alpha who blamed herself for not somehow knowing the unknowable and doing the impossible.

Flynn pulled me down and ravished my mouth with a kiss so deep and thorough it left me dizzy. "And that's one of the reasons I love you. Okay, so it's all or nothing. That's also one of my favorite ways to play."

I nodded. "But Alex isn't remotely ready to talk about the subject, much less act on it. Plus, she may have no interest whatsoever in me—though I think she does in Kam."

Flynn looked like he might argue, so I put a fingertip over his full lips, silencing him.

"If she doesn't want me, we can revisit the subject and figure out what that means for all of us," I said firmly. "But she needs to be part of that conversation, and right now she's not in a position for that. You say *'all or nothing,'* but that's not it, exactly. I'm not a diva. I don't need all of this to be about me. Maybe Kam bridges the gap between Alex and the rest of us. Maybe we have a strategic mating for pack cohesion, even if it's not a love match. Or maybe she never wants to hear the word *'mate'* again. But she needs to have all those choices open."

Flynn gave an easy shrug beneath me. "Course she does. I hear you, Leo. You know me—I'm patient. Just hearing you say yes instead of finding a million words that don't include no makes me happy."

I gave a rueful snort. "Yeah, you were always going to wear me down eventually, weren't you?"

"Yup," he said, taking my waist in his big hands and shifting his hips, drawing a sharp gasp of ecstasy from me.

<hr>

When the weird old butler guy showed up on the morning of the fifth day with an invitation to join our hosts in the west wing of the house, I knew our time of carefree rest was over. It had been an illusion anyway, but a much needed one.

I went in search of the others. Jax and Flynn were easy to find. I eventually heard the sound of trickling water filtering through the half-open door of one of the bathrooms, and followed it to discover Kam and Alex sitting on the floor next to the bathtub. Alex's head was tilted back, her neck resting on the edge of the tub with her long hair trailing into the basin. Kam held a china pitcher from the kitchen filled with water, and was pouring a steady stream over the dark tresses to rinse them.

"This is ridiculous," Alex muttered.

Kam paused. "You want clean hair? Then it isn't ridiculous, you stubborn alpha. You're not getting your hand or your back wet on my watch, so lie back and be pampered, damn it."

I knew I shouldn't be watching like this without announcing my presence, despite the warm, soft feeling the scene engendered. Purposely letting my shoe scuff against the hardwood floor of the hallway, I closed the final two steps to the doorway and knocked lightly on the frame.

"Sorry to interrupt," I said, "but we've been invited into Nikolayev's territory. Hopefully that means Beckett's recovered and it's time to talk."

Alex shot upright like she'd been fired from a cannon, ignoring Kam's huff of irritation as water splashed on the floor. "About bloody time," she said, hauling herself to her feet with her good hand on the tub. Her hair hung in a soaking mass behind her.

"What did I *just* say about getting your back wet?" Kam groused, fumbling for a towel. "We'll be along in a minute, *odama*."

Once everyone was presentable, the butler led us past the grand staircase that divided the two halves of the house, conveying us to the double doors of a beautifully appointed formal receiving room.

"Your guests, sirs," he announced, stepping aside and gesturing at us to enter with his single arm.

We entered to find Kostya Nikolayev standing by the room's massive, unlit fireplace—something which seemed like a bit of an odd feature for a house in the middle of a tropical rainforest. Rhys Beckett sat in an overstuffed chair, wrapped in a flannel dressing gown that practically swallowed his slight frame. He looked drawn, almost frail, but his sea-colored eyes were clear and lucid.

He rose unsteadily at our approach. Nikolayev stepped forward quickly, his hand raised as though to offer support. Beckett waved him away testily.

"Don't hover, Kostya," he said. "It's not as though this was my first heat."

Nikolayev grumbled something inaudible, but backed off—a watchful presence with sharp gray eyes, his long arms folded across his chest.

Beckett immediately turned his attention to us, his expression turning haunted. "Alex. Flynn. I am so incredibly sorry for all of this."

He met us halfway, moving like an old man, and pulled Flynn into a tight embrace. The huge alpha curled around him—a pup with his beloved carrier.

"'S okay, Boss," he said into the smaller man's hair. "No harm done that won't heal. Jax came and rescued us."

"He might have had a *bit* of help with that," Nikolayev put in testily, biting off the words.

"Hush," Beckett said, and I watched in mild amazement from the sidelines as the chairman of the Euro-Soviet Committee hushed.

Beckett released Flynn with a final pat on the back and reached for Alex, taking her good hand in one of his and curling the other around the nape of her neck. "Alex. I'm so sorry. You will have learned about Irina by now, I expect."

Alex leaned down until their foreheads touched and gave a short, wordless nod.

"If I could have thought of a way to tell you without making everything a hundred times more dangerous—" he began.

"It's all right," Alex said hoarsely. "I understand." She eased away. "You're not hurt?"

"No," he said. "No, Alex—I'm fine."

Nikolayev scoffed. "You were kidnapped, drugged, interrogated, tortured psychologically, and thrown into an artificial heat. And I *will* see the one responsible pay in kind."

"We'll get to that part in a minute," Beckett said, letting Alex go. "Jax. Come here."

Jax, too, accepted a hug from the omega who'd been like a parent to him. "Glad you're back, Boss. Not sure I approve in your choice of mates a hundred percent, though. No offense," he added belatedly.

"He's an acquired taste," Beckett replied wryly, "but surprisingly handy to have around in a pinch."

This seemed like as good a time as any to join the conversation.

"When the others said your mate was probably a higher-up in the underground, I'll admit this wasn't quite what I pictured," I told him.

His expression twisted with mild, self-deprecating humor. "Yes. Quite. Though in my defense, it's not as though any of you would have believed the truth."

"About that," I went on, cutting right to the chase. "There are some questions we need answered about dead and tortured alphas and omegas before we go too much further."

"Your sister," Alex said, addressing Nikolayev directly—alpha to alpha. "You faked her death and smuggled her away when she presented as an omega. To protect your own rise to power?"

Nikolayev raised an eyebrow. "My family has been embroiled in the alphomic resistance for generations. Many are betas, holding positions of political and religious power throughout Russia and Eastern Europe. Some, like myself, are alphas hiding in plain sight and embedding ourselves as deeply inside the beta power structure as we can manage. Others are omegas, and have a long history of forging alliances through marriage with other powerful families."

"And the hunts?" I asked. "They weren't real?"

"They were a good way to help fugitives disappear without too many questions being asked." Nikolayev's penetrating gaze pinned me, testing my resolve... seeing if I would give in to my innate omega nature and yield to him. "Dead bodies are not difficult to come by in Russia. And betas do love a good story of bloodthirsty carnage."

"Are you saying that no alphas or omegas have died at the hands of the Euro-Soviet Committee?" Kam asked, standing straight-backed and firm-shouldered beside me. "Because with all due respect, Chairman, I find that very difficult to believe."

"No," Nikolayev replied. "No, I am not saying that at all. I have stood by and watched innocents fall beneath the firing squad, while sharing drinks and handshakes with the guilty. Believe me when I say, if I had the power to wave a wand and end the bloodshed within the Euro-Soviet Confederacy, I would have done so long before now."

Beckett gave a slow clap. "A lovely speech, dearest. Maybe not the *most* reassuring for our guests—but a good, statesmanlike delivery, nonetheless. And it does rather bring us around to the current point," he finished grimly.

"Which is?" I asked, frowning.

"The Nikolayev family and others like them have spent decades getting to this point without being detected." Beckett's eyes flicked to his mate's for a moment, meeting and holding. "Sloane already suspects. He captured me in hopes of blowing the upper levels of the resistance wide open."

"Did you break under interrogation?" Alex asked, with brutal directness.

A low growl rumbled up from Nikolayev's chest, but Beckett waved him off again.

"Not to my knowledge, which is admittedly spotty at best after they started with the drugs,"

Beckett replied, apparently without offense. "But in the end, it may not matter."

"You were rescued by soldiers in helicopters identifying themselves with secure Committee codes," Jax said slowly. "Sloane knows for sure now that there's a rift within his organization." He turned hard blue eyes on Nikolayev. "Does he suspect you specifically?"

The Russian's lips twisted. "Of course he does. He has for years. Despite appearances, the man is not an idiot."

I thought back over Sloane and Nikolayev's history, looking at it through this new lens. "He's been shouting from the rooftops about alphas and omegas infiltrating beta institutions since he first rose to power." I looked to Beckett to confirm what I'd just realized.

"And he's absolutely right about that," Beckett said tartly. "It's a damn good thing he comes across as a fringe lunatic most of the time, or we'd have been in worse trouble than we already are."

"The underground resistance is not ready for all-out war," Nikolayev stated with certainty. "However, whether we are ready or not, that war is coming. It will not be fought with bombs and bullets. At least, not exclusively. It will be fought in the hearts and minds of the people." His eyes landed on me again. "That is why we need all the allies we can get. Especially ones with your… particular skill set."

"Diplomacy?" I hazarded.

"Persuasion," he replied. "That, and I need your contacts. Anyone in a position of power who you believe might harbor alphomic sympathies."

I thought of all the people I'd met over the years in the glittering world of international politics. "I can do that. But that was always the plan, after Beckett rescued me."

"It's more than that now," Beckett said kindly. "Be certain you understand what you're signing up for before you commit."

"Then what are you asking of me?" I asked, frowning.

The energy in the room shifted as all eyes focused on our exchange.

Nikolayev ran a speculative gaze over me. "We are asking you to return to the world stage openly, as a known omega fugitive. We are asking you to risk your life in exchange for all the lives that might be saved if the old order falls."

My heart skipped a beat. Beside me, I heard Kam inhale sharply. I didn't dare turn toward him, choosing instead to lock eyes with Beckett.

Nikolayev's mate reached out and clasped my hand in his. "Leona McCready… we're asking you to be the public figurehead for the alphomic resistance."

End of Book 2

BOOK THREE:

TRUTH OR LIE

ONE

Leona

THE RED LIGHT on the video camera stared at me, unblinking. I stared back, keeping my voice strong and clear as I delivered the carefully scripted speech. My hair and makeup were perfect. My message was vital and just.

"In conclusion, I ask every single one of you who are watching this message to look inside your hearts," I said. "Ask yourself whether allowing alphas and omegas the same basic human rights as betas in any way diminishes your own rights and freedoms. You may find that the opposite is true—that you are not truly free until all human beings are free."

Lifting my chin, I willed the unseen millions of future viewers to think seriously about my words… challenging them to look into my eyes and believe I, as an unregistered omega, wasn't as human as they were.

"That's a wrap," said the cameraman, in his heavy Russian accent.

The red light next to the lens flipped off, and my shoulders slumped from the straight, commanding posture I'd adopted during filming.

"You don't want to do another take?" I asked, already second-guessing some of my choices in delivery and cadence.

A broad-shouldered figure stepped from the shadows, his gray eyes intent. "No, that will suffice. Thank you."

If anyone had tried to tell me six months ago that I'd be looking for approval from Kostya Nikolayev, the Euro-Soviet chairman of the Committee on Alphomic Suppression, I'd have assumed they were off their meds. Of course, if you'd asked me about a lot of things six months ago, I would have given you answers considerably different from the answers I'd give today.

After a lifetime spent concealing my unregistered omega status and working my way up the ranks of the Foreign Service, I was no longer Ambassador Leona McCready of the UFNA. As far as the United Federation of North America was concerned, I was a fugitive. Somehow, I had also become the public face of the Alphomic resistance. It was a position that would ultimately be no less dangerous than hiding in plain sight as an ambassador had been, but it held more of a chance at making a real difference in the world during my lifetime.

I was hiding away with Kameron Patel, my omega packmate, and our three alphas—Flynn, Alex, and Jax. We were staying as guests at Nikolayev's family estate, located southwest of St. Petersburg. Our host, a man I once would have counted as my people's greatest enemy, had turned out to be our most valuable ally. Kostya Nikolayev was an alpha, and yet he'd somehow managed to infiltrate the highest levels of the worldwide beta organization dedicated to crushing our people underfoot.

His family, dedicated to the fight for freedom for generations, had spread its tendrils through the power structure of Russia and Eastern Europe via political maneuvering and strategic marriages within the great families. As an alpha in a public position, Nikolayev's life would have been much simpler if he'd stayed unattached, or perhaps entered into a marriage with a prominent and trustworthy beta woman. Instead, he'd somehow ended up mated to Rhys Beckett, an omega prominent in the UFNA branch of the alphomic underground.

I'd sworn to myself that I'd get that story out of Beckett at some point. But, however it had originally come about, if it weren't for that unlikely mating I'd be dead three times over. Nikolayev had provided intel and logistical support that had saved me on multiple occasions, all of it done from behind the scenes and presumably at great risk to himself.

Most recently, he'd provided soldiers and helicopters to execute a daring rescue of his mate and two of my alphas after Enoch Sloane, the head of the UFNA branch of the Committee, captured them for torture and interrogation. Sloane knew Nikolayev was hiding something, and he'd long held hopes of exposing his rival as an alpha. The Russian's desperate rescue mission to retrieve Beckett, Flynn, and Alex ended up catapulting the hidden conflict between the Committee and the Alphomic underground resistance into the open — ultimately exposing the extent of the underground's infiltration into worldwide beta institutions.

We weren't ready for open warfare with the Committee — but that wouldn't stop the war from coming if Sloane got his way. For now, our best chance was to turn it into a battle of public opinion, preferably before Sloane and his terrorist allies could turn it into a battle of bullets and experimental, alphomic-targeted chemical weapons.

That was where Kam and I came in. Before I was exposed as an unregistered omega, I'd been a high-ranking diplomat, and Kam had been my attaché. We had established connections in international circles. Not only that, but bringing people around to my side of an argument had once been in my *actual job description*. Beckett and Nikolayev had drafted us into their cause in hopes that we could bring those skills and connections to bear on the underground's behalf.

So far, that meant recording videotaped speeches for release to news organizations worldwide while hiding away in Nikolayev's heavily guarded family estate. In many ways, Kam and I were currently safer than we'd ever been in our lives. The answer to the question 'How rich and powerful is the Nikolayev family?' appeared to be 'They own half of the property between St. Petersburg and the Estonian border, and can afford their own private militia.'

This dreamlike time-out-of-time wouldn't last forever. Eventually, I would have to venture out from behind the protective walls and security patrols of Nikolayev's estate, so I could meet with leaders on the world stage in person. After months of laying the groundwork, that time was fast approaching—but first, I would have to deal with something else that was approaching even faster.

My heat cycle.

Twice now, I had entered into a no-strings heat contract with my trio of alpha protectors. At this point, 'no-strings' was basically a joke, and we all knew it. Our relationship had more strings than an entire army of marionettes. I had high hopes that this would be the time when we all stopped pretending that we weren't going to end up mated. As it happened, Kam and I had a meeting planned today to discuss exactly that subject.

For now, though, Nikolayev expected my mind to stay on the job... and that was fair enough.

Kam approached and handed me a glass of water. He eyed the Russian warily, a gazelle assessing a lion. "Has there been any further communication from Secretary Fouchet in Luxembourg?" he asked.

"Not directly," Nikolayev said. "I have, however, received a letter from one of his underlings, requesting clarification of Ms. McCready's status and my own position in the Committee."

"To which you replied…?" I prompted, curious how he was spinning his ongoing brutal vivisection of the Euro-Soviet branch. Across the Atlantic, Enoch Sloane's part of the organization was as rabidly bloodthirsty as ever. However, Nikolayev had managed to plant enough moles inside this branch to effectively neuter it with ousters and political infighting, once the shit hit the fan.

"I replied that the Committee is reassessing its objectives, and you are acting as a liaison to discuss alphomic interests with an eye toward normalizing relations with the beta power structure."

That was as nice a way of saying 'the lunatics are running the asylum' as I was likely to hear. The reality was that we were all running around like headless chickens while we tried to stave off a catastrophic worldwide conflict.

"Fouchet's halfway in love with you, Leo," Kam said. "He'll come through in the end."

I raised an eyebrow. "Maybe we should start contacting all the attachés and assistants you've blatantly flirted with over the years," I told him.

"Oh, *please*. I don't flirt," Kam replied. "I'm the picture of professionalism and decorum, and I always have been."

"Maybe we should start contacting all the attachés and assistants whose blatant flirting you've failed to respond to, in that case." I returned my gaze to Nikolayev's steel-gray eyes. "What about Prime Minister Fairbanks' administration? Any movement there?"

"Not yet." The Russian's expression remained impassive, revealing nothing. "They are in a somewhat difficult position after failing to uncover your unregistered status for so many years, while you were in a high-ranking position within the Foreign Office."

"That's true," I agreed. "I suppose I should be pleased that I didn't end up bringing down the entire coalition government when things went bad. Still, Fairbanks has always been a bit of a sympathizer, at least in subtle ways. I can't help thinking he could be the key. If we could somehow pry him loose, he might bring a lot of other leaders along with him."

Levi Fairbanks, the head of the UFNA government, had risen to power on the back of good looks, charisma, and moderate policies. He'd never risked voter backlash by doing or saying anything overt, but he'd remained a quiet bulwark against some of the more extreme anti-alphomic policies that had taken root elsewhere in the world.

"Perhaps so," was all Nikolayev said.

"How's Beckett doing today?" Kam asked, changing the subject.

"He is currently on bed rest, following the advice of my private physician." Nikolayev's tone didn't invite further inquiry.

During his capture by Enoch Sloane, Rhys Beckett had been drugged in a bid to loosen his tongue during interrogation. He'd reacted badly to the injections and gone into an off-cycle heat. Nikolayev's forces had managed to rescue him before the worst happened, but emotions had been running high in the aftermath of the retrieval mission. Maybe Nikolayev had been too addled by heat pheromones to think about the need for contraception, or maybe he'd simply assumed his mate was already too old to conceive. They were both middle-aged, and Beckett was approaching estropause.

However, 'approaching estropause' wasn't the same thing as 'past estropause.' Now, the Nikolayev family was a couple of months away from welcoming its newest member into the world... assuming Beckett's pregnancy went to term. Unfortunately, that wasn't a foregone conclusion by any means. The fact that he was only pregnant with one pup and not a litter was in his favor, as was the fact that the Nikolayev family had access to alphomic medical specialists. Meanwhile, Beckett's age—especially given the stressful circumstances surrounding the conception—was very much *not* in his favor.

"Tell him we'll visit later if he's feeling up to it," I said, wondering if the poor man was going insane with boredom yet. Given what I knew of him, he probably was.

"I will pass on the message," Nikolayev said. "Now, though, I must take my leave of you both. I have a phone conference this afternoon with the Committee representatives from Kyiv and Moscow."

I winced, not envying him. "Have fun with that."

The slight twitch of his lips in response had more to do with irritation than any attempt at a smile. "Quite," he said, and left us alone with the camera crew packing up their equipment.

Kam rolled his shoulders, releasing some of his tension. "Maybe someday I'll be able to share a room with that man and not feel like he's two seconds away from pulling a knife on me," he said. "Sadly, today is not that day."

I knew what he meant. There was no doubt in my mind that Nikolayev was on the same side we were. That didn't make him any less of a terrifying bastard to deal with.

"Something to aspire to," I told him wryly. "So, are you ready to beard the cheetah in her den?"

Kam's deep brown eyes lit with purpose. "Yes, I bloody well am. This whole thing is getting ridiculous."

"Hey, now," I said, twining my arm through his and tugging him toward the door. "Be fair. Alex has a lot to process, and the kind of trauma she experienced doesn't just disappear in a few months."

Kam sighed. "Of course it doesn't. But if you wall it up and ignore it, then it'll *never* get better. Go on—ask me how I know." The last few words were a low mutter.

I squeezed his arm. "We'll find a chink in her armor. I don't intend to go through another heat cycle with things still in limbo."

Arm in arm, we headed toward the front doors of Nikolayev's palatial manor house—silently girding ourselves to discuss mating bonds with a bereaved alpha. Specifically, an alpha who'd made it crystal clear that she never wanted to hear the word '*mate*' again.

TWO

Leona

SPRING IN RUSSIA near the Gulf of Finland was a capricious thing. Frequently gray, sometimes snowy, occasionally rainy when the temperature crept above freezing. There had been snow blanketing the ground constantly since we'd arrived late in the previous autumn. A steady rainfall two days ago had revealed the first patch of bare earth I'd seen in months.

Today, we'd been blessed with a rare day of brilliant sunshine, pushing the mercury up to something approaching pleasant. I was Colorado born and bred. That, along with years of living in Montreal, had cemented my tolerance for chill, even if I didn't actively enjoy it. Kam, who'd been raised in Kolkata, still despised the cold—but he'd kept a lid on his grumbling when Alex suggested we meet on the balcony of the guesthouse where we'd been staying.

The sheer amount of wealth on display in the Nikolayev estate was staggering. The word *guesthouse* brought to mind a cute little cottage tucked away at the back of someone's property. Nikolayev's guesthouse was a three-story architectural wonder of curving walls, arched windows, stained glass, and modern amenities.

Every room featured a fireplace, and the basement had been dedicated to a massive gym, complete with its own spa. There was a hot tub, a sauna, and even a swimming pool large enough to do laps. I'd counted nine bedrooms, not including the two fully furnished omega nests. The decor was lavish, balancing on the knife's edge of gaudiness. I would never in a million years have associated such a house with the dour Committee chairman.

Not that Nikolayev actually lived here, of course. This was the *guesthouse*. The main house was basically a palace.

Kam and I made our way upstairs to the second floor without meeting either Jax or Flynn. They were probably downstairs making use of the gym, trying to work off some of the frustration of inactivity. Depending on how long it took us to slap sense into Alex, maybe we could join them afterward and watch for a bit.

Kam cut me a sidelong glance. "You're thinking about Flynn and Jax sparring shirtless."

I frowned at him. "Okay, that was mildly creepy. How could you possibly know that?"

He tapped the side of his nose. "You're perfuming."

"Good lord," I muttered. "My heat's not even due for a week yet."

"Welcome to the wonderful world of not taking pheromone suppressors," he said. "You never had a chance to practice modulating your scent when you were young. It will come with practice, I expect."

Kam, a purebred, had grown up with that sort of knowledge. I, on the other hand, had been born to beta parents, and had only presented as an omega at the age of fifteen. After that first, disastrous heat, I'd been on pheromone and heat blockers continuously until last year.

"Damn. That could be a real nightmare during negotiations," I said. "At least, it might be if any of the betas can interpret changes in scent. There's nothing like having every dignitary in the room privy to your innermost thoughts about Adonis belts."

"More like having everybody in the room know that you're horny in general," Kam replied wryly. "It's closer to smoke signals than Morse code, odama. At least it will be to anyone who doesn't know you as well as I do."

"*Smoke signals*?" I echoed, darkly amused by the comparison. "I'm not sure if that's better or worse."

After some discussion, Nikolayev and I had agreed that if we were going to be forced into open conflict with the beta social order, we'd approach it while being what we truly were. Not as the carefully sanitized, beta-friendly version of alphas and omegas, injecting ourselves with a cocktail of drugs so we wouldn't perfume or cycle normally—but rather, as people with complicated lives and relationships, and an equally complicated biology.

Anyone who wished to communicate with me next week would be out of luck, whether they were a king, or a president, or someone's low-level messenger. Next week, I'd be in heat, and therefore unavailable—period, end of sentence.

The idea was mildly terrifying, yet also exhilarating. It was only feasible because I was squirreled away in this impenetrable compound, guarded by armed soldiers and high walls. In a less secure place, it would have been like putting up a neon sign saying *HEY LOOK GUYS, I'M IN HEAT AND TOTALLY HELPLESS — COME AND GET ME.*

Yet, if I couldn't have a heat cycle in peace while staying on the Nikolayev estate in the middle of the Russian wilderness, then I'd never have a heat cycle in peace *anywhere*. I might as well take advantage of the opportunity while I had it.

The guesthouse balcony had been constructed on the roof of the multi-vehicle garage on the ground level. Warmth rising from the heated garage had melted the snow on the balcony's fancy brick floor. Nevertheless, it still would have been a chilly place to meet, if not for the roaring flames coming from a large fire pit situated in the center of the open space.

Three chairs had been pulled into a loose semicircle around the merry blaze. Alex sat in the leftmost seat, staring contemplatively into the fire. Even in such informal surroundings, her shoulders were an unbroken line of tension. Her back was to us, but I harbored no illusions — she already knew we were here. Alex was all alpha, and that included heightened senses. She'd probably heard our approach before we even opened the balcony door. Her obvious tension aside, the fact that she would give us her back like this was a huge compliment.

We crossed to the empty chairs. Kam took the center one, and I took the one farthest from her.

"How was the filming?" Alex asked.

"I think it went well," I said, accepting the neutral conversational gambit. "We might have a nibble from an official in Luxembourg soon."

"Have you spoken with Beckett today?" Kam asked. "Nikolayev said the doctor put him on bed rest. He's probably going to go mental within a week."

"Whelping is dangerous for an omega his age," Alex said, in the carefully flat tone that she used to hide her emotions. "Especially one who's never had pups before. To answer your question, no, I haven't seen him today. I'll go check on him when we're done here."

"We can go together," I told her. "Assuming you don't want to run for the hills after this conversation."

She shifted in her seat. "If it's about your heat, there's really nothing more to say. I've told you before — I can't stop Jax and Flynn from mating you, if the four of you are set on it. Hell—Jax and Kam are technically mated already."

"And we've told *you* before—that isn't the point," I said. I had no intention of losing my temper with Alex… though Kam might, if she pushed him too far. That being said, blunt talk often seemed to be the only way to get her to engage beyond shallow deflections.

Her hard green eyes pinned me. "Then what is the point, Leona? You both want something from me that I'm incapable of giving. That part of me was broken a long time ago."

Alex had mated before, and it had ended tragically. Her former mate was still alive at least—though she was sterilized now, with her mating gland cut out by Committee butchers. I understood that Alex wasn't in any hurry to sign up for a potential repeat of that experience—but that wasn't what we were asking of her.

Or rather, it wasn't what *I* was asking of her.

"Yes," Kam said, his voice low and misleadingly mild. "Please—let's talk about being broken when it comes to mating."

I hid a wince and sat back in my chair, ceding the floor to my packmate. I hadn't expected the gloves to come off quite that fast… yet here we were.

"You more than anyone should appreciate the dangers of this," Alex shot back, never one to back down from a fight.

Kam's brown eyes snapped with reflected firelight. "The dangers? Let's see. Some or all of us might die. Some or all of us might be captured. We might be tortured. We might become victims of the Beta Liberation Front's experimental nerve gas. Perish the thought—I mean, whatever would we do if any of those things happened?"

I suppose I could have warned Alex that when Kam's temper finally reached its tipping point, he played dirty. With the exception of death, everything on that list had already happened to us. And frankly, that no one had died so far was a miracle.

But Kam wasn't done. "And *of course* if you aren't mated to us, you'll be completely blasé about the prospect of our suffering. Just like I didn't give a damn about Jax's wellbeing before I had his bite mark on my shoulder, but now I suddenly care what happens to him because we're *technically fucking mated.*"

This was the reason I usually tried to avoid pissing Kam off. I kept my mouth shut and waited for the fireworks to die down.

"A mating implies an additional expectation of care—" Alex began.

"You've already risked your lives!" Kam's normally quiet voice rose to a shout. "You've done it over and over—for us and for each other! There is *literally nothing more you could sacrifice for us*, simply because we were mated!"

"There's the bond!" Alex's voice rose to match his. "*Damn you*—there's the bond. Another part of my soul that could be ripped out by the roots."

My throat tightened in sympathy at the raw pain in her voice.

"Not with me." Kam's voice had gone quiet again, as he delivered the three devastating words.

His mating gland was still there, but it was useless after what had been done to the rest of his reproductive system in the slave pens. Jax had bitten him during a moment of passion, not realizing that Kam was left-glanded instead of right-glanded. Neither of them regretted the slip… but no psychic bond had formed between them. Kam's body was too damaged.

Alex dragged her gaze away. Her complexion was pale as milk, highlighting the dark circles under her eyes from too many lost nights of sleep.

"I would still feel it," she said.

The flat statement was irrational, in the sense that Kam wasn't magically going to form a functioning mate-bond with Alex any more than he had with Jax. Yet it still cut me to the bone with its utter certainty.

I drew breath to wade into the fray.

"I respect that," I told her. "Mating again—or not—is one hundred percent your own decision. What I need to find out is whether there's a way forward for our two packs. You say you can't stop Jax and Flynn from mating us. But you can—because we're not going to mate members of your pack against your wishes, Alex."

Alex was silent, still looking into the flickering flames rather than at either of us.

"I told the others that you have a say in what happens next, and I meant it," I went on, more gently. "That's why you saying 'I can't stop you' isn't going to be enough for us."

Silence settled over the balcony, broken only by the crackle of burning wood.

"Why do you want this?" Alex asked. "Knowing what you know... knowing how badly things could go wrong... why would you sign up for that kind of pain?"

I did her the courtesy of taking a few moments to think about my answer. Eventually, I spoke, feeling out the words as I went.

"When Beckett was a prisoner of Enoch Sloane, being drugged and tortured... he wasn't alone with his tormenters in that cell," I said slowly. "Nikolayev was living every minute of that horror right along with him, lending him strength even as he mounted a rescue operation. You and Flynn had each other after Sloane captured you, but they could have separated you at any time. And neither of you had anyone on the outside to comfort you. There was no one to tell you help was coming and things were going to be okay."

Alex dragged her eyes away from the fire, looking down at her scarred left hand. She flexed her fingers, bending and straightening them — doubtless taking in the stark red lines etched into her skin where the surgeons had implanted rods and pins to stabilize the crushed bones.

I chewed on my lower lip, aware of how selfish this next part was going to sound. "When the Montreal police dragged me out of my bed in the middle of the night and tossed me into a cell to await Committee extradition, I was more alone than I've ever been in my life. I wanted someone to comfort me more than I wanted my next breath of air. When you came, I didn't believe it was real. If we'd been mated, maybe I would have known that it was."

And if the others hadn't been able to get to me, I would have died a horrible death at the Committee's hands, leaving my mates as distraught as Alex had been after she lost her bond with Irina. Yet I still wanted that connection with a desperate longing.

Like I said — *selfish.*

Kam took my hand and squeezed it.

Finally, Alex looked up. "I can't give you that." Her catlike gaze shifted from me to Kam. "Either of you. But I suppose I also can't begrudge the others a taste of that bond. It's… like a drug, in some ways. I can only hope that they — and you — never find out firsthand what the withdrawal is like when it's unexpectedly taken away."

Kam's hand clutched mine convulsively. I tangled our fingers together and held tight, knowing that Alex's decision wasn't fair to him. Whether he was ready to admit it or not, Kam was falling in love with our recalcitrant female alpha. Her rejection of him had cut him to the quick. I wanted to argue more on his behalf — to drive home the point that she couldn't have that kind of psychic bond with him anyway, so there wouldn't be anything to lose.

Maybe, for her, that wasn't the point. *That part of me was broken a long time ago,* she'd said. Who was I to tell her she was wrong about her own psyche? I ached on my odama's behalf, though.

"I understand," I said, even though it was a lie. How could anyone come to know Kam and not fall in love with him?

"You don't," Alex replied, sounding tired. "And I pray you never do. You should go tell the others the news. I'll check on Beckett and give him your regards."

Kam let my hand drop. "You'll still be there for Leona's heat, though? Won't you?"

Alex shook her head. "I was only present to play referee before—to make sure no one stepped out of line in the passion of the moment. You don't need me around if you're already planning to mate them."

I held my breath. Alex had done a *lot* more than play referee during my last two heats.

"What if we *want* you there?" Kam asked, his tone carefully level.

There was a beat of heavy tension.

"I'm sorry." She rose abruptly, the chair legs scraping on brick. "I can't."

And then she was striding across the balcony, disappearing through the door like a shadow.

"Well, *fuck*," I said, with feeling.

THREE

Kameron

I WATCHED ALEX go with a sense of numbness. Next to me, Leo cursed sharply. Maybe I would have done the same, but I couldn't seem to call the right emotion to hand.

Leo rose and stepped behind my chair, wrapping her arms around me and resting her chin on the top of my head. "I'm sorry," she said. "I'm so sorry, odama. Maybe she'll come around when she's had more time to think about things."

Maybe she would. To be honest, I doubted it.

"We should go and tell the others," I managed. "They'll be relieved she's on board with the rest of it, at least."

I couldn't imagine how awkward it would have been if Alex had been dead set against the others mating us. She was their leader, and Leo never would have forgiven herself if the conflict tore their pack apart.

Personally, I was more worried that the mating bond itself would end up tearing them apart. I'd been young when I was taken away from my purebred family, but not *that* young. I was old enough to be aware of alphomic pack dynamics, and I wasn't aware of any matings where one member of a pack cut themselves off from the rest by failing to join in the psychic bond.

Sure, it had probably happened at some point. For all I knew, it wasn't even that unusual—at age twelve, my sample size was hardly a large one. But did those packs survive afterward? That was the question.

Leo brushed her cheek against mine, scent-marking me. Her lips pressed lightly against my temple a moment later. "Yes. All right," she said. "Let's go tell the others. Maybe they'll decide to take another crack at her, too."

I closed my eyes. "I'm not interested in harassing her into mating either of us when she clearly doesn't want to. I just wish..." The sentence trailed away to nothing, a growing lump in my throat choking off the words.

"That she wanted it on her own?" Leo suggested.

That was *exactly* what I wished for—but I shook my head dismissively and pulled away from her, standing up. We'd held Alex in our arms as she wept for her dead pups. I'd forced care on her when she wouldn't treat her own injuries properly. None of those things obligated her to enter into a mate bond with either of us—especially not when she'd been wounded so badly by a broken bond before.

"It's her decision," I said, with more certainty than I felt.

We went inside, where we'd be warm, if nothing else. I could only imagine what it cost to heat this enormous house during a Russian winter... much less the main house. Good thing money didn't appear to be an issue for the Nikolayev family.

As we headed downstairs, I berated myself for failing to appreciate what we had, simply because of what we couldn't have. We had two alphas who adored us. Both of them would step between us and a bullet without a second thought.

The sound of grunts and thuds reached us from the area of the gym set aside for sparring. All three of the alphas had been struggling a bit during the long months without action, hidden away in relative safety and probably feeling a bit surplus to requirements. They'd all been injured to varying degrees. Flynn had fared the best, though 'best' felt a bit facile when it included being beaten to a pulp and undergoing hours of electrical torture.

Alex's broken hand had healed well, considering. She was still undergoing rehabilitation for it, all these months later. I hadn't seen the whip marks on her back recently, so I had no way of knowing how those had healed.

Jax's bullet graze had ended up being far less of a long-term problem than the experimental nerve agent he'd been exposed to during our earlier capture in Romania. But thanks to alpha toughness, he'd finally overcome most of the intermittent muscle weakness on his left side. He still suffered from headaches, and he probably would for the rest of his life. However, over the last couple of months, he'd worked his body ruthlessly in an attempt to get back to full strength, in a way that made my own gym addiction look like a pleasant walk in the park.

The sparring area was bare except for thick mats on the floor. The alphas were, predictably, shirtless. I'd never been quite sure if that was their preferred way to work out, or if they'd adopted it after seeing Leo's pupils dilate the first time she'd walked in on them.

Not that I was complaining about the half-naked alphas, of course. Omegas were hardwired to respond to alpha strength, alpha muscles, alpha… *alphaness*. And there was plenty of that on display with these two.

Like Alex on the balcony, they would both have been aware of us since the moment we entered the gym, if not before. Even distracted by their sparring session, Leo's scent would be impossible for an alpha to miss — or to ignore. I adored the fact that she was finally off the blockers, maybe for good. And I was sure I wasn't the only one to hold that opinion.

The pair on the mats puffed up, their muscles bulging as they grappled. They were putting on a show for us, and Leo and I were there for it. Bare feet scrabbling for purchase, they shoved at each other like two bulls locking horns.

Flynn had a slight advantage of both height and bulk. His dark skin gleamed beneath the overhead lights, sweat beading on his chest and arms. Jax had the edge when it came to flexibility. His muscle definition was also something to behold. Leo liked to call him her Viking, with his blond hair, blue eyes, and square jaw sharp enough to cut glass.

It was good to see him nearly back to full health.

Flynn readjusted his grip, aiming for better leverage, and Jax took advantage to duck down, lowering his center of gravity and shifting hard to the right. It should have been a perfect takedown move, but Flynn used his heavier weight to roll them, ending up on top. Rather than submit to the pin, Jax twisted his lower body and somehow managed to hook a leg over Flynn's arm. In a flash, he'd grabbed Flynn's wrist and trapped him in a submission hold.

Flynn grunted and tapped out. "Asshole," he grumbled, as Jax rolled to his feet and offered him a hand up.

"Nice moves," Leo said.

Flynn accepted Jax's hand, pulling himself to his feet as well. He stalked Leo with a smile, backing her against the wall by the door and caging her in so he could press his nose to the base of her neck and breathe in deeply. "Is it next week yet? Because I've got some more nice moves I've been dying to show you."

"I can hardly wait," Leo told him, and tilted her face up for a kiss.

Jax grabbed a towel and used it to mop his face as he sauntered over to join me. "What's up, you two? You've got this whole 'good news, bad news' vibe going on."

"It's Alex," I said succinctly, aware that my face probably looked like I'd swallowed a lemon. "Well, also Beckett. But mostly Alex."

He frowned. "Beckett? Did something happen with the pregnancy?"

"The doctor put him on bed rest," Leo said.

Jax relaxed a bit. "Ah. Okay. Next question. What did Alex do?"

"Let me guess," Flynn said. "You tried to pin her down about the mating, and she said she's fine with it as long as she can stay a million miles away from the whole thing."

"Wow, it's like you know her personally or something," Leo said, laying on the irony.

Jax was giving me one of those piercing looks that saw too much. "There's more," he said. "What is it?"

I sighed. "She bailed on Leo's heat. Apparently, if we don't need her to keep either of you from biting us, there's no reason for her to be there—at least, according to her."

Had that come out sounding bitter? Yeah... it probably had.

Blue eyes peered straight through my skull and into my brain, without the need for a psychic mate-bond.

"I will give you a one hundred percent personal guarantee that she didn't stop and think how that would sound before she said it aloud," Jax told me.

"It doesn't matter." I gave myself a mental shake. "Maybe it's for the best if she's not there."

Spoiler alert—it was not, in fact, for the best.

"You want us to gang up on her?" Flynn asked. Leo leaned into him, and he rumbled a purr as his arms came around her, settling her body against his.

"No, please don't," I said. "We said it's her choice, and we meant it."

Jax's blunt fingers touched my jaw, bringing my face up to meet his eyes again. "It's not you. It's not either of you, Kam. You're worthy of love... worthy of being mated and cherished. But we're all broken in different ways. This is just the shape of Alex's jagged edges, and sometimes those jagged edges can be sharp."

"I know. It's fine," I lied.

Now Leo was watching me with a worried gaze as well. *Wonderful.*

"It's fine as long as your pack can take the strain," she clarified. "Alex can run away from us if she wants to. That's her prerogative. But promise us that you won't let her run away from you, too."

Flynn scoffed. "Run away from us? Where would she go?"

"That's what I'm worried about," Leo said.

"It won't come to that," Jax promised, as if he had any way at all of knowing such a thing. "We won't let it."

"Nah," Flynn agreed. "We won't. It'll work out, you'll see."

And oh, how I envied Flynn's simple and straightforward view of the world.

"Of course it will," Jax said. "We've still got a war to win and a world to fix, after all. Alex would never shirk her duties when there's work to do."

"Things will be better when we're not stuck rattling around this place day in and day out," Flynn added. "We're all going a little stir crazy."

"Speak for yourself," Leo said into his chest. "This is the safest I've felt since I was fifteen."

"This is the safest you've *been* since you were fifteen," I pointed out. "So that only makes sense."

"Come on, you two," Flynn said, throwing a possessive arm around me so I was tucked against his left side, and Leo against his right. "Help us get cleaned up so we can all go and bother Beckett for a bit. He must be bored out of his mind, and I need a distraction from thinking about exactly how I'm going to bite both of you."

The little frisson that traveled down my spine was irrational. In the end, it didn't matter whether or not I carried their bite scars over my useless, atrophied mating gland. And yet, that didn't stop me from craving it with single-minded desperation as my packmate's heat approached.

Two mates. It was two more than I ever thought I'd have… and somehow it still wasn't enough.

FOUR

Alex

"GOOD GOD. YOU look like you swallowed a beach ball," I said, pulling up a chair to Beckett's bedside. "Are you sure there's only one pup in there?"

"So the ultrasound technician assures me," Beckett replied with his usual brand of understated, self-deprecating humor. "Though I did have to sign a form stating I'm not allowed to sue him if it turns out I'm carrying sextuplets."

I forced a smile. Being here at all required an act of will, and it took a surprising amount of concentration to shove aside the bone-deep disquiet I felt in response to the proximity of a pregnant omega.

Repressed trauma, a psychiatrist would say, and they'd probably be right about that. But this was Beckett—the man who'd hauled us out of the gutter and given us a life. A *purpose*. I sat down, reflecting that he looked nearly as out of place in this palatial bedroom as I felt. Beckett's left eyebrow climbed—I'd stayed silent too long.

"Something's happened," he said. "Is it anything that will require sedation to keep me in this damned bed once I know about it?"

I shook my head. "Nothing like that. It's a private pack matter."

He settled back, propped against the pile of pillows at the headboard. "Ah. Well, I suppose I can guess what that means. I'd offer to help, but I don't have a leg to stand on when it comes to dangerous and potentially inappropriate mate bonds."

Looking at this fearless omega who'd mated the most powerful kingpin in the alphomic underground, I couldn't disagree.

"Why did you do it, though?" I asked. "You must have had some idea what you'd be getting into? Or was it unplanned?"

A flash of memory assailed me—Irina, begging for my bite as she writhed on my knot… my momentary loss of control in the face of overwhelming instinct and need. Not for the first time, I wondered what was broken inside me that made me lose mastery over myself when other alphas didn't.

"Not precisely unplanned," Beckett replied. "But… ill-advised, maybe." He took a slow breath, as though considering his words. "There's risk inherent in the act of giving yourself freely to another, no matter the circumstances. We all try to delude ourselves that we can somehow control the future by taking certain actions in the present—or by not taking them, as the case may be. But that's just a pretty lie we tell ourselves, mostly to keep from being paralyzed by the fear of what might happen tomorrow, or the next day, or the next."

"By that argument, everyone should do as they please with no thought for the possible consequences," I said, scowling. "Society would crumble."

"Yes, I suppose so," Beckett agreed. "But the fact remains that walling yourself off from the world doesn't magically prevent tragedies from occurring. It merely ensures you'll always be alone."

Somehow, I didn't think that saying '*yes, that's the general idea*' would go over terribly well, so I said nothing.

"Leona's next heat is coming up," Beckett continued, when it became clear I wouldn't be filling the conversational gap. "Are you going to stop the others from mating her and Kameron?"

"I wanted to stop them," I admitted, feeling my lungs constrict. "Why take that kind of risk now, when things are poised to become more dangerous than they've ever been?"

But Beckett only shook his head.

"You're looking at it backwards, Alex. They want to mate now *because* things are about to become even more dangerous," he said simply. "Fear of lost chances is one of the most powerful motivations a human being can experience."

"Is it, though?" I asked.

He gave me a small smile in lieu of an answer, only to wince a moment later, his hand going to the bulge in his abdomen.

I frowned. "Are you all right?"

"Contraction," he said, his expression smoothing out to a blank facade. "Hence the reason for me being stuck in this bed for the next two months. Anyway, my point is this. You already have a pack. You'd die for them. They'd die for you. If that ever happened, heaven forbid, it would rip part of your heart out. As much as you might like to, you don't live in a bubble, Alex."

It was eerily close to the conversation I'd just had with Leona and Kam. I opened my mouth to say something defensive and probably ill-advised, but the sound of the door opening interrupted me.

Nikolayev stalked in, his heavy brows knit together as his piercing gray gaze fell on his pregnant mate. "I felt that. You're in pain. I'll call the doctor back."

Beckett sighed. "Oh my god. *This* is the reason we never lived together, Kostya—not the damned underground. *Just stop.*"

It should have been amusing, watching the head of the Euro-Soviet Committee fussing over an omega who'd doubtless seen far more deadly battles than he ever had. In any other mood, maybe I could have appreciated it.

I rose from my chair. "I'll give you two some privacy."

Nikolayev barely acknowledged me.

Beckett gave me a final, wan smile. "Think about what I said, Alex."

"Sure thing, Boss." The words slid off my tongue as though I actually believed I'd be able to focus on anything else over the coming week until Leona's heat.

Maybe if I asked nicely, Nikolayev could find me a promising suicide mission somewhere, because the idea of being within a hundred miles of Leona and Kam's nest—while knowing that my idiot packmates would have their teeth buried in the pair's flesh—made me feel like I was about to crawl out of my own skin.

Funny how badly I wanted the very thing that would destroy me if I ever let it happen.

FIVE

Leona

SECRETARY FOUCHET finally came through with a proposal for a private meeting with several officials from Luxembourg and Austria. I should have been ecstatic, but I couldn't be bothered to focus on the details because my heat was coming on. In some ways, it was shocking how little I suddenly cared about world events, simply because of a cocktail of hormones rushing through my veins.

The idea that so much of what made me *me* relied on a few milliliters of biologically active chemicals should have been deeply disquieting. Fortunately, I couldn't be bothered to focus on that worry either.

Right now, I was too busy obsessing about the nest. This was the first time I'd ever used the same nest for multiple heats. It should have been instinctually reassuring, but instead, I was hyper-focused on the fact that I didn't know what we were going to do whenever we finally left the haven of Nikolayev's estate.

Kam and I were fugitives. So were the alphas, for that matter. But even if they hadn't already been outed as underground operatives, they had no money to speak of. They'd been subjugated—slaves in all but name. Only the fragile protection of the military alpha program separated them from the thousands upon thousands of victims of the alphomic slave market. Fair payment for their hard and dangerous work wasn't part of that deal. Beckett might have protected them from the more repugnant legal requirements like chemical castration, but I was pretty sure he hadn't been secretly passing them money under the table.

I paced the nest, chewing on a fingernail as I ran through increasingly unlikely scenarios related to where and how we would live, once we were mated and out from under Nikolayev's umbrella of safety and comfort. Would Alex stay with us, wherever we ended up? Or would our mating drive her away from her two packmates?

A hand reached out and snagged my arm as I waded restlessly through the sea of pillows. Kam was seated on the stylish semicircular couch that surrounded half of the sunken nest. He tugged me onto the plush upholstery at his side.

"*Stop*, odama," he said. "Your brain is going to start spewing smoke out your ears like an overheating engine."

I let out a massive sigh. Some of my tension drained out along with the air in my lungs. Curling against Kam's side, I nipped at his neck and tucked my head against the crook of his shoulder. "Sorry."

He stroked my hair back. "Don't be sorry. Just try to focus on the important things, yes? You're going to be mated." He quickly corrected himself when I drew breath to chastise him. "*We're* going to be mated, I mean. Who could have ever foreseen such a thing?"

It was true. I nodded against his neck. "You're right. Good god, Kam—we're going to have a pack. A proper one." I shivered—excitement, nervousness, and anticipation swirling together in my stomach along with the liquid heat of my growing arousal.

"Yes, we are," he agreed. "They'll be here in a few minutes. Want to see if we can shock them?"

The warmth in my belly surged, overtaking my jitters. "You're on." Thinking for a moment, I straightened away from him and tried to put on a commanding expression. "Clothes off. Get naked and kneel on the floor. I want them to find you eating me out when they open the door and walk in."

Kam rose with a dancer's grace and faced me as he started on the buttons of his shirt. "For so many years, I thought I was the depraved one in this relationship, odama."

I smiled, my earlier cares falling away. "If I'd known how things were for you, I would have embraced depravity long ago."

Gooseflesh erupted across my body, and anticipation washed over me as more and more smooth olive skin appeared. Kam was still ethereally beautiful, scars and all. I drank in the sight of him, watching avidly as his trousers and underwear joined the pile of discarded clothing, leaving him bare to my gaze.

He dropped to his knees in front of me, looking up at me through long, dark lashes.

"Hands behind your back," I whispered hoarsely, letting my legs fall open to make space for him. I was wearing nothing but an oversized T-shirt that smelled of alpha sweat, which left me fully exposed to his simmering regard.

Until the alphas, I'd known next to nothing about sex. Or, rather, I'd known nothing about the ways that sex could live inside the mind, rather than in the body. And, in some ways, I'd known nothing about the omega who'd shared my life since we were both wet-behind-the-ears interns at the Foreign Affairs office.

Kameron Patel didn't want to be worshipped. He didn't want to be adored.

No—Kameron Patel wanted to be put on his knees and used over and over until he was a quivering, exhausted wreck. It was the only way he could escape from the awareness of his damaged body and retreat into the place in his mind where he was still whole… still a sexual being.

The first time I'd seen it done to him, I'd been shocked, even though I was trapped beneath the mindless haze of my heat when it happened. Since then, I'd come to understand that if the goal was to give Kam pleasure, I couldn't simply treat him the way I'd want to be treated. I was an omega, but that didn't mean I couldn't help the others use him the way he longed to be used.

With his hands clasped behind him, Kam shuffled forward on his knees until he could kiss his way up my inner thigh. When he got close enough that the pressure of his lips and the rasp of his tongue became a tease rather than a pleasure, I slid my fingers through the thick, dark strands of his hair and fisted it, twisting until I felt him gasp and shudder.

"Get to work, odama," I said, using my grip to move his mouth where I wanted it.

Kam had a talented tongue, and not just in the sense of diplomatic acumen. I moaned approval as he brushed his lips over me, teasing open my folds like someone teasing open a lover's lips in a languid kiss. I was already perfuming in great clouds of honey and orange blossom. Before long, I might be able to catch a hint of Kam's subtle ginger and lemon, as well.

Until then, I relaxed into the nerve-tingling sensation, letting it unknot my muscles even as a new tension grew inside me. My grip on Kam's hair tightened until he whimpered. He redoubled his efforts, lapping up the slick I was churning out and sliding his tongue up to circle my clit. I gave another warning tug, and his lips closed around my sensitive nub, his tongue flicking rapidly. He sucked lightly, and the tightening spring inside me burst free.

I arched and jerked out my first orgasm just as the door to the nest opened, and the scent of two horny alphas wafted in.

"Holy fuck," Flynn said, sounding hoarse.

"I got tired of waiting," I managed, trying for a teasing tone and only managing breathiness.

"If we'd known what we were missing, we'd have been here sooner," Jax said.

Flynn was already stripping. "Jax, get the toys and the lube out for me. Ginger Tea, you are in so much trouble for starting without us. I'm going to make sure you stay filled at both ends until you don't even know which way is up."

Kam made an approving sound against my clit.

Jax set a small case on the table next to the couch and rummaged around in it. "You can keep our cocks warm while we're taking turns with Leona, Kam. But for now, just keep doing what you're doing while this pervert figures out how big of a plug you can take."

"And keep in mind that you'll be taking that asshole's knot before we're done," Flynn added. "So you'll want to be good and loose by then."

Kam made a choked sound as Flynn kicked his knees wider and knelt behind him, lube in hand. But my odama gamely dove into my pussy again, while Jax shed his clothing and peeled me out of my borrowed T-shirt. He sat next to me, his fingers tangling with mine in Kam's hair. I closed my eyes and let my head fall back, baring my throat to the alpha's teasing nips. I could feel Kam's every twitch as Flynn fingered him open with ruthless efficiency, and my pleasure crested again as I fell headlong into the alpha's care.

SIX

Leona

BEING KNOTTED through a heat was, in many ways, indescribable. Even so, Alex's absence from the nest stung like a splinter embedded in flesh—though I suspected that if she'd been here, it would have been miserable for her. Aside from her general angst surrounding our decision to mate, I'd also decreed that a single birth control method—namely, the injection—was plenty, thanks.

Yes, there was a small chance that it would fail, since nothing offered one hundred percent foolproof protection. However, Nikolayev had access to the good stuff when he had a bit of warning to acquire it... and as strange as it felt to contemplate, I was beginning to soften my stance regarding the possibility of pups. It wasn't just me on my own anymore. It wasn't even Kam and me alone against the world, with our tiny, two-person pack.

We were about to mate a pair of trustworthy, responsible alphas, and Kam had always wanted pups desperately. The way I saw it, in the course of the next eight months, we would either have changed the world into something better for alphas and omegas everywhere, or we'd be dead.

It was something of a moot point anyway, since injectable omega birth control was more than ninety-eight percent effective—as long as you didn't end up with counterfeit drugs like Alex and Irina had. There was very little chance of me becoming pregnant during this heat. If I did, we'd deal with it. I might not have been a model carrier-figure, but Kam totally was. I wouldn't be rearing pups alone, if it came to that.

My first peak was already approaching. The warmth of belonging and care swirled together with the heat of my growing lust, everything combining to steal away my higher brain functions. I was safe in my nest, surrounded by people who loved me. The feel of bare flesh against bare flesh, as Flynn slid his massive cock into me in a slow, rolling rhythm, was everything I wanted out of life in this moment.

Well… it was *almost* everything I wanted out of life.

"You gonna beg for my bite when you come, Sweet Thing?" Flynn rumbled.

His big hands framed my hips, controlling my movements as he thrust into me from behind.

"Yes," I said mindlessly, trying to rock back… to speed up his rhythm until we both lost control. "Yes, bite me! Mate me! Flynn, I want your mark on me… oh, god!"

The words tumbled out without anything resembling a brain-to-mouth filter, nearly falling over themselves in my haste to get his teeth on my mating gland. It must have been working, too, because he let out a full-throated growl and knelt up, manhandling me onto his lap with my back to his solid chest. I cried out as his heavy girth shifted inside of me, hitting a place deep inside that made me shudder against him.

Nearby, Jax lifted Kam's head by the hair, pulling Kam's mouth off his dick. "Come here." He lifted Kam onto his lap on the couch. "You'll want to see this."

Kam looked seriously strung out already, his lips wet and swollen as his glassy gaze met mine. A whine escaped his throat as Jax wrapped a large hand over his half-hard omega cock and pressed teeth to the fading bite scar over his mating gland. His eyelids fluttered, his eyes rolling up to show the whites for a moment before he dragged his attention back to me.

My orgasm coiled tight and hot in the cradle of my pelvis. "Bite me... bite me, Flynn—please!" I begged.

"Gonna make you mine, little omega," Flynn said against the nape of my neck. "Make both of you ours, and never, ever give you up."

His tongue rasped over my gland, and I shook apart around him. He groaned, his knot swelling as he spilled inside of me, and in the next instant, teeth clamped down, breaking the skin.

I wailed, the shivery rainbow burst of pain somehow driving my climax even higher. The skin all over my body tightened, flushing hot, then cold, then hot again. My muscles trembled uncontrollably as I writhed, pinned in place between Flynn's teeth and his knot. I could feel his heart pounding against my back like a drum, counterpoint to my own frantic, fluttering pulse.

His lips and tongue covered the bleeding mark, as he swallowed my blood, his saliva entering the wound at the same time. I clenched around his knot, euphoria flooding me even as beads of clammy sweat popped out on my forehead.

Flynn... I could *feel* him. Not just in my body, but in my soul.

His lips pulled away from my abused flesh, and he rested his forehead against my hair. "Oh, my sweet Leona. You're as beautiful on the inside as you are on the outside."

A sob blocked my throat—too much feeling crowded into too small a space. I couldn't speak, so I shoved all my wonder and dawning awareness of him through the nascent bond. His breath puffed out, tickling the nape of my neck.

Flynn was... *wild.* Uncontrolled in some ways, but tightly constrained in others. His mind was in shades of stark black and white, binary and uncompromising.

This is good.

This is bad.

I want this.

I don't want that.

Overlaying all of his other thoughts and feelings was a single, unwavering directive—*protect.* His consciousness formed a reassuringly straightforward presence inside me, but its newness made it overwhelming.

"All right over there, you two?" Jax asked cautiously. He was still supporting Kam, who had emerged from his sex-daze enough to watch us with wide brown eyes.

"He's inside me," I said stupidly, my voice a breathless rasp.

"That he is. Though you should be glad it's me over here watching, and not him," Jax said. "Because that sex joke practically writes itself. Seriously, though—you're both okay?"

"Halfway there, for sure," Flynn said. "It's so good, Jax. *Really* good. Still need to bite someone else today, though."

I could only manage a nod, agreeing with everything he'd said, but completely overcome by what I was feeling.

"Once the bonds settle, you'll be able to learn how to control them better," Kam said. His tone was faintly wistful.

Of course, my purebred odama was the only one here who'd ever been properly educated in such matters. I believed him, though it was hard to picture this runaway sharing of self as ever being *under control.*

But I was still in heat, and mate-bond or no, my body was following a script beyond the scope of willpower. I was sated and knotted, my first peak past.

"Sleepy now," I murmured, letting my head fall back against Flynn's shoulder.

He immediately started purring, his powerful arms encircling me to hold me snug against him. That unassailable sense of protectiveness rose again, settling over me like a blanket.

"Then you should sleep," he said. Alpha strength supported me, barely jostling the place where we were connected as he settled me on my side and spooned me from behind. "I'm not going anywhere. Not ever again."

Kam slid from his place on the couch and crawled through the sea of pillows to reach us. He stretched down, meeting my lips in a chaste kiss. "Congratulations, odama. May your new bond be a light to guide you always."

I stared into his beloved face, feeling Flynn's affection for the omega leaning over me mingling with my own. "Love you," I said, a single tear spilling over to slide down my temple and into my hair. My body throbbed with the pleasure of being filled, and my heart overflowed with the adoration I was giving and receiving in equal measure.

"I love you, too," Kam said, stroking my cheek.

I closed my eyes, allowing exhaustion to overtake me.

⎯⎯⎯⎯◆⎯⎯⎯⎯

If I'd thought sex during my heat was intense before, it was positively mind-melting with a fresh mating bond in place. I'd wondered if Flynn might try to monopolize me, given the chance—but I needn't have worried.

He hadn't been kidding about only being halfway done when it came to biting people. I was currently sprawled across the couch, in that lazy, semi-aware state between the crash following one peak and the rise of the next. Jax's blond head was buried between my thighs, his tongue transporting me unerringly toward nirvana. My head hung over the edge of the seat so I could watch, upside down, as Flynn reduced Kam to a helpless puddle of need.

"You'll take my cock one of these days, won't you?" Flynn asked, sliding a larger plug into Kam's ass.

"Yes, yes, I'll take it! Please... please... I'll do *anything...*"

Something about the desperate edge to Kam's begging kindled a hot surge of need in my gut— never mind that I'd been begging just as abjectly not so long ago. Jax's tongue dragged along my soaked folds, hitting everything *just* right, and I moaned as a powerful release clenched my muscles in fluttering spasms.

Flynn looked up abruptly, his dark eyes catching mine. "Huh. So *that's* what it feels like," he said, before refocusing his attention on Kam. "Nice."

Jax chuckled against my sensitive flesh and repeated the movement, drawing a contented hum from my throat and a rumble of approval from Flynn's.

Meanwhile, Flynn seemed to be intent on talking Kam over the edge with his words alone, taking ruthless advantage of my odama's long-buried thirst for submission and sexual humiliation.

"You know, Ginger Tea," he said, "once we've got you all trained up so you can take an extra-large alpha cock, we might just tie you up in the corner during Leona's heats with your ass on permanent display. Anyone who needed a convenient place to bust a knot could just stick it inside you while they're waiting for the next round. Hell, I could even find Leo a nice strap-on harness with a knotting dildo so she could fuck you, too."

"Oh god," Kam choked.

"Ooh, I want that," I agreed, floating along on the crest of another orgasm. "I'd fuck you so good, Kam."

"We'll definitely have to do that some time," Flynn said with satisfaction. "But right now, I'm going to put my bite mark right over the top of Jax's, and you're going to come so hard for me that you pass out."

Kam made a garbled *nngh* sound as Flynn manhandled him around and dragged his head to one side by the hair, his other hand closing around Kam's dick and jerking him roughly.

"Such a pretty little omega toy." Flynn ran his teeth teasingly over Kam's scar. "Our toy now." He locked eyes with me, then bit down hard.

Kam cried out and arched, writhing and struggling even as clear fluid squirted from his cock. I was close to the edge myself, but too enthralled by what was happening to fully concentrate on my own pleasure. After several seconds of jerking and shuddering, Kam collapsed sobbing in Flynn's grip.

Six months ago, I might have panicked, convinced that something was terribly wrong. But I'd learned more about what made Kam tick since then. I knew how much repressed emotion he'd shoved into the dark, cramped space inside his heart over the decades, and I knew how precious an opportunity it was for him to let some of it escape like this, in safe surroundings and with people he trusted.

Flynn held him close and soothed the livid bite mark with his tongue. Kam grew pliant in his arms by slow degrees, until he was completely limp, not an ounce of tension left anywhere in his body.

"Bet you could take an alpha cock right now without even twitching," Flynn said with clear satisfaction, pressing a final kiss to the mark he'd left. He stilled, a furrow of concentration forming on the dark skin of his forehead as he straightened. "Hang on," he said slowly. "What the hell is that? Leo—do you feel that?"

SEVEN

Kameron

I WAS TOO wrung out to move; too wrung out to think. Yet my omega hindbrain still sat up and took notice when Flynn's spicy scent sharpened. He was saying something... to... someone? But I couldn't make out the words, because there was something wrong inside my head.

Or, maybe wrong wasn't the word?

Someone was whispering in my ear. Possibly two someones? They were so far away, though. It felt like I was standing in a long tunnel, and they were at the far end. My eyes had slipped closed as I tried to focus inward. A slender hand gripped my thigh and I wrenched them open again. Leo's hazel gaze bored into mine.

"Kam?" Her voice trembled on my name.

Jax was standing right behind her. Distantly, I was cognizant of what I must look like, sprawled across Flynn's lap with splatters of fluid drying on my belly and thighs. It didn't matter. Something had just happened, and I couldn't quite trust that I wasn't dreaming.

"That's you, isn't it, Ginger Tea?" Flynn asked, with something like wonder.

"Kam, we can feel you," Leo said.

And... it was *them*. They were the ones standing at the end of the tunnel. My breath stuttered and caught inside my chest. Jax crouched next to us, one hand on Leo's shoulder and one on mine.

"What's happening?" he asked. "You can feel a bond forming?"

"It's faint, but yeah," Flynn said. "You two are already mated. Can't you feel it?"

Jax shook his head. "No, nothing on my end. Kam?"

He expected an answer. I moved my lips a couple of times before words came out. "I don't think so?" My voice sounded strange in my own ears.

Leo's fingers tightened on my leg. Her words were rushed. "Jax. Bite me. Right now."

There was a slight pause, and then Jax said, "You think he's piggybacking off Flynn's mate-bond with you?"

"Maybe," Leo replied, sounding unsure.

"That could make sense," Flynn said. "Just like we think your system uses Leo's heat pheromones to help you perfume, Kam."

Jax leaned in to kiss the top of my head, then the top of Leo's. "A second bite's going to hurt a lot worse than the first, love. I still want you riding a sex-high when it happens, so you don't notice as much, okay?"

Leo rolled her lower lip between her teeth for a long moment before giving a reluctant nod. "Okay."

Behind me, I felt Flynn's chest rise as he breathed in, scenting the air. "It won't be long. You're climbing toward another peak, Sweet Thing."

I breathed in as well, still feeling like something huge and warm was wrapped around my lungs—smothering me, but in a good way. I could track Leo's impatience and Flynn's curiosity as faraway echoes behind my own rampaging emotions. This couldn't really be happening, could it? I was broken—not a proper omega anymore, despite what the others said. I couldn't have a real mate-bond.

Could I?

Leo climbed up to straddle my legs, both of us in a messy tangle on Flynn's lap. Her lips pressed against my forehead, then to each of my eyelids, and finally my lips. This kiss wasn't chaste. It was filthy, and it helped me center myself instead of spiraling out of control.

The others would take care of me, no matter what this impossible thing meant for us in the long term. I was safe. My shoulder throbbed with Flynn's bite, and Leo's throbbed in sympathy through the faraway bond. Flynn's mouth closed over the raw wound again, soothing it with his tongue and sending fresh shivers along my overstretched nerves.

It was okay. We were okay. Maybe this was some kind of post-orgasmic dream and not reality, but at least it was a good dream? Flynn was a sharp-edged shadow in my mind, his details hard to make out. But even at a distance, Leo shone so very brightly. I managed to get enough muscle control back to wrap my arms around her and hold tight, kissing her back with everything I had.

⸺◆⸺

Flynn had, predictably, been right about Leo's next peak. It was hardly anytime at all before her hormones took control again, rendering her mindless with need. Jax put her on her hands and knees. She arched her back, presenting for him, and I watched from the shelter of Flynn's arms as they coupled, raw and wild and joyful.

Flynn purred behind me, churning out happy, protective pheromones as fast as Leo and Jax churned out lustful ones. It was impossible for me to obsess and overanalyze everything under these conditions—doubly so, since my muscles still felt like rubber after the orgasm Flynn had wrung from me earlier.

I closed my eyes, trying to track what was happening through the fragile bond, rather than by sight. I could feel what Leo was feeling, but it was still muffled, like there was a blanket draped over the connection. And then, Jax bit her.

The jolt of pain and pleasure sparked along the bond with more clarity than anything else had so far, ebbing and cresting in a rhythm with her cries and garbled pleas of *yes, more, don't stop.* Suddenly, Jax was just... *there*... as though he'd always been there inside me—a storm half-seen on the horizon, companion to Leo's sun and Flynn's shadow.

"Holy shit," Flynn said, taken aback. "This is so wild. You getting that, Ginger Tea?"

"A bit," I managed, taking in the fact that Leo and I had a *fucking mated pack* now... even if it was currently one person short.

But I couldn't afford to think about that. Not now, not when—

Jax gave a heartfelt moan that almost sounded like relief. "There you are. Both of you."

"*Both*? And what am I, asshole?" Flynn asked. "Chopped liver?"

"You're a headache, just like always," Jax shot back. "Get over here, you two."

I crawled to them, drawn by the prospect of cuddling, and winced a bit as my body protested. The burn from Flynn's selection of anal plugs—now safely removed to let me rest—would be with me for a while yet. Flynn followed close behind me. We burrowed into place next to the knotted pair. I allowed myself to revel in the others' muted pleasure at the intimate contact, as well as my own. I still wasn't one hundred percent convinced this wasn't all a fever dream, but maybe—just maybe—I could begin to hope.

EIGHT

Leona

FOR THE FIRST time since Romania, I resented the way my heat hormones stole away my rational mind in waves, rising and falling with every peak. I needed to be aware for every single minute of this miraculous new bond with Kam, but biology wouldn't allow it. After I was knotted, I was out like a light for hours, my body enforcing rest so I could recover for the next round.

It helped that Kam was curled in my arms for much of that time, and it helped even more that I could kind of, sort of, feel his presence through the mating bond we now shared. He was *softness* inside my head — fur that begged to be stroked, or a fleecy blanket to snuggle. Yet, compared to the alphas, his presence still felt terribly weak and far away.

Jax tucked my tangled hair behind my ear as I stretched, returning gradually to wakefulness.

"Hello, Beautiful," he said. "I've been thinking — "

"Always dangerous," Flynn muttered.

Jax sighed. "I've been *thinking* that you should bite Kam too, Leo."

"*Me*? But I'm an omega. Is that even a thing?" I asked muzzily.

"Not really," Kam said, in a tone of voice that suggested there had been extensive discussion on the subject while I'd been out cold.

I tried to knock some more brain cells together. "But you think it might help strengthen the bond?"

"The way we see it, there's only one way to find out," Flynn said. "Can't hurt, right?"

I pondered that for a bit. We were all lying together in a naked tangle. Kam was helpfully right next to me, opposite Jax, with Flynn on his far side.

"I want to try," I decided. "Roll over, odama."

"I should make you buy me dinner first," Kam muttered.

"You're holding all our money," I pointed out. "So that's going to be difficult. I could do your laundry for a week, though?"

"Now *that's* romance," Flynn said, and Jax snorted a breath of laughter behind me. Flynn sobered a moment later. "Might be better to wait until we can get him nice and horny again, though. It's going to hurt."

But Kam shook his head. "No. Do it now—I need to know." He huffed and rolled over, presenting his left shoulder with its inflamed mating gland, Flynn's bite mark still livid against the olive-colored skin. "God. This is surreal," he said.

I laid a hand on his shoulder, suddenly unsure. "I just sort of… get my teeth around his shoulder and bite down? That's all?"

"That's all," Jax said. "Blood and saliva carry the genetic match, or so I gather."

"Omega blood and *alpha* saliva," Kam retorted.

I gave him a squeeze. "Careful, now. Anyone would think you didn't want my bite. A girl could get a complex."

His tense shoulders relaxed. "It's not that, beloved." He craned around, meeting my eyes over his shoulder. "I'm just trying not to get my hopes up. You know how I am about things."

I did. So many times in Kam's life, the worst of all possible outcomes had materialized just in time to punch him squarely in the face. He still had a surprising amount of optimism for the rest of the world, but he had trouble when it came to optimism for himself.

"No hopes," I promised. "Only possibilities. I can still feel you. Can you feel me?"

His brown eyes glowed. "I can. You shine like a star."

I smiled, tremulous. "And you draw me like a welcoming haven. Maybe we'll feel even more, after this."

He smiled back, uncertain, and turned away, baring his neck to me. As an omega, the idea of being bitten played into long-buried genetic and sexual instincts. But the idea of biting someone else felt foreign. I'd been raised as a beta, and... well... you didn't just go around *biting* people.

But I'd kissed and teased Kam's mating gland countless times over the years, so I started there. He was extra sensitive to my touch after Flynn's bite — just as he had been after Jax bit him, way back in the holding cell in Cuba. Rather than performing the *wham-bam-thank-you-ma'am* version of omega-on-omega mating bites, I took my time, seeing how strung out I could make Kam with only my lips and tongue playing against the juncture of his neck and shoulder.

The answer? *Very* strung out.

Unfortunately, there was no question of making him come again — not so soon after Flynn had taken him apart earlier. It took Kam a couple of days to recover from that, even in a nest full of heat pheromones. Flynn's bite had already stopped bleeding under the power of his healing alpha saliva. I steeled myself, knowing that if I held back and didn't break his skin on my first attempt, I'd just end up bruising him without accomplishing anything else.

"Sorry," I whispered, before clamping my teeth around the raw flesh and biting down until I tasted fresh blood.

Kam stiffened, a faint, choked noise escaping his control—but he didn't jerk away as I pulled bloodied lips away from the wound and started licking away at him. It felt... *odd*. Not nauseating like I might have expected, but the action didn't really raise any buried instincts inside me, either.

"Oh," Kam breathed, and I realized that the soft, warm presence in my head felt a bit closer now... a bit more immediate.

"*That's* what I'm talking about," Flynn said with satisfaction.

"Too bad no one really does alphomic-based research these days," Jax mused. "This is pretty interesting."

"I'm happy not to be someone's lab experiment," Kam said breathlessly. "Thanks all the same." He paused. "Though... I suppose if it could help other omegas in a similar situation..."

"Maybe there will come a day when that kind of science is common again," Jax said.

"If so, we can always revisit it," I agreed. "But, Kam! We're mated. I can hardly believe it's real."

"Still withholding judgment on that part, actually," Kam murmured.

I leaned around him so I could kiss him, heedless of the blood on my lips. He winced as I accidentally brushed against the wound, and I pulled back immediately.

"We'll have to tell this hypothetical future scientist that omega saliva doesn't do much for closing fresh wounds," he said without rancor.

"I'm on it," Jax replied, and eased me out of the way so he could get his mouth over the seeping injury. I scooted around to a better position and went back to kissing Kam like his life depended on it.

⁂

Omega heat stopped for no one, although the flavor of it was noticeably enhanced with the presence of the bond thrumming between the four of us. Peak followed peak, each one growing in intensity. Jax and Flynn grew less carefully controlled as the days passed—they could feel our responses directly now, and that eliminated much of the need for constant checking in regarding our well-being.

It wasn't quite a full-on alpha rut. They were still rational, beneath all the growling and raw physicality. But it was sure as hell pretty intense. Through the tentative bond we shared, I could channel Kam's utter contentment at being so thoroughly dominated. I began to truly understand his feelings from the inside out, rather than the outside in. And while I'd never really thought I would share those desires for myself, I was starting to see the appeal.

Whereas Kam relished truly fighting back and being overpowered, I was enjoying a certain extra spark of satisfaction in playing the omega brat. It was such a cliché in many ways, but it was undeniably fun winding Flynn up, in particular. For one thing, his 'punishments' never failed to be even more enjoyable than the crime had been.

As my final peak approached, Kam did, in fact, end up taking Jax's knot while I took Flynn's. I was pretty sure the intensity of the four climaxes echoing through the bond nearly simultaneously was enough to knock me down a few dozen IQ points—possibly on a permanent basis.

Worth it, I thought, and promptly passed out.

⁂

When I regained consciousness, my heat had broken. I'd been cleaned up and wrapped in blankets, with the nest tidied around me. Two other presences hummed at the back of my mind, projecting reassurance, but with an undertone of sadness.

Two presences.

Not three.

I tried to scramble upright, but my muscles were jelly after our four day long sex marathon. A slender hand grasped my arm, steadying me.

"It's all right, odama," Kam said. "I'm here. I'm fine."

Relief that he was physically all right warred with a terrible sinking feeling in my stomach. "What happened?" I rasped.

A strong arm wrapped around my shoulders, and Jax's woodsy scent surrounded me. "Your heat pheromones faded. We think that's what was boosting the bond," he said.

I could feel Jax's melancholy and disappointment directly. I couldn't feel Kam at all anymore. Not so much as an echo.

Flynn plopped down across from us in the nest. "I bet it comes right back the next time you're in heat. You'll see."

I stared into Kam's face, aware that my eyes were filling with tears.

He cupped my cheeks and brought our foreheads together. "It was always too good to be true, Leo. The last few days have been something I never thought I'd experience in my lifetime. I did, though—and maybe I'll have more of it in the future. Please don't cry for me."

But it was too late. I shook my head helplessly and fell into his arms, clinging tight... weeping the tears that I knew he wouldn't weep for himself.

NINE

Alex

IT HAD BEEN absolutely vital that I get the hell away from the guesthouse during Leona's heat. Fortunately, there were other distractions available — and Nikolayev's main house had something like four dozen bedrooms, so finding an empty one wasn't difficult.

Unfortunately, the most pressing distraction involved an official visit from a Belarusian official and his retinue. This wouldn't have been a problem, in and of itself. We needed potential allies on the world stage. *Desperately*. The problem — if you could call it that — was that this particular Belarusian official happened to be the mate Irina had used to replace me... and she was here, too.

Mate wasn't the right word. They were married, beta-style, and the very idea made my skin crawl. She'd offered herself up as a *fucking bribe*, in order to cement a political alliance. The moment I learned the details, I wanted to kill Dzimitry Polonsky on sight.

He was the People's Commissariat for Social Welfare, a member of the Council of Commissars on the Soviet end of the Euro-Soviet Confederacy. In other words, he was a big deal in international politics, and he was in a position to help our cause immensely.

Ripping Dzimitry Polonsky's spine out through his ass because he'd laid hands on my former mate would not be a smart move. Beckett would look at me with dire disappointment, and Nikolayev would probably have me hauled in front of a firing squad or something. On the positive side, behaving civilly toward the man was exactly the kind of psychological self-flagellation I currently craved.

I stood against the far wall of the room like the leashed guard dog I was — spine straight, hands clasped behind my back. The fingers of my left hand ached in time with my heartbeat. I must have been clenching the muscles unconsciously — what a shock. Against another wall, Polonsky's two-man security team watched me impassively.

I'd found it interesting that Nikolayev would allow armed security into his private sanctum. I assumed that meant he trusted his Belarusian ally. Or maybe it was meant as a demonstration of power and confidence. If Polonsky turned on his host, the presence of two security grunts wouldn't prevent him from ending up as a blood smear on the wall when Nikolayev's private army stormed in.

Without my permission, my thoughts wandered back to the guesthouse, and what was no doubt taking place inside. I wondered if my idiot alefs were mated yet. With an irritated internal headshake, I yanked my attention back to my surroundings.

"I believe the risk involved with a small gathering of officials in Belarus is outweighed by the potential benefits," Polonsky was saying. "Chancellor Shevchenko will certainly attend, and I suspect he can bring others on board from Poland and Hungary."

Shevchenko was the Ukrainian official that Nikolayev's omega sister had married under a new identity after Nikolayev fake-murdered her when she was a teenager... because apparently selling female omegas into political marriages was a thing this family did with some regularity.

Nikolayev sat back and tapped his fingers thoughtfully against the polished surface of the massive table. "I agree," he said at length. "It is time to bring our shadow alliance into the light, if only to normalize the idea that some countries are open to change."

"To breaking publicly with the Committee, you mean," Polonsky said in a dry tone. "Though what that even means these days is something of an open question, now that you've eviscerated half of it."

Nikolayev didn't react, beyond the flicker of a gray eyebrow. "I'm sure I have no idea what you mean, Commissariat. All organizations evolve. The Euro-Soviet Committee has merely evolved to see the error of its ways."

"Leaving a trail of dead officials and destroyed careers in its wake, yes," Polonsky agreed. Irina, seated across from him, failed to stifle a soft snort. I stared at the back of her head, trying to dissect the omega-shaped hole in my mind. I had the distinct impression that if I were somehow magically given the power to plug my former mate back into that hole, she would no longer fit. The idea was disconcerting.

"Evolution is seldom kind to the unfit," Nikolayev was saying. "Very well. I agree in principle to a regional conference where we will discuss ways to move forward within a new framework of laws and treaties."

Polonsky wove his fingers together, leaning forward on his elbows. "And may we expect the presence of your new spokesperson at this conference? I must say, she's been garnering quite a bit of attention in the worldwide media over the past few months."

I perked up. Bringing Leona and Kameron out of hiding and onto the world stage had always been a part of the plan, but the timetable for doing so hadn't been finalized until now.

"Yes," Nikolayev said. "One can hardly have a meaningful dialogue about the future of alphomic policy without the presence of alphomic individuals." His gray gaze moved to Irina.

"Indeed. What a groundbreaking concept," Polonsky said, with the deadpan air of someone who was in on a private joke.

"What about the security considerations?" Irina asked, all business.

Again, I prodded at the gap inside me where the roots of our bond had been torn out, trying to find the pain. It was there, throbbing in time with the bone-deep scars crisscrossing my left hand—but I no longer had the sense that it could be eased by trying to force things back the way they had been before Irina's arrest. I wasn't entirely certain what that meant.

Nikolayev caught my eye and summoned me to the table with a sharp jerk of his chin. I forced a mask of professionalism into place and joined the discussion of how best to keep anyone from getting killed, filling in for Beckett as best I could until Nikolayev and I could consult him directly, inside his posh bedroom prison.

Afterward, Dzimitry Polonsky intercepted me before I could slip away.

"Monsielle Alex, if I might have a word?" he asked in French, using the non-gendered honorific that had once been preferred for addressing unaligned alphas and omegas.

I paused, caught off guard. "Of course, Commissariat Polonsky," I replied in the same language, uncomfortably aware of my earlier gut reaction urging me to wring his beta neck.

Irina watched the exchange intently, but she made no move to join us as Polonsky indicated a door leading to an anteroom off the main conference room. Interestingly, neither did the two security goons—although they were wearing the perfectly blank expressions common to paid guards everywhere who thought their charges were about to do something utterly foolhardy.

Being somewhat familiar with the experience, I could relate.

Nikolayev hadn't missed the exchange either. His expression warned me not to do anything that would endanger the delicate web of diplomacy he'd been weaving. I steeled myself not to react to any potential provocation from Polonsky, desperately hoping this wasn't going to involve some sort of beta breast-beating over the ownership of a woman.

"How can I assist you, Commissariat?" I asked, in a perfectly flat tone, once we were alone.

He waved the words away and gestured me to sit at the small table set in the center of the room. I complied, figuring the symbolic barrier of a piece of furniture separating us could potentially be useful.

"I do not require assistance. Merely a brief conversation," he said, taking the seat across from me. His features weren't classically handsome, though I supposed they were pleasant enough. He had a prominent nose and an aggressive chin beneath sandy hair and light brown eyes. I wondered what Irina saw when she looked at him.

He isn't a constant reminder of a past I would rather forget, she'd told me, the first time we'd spoken after I discovered she was still alive.

"You are Irina's Alex," Polonsky said, wasting no time in going for the jugular.

I pasted on a tight smile in response. It felt like it might split the skin over my cheeks. "Clearly not."

He dipped his head—a gesture of self-effacing acknowledgement. "Forgive me. I know of no good way to say what needs to be said without dredging up old injuries."

"And what is it that you think needs to be said?" I asked, hoping to bring this exchange to a speedy conclusion.

He met my gaze and held it. "I want you to know that I am deeply in love with your former mate. I'm certain I don't need to enumerate all the reasons why. I would like to think she loves me as well—although the rationale on her end is considerably more opaque."

I'm with someone, she'd told me. *I'm in a relationship that makes me happy. He doesn't make me feel as though my lack of a mating gland or a womb makes me somehow incomplete as a person.*

At the time, I hadn't been ready to hear what she was telling me. I still wasn't, but I suddenly seemed to have less choice in the matter.

"She isn't a beta woman, someone to marry in a church and hang off your arm like a trophy," I said sharply, and probably unfairly.

His brows drew together, sadness visible behind his pale brown eyes. "No. Definitely not. She is a proud omega. One who was treated with utter barbarism by monsters in the guise of men. And since then, she has fought every single day to ensure that at some future date, there will be no more damaged omegas like her. She fights with words and with weapons, with her entire heart and soul. It amazes me daily that she still has room in that boundless heart and soul for me."

I could barely breathe.

Betas lied. They lied all the time—politicians even more fluently than most. But deep in my heart, I didn't think Dzimitry Polonsky was lying.

"As long as she's with you of her own free will, then it's no business of mine," I managed, after too long of a pause.

He smiled—a bit tentative… a bit rueful. "Even if she weren't, she wouldn't need you to snap my neck for me. She already would have done it herself."

And I would *not* find this Euro-Soviet beta politician charming, goddamn it. I *certainly* wouldn't find him likable.

"Then, as I say, it's nothing to do with me," I told him. "I'd tell you to keep her safe, but we both know what a sad joke that would be."

He nodded once, allowing me my fictions. "Sadly, that is true. With great risk comes the potential for great reward, but none of us were ready to have our hands forced so soon. We all do the best we can for those we care about, and fate will take care of the rest." He rose, reaching his right hand out to me. "I won't keep you from your duties any longer. Thank you for agreeing to speak with me."

I shook it—a dry, warm grip—and tried not to wonder who I would be if I didn't have to carry around my guilt over a lost omega and a ruined life.

TEN

Alex

SIX WEEKS LATER we were on Nikolayev's private jet, descending toward a small airport on the outskirts of Minsk. I'd already been proven wrong about one thing. Months ago, when I'd helped Beckett retrieve a broken, red-haired omega from Montreal police custody, I had assumed that Ambassador Leona McCready was gone forever.

While it was true she'd been stripped of her official title the moment she'd been arrested as a fugitive omega, the self-assured, put-together diplomat was back with a vengeance, with her trusty attaché at her side. And god help me, I could hardly seem to look away.

Nikolayev's bottomless pockets had provided a new wardrobe and personal stylists for the pair. Leona was dressed to kill from the top of her stylish chignon to the razor-sharp points of her four-inch stilettos. Kameron's carefully cultivated anchor-style fringe of beard was shaped and edged with precision. His understated but perfectly tailored suit was chosen to complement Leona's attention-grabbing beauty, but not compete with it. Both of them looked like greyhounds eyeing the mechanical hare at the starting gate, ready to spring.

Even so, their intensity covered a hint of melancholy. I knew why. Jax had ensured I knew about what had happened during their mating. He hadn't delivered the report with the kind of cruelty I probably deserved — instead framing it both as pack business and information relevant to our ongoing security.

Kam had been able to form a bond within the heat nest, only to have it slip away when Leona's pheromone production declined. I hoped with all sincerity the pain of feeling that bond evaporate had been mitigated by the knowledge that the others were still safe and physically nearby.

I hadn't been brave enough to ask him. Perhaps I didn't feel as though I had the right.

Leona's bonds with the others had remained intact, of course—but I got the impression she would never be fully happy unless Kam was also part of that connection. At least Jax had probably been correct that Kam's connection would reappear whenever Leona was in heat. We just had to keep everybody alive that long.

Minsk was supposed to be a test run. Outside of Nikolayev's stomping grounds near St. Petersburg, the Eastern Bloc was likely to be the closest thing to friendly territory that we'd find. The underground had a network of sympathizers already embedded in the power structure in this part of the world. Additionally, many of those in power who weren't already sympathizers might be persuaded to join our cause with the lure of gaining prestige and prominence in a new post-Committee world order.

The trick would be extending our network of sympathizers into Western Europe, and eventually, the UFNA. If those two global superpowers turned our way, the rest of the world would follow. The Committee was a relatively weak presence in Africa, South America, and Australia to start with. Meanwhile, Asia's policy was usually heavily tied to its trading partners'.

The jet touched down in a jolt of squealing tires, the engines whining as they labored to slow the plane. A couple of turnings onto smaller taxiways, and the aircraft rolled to a stop next to a collection of sleek black vehicles that included a stretch limo. I'd have bet money that the cars were heavily armored and the glass bulletproof.

"Come. Commissariat Polonsky has arranged for our security escort to the hotel," Nikolayev said, leading the way as we deplaned and entered the limo.

Rhys Beckett had nearly burst an aneurysm when he found out that we'd be relying on outside security during this conference. I'd thought for a minute that we'd be scraping Nikolayev's innards off the ceiling of the sick room. Beckett wasn't someone whose bad side I'd ever wanted to get on, but an angry Beckett during late-term pregnancy was fucking terrifying.

The fact that he was stuck on bed rest and unable to accompany us had led to a closed-door argument with Nikolayev—one that had risen to a truly impressive volume of yelling.

The interior of the limo was dark and elegant. Frankly I would have been more comfortable riding with the armed guards at the front of the convoy than sitting across from this pair of glittering omegas who'd practically begged me to make them mine. No one said much as the vehicles rolled out, heading for central Minsk. Flynn and Jax were in guard-dog mode. Nikolayev spent the journey looking out of the window as the convoy entered the city. Leona and Kam appeared completely absorbed in a folder of handwritten notes.

The Hotel Europa was old, expensive, and an intriguing mix of classical and modern. It had completely escaped the brutalist and constructivist architectural crazes that had struck this part of the world in the middle of the century. We stopped there only long enough to drop off our luggage—not even bothering to sweep for bugs yet, since we wouldn't be in the rooms for the next several hours anyway.

If the staff had any issues with extending service to two omegas and their alpha mates sharing one massive suite, they kept it to themselves. I placed my single suitcase in my single room, and tried to ignore the burn of acid in my throat at the knowledge that I could be in there with them. It would only take a handful of words.

Please, I want in.

I don't want to be alone.

Words I must never speak. Someone in this pack needed a clear head, because things were about to get dangerous. That someone was me. Despite the odds against us, I was determined that the others would never know what it felt like to lose a mate forever.

In no time at all, we reconvened in the hotel hallway and returned to the cars, heading for Independence Square, located a few blocks away. After some discussion, the decision had been made to hold this informal conference inside the so-called Government House, seat of the Belarusian unicameral parliament. We could have gone smaller — rented someplace private, or even used the nearby university — but Nikolayev didn't want 'small.' Nikolayev wanted the world's eyeballs on us.

The massive administrative building sat behind a twenty-foot-tall statue of Vladimir Lenin. It was composed of acres of elegant white stone, glass, and sharp right angles that reached unapologetically for the sky. Its aggressive modernity squared off with the classical architecture of the church and government buildings on the opposite side of the huge plaza. Everything here was designed to overwhelm the individual with its sheer scale.

The state is bigger than you, it said. *You don't stand a chance, little citizen.*

There was press waiting for us—unusual in this part of the world, to say the least. I sensed Nikolayev's hand in their presence, or possibly Polonsky's. Immediately, my instincts were on edge. More people meant more potential aggressors. Camera equipment and microphones meant it would be harder to spot hidden weapons. I sensed Jax and Flynn tensing as well.

All three of us were armed—heavily so. But we couldn't exactly open fire in a crowd full of journalists.

Across from me, Leona McCready straightened her shoulders and donned an aura of cool professionalism like a cloak. Kam's face was an unreadable mask; the same mask that had kept him from being discovered as an unregistered omega for nearly two decades spent in public life.

Unlike Leona, he might still pass as beta. The physical build. The beard. Both were thanks to testosterone injections, which he'd apparently continued during the months spent under Nikolayev's protection. But anyone with a nose would be able to tell that Leona was an omega. She'd been off pheromone suppressors since Cuba, presumably as a way to further torture me.

No one—betas included—could mistake the visceral punch behind that orange blossom and honey scent for artificial perfume.

Flynn, Jax, and I exited the limo, scoping out the crowd before parting to allow Nikolayev, Leona, and Kam out behind us. At Leona's appearance, the scrum of reporters burst into a confusion of Russian.

Nikolayev raised a quelling hand. "Questions in French and English only, please," he said.

"Is it true that the Committee intends to recognize equal rights for alphas and omegas?" asked a woman in heavily accented French.

"The Euro-Soviet branch now recognizes alphomic rights," Nikolayev replied. "The UFNA branch is still mired in decades of propaganda and corruption, under the leadership of the war criminal Enoch Sloane."

A male reporter shoved to the front. "You call Sloane a war criminal, yet you brutally murdered your own sister for being an omega?"

"Not true," Nikolayev said. "When she presented as an adolescent, my family and I faked her death in order to move her to an undisclosed location for her own safety."

"So she's still alive?" the man pressed. "That's quite a claim. Where is she? Can we speak with her?"

Nikolayev raised an eyebrow. "Perhaps you should investigate the definition of the word 'undisclosed.'"

"Isn't Leona McCready a wanted international fugitive?" called another journalist.

Leona stepped forward to speak for herself. I felt Jax and Flynn tense, their hard eyes raking the assembled group for threats.

"I do not acknowledge the validity of so-called laws designed to violate the human rights of a marginalized group." Leona met the reporter's gaze, refusing to back down as she continued. "My parents risked jail to protect me from slavery or forced sterilization as a child. A few months ago, I was pulled from my bed at three a.m. by an armed SWAT team who broke down my door without offering any sort of identification, or presenting a warrant for my arrest. That isn't the rule of law. That's fascism."

Silence fell, broken only by the frantic scratch of pens against notepads.

"Where are your parents now?" someone asked. "Do you have contact with them?"

"My parents are deceased," Leona said without breaking expression—a blatant lie, but I couldn't blame her for holding that card close to her chest.

"We are due inside for meetings," Nikolayev said. "Good day."

He ushered us toward the statue of Lenin and the massive doors beyond, ignoring the overlapping babble of questions chasing us. It remained to be seen how the press would spin our presence here, but on the positive side, at least none of them had been undercover assassins with guns hidden in their camera bags.

<hr>

The conference dragged on for days, boring and surprisingly free of drama. I'd been surprised to find that there were other alphas here, working as security for some of the attendees. Other than that, it was in many ways reminiscent of all the times our team had acted as security for one diplomat or another during overseas summits. Beckett's presence would have been reassuring, but so far it had been quiet duty.

I could only follow the parts of the debate that happened within my immediate vicinity, and then, only if the speakers were using French rather than rapid-fire Russian. The goal had been to gain commitments from as many officials as possible to introduce new laws related to alphomic rights into their various legislatures. As far as I could tell, roughly half of those present had agreed, or were at least receptive to further talks.

In other words, it was going to be a painful slog—unless Leona and Nikolayev managed to shake some big names free in Western Europe. And once again, thinking like that was the reason I was standing against the wall with a shoulder holster under my black suit jacket, rather than determining policy somewhere. When it came to saving alphas and omegas, I simply wasn't that patient.

Personally, I would have been more inclined to fuel up those Black Hawk helicopters Nikolayev had somehow acquired in Cuba and go lob a few missiles at Sloane's house.

This was the third day we'd been here, and every day it grew just a little bit harder to wrench my attention away from Leona and Kameron as they worked the room. Yes, I was supposed to be watching them — but only in the sense of making sure none of the people around them posed a threat. Definitely not in the sense of ogling the way Kam's mouth curved when he offered someone a polite smile, or trying to catch a glimpse of the silvery bite scars at the juncture of Leona's neck and shoulder.

Shit.

A server passed, pausing to offer me a drink from his silver tray. I took one of the glasses and sipped at it mindlessly, needing something to both cool me down in the stuffy room and act as a distraction from my unwanted thoughts.

I nursed the clear sparkling water for a few minutes before tipping the rest of it back and returning the glass to another server's tray. It was growing late. I got the sense that things were winding down for the evening, and still without a satisfactory conclusion. There had been talk of extending the talks for one more day, but after that, we would leave.

Even this deep in Euro-Soviet territory, Nikolayev was unwilling to tempt Enoch Sloane or the Beta Liberation Front into attempting something rash. It was probably the right call. By all accounts, Sloane's frustration at his own impotence was spilling over into fits of temper and unhinged screaming at his staff. As for the BLF, there was almost no useful intelligence available about them, leaving the terrorist organization an unpredictable and potentially deadly threat—as Jax could attest firsthand.

Something crashed from across the room, setting my instincts alight. An unintentional growl rose in my throat as I methodically scanned the venue, trying to localize the source of the disturbance while also keeping watch for anyone who might be intending to use the noise as a distraction for something more sinister.

My earpiece crackled. *"Assailant near the north entrance to the hall,"* Jax reported. *"It's one of the alpha security grunts."*

I craned to see. A large figure near the door roared, throwing a clumsy roundhouse punch that didn't seem to be directed at anyone in particular. People scuttled away, opening a bubble of space around the crazed alpha.

"What the fuck?" That was Flynn in my ear.

I was already moving toward Leona and Kam when the source of Flynn's shock grew clear. A second alpha across the room snarled and pulled a gun, only to be immediately tackled by several of his fellows. A shot rang out, followed by a trickle of plaster dust falling from the ceiling where the bullet had impacted.

Flynn appeared, his body acting as a physical barrier between the omegas and the threats. My heartbeat thundered. Sudden rage filled me at the idea that he alone should get to gather the pair up and hustle them toward the south door. Goddamn it—I *wanted* those omegas. I was the pack leader. I was the stronger one. Those omegas should be mine. They *would* be mine.

My clit throbbed in its sheath as a wave of lust slammed over me. My jaw ached with the sudden urge to bite, to claim. Jax was approaching now with

Nikolayev, both of them grim-faced and angry. I needed to act before I was outnumbered. Boiling rage flooded my veins as I reached into my jacket, my fingers closing around the grip of my weapon.

I drew the Makarov and aimed it at my rival. Flynn's eyes fell on me and widened.

Flynn's eyes.

Flynn.

With a gasp, I flung the handgun away as if it had suddenly become red hot, staggering backward. With a shaking hand, I pressed a finger to my earpiece.

"I'm compromised," I croaked. "You need to subdue me before I lose control like the others.

My hip impacted the edge of a table, stopping my backward momentum and sending a half-empty punchbowl and trays of glasses dancing. I saw Flynn exchange a wide-eyed look with Jax, before they both converged on me.

As two rivals charged me, my hindbrain rose up and swallowed my rational awareness. I screamed in rage and sprang at them, ready to snap necks and claw out eyeballs. My nails raked dark skin, just missing my assailant's left eye. The second alpha took advantage of my failed attack and dodged right. Before I could block his swing, something heavy and solid slammed into my temple.

The impact rang through my skull, sending me crashing to my knees. A second blow followed before I could straighten. The darkness swirling at the edge of my vision rushed inward, chasing me into the black.

ELEVEN

Leona

KAM AND I clutched each other in shock as Alex drew a gun on Flynn, only to gasp as if in pain and throw it away a moment later. She staggered backward, saying something I couldn't make out over the shouts and screams of the panicking crowd. Another gunshot shattered the air behind us, and I flinched, trying to stay low.

Flynn had been attempting to shelter us with his body. With a sharp curse, he sprang toward his pack leader. A familiar blond form rushed past us at almost the same instant, yelling at us to take cover. Jax converged on Alex just as she lunged for Flynn, attacking him viciously. Through the bond, I could feel my mates' utter, confused horror at what was happening.

Before I could react, a tall form grabbed me by the shoulder and bore me down, forcing me roughly to my hands and knees between two tables. Kam landed next to me with a pained grunt. For the barest of moments, I was thrown back to the raid at my apartment—strong hands shoving me to the floor. But then Nikolayev appeared, crouching in front of us—watching the room with a tactical eye.

"Can I assume that your female alpha hasn't turned traitor voluntarily?" he asked, with acid in his tone.

"Of course she hasn't," Kam snapped, evidently forgetting his bone-deep fear of the Russian alpha in the face of the implied accusation against Alex's character.

Before Nikolayev could respond, Jax appeared with Alex's unconscious form slung over his shoulders. Flynn was with him, a hand on Jax's arm as they scanned the room for imminent threats. Four jagged lines of blood ran down the side of Flynn's face.

"What the hell is going on?" I demanded, my voice emerging high-pitched and panicky.

"We need to get out," Flynn said.

"Alex said something about being compromised," Jax put in. "That's all we know."

"Drugs," Nikolayev muttered. "Did she drink anything? Eat anything?"

"No idea," Flynn said. "Not really the most pressing problem right now. South door's clear. *Move.*"

Nikolayev pulled Kam and me to our feet, backing off without comment when Flynn snarled and moved in to replace him as our bodyguard. Kam grabbed my hand and we made for the stream of people hurrying toward the double doors. No more gunshots sounded from behind us, so hopefully the armed alpha had been restrained.

I cursed the impractical stiletto heels I'd chosen in an attempt to give myself an impression of added height and authority. Flynn's alpha bristling kept us from being jostled too badly by the crowd, but there was still a growing crush of people at the bottleneck formed by the doorway.

My mind spun, trying to make sense of what had just happened. *Drugged*, Nikolayev had said. A drug that made alphas act crazy?

"This feels like sabotage—something that anti-alphomic interests can use as propaganda," Kam said, as we squeezed through the door and into the grand hallway beyond. "*Dangerous alphas disrupting a meeting of bleeding-heart betas who were only trying to help them* — that kind of thing."

"If Alex and the others were drugged, someone needs to round up the staff and servers so they can be questioned." Jax's strain was barely audible in his voice, but clear as day through the bond.

"Yes," Nikolayev said through gritted teeth. "They certainly do."

More security guards jogged toward us from elsewhere in the building, all of them armed with automatic weapons. I recognized Dzimitry Polonsky hurrying toward them with his hand raised.

"No weapons, please! I believe the situation is under control now," the Commissariat called out.

Nikolayev left to join him, shouting something about making sure the service entrances were locked down. Flynn urged us over to an empty stretch of wall and stood in front of us protectively. Kam immediately moved to check Alex's pulse and pupillary reaction as she hung limp in Jax's grip.

"We need to get her proper medical help," I said, when Kam gave me a nod indicating she didn't seem to be in immediate danger. "Do we have any idea what kind of drug this might have been? Something psychotropic, maybe?"

"I can tell you this much," Jax said grimly. "Her clit's poking me in the shoulder like a steel rod."

"She didn't just start attacking people around her randomly," Flynn said, not sounding any happier about things than Jax was. "She aimed that gun straight at my head."

"And you were protecting Leo and Kam at the time," Jax finished. "She looked at you and saw a sexual rival for omegas she wants."

"Maybe, yeah." Flynn prodded gingerly at the livid scratch marks on his face.

"You're saying someone gave these alphas some kind of substance that forced them into a rut?" Kam asked, looking ill.

Jax opened his mouth, but closed it without saying anything and clamped his jaw in frustration instead.

"Did either of you drink or eat anything?" I asked.

"No," Jax said. Flynn shook his head, indicating that he hadn't, either.

Nikolayev returned and ran an assessing gaze over us. "We're leaving. For the moment, the security forces believe your alpha was injured during the confusion — but if other officials dispute that and say she was waving a gun around, things could become complicated."

"She needs medical assistance," I said, my gaze heated as I pinned the Russian alpha's.

"No doubt she does." Nikolayev didn't back down. "And I would prefer she get it from doctors I trust, in a setting I can control. Not in the same city that just orchestrated a rather neat plot to undermine seven months' worth of our plans. We can be back at my family's private airstrip in Russia in two-and-a-half hours if we hurry."

I felt Jax and Flynn's ambivalence echoing through my thoughts. I shared it. Nikolayev was right about the risks involved in trying to get Alex help in Minsk. Yet none of us were happy with the idea of dumping her on a plane in her current condition and hoping for the best.

"She's tough," Kam said quietly. "But we'll need to restrain her during the flight, in case she regains consciousness and tries to attack again."

I didn't have a decent argument against the bald statement, and apparently neither did Flynn or Jax.

"Yes. Come," Nikolayev said. "We will return to a place of safety and assess the impact of this debacle from there."

He flagged down Commissariat Polonsky, who escorted us back to the waiting limo, using his influence to smooth the way past various hastily erected checkpoints inside the building. The crowd of journalists outside was conspicuous by its absence as we left, and I wondered who'd been responsible for that.

It was approaching nine p.m. local time—fully dark outside except for Minsk's glittering city lights.

"We'll drive directly to the airport," Nikolayev said, his tone clipped. "The Commissariat will see that our belongings are sent on from the hotel."

I spared a thought for whoever ended up with the job of packing and shipping Flynn's sex toys. Jax manhandled Alex's limp body into the back of the limo, before he and Flynn squeezed in as well, flanking her. Nikolayev wisely decided to ride in one of the other vehicles rather than risk being in an enclosed space with Alex, on the off chance that she woke up during the trip to the airport at the edge of the city.

His gray eyes landed on me before I could enter the limo with the alphas. "You and Mr. Patel should take one of the other cars as well."

I opened my mouth to argue, but Kam touched my wrist. "He's right. If she's in a chemically induced rut, our presence will only make things worse by rousing her territorial instincts."

My jaw clenched. I hated this. *Hated it.*

"We'll watch over her," Flynn said from the plush leather seat. "Let's just get where we're going so she can get some proper help, yeah?"

"Yeah," I whispered, and turned on my impractical heels—stalking toward the car parked behind the limo. Kam was right behind me, slipping into the back seat as well. I followed the mating bond inward, knowing that if anything alarming happened during the drive, I'd be able to tell.

"What a disaster," Kam said with a heavy sigh, as the convoy headed out. His head fell back, his eyes trained on the sedan's burgundy headliner. "If anyone was seriously hurt or killed back there, it'll make prime paranoia fodder for the bigots."

I closed my eyes for a moment in an attempt to center my thoughts, breathing in and out slowly. "Only if it gets out," I said eventually. "And if we can get ahead of it with the real narrative—that someone is intent on drugging and poisoning innocent people—maybe it will work in our favor."

Kam rolled his head from side to side to ease the muscles of his neck, his vertebrae popping audibly. "So, who do you think it was? The Beta Liberation Front? Or Sloane?"

"Or maybe both, since there's some evidence the BLF already has connections to the UFNA branch of the Committee," I offered listlessly. As far as we'd been able to determine, that connection was the only conceivable way the authorities in Montreal could have discovered I was an unregistered omega. No one had known except for a handful of BLF terrorists who'd escaped the cave in Romania when Kam, Jax, and I had been rescued.

"Or it could be someone else that we don't even know about yet." Kam thumped the back of his skull lightly against the rear headrest.

"Possibly," I said, not in any hurry to entertain that particular prospect. "Let's worry about Alex now, and leave the rest of it for later."

"Agreed," Kam said. "Leo, we need to be thinking about how far we're willing to go to help her through this, if she doesn't snap out of it naturally."

I knew exactly what he was implying, but I had no desire to discuss the details in the presence of our car's driver and the stoic security guy riding in the passenger seat. I nodded instead, acknowledging that we would have that conversation as soon as we could do so privately.

If Alex had genuinely been thrown into a rut, it would be no different than when I'd gone into heat while trapped in that Romanian terrorist cell. Jax and Kam had helped me then. Kam and I were the most logical options to help Alex now — or at least, we would be once we got someplace physically safe.

Rut for alphas wasn't a biological imperative like heat was for omegas. Everything I'd been able to find on the subject implied that it was a holdover from earlier times — an evolutionary trait that was slowly on its way out. The idea of someone weaponizing an alpha's mating frenzy sparked a slow-burning rage in my chest.

Knowing that Jax and Flynn would be able to feel the emotion, I tamped it down as best I could. It wasn't that I didn't think they'd understand why I was so upset, but they didn't need the extra distraction right now. I only hoped Alex didn't wake up during the trip. Alpha skulls were hard, and alphas healed fast — but it would be best for everyone involved if Flynn and Jax didn't have to clock Alex again to keep her out cold.

The ride continued in silence, broken only by occasional exchanges in Russian over a walkie-talkie in the front seat. We arrived at the small airport to find very little activity. The convoy of vehicles pulled up to a hangar and parked outside after another exchange over the two-way radio.

The security guy craned around to look at us from the front seat. "The boss says stay here until the female alpha is safely restrained on the aircraft," he said, in heavily Russian-accented French.

Kam nodded acknowledgement, wrapping his fingers tightly around mine when I brushed fingertips against his hand. This whole thing was getting way too reminiscent of the *first* occasion Kam and I had been passengers on a plane belonging to Kostya Nikolayev.

"Things worked out surprisingly well the last time we did this," Kam murmured, effortlessly interpreting my thoughts without the need for an active mate-bond.

I squeezed his hand and gave a single nod. "Guess so."

Unfortunately, I didn't see any obvious way that this mess could result in a happy ending for anyone involved. Poor Alex. How she'd hate this.

Time dragged. According to Kameron's watch, it was only about twenty minutes until the radio crackled to life again, and the security guy waved us out of the vehicle. It felt like an eternity.

We cautiously boarded the plane. I was unsure what to expect, but the sight of Alex cuffed hand and foot to one of the airplane seats stopped me cold. It was exactly how Nikolayev's troops had restrained Jax during the flight to Cuba. Jax—currently seated in the row behind Alex—must have felt my pulse of alarm. He sent comfort through the link, catching my eyes in his summer-blue gaze.

"This was a pretty damned effective means of restraint, as much as I hate to say it," he said. "It's only for a couple of hours, and then we'll get her the help she needs."

I forced my body back into motion and took a seat, sitting two rows in front of Alex. Kam slipped in beside me. Nikolayev was already seated at the front of the plane, along with the handful of support staff that had accompanied us to the conference.

The preflight checks dragged every bit as badly as the wait in the car, but eventually we taxied onto the runway and took off, the acceleration pressing me against the seatback. Complete darkness lay beyond the small window until the small jet banked, revealing the twinkling lights of Minsk far below. The aircraft leveled out, and we were on our way back to safety.

Ninety minutes, I thought. *Please, Alex — just stay unconscious for another ninety minutes until we land.*

TWELVE

Kameron

ALEX STAYED unconscious for slightly less than thirty minutes—and then the screaming started. Not screams of fright, but screams of rage, interspersed with feral growling. There was *so much fury* in those sounds... a banshee railing against the unfairness of the world.

Leo sat stiff and unmoving in the seat next to me. I know that she was fighting the same gut-deep need that I was—the need to go to Alex and comfort an alpha in distress. An alpha we both desperately cared for.

Flynn, seated in the row behind us and in front of Alex, must have felt the urge through his bond with Leo. He reached around the seatback to grasp her shoulder. "Don't. It won't help. You two need to know that if you get within range of her teeth, she'll bite you. If she somehow got free of her restraints, she'd try to rape you. There's not a single thought in her head right now except *get to the omegas.*"

It wouldn't be rape, I thought, and I sensed Leo clenching her jaw to hold back similar words. This wasn't a discussion I was willing to have in front of Nikolayev and the gaggle of terrified support staff, but we *would* be having it once we landed.

Leo craned around the edge of the seat, and Alex's wild green gaze locked on her. The alpha lunged, getting her upper body partway into Flynn's row before the metal around her wrists pulled her up short. Spittle flew as she snapped at the air.

"*Fuck!*" Flynn ducked out of range, and Alex fell back, panting and snarling.

The flight was horrible. Alex's shrieks of frustrated anger grew hoarse with exhaustion as time went on. The metal frame of the seat creaked and clattered as she jerked against her restraints convulsively. I wanted to find whoever had done this to her, so I could watch Jax and Flynn beat them within an inch of their worthless, miserable lives.

By the time the plane descended toward the runway at Nikolayev's secure compound, it was after midnight. The Russian had remained stoic as a marble statue throughout the tortuous journey—but as we shed altitude, he stood and made his way to the cockpit.

He returned after only a couple of minutes and sat down again, pulling his seatbelt across his lap. "I've instructed the pilot to radio ahead and ensure medical staff are waiting with an appropriate dose of tranquilizer," he said, pitching his voice to be heard over Alex's wails of distress.

Alex lunged again, only to crash shoulder-first into the bulkhead when the plane banked for its final descent. I faced forward and closed my eyes, gripping my seat arms in an attempt to block out her obvious torment. It must have been windy outside, because the landing was rough, setting my already nauseated stomach roiling.

After an endless few minutes, the plane rolled to a stop, its engines powering down with a whine. The cabin's low lights brightened, turning everything gleaming and white. The unfortunate staff members who'd been stuck on this flight from hell wasted no time in disembarking. They were replaced almost immediately by the doctor who'd been attending Beckett during his pregnancy, along with a burly man dressed as an orderly.

"You believe she was drugged?" the doctor asked.

"That's the current theory," Nikolayev replied tightly. "An unknown substance delivered orally via food or drink to induce a state of alpha rut."

'Well, *fuck*," said the doctor. "That's all the world needs right now. We'll definitely have to sedate her in order to remove her from the plane safely."

He gestured Jax and Flynn to vacate their seats in front of and behind Alex. Setting his medical bag on an empty seat nearby, he withdrew a pre-loaded hypodermic needle and tapped it to release the air bubbles. "She's probably close to exhaustion by now. Vasiliev, restrain her from behind long enough for me to get this into her arm."

I watched with deep misgivings as Vasiliev headed for her. Alex roared and jerked against the cuffs with her full strength. With a sharp, metallic crack, the welds on the seat arm gave way. She took a wild swing at the orderly, the angled hunk of metal arcing out like a weapon, still attached to the other end of the handcuff. Vasiliev cursed and stumbled backward, the heavy length missing his head by barely an inch.

"What the hell is going on in here?" A familiar voice, breathless with exertion, echoed from just outside the cabin door. In our relatively short acquaintance, I'd come to associate that voice with safety and stability. Rhys Beckett stormed onto the plane, one hand wrapped protectively over his swollen belly and his pale eyes snapping fire.

Nikolayev was halfway to him before I could so much as blink. "*Solnishko,* you should not be out of bed!"

"If you wanted me to stay in my fucking bed, you should have done a better job of dampening your worry through the bond." Beckett's growl was worthy of any alpha. "Jax—report, damn it!"

Jax practically snapped to attention beneath the whip-crack order. "She's in full rut, sir. The doctor wants to sedate her so we can move her, but we can't get close to restrain her."

Beckett's gaze raked over the small collection of people left in the cabin. "Everyone get off the plane. Doctor, give me the sedative." His attention fell on me, assessing. "Kam, you've got no pheromones to rile her up. You can stay."

Nikolayev straightened to his full height. "This isn't safe for you. The pregnancy—"

Beckett's lips pulled back in a silent snarl of warning. "*Get. Off. The damned. Plane.*"

Nikolayev took an involuntary step backward. Apparently, no one had warned him about trying to steamroll a pregnant omega.

Beckett softened almost imperceptibly. "I already have pups, Kostya. You know that. And one of them needs me right now."

As if to punctuate the statement, Alex shrieked again. The broken chair arm flew through the air and cracked sharply against the tiny airplane window, still attached to the handcuff chain.

Nikolayev stared Beckett down for a long moment before giving a single, sharp nod. "Do as he says."

Leo gave me a pleading look as I rose to let her squeeze past me into the aisle. "Be careful, odama."

I pressed a kiss to her temple. "Always. We'll figure out what to do next, just as soon as she's someplace safe."

Jax and Flynn followed Leo toward the cabin door, each of them resting a hand on my shoulder as they shuffled past me in a brief gesture of support. I doubt they would have willingly left Alex alone on anyone else's orders, but one word from Beckett was all it took.

The doctor handed over the loaded syringe to his pregnant patient. He didn't look pleased, but there was resignation in his tone when he said, "I'll be waiting outside. You already know this is ill-advised, yes?"

"I've made a successful career out of doing things that are ill-advised," Beckett replied. "I'll send Kameron out to inform you once she's safely out cold."

The man shook his head ruefully, but he didn't argue. With a sharp gesture to his assistant, he led the way to the exit. Once we were alone with Alex, Beckett's tense shoulders slumped. A heartbeat later, he grunted and curled forward, his teeth gritted as he clutched at his distended abdomen for a long moment before straightening cautiously.

A sinking sensation took up residence in my gut. "You're going to bring on your labor prematurely," I said.

He took a couple of deep breaths and let his hand fall to his side. "Can't be helped. And I'm only a couple weeks out from my due date." He indicated Alex, whose violent outburst had subsided into low growls. "The faster we get her the support she needs, the faster I can get back in that blasted, ridiculous bed."

I nodded. "You think your pregnancy pheromones will calm her?"

It was unclear if that was what had halted Alex's rampage, or if it was merely the fact that almost everyone had left the cabin.

"It should help." Beckett quickly checked the syringe. "Alphas tend to get very protective around pregnant omegas. Stay back until I call for you. I'm guessing you know your way around a needle from testosterone injections, yes?"

"As long as it's intramuscular, I can do it," I said.

"Good." He handed me the syringe. "I'll hold her and try to keep her calm. When I tell you it's safe, come stand in the row behind her and inject her in the shoulder. Watch out for that loose seat arm."

"All right," I said. "But for the love of god, try not to get brained, bitten, or otherwise damaged. Your mate would wring my neck with his bare hands."

"Actually, he's partial to firing squads," Beckett replied. "Stay here."

I stared after him. It was probably meant as a joke.

Probably.

Alex sat hunched in her broken seat, panting rapidly. Her curtain of dark hair obscured her expression, but low snarls still emerged from her lips every few seconds. Beckett approached her slowly, his posture open. *Look at me,* it said. *I'm totally harmless. Just a defenseless pregnant omega, no threat to you at all.*

In Beckett's case, that body language was deeply misleading—but it worked well enough to keep Alex from erupting into fresh violence as he moved closer.

"*Alex,*" he said—a beloved carrier soothing a distraught pup.

My throat tightened, long-buried memories of family and loving arms holding me bubbling to the surface. Alex peeked out from the shelter of her hair. She snarled again, baring her teeth, but the sound choked off in a whimper. I held my breath as Beckett closed the final distance separating them, half-expecting the metal seat arm to go flying toward his head.

It didn't, although it did clatter as she raised her freed hand, reaching for him. A terrible, keening moan rose from her throat—the weak cry of an injured animal caught in a trap. Beckett angled his unwieldy belly into the cramped space in front of her and let her clutch at him.

"All right," he said, wrapping an arm around her heaving shoulders and placing a steadying hand on the nape of her neck. "We've got you now. You're going to be okay, you hear me? Kam's here, too. He's going to give you a shot in your left shoulder that will make you sleep. And when you wake up, things will be better."

Beckett met my eyes and gave a beckoning jerk of his chin.

"We're all safe now," I said, approaching with the same unthreatening omega body language Beckett had used. "We're back at Nikolayev's compound, so it's fine to rest for a bit. Everything's okay, but I do need to give you this injection. I'd say something about a little prick, but that would be crass since there are two male omegas present."

Beckett snorted in dark amusement.

I slipped into the space behind Alex's seat, giving the syringe a final check and popping the protective cap off the needle. "Don't laugh. You probably haven't seen your own prick in months, Mr. Preggo," I said, and slid the needle in, depressing the plunger.

I'd been on high alert, prepared to duck an attack and praying Beckett could also move quickly if he needed to. Alex only jerked—letting out a low warning growl, but not moving from his protective hold.

"There, now," he said, stroking her hair. "Let's give that a minute or two to kick in, shall we?"

I capped the spent needle and moved into the aisle, ready to retreat again. To my surprise, Alex reached for me with her freed arm, her fingers outstretched and grasping. Caught out, I sent Beckett a questioning look. He nodded. After setting the syringe safely out of the way, I took Alex's hand and pressed it between both of mine.

Her wrist was horribly bruised from the cuff, and the broken seat arm clanked against the chair frame as we stood there in the deserted private jet—me in the aisle, and Beckett still jammed awkwardly into the gap between seat rows. Alex rocked restlessly in our grips, her body quieting by gradual degrees until a long sigh escaped her lungs and she slumped forward.

Beckett, looking decidedly pasty, eased her back and half-collapsed into the seat next to her. His jaw clenched, and his arm returned to clutch at his belly.

"We need to discuss what will happen if I'm not in a position to stay with her until she's better," he said tightly.

And… *balls*. I'd been right. He was going into labor.

"I haven't spoken with Leo yet, but I'm open to helping Alex with this," I said, ignoring the elephant-sized baby belly in the room—at least for now.

Beckett looked up at me. Sweat beaded his brow. "And you understand what that will mean? Truly?"

"Yes," I said.

His pain-filled gaze didn't let up. "She'll try to bite you. But in her right mind, she wouldn't want that."

"I know," I snapped. It wasn't as though the implications had escaped me. All I'd have to do was get my neck near Alex's teeth, and I'd have that third mating bite I'd craved so badly. All it would take was compromising my morals and taking advantage of a helpless sex partner trapped in a chemical rut.

"Right. Of course you do." Beckett sounded apologetic. "God, what a fucking mess."

He went suddenly very still, and looked down at his lap. I followed his gaze to find his loose cotton pajama pants soaked along the inner thighs. The smell of blood hit me an instant later. The fabric was tinged red where his water had broken.

"Damn and blast," Beckett said. "I suppose you'd better go and get the doctor in here now."

THIRTEEN

Leona

I STOOD BETWEEN Jax and Flynn's reassuring bulk, feeling the minutes tick by like molasses as Beckett and Kam did whatever they were doing to try and calm Alex enough to sedate her. Not for the first time, I was struck by the alphas' unyielding faith in Beckett's ability to fix any given situation, no matter how badly screwed up it was.

Tension crackled off Nikolayev in waves, as he, too, awaited word. Unlike us, he had a direct line to whatever was happening inside the plane via his mating bond. As it did at odd moments, the utter unfairness of Kam's situation hit me. We were bonded, but not really. Not when it counted.

Flynn put his arm around my shoulders and stroked me, soothing.

"They'll take care of it," Jax said. "Don't worry."

Nikolayev stiffened. A moment later, his chest rumbled with a warning growl and he headed for the metal steps leading to the door of the aircraft. My anxiety spiked.

He was halfway up when Kam appeared in the doorway. "Alex is down for the count, but Beckett's water just broke," he called down. "Doctor, we need you in here."

Nikolayev broke into a run, taking the steps three at a time. Kam's eyes widened in alarm, and he ducked out of the way just in time to avoid being bowled over.

"You gonna need help, doc?" Jax asked. "You've only got one gurney."

The grim-faced doctor eyed the rolling cot. "Yes. Assuming she's otherwise uninjured, if one of you can carry your alpha, we'll put Mr. Beckett on the gurney. I should warn you, if this is a true rut, there's not really much to be done for your pack member beyond the obvious."

I had a pretty good idea of what was meant by 'the obvious.' We'd be facing that topic soon enough—but it needed to be a decision we made together.

Flynn followed the doctor and his orderly onto the plane. Once the way was clear, Kam jogged down to join us on the ground. Probably a good thing, since the last thing the others needed was more people underfoot inside the cramped interior of the jet.

"Alex calmed down enough that we were able to sedate her without anyone getting hurt," Kam said quietly. "But Beckett's labor just started two weeks early, and he's bleeding."

"Oh, no," I whispered. All the talk of his pregnancy being high-risk had been yet another background worry in my mind, but I'd mostly managed to avoid thinking about the reality of the danger to him and his unborn pup. The idea that he might be bleeding out from a ruptured placenta less than a hundred feet away from us made bile rise in my throat.

"At least there's qualified medical staff here," Kam offered.

Nikolayev appeared with Beckett in his arms. Both of their faces were gray with strain. I held my breath as the pair descended the narrow rolling staircase, but Nikolayev never missed his footing. He made a beeline for the gurney and laid his mate on it. Beckett had rushed to the plane in the clothing he'd been wearing while on bed-rest. The thin pajama pants were soaked with clear fluid and tinged with blood, but thankfully not stained bright scarlet.

Please let him be okay, I sent to any deity that might be listening. *Please let the pup be alive.*

Flynn followed with Alex in his arms. The metal cuffs still hung from her wrists and ankles. I had a nasty feeling this was because we might need to restrain her again when we got her to wherever we were going. In no time, the nine of us were heading for the main house—the orderly pushing the gurney at a brisk pace while the doctor jogged alongside, checking Beckett's pulse and blood pressure.

It wasn't a short trek to get to the main house, but it wouldn't have saved much time to try and use a car. Considering the difficulty of moving the patients in and out of a vehicle, it made sense to travel on foot, making use of the concrete walkways wending around the property. When we finally arrived at the palatial house, the doctor helped the orderly get the gurney up the low steps leading to the massive front doors.

Inside, he led the way to a large elevator, and we descended to the basement level. It was the first time I'd had cause to come down here, but it came as little surprise that Nikolayev had a pretty decent medical clinic tucked away inside his massive family home. I wondered if Irina had recovered in one of these small, white rooms after Nikolayev had rescued her from the UFNA branch of the Committee.

Nikolayev and the doctor disappeared into one room with Beckett. The orderly gestured Flynn to bring Alex into another and put her on the bed, where he immediately fastened the handcuffs to the metal bed frame. Jax, Kam, and I huddled outside the door, not wanting to be in the way given the room's limited space.

"The physician will be in to take her vitals and draw blood as soon as he can," the orderly—

Vasiliev—told us. "Like he said before, there's probably not much to be done medically. You, uh, might want to talk about other options, if that's on the table. If you need help, we're next door."

He checked Alex's cuffs to make sure they were secure, and then squeezed past us with a nod before disappearing into Beckett's room. Once he was gone, I exchanged looks with Kam and Jax. We joined Flynn inside the modest room, and Jax closed the door behind us. Kam moved to take Alex's cuffed wrist in his hand, his fingers on her pulse point. With his other hand, he peeled back her eyelids to check her pupils.

I understood that Beckett's condition was more of an emergency right now, and I didn't begrudge him the doctor's attention—but it did feel like Alex was something of an afterthought at the moment.

"Time for real talk," Jax said.

Kam nodded. "Beckett was able to calm her down—probably due to his pregnancy pheromones. Unfortunately, he's not in a position to help now. I know this is complicated by the fact that the four of us are mated and she isn't part of that, but I intend to help her if there's nothing the doctor can do medically to interrupt the rut."

Flynn shifted uncomfortably in place. "It's complicated, all right. Alex is still pack, though—even if she won't admit it to herself. But, Ginger Tea, you've only got one place for that knot to go… and it's not a place that's gonna stand up well to an alpha in full rut. She'll tear you up bad."

"We'll tag team her," I said without hesitation. "I can try to take the brunt of it. Does anyone here know how long this is likely to last?"

Please, let it not be days on end, like an omega heat.

There was a longish silence, broken only by Alex's ragged breathing from the bed.

"I'm not sure we can predict it with any accuracy, since it's not a natural rut," Kam said eventually. "And honestly, these days ruts are more of an urban legend than anything else."

"I've only ever heard about them happening during the last day of a heat coupling," Jax said. "And to be fair, things *can* get pretty intense around that time."

"So, maybe a day or so, but we don't really know for sure," I summarized. "It's already been three hours, and the sedative will keep her under for a while. I mean… I don't suppose the doctor could just keep her sedated through the whole thing?"

That would almost certainly be the best option, at least for Alex's peace of mind afterward. I wasn't at all sure how she'd react to having been fucked without her consent—even by Kam and me.

Who was I kidding? *Especially* by Kam and me.

"You can't drug an omega through a heat," Kam said dully. "The required dose just keeps getting higher and higher, until eventually it would kill them to keep trying. This is probably similar."

Well, shit. I tried to recenter my brain around logistics rather than emotions. "We'll need a way to ensure she can't bite." I saw Kam's small flinch, quickly hidden. He'd clearly thought about that possibility already. "We might want to be mated to her," I said, more gently, "but she's made it clear she doesn't want to be mated to us. We have to make sure it can't happen accidentally."

"I've got something for that," Flynn said in a flat tone.

I didn't waste any time being incredulous over Flynn's vast stockpile of sex aids, opting instead for practicality. "You mean you've got something here? Not in our luggage in Belarus?"

"It's here," Flynn said, unrepentant as always when it came to his sex toy collection. "Got it for

Kam in case he might like it, but it'll work for this, too."

"She'll need to be restrained the whole time, so she can't hurt you," Jax said, sounding like the idea made him sick. "You have to be able to get away from her if you need to."

"And we're going to be present, in case something happens and you need muscle." Flynn didn't make it seem like a negotiable point.

"Having other alphas in the room could enrage her," Kam said. He sounded every bit as queasy about the whole thing as Jax had.

"As opposed to how mellow and chill she's gonna be if we're not there?" Flynn asked pointedly.

"He's right," Jax said. "We won't bend on this one, you two. Alex is our pack, but she doesn't get to hurt you. Period."

A faint rumble of a growl sounded from the bed. We turned as one to look at Alex, but she subsided after a moment and lay unmoving.

"Sounds like we're not gonna have loads of time to iron out the details here," Flynn said unhappily.

Kam sighed. "I'll go and let the doctor know she's stirring. Hopefully he can leave Beckett long enough to at least run some basic tests on her."

He ducked out. Once the door swung closed behind him, Jax turned to look at me.

"He's thinking about taking advantage of Alex's condition to mate her," he said, keeping his tone even.

"Everyone in this room has thought about it," I shot back, a pulse of reproach escaping me to thrum through the bond. "And that doesn't mean any of us would actually act on it—Kam included."

The doctor bustled into the room, with Kam in his wake. He wasted no time undoing the top few buttons on Alex's rumpled white shirt and pressing a stethoscope to her chest. He checked her pupils as

Kam had done, strapped a blood pressure cuff to her arm, and finally drew a vial of blood. When the needle slid into her vein, Alex whined and jerked weakly before subsiding again.

"I can't rule out a mild concussion from that bruise on her temple," the doctor said. "Her pulse and blood pressure are elevated, but that's to be expected. You understand there's not a whole lot I can do for her, and I've got an emergency on my hands in the other room."

He looked at the four of us, his expression grave. "If you can do so safely, and if everyone's willing, take her somewhere and keep her restrained so your omegas can help her through this without anyone getting hurt. If that's not an option, she'll just have to stay here under observation and tough it out. I'll monitor her for dangerously high blood pressure readings, but that's about all I can do."

"We'll help her," I said firmly, choosing to look past the 'your omegas' language.

"We can take her to the nest in the guesthouse," Flynn said. "Maybe that will help calm her down."

"How's Beckett doing?" Jax asked.

"His condition is precarious," said the doctor. "As is the pup's condition. I apologize if I seem dismissive of your alpha's situation. But frankly, I can be of much more use to my other patient right now than I can be to this one. I'll run the blood tests as quickly as I can, and if that yields anything useful I'll let you know."

"As long as it's only a rut, she'll live," Flynn said. "Although she probably won't enjoy it for the next little while."

"If we're moving her, let's go." Kam shot Alex a nervous look. "I just saw her hand twitch again."

"I think we can risk one more sedative shot," the doctor said. "It won't last as long as the first, but it will give you time to get her to your nest." He went to a small refrigerator in the corner of the room and retrieved a syringe and a vial, drawing up another dose of drugs and injecting Alex in the hip.

A cry of pain filtered through to us from the room next door.

The doctor straightened and sighed. "I must leave you now."

"We've got her from here." Flynn reached in his pocket and retrieved the key to the handcuffs.

"We'll call you if there are any problems we can't handle," Jax added. "Do your best for Beckett's pup, all right?"

The man nodded and left. I wondered if the others had truly realized that Beckett's own life was in danger—not just his pup's. I tamped the thought down before it could go further. We couldn't help Beckett right now. We *could* help Alex. I'd been where she was before—feeling my body betraying me and being unable to do anything about it. If Kam and I could help it, Alex wouldn't have to suffer in that terrible purgatory for long.

FOURTEEN

Alex

THERE WAS AN omega in the room. The scent of sweet orchards and honey penetrated the overwhelming haze that had weighed down my mind and body, shrouding me in burning darkness. My clit throbbed, pulsing with painful need.

But we weren't alone. *Rivals.* The heavy odor of other alphas sent my hindbrain galloping with the desire to fight, to kill, to *claim*. Spicy musk and mossy cedar filled my nose. Familiar, but still my enemies. They would stand between me and the omega… or, maybe there had been two omegas? I thought there had been two before.

It didn't matter. They would try to keep me from taking what should be mine, and I would have to kill or maim them to get what I wanted.

My body felt too heavy, like something was sitting on my chest. Like my arms and legs were pinned down. Alarm thrummed through my veins. If I couldn't kill the alphas first, they'd kill me and keep the omegas for themselves. The burst of adrenaline woke my nerves and lent fresh strength to my muscles.

"Alex?" The voice was soft. Female. Close. The scent of sweet orange blossoms smothered me. I tried to pounce and snap my teeth, the desire to bite and mark and fuck making my head spin.

There was something in my mouth. It tasted of rubber and I couldn't spit it out—a tough cylinder stretching my lips back like a bit and bridle strapped onto a horse. I couldn't bite through it or push it out with my tongue. I tried to reach up with my hands and rip it off, but I couldn't move my arms. Rope tugged at my wrists. I thrashed and snarled, the sound distorted and muffled around the rubber gag. My legs were trapped, too.

Animal panic flooded me. I had to get free... I couldn't be helpless when the alphas came to kill me. I shrieked and flailed, desperate to escape before rough hands closed around my throat to snap my neck and take the omegas away forever.

They couldn't, *they couldn't*! I had to breed... I had to put pups inside those omegas or the world would end!

"*Alex*!" A different voice—this one male and sounding near to tears, as I screamed through the gag and wrenched at the ropes. "Alex, please! You'll hurt yourself! We're here; we're going to help. Oh, Alex, I'm so sorry..."

Hands landed on me, but they were soft. Not the alphas, ready to kill me. If I was fast enough, if I could only get free, maybe I could still breed this one before the other alphas could stop me. The ache in my clit was growing unbearable.

"Alex." It was the female again. Gentle hands tugged at the closures of my pants. Fingers brushed against my erection, and I arched off the soft surface beneath me as though I'd been electrocuted.

"I've been where you are, okay?" the voice continued. "I know you don't need coddling and reassurance. You just need to be knotting us. But if you can understand me at all, I swear to you that things will be all right afterward. Nothing will change between us unless you want it to."

Fingers were tugging my slacks over my hips... pulling my underwear down enough to free my hard, hypersensitive clit.

"We're going to take turns with you," said the male voice. "We promise, we won't let you be without one or the other of us. You can probably smell the other alphas, but they're not going to stop us or hurt you."

That was bullshit. The alphas wouldn't let these perfect, delectable omegas mate someone else without a fight. *I* would fight. I'd punch and kick and claw and rip—

Honey and orange blossoms crawled on top of me, straddling my hips. I keened, arching up again, trying to push the omega where I needed her.

"Easy." The male omega's hand stroked my forehead, pushing my sweat-soaked hair away from my face. "We've got you, Alex. We've got you."

Slick folds dragged along my length, positioning me. I was already burning up, lava running through my veins, but sliding into the omega's passage was like falling into the sun. I sobbed, and snarled, and tried again to bite through the infuriating gag preventing me from getting my teeth into the female omega's flesh.

It wasn't enough. It could never be enough—but she rode me, and the male omega twined his fingers with mine. I grabbed hard and held, my nails digging into skin as my teeth longed to do. I would breed them, and breed them, and *breed* them, over and over until the other alphas stopped me. I would fill them full of my spunk and knot them so none of it could spill out. I would take them both; have them both, again and again until our pups took over the entire world.

My shirt was half undone at the top. The female made soothing, shushing noises over the sound of my growling and snarling. Her small hand delved inside the rumpled fabric, smoothing over my flat breast and thumbing the nipple. I snapped my hips into her with wild abandon, lifting her body with every violent thrust. She gasped and pinched the pebbled peak hard enough to hurt. The pulse of pain went straight to my clit, and just like that I was coming, coming—shooting inside her with spurt after agonizing spurt.

She groaned in the way that only a well-fucked omega can, her body clamping around me as my knot swelled, locking us together.

It should have been a relief, but it wasn't. Not remotely. The alphas were still here, and now I was even more helpless than before—locked with my mate, pinioned and unable to get free. I couldn't bite her and cement the mating bond. I had to guard the nest. I *couldn't* guard the nest. A whimper of distress escaped me. This was *terrible*.

Hands and voices soothed me… but they were lies. This was the end of the world. I hadn't even bred the other omega yet. My knot ached, pulsing in time with my frantic heartbeat. The female omega smelled distressed. I couldn't smell the male omega at all. I'd been right—something was wrong. *Everything* was wrong. This was wrong, and I was wrong, and I couldn't *fix* any of it because I couldn't *move*.

Tears of frustration trickled down my face, and I *hated* them. The only thing that was right was my seed trapped inside the omega's passage, and her muscles clamping around my knot like she wanted it there.

Minutes ticked by, marked by the thumping beat of my heart. Time marched endlessly, until finally her body released mine and my knot subsided. My erect clit didn't. I needed to fuck, and keep fucking, like doing so could somehow stave off the huge, horrible *something* hanging over my head.

The female slid off me with a groan, but before I could panic again, she curled up with her head on my shoulder. And then, the male was there. He was lithe and pretty and oddly familiar, but it drove me mad not to be able to scent him properly. I squirmed, trying to get lined up because he kept trying to put my clit in the wrong place. I couldn't get any leverage though, and he was insistent in his movements. With a hiss, he guided me inside him. It was tight, and hot, and satiny smooth, making me forget in a flood of sensation that I wouldn't be able to get him pregnant like this.

Instinct took over, and I thrust up, drawing a yelp from him.

"Kam?" It was an alpha voice, low and wary.

I growled my deepest warning growl, having momentarily forgotten about the other alphas who would try to stop me from having this omega. Frustration had me jerking fruitlessly at my bonds again.

"It's all right," said the omega, his voice tight and high-pitched. "Stay back, both of you. I'm all right."

He didn't sound all right. I jerked my hips into him sharply to make him forget whatever was bothering him, and he gasped.

"Easy. *Easy* now, Alex." The female murmured her words against the crook of my neck, but I didn't *want* easy. I wanted to fuck.

I chewed at the infuriating rubber in my mouth, my jaw muscles straining as I continued to drive into the male omega's ass. His soft hands splayed palm-down on my shoulders as he braced himself against my body and took the pounding I was giving him. The female's clever fingers returned to tease my nipples. When her little omega teeth nipped sharply at the tendon running down the side of my neck, I shouted and came again.

The male cried out in counterpoint, clenching. For the second time, I popped a knot inside a hot passage. I fell back, panting.

"Kam," the female said, her distressed pheromones choking the air around us. "Talk to us."

The male was shaking. "It's okay. I'm okay. She can't help being rough."

I didn't want him shaking like that. I wanted him sated and pregnant. I wanted him *claimed*. I gnashed my teeth furiously against the gag.

"Let one of the others check you out once she lets you go," said the female, her scent still sour with worry. "I want to make sure you're not bleeding."

"I will," the male replied. "Please try not to worry. She can smell it on you."

"Sorry," the female said, sounding contrite. Her scent moderated to something more neutral as the minutes passed, and I relaxed a bit.

I couldn't understand why the alphas weren't intervening. At first, I thought maybe they were also restrained like I was — but they didn't seem to be. No one in the room was happy, but as the hours dragged on, I always had an omega to fuck and knot. It was impossible not to let my guard down, at least a little.

It was the female riding me, mostly, but I still knotted the male three times. My clit felt like it was about to snap off at the root from overuse, but I couldn't stop. The world would implode if I stopped. The omegas grew ever more pliant and yielding as time passed, sprawling bonelessly over my body whenever we were tied together. The scent of distress gave way to a scent of exhaustion. I liked that better, even if it still wasn't right. I liked the way they felt when they trusted their weight to me, pressing me into the softness of the mattress at my back.

Maybe that part was almost as good as fucking. Maybe it would be okay to have the weight of drowsy omegas on me without having my clit buried deep inside them. As if the thought had flipped some kind of a switch inside my mind, darkness washed over me and I tumbled into sleep.

FIFTEEN

Alex

SOMEONE WAS STABBING an ice pick through my right eye. I tried to swallow and lick my lips. My jaw hurt. My tongue hurt. Not like I'd accidentally bitten it, though. More like I'd been using it to do dumbbell curls.

I was lying on a bed. The room was dim — soothingly lit with warm, reddish light. *A nest.* My head wasn't the only thing that hurt. My sheathed clit throbbed like someone had kicked me square between the legs with a steel-toed boot. My wrists and ankles felt bruised. The side of my neck was tender.

One of my idiot packmates was sitting in a chair beside the bed. Jax eyed me warily as I groaned and tried to roll into a sitting position, only to fall back on the bed in an ignominious heap.

"Good morning," he said. "What's the last thing you remember?"

There was no world in which a question phrased like that led to anything good. Against my better judgment, I cast my mind back.

"We were—" I began, only to descend into dry coughing.

Jax handed me a cup. I took it and drank, noting in a detached sort of way that my hand was trembling. A dribble of water trickled down my chin.

"We were... in Belarus?" I managed, handing the cup back.

Jax set it aside and returned to his chair. "Yes," he agreed. "At the conference."

The conference. We'd been there with Nikolayev and the omegas, meeting with Irina's mate—*husband*—and several other dignitaries from countries around the region. Things had been going decently well, if not spectacularly so. There'd been talk of extending the meetings for an additional day. I'd been watching Leona and Kam work, berating myself for letting them distract me from scanning for threats like I was supposed to be doing. And then—

I blinked.

Rage. Lust. Terror.

Bodies writhing against mine. Soft words that might as well have been gibberish. Reassurances that I couldn't allow myself to believe. I felt the blood drain from my face so quickly that it made me lightheaded.

"No…" I whispered.

"*Alex.*" Jax's voice cut through my growing panic. "Look at me, alef."

I dragged my gaze to his blue eyes, staring at him past a hazy memory of sighting along my gun barrel at Flynn's head.

"We're back in Russia," Jax said. "No one's injured. You didn't mate either of them. They helped you of their own free will, with the full expectation that it wouldn't change anything afterward."

"I didn't bite them?" The words were a barely audible rasp.

"No one bit anyone." He paused, seeming to rethink the statement. "Correction. No one *mated* anyone. Actually, your neck is a mass of bruises, because apparently Leo has a not-so-secret marking fetish. She didn't break the skin, though."

My body flushed hot, then cold. "And she wasn't in heat." That was right, wasn't it? She hadn't been due for a heat… had she?

"No one's pregnant," Jax said firmly. "And no one's mated to you. Someone at the conference spiked the drinks with a drug that brings on a rut in alphas—probably one of the staff. You and two other alphas got dosed. Nikolayev's doctor ran blood tests on you, and he doesn't seem to think there will be any lasting effects."

"A drug. For alphas," I repeated stupidly, trying to get more neurons firing in sequence.

"If your first thought was *Beta Liberation Front*, so was ours." Jax took a deep breath and let it out in a huff. "It was probably meant as a way to get alphas to hurt or kill people, so the story could be spread over the worldwide news media to reinforce Enoch Sloane's message about the so-called alphomic menace."

I swallowed hard. "Did I..."

"No one at the conference was seriously injured. You pulled a gun on Flynn, but you threw it away an instant later when you realized you were compromised. One of the other alphas in the room got off a few shots, but he didn't hit anybody. I knocked you out. We bundled you onto Nikolayev's plane and brought you back here, where we're secure." He hesitated. "Sorry about pistol-whipping you like that, alef."

They'd kept me from hurting anyone. They'd brought me back. They'd let their precious omega mates fuck me through a rut, and made sure I couldn't bite them or hurt them too badly in the throes of my madness.

Jesus Christ.

"Leave," I said, because I was in danger of falling to pieces and I didn't want him here.

"There's something else," he told me, not rising from his chair. "Beckett whelped a female pup yesterday. It's been touch and go. He's still recovering. The pup's in an incubator, two weeks premature and pretty damned tiny. He'll want to see you as soon you're up to it."

Derailed, I took a moment to try and wrap my brain around that revelation. Nikolayev and Beckett had a daughter? Good god—she'd probably end up ruling the world when she grew up.

I shook my head to dislodge the non sequitur, and regretted it immediately when my eyeballs pulsed like they might roll right out of my skull. "I need to talk to Leona and Kameron," I muttered.

"They're resting at the moment," Jax said, in a carefully neutral tone. "You probably should be, too. I'll let them know you're awake and wanting to see them. I'll also have Flynn bring you something to eat."

My stomach protested the idea of food, but I hadn't eaten in who knew how long, so I nodded.

"Thank you." The words were harder to get out than they should have been.

Jax rose, looking down at me with a troubled expression. "Alex... this thing with Leo and Kam— we need to figure it out. They're dead set on not pressuring you into anything you don't want to do. But, me? I'm starting to worry about what will happen to our pack, long term."

I heard what he wasn't saying. If I'd had a mate-bond with the rest of them, I wouldn't have pulled a gun on Flynn, because I wouldn't have perceived him as a threat. Leo, as an omega, would have been able to soothe my emotions through the psychic link to keep me from losing my shit.

Basically, all of this could have been avoided. My stomach churned harder.

"I hear you, alef," I said. "I do."

He nodded, satisfied—at least for now. "We can talk more later. The doc didn't want to give you any painkillers until you woke up and we saw how you were doing, but there's aspirin on the table next to the water."

Leaning down, he gave my shoulder a squeeze before turning and leaving the room... leaving me alone with my whirling thoughts.

Everyone wanted me mated to Kam and Leona. I'd been helpless during the rut—a slave to my alpha hormones. All they would have needed to do was put a neck in range of my teeth, and the deed would have been done. Instead, they'd made sure things could go back the way they were as soon as I snapped out of the rut. They'd given me the option of pretending it never happened.

I closed my eyes. More bits and pieces of the recent past were filtering into my memory, blurred by the murky pall of madness. I'd been convinced Flynn and Jax were going to kill me. I would have killed *them*, given a chance.

My packmates.

My alefs.

I... I could have killed them.

My thoughts slid unpleasantly sideways, and the passage of time grew hazy. I opened my eyes, but I wasn't seeing the room. I was seeing a memory of Kameron Patel, his brown eyes sparking with frustration as he unleashed his pent-up anger at me.

You've already risked your lives! You've done it over and over—for us and for each other! There is literally nothing more you could sacrifice for us, simply because we were mated!

Jax or Flynn—or both—could easily be dead by my hand. I'd been a hairsbreadth from pulling the trigger on the Makarov and blowing a hole in Flynn's skull. If that had happened, how much comfort would I have taken from the fact that we didn't share a mate-bond through Leona?

A shudder wracked my body, and I wrapped my arms around myself as though I could hold all of my unraveling pieces together. The door opened, and I forced myself straight again. Flynn entered, bearing a plate with a sandwich and a bag of chips on it.

"Heya, alef," Flynn said. "Brought you some food." He set the plate down on the bedside table beside the water and the bottle of aspirin; then he flopped down in the chair Jax had vacated. "You know, you are one seriously terrifying bitch when you're rutting. Will you please mate the omegas now so we don't ever have to do that again?"

A choked sound wrenched free of my throat. In another life, it might have been the bastard offspring of a laugh. *God*, I was losing my fucking mind.

"Did you seriously strap one of your perverted sex toys into my mouth?" I asked in lieu of answering.

He shrugged. "Shit comes in handy sometimes — not that you ever really struck me as the leather-and-floggers type. Next time, leave the bondage gear for the guy who actually enjoys it."

I reached for the sandwich, mostly in self-defense. It was tuna salad — my favorite.

Flynn watched me with his dark eyes that always saw too much. I chewed and swallowed, aware of the heavy weight of the question I hadn't answered.

"I'll talk to them," I said. "Kam and Leona, I mean." The next words caught in my chest, and I had to clear my throat before I could get them out. "I don't want to lose this pack." It was a hoarse rasp.

Flynn blinked at me. "You're not going to lose this pack, alef. Who on earth made you think that?"

The stupid bitch in the mirror, I didn't say. Instead, I looked down and took another bite of my sandwich. "I'll talk to them," I repeated, mumbling the words around a mouthful of food.

As if my words had summoned them, Kam and Leona appeared in the open doorway. Flynn glanced over his shoulder at them before turning back to me.

"You do that," he said.

Leona came over and pressed a kiss to his short-cropped black hair. "Give us some privacy, Big Man," she said.

He caught her wrist and brushed his lips to it. "You bet, Sweet Thing. Get this mess figured out for us, okay?"

Flynn rose, grasping Kam by the nape of his neck and rubbing a possessive thumb over the bite scars at the juncture of his shoulder as he passed. The door closed, and I was alone with the omegas.

I set the sandwich aside.

Leona looked tired, but Kameron looked like absolute shit. And... he wasn't moving right. He was moving like someone in pain.

"They told me you weren't hurt," I said, horror and guilt snaking through me like cold water. How many times had I knotted him? Two? Three? "Kam, you look awful."

"Told you I should have come alone," Leona muttered.

Kam narrowed his eyes at me. "It's impolite to comment on an omega's appearance, *especially* after they help you through a rut. And by the way, you look like a two-day-old corpse yourself."

I opened my mouth. Closed it. Turned my gaze on Leona. "Is he hurt, though?"

"He's sore, because he insisted on letting you knot him three times in twenty-four hours," she said. "There's some minor tearing, but nothing that needed medical treatment. You should probably know that when it comes to you, he's a bit of an idiot."

Kam visibly ground his teeth. "I am standing *right bloody here.*"

"Only because you're too sore to sit." Leona's tone was unapologetic.

"If it's any consolation, I think my clit is broken." I shouldn't be able to joke about this. Not with the dark circles of pain and exhaustion beneath Kam's eyes.

"I bet," he said.

I swallowed, my throat clicking. There was no point in putting this off. "You didn't let me bite you."

Silence settled over the room for a long moment.

"I thought about it," Kam admitted quietly.

"We're not saints," Leona said. "But we're also not monsters."

I could barely breathe. "I almost killed Flynn. I hurt you, Kam. If we'd been mated, none of this would have happened. You could have stopped me... calmed the rut."

"Yes," Leona agreed. "But fear and might-have-beens aren't a good enough reason to mate someone."

I stared at her like she might somehow have the answers I needed — my own personal oracle. "I'm losing my pack." It was a whisper.

She scowled, fierce as a hunting hawk. "*Never.*"

But Kam shook his head. "It's not that simple, Leo." He frowned at me, his sunken-eyed exhaustion doing nothing to blunt the edges of the expression. "You want to lose your pack? Then keep walking away from them like you've been doing for the last six months."

"Kam!" Leo sounded shocked.

"It's true," he said, refusing to break eye contact with me. "You don't want to mate us? Fine. But you'll have to come to terms with the fact that leading your pack now includes us as part of the deal. Of course, the real problem is that you *do* want to mate us. You have all along."

"Of course I fucking do!" The words erupted from me in a frustrated shout. I froze, but it was too late. They hung in the air, irretrievable and indelible.

"We want that, too, Alex," Leona said — the calm to my storm.

They wanted it, and they still hadn't stolen it from me when they'd had the chance. Because they were noble in a way I wasn't, and fearless in a way I desperately wished to be someday.

"I'll be horrible at it," I rasped. "You don't know what kind of a fucked-up bond you're signing up for."

"No offense, but you may be in for a bit of a shock when you get a peek inside Flynn's brain," Leona said. "The word 'twisted' comes to mind, along with a few others."

"And I, of course, am a paragon of mental health and solid coping skills," Kam added. "Though on the positive side, you'll probably only have to experience that part for a few days each quarter, around Leo's heat."

Wait. Had I just agreed to mate them? Had I really just done that? My entire body felt numb.

I licked my lips. "When is your next heat?"

"In six weeks," Leo said. "Well, five and a half now, I guess. So, is it a date?"

I tried to reply, but it took a couple of attempts to get words out. "I... yes."

I'd done it. I'd agreed to mate two omegas — to risk losing them in the future, as long as it also meant having them in the present. And... I'd done it in the crappiest possible way.

Swallowing audibly, I tried to do better. "I'm sorry, that sounds like I'm trying to put it off, but... Kam? Do you know for certain if Leona's heat pheromones were what caused the bond to form for you?"

He shrugged, pretending that the loss of the psychic bond after Leona's heat subsided hadn't broken his heart. "It's all guesswork at this point. But Jax bit me ages ago, and the bond flared to life as soon as he also bit Leo. I don't think I have to take the bite during her heat for it to work."

Leona's brows drew together. "But we don't know what happens if an alpha completes the connection through me when I'm not in heat. I mean—I know it would still work for me, but we don't know if it would make a difference for Kam."

I tried to sort through it with a brain that still felt as thick and useless as porridge. "Then we should wait. This isn't a high school science experiment. If making the connection while you're in heat is what definitely works, then that's what we should do."

This was surreal. Where was the pain? Where was the deep sense of existential dread?

Don't live in the past, Alex. You have a future waiting, too. You just have to reach out and take it.

That was what Irina had told me when I first discovered she was still alive. She'd tried to warn me not to cling to the trauma of our torn bond. I hadn't listened then, but maybe now I was finally ready to hear the truth behind the words.

"That's what we'll do," Leona said. "Kam?"

He nodded. "Agreed. Now, will you please move back here to the guesthouse, Alex? Because there's no more reason for you to stay away from us. Honestly, there never was."

Everything felt like it was crumbling around me—the collapse of a structurally unsound building finally succumbing to gravity. But... was there a possibility I could build something new on the rubble?

"Yes," I said. "If you really want me there, I'll come back."

SIXTEEN

Jax

TO SAY I WAS relieved was an understatement. Alex might still be a bundle of raw nerves, but she wasn't actively imploding anymore. Perhaps more importantly, she was *here*, where we could help.

Twenty-six days after the near-disaster of the conference in Belarus, I still couldn't quite get over the rightness of waking up in the morning as part of a messy, tangled pile of the people I cared about most in all the world.

I'd missed sparring with Alex, even though it usually meant getting my ass kicked. I'd missed the way Flynn's tightly held tension loosened a bit when he knew he could rely on our pack leader to make the hard tactical and ethical decisions. Mostly, I'd missed the security of trusting that our pack structure was stable; that we weren't going to shatter under the next unpredictable blow.

After the retrieval mission to get Beckett and the others out of Sloane's hands, I'd had a taste of what could be our future, and I'd wanted it—badly. Three alphas. Two omegas. A merged pack, with everyone playing to their strengths and bolstering the others' weaknesses.

We were so close—just a few more weeks. And yeah, I was impatient... but I understood and agreed with Alex's reasons for wanting to wait until Leo's heat to finalize the mating. Like her, I wasn't willing to play roulette with Kam's limited ability to bond.

This was how it had successfully worked for him before, so this was how we would do it again.

For now, though, there was the next conference to address. This one was going to be bigger, and I wasn't sure whether that made it more dangerous or less.

Nikolayev had been surprisingly successful in getting ahead of the story about the drinks spiked with the drug targeting alphas. He'd immediately put his pet doctor in front of the cameras, citing the test results from Alex's blood. They'd spun it as a dangerous psychoactive chemical, and hadn't mentioned the word 'rut' at all.

Other reports—originating from the BLF or, just possibly, from Enoch Sloane's branch of the Committee—had tried to float a narrative about rabid, out-of-control alphas attacking betas without provocation, but they were too late. Nikolayev already had his version of the story in place, backed up by science and forensic evidence. That wasn't to say that the fringe crazies weren't buying the BLF's account, but your average person in the street understood what had really happened—assuming they followed the news at all.

The prospect of a previously unknown terrorist organization operating across international borders to physically endanger high-ranking government officials—first in Romania and now in Belarus—had been enough to finally prod the West into action. Luca Fouchet, the guy Leo knew from Luxembourg, apparently had a fair amount of clout with his government. They'd agreed, on surprisingly short notice, to host a larger summit in Luxembourg City, where representatives and heads of state would discuss sweeping changes to alphomic policy. We were still waiting to find out if Prime Minister Fairbanks from the UFNA, or even someone from his Cabinet, would attend.

"They'll need to do a better job of screening the staff this time around." Alex still sounded understandably sour about it.

Alex, Flynn, and I were in the one of the guesthouse's spacious meeting rooms, discussing the security situation while Leo and Kam were off filming another of her press releases with Nikolayev. A knock came against the frame of the open door. I craned around to find Beckett standing there, with a tiny bundle cradled in the crook of his arm.

Flynn lit up like sunshine through the bond, and I didn't try to stop the smile taking over my face. Without a psychic connection, I couldn't be sure what might be going through Alex's mind. I hoped the presence of Beckett's tiny daughter didn't stir up bad associations with her own lost pups. If it did, she hid it well behind her usual cool facade.

"Heya, Boss," Flynn said. "So, the munchkin's finally ready to come out of the oven, huh?"

Anika Nikolayev had spent the first few weeks of her life in a portable neonatal incubator that her sire had ordered brought in as a precaution, when Beckett's pregnancy had begun suffering complications. To my knowledge, while she'd spent short stretches of time outside the incubator with her parents, this was the first time she'd been out of the sterile white room inside Nikolayev's private basement medical clinic.

"She's met her weight goal with an ounce and a half to spare, and her lung function is good," Beckett said, bouncing the tiny pup gently in his arm when she started to fuss. "I thought we'd make our first trip out of the house a short one and meet the rest of the family properly."

"And it also gives you a chance to pick our brains about the summit, because you're about to perish of boredom?" Alex suggested dryly.

"Yes, you got me. I'm slowly going insane in that damned room... so there's that, too," Beckett agreed, deadpan.

Flynn was already on his feet. "Fuck strategy meetings. I want to hold her," he said, approaching Beckett with his arms out.

I rose, too—drawn by the tiny bundle and the intoxicating smell of a new pup. "I'm pretty sure you're supposed to rein in the curse words around newborns," I told him.

"For what it's worth, she's a bit young to pick it up yet. When she does start cursing like a sailor, it will probably be in Russian." Beckett carefully handed his precious burden to Flynn, the pair of them taking care to support her head through the maneuver.

"There we go." Flynn cradled her against his massive chest, a low alpha purr rumbling up. Anika freed one pink arm from the swaddling, waving her fist around.

"Look at you, Little One," I murmured, tweaking the blanket aside an inch or two to reveal her scrunched-up little face.

Alex had also wandered over to look, though not to touch. "If you came for adult conversation, you probably should have left her at the house." Her tone was tart. "I don't think you're going to get much beyond cooing and baby talk from these two for a bit."

"Occupational hazard, apparently," Beckett said without rancor. "Speaking of which... *incoming*."

I focused inward along the bond, where the sense of Leo felt closer than it had a few minutes ago. She and Kam appeared in the doorway, along with our Russian host.

Nikolayev's heavy brows drew together. "Solnishko. Should she be so far from the house?"

"Yes," Beckett said simply. "She should. And you're fussing again."

To his credit, Nikolayev didn't argue further. "So I am. Forgive me." He took a deep breath, visibly refocusing. "The filming went well. I believe our attempts at public messaging are still successfully outstripping our enemies'. Our last sweep of the major news media showed a promising uniformity regarding public condemnation of the terrorist action in Belarus."

He was talking to an audience consisting solely of himself, because Kam and Leo had already joined the rest of us in fawning over Anika. Flynn handed her to Kam, who settled her in his arms and gave her a soft smile that clenched something painfully in my chest.

If ever an omega had been meant to cradle newborn pups in his arms, it was Kameron Patel. I thought achingly of the nameless, faceless offspring I'd doubtless left behind in the breeding pens, and closed my eyes against the upswelling of rage at those who'd taken it on themselves to make human beings into commodities — like livestock to be bred or neutered as convenient.

"Aren't you just the most beautiful little girl who ever was?" Kam asked, as he and Leo bent their heads close together over the swaddled, wriggling infant.

I didn't need a terrorist drug to rouse every alpha instinct I possessed, urging me to take these two somewhere quiet and breed them until we had pups of our own running around the massive three-story guesthouse, filling it with shouts and squeals of youthful laughter. Never mind that it was irrational — Leo wasn't in heat right now, and Kam could never have pups of his own.

It didn't matter. Through the bond, I felt Flynn's thoughts running on parallel tracks to mine. Our eyes met with perfect understanding.

Kam stroked the backs of his fingers against Anika's soft cheek before handing her over to her sire. Nikolayev took her, his body language clearly communicating that no one else would be touching her for the foreseeable future, with the possible exception of his mate.

I wondered if she'd thrown up or peed on any of his suits yet.

"You were saying about the news media?" Alex said, raising an eyebrow.

"Yes, that part's been promising so far," Beckett replied, settling onto a comfortable chair by the fireplace. Like Anika, he'd had a rough time of things. He was still pale and his face appeared gaunt—but there was a sharp glint in his eye as he continued, "Personally, I'm more interested in the possibility of following the BLF trail. The Belarusian secret police succeeded in catching the operative who drugged the drinks. They took him into custody a couple of days ago."

"Did they now?" Alex said, the same light kindling in her green gaze, like a hunter spotting prey.

"I can at least still use a telephone, so I've reached out to some old contacts in Interpol," Beckett went on. "No real shock, but the guy isn't cooperating. Still, we know his identity from fingerprint records, and it makes me wonder what would happen if we started following the money trail."

"He was paid?" I asked.

"He was," Beckett said. "And not in cash, which would have been the smart thing to do. There are bank records. No doubt they'll be opaque as hell—

shrouded in shell corporations and money laundering schemes. It's something, though."

"A lead is a lead," I agreed. "If we could somehow tie the terrorists directly to Sloane's operation—"

"That would be a very neat resolution," Nikolayev agreed. "But also extremely sloppy on his part."

"Plus, it's every bit as likely that the trail will lead back to someone in the Euro-Soviet branch rather than Sloane's branch," Beckett said. "If so, that would complicate matters more than it would simplify them. We need Kostya's wing of the organization to lead world governments toward a more liberal policy outlook."

"It's still better to know than not to know," I said.

Alex nodded. "I agree."

"I'll lay odds that Sloane's got a BLF connection," Leo said with conviction. "That doesn't necessarily mean he was in on the Minsk attack—but the fact remains that the Committee tipped off the Montreal police and let them know I was an unregistered omega. The only people who knew about me at the time were the BLF scientists who escaped in Romania. And—as much as I hate to say it—we may have chased Sloane further into the BLF's arms by hijacking the Euro-Soviet branch of the Committee."

"That's true enough," Kam agreed. "The BLF seems to be based in Eastern Europe. Sloane may see them as the only viable allies he has left on this side of the Atlantic."

"Succinctly put," said Nikolayev, with impressive gravity for someone soothing a fussing infant at the same time. "Our goal, for now, is to draw the Fairbanks administration into negotiations. Just as Sloane may be seeking new allies inside the

Euro-Soviet Confederacy, we will need allies in the UFNA. Going forward, most of our messaging should be targeted toward that end."

"We'll tweak the talking points for the next few videos," Leo said. "For now, though, it's getting late."

"And it sounds like someone's hungry," Kam added, as Anika's fussy cries grew in both insistence and volume.

"She's always hungry," Beckett said wryly. "You're right, though. We'll leave you to your evening. Thanks for the adult conversation, even if it *was* interspersed with cooing and baby talk."

I smiled. "Anytime, Boss. We're just happy to see you up and about."

SEVENTEEN

Kameron

THINGS WERE GOING too well. I paced back and forth in the nest, hopelessly restless even though I wasn't the one going into heat. The dormant mate-bond was stirring into life at the back of my mind as Leo's pheromones thickened. Alex and the others would be here soon, ready to finally complete the circle of our pack of misfits.

Hell, Secretary Fouchet had even contacted us a few days ago to say that he was in talks regarding the summit with a member of Fairbanks' Cabinet. Seriously — things *never* went this smoothly.

"What if Alex changes her mind and backs out?" The words burst free without my volition. I kept pacing, not wanting to stop and look at Leo, radiant in her casual nudity as we awaited the alphas' arrival in the nest.

"At this point?" Leo said. "I imagine Jax and Flynn would cold-cock her again and carry her here."

"It's not a joke!" I paused and tried to focus on my breathing, knowing that it was only my fear making me lash out at her.

A hand grabbed the waistband of my jeans from behind and tugged. I toppled onto the semicircular couch with a grunt. The couch sat at the edge of the sunken nest pit piled with cushions and blankets, ready for use. Additionally, a king-sized four-poster bed with a canopy dominated the far end of the room. Maybe including a beta-style bed in an omega nest was a Russian thing, but I didn't like it. I hadn't liked it before, and I liked it even less now that I'd seen Alex tied to that bed, fighting her bonds for hours and hours until I worried her wrists and ankles would tear and bleed.

"Odama." Leo took my chin in her hand and physically turned my face to look at her. "Have you ever known Alex to say she was going to do something and then not follow through?"

I clamped my mouth shut, because of course the answer was no. I wasn't finished fretting yet, though. She sighed and kissed me. I could feel her growing arousal through the bond... and, more distantly, Jax and Flynn's. Closing my eyes, I let myself fall into it, experiencing my packmate's heat vicariously.

"Sorry," I murmured when she finally pulled away from the kiss.

She bopped my nose with hers. "I love you, odama. We all love you. And before long, we're going to remind Alex what it feels like to be loved— in body and in mind." Her fingers plucked at my shirt collar. "Don't you want to lose the clothes? The others are on their way."

I shook my head. "Flynn enjoys ripping them off me too much."

She snorted. "Whereas you don't enjoy it at all, of course."

"Did I say that?" Despite myself, my paranoia was beginning to fade. I could feel Jax and Flynn's emotions accurately enough to be able to tell that nothing was wrong. If Alex had done a runner, they'd be upset enough for me to feel it through the bond, I was sure.

Leo wrapped me up in a hug, throwing a leg across both of mine for good measure. I buried my face in her soft hair—focusing inward, because it was still such a novelty to feel the others inside my thoughts like this. Although it was difficult, I mostly resisted the temptation to think about the inevitable loss that would come when Leo's heat subsided and my body stopped piggybacking off of her elevated level of bonding hormones. I didn't want to tarnish what time I possessed with grief for something that hadn't happened yet.

A rough voice came from the doorway. "Jesus, I don't know if this is better or worse than walking in to find him eating you out." I looked up to find Flynn leaning an elbow against the doorframe, watching us.

"Is everything all right?" Alex pushed past him, entering the nest. She looked a bit pale in the face, but she was *here*.

"It is now," I said, with complete sincerity.

I felt Leo's smile of happiness before I saw it—a sensation like the sun coming out inside my mind.

"Come in," she said, formally inviting the alphas into the nest.

They did. Jax and Flynn wasted no time in stripping off their clothing and tossing it aside. Alex was dressed in a loose tank top and track pants. Her dark hair was down, and her nipples poked through the thin fabric, tenting it.

Leo's burgeoning lust washed through me. I closed my eyes to savor it, but only for a moment—there was too much to look at. She pressed a final kiss to the hinge of my jaw and untangled from our embrace, giving the others her full attention.

"I'm accelerating from zero to sixty toward heat-brain," she said, with mild, self-deprecating humor. "I blame you three for that. But while I can still think—Alex, I took my birth control injection last night. If you want to use condoms with me, that's fine, but the others won't be. I do draw the line at cervical caps, though. Those things are horrible."

Alex nodded, though something haunted flashed behind her expression. It was no surprise that she found the subject of birth control and pregnancy a difficult one, after the loss of her pups with Irina. We'd already talked about it in a general sense, however. She knew Leo wasn't courting pregnancy, but that she wouldn't be doing cartwheels in an attempt to prevent it, either. Or, at least, she wouldn't be doing cervical caps. Having been press-ganged into helping her remove and replace the damned things during her heat, I could confirm that they were a pain in the, uh, cervix.

"I understand," Alex said.

"I have a request," I said, before I could lose my nerve. "I want you to mate Leo first while I watch."

Alex settled knowing green eyes on me. "You want to make sure I won't back out of the bond. I can't really blame you."

I sighed. So much for trying to play it off as a kink. "Sorry, that sounded horrible, didn't it?"

She was spot on, of course. I couldn't bear the thought of having her bite me when it wouldn't mean anything real. If she bit me first, only to balk at biting Leo, I wouldn't have a true bond with her, only a scar. If she bit Leo first, though, I didn't think she'd hesitate to also bite me. For her, the hard part would already be over.

"No," Alex said. "I deserve that. Rest assured that I'll be mating both of you tonight, but you can watch me mark your odama first."

"Now hang on a minute," Flynn said. His mood through the connection we shared was light and teasing. "Who said you were monopolizing both of them tonight?"

Jax snorted. "You gonna throw down with her for first dibs, asshole? Good luck with that."

"Oh, come on—arm wrestling," Flynn said. "Best three out of five."

"No," Alex told him flatly.

Leo began giggling uncontrollably—proof positive that she was, in fact, starting to lose it as her hormones took over. She slid off the couch and crawled through the sea of pillows to Flynn, who watched with definite interest as she climbed up the length of his body, scaling him like a proverbial tree. When they were nose to nose, she fluttered her eyelashes at him, pouting. "You'll be busy. You have to keep Kam occupied while he's waiting for his turn."

He huffed a laugh, not buying her *innocent* act for a minute. "Guess you're right about that, Sweet Thing. He does seem to have an awful lot of clothes on right now, doesn't he?"

… And that was how I ended up kneeling on the floor, cushioned by a mountain of pillows—with my back braced against the footboard, my arms spread-eagled and my wrists loosely bound to the wooden rails. Flynn took great pleasure in ripping the front of my shirt open, sending buttons flying. He unfastened my fly with slightly more care, made a pleased sort of grunt when he confirmed that I'd gone commando, and pulled my half-hard cock free.

"Got something new for you, Ginger Tea," he said, producing a pair of small metal clamps connected by a chain. The toy had almost certainly come from the bottomless drawer of unspeakable items that he kept in the bedside table.

"Thought you'd sworn off nipple clamps," I managed, attempting valiantly to ignore the anticipatory gooseflesh that rose across my exposed chest.

"For me, yeah. Not for other people," he said, and clamped the first one into place on my left nipple.

I yelped. Then I yelped louder when the second one pinched my right nipple, igniting a phantom ache in the two nipples that were gone. Flynn grinned, pumped my half-hard cock a few times until it stiffened further, and let go, leaving me trapped and panting.

"There ya go. Enjoy the show for a bit." Flynn rose from his crouch and patted me on the head like a dog. "Jax and me will be over to fuck your mouth later if we get bored while we're waiting."

I knew, intellectually, how twisted it was that I got off on things like this. That didn't stop the low pulse of heat at the knowledge that they'd make good on that promise — using me to warm their cocks and otherwise ignoring me, as though I were a fuckable piece of furniture. The heat of excitement stemmed from the idea that I wasn't too broken for them to want to use. The alphas would take pleasure from my body, and it didn't matter in the slightest that I was sterile and scarred.

That knowledge had been enough to get me going even before the mating bond had been in place. Now, I felt like a starving man at a banquet. Other people's lust thrummed through my veins, and it would be like this for *days*. I couldn't physically keep up with it for the whole time, of course — not like Leo could. But she and Jax and Flynn had been learning my limits at the same time I had. They were becoming experts in stringing me along — stringing me out — to wring as much from my body as it could comfortably give.

Now, I hung like a debauched display from the bed frame — shirt and pants gaping, exposed to the others' view with my dick hanging out and my aching nipples clamped and chained. Jax and Flynn were too busy watching Alex and Leo to pay much attention to me now… but I was willing to bet they'd take turns fucking my mouth afterward until I was lightheaded from lack of air. Anticipation sent a new pulse of need through me, trying to further stiffen my omega cock.

In the sunken nest full of pillows, Alex peeled off her thin cotton tank top. I stared at the long, lean lines of her torso, thinking *she's going to be ours... we're finally going to be as we were meant to be. Pack.*

Her loose track pants followed. God—I wasn't ever going to get enough of seeing Leo and Alex together naked. Alex bent down, touching one fingertip lightly to Leo's jaw. She used the contact to draw Leo forward on her hands and knees toward the curved couch. When she reached it, Alex lowered herself onto the seat like a queen and drew up one leg, exposing herself to our gazes. I couldn't see Leo's expression with her back to me, but I could feel her giddy smile lighting me up from the inside.

"You like to mark your alphas?" Alex asked. "In that case, I want a line of love bites up the inside of each leg... right up to the top, little omega."

Leo pounced like an excited kitten with a ball of string, her joy and need shining through the bond like a beacon. Jax, Flynn, and I watched avidly as Leo bit and sucked her way up one hard-muscled leg, paused long enough to tease Alex's clit fully out of its sheath with her tongue, and then abandoned it to repeat the process on the other leg.

"Well done." The praise was practically a purr, and my mouth watered with the need to get my lips and teeth on Alex like Leo just had. *Anywhere.* I didn't care where.

Alex cupped Leo's chin again and directed her onto the couch, where she straddled Alex's lap. Leo cupped Alex's face between her hands, meeting her eyes from inches away.

"Are you doing all right, alef?" Leo asked solemnly, not yet too far gone for words.

Alex's expression made my chest ache.

"I'm terrified," she said. "But I also need my pack."

"You've already got us, Alex," Jax said. "You always did."

"This is going to be so much better, though," Flynn added. "You'll see."

Alex closed her eyes and bowed her head. Leo pressed their foreheads together. "Please fuck me, alpha. I need your knot... I'm so empty, and I want you to fill me up now."

Her perfume was filling the room in great clouds, proclaiming the truth of her need to every alpha in sniffing range. Flynn gave a low groan. Jax leaned back on his pile of pillows and wrapped a hand around his cock, shamelessly jacking off to the show.

Alex released a sharp breath and framed Leo's ribcage with long-fingered hands, bending her backward and leaning down until she could get her mouth on Leo's generous breasts. Leo gasped, her perfume growing sharp and musky as her body sprinted toward her first peak. With a playful, kittenish growl, she wriggled free, scooted up, and impaled herself on Alex's erect clit.

Alex let out a snarl that sounded considerably less playful. She twisted them both, depositing Leo on her back on the couch cushions. Hooking an elbow under Leo's right knee to draw her leg up, Alex set up a rhythm and pounded into her until Leo was gasping obscenities and clawing at her back in desperation.

"Oh, god... oh, *god*! Yes! Bite me, alpha! Knot me, *take me*!"

Alex pulled out, but only long enough to drag Leo down to the floor on her knees and reenter her from behind. I was drunk on Leo's rising peak and the alphas' lust—so much so that I almost missed it when Leo wailed out her first climax, and Alex sunk her teeth into Leo's neck, over her mating gland. The bright spark of pain knifed through the bond, too entwined with pleasure to be easily separated.

Everyone froze. Jax's hand stilled on his cock. The only sound was Leo's desperate panting and Alex's rumble of a growl, slowly modulating to a purr. A grin spread over Flynn's face.

"There you are, alef," he said softly.

"We missed you." Jax sounded deeply gratified.

A great, warm wave of relief washed over me. *The hard part was over.*

Hours later, with my lips swollen and my throat raspy from the others' use… with Alex riding me hard from behind and my capricious orgasm dancing just at the edge of my awareness, it was almost anticlimactic when Alex bit down over the silver marks left by three other sets of teeth.

Of course the five of us were always going to end up here. How could we not? It was meant to be. Pain flared as the skin broke, my blood mixing with her saliva. My body clenched, my mind whiting out with pleasure as I reached my release—and when my scattering thoughts reformed, there she was.

So damaged. So unsure. Her scars were every bit as bad as mine were—they were just hidden on the inside. I wished, as I always did, to be that last little bit closer to them in the psychic bond. But I was close enough. Love echoed through the shared connection, flowing back and forth, through and around—weaving us into a cohesive whole, no matter our individual broken parts and sharp edges.

Pack, at last.

EIGHTEEN

Flynn

THE PALAIS DE LA Cour de Justice in the Kirchberg quarter of Luxembourg City was one hell of a swanky venue. The building was the site of the Euro-Soviet judicial court, and evidently the Confederacy had thrown a fair amount of money at it.

The place was all polished wood, glass, and dark steel, with a weird fucking art installation in the center that looked like a floating yellow jellyfish and took up two entire stories in the main atrium. The summit was taking place in an audience hall that took up most of the second floor. It had the feel of a courtroom, but on a massive scale. A huge, raised area took up the front third of the space, and the rest was filled with long, pew-like benches for the onlookers.

The courtroom of the gods, I thought with a touch of sarcasm.

This was my first time in Luxembourg. Before prepping for this mission, the sum total of my knowledge about it was that it was tiny, and the language was some kind of bastard lovechild between German and French.

Well, that, and the fact that there was a politician here who secretly had the hots for Leona—but I wasn't allowed to corner him and put the fear of alphas in him because he was useful to us, or some shit like that. Didn't mean I wasn't keeping an eye on Secretary Luca Fouchet, though. One wrong move, and he'd learn the hard way that you didn't flirt with a mated omega. Just because he'd apparently been the one to talk Prime Minister Fairbanks from the UFNA into attending the summit wouldn't change that.

Aspects of this whole situation were kind of surreal. I mean, the whole point of going public with the fight against Sloane and his hard-liners in the Committee had been to get the struggle for alphomic rights onto the world stage. But it was still weird seeing alphas and omegas openly mingling with the beta elite, however cautiously.

There were officials here from parts of the world where the Committee held less power—an alpha prince regent from some tiny African nation I'd never heard of; an omega Māori MP from New Zealand; a mixed delegation of human rights advocates from Iceland. Additionally, there were dozens of alphas and omegas from different walks of life who'd been invited here to testify about the atrocities they'd suffered at the hands of the Committee's brutal laws.

Kam was one of those people. He was currently seated at a long table that had been set up on the massive stage in the audience hall, along with nineteen others who were scheduled to speak this afternoon.

Leo and Nikolayev were in the crowd of onlookers, which included delegations from over a hundred countries. Jax and Alex were watching Leo's back, and Beckett had Nikolayev covered.

I was on Kam duty with Irina, which was another bit of weirdness adding to the general sense of unreality surrounding the summit. If someone had told me a year ago that Irina Pasternak was not only still alive, but was also working for Kostya Nikolayev—and that I'd be sharing guard duty with her at an international conference—I'd have laughed in their face.

To be honest, I still wasn't one hundred percent over what she'd done to Alex. But ever since Alex had a heart-to-heart with Irina's beta mate, or husband, or whatever, she'd seemed to be doing better. The bond Alex, Jax, and I shared through Leona meant it was a lot harder for her to hide from us these days. And that was a good thing. She was still pretty messed up in the head, but who was I to say anything? We were all messed up in one way or another.

So, anyway, I could play nice with Irina for something like this summit. She was still one hell of a competent soldier, and it's not like she hadn't gone through a ton of trauma, too. If she'd found happiness—or at least peace—with a beta politician, then more power to her. Her husband, Polonsky, seemed like a guy who mostly had his shit together. He was sitting with Leo and Nikolayev as the current speaker, a middle-aged beta woman, talked in a halting voice about the prison sentence she and her husband had served after failing to register their son when he'd presented as an alpha during puberty.

I wasn't thrilled with the distance separating us from Kam, in case anything went wrong. Private security hadn't been allowed on the stage, so we were down on the main level and off to one side. On a positive note, the staff for the event had been thoroughly vetted this time around. Even the attendees themselves had all gone through metal detectors and had their identities thoroughly checked.

"I didn't expect to see Beckett back on duty for this," Irina said quietly, as the beta woman on the stage wound down, receiving a round of sober applause from the great and the good in the audience.

I raised an eyebrow. "Did you think Nikolayev was going to lock him in the nursery or something?"

She snorted. "It had crossed my mind, yes."

"Nah," I said. "Beckett would have broken out, and then he would have been pissed. Besides, a bunch of Nikolayev's relatives descended on the place. They came to meet the newest addition to the family and got roped into babysitting. I think it's safe to say Anika is just about the safest pup on the planet right now."

Thinking of Anika always got me feeling broody. Well, *horny* and broody. It was still a bit of a sore subject with Alex in particular, but our pack was gradually moving toward the idea of pups. Ever since I'd seen Kam and Leo cooing over Beckett's munchkin, I couldn't get the picture out of my head. I wanted Leo pregnant. Like, *really* wanted it. And Leo hadn't said no.

"Lucky little girl," Irina said, and if she was thinking about her own lost pups, she didn't show it. "She's going to have that whole family wrapped around her little pinky finger."

"Ten bucks says she'll be ruling the world by the time she's thirty-five," I agreed. "She's gonna be terrifying in all the best ways."

I glanced over the crowd during the lull between speakers. Jax saw me looking and sent an *all's good* pulse along the bond. Alex was a watchful presence in the background, and Leo was focused intently on the stage. It was good having that connection with them. Reassuring. Just as it was frustrating as hell not to have it all the time with Kam, who still only completed the connection with the rest of us when Leo's heat hormones were in full swing.

I'd had a couple of thoughts about that, actually. Once things calmed down, I needed to have a word with Beckett, and maybe Nikolayev, too. As if things seemed like they were likely to calm down anytime soon. *Ha.*

Prime Minister Fairbanks was seated in the front row of the audience. His wife and fourteen-year-old daughter had traveled with him, though his younger boy had apparently stayed behind. Jennifer Fairbanks leaned over and put a hand on her husband's knee. They weren't that far away from us, and alpha hearing allowed me to make out her murmured apologies that she needed to take their daughter to the restroom. They left discreetly, a pair of bodyguards peeling away to follow them.

The beta official who'd been introducing each new speaker rose and walked to the podium. "Please return to order. Next, we will hear from Senajit Mandal of Kolkata. Monsielle Mandal is an omega with firsthand experience of the underground railway—a group dedicated to helping alphomic individuals escape from slavery to find new lives with forged documentation and new identities."

I frowned. Kam was also from Kolkata. None of the other people on the stage looked Indian, though. And then, Kam got up from his chair. He crossed to the podium and adjusted the microphone, clearing his throat and settling a sheaf of notes on the lectern.

"Good afternoon," he said. "I must begin by clarifying that my name is no longer Senajit Mandal. For all intents and purposes, Senajit died at the age of twelve, along with the rest of his family."

The crowd murmured.

Kam looked up, his soulful brown eyes playing over the assemblage of politicians and diplomats. "The Mandal family were alphomic purebreds. We traced our ancestry through dozens of generations, and had been influential in the Bengali silk trade since the sixteenth century. We relied on strategic alliances and a fair amount of bribery to maintain cordial relations with the beta-run government, as well as our neighbors in the region. That worked for a surprisingly long time... until the day it didn't."

Silence had settled over the echoing auditorium. Kam looked down, straightening his notes.

"When I was twelve years old, Committee sympathizers arrived at my home, dressed in black and armed with automatic weapons." He lifted his gaze again. His eyes were dry, but I was willing to bet I would have felt his grief through the bond if we'd been connected. "They rounded up all of the adults and took them into the courtyard, where they shot them. Armed men held my littermates and me at gunpoint inside the house, while they stripped us naked one by one to check our alignment.

He paused, swallowing. "My siblings were alphas. Vishaya, who used to love playing rugby. Jaina, who painted the most beautiful pictures with watercolors. Nalak, who was fascinated by our family's business, even at such a young age. At the time, they weren't deemed valuable enough to sell—there wasn't enough demand for alphas who hadn't been raised as slaves from birth. I was the only omega in the litter. I had economic worth as a breeder, so they chained me up, threw me in a cage, and dragged me off to the slave pens."

More murmuring.

Despite the fact that I'd been a slave on a breeding plantation myself before I'd been selected for the military alpha program, I *still* wanted to track down those vigilantes who'd put my Ginger Tea in chains and break every one of their necks.

"Breeding omegas on the plantations are chosen for genetics and temperament," Kam said. "My pedigree might have been impeccable, but evidently I fell short when it came to malleability. After one too many instances of insolence to my handlers, I was taken to a concrete room and strapped to a table. Doctors removed my womb and sewed me shut, ensuring that I would never be able to have normal sexual relations again. They cut out my extra nipples and attempted to remove my mating gland. When I didn't die from blood loss or infection afterward, they threw me onto the auction block, where I was sold at a discount as servant stock."

A few people rose and headed for the exits, looking ill. One woman began openly crying. I swallowed a surge of anger at the fuckers who were acting like this kind of shit was news to them. How oblivious did you have to be, not to know what happened on the production side of the thriving slave industry? Without omega breeders, there would be no docile, chemically castrated alphas to do the betas' unpleasant grunt work. Who the hell did they think was harvesting their vegetables, and processing their meat, and building their shiny buildings? Did they think alphas sprang into being from nothing, already fully formed?

Beside me, Irina was holding herself very, very still.

"Fortunately for me," Kam continued, "the woman who bought me was a member of the alphomic underground. She arranged for me to be sent overseas to the UFNA with a fake beta identity and enough money to start a new life. Senajit Mandal had already been dead for years. When I arrived in my new homeland, Kameron Patel was born. It would give me the greatest satisfaction to see a day when no other omegas ever need to suffer the way I did. I hope that this summit may —"

A hissing noise cut him off in mid-sentence, and for a split second, I thought it must be some problem with the sound system. Then heavy clouds of white vapor began to spew from the ventilation ducts in the walls and ceiling of the vast hall, billowing downward to cover the stage. I was already moving when the first screams reached my ears.

NINETEEN

Flynn

TWO FIGURES tumbled off the raised stage and fell to the floor, twitching. One was a big guy — probably an alpha. I didn't get a good look at the second before the clouds of gas billowed off the stage, obscuring the convulsing body. Then the beta woman who'd spoken before Kam staggered out of the obscuring vapor. She was limping but seemed otherwise unharmed as she ran toward the crowd in the auditorium, shrieking for help.

Irina's hand closed on my bicep, dragging at me until I turned to look at her.

"Stop!" she barked. "It's the VX agent. It has to be! Help the others get Alex and Leona out of here. If you go in there after Patel, you'll die. I'll get him."

Leo's terror and the others' shocked disbelief battered at me through the bond. "You'll die, too," I said stupidly.

"Maybe not," she said. Then she was gone — disappearing into the expanding fog.

I stared after her for the space of a heartbeat, my feet frozen in place. I knew I had to act. Jax would keep Leo from charging after Kam, but Irina was right — if Alex realized that both Irina and Kam were in the gas, she might do something irrational. Jax would need help to get both of them out of here safely.

The gas was only feet away, creeping in white swirls toward my feet. Right on cue, Jax's wordless call for help echoed through the bond. I dragged my body free of its paralysis and sprinted toward the rest of my pack. Most other people in the audience hall were already running toward the exits, but Polonsky charged past me going the other direction... toward where Irina had disappeared into the gas.

For a split second I considered trying to stop him, but I didn't have time and he was a beta. If Irina was right about this being the BLF's experimental gas, he would probably be all right.

Leo was screaming. I thought it had only been inside my head, but no. It was in my ears, too.

"Let me go! Kam! *Kam!*"

Jax held her, and Nikolayev had a restraining hand around Alex's arm—which wasn't going to end well if he kept it there much longer. I charged in and knocked her off balance before she could break the Russian's kneecap and punch him out cold.

"Out!" I snarled. "Get the others out! Polonsky's a beta—he's gone after Kam and Irina!" I gave Alex a shove, knowing that if she fought back with any sort of force we were all going to be screwed.

Beckett appeared, white-faced. "This way," he ordered, in that tone we'd all learned over the years to obey without thought. "*Now.*"

The gas rolled through the cavernous hall, spreading outward. Jax picked Leo up and bodily hauled her after Beckett, who had Nikolayev by the arm and was leading him in the wake of a tight phalanx of dark-suited security goons escorting Prime Minister Fairbanks toward the nearest exit.

I tamped down the mating bond as best I could in an attempt to try and keep my wits about me, but first I sent a silent prayer in Alex's direction—*please don't fight us.* With my hand clamped on her shoulder, I followed the others into the crush of people gathered in front of the double doors. It was exactly like fucking Belarus, except this time the bottleneck at the exit might end up being fatal for anyone stuck at the back, if the gas caught up with them.

A moment later, Beckett's strategy revealed itself. One of the UFNA bodyguards protecting Fairbanks roared, "*Move!*" When the knot of people in front of him didn't immediately clear, he lifted an arm and fired off a single gunshot at the distant ceiling. "*I said move!*"

The crowd around the door heaved forward in panic, erupting through the exit like a champagne cork being shot from a bottle. Beckett stuck to the back of Fairbanks' retinue like glue, and the rest of us followed suit. Bodies battered at me—other panicked attendees being tossed around by the tide of the crowd. I ignored them in favor of keeping a hand on Alex and an eye on Jax and Leona, while simultaneously slamming a heavy mental door closed on thoughts of Kam trapped in the cloud of experimental nerve gas.

If he was dead, there was nothing I could do except grieve him, and try to kill every bastard who'd ever given the Beta Liberation Front the time of day. If he wasn't dead, there was still nothing I could do. Not right now. I had to keep the others alive, and anyway, it would have been physically impossible to turn back and force my way through the press of humanity squeezing through the doors.

Leo's hysteria and Alex's desperate, toxic self-loathing throbbed through the bond despite my best efforts to block them, nearly drowning out Jax's cold determination to keep us safe. Beckett stayed right on the heels of Fairbanks' team, probably assuming that they would be heading for someplace secure.

Alex stumbled in my grip and heaved, upchucking whatever she'd eaten last. With Kam and Irina both possibly dead, I was aware that we were living her worst nightmare in vivid technicolor.

Even so, I didn't release her or let her stop, half-dragging her along with me so we wouldn't lose sight of the others.

I hoped the UFNA goons were planning on getting their charge out of the damned building, because I couldn't stop picturing more clouds of gas erupting from the ventilation ducts above our heads. Fairbanks was shouting about his wife and daughter, demanding to know where they were. I tuned it out.

We eventually spilled out of a side door, and into a paved area beneath a large overhang. I silently congratulated the prime minister's goons on having chosen someplace that would hopefully stymie any terrorist snipers who might be waiting on nearby rooftops to pick off high-value targets as they attempted to escape the gas.

Alex jerked free of my hold and staggered backward against the glass wall of the building, sliding down it to the ground with a hand covering her face. Leo was sobbing in Jax's arms, still trying weakly to turn back the way we'd come as Jax held onto her from behind. Nikolayev's expression might have belonged to Satan himself, and Beckett was wearing a blank mask, his lips bloodless.

One of Fairbanks' bodyguards had two fingers pressed to his earpiece, listening. He looked up. "Sir, a car will be here for you in two minutes."

Fairbanks rounded on him. "I'm not leaving until someone tells me where Jennifer and Samantha are! Get me a damned report on my family — *now*!"

I remembered watching Jennifer Fairbanks excuse herself from the auditorium to take the kid to the restroom, right before Kam started speaking. They'd had security with them, and at least they'd been out of the room before the crowd panicked. Still, who knew if there were BLF operatives hiding elsewhere in the building who might've overpowered the bodyguards and snatched them.

"Prime Minister," Beckett said. His voice sounded hoarse, and he cleared his throat before continuing. "We have reason to believe that the attack used an experimental nerve gas designed to only affect alphas and omegas, not betas. There's every chance that they'll be unharmed, if they were even exposed in the first place."

Fairbanks didn't appear even slightly reassured—but he did pause, taking in Beckett's face for a beat before his gaze landed on Leona. Recognition dawned. "You..." he said. "You're..."

"Former employees of the UFNA government, yes," Beckett finished for him. "Until the Montreal Police Department raided Ambassador McCready's apartment at three in the morning, and threw her in a cell for the crime of having been born an omega."

The prime minister's bodyguards had been keeping a wary watch on us, and it grew even warier at Beckett's words. My packmates' raw emotions were still swirling around me. I did my best to stuff my own feelings in a box until we knew what was what. I felt the moment Leo's agonized fear and grief morphed into incandescent rage. She wrenched free of Jax's loose hold and raised a shaking hand to point directly at Fairbanks' face.

"*This!*" she shouted. "*This is the world you and your damned beta cronies have spawned. Are you fucking happy now?*"

TWENTY

Leona

THE MAN I'D believed in for so many years—the man I'd followed and worked for and *trusted*—gaped at me like a landed fish. Fairbanks' bodyguards closed around him, hands reaching into jackets where they were no doubt grasping their weapons, ready to draw.

Jax wrapped his arms around me again from behind and pulled me back a few steps. But I wasn't finished. I craned to meet Fairbanks' eyes past the wall of men in black suits.

"My closest friend may be *dead*! All because you and your fellow so-called leaders on the world stage couldn't commit to granting basic human rights to a tenth of the world's *fucking* population! You call *us* the threat?" I gestured furiously at the building we'd just escaped. "*That's* the fucking threat!"

Three sleek black cars pulled up to the portico where we were sheltering.

One of the bodyguards put a hand on the prime minister's shoulder and attempted to steer him toward the vehicle. "Sir, you need to get to a secure location."

Fairbanks threw the man's hand off. "I told you, I'm not going anywhere until I know my wife and daughter are safe!"

Beckett stepped between the two groups with a hand raised toward me in silent warning. "There should be a staging area set up somewhere in the complex to coordinate medical care for the injured, and hopefully act as a central hub for information surrounding the attack."

Nikolayev joined him cautiously, eying the twitchy security surrounding the prime minister. "We need to determine if the gas constituted the full extent of the attack, or if there are enemy operatives active in the area."

"Chairman Nikolayev," Fairbanks said, sounding calmer, but equally cautious. "Yes, that makes sense."

"Your transportation could be useful," Nikolayev continued. "Particularly if it's bulletproof transportation—just in case. It would be quicker and safer to drive until we find a checkpoint with radio communication to the venue's security center, rather than to trying to reach them on foot."

Fairbanks hesitated for only an instant, and then gave a single, decisive nod. "Right. Join me, please, Chairman. We'll track down someone who can get us answers." He turned his gaze on the bodyguards. "Keep trying to contact Jennifer's guards. Radio my driver the moment you learn something."

Beckett and Nikolayev exchanged a brief look that contained an entire conversation.

"There's not enough room for the rest of us," Beckett said aloud. "We'll hunker down here for now. Send a couple of cars for us as soon as you know where we need to go."

Nikolayev gave a sharp nod of acknowledgement and followed Fairbanks into the back seat of the middle vehicle. The bodyguards gave us a final mistrustful look and piled into the other two cars. Seconds later, the three black sedans drove off. Beckett let out an audible sigh and scrubbed a hand down the length of his face.

Just like that... there were no more distractions. The enormity of what had happened inside hit me anew, and all the strength left my legs. I would have crumpled to the concrete in a heap beneath the void of Kam's absence, if not for Jax's arms around me.

"Leona, see to Alex, please." Beckett's tone carried the weight of an order, woven through with empathy. "Jax, Flynn—with me. We need to keep a sharp eye out for any further trouble."

Jax supported me over to the glass wall where Alex sat slumped like a broken marionette and eased me down next to her. I was drowning, and so was she. It was all I could do to clutch at the solidity Jax and Flynn were offering us through the mating bond, knowing it was only their need to support us that was keeping them from going under as well.

"We're here for you," Jax murmured against my temple. He reached across and clasped his fingers around Alex's slumped shoulder. After a moment, he straightened and took up a watchful stance in front of us with Flynn and Beckett.

Alex stared into nothing, a terrible expression twisting her drawn features. I knew exactly what she was thinking. *Irina and Kam, both left behind.* If losing Kam was my personal nightmare, this was hers. We were both poised above a great, dark, empty space— suspended for the moment by uncertainty, but fully expecting to fall.

I turned into her, with no idea of how she was likely to react to the contact. The space she occupied in the pack bond was almost as much of a void as the space Kam should have occupied. And, *oh...* was that blank space where I wanted Kam more of a cruelty or a mercy? Outside of my heats, he was absent from our psychic link. If he'd been present like the others, we'd know if he was dead or alive—if he'd suffered and if so, how badly.

The thought was too much. My chest hitched with fresh sobs, my shoulders jerking as I buried my face against Alex's shoulder. Her left hand crossed her body to grab a fistful of my tailored suit jacket, and she turned her head until her cheek was pressed against my hair. A low, terrible noise wrenched free of her throat. Not tears; but rather, the sound of an animal in mortal pain. That sound reached into my very soul, finding its twin inside me.

I fisted handfuls of her clothing with the same awful desperation as she was holding onto mine, and we clung together while the others kept watch around us.

Time felt meaningless, but the angle of the shadows beneath the portico had shifted noticeably by the time a pair of dark gray Mercedes pulled up to us and stopped. Dully, I recognized them as two of the official state vehicles Fouchet had provided us as a courtesy.

Beckett, Jax, and Flynn didn't immediately let their guard down. Alex barely reacted. The driver of the front car got out and exchanged words with Beckett before passing over a folded square of paper. Beckett unfolded it and scanned it quickly before giving a terse nod.

"There's a staging and triage area in the south concourse," he said. "Get in. We'll meet Nikolayev there. No news about our missing people yet—it sounds like things are still chaotic."

"No chance it's a trap?" Jax asked, eyeing the driver.

Beckett shook his head. "I recognize Kostya's appalling handwriting, and more importantly, there's a code phrase. Come on, let's move."

I wasn't sure if knowing Kam and Irina's fates would be better or worse than this all-encompassing uncertain dread, but there wasn't really much choice. We couldn't exactly stay here forever, huddling under an overhang. Jax took my hand and helped me stagger to my feet, swaying on rubbery legs like a newborn colt. To my surprise, it was Beckett who reached down and drew Alex up. Flynn was hanging back, both in my mind and physically. When I tried to catch his gaze, he looked away.

I ended up in the back seat of one car, with Alex in the middle and Beckett squeezed in on her other side. Jax and Flynn rode in the other car. The concourse was on the far side of the complex from the Palais de la Cour de Justice, but it was still only a couple of minutes' drive. We had to stop outside of the parking area, which was packed with ambulances, police cars, and fire trucks.

Covering the final distance on foot was complicated by the fact that I couldn't seem to feel my extremities. I was icy cold despite the perfectly pleasant late afternoon temperature, and it felt like there was a distinct lag time between ordering my muscles to move and getting a response from my body.

Beckett paused, his eyes playing over the chaos. He glanced back at us and jerked his chin, heading toward a large tent or awning that had been erected in one corner of the open area. I followed, clinging to Alex's arm, with Jax and Flynn walking shoulder to shoulder a step behind us.

Nikolayev was waiting for us, standing at the edge of a knot of uniformed police and military officers. Several of them were in animated conversation with Prime Minister Fairbanks, who was still surrounded by his cadre of bodyguards as he railed at them. Nikolayev gestured us to an out-of-the-way corner, where we wouldn't be blocking the flow of official traffic in and out of the tent.

"News?" Beckett asked, in lieu of a greeting.

"There are casualties," Nikolayev replied grimly. "People trampled in the crowd, in addition to several presumed killed by the gas. No names have been released yet, although there has been a report that one of the Icelandic contingent is in critical condition with neurological damage."

His steel-gray gaze landed heavily on me, but I didn't feel the usual alpha pressure urging me to bend and show throat — I was too numb.

"All of the bodies are being taken to the morgue at the Hôpital Kirchberg," he continued carefully. "The most efficient approach might be to go there for identification."

He thought they were dead. *Of course* he thought they were dead. The gas had been specifically designed to kill alphas and omegas, and they'd been at ground zero of the release. But...

"The Icelandic representative is still alive." My voice sounded like rusty nails grinding together.

"And she is also being taken to that same hospital," he replied.

The sick dread ricocheting back and forth through the bond made it nearly impossible to think. Before I could come up with any reason why we shouldn't go to this hospital to look at a bunch of corpses who might be Kam, a disturbance cut through the increasingly angry exchange that was taking place between Fairbanks and the local officials.

"Levi!" It was a female voice.

I turned in a daze to see Jennifer and Samantha Fairbanks hurrying toward the UFNA prime minister, their ever-present bodyguards jogging to keep pace.

"Oh, my god." Fairbanks shoved past his own retinue to rush forward, catching his wife and daughter in his arms. "You're both all right?" He pulled back enough to cup his daughter's face in his hands. "Sammy? You're not hurt? You didn't get near the gas?"

"We didn't even know there *was* gas until a few minutes ago," Jennifer said. "Do you know what's happening? Who's behind this?"

"Sir, we need to get the three of you away from here," one of the security guards interrupted, and a moment later, the retinue headed out.

Irrational anger flared inside me, petty in its vindictiveness. How dare Fairbanks act so worried over his beta wife and child when we'd already told him the gas was designed to only kill alphas and omegas? How dare he get a happy ending while Kam and Irina were presumed dead? I could barely draw breath past the unfairness of it.

Nikolayev was looking after the reunited trio as well. "Pity," he said. "If Fairbanks had lost a family member in the attack, we might have successfully flipped the UFNA against Sloane."

Beckett eyed him. "Tell you what—I'm just going to pretend you didn't say that. Could we focus on the issue at hand, please? I want to make a sweep of the triage area before we leave for this hospital. It's big, but it's not *that* big."

"If you insist," Nikolayev said.

"It would put my mind at ease." Beckett gave Alex a concerned look. "I can go alone and report back."

"No," I said hoarsely.

"We'll all go." Jax sounded firm.

"I'll stay here to keep abreast of any new information regarding the attack," Nikolayev said. "Be as quick as you can."

I didn't actually want to do this, any more than I wanted to take a tour of a hospital morgue. But I trudged after Beckett nonetheless, aware of the others surrounding me. Alex was moving like a sleepwalker. Jax walked at her side with a supportive hand on her arm. Flynn still looked lost inside himself, his presence muted through the bond.

Beckett led us along what I assumed was a logically laid out path through the confusion of the concourse, past knots of people standing around and rows of injured lying on makeshift pallets on the ground, waiting for medical attention. My eyes moved listlessly over the pale, shocked faces—hoping to see a familiar visage, but not really expecting to. Someone had called in a water truck. A line of people waited to be sprayed down with hoses—decontaminated as much as possible after exposure to the gas.

All of them were betas, I was willing to bet.

We'd covered slightly more than half of the crowded area when a gurney carrying a body bag cut a path toward the back of a parked ambulance nearby. My heart lodged in my throat as I watched the black bag juddering over brick pavers on its wheeled cart. I came to an abrupt halt—knowing that we should ask to see the body before it was hauled off to the morgue, but completely unable to move.

"I'll go," Beckett said softly. Before he could, Flynn sucked in a harsh breath.

I turned to look at him, following his gaze to a point some distance past the gurney with its tragic burden. All I could see for a moment was a man in a rumpled dress shirt with his back turned to us, standing near another ambulance. The others turned to look as well.

Beckett cursed sharply. "That's Polonsky. Come on—quickly."

Polonsky turned to look toward the ambulance. The movement revealed the shorter figure he'd been talking to, and my heart skipped a beat, my breath stuttering in my lungs.

Alex gasped.

"*Irina,*" Jax breathed.

TWENTY-ONE

Leona

I WAS RUNNING before I even realized I'd moved. Flynn and Beckett were hard on my heels; Jax and Alex somewhere close behind.

Thank goodness I'd learned my lesson about wearing impractical stiletto heels to places that might be attacked by terrorists, or I probably would have broken an ankle. As it was, I slid to a halt, grabbing Irina by the arm with fingers that felt more like claws.

Polonsky looked alarmed in the instant before he recognized us, but then his shoulders sagged in relief. They were both soaking wet—they must have already been through the decontamination showers.

"Where's Kam?" I demanded, dreading the answer.

Irina took in my crazed appearance, her light-brown eyes dull with exhaustion.

"In the ambulance," she said, and I had a horrible vision of the body bag being transferred behind us. She jerked her head toward the vehicle parked a few yards away. "He was throwing up earlier, but they're giving him atropine to counteract the nerve agent. They think he'll be fine."

I blinked, trying and failing to take that on board. "H-how?" I managed. "How are—?" My voice cut off due to the blockage in my throat.

"How are we alive?" Irina's tone was sour. "It's just a theory, but the gas is designed to affect alphas and omegas. We're both neutered. There's very little left in us that's omega, from a physical or a hormonal standpoint."

"It was still a huge risk going after him," Beckett said quietly.

Irina shrugged a shoulder. "And what isn't, in this life?"

Polonsky had his fingers tangled with hers. "One day, you will do the wrong brave thing and end up dead, *Kachanaja*. And yet, I will still give thanks for whatever time we have together."

"You ran into the gas, too," Irina reminded him.

"Only because you are a terrible influence on me." Polonsky tore his gaze away from her. His eyes landed on Alex, and he frowned. "He is alive, my friends—I promise you. I'm so sorry we weren't able to find a way to contact you more quickly. I don't think the paramedics would appreciate five people cramming into the back of the ambulance, but I imagine they will allow one person to ride along to the hospital."

I'd been paralyzed in place like a statue, terrified that if I made a move toward the ambulance, I'd jerk awake to find that this was all a dream, and Kam was dead. Alex squeezed my hand. I hadn't even realized she'd been holding it.

"You should go." Her words were raspy, but I could feel her mental presence unfolding from its defensive huddle within the bond. There would be psychological fallout from this horrific near miss—not just for Alex, but for all of us.

Now, though, I needed to see my odama and make certain this was, in fact, real. I nodded. "Meet us at the hospital."

"We'll be there," Beckett promised.

I met Jax's blue eyes, and then Flynn's brown ones. Jax's gaze held the relief I expected, but Flynn's expression was still closed off.

"Go," Jax said. "We'll be right behind you."

I nodded, turning and walking toward the back of the ambulance like a zombie. Unsure of the proper protocol, I knocked on the closed metal door. It clanked open a moment later, and a harried woman in scrubs leaned out. She said something in a language that wasn't close enough to German for me to make out the meaning, the sentence rising into a question. Luxembourgish, probably.

"I need to see your patient," I said in French. "Please — I'm a family member."

"Leo? Is that you?" The weak voice came from inside the ambulance, and my heart clenched. I swallowed hard, forcing down a sob.

The paramedic looked over her shoulder, and then back at me. She gave a brisk nod. "Get in," she said, this time in French. "You can sit with him during the journey."

I scrambled into the back without an ounce of grace, where I found Kam lying on a gurney with an IV in one arm and a blood pressure cuff strapped around the other. He was pasty gray beneath his olive complexion, but his eyes were wide open and aware.

"Kam," I croaked, aware that if I broke down and started sobbing into his chest, I'd probably get kicked off the ambulance in short order.

"*Odama*," he said. "Is everyone all right? I'm so sorry I scared you."

I bit my lip hard and nodded, taking the bench seat the paramedic indicated and squeezing Kam's forearm. "They're okay. Just really worried. Irina's okay, too."

"Good." He sighed heavily. "I won't lie. When I saw the gas, I thought it was curtains."

My fingers clenched convulsively. "Irina said it didn't affect you as badly because of what was done to you both."

"Apparently so," he agreed. "She and Polonsky dragged me out of the auditorium. Maybe I took a bigger hit because I still have my mating gland and she doesn't."

It made sense. I also couldn't have cared less about the details right now. "As long as you're going to be okay," I managed.

"So they tell me," he said, as the ambulance rumbled to life and rolled forward. "It's too bad we were so far from help when Jax got dosed in Romania. If he'd gotten atropine sooner, maybe he wouldn't have had such a tough recovery." He let his head roll back, staring at the ambulance ceiling. "God. What is this going to do to the talks?"

"I don't know," I said. I almost added that I didn't care, either—but that wasn't true. I did care, and we'd be dealing with that part of things soon enough. "There are going to be a lot of angry world leaders. Fairbanks' wife and kid were missing in the confusion for more than an hour before they got reunited."

Kam winced. "Ouch. Someone's ass is getting fired over that, I'll wager."

"Probably," I agreed. Something about that reunion was still niggling at me, but it could wait. "The question will be whether all that anger gets directed at the terrorists, or somehow comes back on us."

He closed his eyes, sliding his arm up until I was holding his hand, our fingers intertwining. "That's a question for tomorrow, not today. I expect the doctors will want to keep me in the hospital overnight, at the very least. Are the others following us?"

"They'll meet us there."

He squeezed my hand, and I was relieved that his fingers didn't seem to be shaking or twitching. "Good."

Silence settled, broken only by the paramedic bustling around, taking readings and adjusting the IV drip.

"Is Alex okay, really?" Kam asked into the lull.

I chafed my thumb over his knuckles. "I mean… no, not really. She thought we'd lost both you and Irina. But Irina's okay, and once she sees you for herself, it will help even more. Flynn's struggling, too. Jax was upset before, but now he just feels relieved."

Another deep sigh. "God, I wish this hadn't happened."

"Me, too," I said, and hesitated before continuing. "I, uh, might have cursed out our old boss directly to his face," I admitted. "At extremely loud volume."

Kam opened bloodshot eyes to look at me. "You yelled at Levi Fairbanks?"

"I was upset," I said, by way of defense. "And I'm not sure any of it really penetrated, since he was busy freaking out about Jennifer and Samantha being missing at the time."

Kam mulled that over for a moment. "Well, it's not like he can fire you."

"True."

The ambulance rolled on, toward the hospital with its grim collection of gassed bodies stacking up in the morgue.

***

Kam had been right that the doctors would hold him overnight for observation. I had no idea what strings Beckett and Nikolayev had pulled—or what threats they'd delivered—but he ended up in a private room despite the heavy onslaught of patients in the wake of the attack. More importantly, no one came to kick the rest of us out when visiting hours ended.

There was a television inside the room, but I'd declared a moratorium on any news reports until morning. If something needed doing on that front tonight, it would have to fall to Nikolayev. Beckett had headed out after ensuring that we were settled for the night, leaving the five of us alone except for the regular check-ins from the nursing staff.

Kam had been taken off the IV drip, but was still hooked up to several monitors. A harried doctor had come in at one point to look at Kam's chart, scribble something on it, and inform us that if he continued to improve, he'd be released the following day.

The room only had two chairs for the four of us, but given how overwhelmed the hospital staff must be, no one wanted to make a fuss about it. There were extra blankets, at least, so Jax and Flynn had camped out on the floor.

Alex's mental presence in the bond evened out somewhat as the hours passed, but she was still mostly monosyllabic. She held Kam's hand in hers like it was made of glass, and none of us had tried to push her into talking. I desperately needed a good cry, but somehow this didn't feel like the time for it. The surroundings were too impersonal, and the others were too far away, sitting on the uncomfortable floor.

Flynn was worrying me the most right now. In fact, he was worrying me badly enough that I wasn't willing to let it slide any longer.

"Flynn, will you talk to us, please?" I asked, sending a nudge of concern along the bond. "We're all okay now—or we will be soon, at least. It's worrying me that you don't seem more relieved about that."

"I'm relieved," he said. "Not sure I've been this relieved since we got you back from the Montreal police, Sweet Thing. You don't need to worry about me."

I tried to find a new angle of attack, not buying it for a second. But before I could, Alex spoke up.

"He's beating himself up for not having charged into the gas cloud after Kam and Irina," she said.

My gaze jerked back to Flynn, appalled at the idea that he'd blame himself for that. It would have been suicide.

"Is that true?" Kam asked.

Flynn, who was propped against the wall near the door, shrugged one broad shoulder. "You know how it is. We're supposed to go after the ones who are in trouble. That's the deal."

"If you'd tried to come after me, you'd be downstairs in the morgue right now," Kam said. "I'd still be alive, and then I'd have to live with the knowledge that you threw your life away for me."

Flynn met his eyes, his expression narrowing. "Think I wouldn't die for you, Ginger Tea? Or for anyone else in this room? I would, you know. Hell, I'd do it with a smile on my face."

And what on earth were you supposed to say to something like that?

Alex shifted uncomfortably in her chair. "If you hadn't helped the others drag me out of the auditorium, I might have charged into that gas after them."

"I know," Flynn said. "That's what Irina told me to get me to turn around."

Jax, seated next to Flynn on the floor, drew in a deep breath. "I think… in many ways it's hardwired into us, as alphas, that dying is somehow noble, even if it's a pointless death. I've been in that place before—thinking that there was nothing I could do to protect the omegas in my care, so I might as well do something stupid and violent that would result in me getting killed. As though, by acting recklessly, I could at least ensure that no one would look back and wonder why I didn't do more."

With a pang, I remembered a terrorist cell… an impossible situation. "I told you in Romania that you wouldn't help any of us by getting yourself killed."

"You did," Jax agreed. "And even if I knew it was true, objectively… I still didn't really believe it."

"I wouldn't want your death on my conscience, Flynn," Kam said. "Not ever. But even if I'd died in that gas, I would have wanted you to stay alive so you could help comfort the others while all of you grieved me. Not to die trying to save me."

"I'm supposed to protect you," Flynn said miserably.

"Sure, when you can," Kam agreed. "But sometimes you can't. If you can't, then like I said — I'd want you alive to be with the others, because you're more than just a glorified bodyguard. You're our mate."

Flynn's face twisted. He covered it before I could see the tears, but I knew they were there. Something in the tenor of his thoughts made me think he wouldn't be able to handle it if we all went to comfort him right now. I wanted to go to him anyway, but Alex gave me a small shake of the head. Instead, I watched as Jax scooted closer and slung an arm across his bowed shoulders.

"For what it's worth, asshole… I promise not to give you a hard time if you ever get killed doing stupid alpha shit," he said. "I get it."

"Fuck off," Flynn told him — but he didn't move out from beneath Jax's companionable, one-armed embrace.

The room fell quiet, but it was a comfortable sort of quiet. Exhausted, I leaned forward and laid my head on crossed arms at the edge of Kam's bed, trying not to worry about what tomorrow would bring.

TWENTY-TWO

Leona

THE FOLLOWING DAY brought Kam's release from the hospital, along with the news reports I'd insisted we avoid overnight.

SUSPECTED TERRORIST ATTACK KILLS 23 – DOZENS INJURED.

CHEMICAL WEAPON ATTACK DISRUPTS SUMMIT ON ALPHOMIC RIGHTS.

VIOLENCE HITS ALPHOMIC CONFERENCE – AGAIN. DISTURBING PATTERN EMERGES.

On the hotel room television, a BBC chat show nattered in the background as a man and a woman, both with smart suits and cut-glass vowels, lobbed speculation back and forth.

"At some point, Nigel, we have to start asking why these people are so intent on convincing us they're not a threat, when this kind of violence seems to surround them constantly."

"Now, Josie – that hardly seems fair when most of the victims in this attack were alphas and omegas. Yes, it's true that several betas also died during the panic inside the auditorium, but analysts are saying those deaths were in the nature of collateral damage – they weren't the real targets."

"And how much 'collateral damage' are we as betas going to be expected to take, while this endless debate rages on and on, Nigel? I don't see how we can be expected to..."

I tuned out the infuriating circular argument. Except for Kam, none of us had gotten much in the way of sleep over the course of the last day. Nikolayev and his network of Eastern European cronies were taking point when it came to the media, but sooner or later I'd be expected to release some kind of statement. The amount of makeup required to make me presentable for the camera was going to monumental, as was the self-control I'd need in order to produce anything more nuanced than the same stream of profanity-laced vitriol I'd unleashed on Levi Fairbanks.

At the time, he'd brushed me off with the practiced air of someone who got yelled at a lot in public venues. The thing was, I still felt like something had been off with him yesterday. It had been percolating away in the back of my mind as I dozed at Kam's bedside in the hospital, and also today, as we readied for a meeting with Beckett in what I desperately hoped was a secure hotel room.

When he arrived, it was with the air of a hunting dog on the scent of prey.

"There's news," he said without preamble. "It's significant."

"Let me guess." I couldn't keep the sour note from my voice. "The summit has been put on hold indefinitely due to ongoing security concerns."

"Rather the opposite," Beckett replied. "Fairbanks has been lobbying the other leaders not to leave Luxembourg yet. He's also requested a private meeting with you and Kostya."

I stared at him for a long moment. "Excuse me?"

"You heard right. Tonight at seven p.m., his hotel, no press." Beckett raised an eyebrow. "I would strongly suggest agreeing."

"Well," Kam said. "That's certainly... unexpected."

"Maybe you finally got his attention," Jax said wryly.

"By screaming obscenities at him?" I asked. "If I'd known that would work, I could have done it a year ago."

"Did he specify the reason for the meeting?" Kam said.

"No, although it's a fair guess it has to do with the attack," Beckett replied. "I don't get the impression that the major powers have been taking the BLF seriously until now."

"Well, that's something, I suppose." I tapped a finger against my chin, already plotting ways to maximize the potential benefits of this unexpected good news. "What's Nikolayev's take on this?"

"It's a foot in the door," Beckett said. "Kostya always plays his cards close to his chest until he sees how the other parties are approaching the situation. But the goal remains the same as it has been — drive a wedge between the UFNA and Enoch Sloane; get actual legislation on the table in the UFNA legislature, as well as in Western Europe."

"Right." As Beckett had said, in many ways the attack yesterday had changed nothing. But in others, it might have changed everything if Fairbanks now saw the BLF as an existential threat to be dealt with. "Count me in — as if there were any question. When do I need to be ready to leave?"

Kam frowned. "You mean, when do *we* need to be ready to leave."

"Oh, *hell*, no," I said. "Kam — they let you out of the hospital because they're packed to the gills with casualties, and you're a second-class citizen who isn't on the verge of death. But you were treated for nerve agent exposure less than twenty-four hours ago, and you're not setting foot out of this hotel room until you have *fully recovered*."

He drew breath to argue.

I cut him off. "Also, I intend to use you like a cheap whore when it comes to playing the sympathy card with Fairbanks. *'Oh, Prime Minister – I'm sure you remember Kameron Patel's speech – he was speaking right before the attack. Yes, he's still recovering… it was terrible! We were sure that we'd lost him,'* and so on."

"Damn, I love it when you're a manipulative bitch, Leo," Flynn said. "I am *so* hard right now."

"Too much information, Flynn," Beckett offered. "You're right, though. It could be a useful angle."

"We're going with you, of course," Alex said. "As security."

"If I'm stuck playing invalid, I want Flynn here with me," Kam said firmly. "I'll need security, too, after all."

I met his gaze and raised an approving eyebrow. *Now* who was being manipulative?

"Good idea," I agreed, knowing that the pair needed some time alone. Maybe then, Flynn could reassure himself that Kam really didn't blame him for not running into the gas cloud after him.

This was confirmed when Flynn's brow furrowed in a worried frown. "You sure you want me and not one of the others?"

"If I wanted one of the others, I wouldn't have asked for you," Kam said, with some asperity. "Look at it this way – I know you're still feeling guilty, which means I can make you wait on me hand and foot and you won't complain about it."

Flynn's face cleared. "Oh. Yeah, okay. I can do that."

"If that's settled," I said dryly, "then it looks like I've got a few hours to get some food, get my head on straight, and plaster on enough concealer to make it less obvious that I slept in a plastic hospital chair last night."

Beckett nodded. "We'll be back at six p.m. sharp with a car. Remember to place your room service order through the concierge. He's been thoroughly vetted."

With that, he left. Beckett had been taking every precaution with our security after the drink-spiking incident in Belarus. Our track record with staying one step ahead of the BLF was less than stellar at this point, but I still trusted whatever plans Beckett had personally overseen. We'd had a handful of meals here since arriving in Luxembourg City three days ago, and we hadn't been drugged or poisoned so far.

At this point, that counted as a win in my book.

"Who's hungry?" I asked, girding myself to tackle a private meeting with the man I'd publicly upbraided at full-scale 'shrieking harpy' volume only yesterday.

<hr>

Nikolayev was waiting for me in the back seat of one of the two cars that arrived to pick us up. His expression was a cool mask, giving nothing away. His charcoal suit was impeccable, and his Mephistophelean salt-and-pepper beard had been trimmed to razor-sharp lines.

He looked every inch the terrifying Committee kingpin I'd once believed him to be, and very little like the doting alpha sire who'd bounced a tiny girl-pup in his arms at two in the morning to soothe her colic.

Meanwhile, I probably still looked like an overstressed fugitive omega who'd spent part of the previous day believing one of my soulmates to be dead, followed by a restless night in an overcrowded hospital room wondering if my life's work had just circled the toilet drain and disappeared into the sewer line of history.

But I'd also had a revelation. It had hit me in the middle of my shower, where most of the best ideas come from. I considered telling Nikolayev and decided against it. If I whipped this one out later, I wanted it to pack the greatest possible punch. Conversely, if I was one hundred and eighty degrees off base, it would be better if I was the only one who looked like an idiot, rather than both of us.

We arrived at the prime minister's hotel at six thirty-five. The security checks involved in getting to him were as thorough and involved as one might expect. The five of us were escorted into a small conference room with guards stationed both inside and outside the door. I was confident that the space had been thoroughly checked for bugs as well as any potential threats—including, no doubt, anything hidden in the ventilation ducts.

Fairbanks rose politely as we entered. His day had been somewhat less harrowing than mine had been yesterday, since his family hadn't ended up in a hospital. Still, his practiced public face appeared a bit worn at the edges, and I was pretty sure I wasn't the only one in the room wearing concealer.

"Chairman Nikolayev," he greeted. "Ms. McCready."

"Prime Minister," I replied. "Thank you for inviting us here today."

Some people might have said I should lead with an apology for my outburst the previous day. I had no intention of doing so, for two reasons. First, I'd meant every goddamned word I'd said. And second, if he'd been as offended as all that, one might assume he wouldn't have invited me to this meeting.

Bowing and scraping had never gotten alphas and omegas anywhere. Unless we approached the table as equals, our ambitions of meaningful reform were doomed.

"Prime Minister," Nikolayev greeted—taking the seat Fairbanks indicated, as I did the same. "Your request to speak with us privately was, shall we say, somewhat unexpected. What is it you wish to discuss?"

Alex and Jax took up watchful positions along the back wall. Fairbanks reseated himself across the conference table from us, steepling his fingers before him. "May I be frank, Chairman?"

Nikolayev slanted an eyebrow. "I hope you will be."

Fairbanks gave a single nod, as though to himself. "In that case, I wish to discuss Enoch Sloane."

"A disagreeable subject, but a necessary one," Nikolayev said. "May I assume he contacted your administration before the summit began?"

"He did." Fairbanks tapped his forefingers together, and let his hands fall to rest on the table. "He threatened to topple the current parliamentary coalition if the UFNA agreed to any major pro-alphomic concessions during the talks."

"The Committee threatens the same thing *anytime* there are talks regarding the current laws," I pointed out. "They've done that for years."

"Yes." Fairbanks frowned at us. "But this time, he also had some very specific allegations aimed at you, Chairman. I wanted to speak with you directly for that reason." He squared his shoulders, as though steeling himself. "Are you an alpha, Chairman Nikolayev?"

Nikolayev didn't so much as blink. "If I were, how would that change the course of our discussion?"

Fairbanks drew breath, only to hesitate. "There are reports," he said slowly, "of actions you've taken in the past that seem... at odds with your recent policy changes within the Euro-Soviet branch of the Committee."

That was as diplomatic a way of asking why someone would brutally murder a family member for being an omega, and later crusade for increased alphomic rights, as I was ever likely to hear.

"Reports may sometimes be misleading." Nikolayev's tone was mild. "One wonders what sort of world would voluntarily hand over power to such a murderous individual."

"A troubled one," Fairbanks replied.

The same haunted look I'd noticed yesterday was back in his eyes—and this was the moment. It was time to drag out the heavy artillery and find out if it would explode in my face or not.

"You have a very good reason for wanting to know if the stories about the Chairman are true," I said. "Don't you, Prime Minister?"

Fairbanks' jaw tightened, his closed expression growing rigid.

"For you, it's personal," I continued. "You know, you really are an exceptional actor. I was in your administration for *years*, and I never even suspected."

Now Nikolayev was staring at me as well, his sharp brows drawn together.

I met Fairbanks' eyes and delivered the *coup de grace*. "This hits directly at your family, doesn't it? I saw the way you reacted yesterday, when you thought they might have been exposed to the gas. Your daughter, Samantha, is an unregistered omega."

TWENTY-THREE

Kameron

THE INSTINCT TO soothe upset alphas was hardwired into omegas from the time we were pups. Some betas—and some omegas, for that matter—found the idea demeaning. Maybe it was my purebred upbringing, but I never had. Yes, the urge could rear its head at inappropriate times. So could every other ingrained biological urge one might care to name. That was simply *life*, busily doing its thing at the cellular level while we weren't paying attention.

Personally, I found a certain beauty in the way alphas and omegas meshed. Flynn's reaction to not having thrown his life away in a doomed attempt to drag me to safety was basic *Alpha 101*. Honestly, I'd been surprised by the depth of self-awareness our three alpha mates had shown when discussing it. They understood—intellectually, at least—that getting themselves killed pointlessly and unnecessarily wasn't helpful to anyone. However, understanding something intellectually wasn't an instant cure for feeling like shit about it.

That was where omega soothing came in, and it wasn't as though it was a hardship in this particular case.

I did, in fact, still feel like hell. If Leo hadn't put her foot down, I was sure I could have successfully ridden in a car to the prime minister's hotel and sat at a table for an hour or two. However, it wouldn't have been nearly as enjoyable as lounging on the hotel bed with Flynn, bracketed by his tree-trunk thighs with my back resting against his broad chest while he fed me petit fours by hand.

"Ugh, *mercy*," I said. "Seriously, stop. I'm stuffed."

He set the tray on the bedside table without so much as jostling me, then started stroking my hair away from my temples like someone stroking an exceptionally well-fed cat.

"You don't feel sick again, do you?" he asked.

"Not nauseated or anything like that, no," I assured him. "Just tired, and like my body weighs a ton."

"You didn't eat *that* much," Flynn said.

I snorted. "I think it has more to do with the damned gas than the food. Give me a few days and I'll be right as rain." I shifted with a sigh, pressing my head further into the contact of his rhythmic petting. "Frankly, I'm more worried about the fact that I didn't get a decent sex joke out of you in response the 'stuffed' remark. That opening was as wide open as my asshole after Jax finished knotting me."

His chest shook with silent, surprised laughter. "Didn't really seem like the time, Ginger Tea," he said, his arms coming around me from behind in a hug.

I relaxed into it, thinking for the hundredth time that I'd never expected to have this much out of life. The past few months had been harrowing, but they'd also brought blessings beyond my wildest imaginings.

"Can we talk about something?" Flynn asked, surprising me.

"Anything," I told him. "Always. What do you want to talk about?"

"You," Flynn said. "I was gonna have a word with Beckett first, or maybe the Russian. But now I think that was wrong and I should ask you first."

That sounded a bit alarming, but I only said, "What about me?"

His barrel chest rose and fell behind me, lifting my torso like a ship riding a wave.

"So… they make drugs and stuff for omegas, right? Heat blockers and pheromone suppressors and the like."

"Yes?" I replied cautiously.

"I was just thinking—what if you could get, like, hormone replacement therapy, only for omegas?" he said. "Would you want that?"

I blinked. My mouth opened, but nothing came out. After a moment, I closed it.

"Hormone replacement therapy?" I echoed eventually.

"Well, you take testosterone now, don't you?" Flynn said. "To keep that pretty beta physique. What if, instead, you took the hormones that your body would have been producing, if the beta butchers hadn't caught you as a kid?"

"I… don't know," I replied blankly.

"Like, what if you could take omega hormones, and it meant you were able to stay in the bond all the time instead of just when Leo's in heat? That's what I was thinking."

Again, I paused… struck dumb.

"I don't know," I said again, trying to push past my surprise. "I'm not aware that omega hormones are even available on the black market."

Flynn breathed out. "That's why I wanted to talk to Beckett and Nikolayev. They've got a direct line to the good stuff, so I figured they'd know if it can be done or not."

I lay in the alpha's arms, not sure if it would be too painful to contemplate the what-ifs, in case it wasn't possible to procure omega hormones or they wouldn't work for someone like me.

"Give me some time to think about it," I told him, after long moments had passed in silence.

"'Kay," Flynn said easily. He slipped a hand down to tug at the elastic of my waistband. "Now get these stupid pajamas off. You're all tense. I wanna give you a massage."

"Oh, very well. If I must." My long-suffering air sounded fake enough to draw a snort of amusement from him.

He nudged me forward so that he could slip out from behind me and retrieve a small bottle of massage oil from his luggage. I managed to overcome my heavy limbs long enough to strip off the flannel pajama bottoms and white T-shirt I was wearing by the time he returned.

A massage from Flynn was never going to be PG-rated, but even when his oiled hands wandered to places that made me squirm and gasp, there was no indication that I was expected to do more than relax and enjoy it for what it was—alpha caretaking at its finest.

Within half an hour, I was a puddle in the center of the mattress. Evidently, having absolutely no muscle tone anywhere in my body was somehow conducive to making emotionally fraught decisions.

"Flynn?"

The alpha's big hands stilled on my back. "Yes, Ginger Tea?"

"Talk to Beckett and Nikolayev," I said. "I want to know if it's possible."

TWENTY-FOUR

Leona

"YOUR DAUGHTER Samantha is an unregistered omega." The words landed like bricks in the dead silence of the conference room. I heard Jax and Alex's sharply indrawn breath at the same instant their shock hit me through the bond, and Beckett said, "*Ah,*" in a quiet voice of revelation. Nikolayev's sharp eyes swung to Fairbanks to gauge his reaction.

That reaction was both startling and completely unmistakable. The UFNA prime minister shoved to his feet so abruptly that his chair toppled backward. His hands gripped the edge of the table so tightly that the knuckles turned white.

I saw the moment he realized what a giveaway his response had been. His gaze flew to the blank-faced security guards posted around the room. A couple of them had stepped forward in alarm upon seeing their boss's violent reaction. I had a hysterical moment to wonder if Fairbanks might try to have us arrested—or shot, for that matter—in hopes of preventing the news from leaving this room.

The reality was much less dramatic. His shoulders slumped, his head dipping as though he suddenly lacked the strength to hold it up. His eyes slid closed.

"I thought I could keep her safe," he muttered, the words barely audible. "God help me, I thought we could keep her a secret."

I nodded to myself, achingly aware of all the new possibilities opening up before us. "I'm sure my parents thought much the same thing," I said. "The question is, what happens to all of the other throwback children whose parents *aren't* powerful and well-connected?"

Fairbanks shook his head helplessly, not looking up. Around the room, I caught several of the bodyguards exchanging uncomfortable glances. I wondered how many of these men had guarded young Samantha Fairbanks as she grew from childhood into adolescence. Had any of them suspected?

"Please sit down, Prime Minister," Nikolayev said. "It appears we do, indeed, have much to discuss."

Fairbanks took a single, heaving breath that lifted and lowered his shoulders. Visibly dragging himself together, he reached down and righted his overturned chair before slumping into it. Elbows on the table, he dug the heels of his hands into his eye sockets for a long moment before he spoke. It didn't matter that he was the elected leader of one of the most powerful federations on the planet. In that moment, he was nothing more than a terrified father.

"I didn't dare act openly against the Committee," he began, letting his hands fall limply to the table, where they lay palm up. "I couldn't risk bringing their attention down on my family."

"How long ago did Samantha present as an omega?" I asked, keeping my tone compassionate.

He gave a mirthless laugh. "Two years ago. She was thirteen. We've had her on blockers and suppressors ever since."

Thirteen. That was young for a first heat—the poor girl.

"And yet, you've still done your best to limit the Committee's power inside the UFNA," I said. "You may not realize it, but you're a symbol of hope to alphas and omegas the world over."

It was shameless flattery. It was also true, in a world where the best we'd been able to hope for was someone to slow the ongoing hemorrhage of our human rights.

Heavy silence fell over the room, broken only by the sound of our breathing.

Fairbanks broke it, his voice emerging as a bare rasp — so unlike his usual commanding baritone. "*It's not enough.*"

"No," Nikolayev agreed. "It really isn't. So the question becomes, what are we going to do about it?"

Fairbanks looked like a man gazing into the mouth of hell. "Yesterday... if Jennifer hadn't taken Sammy to the restroom before the gas was released..."

"She could have died at the hands of radical beta supremacists," I finished for him.

He nodded, blank-faced, and then seemed to realize something. "The man who was speaking when the attack started. I recognized him. He used to work with you. Did he survive?"

"He's recovering." I cleared my throat and swallowed, caught off guard by the wave of choking emotion. "Ironically, if the slavers hadn't ripped out his reproductive organs and destroyed his ability to produce omega hormones when he was a kid, he'd be dead like all the others."

Fairbanks stared at me for a long moment. "I can't let my daughter grow up in this twisted excuse for a world."

Hope bloomed in my chest, but I didn't dare trust it yet.

"What do you know of the Beta Liberation Front?" Nikolayev asked.

"I've received intelligence briefings," Fairbanks said dully. "But there's not much information about them. They're a European splinter group, mostly involved in kidnappings and low-level assassinations... at least, until recently."

"And what if I could tie them to Enoch Sloane and his organization?" Nikolayev asked.

Fairbanks' expression sharpened. "*What?*"

"You mentioned kidnappings," Nikolayev replied. "When she was an ambassador, Leona McCready was one of their targets, as you may recall."

The prime minister's gaze flashed to me, and I thought I saw guilt there. "Yes, I do," he said.

"She and her colleagues were successfully retrieved from a stronghold in the Carpathian mountains by a small strike team," Nikolayev continued. "Most of the terrorists were killed in the fighting, but a few got away. Ms. McCready's status as an omega was discovered during her captivity."

I suppressed a shudder, remembering that horrific few days.

"No one else knew her secret besides the terrorists," Nikolayev said. "And yet, a few weeks after her return to Montreal, she was arrested as an unregistered omega after the Montreal police Department received a tip. A tip, I might add, that came directly from a Committee liaison."

Fairbanks blinked at us. I watched as the implication hit home.

He frowned. "That's a tenuous connection at best."

"It is," Nikolayev agreed. "But I have investigations underway to uncover financial links between Sloane and the individual who drugged the drinks at the recent conference in Belarus. Bank records are considerably more useful than hearsay in a court of law."

A fire kindled behind Fairbanks' eyes. "You're telling me Enoch Sloane funded the terrorists who might have killed my little girl?"

"There certainly appears to be a link," Nikolayev told him.

"By god." Fairbanks' right hand closed into a fist. "Get me that proof, and I'll see the pasty-faced Committee rat hauled before an international tribunal before you can say the words *sanctimonious little prick*."

"I would like nothing better," Nikolayev assured him. "And in the meantime?"

"Alphas and omegas are still being bought and sold every day," I said. "Innocent human beings, forced to breed like cattle—or else face involuntary sterilization and second-class status in the eyes of a two-tiered legal system."

"Yes." The prime minister's face settled into sober lines. "Yes—you're absolutely right. I couldn't act before—not unilaterally. One nation can't take on the Committee. But…"

"The Euro-Soviet Committee no longer supports alphomic suppression," Nikolayev finished for him. "I assume there is a question implied in your statement—and the answer is, yes, my branch of the Committee will support you. As will a large bloc of Eastern European and Soviet states."

Fairbanks tapped the fingers of one hand on the table in a thoughtful gesture. "And I think there's growing support among some of the larger Western European states, as well."

"We heard you'd been busy lobbying," I offered. "It sounds like you were already considering an end-run around Sloane and his allies."

He sighed and shook his head. "I wasn't willing to let an upstart terrorist group dictate terms to a meeting of over a hundred nations. Apparently, the fuckers sent in people posing as HVAC maintenance workers to set the gas canisters in place, with remote controls to operate them from a safe distance."

"Practical, I suppose," Nikolayev said blandly.

"As practical as sneaking someone in as a member of the wait staff in Belarus," I added. "I suppose there's no need to be flashy when being pragmatic works so effectively."

"Apparently not." Fairbanks sounded grim. "Very well. If the UFNA were to tackle the subject of alphomic rights in one broad legislative stroke, rather than continuing a policy of lukewarm resistance, what might that look like? I'm open to your thoughts on the matter, Chairman—and yours, Ms. McCready."

I had to take a moment to check in via the mating bond and make absolutely certain this wasn't a dream or a hallucination. Based on Alex and Jax's shocked hope echoing through my thoughts, it wasn't.

"Very well, Prime Minister," I began. "As it happens, we have a package of proposals that we would be more than happy to discuss with you."

TWENTY-FIVE

Leona

WATCHING THE televised perp-walk as Enoch Sloane was led away from his Alabama compound in handcuffs ranked as one of the top three most satisfying experiences of my life. It fell only slightly behind the moment I'd first felt Kam's presence in my mind during the heat when Jax and Flynn had mated us, as well as the moment Alex had finally joined our bond.

Slightly more than six months had passed since we'd met Levi Fairbanks in a hotel conference room and uncovered his most closely guarded secret. He'd been good to his word—risking his tenuous parliamentary coalition by going public with his daughter's omega status... not to mention his intention to lead the world toward a better future where all people received equal rights and protection under the law.

The legislation had been an uphill battle, to put it mildly. There was strong backlash at first, not least from Sloane himself. I'd been utterly convinced that the UFNA progressive coalition would crumble beneath the strain, ushering in something far worse during the next round of elections.

Fortunately for everyone involved, Beckett's deep dive into the financial ties between Enoch Sloane and the Beta Liberation Front had finally hit pay dirt. Confronted with proof that the co-chairman of the Committee was directly responsible for a chemical weapons attack on a gathering of global high-ranking officials, the tide of public opinion turned at a critical moment during the legislative process. Under pressure from voters, the tide of political opinion turned not long after.

Betas had died in that gas attack. Several had been fatally trampled during the mad dash for the exits. A couple more perished of medical complications after the fact—an elderly woman succumbed to a heart attack, and a man died of a burst aortal aneurysm. It was sickening that the deaths of alphas and omegas alone wasn't enough to foster outrage, but there was no denying that the beta casualties had roused public opinion in our favor. Today, we were about to reap the harvest from the seeds of change that we'd sown.

Kam poked his head into the bedroom. "Are you ready, Leo? It's almost time to leave."

We'd been staying in the Russian embassy in Montreal, where Nikolayev's name was enough to secure us a safe haven while the legislative machine ground slowly into motion.

I stopped fussing with my hair and gave myself a final once-over in the mirror. "Yes. Sorry. Just nerves," I said. "Am I holding things up?"

He came in and put his hands on my shoulders from behind. "Not really. I'm just here to give you a five-minute warning."

Clad in a sharp navy suit with a patterned burgundy tie, he looked every inch the suave diplomatic professional. I met his deep brown eyes in the mirror and gave him a tremulous smile.

"This is really happening, huh?" I asked.

He tucked a wayward red curl into place on the back of my head and adjusted a hairpin to keep it there. "Apparently. Though if it's a shared hallucination, at least it's a nice one. Shall we go and join the others?"

"Yes, let's," I said, and took his offered hand.

Tonight, we would witness the presentation of the Alphomic Civil Rights Act to the UFNA Governor General for final approval. If I were more prone to paranoia, I might have become gun-shy about important public functions where large numbers of politicians would be gathering. However, the last six months since the gas attack had seen two vital changes in the world.

First, the Beta Liberation Front's largest source of funding had been cut off, and many of its leaders had been captured or killed. Second, governments had gotten a *lot* more serious about security precautions. Gone were the days when Kam and I had wandered in and out of office parties in the Foreign Affairs building with only a single, bored guard keeping watch at the front door. The Parliament Building — and pretty much every other government installation — had been locked down tight ever since Prime Minister Fairbanks' close call in Luxembourg.

The House of Commons had room for about five hundred spectators in the various viewing galleries above the legislative floor, and it was a fair bet the place would be packed solid. Jax, Flynn, Alex, Kam, and I were attending as Fairbanks' personal guests in the Speaker's Gallery. Beckett and Nikolayev — safely back in Russia with their baby daughter — had declined to travel here and appear in person. They would doubtless be watching the worldwide broadcast on television, despite the seven-hour difference in time zones.

Kam and I exited the bedroom to find the others ready and waiting for us. I'd been prepared for Flynn and Jax in suits, since suits were standard fare in their familiar long-standing roles as bodyguards. I had *not* been prepared for Alex in an evening dress. In fact, I was unprepared enough for Alex in an evening dress that I stopped cold, frozen in place.

She frowned at me. "What?"

I blinked, and then turned my head very deliberately to look at Kam. "You might have warned me about this," I said.

He shrugged, a smile twitching at one corner of his full lips. "I wanted to see your reaction."

Alex was resplendent in a sleeveless, square-neck white satin sheath gown, with her dark hair scraped back in a severe bun. She didn't need makeup to be completely stunning, but I thought I detected a hint of eye shadow, and she was definitely wearing lipstick.

"White suits you," I managed. "And also, Kam and I are going to peel that dress off of you later, so fair warning."

"With our teeth," Kam added helpfully.

Flynn eyed Alex skeptically. "Can you fight in that thing?"

"Probably not without ripping a seam somewhere." Alex didn't look pleased about the admission.

"Maybe we can get through this one official event without imminent danger to life and limb," Jax suggested.

Flynn shrugged. "Maybe. Anyway, we'll be seated in a balcony, so if anyone comes at us, we can just toss 'em over the railing, right?"

"That seems like the simplest strategy," Alex agreed.

I tried not to picture what the newspaper headlines would look like if my alpha bodyguards injured innocent Members of Parliament by dropping terrorists on them from a second-story balcony.

"How about we try to follow Jax's plan of avoiding drama altogether," I said.

A limousine took us to Parliament Square from the Embassy District. The massive Parliament Building was a towering five-story ode to Gothic

Revivalist architecture, all stone arches and slender spires, built near the banks of the St. Lawrence River in Old Montreal. We passed through the various layers of security, emerging into the echoing space of the rotunda. Stone and stained glass stretched above us.

The foyer to the House of Commons marked a transition from the churchlike atmosphere of the building's public spaces to the darker, wood-paneled room where the legislature met to carry out the federation's business. It was still a huge room, overlooked by five galleries to accommodate visitors of various ranks and provenance. In here, however, attention was focused downward toward the parliamentary floor, rather than upward and outward toward the marvels of the surrounding architecture.

The chamber smelled of rich leather, dusty paper, and age. It contained all the trappings of ceremonial power—including a red, throne-like chair at one end, where the Governor General would receive Parliament's petition. The sergeant-at-arms directed us to our seats in the front row of the Speaker's Gallery, where we sat, looking down at the spectacle.

The business of the North American government was steeped in tradition, and aspects of it seemed faintly ridiculous to the outside eye. Even in this day and age, there were a lot of robes involved, a lot of rather silly hats, and an awful lot of formal bowing. Every formal communication on the parliamentary floor was repeated in English, French, and Spanish, making things take three times longer than would otherwise be the case.

We watched, sitting through the endless introductions of various officials and clarification of points of order, until finally, a representative of the House of Commons approached the Governor

General on her red velvet chair, holding an impressively thick stack of bound paper in front of him like an offering.

He bowed respectfully. "May it please Your Excellency, the Senate and the House of Commons have passed the following bills, to which they humbly request Your Excellency's assent. First, a bill to grant full citizenship and rights to all alphomic individuals within the borders of the United Federation of North America."

The Governor General gave a solemn nod.

"Second, a bill outlawing the practice of slavery, and granting monetary compensation to all individuals held in slavery for their time, labor, and any physical or psychological harm that may have been visited upon them in the course of their subjugation."

Murmurs broke out among the onlookers, only to subside beneath stern looks from the sergeants-at-arms.

"Third, a bill outlawing the involuntary sterilization of any individual, either by chemical or surgical means."

Kam shifted in his seat next to me.

"And finally, a bill lifting all restrictions on the manufacture and sale of drugs and medical devices intended for the treatment of alphomic individuals under a doctor's supervision."

His hand brushed mine and I grabbed it, intertwining our fingers and squeezing hard.

The Governor General nodded again and spoke solemnly, the words too soft to carry to the galleries. I held my breath.

Her spokesperson repeated the words for the onlookers' benefit. "Her Excellency the Governor General thanks the parliamentary representatives, accepts their generous benevolence, and assents to these bills. The Alphomic Civil Rights Act is now the law of the land in North America."

My breath whooshed out of my lungs, leaving me lightheaded as the spokesperson repeated the words in French, and finally Spanish. Around us, tentative applause started up, more and more people joining in despite the fact that it was utterly against protocol inside the House chamber. The five of us clapped as loudly as anyone else. Kam rose to his feet, and so did I—the people around us following suit until a thunderous standing ovation rattled the room's ancient timbers.

Hours later, we lay in a naked tangle on the fur rug in front of the living room fireplace in our temporary quarters. My hair was sweaty from exertion. I suspected I had a serious case of raccoon eyes as a result of smeared mascara, and I was definitely going to be sore in some very interesting places tomorrow.

In other words, bliss.

"Can we talk about permanent living arrangements?" Kam asked. He was lying crosswise with his head in my lap and his legs thrown over Alex's hips, staring up at the ceiling in the orange, flickering light of the gas flame.

"Did you have something specific in mind?" Jax replied, the breath from his words tickling the side of my neck.

Kam's dark eyebrows drew together thoughtfully. "I did, yes. When the reparation payments come through, it's going to mean a fairly significant lump sum for the pack. Leo and I will also be putting lawsuits in motion to recover our confiscated assets, and neither of us were exactly poor before all of this started."

"You thinking you might want us to buy a place of our own?" Flynn asked. "Because I kinda like that idea."

"I was thinking of a very specific place, actually." Kam rolled his head, his dark eyes meeting mine. "What would you say to purchasing the safehouse in upstate New York? The one in the woods."

I mulled that over, not having considered the possibility before now.

"We broke all the windows and singed a bunch of the forest around it with Molotov cocktails," Jax pointed out. "After what happened to us there, I'm surprised the place doesn't hold bad associations for the two of you."

"No," I said slowly. "I mean—yes, those things *did* happen, and they were terrifying. But to me, that house will always be the place where I spent my first heat surrounded by people who I knew cared for me." I paused, and then added, "I really miss that nest."

"*Sex furniture*," Kam offered sagely.

"The sex furniture was pretty good, all right," Flynn said.

Jax snorted. "Well, it's nice to see that everyone's got their priorities straight, anyway."

"What about you, Jax?" I asked. "Does that house hold too many bad memories for you?"

"I'm not sure," he said after a long moment. "I failed you there."

"You didn't," Kam said firmly.

"I couldn't protect you," Jax insisted. "But in the end, Nikolayev capturing us was the only thing that saved us. And... to put things in perspective, absolutely nothing bad happened to us in Nikolayev's guesthouse in Russia. The place was ridiculously huge and ridiculously posh—"

"*Gaudy*," Alex muttered.

"—yet I feel more of a connection to the safehouse in New York than I do to that guesthouse."

I nodded. "Same here. For what it's worth, there will be plenty of time to think about it before we'll be in a position to act."

Alex shifted position, rolling onto her side. "It's a good-sized property. Lots of land, natural surroundings." She hesitated, swallowing. "A good place for pups." The words were quiet and hoarse.

My gaze flew to her. She looked pale in the firelight, but she met my eyes and held them without looking away.

"It *would* be good place for pups," I agreed, imagining a pack of littermates running around in the woods, laughing and climbing trees... playing hide and seek.

Flynn perked up, his smile like the sun coming out from behind gray clouds. "We're gonna have pups soon?"

"Your pups will be beautiful, odama," Kam said.

"*Our* pups," I corrected. "I'm not doing this alone."

Jax had stayed very quiet throughout this part of the exchange. Now he looked up, his blue eyes troubled. "I already have pups. Probably a lot of them. I know it's not explicitly part of the new laws, but... I want to try and find them, if I can. Assuming any of them want to be found, I mean. There should be records. The breeders were always very particular about pedigrees."

The last sentence sounded bitter in a way that was unusual for my scarred Viking. I squirmed around until I could get my arms around him.

"Of course we'll try. Oh, Jax..."

"Guess there might be a handful out there with my shitty genes, too," Flynn said. "They used me to breed one time, when there was a gap in the rotation.

I dunno if she got pregnant or not—they never told me."

"Your genes are not shitty," Kam said, sounding deeply offended. "And I say that as a hoity-toity purebred—so there."

"In fact, your genes are in my 'top three' list of potential sperm donor candidates," I added. "So, don't you dare diss them, or else you're basically saying that I have bad taste."

"Hey—you want my genes; they're yours," Flynn said. "You want any part of me, it's yours. Both of yours."

"Good. In that case, we'll take all of you," I said firmly.

Kam nodded. "Seconded."

Flynn shrugged. "Done."

"Have you made a decision about hormone replacement therapy, once it becomes available?" Alex asked Kam, neatly changing the subject.

The new law meant that as of today, omega-specific drugs were no longer contraband items. Of course, some companies had continued to produce them for the black market even after they'd become illegal—that was how I'd managed to obtain blockers for so many years. But they'd always been scarce, expensive, and of widely varying quality.

Flynn had approached Beckett and Nikolayev a few months ago about finding hormone replacement injections for Kam, but omega hormones weren't readily available on the black market like blockers and suppressors were. With tens of thousands of sterilized omegas gaining full rights and medical compensation for what had been done to them, the drug companies would doubtless smell the potential profits and move to fill that gap in the market sooner rather than later. There was shortly going to be a huge demand for alphomic medical specialists in North America, I was betting.

"Yes," Kam said. "I want to try it. Just so you all realize that it will mean saying goodbye to this carefully cultivated and rather amazing beard, though."

"Baby face," I teased in an obnoxious, sing-songy voice.

He scowled at me. "You have no appreciation for the beard, you philistine," he complained, reaching up to flick me on the ear.

I squeaked in surprise and shoved him off my lap, which somehow devolved into a very uneven five-way wrestling match, and from there, to something much more enjoyable. I hadn't felt so light inside in years. Too bad the Russian Embassy's poor, innocent fur rug was never going to be the same after we were through with it.

EPILOGUE

Leona

Five years later

"*AARGH*! GODDAMN IT, I hate every single fucking one of you right now!" Panting rapidly through my nose, I gritted my teeth until the contraction subsided. My hand ached from gripping Kam's so hard that his knuckles ground together. He wisely didn't complain—or reply. I darted a glance to my other side, a bit sheepishly. "I didn't mean you, Mom. Sorry."

My mother let out a soft snort and gave my other hand a reassuring squeeze. "I'll let it slide this once, Pumpkin," she said. "Let's hope your dad is still keeping the twins occupied outside."

"It's probably not the worst thing they've heard," Kam muttered, *sotto voce*.

Patricia McCready, who had been going by the name Victoria Anderson for the past several years, was the source of my Irish complexion and flaming red hair. Unlike mine, her hair was bobbed short, and also shot through with gray. A patchwork of the kind of freckles that I'd largely escaped dusted her pale skin. Laugh lines and frown lines decorated her thin face in equal measure. Her eyes were a striking blue, not dissimilar to Jax's.

I was so relieved to have her here with me that I could have wept.

"Give us another big push on the next contraction, luv," said the midwife. "You're starting to crown."

"*Ugh*." I tried not to focus too much on the fact that this was only the first of two deliveries. If I'd hoped that giving birth to my second set of twins in five years would be easier than the first time around, I was out of luck.

Four familiar presences crowded my mind with love and worry, but I was the only one who could squeeze these pups out. The others would simply have to deal with getting cursed at, both aloud and internally.

"Let's get you up and squatting." The midwife gestured to Kam and my mother. They helped me get in position, despite the fact that my thighs were already shaky from exhaustion.

"Alpha," Kam said softly. "A bit of help over here?"

A moment later, Alex's lean-muscled body settled behind me. Her arms came around me; warm, long-fingered hands resting over my bulge.

"Get ready, odama," she murmured. "Our new pups are almost ready to enter this world and say hello."

I grunted in response, feeling my internal muscles gearing up for another strong contraction. We were in the nest, with its soothing, red-tinged light and mountains of pillows. It was where these pups had been conceived, and where they would take their first breaths. The old house in the woods had been transformed over the past few years. Once a safe haven for alphas and omegas in need, it was now our home.

Our pack house.

As we'd dreamed, the forest outside echoed with the sound of youngsters at play. Matthew and Kristen had been born four years ago, only a couple of months after we'd finalized the purchase of the property and moved in. Kristen had Flynn's unmistakable looks, as well as his stubbornness. Matthew had Alex's green eyes and a hint of red highlights in his dark brown hair. Between them, they'd filled our lives with love and hope for the future.

The overwhelming need to push washed through me, even as my muscles screamed in exhausted protest. I squeezed my eyes shut and bore down, an undignified, high-pitched shriek escaping my throat as things down below stretched past their limits.

I knew that feeling. It was happening—I was pushing the first of our new arrivals out into the world.

"Looking good, Leona," said the midwife. "Just one more push."

Shaking, I clung to the hands holding mine and leaned against Alex's steady strength.

"Almost there, *ma cocotte*," she whispered.

I rallied for a final push, feeling the weight of our new pup slip free, into the midwife's waiting hands. A weak cry came a moment later, followed by a momentary pause, and then a much stronger wail.

"It's a girl," the midwife reported wryly. "And I'm happy to report that she apparently has lungs."

Kam kissed my temple and let go of my hand, taking the little girl in his arms so the midwife could cut the cord. I blinked sweat out of my eyes and looked down at the tiny, scrunched face with something like awe.

"She's beautiful, Pumpkin," my mother crooned, reaching down with her free hand to stroke the downy head. "Do you have a name picked out?"

"Natasha," I said. "She looks like a Natasha, don't you think?"

A single, damp golden curl proclaimed her likely sire.

"Jax will be thrilled," Kam said. "I wonder if she got the blue eyes, too?"

I started to answer, but broke off with a groan when a new contraction hit.

"Here we go again," said the midwife. "Be glad you're not a purebred, or you might have ended up with two or three more left in the chute."

"Have I mentioned that I hate everyone in this room except my mom and my new daughter?" I managed, before the business of delivering Natasha's littermate demanded my full attention.

⚬

Thirty minutes later, I lay exhausted in a nest of cushions, with baby Dana cradled in my arms. I had two tiny new girl pups, and the contented hum of the pack-bond thrummed in my mind.

Kam sat next to me with his back propped against the front of the overstuffed sectional sofa that surrounded the sunken nest. He'd unbuttoned his shirt, and was trying to get Natasha latched onto a nipple. Dana was already suckling greedily at my left breast.

"There you go, little one," he said, as Natasha finally stopped fussing and started feeding. "Good to know all that time spent in the lactation consultant's office wasn't totally wasted."

Kam had spent the last six months on a hormone and galactagogue regimen to induce lactation, and he had quite a bit to say on the subject of breast pumps these days. He'd been on omega hormone replacement therapy for almost five years now, his body restored to as close to what it might have been as modern medicine could manage.

The beard he'd been so proud of was long gone, and some of the muscle definition he'd worked so hard to maintain was now hidden under a sleek layer of fat. After a considerable amount of research and discussion, he'd opted not to seek reconstructive surgery on his scarred and sealed birthing passage, choosing instead to maintain his existing sexual function, such as it was. The hormones helped, and so did the huge reduction of stress in our lives since the new civil rights laws had gone into effect. The near-constant dark circles were gone from beneath Kam's soulful brown eyes, and his shoulders were no longer knotted with long-held tension.

His presence had ghosted its way into the mating bond a few weeks after he started the hormone regimen. Gone were the days when his connection with us faded following my heat cycles. The five of us were together as we were meant to be — bound in mind, body, and soul.

I'd been the one to prod Kam into seeing the lactation consultant. Even male betas could produce milk with the help of the right drugs. It was considerably more straightforward for an omega. I figured there was no reason why Kam couldn't share the burden of nursing twins this time around. I'd still have to do the bulk of the feeding for the first couple of weeks, since I was the only one producing colostrum. But after that, it would free me up to return to work without the need to rely so heavily on bottles.

It was purely practical, obviously — and had nothing to do with my desire to see Kam with a pup to his chest and love shining from his eyes like a beacon. Nothing at all.

Alex was busy guarding the nest from threats that didn't exist, her green eyes intermittently straying to us with the same dazed, *how-is-this-real* look that I saw on the others' faces from time to time.

I could relate. The world beyond our little oasis of peace was far from perfect, or even safe. There were still vocal proponents for beta supremacy and alphomic suppression—the difference was, they were the illegal ones now… not us.

Our cozy pack house in the woods had security cameras and tall fences surrounding it. I still woke sometimes in the middle of the night, convinced that a SWAT team was at the door. But none of us were willing to let the past overshadow the present… or the future. We were mated. We had beautiful pups. We'd helped shape a world that was better than it had been five years ago.

It was enough. Better than enough, it was more than any of us had dared dream.

I felt Jax and Flynn's approach through the bond, and sent a pulse of wordless welcome. The door to the nest creaked open, and our other two mates slipped in, with Krissy and Matt clinging to them like limpets. My father followed a second later.

"Hello," I said. "Come and meet the new family members."

Matt's eyes were very wide as he approached cautiously and looked down at the two red-faced bundles. "Are you okay, Mama?" he asked in a tiny voice. "We heard you yelling."

"I'm fine, sweetheart," I told him, smiling. "Just really tired. Whelping is a lot of work, that's all. You know when Flynn lifts weights, and sometimes he grunts and makes noise when it's extra heavy?"

Matt nodded.

"Well, it's kind of like that," I said.

"Only with added cursing and personal abuse," Kam added helpfully. "Here, do you want to hold your little sisters?"

Kam and my mother helped the two youngsters take their new siblings. Jax and Flynn squatted next to me, pressing kisses against my temple in turn.

Then, they staked out spots on the sofa where they could watch the others and wait their turn to hold the pups. My dad took a seat across from us and gave me a critical onceover.

"How are you doing, Leo?" he asked.

I smiled, the expression exhausted but heartfelt. "Never better. I'm so glad you and Mom could make it up. Are you still thinking of moving back to the mainland permanently?"

Krissy perked up. "You're going to live here, Grandpa?"

Dad grinned. "Maybe for half the year, Cupcake. I won't lie—at our age, winters in Jamaica are a lot more appealing than winters in upstate New York."

"Seconded," Kam said. "Can I come and stay with you in the winter?"

I mock-scowled at him. "Traitor."

"Of course you can," my mother said, without a second's hesitation. "Bring the kids with you. We'll play on the beach and drink margaritas while these goofs shiver in the cold."

"I feel like you, as my parents, shouldn't be ganging up on me when I've just given you two new granddaughters," I pointed out.

My mother winked at me. "Oh, very well. I suppose you and your alphas can come along, too."

"Gee, thanks," I told her, without heat.

The new pups had made the rounds while we talked. Alex handed me Dana, while Flynn handed Natasha to Kam. The midwife was busily cleaning things up in preparation for leaving. I dozed a bit, letting the bustle ebb and flow around me, with Dana a comforting weight on my chest and Kam a familiar presence at my side.

Time passed, and Jax nudged me through the bond. "Hey, beautiful," he said, when I blinked back to awareness. The pup in my arms squirmed, yawned, and then settled again.

"What's up?" I slurred, still half-asleep.

Jax held up the cordless phone handset. "Beckett's on the line. I called him to let him know the good news. Want to talk to him for a minute?"

I reached for the phone with my free hand, and he passed it to me.

"Hello?" I said.

"*Hello, Leona.*" The international line crackled with static and distance, but the reassuring voice that had shepherded us through so many crises was unmistakable. "*I just wanted to pass on my congratulations. Kostya sends his regards, as well.*"

"It's good to hear from you," I said, with all sincerity. "How's Anika doing?"

"*Plotting world domination, in between charming every person she meets.*" Humor laced the words. "*The three of us will be in your neck of the woods in a few weeks. I'm hoping we can meet up for a visit. Meanwhile, Kostya is hoping he can pressgang you into helping him woo the German Chancellor into broader concessions on a new pan-European treaty.*"

I groaned. "Tell him to ask me nicely, preferably sometime when I haven't just given birth to twins. But either way, I look forward to seeing the three of you. And as it happens, a group of Jax's pups will be visiting around that time, too. Maybe Anika can keep the rest of them out of trouble for a few hours."

"*Highly doubtful, but it might still be amusing to watch. I'll pass on the message, and we'll let you know when our travel plans are a bit firmer. Get some rest, Leona — it was good to talk to you.*"

"And you," I said, before handing the phone back to Jax.

"Let me guess," Kam said, nudging my shoulder. "Nikolayev wants you to charm someone for him?"

"Something like that," I replied, yawning. "Did my parents head out while I was dozing?"

"Grocery shopping," he told me. "They said to make sure you get some proper rest, and they'd take care of provisions for the next few days."

"That sounds amazing." I yawned again, wider this time.

Jax returned, this time without the phone. Alex and Flynn weren't far behind, and they had a freshly bathed pair of four-year-olds in tow.

"Alex says we can nap pack style!" Krissy said.

"That's right," Jax confirmed. "We're all going to welcome your new siblings into the pack. In a few hours, your grandma and grandpa will have dinner for us. Sound good?"

Matt and Krissy nodded solemnly.

"And at some point in the near future, I'll introduce you and your brother to the wonderful world of changing diapers," Kam told them.

"Eww." Matt wrinkled his nose in disgust.

I laughed softly, only to wince as my abused uterus registered a complaint with the management. "Ouch."

"Less talking. More snoozing," Flynn said, arranging the pillows and blankets to make a cozy nest for all of us.

"I'll keep watch," Alex said, settling in.

The others carefully fitted themselves around Kam and me, with our precious burdens sleeping peacefully against our chests. When we were arranged in a warm, comfortable pile, Flynn reached across and smoothed my hair away from my cheek—a tender gesture.

"Love you, Sweet Thing," he said. "You, too, Ginger Tea. And you, munchkins."

I let happiness and contentment flow through me like a warm tide, flooding the bond—feeling it wash back over me, multiplied a hundredfold.

"I love all of you," I whispered. "So much."

"So much," Kam echoed.

The others didn't have to reply aloud. I felt it. We all did. With our pups snuggling against us, I closed my eyes and let sleep slide over me, secure in the knowledge that my family would be here when I woke up.

Pack, forever and always.

finis

Discover more books by this author at
www.rasteffan.com